NEW TOEIC

新制

聽力超高分

最新多益改版黃金試題1000題

作者 ● Ki Taek Lee

審訂 ● Helen Yeh

MP3

寂天雲 APP

如何下載 **MP3** 音檔

❶ **寂天雲 APP 聆聽**：掃描書上 QR Code 下載
「寂天雲 – 英日語學習隨身聽」APP。加入會員
後，用 APP 內建掃描器再次掃描書上 QR
Code，即可使用 APP 聆聽音檔。

❷ **官網下載音檔**：請上「寂天閱讀網」
（www.icosmos.com.tw），註冊會員／登入後，
搜尋本書，進入本書頁面，點選「MP3 下載」
下載音檔，存於電腦等其他播放器聆聽使用。

目錄 Contents

多益測驗改制介紹
&
高分戰略

多益測驗的出現

TOEIC 多益測驗（Test of English for International Communication）是針對非英語人士所設計的英語能力測驗。多益測驗的內容主要與職場環境的英語使用有關，能測驗一個人在工作場合上使用英語與人溝通的能力，故有「商業托福」之稱。多益測驗在許多國家施行多年，如今已經成為「職場英語能力檢定」的國際標準。

多益英語測驗是由「美國教育測驗服務社」（Educational Testing Service, ETS）所研發出來。ETS 於 1947 年成立，總部位於美國紐澤西州，是全球最大的私立教育考試機構。ETS 提供標準化的考試和測評服務，除了多益測驗，還包括托福（TOEFL）、GRE 和 GMAT 等等。ETS 在 1979 年時，應日本企業領袖的要求，制定出一套可以用來評估員工英語能力的測驗，以了解員工在貿易、工業和商業領域上所具備的英語程度，以利人力規劃與發展。

如今，多益測驗是全球最通行的職場英語能力測驗，共有超過 165 個國家在施行多益測驗，每年的測試人口超過五百萬。此外，許多校園也要求畢業生須接受多益測驗，而且成績須達一定的分數，以幫助學生在畢業後能更加順利地進入職場。

多益測驗考哪些內容？

多益測驗的研發者強調「國際英語」，而不以「美式英語」和「英式英語」來區分，並重著於測驗非英語人士對母語人士的英語溝通能力。多益的測驗內容不會考專業知識或詞彙，而是測試在日常生活中使用英文的能力。2006 年改版的新多益測驗，還特別加入了四種不同的英語口音，包括：

1 美式英語
2 英式英語
3 澳洲英語
4 加拿大英語

多益題目的設計，以「職場需求」為主，測驗題目的內容則是從全球各地職場的英文資料中蒐集而來，題材多元（但考生毋需具備專業的商業與技術辭彙），包含各種地點與狀況：一般商務、製造業、金融／預算、人事、企業發展、辦公室、採購、技術層面、房屋／公司地產、旅遊、外食、娛樂、保健等主題大類。

多益測驗的方式

1	考試方式	「紙筆測驗」
2	出題方式	所有試題皆為「選擇題」
3	題目類型	聽力測驗（又細分成 4 大題） 閱讀測驗（又細分成 3 大題）
4	考試題數	總共有 200 題（聽力 100 題，閱讀 100 題）
5	作答	考生選好答案後，要在與題目卷分開的「答案卷」上劃卡
6	考試時間	總計 2 小時（聽力考 45 分鐘，閱讀考 75 分鐘，兩者分開計時）

＊但在考試時，考生尚須在答案卷上填寫個人資料，並簡短的回答求學與工作經歷的問卷，因此真正待在考場內的時間會比較長。

多益計分方式

多益測驗沒有「通過」與「不通過」之區別——考生用鉛筆在電腦答案卷上作答，考試分數由答對題數決定，將聽力測驗與閱讀測驗答對之題數換算成分數，聽力與閱讀得分相加即為總分；答錯並不倒扣。聽力得分介於 5-495 分、閱讀得分介於 5-495 分，兩者加起來即為總分，範圍在 10 到 990 分之間。

答對題數	聽力分數	閱讀分數	答對題數	聽力分數	閱讀分數	答對題數	聽力分數	閱讀分數	答對題數	聽力分數	閱讀分數
100	495	495	85	465	420	70	365	320	55	295	230
99	495	495	84	455	415	69	360	315	54	290	225
98	495	495	83	450	410	68	355	310	53	280	220
97	495	490	82	445	400	67	350	300	52	275	215
96	495	485	81	440	395	66	350	295	51	265	210
95	495	480	80	435	385	65	345	290	50	260	205
94	495	475	79	430	380	64	340	285	49	255	200
93	490	470	78	425	375	63	335	280	48	250	195
92	490	465	77	420	370	62	330	270	47	245	190
91	490	460	76	410	365	61	325	265	46	240	185
90	485	455	75	400	360	60	320	260	45	230	180
89	485	450	74	390	350	59	315	255	44	225	175
88	480	440	73	385	345	58	310	250	43	220	170
87	475	430	72	380	335	57	305	245	42	210	165
86	470	425	71	375	330	56	300	240	41	205	160

＊此表格僅供參考，實際計分以官方分數為準。
＊分數計算方式，例如：聽力答對 70 題，閱讀答對 78 題，總分為 365+375=740 分。

2018年新制多益變革表

多益英語測驗有什麼改變？為什麼？

為確保測驗符合考生及成績使用單位之需求，ETS 會定期重新檢驗所有測驗試題。本次多益英語測驗題型更新，反映了全球現有日常生活中社交及職場之英語使用情況。測驗本身將維持其在評量日常生活或職場情境英語的公平性及可信度。其中一些測驗形式會改變，然而，**測驗的難易度、測驗時間或測驗分數所代表的意義不會有所更動**。

新舊制多益測驗結構比較

聽力測驗 Listening Comprehension　45 分鐘　100 題　495 分
測驗總題數、整體難易程度及測驗時間不變

Part	題型	舊制題數	新制題數	題型題數變更說明
1	**Photographs** 照片描述	10 題	6 題	題型不變，題數減少 4 題。
	說明：從四個選項當中，選出一個和照片最相近的描述，問題與選項均不會印在試卷上。			
2	**Question-Response** 應答問題	30 題	25 題	題型不變，題數減少 5 題。
	說明：從三個選項當中，選出與問題最為符合的回答，問題與選項均不會印在試卷上。			
3	**Conversations** 簡短對話	30 題 3 題 X 10 組	39 題 3 題 X 13 組	加入三人對話、加入圖表，題數增加 9 題。
	說明：從四個選項中，選出與問題最為符合的回答，對話內容不會印在試卷上。 　　　對話中將會有較少轉折，但來回交談較為頻繁。 　　　部分對話題型將出現兩名以上的對談者。			
4	**Talks** 獨白	30 題 3 題 X 10 組	30 題 3 題 X 10 組	新增圖表作答題型，題數不變。
	說明：從四個選項中，選出與問題最為符合的回答，獨白內容不會印在試卷上。			

◆ 聽力測驗將包含母音省略（elision，如：going to → gonna）和不完整的句子
（fragment，如：Yes, in a minute. / Down the hall. / Could you? 等省去主詞或動詞的句子）。

◆ 配合圖表，測驗考生是否聽懂對話，並測驗考生能否理解談話背景與對話中隱含的意思。

閱讀測驗 Reading Comprehension　75 分鐘　100 題　495 分
測驗總題數、整體難易程度及測驗時間不變

Part	題型	舊制題數	新制題數	題型題數變更說明
5	**Incomplete Sentences** 句子填空	40 題	30 題	題型不變，題數減少 10 題。
	說明：從四個選項中，選出最為恰當的答案，以完成不完整的句子。			
6	**Text Completion** 段落填空	12 題 4 題×3 篇	16 題 4 題×4 組	加入將適當的句子填入空格的題型，題數增加 4 題。
	說明：從四個選項中，選出最為恰當的答案，以完成文章中不完整的句子。 　　　選項類別除原有之片語、單字、子句之外，另新增完整句子的選項。			
7	**Reading Comprehension–Single Passage** 單篇文章理解	28 題 共 9 篇 每篇 2 到 5 題	29 題 共 10 篇 每篇 2 到 4 題	題型不變，題數增加 1 題。
	Reading Comprehension– Multiple Passage 多篇文章理解	20 題 雙篇閱讀共 4 篇 每篇 5 題	25 題 雙篇閱讀 2 篇 三篇閱讀 3 篇 每篇 5 題	少 2 篇雙篇閱讀文章，加入 3 篇三篇閱讀文章。
	說明：閱讀單篇或兩或三篇內容相關的文章，從四個選項中，選出最為恰當的答案以回答問題。 　　　加入篇章結構題型，測驗考生能否理解整體文章結構，並將一個句子歸置於正確的段落。			

◆ 閱讀測驗將包含文字簡訊、即時通訊，或多人互動的線上聊天訊息內容。
◆ 新增引述文章部分內容，測驗考生是否理解作者希望表達之意思。

◆ 為新制題型說明

資料來源：ETS 官方網站
http://www.toeic.com.tw/2018update/info.html

各大題答題技巧戰略

聽力部分答題技巧

第一大題	照片描述 （6 題）	這個部分是要考你看圖片、選答案的能力。你可以用以下的方法來練習：自己找一些照片來看，並思索根據照片的內容，有哪些問題可以提問。
第二大題	應答問題 （25 題）	這個部分是提出各種問題，問題的開頭——What、How、Why、When、Where、Who 六大問句——可以提示我們需要什麼樣的答案。
第三大題	簡短對話 （39 題）	這個部分會先播放簡短的對話，再考你對對話的理解程度。回答技巧是你可以先看問題、答案選項和圖表，然後再聽對話內容，這樣你在聽的時候會比較知道要專注答案的線索。
第四大題	獨白 （30 題）	這個大題可以說是聽力測驗中最難的部分，平時就需要多聽英文對話和廣播等來加強聽力能力。

聽力題目前的英文指示 & 高分戰略

In the Listening test, you will be asked to demonstrate how well you understand spoken English. The entire Listening test will last approximately 45 minutes. There are four parts, and directions are given for each part. You must mark your answers on the separate answer sheet. Do not write your answers in your test book.

聽力測驗在測驗考生聽懂英語的能力。整個聽力測驗的進行時間約 45 分鐘，共分四大題，每一大題皆有做答指示。請把答案寫在另一張答案卡上，而不要把答案寫在測驗本上。

I. Photographs 第一大題：照片描述

Part 1

Directions: For each question in this part, you will hear four statements about a picture in your test book. When you hear the statements, you must select the one statement that best describes what you see in the picture. Then find the number of the question on your answer sheet and mark your answer. The statements will not be printed in your test book and will be spoken only one time.

Look at the example item below. Now listen to the four statements.

(A) They're pointing at the monitor.
(B) They're looking at the document.
(C) They're talking on the phone.
(D) They're sitting by the table.

Statement (B), "They're looking at the document," is the best description of the picture, so you should select answer (B) and mark it on your answer sheet.

第一大題

指示：本大題的每一小題，在測驗本上都會印有一張圖片，考生會聽到針對照片所做的四段描述，然後選出最符合照片內容的適當描述，接著在答案卡上找到題目編號，將對應的答案選項圓圈塗黑。描述的內容不會印在測驗本上，而且只會播放一次。

（A）他們正指著螢幕。
（B）他們正在看文件。
（C）他們正在講電話。
（D）他們正坐在桌子旁。

描述 (B)「他們正在看文件」是最符合本圖的描述，因此你應該選擇選項 (B)，並在答案卡上劃記。

高分戰略

❶ 以人物為主的照片，要注意該人物的動作特徵。

照片題中有 70 ～ 80％的題目是以人物為照片主角，這些照片時常會考人的動作特徵，因此要先整理好相關的動作用語。舉例來說，一看到人在走路的照片，就立刻想到 walking、strolling 這些和走路有關的動詞，聽題目的時候會更有幫助。

❷ 以事物為中心的照片，要注意事物的狀態或位置。

以事物為中心的照片，其事物的狀態或位置是出題的要點。所以，表示「位置」時經常會用到的介系詞，還有表現「狀態」的片語，要先整理好。舉例來說，在表示位置「在……旁邊」時，要整理出 next to、by、beside、near 等用語，最好整個背下來。另外，多益時常出現的事物名稱，也要事先準備好。

❸ 要小心出人意料之外的問題。

不同於過往題型，題目的正確答案可能會出現描寫事物，這已成為一種出題趨勢。舉例來說，照片是一個男人用手指著掛在牆上的畫，按照常理，會想到是要考這個人的動作，要回答 pointing 這樣的動詞。但意外地，本題以掛在牆上的畫當作正確答案（The picture has been hung on the wall.）。所以出現人的照片時，不僅要注意人的動作，連周邊事物也必須要注意一下。只有提到照片中出現的內容，才會是正確答案；想像的內容絕對不會是正確答案。

II. Question-Response 第二大題：應答問題

高分戰略

❶ 新制有言外之意的考題增加

PART 2 少了五題，但命題方式變得更巧妙、難度也隨之提升。有言外之意的考題增加，考生必須要聽出背後的含意才能找出答案。碰到此類題型時，在聽完題目後，需要思考一番，才能挑出正確的答案。只要稍不留神，很容易就錯失下一題的解題機會。請務必勤加練習，熟悉此類題型的模式。

❷ 沒聽清楚題目最前面的疑問詞，很可惜。

大部分 Part 2 出現的疑問句都會在最前面提示核心要點，尤其是以疑問詞（Who、What、Where、When、Why、How）開頭的疑問句題目，會出約 9 ～ 10 題。這些題目只要聽到句首的疑問詞，幾乎就能找到正確答案，所以平常要常做區分疑問詞的聽力練習。

❸ 利用錯誤答案消去法。

Part 2 是最多陷阱的部分，所以事先把常見的陷阱題整理起來，是很重要的。舉例來說，以疑問詞開頭的疑問句題目，用 yes 或 no 回答的選項，幾乎都是錯誤答案，可以先將其刪除。另外，重複出現題目中的單字，或出現與題目中字彙發音類似的單字，如 copy 與 coffee，也是常出的錯誤答案模式。平常一邊做題目，一邊將具代表性的陷阱題整理好是必要的。

❹ 常考的片語要整個背起來。

多益中常出現的用語或片語，最好當作一個單字一樣地整個背起來。舉例來說，疑問句「Why don't you . . .？」的用法並非要詢問原因，而是「做……好嗎？」的代表句型。像這樣的用語，時常會快速唸過，所以事先整個背起來，考聽力時會很有幫助。

因此平常花功夫多做聽力訓練，並跟著一起唸，把重要的用語整段背下來，征服 Part 2 之路就不遠了。

III. Conversations 第三大題：簡短對話

Part 3

Directions: You will hear some conversations between two or more people. You will be asked to answer three questions about what the speakers say in each conversation. Select the best response to each question and mark the letter (A), (B), (C), or (D) on your answer sheet. The conversations will not be printed in your test book and will be spoken only one time.

第三大題

指示：考生會聽到一些兩個人或多人的對話，並根據對話所聽到的內容，回答三個問題。請選出最符合播放內容的答案，在答案卡上將 (A)、(B)、(C) 或 (D) 的答案選項塗黑。這些對話只會播放一次，而且不會印在測驗本上。

高分戰略

❶ 一定要先瞄題目，以找出要聆聽的重點。

Part 3 是兩到三人的對話，每組對話要回答三道題，所以**事先把題目快速掃描過**，找出重點，是很重要的。若不事先看題目，就不知道要把注意力集中在哪裡，而必須理解並記下整個對話，十分吃力。所以事先看一下題目問什麼，會對接下來的對話有概念，並知道要注意聽哪些地方。

有關圖表的試題，要**先看一下圖表訊息**，再綜合試題和選項後，仔細聽對話的內容。有策略地去聽是很重要的。

❷ 一面聽一面找答案！

即使先掃描過了題目，卻沒有練習邊聽邊找答案，容易會出現漏掉正確答案的情況。因為即使之前非常注意聽的對話，但有些細微的訊息，之後可能會記不起來，尤其是新制多益中，出現三個人的對話，所以談話者的性別，及彼此間的關係會更加複雜。所以一聽到答案出現，立刻作答，是最有利的。這麼做剛開始可能有點困難，但只要勤奮地練習，以後瞄過題目就大概就能猜出答案

❸ 千萬不要錯失對話開頭！

在 Part 3 中，時常出現問**職業、場所或主題**的問題，這些問題的答案時常會出現在對話開頭。要快速掌握對話一開始揭示的主題，才能判斷出接下來會出現什麼內容，對解其他的題目很有幫助。所以要勤加練習，把對話開頭確實聽清楚。

IV. Talks 第四大題：簡短獨白

Part 4

Directions: You will hear some talks given by a single speaker. You will be asked to answer three questions about what the speaker says in each talk. Select the best response to each question and mark the letter (A), (B), (C), or (D) on your answer sheet. The talks will not be printed in your test book and will be spoken only one time.

第四大題

指示：考生會聽到好幾段單人獨白，並根據每一段話的內容，回答三個問題。請選出最符合播放內容的答案，在答案卡上將 (A)、(B)、(C) 或 (D) 的答案選項塗黑。每一段話只會播放一次，而且不會印在測驗本上。

高分戰略

❶ 要事先整理好常考的詢問內容！

和 Part 3 不同，Part 4 的談話種類是有一定類型的。也就是說，會重複聽到有關**交通廣播、天氣預報、旅行導覽、電話留言**等的談話，內容大同小異。所以只需要按這些談話種類，整理出常考的問題類型即可。舉例來說，跟電話溝通相關的主題，時常都在談話一開始出現「I'm calling to . . .」，聽到這個敘述後，要找出正確答案就容易多了。

❷ 具備背景知識的話，答題會更加容易上手。

Part 4 的談話種類是有固定框架的，會感覺好像談話的內容及題目都很類似。所以即使不聽談話，光看題目，就能推測出答案是什麼。舉例來說，若是機場的情境談話，也許會出有關飛機誤點或取消的問題。這時誤點或取消的原因，最常出現的可能是天候不佳。這就是多益的背景知識，即使沒聽清楚，光看題目，也能選出最接近正確答案的選項。所以平常要努力累積多益常考題型的背景知識，不能懶惰。

❸ 要花功夫訓練自己找出問題的要點。

和 Part 3 一樣，Part 4 也是每段談話出三道題，所以要養成先掃描過題目和表格並整理出重點的習慣。由於 Part 4 的談話內容更長，不太可能把全部內容聽完後再答題。因此可以先找出題目的要點，利用背景知識，在試題本上推敲正確答案。不像 Part 3，Part 4 的答案通常會按照題目的順序，一一出現在對話中，答案逐題出現的機率很高。

閱讀部分答題技巧

第五大題	句子填空 （30 題）	在第五大題中，字彙和文法能力最重要。其所考的字彙大都跟職場或商業有關，平時就要多背誦單字。
第六大題	段落填空 （16 題）	除了單字，也需要將比較長的片語或子句，甚至是一整個句子填入空格中，要掌握整篇文章來龍去脈才能找出最合適的答案。
第七大題	單篇文章理解 （29 題） 多篇文章理解 （25 題）	第七大題比較困難，你需要知道有哪幾類的商業文章，像是公告或備忘錄等。平時就要訓練自己能夠快速閱讀文章和圖表，並且能夠找出主要的內容。當然，在這個部分字彙能力也是很重要的。

閱讀題目前的英文指示 & 高分戰略

In the Reading test, you will read a variety of texts and answer several different types of reading comprehension questions. The entire Reading test will last 75 minutes. There are three parts, and directions are given for each part. You are encouraged to answer as many questions as possible within the time allowed.

You must mark your answers on the separate answer sheet. Do not write your answers in your test book.

在閱讀測驗中，考生會讀到各種文章，並回答各種型式的閱讀測驗題目。整個閱讀測驗的進行時間為 75 分鐘 。本測驗共分三大題，每一大題皆有做答指示。請在規定的時間內，盡可能地作答。

請把答案寫在另一張答案卡上，而不要把答案寫在測驗本上。

Incomplete Sentences 第五大題：單句填空

Part 5

Directions: A word or phrase is missing in each of the sentences below. Four answer choices are given below each sentence. Select the best answer to complete the sentence. Then mark the letter (A), (B), (C), or (D) on your answer sheet.

第五大題

指示：本測驗中的每一個句子皆缺少一個單字或詞組，在句子下方會列出四個答案選項，請選出最適合的答案來完成句子，並在做答卡上將 (A)、(B)、(C) 或 (D) 的答案選項塗黑。

高分戰略

❶ 要先看選項。

試題大致可分為**句型**、**字彙**、**文法**以及**慣用語**四種試題。要先看選項，掌握是上述四種題型中的哪一種，便能更快速解題。所以，要練習判斷題型，並正確掌握各題型的解題技巧。

❷ 找出意思最接近的單字。

Part 5 是填空選擇題，若能找出和空格關係最密切的關鍵字彙，便能快速又正確地解題。所以，要練習**分析句子的結構**，並找出和空格關係最密切的字彙作為答題線索。一般來說，**空格前後的單字，就是線索**。舉例來說，如果空格後有名詞，此名詞就是空格的線索單字，以此名詞可以猜想出空格可能是個形容詞。

❸ 要盡力廣泛地蒐羅字彙。

多益會拿來出題的字彙，通常以**片語**形式出現。最具代表的是：動詞和受詞、形容詞和名詞、介系詞和名詞、動詞和副詞等。有些詞組中每個單字都懂，但合起來就很難猜出它的中文意思，所以不要直接用中文而要用英文去理解。因此，平日要養成將這些片語詞組視為整體一起背下來的習慣。

舉例來說，中文說「打電話」，但英文是「make a phone call」；而付錢打電話不能用「pay a phone call」，要用「pay for the phone call」。但是多益中 Part 5 考「pay for the phone call」的 可能性很低，因為多益大多出常見用語，而這句不是。所以，要用英文去理解常見用語，要整個背起來，不要直接用中文理解，因為這是得高分最大的障礙。

VI. Text Completion 第六大題：短文填空

Part 6

Directions: Read the texts that follow. A word, phrase, or sentence is missing in parts of each text. Four answer choices for each question are given below the text. Select the best answer to complete the text. Then mark the letter (A), (B), (C), or (D) on your answer sheet.

第六大題

指示：閱讀本大題的文章，文章中的某些句子缺少單字、片語或句子，這些句子都會有四個答案選項，請選出最適合的答案來完成文章中的空格，並在做答卡上將 (A)、(B)、(C) 或 (D) 的答案選項塗黑。

高分戰略

❶ 要研究空格前後句子連結關係，掌握上下文。

Part 5 和 Part 6 不同的地方是，Part 5 只探究一個句子的結構，而 Part 6 要探究句子和句子間的關係，因此要練習觀察空格前後句子彼此的連結關係。如果有空格的句子是第一句，要看後一句來解題；如果有空格的句子是第二句，就要看前一句來解題。偶爾，也有要看整篇文章才能作答的題目。

PART 6 最難處在於要從選項的四個句子中，選出適當的句子填入空格中。此為新制增加的題型，不僅要多費時解題，平時也得多花功夫如何掌握上下文意上。

❷ Part 6 的動詞時態問題

Part 5 的動詞時態問題，只要看該句子內的動詞是否符合時態即可，但 Part 6 的動詞時態，要看其他句子才能決定該句空格中的時態。大部分的時態題目都區分為：已發生的事或尚未發生的事。從上下文來看，已發生的事，要用現在完成式或過去式；尚未發生的事，就選包含 will 等與未來式相關的助動詞（will、shall、may 等）選項，或用「be going to . . .」。針對 Part 6 的時態問題，多練習區分已發生的事和尚未發生的事便能順利答題。

❸ Part 6 的連接副詞

所謂的連接副詞，是指翻譯時要和前面的內容一起翻譯的副詞。一般來說，這不會出現在只考一句話的 Part 5，而會出現在考句間的關係的 Part 6。舉例來說，副詞 therefore 是「因此」的意思，所以若前後句的內容有因果關係，用它就對了。若是轉折語氣的話，用有「然而」含意的 however 準沒錯。此外，連接副詞還有 otherwise（否則）、consequently（因而導致）、additionally（此外）、instead（反而）等。另外，連接詞用於連接句子，而介系詞是連接名詞，連接副詞是單獨使用的，這是區分它們最便捷的方法。

Part 7

Directions: In this part you will read a selection of texts, such as magazine and newspaper articles, emails, and instant messages. Each text or set of texts is followed by several questions. Select the best answer for each question and mark the letter (A), (B), (C), or (D) on your answer sheet.

第七大題

指示：這大題中會閱讀到不同題材的文章，如雜誌和新聞文章、電子郵件或通訊軟體的訊息等。每篇或每組文章之後會有數個題目，請選出最適合的答案，並在做答卡上將 (A)、(B)、(C) 或 (D) 的答案選項塗黑。

高分戰略

❶ 要熟記類似的字彙及用語。

做 Part 7 的題目，字彙能力最為重要，它能幫助你正確且快速地找出與題目或文章用語最接近的選項。一邊研究 Part 7 的題目，一邊整理並熟記意思相似的字彙或用語，能快速增加字彙。

❷ Part 7 的問題也是有類型的。

Part 7 的題目乍看好像很多元，事實上可以分作幾種類型，如：

① **具體訊息類型**：詢問文章的一些訊息。
② **主題類型**：要找出文章主題。
③ **NOT 類型**：提供的選項中有三項是對的，而要找出錯誤項目。
④ **邏輯推演類型**：從一些線索中推知內容。
⑤ **文意填空類型**：閱讀段落，將題目中的句子填入文中適當的地方。

解題時先將題目分類，再來研究該如何解題，速度會快很多。

❸ 要注意複合式文章題目。

從 176 題開始，是由兩篇到三文章組成的複合式文章類型，有許多問題出自多篇文章內容的相關性。所以在這部分，相關或相同的地方要連貫起來作答。出這種相關連帶問題時，要注意文章的共通點是以何種方式連接。

❹ 培養耐力。

Part 7 是最後一個單元，解題實力雖然重要，但長時間解題能否集中注意力也是勝負的關鍵。平常要訓練自己，至少要持續一個小時不休息地解題，時常以這種方式來訓練閱讀十分重要。多做解題耐力練習，是考高分的必要條件。

ACTUAL TEST

LISTENING TEST

In the Listening test, you will be asked to demonstrate how well you understand spoken English. The entire Listening test will last approximately 45 minutes. There are four parts, and directions are given for each part. You must mark your answers on the separate answer sheet. Do not write your answers in your test book.

PART 1

Directions: For each question in this part, you will hear four statements about a picture in your test book. When you hear the statements, you must select the one statement that best describes what you see in the picture. Then find the number of the question on your answer sheet and mark your answer. The statements will not be printed in your test book and will be spoken only one time.

Example

Sample Answer

Statement (B), "They're looking at the document," is the best description of the picture, so you should select answer (B) and mark it on your answer sheet.

1.

2.

GO ON TO THE NEXT PAGE

3.

4.

5.

6.

GO ON TO THE NEXT PAGE →

PART 2 02

Directions: You will hear a question or statement and three responses spoken in English. They will not be printed in your test book and will be spoken only one time. Select the best response to the question or statement and mark the letter (A), (B), or (C) on your answer sheet.

7. Mark your answer on your answer sheet.

8. Mark your answer on your answer sheet.

9. Mark your answer on your answer sheet.

10. Mark your answer on your answer sheet.

11. Mark your answer on your answer sheet.

12. Mark your answer on your answer sheet.

13. Mark your answer on your answer sheet.

14. Mark your answer on your answer sheet.

15. Mark your answer on your answer sheet.

16. Mark your answer on your answer sheet.

17. Mark your answer on your answer sheet.

18. Mark your answer on your answer sheet.

19. Mark your answer on your answer sheet.

20. Mark your answer on your answer sheet.

21. Mark your answer on your answer sheet.

22. Mark your answer on your answer sheet.

23. Mark your answer on your answer sheet.

24. Mark your answer on your answer sheet.

25. Mark your answer on your answer sheet.

26. Mark your answer on your answer sheet.

27. Mark your answer on your answer sheet.

28. Mark your answer on your answer sheet.

29. Mark your answer on your answer sheet.

30. Mark your answer on your answer sheet.

31. Mark your answer on your answer sheet.

PART 3 ◖03◗

Directions: You will hear some conversations between two or more people. You will be asked to answer three questions about what the speakers say in each conversation. Select the best response to each question and mark the letter (A), (B), (C), or (D) on your answer sheet. The conversations will not be printed in your test book and will be spoken only one time.

32. What are the speakers mainly discussing?

(A) A training seminar
(B) The installation of a television
(C) The date of a presentation
(D) A software upgrade

33. What is the problem?

(A) The necessary tools are unavailable.
(B) The office is closed.
(C) The wall is too weak.
(D) The phone number was wrong.

34. What most likely will the man do first tomorrow?

(A) Order a replacement part
(B) Consult an instruction manual
(C) Contact the woman
(D) Fill out a work order

35. What position is the man applying for?

(A) Lecturer
(B) Editor
(C) Journalist
(D) Superintendent

36. What makes the man qualified for the position?

(A) His academic background
(B) His work experience
(C) His popularity
(D) His eloquence

37. What extra benefit does the woman mention?

(A) Health insurance
(B) Flexible hours
(C) A lot of free time
(D) Regular incentives

GO ON TO THE NEXT PAGE ➡

38. What are the speakers mainly discussing?

(A) An interior renovation
(B) A product launch
(C) A luncheon reservation
(D) A budget proposal

39. What does the man say about the dining room?

(A) It needs more lighting.
(B) It is quite cold.
(C) It is spacious.
(D) It is too loud.

40. What does the man suggest the woman do?

(A) Repaint the walls a brighter color
(B) Compensate guests who have reservations
(C) Draft a budget proposal
(D) Open a bank account

41. What is the man concerned about?

(A) Getting his camera fixed
(B) Receiving sick leave from work
(C) Preparing for a party
(D) Introducing a client

42. According to the man, why does Greg like his new job?

(A) It offers better vacation time.
(B) It pays a higher salary.
(C) It matches his abilities.
(D) It provides health benefits.

43. What most likely will the woman do next?

(A) Take a group photo
(B) Attend a Christmas party
(C) Contact Greg
(D) Send an email attachment

44. What is the man concerned about?

(A) Finishing a project on time
(B) Paying for his new mobile phone
(C) Repairing a piece of equipment
(D) Learning a new skill

45. Where do the speakers work?

(A) At a repair shop
(B) At an electronics store
(C) At a marketing firm
(D) At a design company

46. What does the woman offer to do?

(A) Provide assistance
(B) Pay in cash
(C) Fill in for the man
(D) Email a user manual

47. Who most likely is the man?

(A) A shop owner
(B) A construction worker
(C) A local resident
(D) A market researcher

48. What does the woman mention about the mall?

(A) It was recently renovated.
(B) It has sufficient parking space.
(C) It is attracting many tourists.
(D) It is located outside of town.

49. Why does the woman usually visit the mall?

(A) To purchase groceries
(B) To meet with her clients
(C) To buy clothing
(D) To deliver products

50. What are the speakers discussing?

(A) Orders for office supplies
(B) Equipment for a conference
(C) The budget reports
(D) Their colleague

51. Why does the man mention to the woman when the supply company closes?

(A) To inform her of the business hours
(B) To let her know she can't order anything
(C) To explain that the second order would be late
(D) To imply that new equipment can't be ordered tomorrow

52. What does the woman offer to do?

(A) Pay for the new order
(B) Order the supplies herself
(C) Cancel a meeting
(D) Speak to their colleague

53. What is the problem?

(A) The plane tickets were not booked
(B) A meeting had to be rescheduled
(C) The meeting was a failure
(D) A deadline has been changed

54. Which part of the business trip will be postponed?

(A) The meeting in New York
(B) The meeting in Wisconsin
(C) The meeting in Washington
(D) The meeting in Westboro

55. What does the man mean when he says, "that's not a bad idea"?

(A) He thinks it is a bad idea.
(B) He agrees with the proposed solution.
(C) He wants to hear other ideas.
(D) He disagrees with the solution.

56. What was the woman doing in Australia?

(A) Conducting business
(B) Studying abroad
(C) Taking a vacation
(D) Searching for employees

57. What does the woman imply when she says, "is this Robert Wilder's application"?

(A) She is surprised to see the application.
(B) She will reject the application.
(C) She doesn't understand something.
(D) She agrees with the application.

58. How does the woman know Robert Wilder?

(A) They went to college together.
(B) They work in the same department.
(C) They play baseball together.
(D) They play tennis together.

59. What is the woman concerned about?

(A) Getting extra vacation
(B) Doing too much work
(C) Not having time for her children
(D) Preparing a report

60. What does the man suggest?

(A) Fire the manager
(B) Wait until their vacation
(C) Hire a new employee
(D) Have some extra vacation days

61. What does the woman say she will have to do?

(A) Hire a babysitter
(B) Go to another company
(C) Ask her husband
(D) Finish her sales reports

GO ON TO THE NEXT PAGE

Conference Table Price List	
Pine	$165
Maple	$195
Walnut	$225
Cherry	$307

62. What does the woman have on Friday?

(A) A dinner
(B) A seminar
(C) A meeting
(D) An office party

63. Look at the graphic. How much will the woman pay for the furniture?

(A) $165
(B) $195
(C) $307
(D) $614

64. What does the man say he will do?

(A) Arrange free delivery
(B) Deliver the furniture in the evening
(C) Send a confirmation
(D) Deliver the table himself

Airline Mileage Redemption Points	
To East Asia	50,000
To Southeast Asia	60,000
To the Middle East	70,000
To Europe	80,000

65. Why does the woman call?

(A) To get an upgrade
(B) To book a flight to Korea and Japan
(C) To cancel her flight to Singapore
(D) To sign up for a mileage card

66. Look at the graphic. How many points will the woman use?

(A) 50,000
(B) 60,000
(C) 70,000
(D) 80,000

67. What suggestion does the man give the woman?

(A) Upgrade her flight to Korea
(B) Make the request after her trip to Korea and Japan
(C) Book a different flight
(D) Cancel her reservation

68. What are the speakers discussing?

   (A) Their GPS systems
   (B) Which coffee shop to visit
   (C) How far Cambridge is from their
        apartments
   (D) The fastest route to work

69. What does the woman want to do?

   (A) Keep losing the game
   (B) Make more money than the man does
   (C) Get to work faster than the man does
   (D) Participate in a car race

70. Look at the list. Which shop does the man
    most likely stop at?

   (A) Coffee Bean
   (B) Tea Shop
   (C) Java the Cup
   (D) Jake's Diner

GO ON TO THE NEXT PAGE

PART 4 (04)

Directions: You will hear some talks given by a single speaker. You will be asked to answer three questions about what the speaker says in each talk. Select the best response to each question and mark the letter (A), (B), (C), or (D) on your answer sheet. The talks will not be printed in your test book and will be spoken only one time.

71. Where most likely does the speaker work?

    (A) At a theater
    (B) At a car dealership
    (C) At a retail store
    (D) At a library

72. What is the listener asked to double-check?

    (A) Accurate pricing
    (B) Sales figures
    (C) Business hours
    (D) Name tags

73. When should the listener contact the speaker?

    (A) If an employee is late for work
    (B) If a technical problem occurs
    (C) If an item is out of stock
    (D) If a customer is dissatisfied

74. What is the announcement about?

    (A) An opening of a public building
    (B) A commemorative statue
    (C) A singing contest
    (D) A survey result

75. Who is Jim Neilson?

    (A) A mayor
    (B) An instructor
    (C) A musician
    (D) An architect

76. What are attendees asked to do?

    (A) Reserve seats in advance
    (B) Complete a survey
    (C) Subscribe to a newsletter
    (D) Contribute to a fundraiser

77. Who most likely is the speaker?

   (A) A scholar
   (B) A producer
   (C) A pilot
   (D) A programmer

78. Who most likely are the listeners?

   (A) Potential investors
   (B) Actors
   (C) Homemakers
   (D) University students

79. What will the listeners do in the meeting room?

   (A) Participate in a raffle
   (B) Watch a video
   (C) Enroll in a class
   (D) Attend an interview

80. What is the purpose of the broadcast?

   (A) To announce the results of a soccer match
   (B) To promote a store's grand opening
   (C) To advertise a new product
   (D) To inform the listeners of a special event

81. What does the speaker suggest doing?

   (A) Wearing comfortable clothing
   (B) Exercising on a regular basis
   (C) Bringing personal belongings
   (D) Booking a ticket in advance

82. What does the speaker say about the summer camp?

   (A) It is free of charge.
   (B) It will last three months.
   (C) It has a restricted number of participants.
   (D) It will be sponsored by Dave's Sport Shop.

83. What does the speaker mention about her company?

   (A) They have merged with another company.
   (B) They are manufacturing a new product.
   (C) They are creating new policies.
   (D) They had record profits.

84. Why does the woman say, "my schedule is too tight to do that"?

   (A) Because the email is secure
   (B) To sign a new contract
   (C) She needs some help.
   (D) She doesn't have time.

85. What will they be sending a lot of?

   (A) Portfolios
   (B) Contract forms
   (C) Vital data
   (D) Building plans

86. What is *The Tempest* about?

   (A) The evolution of man
   (B) A love affair between a man and a woman
   (C) A ghost ship
   (D) Magic and illusion

87. Why does the speaker say, "remember, last year the Bromley Actors Guild won first place at this event"?

   (A) To suggest that they are impressive
   (B) To recommend that you join them
   (C) To explain why they are here
   (D) To excuse a poor performance

88. What will most likely happen after the performance?

   (A) Dinner and drinks
   (B) Question time with the actors
   (C) DVDs will be sold.
   (D) The actors will sign autographs.

GO ON TO THE NEXT PAGE

89. What types of products are being discussed?

(A) Cell phone cases and selfie sticks
(B) Cell phones and MP3 Players
(C) Selfie sticks and headphones
(D) Software programs

90. Why does the speaker say, "I wonder if the cost is too high compared to the other products on the market"?

(A) To ask for assistance
(B) To offer help
(C) To suggest a change
(D) To create some new products

91. What will the listeners most likely do after lunch?

(A) Review a safety policy
(B) Attend a seminar
(C) Go back to work
(D) Have a conference call

ORDER FORM

Item	Quantity in stock	Quantity to order
Office Table	13	0
Whiteboard	0	12
Office Chair	0	20
Drafting Table	6	0

92. Look at the graphic. Which items need to be ordered?

(A) Office tables and chairs
(B) Chairs and drafting tables
(C) Whiteboards and office chairs
(D) Whiteboards and drafting tables

93. What does the speaker anticipate about the company?

(A) It won't need any more furniture.
(B) It will have more staff in their building.
(C) The boardrooms will be renovated.
(D) Their staff are moving offices.

94. What is the listener asked to do before making any orders?

(A) Sign them herself
(B) Make sure the manager signs them
(C) Bring some extra paper
(D) Prepare a delivery receipt

MARKET SHARE

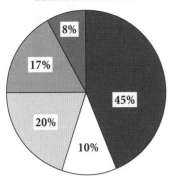

- ■ Future Tech Studios
- ■ AK Gaming
- ■ Seven Strings Technologies
- □ Slight Line, Inc.
- □ Others

95. Which industry does the speaker work in?

(A) Computer hardware
(B) Computer games
(C) Computer software
(D) Computer microchips

96. Look at the graphic. What company does the speaker work for?

(A) Future Tech Studios
(B) Slight Line Inc.
(C) Seven Strings Technologies
(D) AK Gaming

97. According to the speaker, what will the company do in the next quarter?

(A) Give away gifts
(B) Give away expansion packs
(C) Offer free software with new products
(D) Install a new security system

Training Schedule

Tuesday	Wednesday	Thursday	Friday
Basic knife skills and food preparation	Health and safety in the kitchen	Food safety and hygiene	Time management
	Team lunch		Evaluation

98. What are the listeners training to be?

(A) Factory workers
(B) Store owners
(C) Restaurant chefs
(D) Medical workers

99. According to the speaker, what will the listeners enjoy doing?

(A) Working with the celebrity chefs
(B) Becoming a celebrity chef
(C) Using the kitchen tools
(D) Working with each other

100. Look at the graphic. On which day will the listeners learn food safety and hygiene?

(A) Tuesday
(B) Wednesday
(C) Thursday
(D) Friday

This is the end of the Listening test.

LISTENING TEST (05)

In the Listening test, you will be asked to demonstrate how well you understand spoken English. The entire Listening test will last approximately 45 minutes. There are four parts, and directions are given for each part. You must mark your answers on the separate answer sheet. Do not write your answers in your test book.

PART 1

Directions: For each question in this part, you will hear four statements about a picture in your test book. When you hear the statements, you must select the one statement that best describes what you see in the picture. Then find the number of the question on your answer sheet and mark your answer. The statements will not be printed in your test book and will be spoken only one time.

Example

Sample Answer

Ⓐ ● Ⓒ Ⓓ

Statement (B), "They're looking at the document," is the best description of the picture, so you should select answer (B) and mark it on your answer sheet.

1.

2.

GO ON TO THE NEXT PAGE ➔

3.

4.

5.

6.

GO ON TO THE NEXT PAGE

PART 2 (06)

Directions: You will hear a question or statement and three responses spoken in English. They will not be printed in your test book and will be spoken only one time. Select the best response to the question or statement and mark the letter (A), (B), or (C) on your answer sheet.

7. Mark your answer on your answer sheet.

8. Mark your answer on your answer sheet.

9. Mark your answer on your answer sheet.

10. Mark your answer on your answer sheet.

11. Mark your answer on your answer sheet.

12. Mark your answer on your answer sheet.

13. Mark your answer on your answer sheet.

14. Mark your answer on your answer sheet.

15. Mark your answer on your answer sheet.

16. Mark your answer on your answer sheet.

17. Mark your answer on your answer sheet.

18. Mark your answer on your answer sheet.

19. Mark your answer on your answer sheet.

20. Mark your answer on your answer sheet.

21. Mark your answer on your answer sheet.

22. Mark your answer on your answer sheet.

23. Mark your answer on your answer sheet.

24. Mark your answer on your answer sheet.

25. Mark your answer on your answer sheet.

26. Mark your answer on your answer sheet.

27. Mark your answer on your answer sheet.

28. Mark your answer on your answer sheet.

29. Mark your answer on your answer sheet.

30. Mark your answer on your answer sheet.

31. Mark your answer on your answer sheet.

PART 3 (07)

Directions: You will hear some conversations between two or more people. You will be asked to answer three questions about what the speakers say in each conversation. Select the best response to each question and mark the letter (A), (B), (C), or (D) on your answer sheet. The conversations will not be printed in your test book and will be spoken only one time.

32. What are the speakers discussing?

(A) A business trip
(B) A budget proposal
(C) An upcoming conference
(D) A package delivery

33. What problem does the woman mention?

(A) The address is no longer relevant.
(B) A company has gone bankrupt.
(C) A budget must be revised.
(D) A flight has been canceled.

34. What does the woman say she will do?

(A) Review a contract
(B) Go to Tokyo
(C) Visit the post office
(D) Ask for compensation

35. Who most likely is the woman?

(A) A radio host
(B) A professor
(C) A business owner
(D) An athlete

36. What did the woman want to do?

(A) Make use of her education
(B) Open a fitness center
(C) Appear on radio
(D) Teach food and nutrition

37. According to the woman, what is the main reason for her success?

(A) Effective advertisements
(B) Considerable interest in nutrition
(C) Long-term investments
(D) Government policies

GO ON TO THE NEXT PAGE

38. Where most likely are the speakers?

(A) At a children's hospital
(B) At a university
(C) At a music store
(D) At a concert hall

39. What does the woman suggest doing?

(A) Purchasing a piano
(B) Writing a birthday card
(C) Playing string instruments
(D) Attending advanced classes

40. What does the woman give the man?

(A) A receipt
(B) A business card
(C) A map
(D) A pamphlet

41. Who most likely are the speakers?

(A) Show hosts
(B) Advertisers
(C) Television producers
(D) Viewers

42. According to the woman, what is the reason for the problem?

(A) A new product was recalled.
(B) An actor was injured.
(C) A television show was canceled.
(D) A new host is not well-liked.

43. What solution does the man suggest?

(A) Rewriting the script
(B) Replacing the host
(C) Conducting a survey
(D) Placing an advertisement

44. What does the man ask about?

(A) The reason the woman arrived early
(B) The date of the woman's wedding
(C) The name of a client
(D) Directions to the office

45. What will the woman do after work?

(A) Organize a party
(B) Try on a dress
(C) Attend a wedding
(D) Purchase office supplies

46. What will the man probably do next?

(A) Reply to an invitation
(B) Write an email
(C) Order a supply closet
(D) Go to the second floor

47. Where do the speakers work?

(A) At an electronics store
(B) At a software company
(C) At a clothing store
(D) At a photography studio

48. What does the man want to do with the website?

(A) Make the interface easier to use
(B) Enlarge the font
(C) Change the colors
(D) Increase the number of menus

49. What does the woman suggest doing?

(A) Hiring a professional
(B) Lowering the prices
(C) Changing the color scheme
(D) Including more images

50. What does the man talk about?

(A) His upcoming business trip
(B) His co-worker's wedding
(C) Where the conference should be
(D) His unfinished reports

51. What does the woman mention about the venue?

(A) They provide excellent services.
(B) She had her wedding at the venue.
(C) The venue may be booked quickly.
(D) They don't have enough rooms.

52. What does the woman offer to do?

(A) Send out emails.
(B) Work on newsletters.
(C) Contact co-workers.
(D) Help with organizing an event.

53. What are the speakers mainly discussing?

(A) An issue with the new contract
(B) The new contract states a longer vacation period
(C) A vacation in America
(D) Flights and accommodation

54. What does the woman mean when she says, "I'm on my way to an appointment"?

(A) She has a lunch meeting.
(B) She doesn't have much time to talk.
(C) She wants the man to sign the contract.
(D) She has a lot of time to talk.

55. What does the woman want to know?

(A) If he will sign the new contract
(B) If he can come to her office at 3 p.m.
(C) If he is going to Europe for vacation
(D) If he has paid for his trip already

56. What does the man imply when he says, "Some of us from the accounting department are going to Dreamworld on Saturday for a team bonding day"?

(A) He is recommending the theme park.
(B) He needs some documents signed.
(C) He wants the sales figures for this month.
(D) He is inviting her to join them.

57. What does the woman say about her plans?

(A) She can't change them.
(B) She can change them.
(C) They've been cancelled.
(D) They've been postponed.

58. What does the woman offer to do?

(A) Pick everyone up in her car
(B) Meet them at the amusement park
(C) Book the tickets online
(D) Pay for the tickets with cash

59. Where are the speakers planning to go?

(A) To the cinema
(B) To a restaurant
(C) To a friend's house
(D) To a Broadway show

60. What does the woman offer to do?

(A) Buy the tickets
(B) Call John and tell him something
(C) Pick John up in her car
(D) Send John a text message

61. What does the man offer to give to the woman?

(A) Money for parking
(B) A text message
(C) A bottle of champagne
(D) A ride to the show

GO ON TO THE NEXT PAGE

Maxx Cosmetics
Gift Card

10% off any purchase over $50

Expires March 1

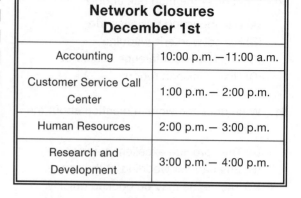

Network Closures December 1st	
Accounting	10:00 p.m.—11:00 a.m.
Customer Service Call Center	1:00 p.m.— 2:00 p.m.
Human Resources	2:00 p.m.— 3:00 p.m.
Research and Development	3:00 p.m.— 4:00 p.m.

62. What does the woman ask the man?

(A) If the body wash is on sale
(B) If he has a loyalty card
(C) If he wants to use a credit card
(D) If the body wash is good

63. Look at the graphic. Why is the gift card rejected?

(A) Because he is in the wrong store
(B) It has already been used too many times.
(C) He doesn't have items over $50.
(D) It has expired.

64. What does the woman offer to do?

(A) Find some other products
(B) Give him a new card
(C) Get her manager
(D) Hold his products at the counter

65. What is happening next month?

(A) An annual software convention
(B) Their software is being upgraded.
(C) The software will be sold early.
(D) The monthly hardware update

66. Look at the graphic. Which department is on the 2nd floor?

(A) Accounting
(B) Human Resources Department
(C) Research and Development
(D) Customer Service Call Center

67. What does the man suggest the woman do?

(A) Call Human Resources
(B) Call her manager
(C) Call the sales department
(D) Call the software company

Airline Mileage Redemption Points ✈	
To East Asia	60,000
To North America	80,000
To South America	90,000
To Europe	70,000

68. Why does the woman call?

(A) To cancel a flight
(B) To register a membership
(C) To use her mileage points
(D) To confirm an appointment

69. Look at the graphic. How many points does the woman currently have?

(A) 20,000 points
(B) 40,000 points
(C) 50,000 points
(D) 70,000 points

70. What does the man ask the woman to tell him?

(A) Her plane ticket
(B) Her membership number
(C) Her cell phone number
(D) Her flight itinerary

GO ON TO THE NEXT PAGE

PART 4 (08)

Directions: You will hear some talks given by a single speaker. You will be asked to answer three questions about what the speaker says in each talk. Select the best response to each question and mark the letter (A), (B), (C), or (D) on your answer sheet. The talks will not be printed in your test book and will be spoken only one time.

71. Who is the message probably for?

    (A) A carpenter
    (B) A store manager
    (C) A furniture designer
    (D) A bank teller

72. According to the speaker, when does he think he lost his wallet?

    (A) When he used a dressing room
    (B) When he visited a bookstore
    (C) When he presented his ID card
    (D) When he tried some furniture

73. What does the speaker plan to do?

    (A) Replace an item
    (B) Call the police
    (C) Go to the store again
    (D) Stop by the listener's home

74. Who most likely is the speaker?

    (A) A historian
    (B) An artist
    (C) An antiques dealer
    (D) A museum guide

75. What is mentioned about the exhibit?

    (A) It is sponsored by the Egyptian government.
    (B) Most of its artifacts had not been seen by the public.
    (C) It will run until the end of the month.
    (D) It includes works from modern Egyptian artists.

76. According to the speaker, how can listeners receive more information?

    (A) By reading a sign
    (B) By searching online
    (C) By purchasing a publication
    (D) By listening to a presentation

77. What has caused the problem?

   (A) A traffic accident
   (B) A heavy workload
   (C) Bad weather
   (D) A vehicle malfunction

78. According to the speaker, around what time will the bus arrive at the destination?

   (A) 4:00 p.m.
   (B) 5:00 p.m.
   (C) 6:00 p.m.
   (D) 7:00 p.m.

79. What does the bus provide to passengers?

   (A) Free Internet access
   (B) A discounted ticket
   (C) A complimentary meal
   (D) A comfortable connecting bus service

80. Who is being introduced?

   (A) A chef
   (B) A backpacker
   (C) A critic
   (D) A producer

81. What is the documentary about?

   (A) World-famous restaurants
   (B) Traditional Chinese cuisine
   (C) A celebrity's life
   (D) Popular recipe books

82. According to the speaker, what can listeners find on the website?

   (A) A review
   (B) A menu
   (C) A preview
   (D) An interview

83. What type of products are being discussed?

   (A) Computer parts
   (B) Hair products
   (C) Beauty products
   (D) Cell phones

84. According to the speaker, what happened last month?

   (A) Sales went down.
   (B) A product launch went better than expected.
   (C) Their products were featured in a magazine.
   (D) Another company took over their contract.

85. What does the woman mean when she says, "How about that?"

   (A) She doesn't understand the situation.
   (B) She expected a customer return policy.
   (C) She wants to purchase some products.
   (D) She is happy with the company's progress.

GO ON TO THE NEXT PAGE

86. According to the speaker, why are changes being made?

   (A) Because of poor working condition
   (B) To save the company money
   (C) So that they can afford a Christmas party
   (D) He expected a better contract.

87. What does the speaker imply when he says, "when the software is installed I don't think you will need any training"?

   (A) The new system is easy to learn.
   (B) He doesn't want to train people.
   (C) There is no budget for training.
   (D) Everyone must attend a meeting.

88. What does the speaker tell the listeners they will have to start bringing to work?

   (A) Extra uniforms
   (B) Other people's lunch
   (C) Their own lunch
   (D) A new contract

---

89. What position is being advertised?

   (A) Legal assistant
   (B) Dental assistant
   (C) Foreign coordinator
   (D) Bank manager

90. What does the man imply when he asks, "Have you seen the criteria for the dental assistant position?"

   (A) He is looking at some forms.
   (B) He is asking if Julia is familiar with the requirements.
   (C) He needs some extra work done.
   (D) He wants to apply for the job.

91. Why does the man want to meet the woman?

   (A) To show him the criteria
   (B) To make some changes to his office
   (C) To sign the contract
   (D) To change the criteria

IN-HOUSE DIRECTORY

Extension	Name
10	John Trizz
11	Don Trenton
12	Shubert Mendez
13	Sally Howle

92. Who most likely is the speaker?

   (A) A content developer
   (B) A secretary
   (C) A company manager
   (D) A police officer

93. Why most likely is the speaker calling?

   (A) To confirm the size of an order
   (B) To request some delivery information
   (C) To send an extra gift
   (D) To purchase a new set of cards

94. Look at the graphic. What is the planner's extension number?

   (A) 10
   (B) 11
   (C) 12
   (D) 13

BEST-SELLING ALBUMS

Rank	Name
1	Talk Down
2	Valleys of Fire
3	Tunnel Vision
4	Step It Up

GRANGE RIVER TOWER DIRECTORY

Floor	Name
3rd Floor	Corporate Suites
4th Floor	Rosella Ballroom
5th Floor	Gloria Westwood Ballroom
6th Floor	Main Office

95. Look at the graphic. What is the name of the guest's new album?

(A) Valleys of Fire
(B) Step It Up
(C) Tunnel Vision
(D) Talk Down

96. What does the speaker say has influenced the guest's music?

(A) Getting married
(B) Moving to America
(C) Moving to London
(D) Meeting Joey Denton

97. What will the guest most likely do next?

(A) Move back to his hometown
(B) Get engaged to his girlfriend
(C) Release a new album
(D) Get married to his girlfriend

98. Look at the graphic. Where is the celebration taking place?

(A) 3rd floor
(B) 4th floor
(C) 5th floor
(D) 6th floor

99. What is the reason for the celebration?

(A) To introduce a new employee
(B) Mr. Jang's birthday
(C) The retirement of Mr. Jang
(D) A wedding anniversary

100. Who is Mr. Hopkins?

(A) Mr. Jang's nephew
(B) An employee of Mr. Jang
(C) The owner of the company
(D) A waiter

This is the end of the Listening test.

LISTENING TEST

In the Listening test, you will be asked to demonstrate how well you understand spoken English. The entire Listening test will last approximately 45 minutes. There are four parts, and directions are given for each part. You must mark your answers on the separate answer sheet. Do not write your answers in your test book.

PART 1

Directions: For each question in this part, you will hear four statements about a picture in your test book. When you hear the statements, you must select the one statement that best describes what you see in the picture. Then find the number of the question on your answer sheet and mark your answer. The statements will not be printed in your test book and will be spoken only one time.

Example

Sample Answer

Ⓐ ● Ⓒ Ⓓ

Statement (B), "They're looking at the document," is the best description of the picture, so you should select answer (B) and mark it on your answer sheet.

1.

2.

GO ON TO THE NEXT PAGE ➡

3.

4.

5.

6.

GO ON TO THE NEXT PAGE

PART 2

Directions: You will hear a question or statement and three responses spoken in English. They will not be printed in your test book and will be spoken only one time. Select the best response to the question or statement and mark the letter (A), (B), or (C) on your answer sheet.

7. Mark your answer on your answer sheet.

8. Mark your answer on your answer sheet.

9. Mark your answer on your answer sheet.

10. Mark your answer on your answer sheet.

11. Mark your answer on your answer sheet.

12. Mark your answer on your answer sheet.

13. Mark your answer on your answer sheet.

14. Mark your answer on your answer sheet.

15. Mark your answer on your answer sheet.

16. Mark your answer on your answer sheet.

17. Mark your answer on your answer sheet.

18. Mark your answer on your answer sheet.

19. Mark your answer on your answer sheet.

20. Mark your answer on your answer sheet.

21. Mark your answer on your answer sheet.

22. Mark your answer on your answer sheet.

23. Mark your answer on your answer sheet.

24. Mark your answer on your answer sheet.

25. Mark your answer on your answer sheet.

26. Mark your answer on your answer sheet.

27. Mark your answer on your answer sheet.

28. Mark your answer on your answer sheet.

29. Mark your answer on your answer sheet.

30. Mark your answer on your answer sheet.

31. Mark your answer on your answer sheet.

Directions: You will hear some conversations between two or more people. You will be asked to answer three questions about what the speakers say in each conversation. Select the best response to each question and mark the letter (A), (B), (C), or (D) on your answer sheet. The conversations will not be printed in your test book and will be spoken only one time.

32. Which department does the man most likely work in?

(A) Human Resources
(B) Accounting
(C) Marketing
(D) Technical Support

33. What is the woman unable to do?

(A) Contact a client
(B) Write an email
(C) Access a file
(D) Purchase a laptop computer

34. What does the man suggest doing?

(A) Stopping by his office
(B) Enrolling in a class
(C) Replacing a part
(D) Reading a manual

35. Why is the man calling?

(A) To request a payment
(B) To confirm an order
(C) To offer a room upgrade
(D) To advertise a product

36. What does the woman inquire about?

(A) Difference in price
(B) Valet parking
(C) Local entities
(D) A warranty period

37. What does the woman say she will do?

(A) Pay by credit card
(B) Compare options
(C) Take pictures
(D) Rearrange her schedule

ACTUAL TEST

03

GO ON TO THE NEXT PAGE

38. Why is the man calling?

(A) To cancel an order
(B) To ask for advice
(C) To purchase an air conditioner
(D) To schedule an appointment

39. How long has the man most likely used the air conditioner?

(A) About a day
(B) About a week
(C) About a month
(D) About a year

40. What information does the woman request?

(A) The year of production
(B) Contact information
(C) A model number
(D) The date of purchase

41. What type of event are the speakers discussing?

(A) A fundraiser
(B) A workshop
(C) An anniversary
(D) A music festival

42. What is the woman concerned about?

(A) Reserving tickets
(B) Finding a parking space
(C) Arriving on time
(D) Accommodating more attendees

43. How is the event different from the one held last year?

(A) There will be a family ticket option.
(B) A shuttle bus will be available.
(C) No cameras will be allowed.
(D) A different place will be used.

44. How did the man find out about the yoga class?

(A) From a public posting
(B) From a coworker
(C) From the woman
(D) From a company's website

45. Why can't the woman attend the yoga class?

(A) She hurt her back.
(B) She can't afford the fee.
(C) She has to take care of her children.
(D) She must attend a different class.

46. What will the woman do next month?

(A) Apply for a new job
(B) Watch the man's jazz dance
(C) Appear in a performance
(D) Register for a class

47. Who most likely is the woman?

(A) A customer service representative
(B) A travel agent
(C) A fashion designer
(D) An event coordinator

48. According to the woman, why can't the item be refunded immediately?

(A) A computer system is not working.
(B) A manager is absent.
(C) It has already been sent.
(D) The man is not eligible for a refund.

49. What does the woman say she will do?

(A) Offer a discount
(B) Send an email
(C) Provide a product catalog
(D) Contact a manager

50. Why is it hot inside the office?

   (A) The air conditioner was on.
   (B) The air conditioner was broken.
   (C) There is no air conditioning.
   (D) The air conditioner had been off.

51. What is the man's problem with the office?

   (A) There is no public transport close by.
   (B) The carpet is not clean.
   (C) The contract is not signed.
   (D) The office is too small.

52. How does the woman respond to the man's problem?

   (A) She tells him they are putting in new carpets.
   (B) She tells him that the carpets aren't dirty.
   (C) She prepares the contract for tomorrow.
   (D) She shows him another office.

53. What are the speakers discussing?

   (A) A real estate deal
   (B) The condition of the property
   (C) The terms of a contract
   (D) Renovating the property

54. Why does the woman say, "I've had several other offers that are higher than that from other real estate agents"?

   (A) To offer a contract
   (B) To negotiate a higher price
   (C) To settle a deal
   (D) To recommend a realtor

55. Why is the woman pleased?

   (A) Because she completed her work.
   (B) The renovations will go ahead.
   (C) She found a new realtor.
   (D) The buyer will pay more money.

56. Where do the speakers most likely work?

   (A) A research facility
   (B) A legal firm
   (C) A construction company
   (D) A pharmacy

57. What does the man mean when he says, "I've been meaning to visit him"?

   (A) He has already visited him.
   (B) He knows that he should have visited him.
   (C) He will visit him tonight.
   (D) He forgot about it.

58. What will the woman include in her email?

   (A) When to visit Joseph
   (B) The contract details
   (C) Joseph's phone number
   (D) The lawyer's documents

59. What kind of work are the men doing?

   (A) Remodeling the foyer
   (B) Renovating the bathrooms
   (C) Repainting the foyer
   (D) Renovating the kitchen

60. What does the man explain to the woman?

   (A) Why she has a low budget
   (B) Why the price is above her budget
   (C) Why the foyer isn't ready to be painted
   (D) Why the paint in the foyer is peeling

61. When does the woman want the men to begin work?

   (A) The second week of September
   (B) Anytime during August
   (C) After August
   (D) The first Saturday of August

GO ON TO THE NEXT PAGE

Nutrition Information	
Serving Size: 150 g	
Calories	**200**
Fat	5 grs
Protein	10 grs
Sugar	28 grs

Frankie's Dry Cleaning	
Fabric	Price
Polyester	$10
Cotton	$12
Wool	$20
Silk	$30

62. What is the woman trying to do?

(A) Gain some weight
(B) Eat foods with more sugar
(C) Skip breakfast
(D) Lose some weight

63. Look at the graphic. Which content is the woman concerned about?

(A) Fat
(B) Sugar
(C) Protein
(D) Eggs

64. What does the man recommend the woman do?

(A) Have some bacon and eggs
(B) Just drink coffee in the morning
(C) Don't eat breakfast
(D) Have coffee and eggs

65. What does the man say he will do on the weekend?

(A) Go on a vacation
(B) Host a business lunch
(C) Go on a business trip
(D) Get some new suits

66. Look at the graphic. What is the suit made of?

(A) Polyester
(B) Silk
(C) Cotton
(D) Wool

67. What does the woman say she will do?

(A) She won't do it for twenty dollars.
(B) She will charge the man the original price.
(C) She will do it for more than twenty dollars.
(D) She will do it by next week.

Franklin Towers

First floor: Trinity Construction
Second Floor: Mullberry & Co.
Third Floor: Olive Cosmetics
Fourth Floor: Torrenz Inc.

68. Who most likely are the speakers?

(A) Plumbers
(B) Office workers
(C) Electricians
(D) Carpet cleaners

69. Look at the graphic. Where is the woman currently working?

(A) Trinity Construction
(B) Mullberry & Co.
(C) Olive Cosmetics
(D) Torrenz Inc.

70. What does the woman ask the man to do?

(A) Install some piping in the wall
(B) Install some cables in the ground
(C) Install some cables in the roof
(D) Install some new software on the computers

GO ON TO THE NEXT PAGE

PART 4 🎧 12

Directions: You will hear some talks given by a single speaker. You will be asked to answer three questions about what the speaker says in each talk. Select the best response to each question and mark the letter (A), (B), (C), or (D) on your answer sheet. The talks will not be printed in your test book and will be spoken only one time.

71. Why is the speaker calling?

(A) To order food delivery
(B) To advertise a cooking class
(C) To report a problem
(D) To make a reservation

72. What will the speaker celebrate next week?

(A) A birthday
(B) A promotion
(C) A retirement
(D) A wedding

73. What does the speaker want the listener to do?

(A) Contact some guests
(B) Decorate a space
(C) Meet special dietary needs
(D) Prepare an estimate

74. What does the factory produce?

(A) Appliances
(B) Clothes
(C) Toys
(D) Shoes

75. What is special about the factory?

(A) Its size
(B) Its production method
(C) Its automated machines
(D) Its location

76. What will listeners do at the end of the tour?

(A) Participate in a hands-on experience
(B) Receive a free product
(C) Have refreshments
(D) Return to the tour bus

77. What will happen next week?

(A) A budget proposal
(B) A business event
(C) A performance evaluation
(D) A shareholders' meeting

78. What benefit does the speaker mention?

(A) Fewer complaints
(B) Reduced travel time
(C) Access to clients
(D) Strengthened security

79. What are the listeners asked to do?

(A) Delete unnecessary data
(B) Submit a report
(C) Contact clients directly
(D) Email an order confirmation

80. Who most likely are the listeners?

(A) Professional novelists
(B) University professors
(C) Potential writers
(D) Prospective clients

81. What are the listeners asked to do?

(A) Fill out a questionnaire
(B) Attach a name tag
(C) Introduce themselves
(D) Read a book

82. Who is Natasha Marsh?

(A) An athlete
(B) A children's author
(C) An event organizer
(D) A guest speaker

83. According to the speaker, what is happening?

(A) A new product is being released.
(B) The store is closing down.
(C) Their staff are all quitting.
(D) The company is shooting a commercial.

84. What does the speaker mean when she says, "you'd think they were giving the shoes away"?

(A) The store is giving the shoes away.
(B) There are a lot of people waiting to buy the product.
(C) They ran out of stock.
(D) A few people were upset about the product.

85. According to the speaker, what is WingTip offering the first 100 customers?

(A) 10% discount
(B) A new pair of headphones
(C) Free shoes
(D) Special edition shoes

GO ON TO THE NEXT PAGE

86. According to the speaker, how can we see the value of Mr. Hardwell's work?

    (A) By looking at all the paintings on his walls
    (B) By looking at all the pictures on his walls
    (C) By looking at all the fan mail in his office
    (D) By looking at all the special awards on his desk

87. Why does the speaker say, "I think it's safe to say Mr. Hardwell should leave some room on his walls"?

    (A) To discuss another issue
    (B) To suggest he is going to continue doing more work
    (C) To recommend a friend to him
    (D) To make sure the audience is familiar with him

88. What will Mr. Hardwell do today?

    (A) Share some of his business knowledge
    (B) Preview the book and show some video
    (C) Read some excerpts from his book
    (D) Read a chapter from his book

---

89. Where does the speaker most likely work?

    (A) In a law office
    (B) In a fashion company
    (C) In an airline company
    (D) In an accounting firm

90. Why does the speaker say, "I was out of town on a business trip"?

    (A) To explain why she hadn't called
    (B) To arrange an appointment
    (C) To sign the contract
    (D) To discuss the building plan

91. What does the speaker offer to the woman?

    (A) A free plane ticket
    (B) Another portfolio
    (C) A deposit for rent
    (D) A possible contract

Order Form 5521673 Customer: Winbox Computers	
Item	**Quantity**
Cold meat tray	3
Mixed salad plates	5
12 pack bread rolls	2
Cutlery sets	10

92. What type of event is being catered?

    (A) A business dinner
    (B) A business luncheon
    (C) A corporate breakfast
    (D) An annual picnic

93. Look at the graphic. Which items were not changed?

    (A) Cold meat trays and mixed salad plates
    (B) 12 pack bread rolls
    (C) Cutlery sets
    (D) Cutlery sets and bread rolls

94. What is the listener asked to do?

    (A) Send an email confirmation
    (B) Call the man to confirm the changes
    (C) Not to change the order
    (D) Cancel the whole order

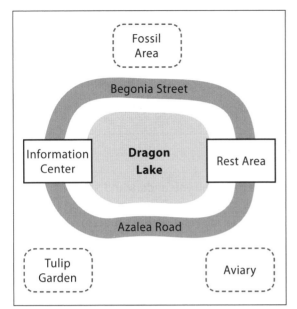

HEIRLOOM TOMATOES!
Prices are per pound~

Black Cherry	$1.09
Brandywine	$1.39
Black Krim	$2.64
Amana Orange	$1.30

98. When will the special sale be over?

(A) Monday
(B) Saturday
(C) Sunday
(D) It is weekly.

99. What is indicated about Granville Produce?

(A) They have a wide variety of potatoes.
(B) They highlight their heirloom tomatoes.
(C) They are an inexpensive grocer.
(D) They have been in business for several years.

100. Look at the graphic. Why is the Brandywine such a good deal?

(A) It is cheaper than the Black Krim.
(B) It is a delicious tomato.
(C) It is normally over a dollar more expensive per pound.
(D) It is normally not in season.

95. Who most likely is the speaker?

(A) President of the Maryland Florist Association
(B) President of the annual florist convention
(C) President of Tulip Garden
(D) President of the rest area

96. Look at the graphic. Where will the listeners go first?

(A) The Aviary
(B) Begonia Street
(C) Dragon Lake
(D) Azalea Road

97. What does the speaker encourage listeners to do before they leave?

(A) Visit the Tulip Garden
(B) Buy some flowers
(C) Pick some roses
(D) Visit the Aviary

This is the end of the Listening test.

LISTENING TEST

In the Listening test, you will be asked to demonstrate how well you understand spoken English. The entire Listening test will last approximately 45 minutes. There are four parts, and directions are given for each part. You must mark your answers on the separate answer sheet. Do not write your answers in your test book.

PART 1

Directions: For each question in this part, you will hear four statements about a picture in your test book. When you hear the statements, you must select the one statement that best describes what you see in the picture. Then find the number of the question on your answer sheet and mark your answer. The statements will not be printed in your test book and will be spoken only one time.

Example

Sample Answer

Statement (B), "They're looking at the document," is the best description of the picture, so you should select answer (B) and mark it on your answer sheet.

1.

2.

GO ON TO THE NEXT PAGE ➡

3.

4.

5.

6.

GO ON TO THE NEXT PAGE

PART 2 🎧 14

7. Mark your answer on your answer sheet.

8. Mark your answer on your answer sheet.

9. Mark your answer on your answer sheet.

10. Mark your answer on your answer sheet.

11. Mark your answer on your answer sheet.

12. Mark your answer on your answer sheet.

13. Mark your answer on your answer sheet.

14. Mark your answer on your answer sheet.

15. Mark your answer on your answer sheet.

16. Mark your answer on your answer sheet.

17. Mark your answer on your answer sheet.

18. Mark your answer on your answer sheet.

19. Mark your answer on your answer sheet.

20. Mark your answer on your answer sheet.

21. Mark your answer on your answer sheet.

22. Mark your answer on your answer sheet.

23. Mark your answer on your answer sheet.

24. Mark your answer on your answer sheet.

25. Mark your answer on your answer sheet.

26. Mark your answer on your answer sheet.

27. Mark your answer on your answer sheet.

28. Mark your answer on your answer sheet.

29. Mark your answer on your answer sheet.

30. Mark your answer on your answer sheet.

31. Mark your answer on your answer sheet.

PART 3 ◀15▶

Directions: You will hear some conversations between two or more people. You will be asked to answer three questions about what the speakers say in each conversation. Select the best response to each question and mark the letter (A), (B), (C), or (D) on your answer sheet. The conversations will not be printed in your test book and will be spoken only one time.

32. What did the man recently do?

(A) Purchased a house
(B) Went on a business trip
(C) Signed up for a service
(D) Installed a television

33. Why must the man pay a fee?

(A) He wants to change his schedule.
(B) He returned an item late.
(C) He lost his membership card.
(D) He needs an additional service.

34. What will the woman include in an email?

(A) A receipt
(B) Log-in information
(C) A membership contract
(D) Driving directions

35. What does the woman say caused the problem?

(A) A repair cost has increased.
(B) A reservation has been canceled.
(C) A client arrived too late.
(D) A tire needed to be replaced.

36. Why is the man concerned?

(A) He lost an important receipt.
(B) He needs a car to greet a client.
(C) He has to reschedule a meeting.
(D) He was unable to contact a client.

37. What does the woman suggest?

(A) Preparing an alternative plan
(B) Ordering a replacement part
(C) Attending a conference
(D) Reserving a less expensive ticket

GO ON TO THE NEXT PAGE

38. What problem is the woman reporting?

    (A) An accounting error has been made.
    (B) A printer is out of order.
    (C) Some office supplies have run out.
    (D) A document has been lost.

39. What does the man ask the woman to do?

    (A) Check some product information
    (B) Install new equipment
    (C) Update customer information
    (D) Stop by his office

40. What is mentioned about Mr. Hills?

    (A) He is in charge of a new project.
    (B) He is in the same department as the
        woman.
    (C) He has recently ordered a new item.
    (D) He wrote a hardware list.

41. How did the man learn about the store?

    (A) By watching television
    (B) By talking to a friend
    (C) By reading a brochure
    (D) By listening to the radio

42. According to the woman, what is being
    offered this month?

    (A) A discount coupon
    (B) A reduced membership fee
    (C) Free delivery
    (D) A lifetime warranty

43. What does the woman suggest doing?

    (A) Paying in advance
    (B) Getting measurements taken
    (C) Submitting a proposal
    (D) Hiring an assistant

44. What kind of services are the speakers
    discussing?

    (A) Catering for company events
    (B) Business consultation
    (C) Workforce training
    (D) Delivery services

45. Why has the man NOT used Rose and Lily
    Co.'s services before?

    (A) He was unaware of them.
    (B) He was reluctant to pay a membership
        fee.
    (C) He was on bad terms with the owner.
    (D) He did not realize their availability.

46. What does the man ask the woman to do?

    (A) Try some food and beverages
    (B) Send a catalog
    (C) Provide a sample
    (D) Expedite an order

47. What does the woman say she has heard
    about?

    (A) The joining of two businesses
    (B) The construction of a factory
    (C) An international conference
    (D) A highway expansion project

48. What benefit does the man mention?

    (A) Lower insurance costs
    (B) Increased vacation days
    (C) International competitiveness
    (D) Updated equipment

49. What does the man suggest the woman
    do?

    (A) Visit his office
    (B) Post an advertisement
    (C) Submit a proposal
    (D) Check job listings

50. What is the reason for Joseph's call?

(A) To relate a problem concerning the apartment
(B) To sign the contract for the apartment
(C) To discuss another apartment
(D) To discuss the price of rent

51. What does Joseph say about the Kahlua Apartment?

(A) It's ready to be occupied anytime.
(B) There are renovations occurring.
(C) It is near a new fitness center.
(D) There is a major pest problem.

52. What does Joseph offer to do?

(A) Find a new apartment at Graceville Towers
(B) Arrange all of the moving
(C) Move her furniture personally
(D) Move into the Kahlua Apartment building

53. Why is the woman calling the man?

(A) To ask a favor of him
(B) To order some flowers
(C) To find a rental property
(D) To rent a house

54. What does the woman say she has done recently?

(A) Been promoted at her company
(B) Closed down her business
(C) Got a new job
(D) Opened her own business

55. Why does the man say, "What's your afternoon like"?

(A) To figure out when they can meet
(B) To ask her to dinner
(C) To explain rental conditions
(D) To get some keys for the office

56. What did the company do recently?

(A) Renovated the lobby
(B) Built new research facilities
(C) Hired new staff
(D) Built new offices

57. What does the woman mean when she says, "it's about time"?

(A) She thinks the company deserves to have new offices.
(B) She thinks construction has taken too long.
(C) She doesn't like the new offices.
(D) She wants a raise in her salary.

58. What does the woman imply about the company?

(A) They have been very lucky to grow so fast.
(B) Some of the staff is not working hard.
(C) The company worked hard to grow fast.
(D) The new offices aren't very nice.

59. What are the speakers mainly discussing?

(A) Getting ready for a work party
(B) Getting the sales report ready
(C) Getting ready for a promotion
(D) Getting ready to finish the quarter

60. What does the man say about Andrew?

(A) That he left work early the night before
(B) That he thinks Andrew isn't a hard worker
(C) That he worked late the night before
(D) That he had a good quarter

61. What does Roger tell Andrew to do?

(A) Send a letter to Roger when he is finished
(B) Bring the email to the meeting
(C) Not to come to the meeting
(D) Send an email when he is finished

GO ON TO THE NEXT PAGE

ACTUAL TEST

04

Part A — 90 mm Bolts

Part B — 25 mm Wood Screws

Part C — Barrel Nuts x 6

Part D — Long Allen Key x 1

Bridge closed until
Jan. 12 due to upgrade of
infrastructure

62. Where does the man most likely work?

(A) At a university
(B) At a furniture store
(C) At a bedding store
(D) At a technical college

63. Look at the graphic. What is the woman missing?

(A) 90 mm Bolts
(B) Wood Screws
(C) Barrel Nuts
(D) Allen Key

64. What does the man offer to do?

(A) Deliver the parts to her house by post
(B) Deliver the parts to her house in person
(C) Have the parts delivered by his staff
(D) Leave the parts at the front counter

65. According to the woman, what is causing people to arrive late to work?

(A) A meeting was postponed.
(B) The bridge was very busy.
(C) The bridge was closed.
(D) They had car problems.

66. Look at the graphic. Where is the sign most likely located?

(A) The Brooklyn Bridge
(B) The Tower Bridge
(C) The East Bay Tunnel
(D) The Express Tunnel

67. What does the woman recommend to the man?

(A) Take the bus to work
(B) Share a taxi to work
(C) Take the subway to work
(D) Take the Express Tunnel

Fisherman's Wharf
Discount Coupon

10% off any order above $100

Expires November 1st

68. Where most likely are the speakers?

(A) In a hospital
(B) In a restaurant
(C) In a bar
(D) In a hotel

69. Look at the graphic. Why is the coupon rejected?

(A) The order was above $100.
(B) It is expired.
(C) Their order was below $100.
(D) The coupon didn't have credit on it.

70. What does the woman offer to do?

(A) Give them a new card
(B) Put the coupon in the computer system
(C) Hold the card for them
(D) Provide a refund

GO ON TO THE NEXT PAGE

PART 4 (16)

Directions: You will hear some talks given by a single speaker. You will be asked to answer three questions about what the speaker says in each talk. Select the best response to each question and mark the letter (A), (B), (C), or (D) on your answer sheet. The talks will not be printed in your test book and will be spoken only one time.

71. What is causing the delay?

    (A) Bad weather
    (B) A canceled flight
    (C) A scheduling error
    (D) A technical difficulty

72. According to the speaker, after how long will the presentation begin?

    (A) 5 minutes
    (B) 30 minutes
    (C) 45 minutes
    (D) 60 minutes

73. What will happen when it's time for the presentation to begin?

    (A) An announcement will be made.
    (B) Lighting will be adjusted.
    (C) A keynote speaker will appear on the stage.
    (D) Refreshments will be served.

74. What is the radio broadcast about?

    (A) The opening of a pet store
    (B) A newly introduced law
    (C) A new council hall
    (D) An upcoming election

75. According to the speaker, what did Tim Kellerman do recently?

    (A) He ran for office.
    (B) He won an award.
    (C) He selected a pet.
    (D) He paid a fine.

76. What will listeners most likely hear next?

    (A) A weather forecast
    (B) Some breaking news
    (C) Community members' opinions
    (D) A telephone interview

77. Where should listeners get carts?

(A) In the parking lot
(B) At the entrance
(C) Near the lobby
(D) From a cashier

78. According to the speaker, who is wearing green vests?

(A) Cashiers
(B) Store managers
(C) Additional staff
(D) Parking lot attendants

79. What will the speaker most likely do at the end of the day?

(A) Announce winners
(B) Collect donations
(C) Give a demonstration
(D) Purchase an item

80. What business is being advertised?

(A) A computer retailer
(B) An electronics repair shop
(C) An office supply store
(D) A cosmetics store

81. What service is available in April?

(A) Installment payments
(B) Express shipping
(C) Online assistance
(D) Free installation

82. How can listeners get a discount?

(A) By bringing a coupon
(B) By buying in bulk
(C) By becoming a regular customer
(D) By signing up for a newsletter

83. According to the speaker, why are changes being made?

(A) The government took the company to court
(B) To conform to government regulations
(C) To enact a new labor law
(D) To arrange lower-paying contracts

84. What does the speaker imply when she says, "it's a very simple device; you just attach it to your work belt and it will do the rest, so you won't need any training with that"?

(A) The new system requires no training.
(B) She doesn't like the new system.
(C) There is no budget for staff uniforms.
(D) Everyone needs training.

85. What does the speaker tell the listeners they will have to start bringing to work?

(A) Extra pairs of work pants
(B) Other people's helmets
(C) Their own boots and helmets
(D) A new financial plan

GO ON TO THE NEXT PAGE →

86. According to the man, what did the company recently do?

    (A) Began operating out of Beijing
    (B) Began operating in India
    (C) Hired some new designers
    (D) Created some special dishes

87. What most likely will the Xinhua Fashion magazine do next Thursday?

    (A) Interview the models
    (B) Make a video of the street outside
    (C) Photograph clothing
    (D) Sign a new contract

88. What does the man mean when he says, "our success is going to skyrocket"?

    (A) Their business is going to grow quickly
    (B) They will discuss the future plan
    (C) They will prevent the photo shoot
    (D) They will transfer some documents via mail

89. According to the speaker, who is introducing the new regulations?

    (A) The Board of Directors
    (B) Head Office
    (C) Management
    (D) The secretary

90. What does the speaker imply when she says, "we really need to stay on top of this, or some people might get fired"?

    (A) There is a lot of work to do.
    (B) It isn't that important.
    (C) They can wait a week to start.
    (D) The project will begin soon.

91. What does the speaker tell the listeners to do?

    (A) Bring their lunch to work
    (B) Occasionally work on Saturdays
    (C) Work every Sunday
    (D) Have some time off on Saturday

This Weekend's Events in Columbia

Afternoon Theater
Columbia's own theater troupe stages short versions of classic plays for free in Central Park every Thursday at noon.

Friday Night Concert in the Park Series
The show begins at 8:30 P.M. and lasts until 10:30 P.M.!

Midnight Wine Tasting
Regional wines sampled under the stars at the Black Cat, every Friday and Saturday night!

Appropriate for all ages!

92. What kind of transportation company is Continental Lines?

    (A) Bus
    (B) Train
    (C) Limousine
    (D) Taxi

93. What is the last stop for Continental Lines this trip?

    (A) Charleston
    (B) Columbia
    (C) Eastport
    (D) Chesterville

94. Look at the graphic. What activity will still be available for the passengers to participate in when they arrive in Columbia?

    (A) None
    (B) Friday Night Concert in the Park
    (C) Afternoon Theater
    (D) Midnight Wine Tasting

Customer Service FAQ Analysis

Disputed Long Distance/Overcharges	37%
Disputed Data Charges	36%
Service Plan Change	11%
Dropped Calls	9%
Replacement Phones	5%
Miscellaneous	2%

95. What is indicated about Monster Telecom?

(A) They are having customer service problems.
(B) There are too many calls for the number of employees.
(C) Customer service is not important to them.
(D) They need to hire more people.

96. Look at the graphic. What areas should the leaders focus their training on?

(A) How to deal with upset customers by overcharges
(B) Knowledge of all of the service plans
(C) Helping customers replace phones
(D) Knowledge of Monster Telecom's cellular coverage area

97. What is the goal for Monster Telecom?

(A) Reduce the number of dropped calls
(B) Expand their coverage area
(C) Add new cellular phone options
(D) Reduce the number of customer calls they receive by 50%

LAP POOL SIGN-UP SHEET

LANE	9:00 a.m.	10:00 a.m.	11:00 a.m.	12:00 p.m.	1:00 p.m.	2:00 p.m.	3:00 p.m.	4:00 p.m.	5:00 p.m.
1									
2									
3									

98. What is indicated about Springdale Fitness Club?

(A) They have a tennis court.
(B) They take pride in their customer service.
(C) They specialize in children's pool parties.
(D) They have a variety of swimming facilities.

99. Look at the graphic. What are the hours of the lap pool?

(A) 8 a.m. to 5 p.m.
(B) 9 a.m. to 5 p.m.
(C) 9 a.m. to 6 p.m.
(D) 8 a.m. to 6 p.m.

100. What does Springdale Fitness Club say about the new lap pool?

(A) It is Olympic size.
(B) It has four lanes.
(C) It's for serious swimmers.
(D) It will host weekly races.

This is the end of the Listening test.

LISTENING TEST

In the Listening test, you will be asked to demonstrate how well you understand spoken English. The entire Listening test will last approximately 45 minutes. There are four parts, and directions are given for each part. You must mark your answers on the separate answer sheet. Do not write your answers in your test book.

PART 1

Directions: For each question in this part, you will hear four statements about a picture in your test book. When you hear the statements, you must select the one statement that best describes what you see in the picture. Then find the number of the question on your answer sheet and mark your answer. The statements will not be printed in your test book and will be spoken only one time.

Example

Sample Answer

Ⓐ ● Ⓒ Ⓓ

Statement (B), "They're looking at the document," is the best description of the picture, so you should select answer (B) and mark it on your answer sheet.

1.

2.

GO ON TO THE NEXT PAGE ⟶

ACTUAL TEST

05

3.

4.

5.

6.

GO ON TO THE NEXT PAGE

PART 2 🎧 18

7. Mark your answer on your answer sheet.

8. Mark your answer on your answer sheet.

9. Mark your answer on your answer sheet.

10. Mark your answer on your answer sheet.

11. Mark your answer on your answer sheet.

12. Mark your answer on your answer sheet.

13. Mark your answer on your answer sheet.

14. Mark your answer on your answer sheet.

15. Mark your answer on your answer sheet.

16. Mark your answer on your answer sheet.

17. Mark your answer on your answer sheet.

18. Mark your answer on your answer sheet.

19. Mark your answer on your answer sheet.

20. Mark your answer on your answer sheet.

21. Mark your answer on your answer sheet.

22. Mark your answer on your answer sheet.

23. Mark your answer on your answer sheet.

24. Mark your answer on your answer sheet.

25. Mark your answer on your answer sheet.

26. Mark your answer on your answer sheet.

27. Mark your answer on your answer sheet.

28. Mark your answer on your answer sheet.

29. Mark your answer on your answer sheet.

30. Mark your answer on your answer sheet.

31. Mark your answer on your answer sheet.

PART 3 🎧 19

Directions: You will hear some conversations between two or more people. You will be asked to answer three questions about what the speakers say in each conversation. Select the best response to each question and mark the letter (A), (B), (C), or (D) on your answer sheet. The conversations will not be printed in your test book and will be spoken only one time.

32. What is the woman's problem?

    (A) A meeting room is occupied.
    (B) A piece of equipment is out of stock.
    (C) An appointment has been canceled.
    (D) Some software is not installed.

33. Why does the man mention a system malfunction?

    (A) To apologize for an incorrect charge
    (B) To explain a scheduling error
    (C) To warn of security threats
    (D) To change a company policy

34. What does the man say he will do?

    (A) Fix a computer
    (B) Provide an alternative
    (C) Attend a meeting
    (D) Check the employee manual

35. What does the woman ask the man about?

    (A) How to write a report
    (B) Whether a document is finished
    (C) How to reserve a meeting room
    (D) Whether a client has been contacted

36. What does the man say he will do?

    (A) Prioritize the woman's request
    (B) Extend a deadline
    (C) Draft a budget
    (D) Visit the woman's office

37. What does the woman need?

    (A) A list of clients
    (B) A sample product
    (C) Meeting materials
    (D) A revised itinerary

38. What career is the woman interested in?

    (A) College professor
    (B) Web programmer
    (C) Dental assistant
    (D) Financial adviser

39. What does the woman say she will do?

    (A) Submit an application
    (B) Inquire about a loan
    (C) Consult a doctor
    (D) Apply for a scholarship

40. According to the man, what advantage does the college offer?

    (A) Convenient class times
    (B) Small class sizes
    (C) Advanced level courses
    (D) Reduced tuition

41. Where most likely do the speakers work?

    (A) At a software company
    (B) At a marketing firm
    (C) At a travel agency
    (D) At a graphic design company

42. What is the woman's complaint about the training session?

    (A) There were not enough seats.
    (B) The registration fee was too high.
    (C) There was no time for inquiries.
    (D) The instructor's presentation was lengthy.

43. What does the man suggest?

    (A) Attending another training session
    (B) Transferring to a new department
    (C) Reviewing a training manual
    (D) Contacting the instructor

44. What is the topic of the conversation?

    (A) A pay raise
    (B) An upcoming deadline
    (C) A prescription for the flu
    (D) A new work procedure

45. What does the woman ask about?

    (A) Pay compensation
    (B) Promotion opportunities
    (C) Sick leave availability
    (D) Official forms

46. What will the man most likely do next?

    (A) Send an email
    (B) Revise a budget
    (C) Deliver a document
    (D) Call a doctor

47. Where most likely does the man work?

    (A) At a real estate agency
    (B) At a bank
    (C) At an art gallery
    (D) At a landscaping agency

48. How long does the man say the woman will have to wait?

    (A) For a day
    (B) For a week
    (C) For a month
    (D) For two months

49. What information will the man send the woman?

    (A) A job opening
    (B) An itinerary
    (C) A price quote
    (D) A meeting agenda

50. What does the man ask about?

(A) A lunch meeting location
(B) The schedule for the week
(C) The budget reports
(D) A client list

51. What does the woman remind the man about?

(A) A dinner meeting
(B) A restaurant reservation
(C) A presentation
(D) A client's demands

52. What does the woman offer to do?

(A) Meet with a colleague
(B) Talk to a client
(C) Call some coworkers
(D) Organize the reports

53. What is the problem?

(A) The man forgot to book his plane ticket.
(B) The flight is delayed.
(C) The flight is canceled.
(D) The man lost his ticket.

54. What solution does the woman propose?

(A) To book a bus for the man
(B) To pay for his hotel room
(C) To send him documents
(D) To call his client in Vancouver

55. What does the man mean when he says, "that's not a bad idea"?

(A) He wants a better solution.
(B) He agrees with the proposed solution.
(C) He would like to hear more options.
(D) He wants to keep the plane ticket.

56. What was the woman doing in New York?

(A) Taking a vacation
(B) Visiting family
(C) Looking for new staff
(D) Meeting clients

57. What does the woman imply when she says, "are they real"?

(A) The flowers look really bad.
(B) The flowers look fake.
(C) She is surprised to see them.
(D) She thinks they are real.

58. What does the man offer to do?

(A) Give her a promotion
(B) Send her a gift card
(C) Have flowers delivered to her office
(D) Send her to New York

59. Why is the man calling Jennifer?

(A) To ask about her vacation
(B) To transfer her to another department
(C) To ask about a money transfer
(D) To talk to Mr. Woods

60. What does Grace say about the bank?

(A) They were closed when she got there.
(B) They are having problems with their computers.
(C) She emailed the receipt.
(D) She couldn't find the location.

61. What does the man say he needs?

(A) The transfer receipt
(B) The bank check
(C) The company credit card
(D) The transfer system

GO ON TO THE NEXT PAGE →

Subway Closures September 24th	
Line 2	6:00 a.m. – 10:00 a.m.
Line 4	10:00 a.m. – 11:00 a.m.
Line 6	11:00 a.m. – 12:00 p.m.
Line 7	1:00 p.m. – 2:00 p.m.

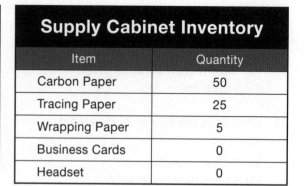

Supply Cabinet Inventory	
Item	Quantity
Carbon Paper	50
Tracing Paper	25
Wrapping Paper	5
Business Cards	0
Headset	0

62. Why is the subway being closed on September 24th?

(A) To upgrade the audio system
(B) Because the drivers are striking
(C) There is a safety issue
(D) Problems with the air conditioner

63. Look at the graphic. Which subway line do the speakers need to take?

(A) Line 6
(B) Line 7
(C) Line 2
(D) Line 4

64. What does the man suggest doing?

(A) Taking the subway
(B) Using the taxi service
(C) Taking the bus
(D) Driving his car

65. Why do they need to send the order today?

(A) Because the company is closing for Christmas
(B) Because the company is closing for New Years
(C) The company doesn't have the item.
(D) They have delayed the order.

66. Look at the graphic. What will the man NOT order for the woman?

(A) Wrapping paper
(B) A headset
(C) Business cards
(D) Carbon paper

67. What does the woman ask the man to do?

(A) Send her the order form
(B) Send her a headset
(C) Revise the memo
(D) Send a receipt

Nutrition Information	
Serving Size: 150 g	
Calories	**173**
Fat	5 g
Protein	10 g
Sugar	22 g
Sodium	60 mg
Caffeine	80 mg

68. Why is the man looking for a certain product?

(A) He is on a diet.
(B) He doesn't like sugar.
(C) He will compete in a race.
(D) He has a test soon.

69. Look at the graphic. Which of the ingredients is the man interested in?

(A) Fat
(B) Sugar
(C) Caffeine
(D) Protein

70. What does the woman suggest the man do?

(A) Drink a lot of caffeine before taking the gel
(B) Don't drink a lot of caffeine before taking the gel
(C) Drink some caffeine before bed
(D) Drink some caffeine in the morning

GO ON TO THE NEXT PAGE

PART 4 (20)

Directions: You will hear some talks given by a single speaker. You will be asked to answer three questions about what the speaker says in each talk. Select the best response to each question and mark the letter (A), (B), (C), or (D) on your answer sheet. The talks will not be printed in your test book and will be spoken only one time.

71. Where does the speaker work?

(A) At a retail store
(B) At a bank
(C) At a gift shop
(D) At a shipping company

72. What does the speaker apologize for?

(A) A delivery mistake
(B) An incorrect charge
(C) A scheduling error
(D) A defective product

73. What does the speaker ask the listener to do?

(A) Return a call
(B) Renew his credit card
(C) Get rid of the recently delivered card
(D) Sign an application form

74. Where is the announcement being made?

(A) In a subway station
(B) In a conference hall
(C) In a shopping mall
(D) In a baggage claim area

75. What are the listeners asked to do?

(A) Proceed to the checkout immediately
(B) Register for a workshop
(C) Search for a missing item
(D) Visit a different location

76. Why should Ms. Goya go to the front desk?

(A) To pay a membership fee
(B) To recover a lost item
(C) To receive a voucher
(D) To return an item

77. What business created the message?

    (A) A glassware factory
    (B) A pharmacy
    (C) An eyeglasses store
    (D) An insurance company

78. According to the speaker, what service does the business offer?

    (A) Free eye examinations
    (B) Online purchases
    (C) Special discounts for regular customers
    (D) Free delivery on large orders

79. Why would listeners press 2?

    (A) To cancel an order
    (B) To change delivery information
    (C) To schedule an appointment
    (D) To leave a message

---

80. What special feature of the new laptop does the speaker mention?

    (A) It is the lightest in the market.
    (B) It has a built-in high-definition camera.
    (C) It is water resistant.
    (D) It is convenient to carry.

81. How can customers purchase the new laptop?

    (A) By accessing a website
    (B) By stopping by the speaker's office
    (C) By visiting a local store
    (D) By calling a customer service hotline

82. What can customers receive this week?

    (A) An additional battery
    (B) A carrying case
    (C) A portable speaker
    (D) A small printer

83. What is the reason for the meeting?

    (A) To announce a new partnership
    (B) To introduce a new manager
    (C) To propose a budget plan
    (D) To announce her retirement

84. What does the woman imply when she says, "and why wouldn't we"?

    (A) To suggest the partnership is good
    (B) To review some materials
    (C) To recommend a new method
    (D) To offer a training program

85. What does the woman suggest the studio staff do?

    (A) Go on vacation
    (B) Continue using the old equipment
    (C) Produce a movie
    (D) Study the new equipment

---

86. What problem does the speaker mention?

    (A) A shipment was missed.
    (B) The order was wrong.
    (C) The center will have no hot water.
    (D) There will be no water.

87. What does the speaker imply when he says, "you might want to hold off until later"?

    (A) Members of the center should come in the afternoon.
    (B) Members of the center shouldn't come.
    (C) There will be a meeting in the morning.
    (D) The center is closed in the afternoon.

88. What does the speaker say he will do?

    (A) Send a text message
    (B) Send an email
    (C) Make a phone call
    (D) Post a letter

GO ON TO THE NEXT PAGE

89. Where does the speaker work?

   (A) At a market
   (B) At a clinic
   (C) At a restaurant
   (D) At a factory

90. What problem does the speaker describe?

   (A) Extra items were delivered.
   (B) The delivery is late.
   (C) The business was closed.
   (D) There is a special event planned.

91. What does the woman mean when she says, "I have to finish the kitchen inventory by 11 a.m."?

   (A) She would like a response soon.
   (B) She doesn't need to know soon.
   (C) She needs some help with the new menu.
   (D) They have the right ingredients.

Training Schedule

Monday	Tuesday	Wednesday	Thursday
Meet and greet	Machine training	Machine training	Machine training
Factory tour			Lunch meeting with president

92. What are the listeners training to be?

   (A) Airline attendants
   (B) Military soldiers
   (C) Assembly line workers
   (D) Computer programmers

93. According to the speaker, what will the listeners enjoy doing?

   (A) Learning their job
   (B) Assembling products
   (C) Producing quality materials
   (D) Going to company events

94. Look at the graphic. On what day will the listeners meet with the company president?

   (A) Monday
   (B) Tuesday
   (C) Wednesday
   (D) Thursday

FOCUS GROUP QUESTIONAIRE RESULTS:
Majority respondents selected the following

Alright Ales New Styles	Do you like the label?	Do you like the flavor?	Would you choose this again?	Would you recommend this beer?
Dark Ale	Yes	No	Maybe	Maybe
Red Ale	No	Yes	Yes	Yes
Belgium Style	Yes	No	No	No
Wheat Ale	Yes	Yes	Yes	Yes

Zone 1 — Board Games and Video Games

Zone 2 — Action Figures and Dolls

Zone 3 — Sports Equipment

Zone 4 — Learning and Education Games

Toy List
Z1 Laughing Logs, **Z2** Macho Man, **Z2** Lovely Lady, **Z3** Soccer Ball, **Z3** Golf Clubs, **Z4** Animal ID, **Z1** Business Tycoon, **Z1** Fighting Forces.

95. Why is Alright Ales worried?

(A) They have a new competitor.
(B) They are nervous about their new beers.
(C) They are not in the top 5 of the market share in Northcut.
(D) They will have to cut staff.

96. What will the company likely do with the results of the survey?

(A) Change the label of the Red Ale
(B) Work on the Belgium Style
(C) Begin marketing the chosen beers
(D) Start working on a new style of beer

97. Look at the graphic. What beer is least likely to be part of Alright Ales' new product line?

(A) Wheat Ale
(B) Dark Ale
(C) Red Ale
(D) Belgium Style

98. What is indicated at the orientation?

(A) Big Toys will be a boring job.
(B) Big Toys has a large selection of products.
(C) Their inventory system is confusing.
(D) The managers will be very critical of mistakes.

99. Look at the graphic. Where will the trainees spend most of their time during the training exercise?

(A) Zone 1
(B) Zone 2
(C) Zone 3
(D) Zone 4

100. How quickly should the trainees complete their exercise?

(A) 2 hours
(B) 45 minutes or less
(C) 1.5 hours
(D) 1 hour or less

This is the end of the Listening test.

LISTENING TEST

In the Listening test, you will be asked to demonstrate how well you understand spoken English. The entire Listening test will last approximately 45 minutes. There are four parts, and directions are given for each part. You must mark your answers on the separate answer sheet. Do not write your answers in your test book.

PART 1

Directions: For each question in this part, you will hear four statements about a picture in your test book. When you hear the statements, you must select the one statement that best describes what you see in the picture. Then find the number of the question on your answer sheet and mark your answer. The statements will not be printed in your test book and will be spoken only one time.

Example

Sample Answer

Ⓐ ● Ⓒ Ⓓ

Statement (B), "They're looking at the document," is the best description of the picture, so you should select answer (B) and mark it on your answer sheet.

1.

2.

GO ON TO THE NEXT PAGE

3.

4.

5.

6.

GO ON TO THE NEXT PAGE

Directions: You will hear a question or statement and three responses spoken in English. They will not be printed in your test book and will be spoken only one time. Select the best response to the question or statement and mark the letter (A), (B), or (C) on your answer sheet.

7. Mark your answer on your answer sheet.

8. Mark your answer on your answer sheet.

9. Mark your answer on your answer sheet.

10. Mark your answer on your answer sheet.

11. Mark your answer on your answer sheet.

12. Mark your answer on your answer sheet.

13. Mark your answer on your answer sheet.

14. Mark your answer on your answer sheet.

15. Mark your answer on your answer sheet.

16. Mark your answer on your answer sheet.

17. Mark your answer on your answer sheet.

18. Mark your answer on your answer sheet.

19. Mark your answer on your answer sheet.

20. Mark your answer on your answer sheet.

21. Mark your answer on your answer sheet.

22. Mark your answer on your answer sheet.

23. Mark your answer on your answer sheet.

24. Mark your answer on your answer sheet.

25. Mark your answer on your answer sheet.

26. Mark your answer on your answer sheet.

27. Mark your answer on your answer sheet.

28. Mark your answer on your answer sheet.

29. Mark your answer on your answer sheet.

30. Mark your answer on your answer sheet.

31. Mark your answer on your answer sheet.

PART 3 ◖23◗

Directions: You will hear some conversations between two or more people. You will be asked to answer three questions about what the speakers say in each conversation. Select the best response to each question and mark the letter (A), (B), (C), or (D) on your answer sheet. The conversations will not be printed in your test book and will be spoken only one time.

32. Why is the woman calling?

(A) To extend a rental period
(B) To confirm an appointment
(C) To offer an assignment
(D) To accept a proposal

33. What does the man ask the woman to do?

(A) Interpret for her supervisor
(B) Send an advance payment
(C) Submit an official request
(D) Provide a work space

34. What will the woman inform the man about?

(A) A requirement
(B) A deadline
(C) A meeting time
(D) A company policy

35. What did the woman make a copy of?

(A) A receipt
(B) A meeting schedule
(C) An expense report
(D) A prescription

36. What does the man ask the woman to do?

(A) Sign a contract
(B) Write a message
(C) Contact a receptionist
(D) Go on a business trip to Tokyo

37. What does the man plan to do?

(A) Visit his co-worker
(B) Submit a report
(C) Make a new reservation
(D) Work overtime

GO ON TO THE NEXT PAGE

38. What field do the speakers work in?

(A) Education
(B) Manufacturing
(C) Product development
(D) Interior design

39. What does the man plan to do?

(A) Choose different furniture
(B) Share a building plan
(C) Change a color scheme
(D) Place an order for wallpaper

40. According to the woman, why will the speakers have to wait?

(A) A shipment has been delayed.
(B) A contract has not been signed yet.
(C) Authorization must first be obtained.
(D) Some equipment is out of order.

41. Where most likely are the speakers?

(A) At a pet shop
(B) At a catering company
(C) At a fire station
(D) At an animal shelter

42. What aspect of the woman's needs is mentioned?

(A) The price
(B) The size
(C) The age
(D) The color

43. According to the man, what does the woman have to do?

(A) Make an advance payment
(B) Bring her identification
(C) Fill out some documents
(D) Submit a letter of reference

44. Who most likely is the man?

(A) A photographer
(B) A talent agent
(C) A performer
(D) A receptionist

45. Why is the man calling?

(A) To buy a ticket in advance
(B) To confirm a reservation
(C) To provide a reminder
(D) To inquire about an advertisement

46. What does the woman offer to do?

(A) Restrict backstage access
(B) Take pictures of Mr. Jackson
(C) Show the man a list of guests
(D) Make an official announcement

47. What is mentioned about the product?

(A) It is affordable.
(B) It is superior to competitors'.
(C) It is safe for children to use.
(D) It is simple to install.

48. According to the man, what will the advertisement help to do?

(A) Promote new products
(B) Increase stock value
(C) Encourage innovations
(D) Reduce customer complaints

49. What will the man do next?

(A) Create a website
(B) Buy a magazine
(C) Revise an article
(D) Contact an agency

50. Why is the woman calling?

   (A) She hasn't received her product.
   (B) She was overcharged for the item.
   (C) She wants a product exchanged.
   (D) She wants to return a product.

51. Why does Michael transfer the call?

   (A) He is busy with another customer.
   (B) The woman requested another representative.
   (C) The woman called the wrong department.
   (D) The manager is unavailable.

52. What does Brian ask the woman for?

   (A) The tracking number
   (B) Her receipt
   (C) Her full name
   (D) The product name

53. What are the speakers mainly discussing?

   (A) Merging with another company
   (B) Last month's sales reports
   (C) The woman's anniversary party
   (D) When the band will arrive

54. What does the man mean when he says, "But it's your fifth anniversary party"?

   (A) He wants her to change her schedule.
   (B) He thinks it's not important.
   (C) He will tell the band not to come.
   (D) He wants her to go to the meetings.

55. What solution does the woman provide?

   (A) She will cancel the band.
   (B) She will cancel the dinner service.
   (C) She will cancel her meeting.
   (D) She will fire the man.

56. Why is the man calling the woman?

   (A) To check the sales figures
   (B) To check if she received the flowers
   (C) To check if she wanted to go to dinner
   (D) To check if the documents were ready

57. What does the woman say he should do?

   (A) Take her to the hospital
   (B) Pay her hospital bills
   (C) Take her out for dinner
   (D) Buy her more flowers

58. Why does the man say, "I thought you would like them"?

   (A) To express disappointment
   (B) To show appreciation
   (C) To show respect
   (D) To show he thinks it's funny

59. What is the main problem the speakers are discussing?

   (A) What they should eat for lunch
   (B) Going out for dinner
   (C) High entertainment expenses
   (D) Getting more customers

60. What does the woman suggest they do?

   (A) Stop going out for dinner
   (B) Reduce client numbers
   (C) Stop having lunches
   (D) Pay for their own lunches

61. What does the woman say she will send the man?

   (A) A monthly budget plan
   (B) This month's sales report
   (C) The old budget plan
   (D) Last month's marketing materials

GO ON TO THE NEXT PAGE ➡

Lifts will be out of order	
North Wing	8:00 a.m. – 9:00 a.m.
East Wing	11:00 a.m. – 12:00 p.m.
South Wing	1:30 p.m. – 2:30 p.m.
West Wing	3:00 p.m. – 4:00 p.m.

62. What did Harriet see last week?

(A) Technicians in the building next door
(B) Technicians posting about lift repairs
(C) Some technicians installing lighting
(D) Her boss having a meeting with some technicians

63. Look at the graphic. Which is the busiest wing in the hospital?

(A) West
(B) East
(C) North
(D) South

64. What does the man suggest the woman do?

(A) Cancel the repairs immediately
(B) Talk to Dr. Franklin
(C) Ask Dr. Franklin to lunch
(D) Close the North Wing

Camping Pack

4 Rectangular Sleeping Bags
4 Camping Mats
Carry Bag
Portable Gas Stove

65. Where does the woman likely work?

(A) A camping store
(B) A hardware store
(C) A medical clinic
(D) A shipping company

66. Look at the graphic. What is the man missing?

(A) Carry bag
(B) Portable gas stove
(C) Camping mats
(D) Sleeping bags

67. What does the woman offer to do?

(A) Give him a full refund
(B) Give him a 15% discount voucher
(C) Give him a 15% refund
(D) Give him a free tent

Henson's Corporate Cleaners	
Carpet Cleaning	
Frieze	$100 per room
Shag Pile	$150 per room
Velvet	$250 per room
Woven Carpet	$400 per room

68. What does the man say he is planning on doing with his office?

(A) Renovate it
(B) Sell it
(C) Clean it
(D) Repaint it

69. Look at the graphic. What is the carpet made of?

(A) Frieze
(B) Shag Pile
(C) Velvet
(D) Woven Carpet

70. What does the man say he will do?

(A) Buy the carpet today
(B) Ask his wife about it
(C) Tell his manager
(D) Think about it and come back

GO ON TO THE NEXT PAGE

PART 4 (24)

Directions: You will hear some talks given by a single speaker. You will be asked to answer three questions about what the speaker says in each talk. Select the best response to each question and mark the letter (A), (B), (C), or (D) on your answer sheet. The talks will not be printed in your test book and will be spoken only one time.

71. What is the announcement about?

(A) An opinion survey
(B) An upcoming election
(C) An election outcome
(D) A website update

72. What can listeners do on the website?

(A) Register as a candidate
(B) Cast their vote
(C) Find some information
(D) Enter a contest

73. What are listeners encouraged to do?

(A) Participate in an official occasion
(B) Reserve a ticket in advance
(C) Exercise on a daily basis
(D) Listen to an upcoming announcement

74. What is the outlet store celebrating?

(A) An anniversary
(B) A festival
(C) An opening
(D) A holiday

75. What must customers do to receive the promotional offer?

(A) Become a member
(B) Purchase a certain amount
(C) Recommend some brands
(D) Trade in a television

76. When does the promotion end?

(A) At the beginning of next month
(B) At the end of the year
(C) On the second Sunday of the month
(D) At the end of the month

77. Who most likely are the listeners?

(A) Environmentalists
(B) Instructors
(C) Factory workers
(D) Factory consultants

78. What document has the speaker reviewed?

(A) An employee roster
(B) An annual budget
(C) A project overview
(D) Accident reports

79. What does the speaker suggest listeners do?

(A) Get enough rest
(B) Work a day shift
(C) Receive more training
(D) Read a handout

80. What is the purpose of the trip to Moscow?

(A) To finalize a contract
(B) To visit a factory
(C) To give a product demonstration
(D) To renovate a building

81. What is the reason for the postponed departure?

(A) A necessary document is not ready.
(B) Some construction is underway.
(C) A company has gone out of business.
(D) Building materials have not arrived yet.

82. What does the speaker say she will send to the listener?

(A) A copy of her passport
(B) A plane ticket
(C) An itinerary
(D) A blueprint

83. What is the purpose of the speech?

(A) To announce a discovery
(B) To announce a retirement
(C) To accept a promotion
(D) To accept an award

84. Why does the speaker say: "I could not have done this without highly skilled crew"?

(A) She wants to thank her team.
(B) She hasn't worked on a team before.
(C) She dislikes her coworkers.
(D) She wants to accept the award.

85. Where most likely does the speaker work?

(A) At a hotel
(B) At a travel agency
(C) At a restaurant
(D) At a warehouse

86. Why is the woman calling?

(A) To express her gratitude
(B) To discuss a recipe
(C) To report some news
(D) To make a complaint

87. What does the woman imply when she says, "you have to show me the recipe"?

(A) She didn't enjoy it.
(B) She wants to recommend a different ingredient.
(C) She wants to cook the dish herself.
(D) She wants her friend to try it.

88. Why is the woman looking forward to next week?

(A) She is going to the movies.
(B) She is taking her son to school.
(C) Some new project will be completed.
(D) They will work together again.

GO ON TO THE NEXT PAGE

89. Who most likely is the speaker?

(A) A news editor
(B) A filmmaker
(C) A news reporter
(D) A movie star

90. What is Bernberg Studios looking for?

(A) An actress
(B) A filming location
(C) A new script
(D) More ideas for movies

91. What does the speaker imply when she says, "After all, this is Robert Holloway we are talking about"?

(A) Robert Holloway is very famous.
(B) Robert Holloway owns the house.
(C) She will interview him next.
(D) She doesn't know who Robert Holloway is.

MAMA SAN premium pillows

Beauty Sleep	£ 30.00
Soft Night	£ 35.00
Dreamtime	£ 42.00
Lovely Rest	£ 50.00

92. Look at the graphic. How much can a shopper purchase the Dreamtime Pillow for before Friday?

(A) £15.00
(B) £11.50
(C) £21.00
(D) £50.00

93. What is indicated about Happy Day?

(A) They have a wide variety of toys.
(B) They are bringing in more merchandise.
(C) They specialize in low-end furniture.
(D) They are going out of business this Friday.

94. What service does Happy Day offer?

(A) Personalized interior design advice
(B) Free shipping
(C) Home installation
(D) Wall papering services

ORDER FORM OF BLANDERS & CO.	
	14 March
Product	**Quantity**
Case binders	30
Envelopes	20
Flags & Tabs	40
Legal pads	10

MIDNIGHT CRUISE ITINERARY	
5 p.m.	Captain's address
6 p.m.	Cocktails and dinner
7 p.m.	Constellation orientation
8 p.m. — 10 p.m.	Social mixer
10 p.m.	Port Lewis for champagne toast
11 p.m.	Cast off and back to Billing's Bay
12 a.m.	Midnight constellation lesson and meteor shower on Top Deck

95. Look at the graphic. How many items were not delivered in total?

(A) 40
(B) 30
(C) 20
(D) 10

96. According to the speaker, why are the case binders important?

(A) To look professional in the office
(B) To look professional in court
(C) To organize their financial record
(D) To maintain the deadline

97. Where does Trent Herrington most likely work?

(A) At an accounting firm
(B) At a law firm
(C) At a patenting firm
(D) At a catering business

98. Where will the cruise spend most of its time?

(A) Eagle Island
(B) Port Lewis
(C) Billing's Bay
(D) Socializing

99. Who is Star Master Jenkins?

(A) Host
(B) Captain
(C) Bartender
(D) Security guard

100. Look at the graphic. How long will the cruise stop at Port Lewis?

(A) All evening
(B) 3 hours
(C) 2 hours
(D) 1 hour

This is the end of the Listening test.

LISTENING TEST 🎧25

In the Listening test, you will be asked to demonstrate how well you understand spoken English. The entire Listening test will last approximately 45 minutes. There are four parts, and directions are given for each part. You must mark your answers on the separate answer sheet. Do not write your answers in your test book.

PART 1

Directions: For each question in this part, you will hear four statements about a picture in your test book. When you hear the statements, you must select the one statement that best describes what you see in the picture. Then find the number of the question on your answer sheet and mark your answer. The statements will not be printed in your test book and will be spoken only one time.

Example

Sample Answer

Ⓐ ● Ⓒ Ⓓ

Statement (B), "They're looking at the document," is the best description of the picture, so you should select answer (B) and mark it on your answer sheet.

1.

2.

GO ON TO THE NEXT PAGE ➡

3.

4.

5.

6.

GO ON TO THE NEXT PAGE →

Directions: You will hear a question or statement and three responses spoken in English. They will not be printed in your test book and will be spoken only one time. Select the best response to the question or statement and mark the letter (A), (B), or (C) on your answer sheet.

7. Mark your answer on your answer sheet.

8. Mark your answer on your answer sheet.

9. Mark your answer on your answer sheet.

10. Mark your answer on your answer sheet.

11. Mark your answer on your answer sheet.

12. Mark your answer on your answer sheet.

13. Mark your answer on your answer sheet.

14. Mark your answer on your answer sheet.

15. Mark your answer on your answer sheet.

16. Mark your answer on your answer sheet.

17. Mark your answer on your answer sheet.

18. Mark your answer on your answer sheet.

19. Mark your answer on your answer sheet.

20. Mark your answer on your answer sheet.

21. Mark your answer on your answer sheet.

22. Mark your answer on your answer sheet.

23. Mark your answer on your answer sheet.

24. Mark your answer on your answer sheet.

25. Mark your answer on your answer sheet.

26. Mark your answer on your answer sheet.

27. Mark your answer on your answer sheet.

28. Mark your answer on your answer sheet.

29. Mark your answer on your answer sheet.

30. Mark your answer on your answer sheet.

31. Mark your answer on your answer sheet.

PART 3 (27)

Directions: You will hear some conversations between two or more people. You will be asked to answer three questions about what the speakers say in each conversation. Select the best response to each question and mark the letter (A), (B), (C), or (D) on your answer sheet. The conversations will not be printed in your test book and will be spoken only one time.

32. What does the woman ask the man to do?

(A) Introduce a new client
(B) Help to prepare a presentation
(C) Repair malfunctioning equipment
(D) Look for an instruction manual

33. Why is the man unable to help?

(A) He has to meet a major client soon.
(B) He finds the problem too complicated.
(C) He isn't nearby at the moment.
(D) He doesn't have the necessary tools.

34. What will the woman do next?

(A) Attempt to solve the problem herself
(B) Cancel an appointment
(C) Print out a document
(D) Have a meeting with a client

35. What problem does the woman mention?

(A) The advertisements are not widely circulated.
(B) The store inventory is inadequate.
(C) The discounted price is not competitive.
(D) The product is not selling well.

36. What does the woman say about this month's sales figures?

(A) They are beginning to decrease.
(B) They are similar to last month's figures.
(C) They are unusually high.
(D) They are impossible to predict.

37. What does the man ask the woman to do?

(A) Extend the length of the promotion
(B) Direct customers to the online store
(C) Secure more advertising space
(D) Offer customers a bigger discount

GO ON TO THE NEXT PAGE ➡

38. Where most likely does the man work?

    (A) At a hospital
    (B) At a factory
    (C) At a clothing store
    (D) At a restaurant

39. Why does the woman think she is qualified for the job?

    (A) She completed a training course.
    (B) She has worked similar jobs before.
    (C) She likes interacting with people.
    (D) She majored in a related field.

40. What will the speakers discuss next?

    (A) Work hours
    (B) An annual salary
    (C) Job qualifications
    (D) Previous jobs

41. Where most likely does the woman work?

    (A) At a wedding hall
    (B) At a bakery
    (C) At a clothing store
    (D) At a shipping company

42. Why is the man unable to visit the woman's workplace?

    (A) He has urgent arrangements to make.
    (B) He must attend a wedding today.
    (C) He is not feeling well.
    (D) He has to prepare an order.

43. What information will the man probably provide?

    (A) Directions to a location
    (B) An individual's name
    (C) His home address
    (D) His phone number

44. Where most likely do the speakers work?

    (A) At a souvenir shop
    (B) At a language school
    (C) At a restaurant
    (D) At a travel agency

45. What does the man recommend doing?

    (A) Hiring bilingual staff
    (B) Opening a second location
    (C) Taking language classes
    (D) Planning a vacation

46. What has the woman done?

    (A) Contacted a translation agency
    (B) Scheduled job interviews
    (C) Extended operating hours
    (D) Hired new employees

47. Why did Jessica leave work early?

    (A) She had a prior engagement.
    (B) She wasn't feeling well.
    (C) Her doctor called.
    (D) She had to attend a wedding.

48. What does the man ask the woman to do?

    (A) Work another person's shift
    (B) Clean the store tomorrow morning
    (C) Deliver a presentation at a meeting
    (D) Calculate sales figures

49. What will the woman do next?

    (A) Fill out a form
    (B) Distribute paychecks
    (C) Go to the hospital
    (D) Call her coworkers

50. What problem does the man mention?

    (A) The fridge is not working.
    (B) The temperature is too low.
    (C) The freezer temperature is too high.
    (D) Water is leaking from the fridge.

51. What does the woman mention about the fridge?

    (A) It is a very old model.
    (B) It is no longer manufactured.
    (C) It is not from their company.
    (D) It is a popular model.

52. What does the woman offer to do?

    (A) Give him a new manual
    (B) Give him a link to a website
    (C) Let him get a replacement
    (D) Send a technician over to him

53. Where do the speakers most likely work?

    (A) At a plumbing company
    (B) At an electrical company
    (C) At a construction company
    (D) In an office

54. What does the woman mean when she says, "I intended to call them today"?

    (A) She wasn't going to call them.
    (B) They were going to call her back.
    (C) She was going to call them that day.
    (D) She was going to send them an email.

55. What is the problem?

    (A) They can't install the electrical system.
    (B) The plumbing is already installed.
    (C) There is some problem with the payment.
    (D) They may need to dig deeper to install the plumbing.

56. What does the man mean when he says, "Are you serious"?

    (A) He believes the woman is correct.
    (B) He thinks the woman made a mistake.
    (C) He is going to pay by card.
    (D) He will pay with cash.

57. What does the woman want to know?

    (A) How much room service he ordered
    (B) Which room he is staying in
    (C) His credit card number
    (D) Whether he ordered room service

58. What does the woman offer to do?

    (A) Give him his room for free
    (B) Give him a discount on his next visit
    (C) Give him free room service
    (D) Give him a gift certificate

59. What is Robert Porter's position?

    (A) Lead repairer
    (B) Head engineer
    (C) Main engineer
    (D) Main repairer

60. What problem does Susan Sherman describe?

    (A) Some of the measurements weren't done.
    (B) Some of their receipts are missing.
    (C) Some of their equipment is missing.
    (D) A piece of equipment is still in the office.

61. Why did Robert take the equipment away?

    (A) To review it further
    (B) For special repairs
    (C) For replacement
    (D) To evaluate its condition

GO ON TO THE NEXT PAGE

Discount Voucher
10% off any order over $100

Valid until December 31st

No Parking After 9 A.M.

62. Where most likely are the speakers?

    (A) At a stand

    (B) At a café

    (C) At a restaurant

    (D) At the airport

63. Look at the graphic. Why is the voucher invalid?

    (A) Their bill is under $100.

    (B) The food was not good.

    (C) Their bill was over $100.

    (D) The voucher is expired.

64. What does the man ask the woman?

    (A) If they can have more food

    (B) If they can have more drinks

    (C) If they can have a refund

    (D) If they can come back another time

65. According to the man, why are people arriving late to work?

    (A) The parking lot on Swan Street was closed.

    (B) The Franklin Avenue parking lot was closed.

    (C) Everyone was feeling sick.

    (D) The traffic was bad.

66. Look at the graphic. Where is the sign most likely located?

    (A) On Franklin Avenue

    (B) On Swan Street

    (C) In front of the building

    (D) On Swanson Avenue

67. What does the woman recommend to the man?

    (A) Take the subway

    (B) Take a bus

    (C) Take a taxi

    (D) Drive his car

Laptop Package

1 laptop computer
Wireless mouse
Wireless keyboard
Office software
Detachable webcam
Free 8 gigabyte USB stick

68. Where does the woman most likely work?

(A) At a hardware store
(B) At an online store
(C) At a home appliance store
(D) At an electronics store

69. Look at the graphic. What is missing from the man's laptop package?

(A) Office software
(B) An 8 gigabyte USB stick
(C) A wireless keyboard
(D) A wireless mouse

70. What does the woman offer to do?

(A) Send a delivery driver the next day
(B) Give him a coupon
(C) Have him come and pick the gift up
(D) Deliver the gift in person

GO ON TO THE NEXT PAGE

PART 4 (28)

Directions: You will hear some talks given by a single speaker. You will be asked to answer three questions about what the speaker says in each talk. Select the best response to each question and mark the letter (A), (B), (C), or (D) on your answer sheet. The talks will not be printed in your test book and will be spoken only one time.

71. What is the advertisement about?

(A) A martial arts class
(B) An athletic contest
(C) A city tour bus
(D) A downtown festival

72. Who is the special offer directed at?

(A) Senior citizens
(B) Beginners
(C) Children
(D) Local residents

73. What does the speaker say about the advertised location?

(A) It is accessible by public transportation.
(B) It has no parking space available.
(C) It is near a train station.
(D) It is in the same building as Geller Bank.

74. Where is the introduction taking place?

(A) At a school
(B) At a museum
(C) At a radio station
(D) At a community center

75. Who is George Butler?

(A) A computer technician
(B) A mechanical engineer
(C) An electrician
(D) A technology expert

76. What is offered to teenage students?

(A) Hands-on experience
(B) A weekly after-school class
(C) A complimentary souvenir
(D) A discounted ticket price

77. What has caused the change in plans?

    (A) Broken kitchen equipment
    (B) The absence of some clients
    (C) A late delivery
    (D) Traffic congestion

78. What will listeners receive?

    (A) A conference schedule
    (B) A meal voucher
    (C) A lunch menu
    (D) A name tag

79. What will begin at 1:00 p.m.?

    (A) A software demonstration
    (B) A leadership workshop
    (C) A luncheon
    (D) A client meeting

80. What is the purpose of the planning committee?

    (A) To tighten some regulations
    (B) To supervise a construction project
    (C) To review employee performance
    (D) To develop a new curriculum

81. What does the volunteer need to do?

    (A) Pick up a client
    (B) Introduce a guest
    (C) Write down an agenda
    (D) Give a presentation

82. What will listeners do next?

    (A) Go on a business trip
    (B) Participate in a workshop
    (C) Introduce themselves
    (D) Select a group leader

83. Who most likely are the listeners?

    (A) Factory workers
    (B) Lawyers
    (C) Accountants
    (D) Web developers

84. What does the woman mean when she says, "I know that you have all been overworked"?

    (A) She recognizes the listeners concerns.
    (B) She doesn't really mind what they think.
    (C) She wants them to work less.
    (D) She is inviting them to a meeting.

85. What task does the speaker assign to the listeners?

    (A) Prepare some instructions
    (B) Prepare a new budget
    (C) Revise some training materials
    (D) Hire new staff

86. What is *Beyond the Blue* about?

    (A) Online bullying
    (B) The ocean
    (C) Whales and sharks
    (D) Sea water

87. Why does the speaker say, "Remember, this is the first film Mr. Harris has made"?

    (A) To suggest that he is an impressive director
    (B) To suggest the film will be poor
    (C) To recommend him as a good worker
    (D) To suggest they shouldn't watch the film

88. What is going to happen after the film?

    (A) They will give away free DVDs.
    (B) They will watch it again.
    (C) The director will have a short Q&A.
    (D) An actor will sign autographs.

GO ON TO THE NEXT PAGE

89. According to the speaker, what has happened to the company in the last year?

(A) Their products have gained global success.
(B) Their sales have gone down.
(C) The quality of the products has changed.
(D) Their CEO has changed many times.

90. What most likely are the CNU reporters doing on Wednesday?

(A) Interviewing some office workers
(B) Interviewing the president
(C) Making a music video
(D) Promoting their new web series

91. Why does the man say, "you realize what this means"?

(A) To discuss future renovations
(B) To make a point clear
(C) To highlight that the company will grow
(D) To give staff some bonuses

SAM'S SALON PRICING FOR THE HOMELESS BENEFIT	
Men's trim	$10
Men's full cut and shave	$25
Women's trim	$20
Women's styling	$45
Sorry! No coloring or perms for this Saturday's benefit!	

92. What is indicated in the article?

(A) Sam's Salon is just starting to interact with the homeless.
(B) Sam's Salon has been involved with improving the lives of homeless people.
(C) Sam's Salon employs a high quality manicurist.
(D) Sam's Salon is trying to make extra money from coloring and perms.

93. Look at the graphic. What is true about the benefit?

(A) People should get their hair colored another time.
(B) Women's trim is expensive.
(C) Most men will choose a trim.
(D) Homeless people need to shave.

94. How much does Sam's Salon charge the homeless for a shampoo, shave, and a haircut?

(A) $25
(B) $45
(C) $10
(D) Nothing; its free

	Option 1	Option 2	Option 3	Option 4
Price	$1,000	$1,200	$1,300	$2,000
Back-up System	yes	no	no	no
Data Archive	1 week	10 weeks	30 weeks	52 weeks

95. Where does the talk most likely take place?

(A) The cafeteria
(B) The conference room
(C) The new break room
(D) The new foyer

96. Look at the graphic. Which option does the speaker recommend?

(A) Option 1
(B) Option 2
(C) Option 3
(D) Option 4

97. Why is Option 4 more expensive than the others?

(A) It has state-of-the-art surveillance.
(B) It has video cameras.
(C) It includes a one-year data archive.
(D) It offers a back-up system.

**A LETTER
TO MILTON'S DINER**

Dear Milton's Staff,

My name is Jerome and I am a long haul trucker. I saw the sign from the highway, "Milton's Diner, home of classic pies," and thought, you know what, I am going to treat myself. I was exhausted, but as soon as I walked into the diner and smelled the pies, saw all the decorations, and was greeted by the hostess, I just felt so good. You really made my weekend special, and I wanted to thank you with all sincerity. Happy Holidays,

Jerome Simmons

98. Who is speaking to the staff?

(A) Milton
(B) The manager
(C) The chef
(D) Jerome Simmons

99. Look at the letter. What do you think Milton's Diner prides itself on?

(A) Cakes
(B) Pies
(C) Drinks
(D) Steaks

100. What effect did Jerome's letter have?

(A) The staff will get a day off.
(B) Everyone will get to take home a pie.
(C) Everyone will get holiday gift cards.
(D) The staff will receive an extra holiday bonus.

This is the end of the Listening test.

LISTENING TEST

In the Listening test, you will be asked to demonstrate how well you understand spoken English. The entire Listening test will last approximately 45 minutes. There are four parts, and directions are given for each part. You must mark your answers on the separate answer sheet. Do not write your answers in your test book.

PART 1

Directions: For each question in this part, you will hear four statements about a picture in your test book. When you hear the statements, you must select the one statement that best describes what you see in the picture. Then find the number of the question on your answer sheet and mark your answer. The statements will not be printed in your test book and will be spoken only one time.

Example

Sample Answer

Ⓐ ● Ⓒ Ⓓ

Statement (B), "They're looking at the document," is the best description of the picture, so you should select answer (B) and mark it on your answer sheet.

1.

2.

GO ON TO THE NEXT PAGE

3.

4.

5.

6.

GO ON TO THE NEXT PAGE ➡

PART 2 (30)

7. Mark your answer on your answer sheet.

8. Mark your answer on your answer sheet.

9. Mark your answer on your answer sheet.

10. Mark your answer on your answer sheet.

11. Mark your answer on your answer sheet.

12. Mark your answer on your answer sheet.

13. Mark your answer on your answer sheet.

14. Mark your answer on your answer sheet.

15. Mark your answer on your answer sheet.

16. Mark your answer on your answer sheet.

17. Mark your answer on your answer sheet.

18. Mark your answer on your answer sheet.

19. Mark your answer on your answer sheet.

20. Mark your answer on your answer sheet.

21. Mark your answer on your answer sheet.

22. Mark your answer on your answer sheet.

23. Mark your answer on your answer sheet.

24. Mark your answer on your answer sheet.

25. Mark your answer on your answer sheet.

26. Mark your answer on your answer sheet.

27. Mark your answer on your answer sheet.

28. Mark your answer on your answer sheet.

29. Mark your answer on your answer sheet.

30. Mark your answer on your answer sheet.

31. Mark your answer on your answer sheet.

Directions: You will hear some conversations between two or more people. You will be asked to answer three questions about what the speakers say in each conversation. Select the best response to each question and mark the letter (A), (B), (C), or (D) on your answer sheet. The conversations will not be printed in your test book and will be spoken only one time.

32. Who is the man?

(A) A hotel guest
(B) A janitor
(C) A night manager
(D) A receptionist

33. Why is Mr. Carter unavailable?

(A) He is meeting a client.
(B) He is on vacation.
(C) He has not arrived at work yet.
(D) He is giving a presentation.

34. What will the man do next?

(A) Watch training videos
(B) Conduct an interview
(C) Contact Mr. Carter
(D) Fill out paperwork

35. What are the speakers discussing?

(A) Preparations for a meeting
(B) A keynote speech
(C) A seminar agenda
(D) Meeting locations

36. What does the man say he is relieved about?

(A) A product is selling well.
(B) A trip was not delayed.
(C) A new employee was hired.
(D) A meeting room is available.

37. What does the woman offer to do?

(A) Act as an interpreter during a meeting
(B) Call before she arrives
(C) Call Mr. Takahashi's secretary
(D) Listen to a weather report

ACTUAL TEST

08

GO ON TO THE NEXT PAGE

38. What does the woman ask the man about?

   (A) The status of a project
   (B) The location of a store
   (C) The list of clients
   (D) The cause of a problem

39. Why was the man unable to complete his work?

   (A) He didn't have enough time.
   (B) His car wouldn't start.
   (C) He was busy with other projects.
   (D) His computer malfunctioned.

40. What is the woman planning to do?

   (A) Terminate a contract
   (B) Ask for a deadline extension
   (C) Meet with a company executive
   (D) Hire a new designer

41. What problem does the man report?

   (A) Internet access has been disconnected.
   (B) A delivery has not arrived yet.
   (C) A power outage occurred.
   (D) Some equipment has malfunctioned.

42. Where most likely does the woman work?

   (A) At an electronics store
   (B) At a power company
   (C) At a toy factory
   (D) At a communications provider

43. What does the woman suggest the man do?

   (A) Take shelter elsewhere
   (B) Report the incident to the police
   (C) Restart his computer
   (D) Arrive ahead of schedule

44. Where does the man work?

   (A) At an immigration office
   (B) At a public school
   (C) At a post office
   (D) At a travel agency

45. Why is the woman in a hurry?

   (A) She is late to work.
   (B) She forgot an important event.
   (C) She must meet a deadline.
   (D) She has another appointment.

46. What does the man recommend?

   (A) Making a phone call
   (B) Visiting a different business
   (C) Sending an email
   (D) Canceling a subscription

47. What type of business does the man work for?

   (A) An auto repair shop
   (B) An insurance company
   (C) An automobile dealership
   (D) A construction contractor

48. What does the woman say is her top priority when she makes a purchase?

   (A) Affordability
   (B) Popularity
   (C) Design
   (D) Safety

49. What does the man suggest doing?

   (A) Replacing a broken part
   (B) Evaluating a different model
   (C) Visiting a new branch
   (D) Paying a deposit

50. What are the speakers mainly discussing?

    (A) High sales figures
    (B) A staff conflict
    (C) Low sales figures
    (D) A new training manual

51. What does the woman mean when she says, "I'm actually on my way to a meeting"?

    (A) She doesn't have a lot of time to talk.
    (B) She can stay and chat for a long time.
    (C) She is asking the man out to lunch.
    (D) She will send him an email later on.

52. What possible solution does the man suggest?

    (A) To employ more staff members
    (B) That the woman should be fired
    (C) They should have lunch together.
    (D) The woman might have to fire someone.

53. What is the problem?

    (A) The person who was supposed to give the speech is sick.
    (B) The person who was supposed to give the speech doesn't want to do it now.
    (C) There is no keynote speech anymore.
    (D) The keynote speaker is late.

54. What does the woman say to the man?

    (A) To find someone to do the speech.
    (B) She will deliver the speech.
    (C) To deliver the keynote speech.
    (D) The board is not happy.

55. What does the man imply when he says, "thanks, but I'll have to pass on it"?

    (A) He will deliver the speech.
    (B) He doesn't want to deliver the speech.
    (C) He will talk to the board of directors.
    (D) He needs some more information.

56. Why is the man calling Tristar Logistics?

    (A) To reschedule a delivery
    (B) To cancel his order
    (C) To change his address
    (D) To update his details

57. What does he imply when he says, "that won't work for me"?

    (A) The package contains important documents.
    (B) He will pay with a money order.
    (C) He doesn't want them to leave the package with someone else.
    (D) He wants it left at the office.

58. What does the woman say she wants?

    (A) The office address
    (B) His cell phone number
    (C) The order number
    (D) His building number

59. What are the speakers mainly discussing?

    (A) The delivery of some furniture
    (B) The signing of a rental contract
    (C) The drafting of a document
    (D) The delivery of computer equipment

60. What problem do Ruth and Greg have?

    (A) They don't need the equipment.
    (B) They could miss some important deadlines.
    (C) They need to train their new staff.
    (D) They haven't found the documents.

61. What does the woman suggest she'll do?

    (A) Accept the late order
    (B) Cancel the order
    (C) Call another supplier
    (D) Rent some equipment

GO ON TO THE NEXT PAGE

Office Directory

1st FL   Harlington Accounting
2nd FL Jersey Construction
3rd FL Swanson and Sons
4th FL Grounds Ltd

Harron Dry Cleaning

Fabric	Price
Cotton	$10
Denim	$15
Wool	$20
Silk	$12

62. Who most likely are the speakers?

(A) Store clerks
(B) Artists
(C) Painters
(D) Electricians

63. Look at the graphic. Where is the man currently working?

(A) Swanson and Sons
(B) Harlington Accounting
(C) Jersey Construction
(D) Grounds Ltd

64. What does the woman recommend to the man?

(A) To bring more paint
(B) To bring one ladder
(C) To bring at least three ladders
(D) To paint the roof first

65. What does the woman say she will do tomorrow?

(A) Go out for dinner
(B) Visit her family
(C) Host an award show
(D) Attend an award ceremony

66. Look at the graphic. What is the gown made of?

(A) Cotton
(B) Wool
(C) Denim
(D) Silk

67. What does the woman say she will do?

(A) Pick it up at 9 p.m.
(B) Send her husband to pick it up
(C) Send her daughter to pick it up
(D) Cancel the order

**No Parking
After 8 P.M.**

68. According to the man, what is causing people to arrive late to work?

(A) An electrical storm
(B) A closed parking lot
(C) A protest
(D) Some new traffic rules

69. Look at the graphic. Where is the sign most likely located?

(A) On Swinton Road
(B) At the Cranson Lot
(C) On Menzies Street
(D) On Prunkel Street

70. What does the man suggest they do?

(A) Go home
(B) Buy some parking tickets
(C) Have an early dinner
(D) Walk to work

GO ON TO THE NEXT PAGE

PART 4 (32)

Directions: You will hear some talks given by a single speaker. You will be asked to answer three questions about what the speaker says in each talk. Select the best response to each question and mark the letter (A), (B), (C), or (D) on your answer sheet. The talks will not be printed in your test book and will be spoken only one time.

71. Where does the announcement most likely take place?

   (A) On a train
   (B) On a bus
   (C) On a plane
   (D) On a ship

72. What is the speaker waiting for?

   (A) An itinerary
   (B) Authorization to depart
   (C) Some passengers to board
   (D) A parking permit

73. What does the speaker suggest listeners do?

   (A) Have their tickets reissued
   (B) Transfer to another line
   (C) Stay near a departure gate
   (D) Modify their plans

74. What type of business does the speaker work for?

   (A) An electronics store
   (B) A furniture outlet
   (C) A clothing store
   (D) A theater company

75. What improvement is mentioned?

   (A) Product selection will be increased.
   (B) More staff will be able to help.
   (C) Free parking will be offered.
   (D) Store hours will be extended.

76. When can customers receive a discount?

   (A) On Tuesday
   (B) On Wednesday
   (C) On Thursday
   (D) On Friday

77. What is being advertised?

(A) A security system
(B) A rented house
(C) A gardening tool
(D) An insulating product

78. What is mentioned about the product?

(A) It is domestically produced.
(B) It reduces the cost of living.
(C) It won several awards.
(D) It received positive reviews.

79. What must listeners do to receive a discount?

(A) Buy a certain amount of products
(B) Apply for a membership card
(C) Talk about the advertisement
(D) Make a payment in cash

80. What event is ending?

(A) A grand opening
(B) A consumer electronics expo
(C) A product demonstration
(D) A museum tour

81. What is required of volunteers?

(A) Relevant experience
(B) A degree in engineering
(C) Availability to work on weekends
(D) Fluency in two languages

82. What are potential volunteers cautioned about?

(A) Missing a deadline
(B) Leaking confidential information
(C) Damaging a device
(D) Interrupting a presenter

83. What is the company recruiting?

(A) Programmers
(B) Chefs
(C) Interns
(D) Factory workers

84. What does the man imply when he says, "Have you seen the interview questions we use"?

(A) He is postponing an appointment.
(B) He needs a record of the report.
(C) He wants her to help him with the questions.
(D) He will recruit some accountants.

85. Why does the man want to meet with the woman?

(A) To get some assistance from her
(B) To ask her for some records
(C) To get a new letterhead
(D) To plan an orientation

86. What is the purpose of the announcement?

(A) To announce an achievement
(B) To announce a rise in sales
(C) To announce a new team member
(D) To complete a project

87. What does the woman imply when she says, "so let's keep moving up"?

(A) They need to continue working hard.
(B) They are moving buildings.
(C) She is renovating the office.
(D) They are going on a business trip.

88. What does the woman ask the staff to do?

(A) Study the new handbook
(B) Prepare a report
(C) Study material on corporate law
(D) Write a memo

GO ON TO THE NEXT PAGE

89. Why is the woman calling?

   (A) To say thank you
   (B) To ask a favor
   (C) To discuss travel plans
   (D) To request a form

90. What does the woman imply when she says, "you have to show me the design sometime"?

   (A) She wants to learn how to make it.
   (B) She wasn't sure about the details.
   (C) She needs a dentist recommendation.
   (D) She is writing a design manual.

91. What will the women do next week?

   (A) Plan for the Grayson wedding
   (B) Plan for the Christmas party
   (C) Design a new invitation
   (D) Meet for coffee

**SPRINGDALE MUSIC CLUB'S
SATURDAY CONCERT LINE UP**

5 p.m.—8 p.m.	Barbeque Cookout, bring your own meat!
8 p.m.—9 p.m.	Djubai Djinn, all the way from East Timor
9 p.m.—10 p.m.	Swinging Devils touring from Memphis
10 p.m.—11 p.m.	Rock or Die! Local Heroes
11 p.m.—12 a.m.	Ferocious Four all the way from New York City

92. What is indicated about Springdale Music Club?

   (A) They love all music equally.
   (B) They take pride in their location.
   (C) They specialize in country music.
   (D) They didn't carry world music before.

93. Look at the graphic. What can you infer about the bands?

   (A) They will be great.
   (B) They are jazz musicians.
   (C) The acts following Djubai Djinn play rock and roll.
   (D) They will be loud.

94. Why does Springdale Music Club ask you to bring your money?

   (A) The concert will be expensive.
   (B) There is a bar.
   (C) To help support Djubai Djinn's US tour
   (D) To pay for your meats

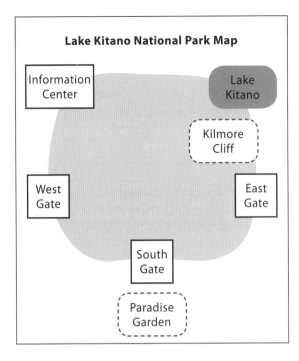

Lake Kitano National Park Map

Order form	
Item	**Quantity**
Desks	1
Chairs	8
File Binders	3

98. Look at the graphic. Which department filled out the order form?

(A) Finance
(B) IT
(C) Public Relations
(D) Human Resources

99. What does the speaker anticipate may happen?

(A) Some departments may go over budget.
(B) The warehouse may not have enough supplies.
(C) The orders may not arrive on time.
(D) The departments may forget some items.

95. Who most likely are the listeners?

(A) Residents
(B) Tourists
(C) Park employees
(D) Forest rangers

96. Look at the map. What place are the listeners unable to go to?

(A) Lake Kitano
(B) East Gate
(C) Kilmore Cliff
(D) Paradise Garden

97. What does the woman mention about Kilmore Cliff?

(A) It is dangerous.
(B) The views are spectacular.
(C) People who fear heights may not enjoy it.
(D) It is 50 meters from the final destination.

100. What does the speaker request of Lima?

(A) To fax over the orders
(B) To file the papers
(C) To arrange a meeting
(D) To contact him

This is the end of the Listening test.

LISTENING TEST

In the Listening test, you will be asked to demonstrate how well you understand spoken English. The entire Listening test will last approximately 45 minutes. There are four parts, and directions are given for each part. You must mark your answers on the separate answer sheet. Do not write your answers in your test book.

PART 1

Directions: For each question in this part, you will hear four statements about a picture in your test book. When you hear the statements, you must select the one statement that best describes what you see in the picture. Then find the number of the question on your answer sheet and mark your answer. The statements will not be printed in your test book and will be spoken only one time.

Example

Sample Answer

Statement (B), "They're looking at the document," is the best description of the picture, so you should select answer (B) and mark it on your answer sheet.

1.

2.

GO ON TO THE NEXT PAGE →

3.

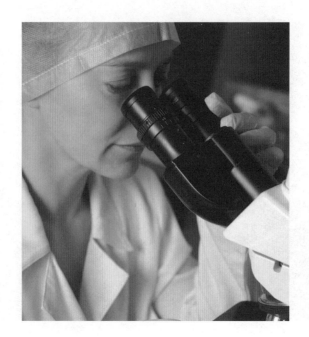

4.

5.

6.

GO ON TO THE NEXT PAGE ➡

PART 2 (34)

Directions: You will hear a question or statement and three responses spoken in English. They will not be printed in your test book and will be spoken only one time. Select the best response to the question or statement and mark the letter (A), (B), or (C) on your answer sheet.

7. Mark your answer on your answer sheet.

8. Mark your answer on your answer sheet.

9. Mark your answer on your answer sheet.

10. Mark your answer on your answer sheet.

11. Mark your answer on your answer sheet.

12. Mark your answer on your answer sheet.

13. Mark your answer on your answer sheet.

14. Mark your answer on your answer sheet.

15. Mark your answer on your answer sheet.

16. Mark your answer on your answer sheet.

17. Mark your answer on your answer sheet.

18. Mark your answer on your answer sheet.

19. Mark your answer on your answer sheet.

20. Mark your answer on your answer sheet.

21. Mark your answer on your answer sheet.

22. Mark your answer on your answer sheet.

23. Mark your answer on your answer sheet.

24. Mark your answer on your answer sheet.

25. Mark your answer on your answer sheet.

26. Mark your answer on your answer sheet.

27. Mark your answer on your answer sheet.

28. Mark your answer on your answer sheet.

29. Mark your answer on your answer sheet.

30. Mark your answer on your answer sheet.

31. Mark your answer on your answer sheet.

PART 3 🎧 35

Directions: You will hear some conversations between two or more people. You will be asked to answer three questions about what the speakers say in each conversation. Select the best response to each question and mark the letter (A), (B), (C), or (D) on your answer sheet. The conversations will not be printed in your test book and will be spoken only one time.

32. What is the woman requesting?

(A) Time off from work
(B) A recommendation letter
(C) A schedule change
(D) A pay raise

33. Why is the woman unsure about the man's question?

(A) She wants to quit her job.
(B) She is waiting for her exam results.
(C) She got a job offer from another restaurant.
(D) She has not registered for classes.

34. What does the man ask the woman to do?

(A) Work overtime this week
(B) Inform him about her availability
(C) Recommend her acquaintance
(D) Create a new menu design

35. Why is the man calling?

(A) To order a product
(B) To postpone an appointment
(C) To book a wedding hall
(D) To hire a photographer

36. What does the man inquire about?

(A) A price quote
(B) A product sample
(C) A list of employees
(D) An event schedule

37. Why does the woman say the service might be quite expensive?

(A) Her services are in high demand.
(B) She will need additional staff.
(C) She uses high-end equipment.
(D) She has to meet a tight deadline.

ACTUAL TEST

09

GO ON TO THE NEXT PAGE

38. Who is Nathan Gates?

    (A) A sales clerk
    (B) A customer
    (C) A private detective
    (D) A product inspector

39. What does the man ask the woman to do?

    (A) Run a training session
    (B) Enforce safety measures
    (C) Introduce a new employee
    (D) Inspect a construction site

40. What will the woman give Mr. Gates?

    (A) A training manual
    (B) Safety gear
    (C) A work schedule
    (D) An identification card

41. What problem are the speakers discussing?

    (A) Unsatisfied customers
    (B) An unexpected drop in sales
    (C) Damaged inventory
    (D) A delayed shipment

42. What caused the problem?

    (A) An electrical fire
    (B) A burst water pipe
    (C) A sudden flood
    (D) A gas leak

43. What will happen on Friday?

    (A) Construction will be completed.
    (B) Stock prices will increase.
    (C) A shipment will arrive.
    (D) A supplier will be changed.

44. What are the speakers discussing?

    (A) A public lecture
    (B) An upcoming exam
    (C) A graduation requirement
    (D) A recent publishing trend

45. Who is Charlie Klein?

    (A) A scientist
    (B) An inventor
    (C) A professor
    (D) A writer

46. Why is the woman planning to visit the man tomorrow?

    (A) To return an item
    (B) To borrow a book
    (C) To meet Mr. Klein
    (D) To sign up for a course

47. Who is Dr. Moran?

    (A) A university professor
    (B) A patient
    (C) A pharmacist
    (D) A medical practitioner

48. What problem does the woman mention?

    (A) An incorrect diagnosis
    (B) A family problem
    (C) Persistent pain
    (D) An outstanding balance

49. What does the man offer to do?

    (A) Provide contact information
    (B) Drive the woman to the hospital
    (C) Set up an appointment
    (D) Offer a free consultation

50. What is the man concerned about?

(A) The messaging system
(B) Cell phone reception
(C) Phone transfer software
(D) A new computer system

51. What does the woman suggest?

(A) Deleting all his software
(B) Getting a new computer
(C) Downloading a movie
(D) Upgrading his software

52. What does the woman say she will do?

(A) Send him a link for a free upgrade
(B) Upgrade his phone model
(C) Revise the schedule
(D) Check with management

---

53. What is the man worried about?

(A) Buying new software
(B) The production rate of the machine
(C) Finding a repair shop
(D) An increase in production

54. What does the man imply when he says, "It doesn't make sense to keep going like this"?

(A) He wants to take action immediately.
(B) He wants to continue business as usual.
(C) He wants to repair the software.
(D) He doesn't agree with the woman.

55. What does the woman say she will do?

(A) Call the software engineer
(B) Contact the IT department
(C) Call the machine repair shop
(D) Buy new software

---

56. What did the man do last weekend?

(A) He went to a conference.
(B) He finished his sales reports.
(C) He gave a presentation.
(D) He visited his family.

57. What does the woman imply when she says, "wow, sounds like you've really made it"?

(A) He failed.
(B) He was successful with his presentation.
(C) His presentation wasn't well received
(D) His book didn't sell well.

58. What does the man plan on doing next year?

(A) Retire from writing
(B) Move to another country
(C) Have a child with his wife
(D) Release another book

---

59. Why most likely is the man calling?

(A) To discuss an issue with the apartment
(B) To offer a lower rental price
(C) To negotiate a contract
(D) To make an appointment

60. What does the man say about the Swiss Tower building?

(A) It is too far away from her office.
(B) It is being renovated at the moment.
(C) It is being closed down.
(D) It is located close to a dry cleaner.

61. What does the man offer the woman?

(A) Give her a lower rental price
(B) Extend the lease
(C) Pay for her hotel costs
(D) Arrange to move her furniture

GO ON TO THE NEXT PAGE

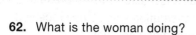

Bernard & Son's Tailors
Gift Certificate

10% off any purchase of $500 or more

Expires March 10

Nutrition Information
Serving Size: 1 Rounded Scoop (29.4g)

Calories	120
Fat	10 grams
Carbohydrate	3 grams
Protein	24 grams
Calcium	10%
Contains milk and soy products	

62. What is the woman doing?

(A) Giving away free suits
(B) Helping a customer
(C) Updating software
(D) Celebrating with friends

63. Look at the graphic. Why is the gift certificate rejected?

(A) It is expired.
(B) Because he is in the wrong store
(C) Because he didn't purchase enough
(D) The certificate is damaged.

64. What does the woman offer to do?

(A) Give him another certificate
(B) Help him try on a suit
(C) Show him some pants
(D) Give him a refund

65. Why is the man looking for a certain product?

(A) He stopped working out.
(B) His trainer told him to.
(C) Because he is a trainer.
(D) He had a favorite brand.

66. Look at the graphic. Which content is the man worried about?

(A) Carbohydrate
(B) Fat
(C) Milk
(D) Protein

67. What does the woman suggest?

(A) Purchasing a milk-based product
(B) Getting a full refund
(C) Using soy beans
(D) Buying a soy-based powder

Park Tower
Office Directory

1st Floor		Farnod Computing
2nd Floor		Chaims & Son
3rd Floor		Raptas
4th Floor		Hecadi Constructing

68. Who most likely are the speakers?

(A) office cleaners
(B) computer repair technicians
(C) telephone operators
(D) athletes

69. Look at the graphic. Where is the woman going next?

(A) Raptas
(B) Farnod Computing
(C) Chaims & Son
(D) Hecadi Constructing

70. What are the speakers going to do when they're finished with the windows?

(A) go home
(B) eat lunch
(C) clean the carpets
(D) leave the building

ACTUAL TEST

09

GO ON TO THE NEXT PAGE

PART 4 (36)

Directions: You will hear some talks given by a single speaker. You will be asked to answer three questions about what the speaker says in each talk. Select the best response to each question and mark the letter (A), (B), (C), or (D) on your answer sheet. The talks will not be printed in your test book and will be spoken only one time.

71. Who most likely is the speaker?

    (A) A potential buyer
    (B) A bank teller
    (C) A real estate agent
    (D) An architect

72. Why would the speaker like to arrange a meeting?

    (A) To discuss a sale
    (B) To renew a contract
    (C) To draw up a budget
    (D) To introduce his coworker

73. What does the speaker suggest doing?

    (A) Updating a website
    (B) Accepting an offer
    (C) Making the house neat
    (D) Lowering a price

74. What is the news report mainly about?

    (A) A weather forecast
    (B) A road construction project
    (C) A traffic accident
    (D) A cooking contest

75. What event has been delayed?

    (A) A sports game
    (B) A live concert
    (C) An opening ceremony
    (D) An orientation

76. What will the winner of the eating contest receive?

    (A) A concert ticket
    (B) A gift certificate
    (C) A cash prize
    (D) A plane ticket

77. Where is the announcement being made?

(A) At a campground
(B) At a movie theater
(C) At a concert hall
(D) At a sports stadium

78. What is being announced?

(A) A new restriction
(B) Operating hours
(C) Price changes
(D) A discount policy

79. What is said about some of the proceeds?

(A) They will be used for a worthy cause.
(B) They will be put toward updating facilities.
(C) They will be saved for a special event.
(D) They will be awarded to some spectators.

---

80. What is the speaker discussing?

(A) A new curriculum
(B) A weather warning
(C) A quarterly report
(D) A travel advisory

81. What has been canceled?

(A) Television programs
(B) Graduation ceremonies
(C) Educational programs
(D) Fundraising events

82. What are local residents advised to do?

(A) Update their anti-virus software
(B) Wear protective gear
(C) Go into a safe place
(D) Take an alternative route

---

83. What is the purpose of the speech?

(A) To accept a nomination
(B) To announce a retirement
(C) To announce a merger
(D) To request funding

84. Why does the speaker say: "I couldn't have done this without my talented team"?

(A) She dislikes her team.
(B) She is asking for some extra awards.
(C) She wants to thank her colleagues.
(D) She wants to offer her services.

85. Where most likely does the speaker work?

(A) At a cell phone shop
(B) At a computer shop
(C) At a shoe store
(D) At a flower shop

---

86. What problem does the speaker mention?

(A) No breakfast service
(B) No dinner service
(C) Missing items on the menu
(D) Rats in the kitchen

87. What does the speaker imply when he says, "you might want to come in the evening"?

(A) He will offer free breakfast.
(B) The dinner menu is better.
(C) Don't come during the day.
(D) They are installing air conditioners.

88. What does the speaker say he will do?

(A) Serve breakfast at night
(B) Charge more
(C) Offer free breakfast
(D) Offer a discount

GO ON TO THE NEXT PAGE

89. Where does the speaker work?

(A) A fashion company
(B) A restaurant
(C) A factory
(D) A clinic

90. What problem does the speaker describe?

(A) The delivery driver is lost.
(B) The delivery is late.
(C) The order is not perfect.
(D) The order has extra items.

91. What does the woman imply when she says, "I need to let head office know what to do by 1 p.m., and it's already midday"?

(A) She would like a response after midday.
(B) She would like a response as soon as possible.
(C) She would like extra time off.
(D) She will call head office now.

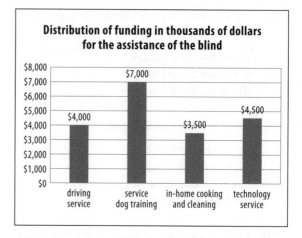

Distribution of funding in thousands of dollars for the assistance of the blind

92. Look at the graphic. What is the largest expense?

(A) Dog training
(B) Technology
(C) Meal preparation
(D) Driving assistance

93. What is the listener asked to do?

(A) Give more money than last year
(B) Listen to some information
(C) Become a volunteer
(D) Become a member of the National Center for the Blind

94. Where does the speaker most likely work?

(A) A hospital
(B) The National Center for the Blind
(C) A church
(D) The local government

FFFS Seminar Schedule and Price Guide

Orlando	"3 Weeks to Riches!"	3 weeks	$1,500
New York	"The Big Apple is Yours"	5 days	$750
Boston	"Revolutionary Wealth"	13 days	$1,200
Seattle	"Prepare for Your Rainy Day"	20 days	$3,000

Common Area Cleanliness Checklist

Area	Monday	Tuesday	Wednesday	Thursday	Friday
Kitchen	Scott W	Scott W	Scott W	Bill T	Bill T
Foyer	Bill T	Bill T	Hillary P	Hillary P	Hillary P
Rec. A	Lawrence P.	Lawrence P.	Lawrence P.	Hillary P	Scott W
Lounge C	Hillary P	Hillary P	Bill T	Scott W	Lawrence P.

95. Look at the graphic. Where will the longest course take place?

(A) Orlando
(B) Boston
(C) New York
(D) Seattle

96. Who most likely are the people attending the seminar?

(A) Wealthy people
(B) People who want to get rich
(C) Those who are bored
(D) Those invited by friends

97. What is the speaker trying to do?

(A) Sell real estate
(B) Sell seminar packages
(C) Sell vacations
(D) Sell small businesses

98. Who is speaking to the staff?

(A) Human Resources
(B) The regional manager
(C) The CEO
(D) The sales manager

99. Look at the graphic. Which employee was given responsibility for two common areas on the same day?

(A) Lawrence P.
(B) Hillary P.
(C) Scott W.
(D) Bill T.

100. What is indicated in the meeting?

(A) The staff will get reprimanded.
(B) The staff will need to work weekends.
(C) Everyone will get a holiday bonus.
(D) There have been a lot of complaints.

This is the end of the Listening test.

LISTENING TEST

In the Listening test, you will be asked to demonstrate how well you understand spoken English. The entire Listening test will last approximately 45 minutes. There are four parts, and directions are given for each part. You must mark your answers on the separate answer sheet. Do not write your answers in your test book.

PART 1

Directions: For each question in this part, you will hear four statements about a picture in your test book. When you hear the statements, you must select the one statement that best describes what you see in the picture. Then find the number of the question on your answer sheet and mark your answer. The statements will not be printed in your test book and will be spoken only one time.

Example

Sample Answer
Ⓐ ● Ⓒ Ⓓ

Statement (B), "They're looking at the document," is the best description of the picture, so you should select answer (B) and mark it on your answer sheet.

1.

2.

3.

4.

5.

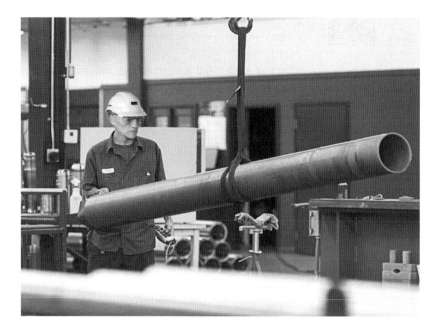

6.

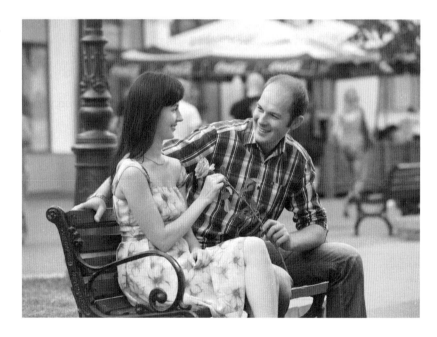

GO ON TO THE NEXT PAGE

ACTUAL TEST

10

PART 2

Directions: You will hear a question or statement and three responses spoken in English. They will not be printed in your test book and will be spoken only one time. Select the best response to the question or statement and mark the letter (A), (B), or (C) on your answer sheet.

7. Mark your answer on your answer sheet.

8. Mark your answer on your answer sheet.

9. Mark your answer on your answer sheet.

10. Mark your answer on your answer sheet.

11. Mark your answer on your answer sheet.

12. Mark your answer on your answer sheet.

13. Mark your answer on your answer sheet.

14. Mark your answer on your answer sheet.

15. Mark your answer on your answer sheet.

16. Mark your answer on your answer sheet.

17. Mark your answer on your answer sheet.

18. Mark your answer on your answer sheet.

19. Mark your answer on your answer sheet.

20. Mark your answer on your answer sheet.

21. Mark your answer on your answer sheet.

22. Mark your answer on your answer sheet.

23. Mark your answer on your answer sheet.

24. Mark your answer on your answer sheet.

25. Mark your answer on your answer sheet.

26. Mark your answer on your answer sheet.

27. Mark your answer on your answer sheet.

28. Mark your answer on your answer sheet.

29. Mark your answer on your answer sheet.

30. Mark your answer on your answer sheet.

31. Mark your answer on your answer sheet.

PART 3 ◀39▶

Directions: You will hear some conversations between two or more people. You will be asked to answer three questions about what the speakers say in each conversation. Select the best response to each question and mark the letter (A), (B), (C), or (D) on your answer sheet. The conversations will not be printed in your test book and will be spoken only one time.

32. How do the speakers know each other?

   (A) They met through a friend.
   (B) They take a class together.
   (C) They live in the same apartment complex.
   (D) They work at the same company.

33. What does the woman suggest that the man do?

   (A) Introduce himself to his coworkers
   (B) Wear a work uniform
   (C) Learn how to make a list of goods
   (D) Have a house-warming party

34. What does the man need to do first?

   (A) Change his clothes
   (B) Attach a name tag
   (C) Contact a warehouse supervisor
   (D) Read an employee handbook

35. Why is the man calling?

   (A) He forgot a document password.
   (B) He needs an important document.
   (C) He wants to apply for a job.
   (D) His computer is not working.

36. When will the woman leave work?

   (A) 4:00 p.m.
   (B) 5:00 p.m.
   (C) 6:00 p.m.
   (D) 7:00 p.m.

37. What does the woman suggest the man do?

   (A) Extend a warranty
   (B) Come to work early tomorrow
   (C) Participate in a survey
   (D) Check his email

ACTUAL TEST

10

GO ON TO THE NEXT PAGE ➡

38. Where does the woman work?

    (A) At a restaurant
    (B) At a hostel
    (C) At a movie theater
    (D) At a hotel

39. Why are the tables and chairs currently unavailable?

    (A) A shipment has not arrived.
    (B) The woman didn't permit their use.
    (C) Other people are using them.
    (D) The storage room is locked.

40. What does the man clarify?

    (A) The expected number of guests
    (B) The location of stored supplies
    (C) The starting time of an event
    (D) The necessary documents

41. What are the speakers mainly discussing?

    (A) A new recipe
    (B) A grand opening
    (C) An interview
    (D) A detailed itinerary

42. What change does the woman mention about the restaurant?

    (A) A menu was expanded.
    (B) An address was changed.
    (C) A document was revised.
    (D) An opening date was delayed.

43. What does the man suggest doing?

    (A) Redecorating the space
    (B) Hiring a Mexican chef
    (C) Meeting at a different time
    (D) Making a reservation

44. Where is the conversation taking place?

    (A) At a hardware store
    (B) At a fish market
    (C) At a pet store
    (D) At an animal shelter

45. What problem does the man mention?

    (A) A piece of equipment is out of order.
    (B) Some fish was not cooked properly.
    (C) A personal item has been lost.
    (D) An extra charge was added.

46. What does the woman say she will do?

    (A) Deliver an item
    (B) Fix a computer error
    (C) Replace a purchase
    (D) Offer a discount

47. Who most likely is the man?

    (A) A recording technician
    (B) A tour guide
    (C) A musician
    (D) A radio host

48. What kind of music does the woman currently play?

    (A) Pop
    (B) Rock
    (C) Folk
    (D) Blues

49. According to the woman, what will be different about her upcoming performance?

    (A) It will begin at midnight.
    (B) It is free to the public.
    (C) It will be broadcast live.
    (D) It will include more performers.

50. Who is Mr. Hyatt?

(A) Building Manager
(B) Funds Manager
(C) Accountant
(D) Construction worker

51. What problem does Mrs. Jasmin mention?

(A) The main branch is closed.
(B) Construction is continuing.
(C) She didn't receive some funds.
(D) The timing was incorrect.

52. What does Mr. Hyatt ask Mrs. Jasmin to do?

(A) Not to message him back
(B) Send him a message back
(C) Review the receipt
(D) Cancel the transfer

---

53. What does the woman say about the restaurant space?

(A) She thinks it's too big.
(B) It has a good location.
(C) The location is not good.
(D) It's a bit far from her office.

54. Why does the woman say, "I've looked at another location up the street that is about 10% cheaper"?

(A) To get a lower rental price
(B) To buy the property
(C) To prepare a new contract
(D) To deny the request

55. What does the man say about the price?

(A) He agrees to reduce it.
(B) He has to ask his co-worker.
(C) He has to ask his manager.
(D) He refuses to reduce it.

---

56. What are the speakers discussing?

(A) Sales results of last quarter
(B) Sales results of last month
(C) Sales of the new range
(D) Sales for the coming month

57. What does the woman imply when she says, "that's interesting"?

(A) She wants to work at the Collingwood store.
(B) She knows their sales are down.
(C) She wasn't listening to the man.
(D) She wants to know why sales are down.

58. What does the man suggest they do?

(A) Visit Head Office
(B) Visit the Woodsdale store
(C) Visit the Collingwood store
(D) Visit their manager

---

59. Where most likely are the speakers?

(A) At an office
(B) At a lawyer's office
(C) At a hardware store
(D) At a restaurant

60. What does the man mention about the delivery?

(A) He isn't getting any equipment delivered to the office.
(B) He is getting the small equipment delivered to the office.
(C) He is getting a drill delivered to the office.
(D) He is getting some documents delivered to the office.

61. What does the man say he needs?

(A) A saw
(B) Some tapes
(C) A shovel
(D) Some nails

GO ON TO THE NEXT PAGE ➡

ACTUAL TEST

10

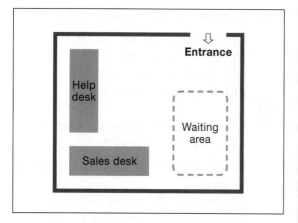

Fire Drill Procedures January 21st		
Level 1	8 a.m. - 9 a.m.	Human Resources Department
Level 2	9 a.m. - 10 a.m.	Accounting Department
Level 3	11 a.m. - 12 p.m.	Customer Service Department
Level 4	12 p.m. - 1 p.m.	Legal Department

62. What did the man recently do?

(A) He met with a photographer.
(B) He met with a sales associate.
(C) He met with an interior decorator.
(D) He met with his supervisor.

63. Why does the man want to move the sales desk?

(A) To increase the company's sales
(B) To make it look nicer
(C) To make more room for the woman to work
(D) To give waiting customers more space

64. Look at the graphic. Where will the sales desk be moved to?

(A) Where the help desk is now
(B) So it is to the right of the entrance
(C) Where the waiting area is
(D) They will move the help desk instead

65. What did the man say about next week?

(A) There will be an inspection.
(B) Some new computers will arrive.
(C) They will have fire drills.
(D) Someone called in sick.

66. Look at the graphic. What department do the speakers work in?

(A) Human Resources
(B) Accounting
(C) Customer Service
(D) Legal

67. What does the woman suggest they do?

(A) Don't say anything
(B) Print out some extra copies
(C) Speak to their supervisor
(D) Put up a sign

1980 Mazda Mikado Plastic Model

Part A - 1:25 scale plastic model kit

Part B - Snap fit tool

Part C - Rubber tires

Part D - Rub-on decals

68. Where does the man most likely work?

    (A) At a stationery shop
    (B) At a hardware store
    (C) At a model shop
    (D) At a medical clinic

69. Look at the graphic. Which part is the woman missing?

    (A) Decals
    (B) Model kit
    (C) Snap fit tool
    (D) Rubber tires

70. What does the man offer to do?

    (A) Deliver it to her
    (B) Give her a refund
    (C) Cancel the order
    (D) Express-post it to her

PART 4 ◖40◗

Directions: You will hear some talks given by a single speaker. You will be asked to answer three questions about what the speaker says in each talk. Select the best response to each question and mark the letter (A), (B), (C), or (D) on your answer sheet. The talks will not be printed in your test book and will be spoken only one time.

71. What did Ms. Jansen offer to do?

(A) Attend a meeting
(B) Go to New York
(C) Take care of the speaker's child
(D) Lend a personal item

72. What will happen in April?

(A) An annual conference
(B) A business merger
(C) A budget review
(D) A town meeting

73. What will the listener most likely inform the speaker about?

(A) The time of arrival
(B) The payment
(C) An event location
(D) A weekend schedule

74. Where most likely is this announcement being made?

(A) In a factory
(B) On an airplane
(C) At a bus terminal
(D) At an airport

75. What can listeners receive at the counter?

(A) A name tag
(B) A receipt
(C) A meal ticket
(D) Some refreshments

76. What are listeners asked to do?

(A) Form a line
(B) Stay nearby
(C) Sign a document
(D) Present a ticket

77. Where most likely is the speaker?

    (A) In a museum
    (B) In a library
    (C) In a lecture hall
    (D) In a gift shop

78. According to the speaker, what is Dr. Simmons famous for?

    (A) Writing best-selling books
    (B) Making important discoveries
    (C) Finding ancient buildings
    (D) Conducting groundbreaking experiments

79. What does the speaker request that listeners do?

    (A) Purchase a day pass
    (B) Turn off a camera
    (C) Refrain from using a flash
    (D) Stay with the group

---

80. What is the speaker mainly discussing?

    (A) A company picnic
    (B) A job opportunity
    (C) A new benefit
    (D) Overseas expansion

81. According to the speaker, what can listeners do online?

    (A) Find out a new payment
    (B) Register for a workshop
    (C) Remit a monthly payment
    (D) Review a proposal

82. Why should some listeners contact Suzie Summers?

    (A) To request a schedule change
    (B) To obtain personal information
    (C) To cancel a subscription
    (D) To congratulate a co-worker

---

83. Who most likely are the listeners?

    (A) Lawyers
    (B) Accountants
    (C) Bankers
    (D) Cashiers

84. What does the woman mean when she says, "I know that you are all very busy"?

    (A) She wants to organize a meeting.
    (B) She needs more printers.
    (C) She is recognizing their concerns.
    (D) She isn't sure what to do.

85. What task does the speaker assign to the listeners?

    (A) Spend a week with the interns
    (B) Not to speak to the interns
    (C) Write a training manual
    (D) Report on sales figures

---

86. What product does the speaker's company sell?

    (A) Electronics
    (B) Software
    (C) Wearable technology
    (D) Automobile

87. According to the speaker, what happened last month?

    (A) Someone was fired.
    (B) Some products sold well.
    (C) The company went bankrupt.
    (D) There was a merger.

88. What does the woman mean when she says, "sit in on the meeting"?

    (A) She will send employees an email.
    (B) She wants employees to prepare a report.
    (C) She wants employees to come to the meeting.
    (D) She will have a conference call.

GO ON TO THE NEXT PAGE

89. What product does the speaker's company sell?

(A) Heating products
(B) Air conditioners
(C) Vacuum cleaners
(D) Magazines

90. According to the speaker, what happened last month?

(A) They signed a special contract.
(B) They bought out another company.
(C) They traded stocks.
(D) Their sales went down.

91. What does the man mean when he says, "How about that?"

(A) He is confused about the situation.
(B) He is pleased with the results.
(C) He isn't happy.
(D) He wants to try to upgrade their computers.

SPRINGFIELD DANCE TROUPE CLASS SCHEDULE							
Class	Mon	Tue	Wed	Thu	Fri	Sat	Sun
Hip Hop	X	X	X	Tiffany 11-2	Tiffany 11-2	Owen 11-2	Owen 11-2
Swing	Beth 11-2	Beth 11-2	Beth 11-2	Beth 11-2	Beth 11-2	X	X
Jazz	Gwen 5-8	X	Gwen 5-8	X	X	Gwen 5-8	X
Ballet	Sally 1-4	Sally 1-4	X	X	X	X	X

92. What is indicated about Springfield Dance Troupe?

(A) They are changing the music they like.
(B) They are moving to a new location.
(C) They want to find a new swing class instructor.
(D) They are changing the courses they will offer.

93. Look at the graphic. What can you infer about the dance classes?

(A) They will be difficult.
(B) They are for beginners.
(C) Dance classes last for three hours.
(D) They are coed.

94. What does Springfield Dance Troupe invite the public to do?

(A) Come to their picnic
(B) See them in the concert hall downtown
(C) Watch them perform a hip-hop dance routine
(D) Say goodbye to Sally Jones

Presidential Tailoring Pricing Structure
FIRST MEASUREMENTS ARE FREE

Men's trousers	$35*
Men's jackets	$150*
Women's ensembles	$130*
Women's gowns	$200*

*Prices may vary by choice and volume of fabric chosen or required.

INVOICE

Item	Quantity	Volume discount
Foot Stools	36	3%
Chairs	12	0%
Small End tables	117	5%
Large End tables	24	5%

95. What is indicated in the advertisement?

(A) Presidential Tailoring is just getting started in their business.
(B) Jeffrey Frye is an experienced American tailor trained overseas.
(C) Presidential Tailoring is having a big sale.
(D) They only have one tailor on staff.

96. Look at the graphic. What is true about the pricing?

(A) It can change based on the material chosen.
(B) Women's gowns are cheaper than women's ensembles.
(C) Women's ensembles cost more than men's jackets.
(D) All of the clothes are 10% off.

97. What can you infer about Presidential Tailoring?

(A) They are a discount clothier.
(B) They work with leather.
(C) Their target market is children.
(D) They take a lot of pride in their work.

98. Look at the graphic. Which item was incorrectly discounted?

(A) Foot stools 3%
(B) Chairs 0%
(C) Small end tables 5%
(D) Large end tables 5%

99. What is Mr. Johnson asked to do with the invoice?

(A) Change the large end table orders to two dozen
(B) Make the invoice match the order
(C) Send the invoice to the factory for completion
(D) Send the invoice to accounting

100. What does the speaker anticipate will happen next?

(A) He will receive his order.
(B) He will receive a new invoice.
(C) He will have to place the order a third time.
(D) He will need to use a different supplier.

GO ON TO THE NEXT PAGE

This is the end of the Listening test.

AUDIO SCRIPT
&
TRANSLATION

ACTUAL TEST ①

PART 1 P. 18–21 01

1. Ⓐ **The woman is talking on the phone.**
   Ⓑ The woman is using her cell phone.
   Ⓒ The woman is typing on the laptop.
   Ⓓ The woman is writing in her notebook.

2. Ⓐ **The woman is cooking some bacon.**
   Ⓑ The woman is baking a cake.
   Ⓒ The woman is preparing for dinner.
   Ⓓ The woman is frying some fish.

3. Ⓐ **The man is holding some seafood.**
   Ⓑ The woman is baking a crab.
   Ⓒ They are scared of the crab.
   Ⓓ The family is shopping for breakfast.

4. Ⓐ The man is using a screwdriver to screw a nail
      into the building frame.
   Ⓑ **The man is hammering something into a
      building frame.**
   Ⓒ The man is making the frame with his hand.
   Ⓓ The man is wearing protective glasses.

5. Ⓐ **There are some tables and chairs outdoors.**
   Ⓑ There are some people sitting at the tables.
   Ⓒ There are plastic umbrellas on the tables.
   Ⓓ There are many flowers in the garden.

6. Ⓐ They are looking at each other.
   Ⓑ The woman is typing on her computer.
   Ⓒ The man is using the calculator.
   Ⓓ **The man is writing something onto the
      notepad.**

PART 2 P. 22 02

7. Where was the company picnic held?
   Ⓐ In April.
   Ⓑ Refreshments will be provided.
   Ⓒ **At a park next to a lake.**

1. Ⓐ 女子正在講電話。
   Ⓑ 女子正在使用手機。
   Ⓒ 女子正在用筆記型電腦打字。
   Ⓓ 女子正在筆記本裡寫字。

2. Ⓐ 女子正在烹煮培根。
   Ⓑ 女子正在烘焙蛋糕。
   Ⓒ 女子正在準備晚餐。
   Ⓓ 女子正在煎某種魚。

3. Ⓐ 男子正拿著海鮮。
   Ⓑ 女子正在烘焙螃蟹。
   Ⓒ 他們都害怕這隻螃蟹。
   Ⓓ 這家人正在購買早餐。

4. Ⓐ 男子正在使用螺絲起子將釘子鎖
      進建築物的框架。
   Ⓑ 男子正在用鐵鎚將某個物件敲進
      建築物的框架。
   Ⓒ 男子正在用手製作框架。
   Ⓓ 男子戴著護目鏡。

5. Ⓐ 戶外有一些桌椅。
   Ⓑ 有些人坐在桌子旁。
   Ⓒ 桌子上有塑膠傘。
   Ⓓ 花園裡有許多花朵。

6. Ⓐ 他們正看著彼此。
   Ⓑ 女子正在用電腦打字。
   Ⓒ 男子正在使用計算機。
   Ⓓ 男子正在記事本上寫字。

7. 公司的野餐在哪裡舉行？
   Ⓐ 在四月。
   Ⓑ 將會供應茶點。
   Ⓒ 在湖邊的公園。

8. Who's working at the front desk today?
   A That's a difficult request.
   B It's Katie Miller.
   C Make room on your desk.

9. Would you like to work together or separately?
   A Actually, I prefer working alone.
   B Let's gather the company's data.
   C Before next Friday.

10. Have you introduced yourself to the new employee?
    A A new reward system will be introduced soon.
    B No, I've been too busy today.
    C Nice to meet you.

11. Where does this bus go to?
    A You need a transit card.
    B The bus stop is over there.
    C It is headed downtown.

12. The elevator has been repaired, right?
    A She works on the third floor.
    B Yes, it is working again.
    C That's not what I saw.

13. What was the cost of replacing the window?
    A I think it was less than 60 dollars.
    B In a department store.
    C It wasn't difficult at all.

14. Will you be checking your email tomorrow?
    A Look at the attachment.
    B Actually, I'll be on vacation.
    C We accept cash or check.

15. Have you considered building a fence?
    A The house is for sale.
    B Yes, we're doing that next.
    C His remarks caused offense.

16. Why did the subway stop running early tonight?
    A Because it's a holiday.
    B Let's get off at the next station.
    C No, I won't be running tomorrow.

17. How was the museum tour?
    A The window faces the street.
    B Between Williams Street and Keller Avenue.
    C It was very informative.

8. 今天是誰站櫃檯？
   A 那是個困難的請求。
   B 是凱蒂‧米勒。
   C 把你的書桌騰出空間。

9. 你想要一起或是個別工作？
   A 其實，我偏好單獨工作。
   B 我們來匯集電腦資料吧。
   C 在下個週五前。

10. 你向新進員工自我介紹了嗎？
    A 很快會推行一個新的獎勵機制。
    B 還沒有，我今天太忙了。
    C 很高興見到你。

11. 這班公車開往哪裡？
    A 你需要一張轉乘卡。
    B 公車站就在那裡。
    C 它開往市區。

12. 電梯已經修好了，對吧？
    A 她在三樓上班。
    B 是的，它又正常運轉了。
    C 我看到的並非如此。

13. 更換窗戶要多少錢？
    A 我想還不到 60 元。
    B 在百貨公司裡。
    C 一點都不困難。

14. 你明天會查看電子郵件嗎？
    A 看附件。
    B 事實上，我將要去度假。
    C 我們接受現金或支票。

15. 你考慮過要圍個籬笆嗎？
    A 房子在出售中。
    B 是的，我們接下來將會那麼做。
    C 他的話語冒犯了人。

16. 地鐵為何今晚提早收班？
    A 因為今天是假日。
    B 我們在下一站下車吧。
    C 不，我明天不會跑步。

17. 博物館之旅怎麼樣？
    A 這扇窗面向街道。
    B 在威廉斯街和凱勒大道之間。
    C 很有教育意義。

18. Why weren't the flyers ready in time for the event?
    A They're not frequent flyers.
    B The copier malfunctioned.
    C It was the company's 40th anniversary.

19. Who's speaking at tonight's opening ceremony?
    A Front row seats.
    B Mr. Gibson will close the door.
    C A famous novelist.

20. When should I turn on the air conditioner?
    A When it reaches 25 degrees.
    B I agree with you.
    C They'll be on air in about an hour.

21. Which seat is mine?
    A It's a comfortable chair.
    B Please sit anywhere.
    C Keep that in mind.

22. I couldn't get a hold of George.
    A Hold the line, please.
    B Some empty boxes.
    C Try calling back later.

23. Shouldn't our food have been served by now?
    A It was delicious.
    B Yes, the service is rather slow tonight.
    C I'll order the tomato pasta.

24. Why don't we take a group picture?
    A Sure, let's do it on the steps.
    B A digital camera.
    C Yes, she looks attractive in this picture.

25. This new coffee maker was very expensive.
    A He has extensive management experience.
    B There's a paper jam in the copy machine.
    C That's why the coffee tastes great.

26. Are you going out for dinner or staying in?
    A I'm going to order delivery.
    B Please bring the bill.
    C At a convenient time.

27. Would you like to borrow this book when I finish reading it?
    A Ms. Watson will be leading the team.
    B I'm going to book a table for dinner.
    C No, I'll get it from the library.

18. 傳單為何沒及時在這場活動前準備好？
    A 它們不是飛行常客。
    B 影印機故障了。
    C 這是公司 40 週年紀念日。

19. 誰要在今晚的開幕典禮演講？
    A 前排的座位。
    B 吉普森先生將會關門。
    C 一位知名的小說家。

20. 我應該什麼時候開空調？
    A 氣溫到達 25 度時。
    B 我同意你的看法。
    C 它們大約一小時後會播出。

21. 哪一個座位是我的？
    A 這是一張舒適的椅子。
    B 請隨意就座。
    C 請謹記在心。

22. 我無法與喬治取得聯繫。
    A 請先別掛電話。
    B 一些空的盒子。
    C 試著稍後再打電話。

23. 現在不是該上我們的餐點嗎？
    A 相當美味。
    B 是的，今晚的服務速度很緩慢。
    C 我要點番茄義大利麵。

24. 我們何不來拍團體照？
    A 好啊，我們在階梯上拍吧。
    B 一台數位相機。
    C 是的，照片裡的她看起來很迷人。

25. 這台新的咖啡機非常貴。
    A 他擁有很廣泛的管理經驗。
    B 影印機卡紙了。
    C 那就是為什麼這咖啡很好喝。

26. 你要外出吃晚餐還是待在家裡？
    A 我要點外送。
    B 請將帳單拿過來。
    C 在方便的時候。

27. 等我讀完這本書時，你想要借閱嗎？
    A 華生女士將會帶領這個團隊。
    B 我將要訂晚餐的桌位。
    C 不，我要去圖書館借。

28. Didn't you receive a paycheck?

   A No, they are distributed next week.

   B Sure, I'll send him an email.

   C She wants to get the promotion.

29. You set up chairs in the conference room, didn't you?

   A I need a reference book.

   B Yes, 200 seats in total.

   C No, I couldn't find the email address.

30. I was very impressed with Alex's singing.

   A I forgot the singer's name.

   B Where is the concert?

   C Yes, he has a wonderful voice.

31. How about renting a larger space for the party?

   A Is that really necessary?

   B I returned the equipment.

   C I'm not a tenant.

28. 你沒有收到薪資支票嗎？

   A 沒有，下星期才會發放。

   B 當然，我會寄電子郵件給他。

   C 她想要獲得晉升。

29. 你在會議室裡擺放了椅子，對吧？

   A 我需要一本參考書籍。

   B 是的，總共 200 個座位。

   C 不，我找不到那個電子郵件信箱。

30. 我對亞力克斯的歌聲印象深刻。

   A 我忘了歌手的名字。

   B 音樂會在哪裡？

   C 是的，他有很棒的聲音。

31. 為這派對租個較大的場地如何？

   A 有這個必要嗎？

   B 我歸還了設備。

   C 我不是房客。

PART 3   P. 23-27

32–34 conversation

M： Hello, I'm Steven from Home Appliance Mart. **(32) I'm here to install the UHD television that you ordered last week.**

W： Yes, come right this way. We would like to mount the television on this wall. We plan to use it for presentations and training seminars.

M： Oh, no. **(33) It looks like I forgot the tools that I need to screw the television to the wall mount.** I'm sorry. I'll have to come back tomorrow morning.

W： Oh, that's all right. **(34) However, please call me before you come tomorrow to make sure that someone is in the office to meet you.**

32–34 對話

男： 您好，我是家用寶超市的史帝芬。**(32) 我是來安裝您上星期訂購的超高畫質電視。**

女： 好的，請往這裡來。我們想要將電視安裝在牆上，我們打算用它來做簡報和培訓研討會。

男： 糟了，**(33) 我似乎忘了帶將電視栓在壁掛上所需的工具。** 很抱歉，我得明天早上再來。

女： 喔，沒關係。**(34) 不過，明天你來之前請打電話給我，以確保辦公室有人能接待你。**

32. What are the speakers mainly discussing?

   A A training seminar

   B The installation of a television

   C The date of a presentation

   D A software upgrade

32. 對話者主要在討論什麼？

   A 培訓研討會

   B 安裝電視機

   C 簡報日期

   D 軟體更新

33. What is the problem?
   Ⓐ The necessary tools are unavailable.
   Ⓑ The office is closed.
   Ⓒ The wall is too weak.
   Ⓓ The phone number was wrong.

34. What most likely will the man do first tomorrow?
   Ⓐ Order a replacement part
   Ⓑ Consult an instruction manual
   Ⓒ Contact the woman
   Ⓓ Fill out a work order

35–37 conversation

W：Hello, Mr. Weaver. **(35) You are one of the final applicants that we are considering for the teaching position at Belmont University.** How do you think your previous jobs have prepared you to teach at our university?

M：**(36) Well, I used to be an editor-in-chief at a literary magazine.** Therefore, I think it has prepared me well to teach in the English literature department at your university. I would be able to help students to become better writers.

W：Well, I think you are right about that. You seem to be qualified for the position. As you may know, we don't pay a lot for this position. **(37) However, if you take the job, you would receive a lot of time off during the summer vacation.**

M：Actually, that's one of the reasons I chose to apply for this job.

35. What position is the man applying for?
   Ⓐ Lecturer
   Ⓑ Editor
   Ⓒ Journalist
   Ⓓ Superintendent

36. What makes the man qualified for the position?
   Ⓐ His academic background
   Ⓑ His work experience
   Ⓒ His popularity
   Ⓓ His eloquence

33. 出了什麼問題？
   Ⓐ 缺少必要的工具
   Ⓑ 辦公室關閉了
   Ⓒ 牆壁太薄弱
   Ⓓ 電話號碼有誤

34. 男子明天最有可能先做什麼？
   Ⓐ 訂購更換的零件
   Ⓑ 查詢說明書
   Ⓒ 聯繫女子
   Ⓓ 填寫工作通知單

35–37 對話

女：您好，威佛先生。**(35) 您是我們考慮要錄取擔任貝爾蒙特大學教職的決選人。**您覺得您先前的工作是如何預備您在我們的大學教書呢？

男：**(36) 嗯，我以前是文學雜誌的主編。**因此我認為這讓我準備好能在貴大學的英國文學系教書。我能幫助學生更擅長寫作。

女：嗯，我想關於這點您說的是對的，您看起來很適合擔任這項職務。您可能知道，我們這個職務的給薪並不高。**(37) 然而，您若接受這份工作，就能在暑假期間享有許多休假。**

男：實際上，這就是我選擇這份工作的原因之一。

35. 男子應徵什麼職務？
   Ⓐ 講師
   Ⓑ 編輯
   Ⓒ 記者
   Ⓓ 主管

36. 什麼使男子符合此項職務的資格？
   Ⓐ 他的學術背景
   Ⓑ 他的資歷
   Ⓒ 他的名氣
   Ⓓ 他的口才

37. What extra benefit does the woman mention?

    A Health insurance

    B Flexible hours

    C A lot of free time

    D Regular incentives

37. 女子提到什麼額外的福利？

    A 健康保險

    B 彈性工時

    C 許多的空閒時間

    D 常態的獎勵

38–40 conversation

W：**(38) Chris, how are the renovations going in the dining room?** Do you think we'll be ready to reopen by this Saturday?

M：No, definitely not. The shipment of floor tiles still hasn't arrived. **(39) Because the floor space is so large, it'll take at least a week to finish the entire project.**

W：Ah, I see. Well, we have a lot of dinner reservations for the weekend. What should I do about that?

M：**(40) Why don't you call everyone who already made a reservation and offer them a 20% discount on their next meal by way of compensation?**

38–40 對話

女：**(38) 克里斯，飯廳的翻修進行得如何？**你認為我們在這週六之前能準備好重新開幕嗎？

男：不，一定不行，地磚還沒有送達。**(39) 因為地板的面積很大，所以至少要花一個星期才能完成整個工程。**

女：啊，我了解了。週末有很多的晚餐訂位。我該怎麼處理？

男：**(40) 你何不打電話給已經訂位的人，並提供他們下次用餐打八折的優惠作為補償？**

---

38. What are the speakers mainly discussing?

    A An interior renovation

    B A product launch

    C A luncheon reservation

    D A budget proposal

38. 對話者主要在討論什麼？

    A 室內整修

    B 產品發表

    C 午餐訂位

    D 預算提案

39. What does the man say about the dining room?

    A It needs more lighting.

    B It is quite cold.

    C It is spacious.

    D It is too loud.

39. 關於飯廳，男子說了什麼？

    A 它需要更多採光

    B 它相當寒冷

    C 它空間寬敞

    D 它太過大聲

40. What does the man suggest the woman do?

    A Repaint the walls a brighter color

    B Compensate guests who have reservations

    C Draft a budget proposal

    D Open a bank account

40. 男子提議女子做什麼？

    A 將牆壁重新油漆為較亮的顏色

    B 補償已經訂位的客人

    C 起草預算提案

    D 開立銀行帳戶

41–43 conversation

M：Hi, Linda. I'm responsible for putting together a slide show for Greg's going-away party this Friday. **(41) However, I can't find many pictures.** Do you happen to have any photos of Greg that you could send to me?

41–43 對話

男：嗨，琳達。我負責籌辦幻燈片秀，要用在本週五葛雷格的歡送派對。**(41) 但是我找到的照片不多。**你是否恰好有葛雷格的一些照片能夠寄給我？

W：What? Greg is leaving the company? I had no idea.

M：Yeah, he is taking a job at a design company. **(42) He said the job is more suited to his skills.**

W：Oh, I'm happy for him. I have a few photos from last year's Christmas party. **(43) I'll find the ones with Greg in them and email them to you.**

女：什麼？葛雷格要離開公司了？我完全不知道。

男：是的，他要去一家設計公司工作。**(42) 他說這份工作更符合他的專長。**

女：喔，我很為他感到高興。我有一些去年聖誕派對的照片，**(43) 我會把裡面有葛雷格的照片找出來並用電子郵件寄給你。**

41. What is the man concerned about?
   A Getting his camera fixed
   B Receiving sick leave from work
   C Preparing for a party
   D Introducing a client

41. 男子在擔心什麼事？
   A 修理他的相機
   B 請病假不去上班
   C 為派對做準備
   D 介紹一名客戶

42. According to the man, why does Greg like his new job?
   A It offers better vacation time.
   B It pays a higher salary.
   C It matches his abilities.
   D It provides health benefits.

42. 根據男子，葛雷格為何喜歡他的新工作？
   A 它提供較好的休假時間
   B 它付給較高的薪資
   C 它符合他的能力
   D 它提供了健康福利

43. What most likely will the woman do next?
   A Take a group photo
   B Attend a Christmas party
   C Contact Greg
   D Send an email attachment

43. 女子接下來最有可能做什麼？
   A 拍團體照
   B 參加聖誕派對
   C 聯繫葛雷格
   D 寄電子郵件附件

44–46 conversation

M：Joanne, did you hear that all employees will be receiving free tablet computers next week? **(44) I'm excited about it, but actually I don't know how to use one.** Even my mobile phone is not a smartphone.

W：Don't worry about it. I have one at home and they are very user-friendly. You won't have any trouble familiarizing yourself with it.

M：I'm glad to hear that. **(45) As a logo design company, we can definitely use the tablet computers to increase work efficiency.**

W：You're right. **(46) If you have any questions, feel free to ask me for help.**

44–46 對話

男：喬安，你有聽說所有員工下星期都會拿到免費的平板電腦嗎？**(44) 我對此感到很興奮，但其實我不知道如何使用平板電腦。就連我的行動電話都不是智慧型手機。**

女：別擔心，我家裡有一台平板電腦，它們非常容易上手。要熟悉平板電腦並不困難。

男：我很高興聽你這麼說。**(45) 作為商標設計公司，我們一定可以使用平板電腦來增加工作效率。**

女：你說得對。**(46) 如果你有任何問題，請儘管找我幫忙。**

44. What is the man concerned about?
- [A] Finishing a project on time
- [B] Paying for his new mobile phone
- [C] Repairing a piece of equipment
- **[D] Learning a new skill**

45. Where do the speakers work?
- [A] At a repair shop
- [B] At an electronics store
- [C] At a marketing firm
- **[D] At a design company**

46. What does the woman offer to do?
- **[A] Provide assistance**
- [B] Pay in cash
- [C] Fill in for the man
- [D] Email a user manual

44. 男子在擔心什麼事？
- [A] 準時完成專案
- [B] 付款買新的行動電話
- [C] 修理一件器材設備
- **[D] 學習新技巧**

45. 對話者們在哪裡工作？
- [A] 在維修店
- [B] 在電子產品店
- [C] 在行銷公司
- **[D] 在設計公司**

46. 女子提議要做什麼？
- **[A] 提供協助**
- [B] 以現金付款
- [C] 為男子代班
- [D] 用電子郵件寄送使用者手冊

47–49 conversation

M： Excuse me. **(47) I'm conducting research on the effect that the new downtown mall is having on local residents' shopping habits.** Do you have a moment to talk to me?

W： Sure, no problem. I can tell you that since the mall was built, I find myself coming downtown a lot more. **(48) I think what I like most is that I never have to struggle to find a parking spot.**

M： I see. What about the variety of shops? Are you satisfied with that?

W： **(49) Well, I usually come to the mall to shop for clothes.** I think there is a wide selection of women's clothes.

47–49 對話

男： 不好意思，**(47)** 我正在進行研究，想了解新的市區商場對於在地居民的購物習慣有什麼影響。請問你有空可以與我談一下嗎？

女： 當然，沒問題。我可以告訴你，自從商場蓋好以來，我發覺自己更頻繁地來市區。**(48)** 我想我最喜歡的一點是，我從不用辛苦找停車位。

男： 我了解。你覺得商店的種類多不多？你對此滿意嗎？

女： **(49)** 我通常去商場買衣服，我認為那邊女性服飾的選擇很多。

---

47. Who most likely is the man?
- [A] A shop owner
- [B] A construction worker
- [C] A local resident
- **[D] A market researcher**

48. What does the woman mention about the mall?
- [A] It was recently renovated.
- **[B] It has sufficient parking space.**
- [C] It is attracting many tourists.
- [D] It is located outside of town.

47. 男子最有可能是什麼人？
- [A] 商店業主
- [B] 建築工人
- [C] 當地居民
- **[D] 市場研究員**

48. 關於商場，女子提到什麼？
- [A] 它才剛翻修過
- **[B] 它有足夠的停車空間**
- [C] 它吸引了許多遊客
- [D] 它座落於城鎮之外

49. Why does the woman usually visit the mall?
- [A] To purchase groceries
- [B] To meet with her clients
- **[C] To buy clothing**
- [D] To deliver products

(NEW)

50–52 conversation

W：**(50) Have you placed the order yet?** Mr. Johnson just called and said he wants two more laptops, and a 50-inch monitor.

M：Well, I already placed the previous order, **(51) but the laptops and monitor will have to wait until tomorrow. The supply company closes at 8 p.m.**

W：Oh, will they be able to deliver to us on the same day? Mr. Johnson was hoping to get everything tomorrow.

M：I'm not sure. I'll call them first thing in the morning and find out.

W：Meanwhile, how much was the total for the order?

M：It came to $12,500. Do we have enough in our budget for more laptops and a monitor?

W：**(52) I'll call Mr. Johnson and ask.** It looks like we've gone over our budget.

50. What are the speakers discussing?
- **[A] Orders for office supplies**
- [B] Equipment for a conference
- [C] The budget reports
- [D] Their colleague

51. Why does the man mention to the woman when the supply company closes?
- [A] To inform her of the business hours
- [B] To let her know she can't order anything
- **[C] To explain that the second order would be late**
- [D] To imply that new equipment can't be ordered tomorrow

52. What does the woman offer to do?
- [A] Pay for the new order
- [B] Order the supplies herself
- [C] Cancel a meeting
- **[D] Speak to their colleague**

49. 女子為何經常逛商場？
- [A] 為了購買雜貨
- [B] 為了與客戶會面
- **[C] 為了購買服飾**
- [D] 為了運送貨品

50–52 對話

女：**(50) 你已經下訂單了嗎？**強森先生剛打電話來，說他還想要兩台筆記型電腦以及一台 50 吋螢幕。

男：我已經下了先前的訂單，**(51) 但是筆記型電腦和螢幕要等到明天。供貨公司晚上八點鐘就關門了。**

女：喔，他們能在同一天把貨送來嗎？強森先生希望明天就收到所有貨品。

男：我不確定，我明天一早就會打電話確認。

女：還有，我想問這份訂單總共多少錢？

男：總計 12,500 元。我們還有足夠的預算可以加購筆記型電腦和一台螢幕嗎？

女：**(52) 我會打電話問強森先生。**看起來我們已經超過預算了。

50. 對話者們在討論什麼？
- **[A] 辦公用品的訂單**
- [B] 會議使用的設備
- [C] 預算報告
- [D] 他們的同事

51. 男子為何跟女子提到供貨公司何時關門？
- [A] 為了告知她營業時間
- [B] 為了讓她知道她無法訂購任何東西
- **[C] 為了解釋第二份訂單將會延遲**
- [D] 為了暗示新的設備明天無法訂購

52. 女子提議她要做什麼事？
- [A] 為新的訂單付款
- [B] 親自訂購用品
- [C] 取消會議
- **[D] 與他們的同事交談**

53–55 conversation

W： Hi, Mr. Jeffries. **(53) Unfortunately our client in New Jersey called and said they have to reschedule the meeting date to the 5th of July.** I went ahead and booked a ticket for the 4th. Is it OK if you go straight to Washington after New Jersey?

M： What about the client in Washington? Were they comfortable with the schedule?

W： Yes. **(54) I explained that we need to postpone the meeting in Washington because of our client in New Jersey.** I think this gives us time to prepare some additional materials for your presentation. I would like to add some more details to your PowerPoint slides about our new products. Let's meet this afternoon and discuss it.

M： **(55) That's not a bad idea. I'll see you this afternoon.**

53–55 對話

女： 嗨，傑佛瑞斯先生。**(53) 很可惜，我們在紐澤西的客戶打電話來，說他們要將會議的日期改到七月五日。** 我直接預訂了七月四日的票，你可以在紐澤西行程後直接前往華盛頓嗎？

男： 華盛頓的客戶怎麼辦？他們可以接受行程安排嗎？

女： 是的。**(54) 我向他們說明，由於紐澤西的客戶改期，所以我們需要將華盛頓的會議延後。** 我想這樣我們有就時間為你的簡報多準備額外的資料。我想要在新產品的投影片上多增加一些細節。我們今天下午會面來討論此事。

男： **(55) 那是個不錯的點子，我們今天下午見。**

---

53. What is the problem?

   Ⓐ The plane tickets were not booked

   Ⓑ A meeting had to be rescheduled

   Ⓒ The meeting was a failure

   Ⓓ A deadline has been changed

54. Which part of the business trip will be postponed?

   Ⓐ The meeting in New York

   Ⓑ The meeting in Wisconsin

   Ⓒ The meeting in Washington

   Ⓓ The meeting in Westboro

55. What does the man mean when he says, "that's not a bad idea"?

   Ⓐ He thinks it is a bad idea.

   Ⓑ He agrees with the proposed solution.

   Ⓒ He wants to hear other ideas.

   Ⓓ He disagrees with the solution.

53. 出了什麼問題？

   Ⓐ 未預訂機票

   Ⓑ 必須重新安排會議時間

   Ⓒ 會議很失敗

   Ⓓ 變更最後的期限

54. 這趟出差的哪個部分將會被推遲？

   Ⓐ 在紐約的會議

   Ⓑ 在威斯康辛的會議

   Ⓒ 在華盛頓的會議

   Ⓓ 在威斯特布路的會議

55. 男子說「那是個不錯的點子」時，指的是什麼意思？

   Ⓐ 他認為那是個壞點子

   Ⓑ 他同意所提出的解決方案

   Ⓒ 他想要聽其他的想法

   Ⓓ 他不同意解決方案

56–58 conversation

M： **(56) Rachel, how was your vacation in Australia?**

56–58 對話

男： **(56) 瑞秋，你在澳洲的假期如何？**

W： It was fantastic! It is a beautiful country, but we did not get to see everything we wanted to see. Maybe we will go back in the future. Have you managed to find a new account manager yet? We are starting to get busy and we need some more staff.

M： Actually, there is someone we are looking to hire. His CV is quite impressive. Here, take a look.

W： (57) **What's this? Is this Robert Wilder's application?** I have known him for years! (58) **We play tennis together on the weekends.** So you are thinking about hiring him?

M： Yeah. The interview went really well and he has all the qualifications. I think he can be a great member of our team.

W： I agree. I have never worked with him, but personally I think he will be an excellent employee. I'm just surprised to see him applying here.

女：假期很棒。澳洲是個美麗的國家，但我們沒看到所有想看的東西。也許我們將來會再去造訪。你找到了新的客戶經理了嗎？我們開始要忙了，需要多一些人手。

男：實際上，我們有個想要僱用的人。他的履歷表相當令人印象深刻。拿去，你看看。

女：(57) 這是什麼？是羅伯‧懷德的應徵函嗎？我認識他好多年了，(58) 我們週末時會一起打網球。你考慮要僱用他嗎？

男：是的。面試進行得很順利，而且他具備所有的條件。我認為他可以成為我們團隊很棒的一員。

女：我同意。我從未與他共事，但就我個人認為，我想他會是很好的員工，我只是很訝異得知他來求職。

56. What was the woman doing in Australia?
- [A] Conducting business
- [B] Studying abroad
- **[C] Taking a vacation**
- [D] Searching for employees

56. 女子在澳洲做什麼？
- [A] 出差
- [B] 留學
- **[C] 度假**
- [D] 找員工

57. What does the woman imply when she says, "is this Robert Wilder's application"?
- **[A] She is surprised to see the application.**
- [B] She will reject the application.
- [C] She doesn't understand something.
- [D] She agrees with the application.

57. 女子說「這是羅伯‧懷德的應徵函嗎」，她在暗示什麼？
- **[A] 她看到這份應徵函感到很驚訝**
- [B] 她將會拒絕這項應徵
- [C] 她不了解某件事
- [D] 她同意這項申請

58. How does the woman know Robert Wilder?
- [A] They went to college together.
- [B] They work in the same department.
- [C] They play baseball together.
- **[D] They play tennis together.**

58. 女子是如何認識羅伯‧懷德的？
- [A] 他們一起上大學
- [B] 他們在相同的部門工作
- [C] 他們一起打棒球
- **[D] 他們一起打網球**

59–61 conversation

M1： Tom and Julie, I need the sales reports for this month ready a bit early. Next month is really

59–61 對話

男1：湯姆和茉莉，我要你們早一點備妥這個月的銷售報告。下個月對我

important for our company, so we need to prepare a bit earlier than usual.

W: Sure. But we will need to do some overtime. **(59) We are really busy at the moment, so it's going to be a lot of extra hours after work, and I have to take care of my children.**

M2: Yeah, that's a lot of extra work. **(60) I think after next month we should get a few days added to our vacation.**

W: That sounds reasonable. **(61) I will need to hire a babysitter while I'm doing the overtime,** so the extra vacation time seems fair.

M1: I agree. OK, we will discuss the details later, but I definitely agree with you.

們公司非常重要,因此我們需要比平常更早一點做好準備。

女:當然,但我們需要加班。**(59) 我們現在真的很忙**,因此在下班後還要多花很多時間,而且我必須要照顧孩子。

男2:是的,那會額外增加很多的工作。**(60) 我認為,下個月之後我們應該要多休幾天假。**

女:這聽起來很合理。**(61) 加班的時候,我需要請保母**,因此多給幾天假似乎很合理。

男1:我同意。好,我們以後再討論細節,但我非常同意你們的看法。

59. What is the woman concerned about?
Ⓐ Getting extra vacation
Ⓑ Doing too much work
Ⓒ Not having time for her children
Ⓓ Preparing a report

59. 女子在意什麼事?
Ⓐ 獲得額外的假期
Ⓑ 做太多的工作
Ⓒ 沒有時間陪孩子
Ⓓ 準備一份報告

60. What does the man suggest?
Ⓐ Fire the manager
Ⓑ Wait until their vacation
Ⓒ Hire a new employee
Ⓓ Have some extra vacation days

60. 男子建議什麼?
Ⓐ 解聘經理
Ⓑ 等到放假再說
Ⓒ 僱用一名新員工
Ⓓ 多放幾天假

61. What does the woman say she will have to do?
Ⓐ Hire a babysitter
Ⓑ Go to another company
Ⓒ Ask her husband
Ⓓ Finish her sales reports

61. 女子說她將必須做什麼?
Ⓐ 僱用一名保母
Ⓑ 去另一家公司
Ⓒ 詢問她的丈夫
Ⓓ 完成她的銷售報告

62–64 conversation

W: Hi, we are renovating our boardroom and I'd like to purchase some cherry wood tables for our conference room. **(62) I am having a meeting with some very important clients on Friday. So I'd like to have them delivered tomorrow.** What is the cost for an emergency delivery?

M: Hold a moment, please. Next day delivery is an extra seventy-five dollars.

62–64 對話

女:嗨,我們正在翻修會議室,我想要為會議室採買一些櫻桃木桌。**(62) 我星期五要與一些很重要的客戶開會,因此我希望桌子能在明天到貨。**急件運費是多少?

男:請稍等,隔日到貨要多收 75 元。

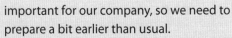

171

W : Really? That is expensive. I thought if my order was over three hundred dollars delivery would be free of charge. **M :** Well, yes. **(63) Are you planning to order the cherry wood tables?** **W :** Yes, I would like two of them. **M :** OK then, **(64) I will make sure that your order arrives tomorrow morning before midday, and delivery will be free of charge.**	**女：**真的嗎？那真是昂貴。我以為如果訂貨超過 300 元就可以免費運送。 **男：**嗯，是的。**(63) 您打算訂購櫻桃木桌嗎？** **女：**是的，我想要兩張。 **男：**好的，那麼，**(64) 我會確保您訂的貨品在明天中午之前送達，並且免運費。**

Conference Table Price List 會議桌價目表	
Pine 松木	165 元
Maple 楓木	195 元
Walnut 核桃木	225 元
Cherry 櫻桃木	307 元

62. What does the woman have on Friday?
    A A dinner
    B A seminar
    C A meeting
    D An office party

(NEW)
63. Look at the graphic. How much will the woman pay for the furniture?
    A $165
    B $195
    C $307
    D $614

64. What does the man say he will do?
    A Arrange free delivery
    B Deliver the furniture in the evening
    C Send a confirmation
    D Deliver the table himself

62. 女子在星期五有什麼事？
    A 晚餐
    B 研討會
    C 會議
    D 公司聚會

63. 參看圖表，女子要為家具付多少錢？
    A 165 元
    B 195 元
    C 307 元
    D 614 元

64. 男子說他會做什麼？
    A 安排免費運送
    B 在夜晚運送家具
    C 寄送確認書
    D 親自運送桌子

(NEW)
65–67 conversation

W : Hi, this is Rachel. **(65) I'm calling to see if I can upgrade from coach to business for my flight to (66) Thailand this June.**

M : OK, can I have your membership number please?
W : Yes, it's EM3985771.

65–67 對話

女：嗨，我是瑞秋。**(65) 我打電話是要了解，我今年六月 (66) 到泰國的班機是否可以從經濟艙升等為商務艙。**

男：好的，可以告訴我您的會員號碼嗎？
女：好的，是 EM3985771。

M：⁽⁶⁷⁾ **I'm sorry. You don't have enough points for this trip. However, I see that you're traveling to Korea and Japan next week. That should give you enough points to upgrade in June. Why don't you call again after your trip?**

W：OK, that's a great idea. I'll call again in two weeks.

男：⁽⁶⁷⁾ 很抱歉，您沒有足夠的點數供這趟旅程使用。但是我看到您下星期將要前往韓國和日本。這樣應該能讓您有足夠的點數在六月進行升等。您何不在這趟旅程後再打電話來？

女：好的，這是個好主意。我兩週後會再打來。

Airline Mileage Redemption Points 航空哩程兌換點數 ✈

To East Asia 到東亞	50,000
To Southeast Asia 到東南亞	60,000
To the Middle East 到中東	70,000
To Europe 到歐洲	80,000

65. Why does the woman call?
- **A To get an upgrade**
- B To book a flight to Korea and Japan
- C To cancel her flight to Singapore
- D To sign up for a mileage card

(NEW)
66. Look at the graphic. How many points will the woman use?
- A 50,000
- **B 60,000**
- C 70,000
- D 80,000

67. What suggestion does the man give the woman?
- A Upgrade her flight to Korea
- **B Make the request after her trip to Korea and Japan**
- C Book a different flight
- D Cancel her reservation

65. 女子為何打電話？
- **A 為了獲得升等**
- B 為了預訂前往韓國和日本的班機
- C 為了取消前往新加坡的班機
- D 為了申請哩程卡

66. 參看圖表，女子將會使用多少點數？
- A 50,000
- **B 60,000**
- C 70,000
- D 80,000

67. 男子給女子什麼建議？
- A 升等她的韓國班機
- **B 在韓日之旅後提出申請**
- C 訂不同的班機
- D 取消她的預訂

(NEW)
68–70 conversation

W：⁽⁶⁹⁾ **You beat me again! You always get to work before I do, even though I leave before you.** How do you do that?

M：Which road do you take?

W：⁽⁶⁸⁾ **I just follow my GPS and it shows that Kinsley Road is the most direct route to work.**

68–70 對話

女：⁽⁶⁹⁾ 你再次贏過我了！你總是比我早來上班，即使我比你早出門。你是怎麼辦到的？

男：你走哪一條路？

女：⁽⁶⁸⁾ 我照 GPS 指示走，它顯示金斯利路是來上班最直接的路線。

M： No, don't follow your GPS. Your route passes through several residential areas and school zones as well as traffic signs, so it takes much longer to get here.

W： Which route do you take then?

M： **(70) I go to Cambridge Street, which takes a bit of a detour from our apartments, but it's practically a highway. I even have enough time to stop for some coffee before work.**

W： Wow, I always thought Cambridge would take much longer.

M： No, it's really quick. I can show you next time.

男：不，別照你的 GPS 走。你走的路線會經過幾個住宅區和學區，還有交通號誌，因此來到這裡要花更久的時間。

女：那麼你走哪一條路線？

男：(70) 我走到康橋街，從我們的公寓出發會需要稍微繞路，但它其實是一條公路。我甚至有足夠的時間停下來，在上班前喝點咖啡。

女：哇，我一直以為走康橋街要更久。

男：不，真的很快。我下次可以帶你走看看。

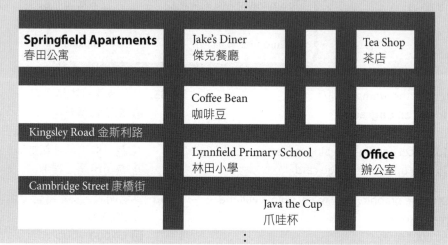

68. What are the speakers discussing?
   A Their GPS systems
   B Which coffee shop to visit
   C How far Cambridge is from their apartments
   D The fastest route to work

69. What does the woman want to do?
   A Keep losing the game
   B Make more money than the man does
   C Get to work faster than the man does
   D Participate in a car race

70. Look at the list. Which shop does the man most likely stop at?
   A Coffee Bean
   B Tea Shop
   C Java the Cup
   D Jake's Diner

68. 對話者們在討論什麼？
   A 他們的 GPS 系統
   B 要造訪哪家咖啡店
   C 康橋街距離他們的公寓有多遠
   D 上班最快速的路線

69. 女子想要做什麼？
   A 持續輸掉比賽
   B 比男子賺更多的錢
   C 比男子更快到公司
   D 參加賽車

70. 參看圖表，男子最有可能去哪一家店？
   A 咖啡豆
   B 茶店
   C 爪哇杯
   D 傑克餐廳

71–73 instructions

M：**(71) Amy, it is your responsibility to check that the store is clean and well-stocked for customers before we open for the day. (72) Most importantly, I would like you to make sure that the proper price tags are displayed in front of their corresponding products.** Customers get really confused and upset when the price of a product is displayed incorrectly. **(73) In the case that a customer ever does get displeased, please let me know right away, so I can come and deal with the problem in person.**

71–73 指示

男：**(71)** 艾美，你的責任是要在當天營業以前，為顧客確保店內清潔並且貨品充足。**(72)** 最重要的是，我希望你能確認正確的價格標籤是放置在它們相對應的商品前面。產品的標價放錯位置時，顧客會很困惑和不悅。**(73)** 若是顧客真的感到不高興，請立即告知我，讓我親自過來處理問題。

71. Where most likely does the speaker work?
  A At a theater
  B At a car dealership
  C At a retail store
  D At a library

71. 發話者最有可能在哪裡工作？
  A 在戲院
  B 在汽車經銷商
  C 在零售店
  D 在圖書館

72. What is the listener asked to double-check?
  A Accurate pricing
  B Sales figures
  C Business hours
  D Name tags

72. 聽者被要求要再確認什麼？
  A 正確的標價
  B 銷售數字
  C 營業時間
  D 名牌

73. When should the listener contact the speaker?
  A If an employee is late for work
  B If a technical problem occurs
  C If an item is out of stock
  D If a customer is dissatisfied

73. 聽者應該何時聯繫發話者？
  A 若員工遲到時
  B 若發生了技術性的問題時
  C 若產品缺貨時
  D 若顧客不滿意時

74–76 announcement

W：**(74) The town of Dayton is excited to announce the opening of a new community center.** The center provides daytime activities for kids and adults of all ages. **(75) For the grand opening, the local band Summer Heat, led by Jim Neilson, will perform a show in half an hour. (76) Afterwards, attendees are encouraged to fill out a survey meant to judge the needs of local citizens.** Thank you.

74—76 宣布

女：**(74)** 德頓鎮很高興宣布，新的社區活動中心開幕了。中心為各年齡層的孩子和成人提供日間的活動。**(75)** 為了慶祝盛大開幕，由吉姆‧尼爾森領銜演出的本地樂團夏季之熱，將在半小時後演出。**(76)** 在那之後，我們希望與會者能填寫問卷，以評估本地人的需求。謝謝您。

74. What is the announcement about?

[A] **An opening of a public building**

[B] A commemorative statue

[C] A singing contest

[D] A survey result

75. Who is Jim Neilson?

[A] A mayor

[B] An instructor

[C] **A musician**

[D] An architect

76. What are attendees asked to do?

[A] Reserve seats in advance

[B] **Complete a survey**

[C] Subscribe to a newsletter

[D] Contribute to a fundraiser

77–79 talk

W：Good morning, everyone. **(77) Welcome to the test screening of our pilot for a new daytime sitcom entitled *Once Upon a Romance.*** Your participation in this focus group is essential for assessing audience reception. **(78) This television show is meant to appeal to middle-aged housewives, and that is why you have all been selected. (79) After watching the pilot, we will take you to a meeting room, where we will conduct an in-depth interview that will help us gather your feedback and responses.** Thank you again for your cooperation.

---

77. Who most likely is the speaker?

[A] A scholar

[B] **A producer**

[C] A pilot

[D] A programmer

78. Who most likely are the listeners?

[A] Potential investors

[B] Actors

[C] **Homemakers**

[D] University students

---

74. 這個宣布與什麼有關？

[A] **公共建築物的開幕**

[B] 紀念雕像

[C] 歌唱比賽

[D] 調查結果

75. 吉姆・尼爾森是什麼人？

[A] 市長

[B] 講師

[C] **音樂家**

[D] 建築師

76. 出席的人被要求做什麼？

[A] 提前訂位

[B] **填寫問卷**

[C] 訂閱電子報

[D] 捐錢給募款者

77–79 談話

女：各位早安。**(77)** 歡迎來到日間情境喜劇《昔日浪漫》的首集試映會。你們來參與此焦點小組的訪談，對於評估觀眾的接受度非常重要。**(78)** 這個電視節目是要迎合中年家庭主婦，這也是各位被選中的原因。**(79)** 觀賞過試播影片後，我們會帶各位到會議室進行深度訪談，以幫助我們收集各位的意見和回應。再次感謝各位的合作。

---

77. 發話者最有可能是什麼人？

[A] 學者

[B] **製作人**

[C] 飛行員

[D] 程式設計師

78. 聽眾最有可能是什麼人？

[A] 潛在投資者

[B] 演員

[C] **家庭主婦**

[D] 大學生

79. What will the listeners do in the meeting room?
[A] Participate in a raffle
[B] Watch a video
[C] Enroll in a class
[D] Attend an interview

79. 聽眾將會在會議室做什麼？
[A] 參與抽獎
[B] 觀賞影片
[C] 報名參加課程
[D] 參與訪談

80–82 radio broadcast

M： **(80) This is a reminder that legendary soccer player Tommy Durant will be signing autographs at Dave's Sport Shop at 1:00 p.m. tomorrow. (81) You are encouraged to bring your own items, such as clothes or books, for Mr. Durant to autograph.** Also at this time, parents will be able to sign their children up for a summer soccer camp that will be run by Tommy Durant. **(82) The camp is limited to twenty children, so anyone who is interested should sign up early.**

80–82 收音機廣播

男： **(80)** 這則廣播是要提醒大家，傳奇足球選手湯米‧杜蘭將於明天下午一點在戴夫運動用品店舉辦簽名會。**(81)** 各位可以帶自己的物品給杜蘭先生簽名，像是衣服和書本等。父母亦可在此時可為子女們報名由湯米‧杜蘭承辦的夏季足球營隊。**(82)** 這個營隊人數限制為 20 名孩童，因此有興趣的人應該盡早報名。

---

80. What is the purpose of the broadcast?
[A] To announce the results of a soccer match
[B] To promote a store's grand opening
[C] To advertise a new product
[D] To inform the listeners of a special event

80. 這則廣播的目的是什麼？
[A] 為了宣布足球比賽的結果
[B] 為了宣傳商店的盛大開幕
[C] 為了廣告新產品
[D] 為了告知聽眾一項特別活動

81. What does the speaker suggest doing?
[A] Wearing comfortable clothing
[B] Exercising on a regular basis
[C] Bringing personal belongings
[D] Booking a ticket in advance

81. 發話者提議做什麼？
[A] 穿著舒適衣物
[B] 規律運動
[C] 攜帶個人物品
[D] 提前訂票

82. What does the speaker say about the summer camp?
[A] It is free of charge.
[B] It will last three months.
[C] It has a restricted number of participants.
[D] It will be sponsored by Dave's Sport Shop.

82. 關於夏令營，發話者說了什麼？
[A] 它是免費的
[B] 它將為期三個月
[C] 它有限制參與人數
[D] 它將會由戴夫運動用品店贊助

83–85 announcement

W： As I'm sure everyone is aware, **(83) we have recently merged with another company that is located in India.** Now that we have become an international corporation, **(85) we will be sending a lot of our most vital data through unsecure email systems.** According to the I.T.

83–85 宣布

女： 我相信各位都知道，**(83)** 我們最近與另外一家位於印度的公司合併了。因為我們已經成為國際企業，**(85)** 我們將透過不安全的電子郵件系統，寄送許多重要資料。根據資訊科技部門的說法，這是無可避免

department this is unavoidable. Unfortunately, this means we have to be very careful with what data we send through email. This afternoon everyone must attend a seminar explaining the new procedures for what data can be sent via email. The rest will be sent using secure air mail. If you don't come to the meeting, then I will have to explain the same thing over and over again and **(84) my schedule is too tight to do that.** So, everyone should come to the 1st floor meeting room at 2:30 p.m.

的。很可惜地，這表示對於要透過電子郵件寄送的資料，我們都必須採取非常謹慎的態度。今天下午所有人都必須出席一場研討會，會中將解釋新程序，是關於哪些資料可以透過電子郵件寄送，而其他的資料將使用安全的航空郵件寄送。如果各位不來開會，那麼我就要反覆解釋相同的東西，但 **(84) 我的行程太緊湊而無法這麼做。** 因此所有人都應該在下午兩點半來到一樓的會議室。

83. What does the speaker mention about her company?
   A **They have merged with another company.**
   B They are manufacturing a new product.
   C They are creating new policies.
   D They had record profits.

(NEW)

84. Why does the woman say, "my schedule is too tight to do that"?
   A Because the email is secure
   B To sign a new contract
   C She needs some help.
   D **She doesn't have time.**

85. What will they be sending a lot of?
   A Portfolios
   B Contract forms
   C **Vital data**
   D Building plans

83. 發話者提到關於她公司的什麼事？
   A 他們已經與另一家公司合併
   B 他們正在生產一項新產品
   C 他們正在制定新政策
   D 他們先前有破紀錄的獲利

84. 女子為何說「我的行程太緊湊而無法這麼做」？
   A 因為電子郵件是安全的
   B 為了簽署一個新合約
   C 她需要一些協助
   D 她沒有時間

85. 他們將會大量寄送什麼？
   A 文件夾
   B 合約表格
   C 重要資料
   D 建築計畫

86–88 speech

W：First of all, I'd like to thank everyone for attending the annual Bob Shilling Short Theater festival. I'm sure you have all enjoyed the performances so far. The actors have put in many nights of rehearsal to bring you some excellent performances! Next up is the Bromley Actors Guild, and they will be doing Shakespeare's play *The Tempest*. **(86) This is a play that focuses on the themes of magic and illusion. (87) Remember, last year the Bromley Actors Guild won first place at this**

86–88 演說

女：首先，我想要感謝各位出席年度的「鮑伯‧先令短劇節」。我想你們都很喜歡目前為止的演出。演員們花了許多晚排練，為各位帶來很棒的演出。接下來上場的是布朗利演員協會，他們將演出莎士比亞的戲劇《暴風雨》。**(86)** 這齣戲的主題集中在魔法及幻覺。**(87)** 還記得，去年布朗利演員協會在這場活動中奪得冠軍，因此各位應該很期待看他們演出這齣佳劇。**(88)** 演出結束

event, so you should look forward to seeing them perform this wonderful play. **(88) After the play finishes, we will have question-and-answer time**, and you can get to know some of the members of the Guild.

後，我們將會有問答時間，屆時各位就有機會認識協會的一些成員。

86. What is *The Tempest* about?
  A The evolution of man
  B A love affair between a man and a woman
  C A ghost ship
  D Magic and illusion

86. 《暴風雨》與什麼有關？
  A 人類進化
  B 男女愛情故事
  C 一艘幽靈船
  D 魔法和幻象

(NEW)
87. Why does the speaker say, "remember, last year the Bromley Actors Guild won first place at this event"?
  A To suggest that they are impressive
  B To recommend that you join them
  C To explain why they are here
  D To excuse a poor performance

87. 為何發話者說「請記得，去年布朗利演員協會在這項活動中奪得冠軍」？
  A 為了表示他們令人印象深刻
  B 為了推薦你加入他們
  C 為了解釋他們為何來到這裡
  D 為了幫差勁的演出找藉口

88. What will most likely happen after the performance?
  A Dinner and drinks
  B Question time with the actors
  C DVDs will be sold.
  D The actors will sign autographs.

88. 在表演之後最有可能發生什麼事？
  A 晚餐和飲料
  B 與演員們的提問時間
  C 將會販售 DVD
  D 演員們將會簽名

89–91 announcement

W：I'm sure you are all aware that the **(89) new line of cell phone cases and selfie sticks we released are selling very well.** For some reason though, our range of portable batteries are selling quite poorly. **(90) I wonder if the cost is too high compared to the other products on the market. We need to develop a strategy to start selling more batteries, so I've consulted with a marketing specialist in regard to changing our prices. (91) This afternoon we will have a conference call, so please come to my office after lunch and sit in on the discussion.**

89–91 宣布

女：我相信各位都知道，**(89) 我們推出的新系列手機殼和自拍棒銷售極佳。**然而，基於某個理由，我們的可攜式電池賣得相當差。**(90) 我在想，其售價與市面上其他產品相比是否太高了。**我們需要制定一項新策略，開始增加電池的銷售量。因此我已經向一位行銷專家請教調整售價的事。**(91) 今天下午我們將進行電話會議，因此午餐後請到我的辦公室來參與討論。**

89. What types of products are being discussed?
- **A Cell phone cases and selfie sticks**
- B Cell phones and MP3 Players
- C Selfie sticks and headphones
- D Software programs

90. Why does the speaker say, "I wonder if the cost is too high compared to the other products on the market"?
- A To ask for assistance
- B To offer help
- **C To suggest a change**
- D To create some new products

91. What will the listeners most likely do after lunch?
- A Review a safety policy
- B Attend a seminar
- C Go back to work
- **D Have a conference call**

89. 是什麼類型的商品正被討論？
- **A 手機殼和自拍棒**
- B 手機和 MP3 播放器
- C 自拍棒和耳機
- D 軟體程式

90. 發話者為何說「我在想，其售價與市面上其他產品相比是否太高」？
- A 為了求助
- B 為了提供幫助
- **C 為了提出一項改變**
- D 為了創造新的產品

91. 聽眾在午餐後最有可能做什麼？
- A 檢視安全政策
- B 參與研討會
- C 返回工作
- **D 進行電話會議**

92–94 telephone message

M：Hi, Susan. I'm calling about the office furniture we delivered to Harmons & Sons recently. They said their first floor looks really good, but they are going to need 20 chairs and 12 whiteboards for their boardrooms upstairs. **(93) They recently merged with another company, so I think they will have a lot more staff in their building soon.** Make sure you check what we have in the warehouse. If we are missing anything, we need to order it today. **(94) Also, before you send the order, please have me sign off on it. As the manager, I need to sign all outgoing orders before they leave the office.** Please let me know when you have the order prepared.

92–94 電話留言

男：嗨，蘇珊。我打電話來，是關於我們最近運送到哈蒙斯家族公司的一批辦公室家具。他們說一樓看起來很不錯，但還需要 20 張椅子和 12 個白板供樓上的會議室使用。**(93) 他們最近與另一家公司合併，因此我認為他們的大樓很快就會增加許多員工。**請務必確認我們倉庫裡有哪些品項，如果有任何缺貨，今天就需要訂購。**(94) 此外，你送出訂單之前，要給我簽名。身為經理，所有訂單離開辦公室之前，都需要由我簽署。**請告知我你何時能將訂單準備好。

ORDER FORM 存貨訂貨表

Item 項目	Quantity in stock 庫存量	Quantity to order 訂貨量
Office Table 辦公桌	13	0
Whiteboard 白板	0	12
Office Chair 辦公椅	0	20
Drafting Table 繪圖桌	6	0

92. Look at the graphic. Which items need to be ordered?
- Ⓐ Office tables and chairs
- Ⓑ Chairs and drafting tables
- **Ⓒ Whiteboards and office chairs**
- Ⓓ Whiteboards and drafting tables

92. 參看圖表，需要訂購哪些品項？
- Ⓐ 辦公桌椅
- Ⓑ 椅子和繪圖桌
- **Ⓒ 白板和辦公椅**
- Ⓓ 白板和繪圖桌

93. What does the speaker anticipate about the company?
- Ⓐ It won't need any more furniture.
- **Ⓑ It will have more staff in their building.**
- Ⓒ The boardrooms will be renovated.
- Ⓓ Their staff are moving offices.

93. 發話者該對公司有何預期？
- Ⓐ 他們不需要更多家具
- **Ⓑ 他們大樓會有更多的員工**
- Ⓒ 會議室將進行翻修
- Ⓓ 員工正在搬遷辦公室

94. What is the listener asked to do before making any orders?
- Ⓐ Sign them herself
- **Ⓑ Make sure the manager signs them**
- Ⓒ Bring some extra paper
- Ⓓ Prepare a delivery receipt

94. 聽者被要求在訂貨之前要做什麼？
- Ⓐ 親自簽名
- **Ⓑ 確保經理簽名**
- Ⓒ 帶來額外的紙張
- Ⓓ 備妥送貨收據

95–97 talk

W：OK, everybody, thank you for coming in. **(95) I received the statistics for this year's software market shares.** Although we are still in the top four, we need to work harder. **(96) Slight Line, Inc. has just moved past us by three percent in one year. We were much bigger than them last year.** Analysts are suggesting that Slight Line's success is due to their giving away a lot of free software updates after people buy their games. **(97) In the next quarter, we are going to begin to offer all of our expansion packs for free download.** I think this can give us the edge we need and help us get back on track.

95–97 談話

女：好的，各位。感謝你們過來。**(95) 我收到了今年度軟體市佔率的統計資料。** 雖然我們仍是排名前四名的公司，我們需要更加努力。**(96) 斯萊特線公司今年才剛超越我們三個百分比，而我們去年的市佔率比他們大得多。** 分析師指出斯萊特線公司的成功，是因為人們購買他們的遊戲之後，他們還會發送許多免費的軟體更新。**(97) 我們在下一季時將開始提供所有的擴充包讓人免費下載。** 我認為這能給我們帶來所需的優勢，並且幫我們重振旗鼓。

MARKET SHARE 市場佔有率

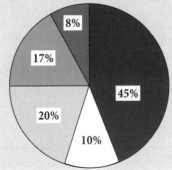

- ■ Future Tech Studios 未來科技工作室
- ■ AK Gaming AK 遊戲
- ■ Seven Strings Technologies 七線科技
- □ Slight Line, Inc. 斯萊特線公司
- □ Others 其他

95. Which industry does the speaker work in?

  A Computer hardware

  B Computer games

  C Computer software

  D Computer microchips

(NEW)

96. Look at the graphic. What company does the speaker work for?

  A Future Tech Studios

  B Slight Line Inc.

  C Seven Strings Technologies

  D AK Gaming

97. According to the speaker, what will the company do in the next quarter?

  A Give away gifts

  B Give away expansion packs

  C Offer free software with new products

  D Install a new security system

95. 發話者從事哪一門行業？

  A 電腦硬體

  B 電腦遊戲

  C 電腦軟體

  D 電腦微晶片

96. 參看圖表，發話者在哪一家公司工作？

  A 未來科技工作室

  B 斯萊特線公司

  C 七線科技

  D AK 遊戲

97. 根據發話者，這家公司在下一季將會做什麼？

  A 送禮物

  B 送擴充包

  C 隨新產品提供免費軟體

  D 安裝新的保全系統

98–100 introduction

M： Hello everyone! **(98) Welcome to your first day at Valencia's Culinary Training Center. Your ability to combine cooking skills with health and safety procedures will be crucial for your future career.** Here's our training schedule for the next four days. Today, we will work on basic knife skills and food preparation. This is an essential first step in becoming a skilled chef. For the rest of the week, each day will have a different theme relating to the most important aspects of working in a kitchen. **(99) We have some celebrity chefs coming in who are highly skilled, and I'm sure you will enjoy working with them.** One more thing to remember is we will have a special team lunch on Wednesday that will be prepared by everyone together.

98–100 介紹

男： 哈囉，大家好。**(98) 歡迎各位首次來到凡妮莎烹飪訓練中心。將烹飪技巧和健康以及安全程序結合，對於你們未來的職涯相當重要。**這裡是接下來四天的訓練時間表。今天我們會進行基本刀工訓練以及食物準備。如果要成為一名專業大廚師，這是必要的第一步。本週其餘的日子，每天皆有不同的主題，與廚房工作的各種層面相關。**(99) 我們請來了一些知名廚師，他們都很技巧純熟，我肯定你們會喜歡與他們共事。**還要記住一件事，就是我們將在星期三將舉辦一場由大家合力準備的特別團隊午餐。

Training Schedule 訓練計劃表

Tuesday 星期二	Wednesday 星期三	Thursday 星期四	Friday 星期五
Basic knife skills and food preparation 基本刀工及食物準備	Health and safety in the kitchen 健康及廚房安全	Food safety and hygiene 食物安全及衛生	Time management 時間管理
	Team lunch 團隊午餐		Evaluation 評量

98. What are the listeners training to be?
  - Ⓐ Factory workers
  - Ⓑ Store owners
  - **Ⓒ Restaurant chefs**
  - Ⓓ Medical workers

99. According to the speaker, what will the listeners enjoy doing?
  - **Ⓐ Working with the celebrity chefs**
  - Ⓑ Becoming a celebrity chef
  - Ⓒ Using the kitchen tools
  - Ⓓ Working with each other

100. Look at the graphic. On which day will the listeners learn food safety and hygiene?
  - Ⓐ Tuesday
  - Ⓑ Wednesday
  - **Ⓒ Thursday**
  - Ⓓ Friday

98. 聽者正在為了成為什麼而受訓？
  - Ⓐ 工廠工人
  - Ⓑ 商店業主
  - **Ⓒ 餐廳廚師**
  - Ⓓ 醫療工作者

99. 根據發話者，聽者將會喜愛什麼事？
  - **Ⓐ 與名廚合作**
  - Ⓑ 成為名廚
  - Ⓒ 使用廚房器具
  - Ⓓ 與彼此合作

100. 參看圖表，聽者將在哪一天學習食物安全與衛生？
  - Ⓐ 星期二
  - Ⓑ 星期三
  - **Ⓒ 星期四**
  - Ⓓ 星期五

PART 1   P. 32-35   🎧 05

1. Ⓐ **The plane is docked at the airport.**
    Ⓑ There is luggage being put onto the plane.
    Ⓒ There are many people boarding the plane.
    Ⓓ There are maintenance workers fixing the plane.

2. Ⓐ **The woman is drinking a cup of coffee.**
    Ⓑ The woman is listening to music.
    Ⓒ The woman is talking on her cell phone.
    Ⓓ The woman is looking at the newspaper.

3. Ⓐ She is fixing the wheel on her bike.
    Ⓑ **She is changing the tire on her car.**
    Ⓒ She is putting oil into her car.
    Ⓓ She is standing behind the windmill.

4. Ⓐ They are very close to the chairlift.
    Ⓑ They are making snow.
    Ⓒ **The people are skiing down the mountain.**
    Ⓓ All of the skiers are wearing helmets.

5. Ⓐ The people are drinking glasses of juice.
    Ⓑ She is giving a presentation about September's sales figures.
    Ⓒ All of the women are sitting down.
    Ⓓ **One of the women is giving a business presentation on a whiteboard.**

6. Ⓐ The men are adjusting headsets.
    Ⓑ **The women are wearing headsets.**
    Ⓒ The men are using a mouse with the laptop.
    Ⓓ The women are talking to each other.

PART 2   P. 36   🎧 06

7. Where should I put the extra extension cords?
    Ⓐ **In the top drawer.**
    Ⓑ The deadline is strict.
    Ⓒ After today's meeting.

8. How often should the windows be washed?
    Ⓐ Please pass me my glasses.
    Ⓑ **At least twice a year.**
    Ⓒ Friday, March 3.

1. Ⓐ **這架飛機停靠在機場。**
    Ⓑ 有行李正被放上飛機。
    Ⓒ 有許多人在登機。
    Ⓓ 有維修工人在修理飛機。

2. Ⓐ **女子正在喝一杯咖啡。**
    Ⓑ 女子正在聆聽音樂。
    Ⓒ 女子正在講手機。
    Ⓓ 女子正看著報紙。

3. Ⓐ 她正在修理腳踏車的輪子。
    Ⓑ **她正在換汽車的輪胎。**
    Ⓒ 她正在為汽車加油。
    Ⓓ 她正站在風車的後方。

4. Ⓐ 他們很靠近滑雪升降椅。
    Ⓑ 他們正在造雪。
    Ⓒ **人們正在滑雪下山。**
    Ⓓ 所有的滑雪者都戴著頭盔。

5. Ⓐ 人們正在喝杯裡的果汁。
    Ⓑ 她正在做九月分銷售數字的簡報。
    Ⓒ 所有的女子都坐著。
    Ⓓ **其中一名女子正在白板上進行商務簡報。**

6. Ⓐ 男子們正在調整頭戴式耳機。
    Ⓑ **女子們正帶著頭戴式耳機。**
    Ⓒ 男子們在使用連接筆電的滑鼠。
    Ⓓ 女子們正在與彼此交談。

7. 我應該把多的延長線放在哪裡？
    Ⓐ **在最頂層的抽屜。**
    Ⓑ 截止期限很嚴格。
    Ⓒ 在今天的會議後。

8. 這些窗戶應該多久洗一次？
    Ⓐ 請幫我把眼鏡傳過來。
    Ⓑ **至少一年兩次。**
    Ⓒ 三月三日，星期五。

9. I'd be happy to make you dinner.
  A Thanks, but let's go out.
  B At most 50 dollars.
  C It was wonderful.

10. Which shoes fit you the best?
  A He's physically fit.
  B Make sure to tie them tight.
  C The striped ones.

11. Is this the theater box office?
  A The head office is in Chicago.
  B Yes, you can buy tickets here.
  C The play was impressive.

12. Where is the entrance to the parking garage?
  A It's $10 per hour.
  B Take a right turn up ahead.
  C The entrance exam was difficult.

13. Do you have the key to the meeting room or should I ask someone else?
  A The meeting will last over an hour.
  B I think I have it in my desk.
  C It's a key factor.

14. Did Mark submit a proposal yet?
  A Yes, he's in charge of waste disposal.
  B Print it double-sided.
  C No, he is still working on it.

15. Would you please help Janet move that table?
  A Where should we put it?
  B Yes, she made a great impression.
  C On the third floor.

16. What style of dress do you want to buy?
  A In the dressing room.
  B I'd like to try this on.
  C Something appropriate for summer.

17. When is the new department store scheduled to open?
  A In time for Christmas.
  B I never opened it.
  C Yes, you can use a shopping cart.

9. 我會很樂意為你做晚餐。
  A 謝謝,但我們出去吃吧。
  B 最多 50 元。
  C 那很不錯。

10. 哪雙鞋子最適合你?
  A 他體格很好。
  B 務必要把它們綁緊。
  C 有條紋的那雙。

11. 這是戲院的售票處嗎?
  A 總部在芝加哥。
  B 是的,你可以在這裡買票。
  C 這齣戲很令人印象深刻。

12. 停車場的入口處在哪裡?
  A 每小時十元。
  B 在前面右轉。
  C 入學考試很困難。

13. 你有會議室的鑰匙嗎,或者我該問別人?
  A 會議將超過一小時。
  B 我想我把它放在桌子裡。
  C 這是一項關鍵因素。

14. 馬克繳交提案了嗎?
  A 是的,他負責處理廢棄物。
  B 將它雙面印刷。
  C 不,他還在處理。

15. 可以請你們幫珍妮搬那張桌子嗎?
  A 我們該把它放在哪裡?
  B 是的,她讓人留下好印象。
  C 在三樓。

16. 你想要購買哪種風格的洋裝?
  A 在更衣室裡。
  B 我想試穿這一件。
  C 適合夏天穿的。

17. 新的百貨公司預計何時開幕?
  A 趕在聖誕節前。
  B 我從來沒有將它打開過。
  C 是的,你可以使用購物推車。

18. The advertisement has been effective, hasn't it?
    A No, it was an Internet advertisement.
    B Yes, sales have increased.
    C Turn on the television.

19. How can I help out?
    A I was inside the room.
    B It was helpful.
    C You could wash the dishes.

20. Why hasn't the delivery person come all this week?
    A I heard he was sick.
    B No, I read it in the newspaper.
    C I think it's $5.

21. I don't expect to be able to finish this work in time.
    A A finished product.
    B Maybe you should ask for help.
    C We should inspect the equipment.

22. Shall we ship this package at an express or normal rate?
    A It's not an urgent shipment.
    B It was a very large ship.
    C Due to the high unemployment rate.

23. Why don't you buy a new suit for the presentation?
    A Did you win the award?
    B Hmm . . . I'll follow your advice.
    C It'll suit your company's needs.

24. Where can I call a taxi?
    A At the intersection over there.
    B Today at 3:00 p.m.
    C No, there is no tax on this.

25. We had dinner at the new Italian restaurant last night.
    A You will have a good time.
    B Yes, he's a chef from Milan.
    C I still haven't been there.

26. The merger hasn't been finalized yet, has it?
    A They exceeded the initial sales forecast.
    B No, but it will be soon.
    C I'll return it by the end of the day.

18. 這則廣告很有效，不是嗎？
    A 不，它是網路的廣告。
    B 是的，銷售量增加了。
    C 打開電視。

19. 我能幫什麼忙？
    A 我在房間裡。
    B 這很有幫助。
    C 你可以洗餐盤。

20. 為何那名快遞整個星期都沒來？
    A 我聽說他生病了。
    B 不，我在報紙裡讀到的。
    C 我想它要價五元。

21. 我不指望能及時完成這項工作。
    A 一件完成的商品。
    B 也許你該尋求協助。
    C 我們應該檢查這個設備。

22. 我們要將這個包裹用限時快遞或普通郵件寄送？
    A 這不是急件。
    B 這是一艘很大的船。
    C 因為高失業率。

23. 你何不為做簡報買件新的西裝？
    A 你贏得這個獎了嗎？
    B 嗯……我會聽從你的建議。
    C 這會很符合你公司的需求。

24. 我可以在哪裡叫計程車？
    A 在那裡的十字路口。
    B 今天下午三點。
    C 不，這不含稅。

25. 我們昨晚在那家新開的義大利餐廳吃晚餐。
    A 你們將有愉快的時光。
    B 是的，他是來自米蘭的廚師。
    C 我還沒有去過那裡。

26. 這個合併案還沒有定案，不是嗎？
    A 它們超過原本的銷售預估。
    B 還沒有，但很快就會了。
    C 我會在今天結束前歸還。

27. Who reserved the convention center?
　　A It is located near a subway station.
　　B She deserved the award.
　　C An election candidate.

28. Don't you need to get to the airport at least three hours early?
　　A I need a few hours to read it.
　　B No, that's unnecessary.
　　C She lost her boarding pass.

29. Why don't we take a tour of the house?
　　A No, I already saw this exhibit.
　　B Sure, I'd like to take a look, too.
　　C Because the tenant will be moving out soon.

30. How long has this company been in business?
　　A It was founded in 1958.
　　B The meeting is at 5 o'clock.
　　C It's around 5 meters, I guess.

31. Jonathan knows the sales figures.
　　A Enter the figures in the spreadsheet.
　　B Is he in the office now?
　　C I can't figure out what's going on.

27. 誰訂走會議中心？
　　A 它位於地鐵車站附近。
　　B 她應得這個獎。
　　C 一位選舉候選人。

28. 你不是需要提早至少三小時到達機場嗎？
　　A 我需要幾小時來閱讀它。
　　B 不，那沒有必要。
　　C 她遺失了她的登機證。

29. 我們何不參觀這間房子？
　　A 不，我已經看過這個展覽了。
　　B 好啊，我也想要看看。
　　C 因為房客很快就要搬出去了。

30. 這間公司營運多久了？
　　A 它成立於 1958 年。
　　B 會議在五點鐘舉行。
　　C 我猜想，大約五公尺吧。

31. 強納森知道銷售額。
　　A 在試算表中輸入這些數字。
　　B 他現在在辦公室嗎？
　　C 我不知道到底正在發生什麼事。

TEST 2

PART 3

07

PART 3　P. 37-41　07

32-34 conversation

M：**(32) Ms. Potter, the package that you sent to the advertising agency in Tokyo was returned today.** It seems that you sent it to the wrong address.

W：**(33) Actually, I received an email from the Tokyo office today informing me that they relocated their office yesterday.** I wish they had told me earlier.

M：Well, that's unfortunate. It seems unfair that you had to pay for the postage. It must have been expensive to send such a large package.

W：Yes, it was. **(34) I'm going to request that the company in Tokyo pay me back.**

32. What are the speakers discussing?
　　A A business trip
　　B A budget proposal
　　C An upcoming conference
　　D A package delivery

32-34 對話

男：(32) 波特女士，你寄到東京廣告代理商的包裹今天被退回來了。你似乎寄到錯誤的地址了。

女：(33) 其實，我今天收到東京辦公室的電子郵件，告知我他們辦公室昨天搬遷。真希望他們能提早告訴我。

男：那還真倒楣，要你付郵資似乎並不公平，寄那麼大的包裹一定很貴吧。

女：沒錯，的確如此。(34) 我將會要求那家在東京的公司退我錢。

32. 對話者們在討論什麼？
　　A 出差旅行
　　B 預算提案
　　C 即將舉辦的會議
　　D 包裹寄送

187

33. What problem does the woman mention?

    A The address is no longer relevant.

    B A company has gone bankrupt.

    C A budget must be revised.

    D A flight has been canceled.

34. What does the woman say she will do?

    A Review a contract

    B Go to Tokyo

    C Visit the post office

    D Ask for compensation

35-37 conversation

M：This is Mike Judge, your host for the morning news here at QQBC 99.5. Today our guest is business leader Karen Chambers. **(35) She recently opened a chain of health food stores across the state.** How did you get the idea, Ms. Chambers?

W：Well, I majored in food and nutrition and I minored in business administration. **(36) So, my goal was to utilize what I learned in college to open a successful company.**

M：Ah, I see. What factor do you think has contributed most to the success of your chain of stores?

W：**(37) I think it's due to the recent trend of people showing enormous interest in health and fitness.**

35. Who most likely is the woman?

    A A radio host

    B A professor

    C A business owner

    D An athlete

36. What did the woman want to do?

    A Make use of her education

    B Open a fitness center

    C Appear on radio

    D Teach food and nutrition

37. According to the woman, what is the main reason for her success?

    A Effective advertisements

    B Considerable interest in nutrition

    C Long-term investments

    D Government policies

33. 女子提到什麼問題？

    A 地址不再適用

    B 公司已經破產

    C 必須重新編預算

    D 班機被取消了

34. 女子說她將要做什麼？

    A 檢視合約

    B 去東京

    C 去郵局

    D 要求賠償

35–37 對話

男：我是麥克・賈奇，QQBC 99.5 晨間新聞的主持人。今天我們的來賓是企業領導者凱倫・錢伯斯。**(35) 她最近在全國各地開了健康食品連鎖店。**您是如何有這個想法的，錢伯斯女士？

女：我以前主修食物和營養，副修企業管理。**(36) 因此，我的目標是利用大學所學開一家成功的公司。**

男：啊，原來如此。您認為什麼是讓您連鎖店成功最大的因素？

女：**(37) 我認為這是因為近來人們對健康和體適能很有興趣的趨勢。**

35. 女子最有可能是什麼人？

    A 廣播主持人

    B 教授

    C 企業主

    D 運動員

36. 女子想要做什麼？

    A 利用她受的教育

    B 開設健身中心

    C 上廣播節目

    D 教授食物和營養

37. 根據女子的說法，她成功的主因為何？

    A 有效的廣告

    B 對營養有強烈興趣

    C 長期投資

    D 政府政策

38-40 conversation

M : **(38) Hello, I'm here because I'm interested in buying an instrument.** My son just turned seven years old today and I thought it would be a great birthday present. Could you give me some advice on what to buy?

W : **(39) Well, I usually suggest that children start by learning the piano.** String instruments such as guitars or violins can be difficult for children to hold. On the other hand, a piano is fine for children and they can learn musical principles easily.

M : I see. However, do you think my son is too young to begin learning an instrument?

W : Not at all. Actually, children can learn as young as three years old. **(40) Here is a pamphlet that will give you some information about the lessons for children that we offer.**

38. Where most likely are the speakers?
  - A At a children's hospital
  - B At a university
  - **C At a music store**
  - D At a concert hall

39. What does the woman suggest doing?
  - **A Purchasing a piano**
  - B Writing a birthday card
  - C Playing string instruments
  - D Attending advanced classes

40. What does the woman give the man?
  - A A receipt
  - B A business card
  - C A map
  - **D A pamphlet**

41-43 conversation

W : **(41) Steve, did you notice that this month there was a slight decrease in the number of viewers for our show? (42) I'm worried our new host, Jim Cruz, isn't very popular with viewers.**

M : I know. I was expecting a lot more viewers. **(43) I think we need to spend more money on advertising.**

38–40 對話

男：**(38)** 哈囉，我來這裡是因為我想買樂器。我的兒子今天剛滿七歲，我覺得樂器會是很好的生日禮物。你可以建議我該買什麼嗎？

女：**(39)** 我通常會建議兒童先從學鋼琴開始。吉他和小提琴這類的弦樂器，兒童很難握住。相對的，鋼琴則很適合兒童，而且他們很容易就能學會樂理。

男：我懂了。但是你會不會覺得我兒子太小，還不適合開始學樂器？

女：一點也不。其實孩子三歲就可以學樂器了。**(40)** 這裡有一本手冊，能給您一些我們兒童課程開課的相關資訊。

38. 對話者們最有可能在什麼地方？
  - A 在兒童醫院
  - B 在大學
  - **C 在樂器行**
  - D 在音樂廳

39. 女子提議要做什麼？
  - **A 購買一架鋼琴**
  - B 寫生日卡片
  - C 演奏弦樂器
  - D 參加進階課程

40. 女子給男子什麼？
  - A 收據
  - B 名片
  - C 地圖
  - **D 手冊**

41–43 對話

女：**(41)** 史蒂夫，你有注意到這個月我們節目的收視人數有些微下滑嗎？**(42)** 我擔心我們的新主持人吉姆‧克魯茲不太受觀眾歡迎。

男：我知道，我原本預期會有更多觀眾。**(43)** 我認為我們需要多花錢做廣告。

W : I see. Maybe a lot of people are just unaware of the show. I'll get in touch with an advertising agency right away.

M : Thanks. Tell me if you need any assistance.

女：我知道了。也許很多人只是不知道有這個節目。我會立刻與廣告公司聯絡。

男：謝謝你。若需要協助，請告訴我。

---

41. Who most likely are the speakers?
   A Show hosts
   B Advertisers
   C Television producers
   D Viewers

42. According to the woman, what is the reason for the problem?
   A A new product was recalled.
   B An actor was injured.
   C A television show was canceled.
   D A new host is not well-liked.

43. What solution does the man suggest?
   A Rewriting the script
   B Replacing the host
   C Conducting a survey
   D Placing an advertisement

41. 對話者最有可能是什麼人？
   A 節目主持人
   B 廣告客戶
   C 電視製作人
   D 觀眾

42. 根據女子所言，問題的原因是什麼？
   A 新產品被召回
   B 演員受傷了
   C 電視節目被取消了
   D 新的主持人不受喜愛

43. 男子提出什麼解決方法？
   A 重寫劇本
   B 更換主持人
   C 進行調查
   D 做廣告

44-46 conversation

M : Good morning, Ms. Spencer. **(44) Why did you come to work particularly early today?** Usually I'm the only one here at this time.

W : **(45) Well, I have to leave work early today in order to attend my sister's wedding, so I came in early.** By the way, do you think you could do me a favor?

M : Sure, I'd be happy to. What seems to be the problem?

W : The stapler ran out of staples. **(46) Do you think you could bring me some more from the supply closet on the second floor?** I have something to do right now.

44–46 對話

男：早安，史本瑟女士。**(44) 你今天為何特別早來上班？** 通常在這個時候，我是唯一到班的人。

女：**(45) 我今天必須提早下班去參加我妹妹的婚禮，因此我提早來上班。** 對了，你覺得你可以幫我個忙嗎？

男：當然，我很樂意。有什麼問題？

女：釘書機沒有釘書針了。**(46) 你想你可以從二樓的用品櫃幫我多拿一些過來嗎？** 我現在得處理一些事情。

---

44. What does the man ask about?
   A The reason the woman arrived early
   B The date of the woman's wedding
   C The name of a client
   D Directions to the office

44. 男子詢問什麼事？
   A 女子提早到班的原因
   B 女子婚禮的日期
   C 客戶的姓名
   D 到辦公室的路

45. What will the woman do after work?
- A Organize a party
- B Try on a dress
- **C Attend a wedding**
- D Purchase office supplies

46. What will the man probably do next?
- A Reply to an invitation
- B Write an email
- C Order a supply closet
- **D Go to the second floor**

47-49 conversation

W: Marcus, have you finished designing the layout for our new online clothing store? **(47) I'm really excited to start selling our clothes online as well as at the offline store.** Can I see the website?

M: Sure, but there are still a few changes I would like to make. I'm worried that some customers might get confused while navigating the website. **(48) I think I need to simplify the interface more.** What do you think?

W: Actually, I like it the way it is. I don't think it's too confusing. **(49) However, I think we need to add more photographs of the products.** If customers can't see exactly how the products look, they might be discouraged from making a purchase online.

47. Where do the speakers work?
- A At an electronics store
- B At a software company
- **C At a clothing store**
- D At a photography studio

48. What does the man want to do with the website?
- **A Make the interface easier to use**
- B Enlarge the font
- C Change the colors
- D Increase the number of menus

49. What does the woman suggest doing?
- A Hiring a professional
- B Lowering the prices
- C Changing the color scheme
- **D Including more images**

---

45. 女子下班後將要做什麼？
- A 籌劃派對
- B 試穿洋裝
- **C 參加婚禮**
- D 購買辦公用品

46. 男子接下來也許會做什麼？
- A 回覆邀請
- B 寫電子郵件
- C 訂購用品櫃
- **D 去二樓**

47–49 對話

女：馬可斯，你是否已經完成我們新線上服飾店的版型設計？**(47) 我很興奮能開始在網路商店和實體店面同時販售我們的衣服。** 我可以看看網站嗎？

男：當然，但是我還想要做一些改變。我擔心一些顧客在瀏覽網站時可能會感到困惑，**(48) 我認為我需要再簡化介面**，你覺得呢？

女：其實，我喜歡現在的樣子。我不認為這會太令人困惑。**(49) 不過，我認為我們需要增加商品的照片。** 如果顧客無法確切看見商品的樣子，他們也許會不想在網路上購買。

47. 對話者在哪裡工作？
- A 在電子用品店
- B 在軟體公司
- **C 在服飾店**
- D 在攝影工作室

48. 男子想要如何處理網站？
- **A 使介面更好用**
- B 放大字體
- C 改變顏色
- D 增加選單數量

49. 女子提議要做什麼？
- A 僱用專業人士
- B 降低售價
- C 改變配色設計
- **D 囊括更多圖片**

50-52 conversation

M：Hi, Sarah. **(50) I'm making plans for the next business conference in the summer. What venues would you recommend?**

W：(51) I think Highwind Hotel has great conference rooms and all the equipment you might need. I've planned seminars as well as weddings there, and they always do a great job.

M：All right, I'll give them a call and reserve their spaces today.

W：Did you release a newsletter about it yet?

M：No, I just want to confirm the venues first and then we'll start sending out emails and newsletters.

W：Great, **(52) let me know if you need any help.**

M：Thanks, in fact, can you take a look at a draft I'm working on? I'd like your opinion on it.

50-52 對話

男：嗨，莎拉。**(50)** 我正在規劃下次的夏季商務會議。你會推薦哪些地點？

女：(51) 我認為疾風飯店有很好的會議室以及你可能需要的一切設備。我曾經在那裡籌劃研討會以及婚禮，他們一職辦得不錯。

男：好吧，我今天會打電話給他們並且預訂場地。

女：你已經發出電子報了嗎？

男：還沒有，我想要先確認地點，然後我們就會開始寄出電子郵件以及電子報。

女：很好。**(52)** 若你需要任何協助，請告知我。

男：謝謝。實際上，你可以看看我正在處理的草案嗎？我想聽聽你對它的看法。

---

50. What does the man talk about?
    A His upcoming business trip
    B His co-worker's wedding
    C Where the conference should be
    D His unfinished reports

51. What does the woman mention about the venue?
    A They provide excellent services.
    B She had her wedding at the venue.
    C The venue may be booked quickly.
    D They don't have enough rooms.

52. What does the woman offer to do?
    A Send out emails.
    B Work on newsletters.
    C Contact co-workers.
    D Help with organizing an event.

50. 男子在談論什麼？
    A 他近期的出差
    B 他同事的婚禮
    C 會議應該要在哪裡舉行
    D 他未完成的報告

51. 關於地點，女子提到了什麼？
    A 他們提供很好的服務
    B 她之前在該地點舉辦婚禮
    C 場地可能很快就被訂走
    D 他們沒有足夠的空房

52. 女子提議要做什麼？
    A 寄電子郵件
    B 處理電子報
    C 聯繫同事
    D 協助籌辦活動

53-55 conversation

M：Excuse me, Mrs. Stevenson. **(53) Do you have a minute to discuss the new contract you offered me?**

53-55 對話

男：不好意思，史蒂文生太太。**(53)** 你有空可以討論一下你給我的新合約嗎？

W : (54) **Actually, I'm on my way to an appointment. Is there a problem with the contract?**

M : Actually there is. The vacation time is much shorter on the new contract, and I had planned a trip to Europe this summer.

W : I see. (55) **Have you already paid for your flights and accommodation?**

M : Yes, I have. I had been planning it for months. It is a large amount of money.

W : I see. I'm sure we can work it out. I think I can extend your old contract until after your vacation. I don't want you to lose your money. Come to my office at around 3 p.m. today and we will try to work something out.

女：(54) 其實我正要去赴約，合約有什麼問題嗎？

男：的確有。新合約的休假時間短很多，而我已經計劃今年夏季要到歐洲旅遊。

女：這樣啊。(55) 你已經支付班機和住宿的費用了嗎？

男：是的，我付了。我已經計劃好幾個月了，那可是一筆大錢。

女：我了解，我想我們可以想辦法解決。我想我可以把你的舊合約延到你假期結束，我不想讓你虧錢。今天下午三點左右到我辦公室來，我們試著想辦法解決。

---

53. What are the speakers mainly discussing?

 A **An issue with the new contract**

 B The new contract states a longer vacation period

 C A vacation in America

 D Flights and accommodation

53. 對話者主要在討論什麼？

 A **新合約的問題**

 B 新合約的休假較長

 C 在美國的假期

 D 班機及住宿

(NEW)

54. What does the woman mean when she says, "I'm on my way to an appointment"?

 A She has a lunch meeting.

 B **She doesn't have much time to talk.**

 C She wants the man to sign the contract.

 D She has a lot of time to talk.

54. 女子說「我正在去赴約的路上」，她指的是什麼？

 A 她有一場午餐會議

 B **她沒有太多時間講話**

 C 她想要男子簽署合約

 D 她有很多時間講話

55. What does the woman want to know?

 A If he will sign the new contract

 B If he can come to her office at 3 p.m.

 C If he is going to Europe for vacation

 D **If he has paid for his trip already**

55. 女子想要知道什麼？

 A 他是否會簽署新合約

 B 他是否可以在下午三點來到她的辦公室

 C 他是否要去歐洲度假

 D **他是否已經付旅遊費了**

(NEW)

56-58 conversation

M : Hi, Beth. Do you like amusement parks?

W : Yeah! I really like them.

M : (56) **Some of us from the accounting department are going to Dreamworld on Saturday for a team bonding day.**

W : Oh really? I've never been there before. (57) **I had some plans this Saturday but I can easily change them.** What time were you thinking of going?

56–58 對話

男：嗨，貝絲。你喜歡遊樂園嗎？

女：是的！我真的很喜歡。

男：(56) 我們會計部門有些人要在星期六的團隊聯誼日去夢幻世界。

女：喔，真的嗎？我從來沒有去過那裡。(57) 我這星期六已有安排一些計劃，但我很容易就能改變計劃。你們想要幾點去？

M : We should meet around 10 a.m. at Central Station. It will be much easier to take the subway because it's hard to find parking at the amusement park.

W : OK. Sounds good. **(58) I will book all of the tickets on my credit card online so we don't have to wait in the line.**

男：我們應該會於上午十點在中央車站會面。搭地鐵會容易得多，因為在遊樂園很難找到停車位。

女：好的，聽起來不錯。**(58) 我會用信用卡在網路上訂所有的票，這樣我們就不用排隊。**

(NEW)

56. What does the man imply when he says, "Some of us from the accounting department are going to Dreamworld on Saturday for a team bonding day"?
   A He is recommending the theme park.
   B He needs some documents signed.
   C He wants the sales figures for this month.
   D He is inviting her to join them.

56. 男子說「我們會計部門有些人要在星期六的團隊聯誼日去夢幻世界」時，在暗示什麼？
   A 他推薦這個主題樂園
   B 他需要有人簽署一些文件
   C 他想要本月的銷售數字
   D 他在邀請她加入他們

57. What does the woman say about her plans?
   A She can't change them.
   B She can change them.
   C They've been cancelled.
   D They've been postponed.

57. 關於她的計劃，女子說了什麼？
   A 她無法改變計劃
   B 她可以改變計劃
   C 計劃被取消了
   D 計劃被延後了

58. What does the woman offer to do?
   A Pick everyone up in her car
   B Meet them at the amusement park
   C Book the tickets online
   D Pay for the tickets with cash

58. 女子提議做什麼？
   A 開她的車去接大家
   B 與他們在遊樂園碰面
   C 在網路上訂票
   D 用現金付款買票

(NEW)

59-61 conversation

W : Are you guys ready? We need to leave shortly because the show starts in an hour. The traffic will be very heavy.

M1 : Yeah, we better go soon. I'm so excited! **(59) I've never seen a Broadway show before.** I'll call John and see if he is ready to go or not.

W : **(60) Tell him I can pick him up with my car on the way there.** Otherwise, he has to take the subway and that will take a long time.

M2 : Yeah, you're right. I will text him and let him know we are on our way.

M1 : Do not text him. I will just call him now and let him know. **(61) Oh, and Judy, I will give you some money for parking because it is quite expensive in that area.**

59-61 對話

女：你們準備好了嗎？我們馬上就得出發了，因為表演一小時後就要開始。交通很繁忙。

男1：是的，我們最好快點走。我超興奮的！**(59) 我以前從來沒看過百老匯的表演。**我打電話給約翰看看他是否準備好要出發了。

女：**(60) 告訴他我可以開車順路去接他。**否則他就得搭地鐵，那樣要很久。

男2：沒錯，你說的對。我傳簡訊給他讓他知道我們上路了。

男1：別傳簡訊給他。我現在就打電話並跟他說。**(61) 對了，茱蒂，我會給你一些停車的費用，因為在那地區停車相當昂貴。**

59. Where are the speakers planning to go?
　　A To the cinema
　　B To a restaurant
　　C To a friend's house
　　D To a Broadway show

60. What does the woman offer to do?
　　A Buy the tickets
　　B Call John and tell him something
　　C Pick John up in her car
　　D Send John a text message

61. What does the man offer to give to the woman?
　　A Money for parking
　　B A text message
　　C A bottle of champagne
　　D A ride to the show

59. 對話者們正打算要去哪裡？
　　A 去電影院去
　　B 去餐廳
　　C 去朋友的家
　　D 去看百老匯的表演

60. 女子提議要做什麼？
　　A 買票
　　B 打電話給約翰並告知他某件事
　　C 開她的車載約翰
　　D 傳簡訊給約翰

61. 男子提議要給女子什麼？
　　A 停車費
　　B 簡訊
　　C 一瓶香檳
　　D 載她去看表演

(NEW)
62-64 conversation

W : OK, **(62) the body wash set on special today is $48. Do you have a customer loyalty card?**

M : I have a discount coupon I want to use while it's still valid. It's in my bag . . . here it is.

W : OK. Hmm, it's not registering on the computer. Let me try to figure this out.

M : Wait a minute . . . Oh, I see what the problem is. **(63) I don't have enough items.** Let me get some more things and I will be right back.

W : No problem. **(64) I will hold this stuff at the counter for you while you take a look.**

62–64 對話

女：好的，**(62) 今日特價的沐浴組要 48 元。你有會員卡嗎？**

男：我有一張折價券，想趁它還在有效期限內使用。它在我的包包裡……找到了。

女：好的，嗯，電腦無法讀取。我來想辦法處理。

男：等等……喔，我知道問題出在哪了。**(63) 我購買的品項不夠多，**讓我再多拿幾樣東西，我很快就會回來。

女：沒問題。**(64) 你去逛的時候，我會把這些物品保留在櫃台。**

Maxx Cosmetics 麥克斯化妝品
Gift Card 折價券

10% off any purchase over $50 消費滿 50 元可打九折

Expires March 1 三月一日到期

62. What does the woman ask the man?
  A If the body wash is on sale
  B If he has a loyalty card
  C If he wants to use a credit card
  D If the body wash is good

63. Look at the graphic. Why is the gift card rejected?
  A Because he is in the wrong store
  B It has already been used too many times.
  C He doesn't have items over $50.
  D It has expired.

64. What does the woman offer to do?
  A Find some other products
  B Give him a new card
  C Get her manager
  D Hold his products at the counter

62. 女子詢問男子什麼？
  A 沐浴乳是否在特價
  B 他是否有會員卡
  C 他是否想要使用信用卡
  D 沐浴乳是否好用

63. 參看圖表，這張折價券為何不能用？
  A 因為他來錯商店
  B 它已經被使用過太多次了
  C 他沒有買超過 50 元的商品
  D 它已經過期了。

64. 女子提議要做什麼？
  A 找一些別的產品
  B 給他一張新的卡
  C 找她的經理來
  D 把他要買的商品留在櫃台

65-67 conversation

W: Did you hear about the network closures next week?

M: Mr. Bronson got the email about this yesterday. **(65) They need to upgrade our network so we can update our software next month.**

W: Oh, ok. But **(66) why would they put the 2nd floor offline at 1 o'clock?** They are usually so busy during that period. I don't understand why they would schedule it like that. They should do it on their lunch break.

M: Hmm . . . **(67) Good point. You should go talk to the manager. I'm sure he will agree with you, and then he can get the schedule changed.**

W: Yeah, I will. I think I better tell him now so we can arrange it.

65-67 對話

女：你聽說了下個星期網路會斷線的事了嗎？

男：布朗森先生昨天有收到關於此事的電子郵件。**(65) 他們需要升級我們的網路，以便我們在下個月更新軟體。**

女：好的，但是 **(66) 他們為何要在一點時關閉二樓的網路？** 他們在那段時間通常很忙。我不懂為何他們要這樣子安排時間，他們應該要在午休時這麼做。

男：嗯，**(67) 說得好。你應該去和經理談談，我相信他會同意你的看法，然後他就可以更改計劃。**

女：好的，我會去談談。我認為我最好現在就告知他，以便我們安排此事。

Network Closures 網路斷線 December 1st　12 月 1 日	
Accounting 會計部	10:00 p.m. — 11:00 a.m. 晚上 10 點－早上 11 點
Customer Service Call Center 電話客服中心	1:00 p.m. — 2:00 p.m. 下午 1 點－下午 2 點
Human Resources 人資部	2:00 p.m. — 3:00 p.m. 下午 2 點－下午 3 點
Research and Development 研發部	3:00 p.m. — 4:00 p.m. 下午 3 點－下午 4 點

65. What is happening next month?
- A An annual software convention
- **B Their software is being upgraded.**
- C The software will be sold early.
- D The monthly hardware update

(NEW)

66. Look at the graphic. Which department is on the 2nd floor?
- A Accounting
- B Human Resources Department
- C Research and Development
- **D Customer Service Call Center**

67. What does the man suggest the woman do?
- A Call Human Resources
- **B Call her manager**
- C Call the sales department
- D Call the software company

(NEW)

68-70 conversation

W：Hello, I'm travelling to Barcelona, Spain on business next month. **(68) I'd like to use my mileage points to upgrade my seat.**

M：Of course, **(70) can you please tell me your JenAir membership number?**

W：OK, it's JA388739.

M：Give me a minute as I bring up your information. Oh, I'm sorry. You don't have enough points to upgrade for this trip.

W：Oh, that's too bad. How many more points do I need?

M：**(69) About 20,000 more points. You should have enough to upgrade after your trip to Spain, however.**

W：Oh, that's so disappointing. I'll have to come to terms with waiting another few months before that upgrade then.

---

65. 下個月會發生什麼事？
- A 年度的軟體會議
- **B 他們的軟體將被升級**
- C 他們的軟體將會提早販售
- D 每個月的硬體更新

66. 參看圖表，在二樓的是哪一個部門？
- A 會計部
- B 人資部
- C 研發部
- **D 電話客服中心**

67. 男子提議女子做什麼？
- A 打電話給人資部
- **B 打電話給她的經理**
- C 打電話給業務部
- D 打電話給軟體公司

68-70 對話

女：哈囉，我下個月要到西班牙巴塞隆納出差。**(68) 我想要使用我的里程點數來升級座位。**

男：當然，**(70) 可以請您告訴我您的珍航會員號碼嗎？**

女：好的，號碼是 JA388739。

男：請稍待，讓我找出你的資訊。很抱歉，你這趟旅行沒有足夠的點數可以升級。

女：太可惜了。我還需要多少點數？

男：**(69) 大約還要 20,000 點，不過你去西班牙之後應該就有足夠的點數可以升級了。**

女：喔，真令人失望。我也只好接受再多等幾個月才能升級。

Airline Mileage Redemption Points 航空哩程兌換點數	✈
To East Asia 到東亞	60,000
To North America 到北美	80,000
To South America 到南美	90,000
To Europe 到歐洲	70,000

68. Why does the woman call?
    A To cancel a flight
    B To register a membership
    C To use her mileage points
    D To confirm an appointment

(NEW)

69. Look at the graphic. How many points does the woman currently have?
    A 20,000 points
    B 40,000 points
    C 50,000 points
    D 70,000 points

70. What does the man ask the woman to tell him?
    A Her plane ticket
    B Her membership number
    C Her cell phone number
    D Her flight itinerary

68. 女子為何打電話？
    A 為了取消班機
    B 為了註冊會員身份
    C 為了使用她的哩程點數
    D 為了確認一場會面

69. 參看圖表，女子目前有多少點數？
    A 20,000 點
    B 40,000 點
    C 50,000 點
    D 70,000 點

70. 男子要求女子告訴他什麼？
    A 她的機票
    B 她的會員編號
    C 她的手機號碼
    D 她的航班行程資訊

PART 4   P. 42-45   🎧 08

71-73 telephone message

M：Hello, my name is Rick Dunn. **(71) I was in your store today and I'm worried I may have left my wallet there.** Earlier today I was in the home furniture section looking at some couches. **(72) I think my wallet may have slipped out of my pocket while sitting on one of the couches.** If you could please look for it, I would really appreciate it. **(73) I'd like to stop by your store when you open it at 9:00 a.m. tomorrow.** I hope you have good news for me. My phone number is 023-555-6541. Thank you in advance.

71-73 電話留言

男：哈囉，我的名字是李克・鄧恩。**(71) 我今天去了你的店，我擔心我可能把皮夾留在那裡了。** 今天稍早我在家具區看一些沙發椅。**(72) 我想當我坐在其中一張沙發椅時，皮夾可能滑出口袋了。** 可以的話，請你幫我找找，我會很感激的。**(73) 我想在你明天早上九點開門時到你店裡。** 我希望你能給我好消息。我的電話號碼是 023-555-6541。那就先謝謝你了。

71. Who is the message probably for?
    A A carpenter
    B A store manager
    C A furniture designer
    D A bank teller

72. According to the speaker, when does he think he lost his wallet?
    A When he used a dressing room
    B When he visited a bookstore
    C When he presented his ID card
    D When he tried some furniture

71. 這則留言可能是要給誰的？
    A 木匠
    B 商店經理
    C 家具設計師
    D 銀行櫃員

72. 根據發話者所言，他認為他何時遺失皮夾的？
    A 當他使用更衣室時
    B 當他去書店時
    C 當他拿出證件時
    D 當他試用某件家具時

73. What does the speaker plan to do?
  A Replace an item
  B Call the police
  C Go to the store again
  D Stop by the listener's home

73. 發話者打算做什麼？
  A 換貨
  B 報警
  C 再去商店
  D 去聽者的家

74-76 introduction

W: Welcome to the Gould Museum of Ancient Artifacts. **(74) I'll be your guide today for the Ancient Egypt exhibit. (75) The majority of the artifacts you will see today are being put on public display for the first time.** In particular, this exhibit features the everyday objects used by ancient Egyptian people. These items include jewelry, pots, and kitchen utensils. **(76) After this tour, you can purchase a book in our gift shop that includes photographs of the artifacts with more detailed background information explaining their origins.**

74–76 介紹

女：歡迎來到古爾德古代工藝品博物館。**(74) 今天由我擔任各位的古埃及展的導覽。(75) 各位今天所見的文物大多都是首度參展。**尤其，這個展覽的主題是古埃及人的日常用品。這些物品包含珠寶、盆器以及廚房用品。**(76) 導覽過後，各位可以在禮品部買書，書裡有展品的照片，及更詳細的背景資料，解釋這些展品的來源。**

---

74. Who most likely is the speaker?
  A A historian
  B An artist
  C An antiques dealer
  D A museum guide

74. 發話者最有可能是什麼人？
  A 歷史學家
  B 藝術家
  C 古董經銷商
  D 博物館導覽人員

75. What is mentioned about the exhibit?
  A It is sponsored by the Egyptian government.
  B Most of its artifacts had not been seen by the public.
  C It will run until the end of the month.
  D It includes works from modern Egyptian artists.

75. 關於這個展覽，有提到什麼？
  A 展覽是由埃及政府贊助的
  B 大部分的展品先前未曾公開展出
  C 展覽將持續到月底
  D 展品包含現代埃及藝術家的作品

76. According to the speaker, how can listeners receive more information?
  A By reading a sign
  B By searching online
  C By purchasing a publication
  D By listening to a presentation

76. 根據發話者所言，聽者要如何獲得更多資訊？
  A 藉由閱讀解說告示
  B 藉由上網搜尋
  C 藉由購買出版品
  D 藉由聆聽簡報

77-79 announcement

W: Attention, passengers. Our arrival in Chicago is expected to be somewhat behind schedule. **(77) Due to the heavy snowfall, our bus driver must use appropriate caution and drive at a slower speed. (78) Therefore, we will probably be arriving an hour later than our scheduled arrival time, which was 5:00 p.m.** Although these circumstances are out of our control, we do apologize for any inconvenience it may cause you. **(79) We would like to remind passengers that this bus offers free Wi-Fi connection.** This is just one of the amenities that make riding with us more comfortable than with our competitors.

77-79 宣布

女：各位乘客請注意。我們抵達芝加哥的行程預計會有些延後。**(77) 因為這場大雪，我們的巴士司機必須謹慎以對，用較慢的速度行駛。(78) 因此，我們也許會比原定下午五點鐘的抵達時間晚一小時到達。**雖然這些情況並非我們所能控制，我們仍要為造成您的不便致歉。**(79) 我們想要提醒乘客，這輛巴士提供免費的無線網路。**這只是其中一項便利設施，讓搭乘本公司的車，比搭乘同業的車更為舒適。

77. What has caused the problem?
 A A traffic accident
 B A heavy workload
 C Bad weather
 D A vehicle malfunction

78. According to the speaker, around what time will the bus arrive at the destination?
 A 4:00 p.m.
 B 5:00 p.m.
 C 6:00 p.m.
 D 7:00 p.m.

79. What does the bus provide to passengers?
 A Free Internet access
 B A discounted ticket
 C A complimentary meal
 D A comfortable connecting bus service

77. 什麼導致了這個問題？
 A 交通事故
 B 繁重的工作量
 C 天候不佳
 D 車輛故障

78. 根據發話者所言，巴士將大約在幾點到達目的地？
 A 下午四點
 B 下午五點
 C 下午六點
 D 下午七點

79. 巴士為乘客提供了什麼？
 A 免費上網
 B 打折車票
 C 免費餐點
 D 舒適的接駁車服務

80-82 radio broadcast

M: Good afternoon, dedicated listeners. You are listening to the weekly broadcast of *World Table*, the program that explores culinary traditions from all around the world. **(80) On today's show, our guest is Cindy Mills, a renowned documentary producer.** Ms. Mills is going to speak about her new documentary,

80-82 收音機廣播

男：午安，各位忠實聽眾。你們收聽的是每週播出的廣播節目《世界餐桌》，本節目探索世界各地的烹飪傳統。**(80) 在今天的節目裡，我們的來賓是辛蒂·米爾斯，她是知名的紀錄片製作人。**米爾斯女士將要談論她的新紀錄片《中國的飲食和

Food and Life of China. **(81) She produced the documentary while visiting traditional Chinese restaurants and interviewing chefs and restaurant patrons. (82) If you visit the website at www.tmostation.com, you can view a trailer for the documentary.**

生活》。**(81) 她製作這部紀錄片的期間，造訪傳統的中國餐館，並採訪廚師和餐廳主顧。(82) 若你上網站 www.tmostation.com，可以看到這部紀錄片的預告。**

08

80. Who is being introduced?
  A A chef
  B A backpacker
  C A critic
  D A producer

80. 正在介紹的是什麼人？
  A 廚師
  B 背包客
  C 評論家
  D 製作人

81. What is the documentary about?
  A World-famous restaurants
  B Traditional Chinese cuisine
  C A celebrity's life
  D Popular recipe books

81. 這部記錄片與什麼有關？
  A 世界知名餐廳
  B 傳統中國菜餚
  C 名人生活
  D 受歡迎的食譜書

82. According to the speaker, what can listeners find on the website?
  A A review
  B A menu
  C A preview
  D An interview

82. 根據發話者所言，聽眾可以在網站上找到什麼？
  A 評論
  B 菜單
  C 預告片
  D 訪談

83-85 excerpt from a meeting

W：Great news everybody! Quarterly profits are up 23%. **(83) The introduction of our new range of body washes has exceeded all of our expectations.** Our other products have continued to sell well, particularly our facial creams and hand creams. **(84) Last month our products were featured in *En Vogue* magazine, and they had a three-page story on the quality of our manufacturing process.** This must have helped with our sales increase. We are expecting more media exposure in the following months, and the release of several new products. **(85) How about that? I'm proud of all the work you have put into this quarter.** Let's keep it up!

83-85 會議摘錄

女：各位，有好消息！季度的獲利增加了 23%。**(83) 我們推出的新沐浴乳系列表現超越預期。** 我們其他的產品持續暢銷，尤其是面霜和護手乳。**(84) 上個月我們的產品受到《風尚》雜誌的報導，他們用了三頁來報導我們生產過程的品質。** 這肯定有助於我們銷售量的增加。我們預期在接下來幾個月中有更多的媒體曝光機會，還有幾項新產品的上市。**(85) 你們覺得如何？我對於你們這一季的努力感到驕傲。** 我們繼續保持下去吧！

83. What type of products are being discussed?

    A Computer parts

    B Hair products

    C Beauty products

    D Cell phones

84. According to the speaker, what happened last month?

    A Sales went down.

    B A product launch went better than expected.

    C Their products were featured in a magazine.

    D Another company took over their contract.

(NEW)

85. What does the woman mean when she says, "How about that?"

    A She doesn't understand the situation.

    B She expected a customer return policy.

    C She wants to purchase some products.

    D She is happy with the company's progress.

86-88 announcement

M：Hello, everyone. **(86) I'd like to announce a few changes in our procedure that are designed to save us money.** Firstly, we will no longer be sending statements to clients through the post. We'll be using email to send monthly statements. **(87) It is a simple procedure, and when the software is installed I don't think you will need any training. The system is very straightforward.** We are also renting out the catering room, and installing some refrigerators in the cafeteria, **(88) so you will have to start bringing your own lunches to work.**

86. According to the speaker, why are changes being made?

    A Because of poor working condition

    B To save the company money

    C So that they can afford a Christmas party

    D He expected a better contract.

---

83. 討論的是什麼類型的產品？

    A 電腦零件

    B 美髮用品

    C 美容產品

    D 手機

84. 根據發話者所言，上個月發生了什麼事？

    A 銷售下滑

    B 產品發表會比預期更好

    C 他們的產品受到雜誌的報導

    D 另一家公司接手了他們的合約

85. 女子說「你們覺得如何」，她指的是什麼？

    A 她不了解情況

    B 她預期有顧客退貨政策

    C 她想要購買一些產品

    D 她對於公司的進步感到滿意

86–88 宣布

男：哈囉，大家好。**(86) 我想宣布程序上的幾項改變，其目的是要節省開銷。** 首先，我們不再透過郵件寄送報表給客戶，我們將使用電子郵件來寄月報表。**(87) 這是很簡單的程序，等軟體安裝完成後，我認為你們不會需要任何訓練，該系統非常簡明易懂。** 我們也將出租餐廳，並且在自助餐廳裡安裝幾台冰箱。**(88) 因此，你們必須開始帶自己的午餐來上班。**

86. 根據發話者，為何做出這些改變？

    A 因為不良的工作環境

    B 為了節省公司的錢

    C 這樣他們就能負擔得起聖誕派對

    D 他預期會有更好的合約

87. What does the speaker imply when he says, "when the software is installed I don't think you will need any training"?

A The new system is easy to learn.
B He doesn't want to train people.
C There is no budget for training.
D Everyone must attend a meeting.

88. What does the speaker tell the listeners they will have to start bringing to work?

A Extra uniforms
B Other people's lunch
C Their own lunch
D A new contract

89-91 telephone message

M： Hi, Julia, This is Frank Walton from Human Resources. **(89) We need to post an ad this week for a new dental assistant.** A colleague told me you are really good at making job application ads. **(90) Have you seen the criteria for the dental assistant position?** This is my first time recruiting new staff, so I'm a little unfamiliar with some of the questions. **(91) I would really appreciate it if you could come by my office today and show me the criteria.** Thanks.

---

89. What position is being advertised?

A Legal assistant
B Dental assistant
C Foreign coordinator
D Bank manager

90. What does the man imply when he asks, "Have you seen the criteria for the dental assistant position?"

A He is looking at some forms.
B He is asking if Julia is familiar with the requirements.
C He needs some extra work done.
D He wants to apply for the job.

---

87. 發話者説「等軟體安裝完成後，我認為你們不會需要任何訓練」，他在暗示什麼？

A 新的系統很容易上手
B 他不想訓練員工
C 沒有訓練的預算
D 大家都必須出席會議

88. 發話者告訴聽眾他們必須開始帶什麼來上班？

A 額外的制服
B 其他人的午餐
C 自己的午餐
D 新的合約

89–91 電話留言

男： 嗨，茉莉亞。我是人力資源部的法蘭克·沃頓。**(89) 我們這星期需要張貼一則徵才廣告，要找新的牙醫助理。** 有個同事告訴我你很擅長製作徵才廣告。**(90) 你是否看過牙醫助理一職的資格條件？** 這是我第一次招募新員工，因此我對於當中的一些問題不太熟悉。**(91) 若你今天能到我辦公室來並告訴我這些資格條件，我會很感激的。** 謝謝。

---

89. 這是什麼職務的廣告？

A 法律助理
B 牙醫助理
C 國外協調員
D 銀行經理

90. 男子問説「你是否看過牙醫助理一職的資格條件」，他在暗示什麼？

A 他正在看一些表格
B 他在問茉莉亞是否熟悉這些條件
C 他需要有人做一些額外的工作
D 他想要應徵這份工作

91. Why does the man want to meet the woman?
- **A To show him the criteria**
- B To make some changes to his office
- C To sign the contract
- D To change the criteria

91. 為何男子想與女子見面？
- **A 請女子告訴他這些資格條件**
- B 要變動他的辦公室
- C 要簽署合約
- D 要改變資格條件

92-94 telephone message

W：Hi, this message is for Ronald Benson. **(92) My name is Amy Lawson, the manager at Rosewood Printing Company.** We just received an online order from you for 2000 wedding invitations with lace and gold fabric wrappings. **(93) I'm calling just to confirm your order is for 2000 invitations and not 200.** It is unusual to get such a large order so I just want to make sure it is correct. Please call me back to confirm when you have a chance. We will not proceed with the order until you confirm. **(94) Also, if you are planning such a large event, we have an excellent planner in the office named Shubert Mendez. If you want to speak with him, I will make sure he gives you a free consultation.**

92-94 電話留言

女：嗨，這則留言是要給羅納德‧班森的。**(92) 我的名字是艾咪‧洛森，我是羅斯伍德印刷公司的經理。** 我們剛收到您寄來的一份線上訂單，要印製 2000 份有蕾絲和金色織品包裝的婚禮邀請函。**(93) 我打電話是要確認你的訂單是要 2000 份邀請函而不是 200 份。** 那麼大筆的訂單很不尋常，因此我想要確認訂單是正確的，請您有空的時候回電給我進行確認，在您確認之前我們不會開始處理這份訂單。**(94) 此外，如果你正在籌劃這麼大型的活動，我們公司有位很優秀的婚禮規劃師，名叫舒伯特‧曼德茲。如果您想與他洽談，我會請他提供您免費諮詢。**

IN-HOUSE DIRECTORY 同事通訊錄

Extension 分機	Name 姓名
10	John Trizz 約翰‧特利斯
11	Don Trenton 唐‧德蘭頓
12	Shubert Mendez 舒伯特‧曼德茲
13	Sally Howle 莎莉‧荷伊

92. Who most likely is the speaker?
- A A content developer
- B A secretary
- **C A company manager**
- D A police officer

92. 發話者最有可能是什麼人？
- A 網頁內容開發者
- B 秘書
- **C 公司經理**
- D 警官

93. Why most likely is the speaker calling?

A **To confirm the size of an order**

B To request some delivery information

C To send an extra gift

D To purchase a new set of cards

94. Look at the graphic. What is the planner's extension number?

A 10

B 11

C **12**

D 13

93. 發話者最有可能是為了什麼打電話？

A **為了確認訂單的數量**

B 為了請求某些運送資訊

C 為了寄送附加贈品

D 為了購買一套新卡片

94. 參看圖表，籌辦者的分機為何？

A 10

B 11

C **12**

D 13

95-97 radio broadcast

M：Hi everybody, this is the late shift with Joey Denton on Free Net Radio. **(95) Today we have George Farrelli in the studio to talk about his hit new album, which has been number one on the charts for six weeks.** Earlier today, **(96) George was telling me how his album was heavily influenced by his recent move to London**, and the growing rock-and-roll scene there. You can definitely hear the British influence in the title track "Frankly Speaking." **(97) Coming up next, we will discuss George's up and coming marriage to his longtime girlfriend Cindy Pullman.** Thanks for joining us today George.

95–97 廣播節目

男：大家好，這裡是免費網路廣播電台晚班的喬伊‧丹頓。**(95) 今天我們特別邀請到喬治‧法拉利來到錄音室，要談論他新的暢銷專輯，此專輯已蟬聯六週的排行榜冠軍。**今天稍早，**(96) 喬治告訴我，他最近搬遷到倫敦及該地日漸盛行的搖滾氛圍，皆對他的專輯產生深遠的影響。**各位在主打歌〈老實說〉當中一定能聽出英倫風格的影響。**(97) 接下來，我們會討論喬治與愛情長跑的女友辛蒂‧普曼即將舉行的婚禮。**感謝你今天加入我們，喬治。

BEST-SELLING ALBUMS 暢銷專輯

Rank 排名	Name 名稱
1	Talk Down《高聲駁倒》
2	Valleys of Fire《火焰之谷》
3	Tunnel Vision《狹隘之見》
4	Step It Up《向上提升》

95. Look at the graphic. What is the name of the guest's new album?

A Valleys of Fire

B Step It Up

C Tunnel Vision

D **Talk Down**

95. 參看圖表。來賓的新專輯名稱為何？

A 《火焰之谷》

B 《向上提升》

C 《狹隘之見》

D **《高聲駁倒》**

96. What does the speaker say has influenced the guest's music?

Ⓐ Getting married
Ⓑ Moving to America
Ⓒ Moving to London
Ⓓ Meeting Joey Denton

97. What will the guest most likely do next?

Ⓐ Move back to his hometown
Ⓑ Get engaged to his girlfriend
Ⓒ Release a new album
Ⓓ Get married to his girlfriend

96. 發話者説什麼影響了來賓的音樂？

Ⓐ 結婚
Ⓑ 搬遷到美國
Ⓒ 搬遷到倫敦
Ⓓ 與喬伊・丹頓會面

97. 來賓接下來最有可能做什麼事？

Ⓐ 搬遷回故鄉
Ⓑ 與女友訂婚
Ⓒ 發表新專輯
Ⓓ 與女友結婚

98-100 introduction

M： Hi, everybody. **(99) Welcome to the retirement celebration of our long-time president Mr. Jang.** Mr. Jang has served as president for the last 22 years and has helped build our business from its humble beginnings to a fortune 500 company. **(98) It's a pleasure to host this special event in the famous Gloria Westwood Ballroom.** I consider it an indication of the success we have experienced. **(100) My name is Bob Hopkins, and I've worked for Mr. Jang for over 20 years.** I consider him to be one of the most talented, honest, and hardworking people I know, and I feel privileged to call him my friend. So, with no further ado, please put your hands together for Mr. Jang.

98–100 介紹

男：嗨，大家好。**(99) 歡迎來到常任董事長張先生的退休歡送會。** 張先生在過去22年以來一直擔任董事長，協助公司從草創初期，發展成如今的全球五百大企業。**(98) 我很榮幸能在著名的葛洛莉・威斯伍德宴會廳主持這場特別的活動**，我認為這代表了我們擁有的成功。**(100) 我的名字是鮑伯・霍普金斯，我在張先生的旗下超過20年了。** 我認為他是我所認識最聰明、最誠實和最努力的人，我有幸稱他為我的朋友。那麼，廢話不再多説，請大家鼓掌歡迎張先生。

GRANGE RIVER TOWER DIRECTORY 格蘭治河大樓名錄

Floor 樓層	Name 名稱
3rd Floor 三樓	Corporate Suites 公司套房
4th Floor 四樓	Rosella Ballroom 羅賽拉宴會廳
5th Floor 五樓	Gloria Westwood Ballroom 葛洛莉・威斯伍德宴會廳
6th Floor 六樓	Main Office 主要辦公室

98. Look at the graphic. Where is the celebration taking place?

   Ⓐ 3rd floor

   Ⓑ 4th floor

   Ⓒ 5th floor

   Ⓓ 6th floor

99. What is the reason for the celebration?

   Ⓐ To introduce a new employee

   Ⓑ Mr. Jang's birthday

   Ⓒ The retirement of Mr. Jang

   Ⓓ A wedding anniversary

100. Who is Mr. Hopkins?

   Ⓐ Mr. Jang's nephew

   Ⓑ An employee of Mr. Jang

   Ⓒ The owner of the company

   Ⓓ A waiter

98. 參看圖表，慶祝會在哪裡舉行？

   Ⓐ 三樓

   Ⓑ 四樓

   Ⓒ 五樓

   Ⓓ 六樓

99. 開慶祝會的原因是什麼？

   Ⓐ 介紹一名新員工

   Ⓑ 張先生的生日

   Ⓒ 張先生的退休

   Ⓓ 婚禮週年紀念

100. 霍普金斯先生是誰？

   Ⓐ 張先生的外甥

   Ⓑ 張先生的員工

   Ⓒ 企業主

   Ⓓ 服務生

PART 1 P. 46-49

1. Ⓐ The woman is looking at some menu.
   Ⓑ There is a measuring tape around her neck.
   Ⓒ She is holding a pair of scissors.
   Ⓓ She is making some curtains with her measuring tape.

2. **Ⓐ She is looking at the laptop.**
   Ⓑ The vegetables are behind the laptop.
   Ⓒ She is writing an email.
   Ⓓ She is cutting some cucumber and carrot.

3. Ⓐ All of the men are wearing glasses.
   Ⓑ All of the people are looking at the laptop.
   Ⓒ There are glasses of water on the table.
   Ⓓ All of the men are leaning over the table.

4. Ⓐ The man is throwing a snowball at the wood.
   Ⓑ They are making a snowman.
   Ⓒ The man is breaking the snowball.
   Ⓓ They are having a snowball fight.

5. **Ⓐ All of the chairs are the same.**
   Ⓑ There are a lot of people swimming in the water.
   Ⓒ The pool is nearby the sea.
   Ⓓ The umbrellas are closed.

6. Ⓐ She is at the supermarket.
   Ⓑ She is selecting a pot of flowers.
   Ⓒ She is with her best friend.
   Ⓓ She is paying for a pot of flowers.

PART 2 P. 50

7. Where are the training materials being distributed?
   Ⓐ Please pass me the stapler.
   Ⓑ In Room 403.
   Ⓒ On-the-job training.

8. Is this the last train?
   Ⓐ Yes, it's the nature trail I visited a month ago.
   Ⓑ It'll last two hours.
   Ⓒ No, there will be another.

---

1. Ⓐ 女子正在看菜單。
   Ⓑ 她的脖子上掛著一條捲尺。
   Ⓒ 她正拿著一把剪刀。
   Ⓓ 她正用捲尺製作一些簾幕。

2. **Ⓐ 她看著筆記型電腦。**
   Ⓑ 蔬菜在筆記型電腦的後方。
   Ⓒ 她在寫電子郵件。
   Ⓓ 她在切一些小黃瓜和紅蘿蔔。

3. Ⓐ 男子們全都帶著眼鏡。
   Ⓑ 所有人都看著筆記型電腦。
   Ⓒ 桌上有數杯水。
   Ⓓ 男子們全都倚靠著桌子。

4. Ⓐ 男子正在對著木頭丟雪球。
   Ⓑ 他們正在堆雪人。
   Ⓒ 男子正在打破雪球。
   Ⓓ 他們正在打雪仗。

5. **Ⓐ 這些椅子全都相同。**
   Ⓑ 有很多人在水中游泳。
   Ⓒ 這個水池在海邊。
   Ⓓ 傘是收起來的。

6. Ⓐ 她在超級市場。
   Ⓑ 她正在挑選一盆花。
   Ⓒ 她和最好的朋友在一起。
   Ⓓ 她正在付錢購買一盆花。

7. 訓練教材正在哪裡發放？
   Ⓐ 請將訂書機傳來給我。
   Ⓑ 在 403 室。
   Ⓒ 在職訓練。

8. 這是最後一班火車嗎？
   Ⓐ 是的，這就是我一個月前走過的天然步道。
   Ⓑ 它將持續兩小時。
   Ⓒ 不，還有另一班。

9. Jesse left an envelope for me, didn't he?
   A **It's at the front desk.**
   B No, turn right at the corner.
   C Yes, he will develop a new product.

10. When will the construction be completed?
    A **In three months.**
    B They're building a bridge.
    C It was too complicated.

11. Won't you try the dessert?
    A Try on this one.
    B The area is mostly desert.
    C **Sorry, but I'm full.**

12. Why didn't you call our client today?
    A I saw it yesterday.
    B **I emailed her instead.**
    C Thank you for calling us.

13. Who still hasn't arrived yet?
    A **I'll ask Mr. Simpson.**
    B He arrived an hour ago.
    C The train has been delayed.

14. What do you think about our new television advertisement?
    A I watched the show yesterday.
    B Through the advertising agency.
    C **It's very eye-catching.**

15. Where are the stairs to the basement?
    A He stared at the sign.
    B **At the end of the hall.**
    C There's no elevator in the building.

16. Can you give me a hand now, or should I ask again later?
    A Please hand out these flyers.
    B **How about after lunch?**
    C It's my pleasure.

17. Should we hire a new employee to handle this project?
    A **Yes, we'll need help.**
    B Turn the handle.
    C A little higher, please.

9. 傑西留了一個信封給我，對不對？
   A 它在櫃台。
   B 不，在街角右轉。
   C 是的，他將開發一個新產品。

10. 這項工程何時會完工？
    A 三個月內。
    B 他們正在建造橋樑。
    C 它太複雜了。

11. 你不試試這個甜點嗎？
    A 試穿這一件。
    B 這個地區大多是沙漠。
    C 抱歉，但我飽了。

12. 你今天為何沒有打電話給我們的客戶？
    A 我昨天看見它了。
    B 我改成寄電子郵件給她。
    C 感謝你打電話給我們。

13. 誰還沒到？
    A 我來問辛普森先生。
    B 他一小時前就到了。
    C 這列火車誤點了。

14. 你覺得我們新的電視廣告怎麼樣？
    A 我昨天看了這個節目。
    B 透過這家廣告代理商。
    C 它非常吸睛。

15. 通往地下室的樓梯在哪裡？
    A 他盯著這個號誌看。
    B 在走廊的盡頭。
    C 這棟大樓裡沒有電梯。

16. 你現在可以幫我嗎，或是我晚點再問你？
    A 請發這些傳單。
    B 午餐之後如何？
    C 我很樂意。

17. 我們應該僱用一名新員工來處理這個專案嗎？
    A 是的，我們將需要協助。
    B 轉動這個把手。
    C 請稍微高一點。

18. The concert isn't sold out already, is it?
- A The guitarist is Andy Gordon.
- **B No, tickets just went on sale today.**
- C I sold my vehicle.

19. I'm here to return some shoes.
- **A Do you have the receipt?**
- B They fit perfectly.
- C Before the race starts.

20. Have you tested the product?
- A Yes, it was an aptitude test.
- B I saw it on the news.
- **C No, should I?**

21. Who had lunch delivered to the office today?
- A Ms. Adams will.
- **B I don't know, since I just arrived.**
- C In the meeting room.

22. What's the address of our buyer in Hong Kong?
- **A Check the client database.**
- B From the shipping company.
- C Fragile contents.

23. Would you like to go through the quarterly report?
- **A I already did.**
- B How about through the consulting firm?
- C According to the news report.

24. Did you purchase tickets for the performance?
- A No, it's a one-way ticket.
- **B We could watch it live on television.**
- C The band is world-famous.

25. Do you remember the name of the presenter?
- A No, I didn't present my ID card.
- **B It's written in the program.**
- C He was named after his grandfather.

26. How did you find my wallet?
- A It was less than $50.
- B He paid in cash.
- **C I asked at the lost and found.**

27. Why didn't Sam publish his book yet?
- **A He is still revising it.**
- B The library is closed today.
- C I'll book a flight.

18. 音樂會的票還沒賣完，對嗎？
- A 吉他手是安迪‧歌頓。
- **B 還沒有，票今天才開賣。**
- C 我賣了我的車。

19. 我是來退還鞋子的。
- **A 你有收據嗎？**
- B 它們很合身。
- C 在賽跑開始之前。

20. 你測試過這項產品了嗎？
- A 是的，這是性向測驗。
- B 我在新聞上看到它。
- **C 還沒有，我該這麼做嗎？**

21. 今天是誰叫了午餐外送到辦公室？
- A 將會是亞當斯女士。
- **B 我不知道，因為我才剛來。**
- C 在會議室。

22. 我們香港買家的地址是什麼？
- **A 查閱客戶資料庫。**
- B 從貨運公司。
- C 易碎的內容物。

23. 你想要檢視季度報告嗎？
- **A 我已經這麼做了。**
- B 透過這家顧問公司怎麼樣？
- C 根據新聞報導。

24. 你買了這場表演的門票了嗎？
- A 不，這是單程票。
- **B 我們可以看電視直播。**
- C 這個樂團世界知名。

25. 你記得簡報者的姓名嗎？
- A 不，我沒有拿出證件。
- **B 它就寫在活動大綱中。**
- C 他是以他祖父的名字命名的。

26. 你是怎麼找到我的皮夾的？
- A 不到 50 元。
- B 他用現金付款。
- **C 我去失物招領處詢問。**

27. 為何山姆還沒有出版他的書？
- **A 他還在修改它。**
- B 圖書館今日不開放。
- C 我將會訂機票。

28. Could you post this announcement on the front door?
  A Sure, wait a minute.
  B Yes, he applied for the post.
  C They made an announcement yesterday.

29. Didn't the courier already come today?
  A I replaced the broken part.
  B No, he usually arrives after lunch.
  C It was an international carrier.

30. We can't accept credit cards at our store for now.
  A It was on sale.
  B The last four digits of my credit card.
  C What about checks?

31. Why don't you bring a camera along?
  A In a frame.
  B An amateur photographer.
  C Actually, I don't have one.

28. 你可以將這個布告張貼在前門嗎？
  A 當然可以，請稍等。
  B 是的，他應徵了這個職位。
  C 他們昨天宣布了。

29. 快遞今天不是來過了嗎？
  A 我更換了壞掉的零件。
  B 不，他通常在午餐之後來。
  C 這是一家國際運輸公司。

30. 本店暫時無法接受信用卡。
  A 它在特價中。
  B 我信用卡的最後四碼。
  C 那用支票可以嗎？

31. 你為何不帶著相機？
  A 在相框裡。
  B 業餘攝影師。
  C 其實我沒有相機。

PART 3　P. 51-55

32-34 conversation

W：Hello, this is Julia Kramer calling from Human Resources. **(32) I gave your department a laptop computer to be fixed last week, and I still haven't received an update**. The keyboard needed to be replaced.

M：Ah, yes, Ms. Kramer. We have had a lot of work orders lately, so we are a little behind with repairs. Is the matter urgent?

W：**(33) Well, I just forgot to copy an important file off the hard drive that I need for my work**.

M：I can transfer that file onto a storage device for you. **(34) Come to my office at your convenience.**

32-34 對話

女：哈囉，我是人力資源部門的茱莉亞‧克萊門。**(32) 我上星期拿了一台筆記型電腦到你的部門修理，而我還沒有被告知目前的進度**。鍵盤需要更換。

男：是的，克萊門女士。我們最近接到許多工單，因此維修進度有點落後。是很緊急的事情嗎？

女：**(33) 我只是忘了從硬碟複製工作需要的重要檔案。**

男：我可以幫你將檔案傳輸到儲存裝置。**(34) 你方便時請到我的辦公室來。**

32. Which department does the man most likely work in?
  A Human Resources
  B Accounting
  C Marketing
  D Technical Support

32. 男子最有可能在哪個部門工作？
  A 人力資源部
  B 會計部
  C 行銷部
  D 技術支援部

33. What is the woman unable to do?
- [A] Contact a client
- [B] Write an email
- **[C] Access a file**
- [D] Purchase a laptop computer

34. What does the man suggest doing?
- **[A] Stopping by his office**
- [B] Enrolling in a class
- [C] Replacing a part
- [D] Reading a manual

35-37 conversation

M：Hello, Ms. Turner. This is Michael Schmidt calling from the Yorkshire Seaside Hotel. It says here that you would like to be informed if a seaside room becomes available. **(35) Well, someone has just canceled, so if you would like to upgrade, you may.**

W：Oh, great. Thanks so much for informing me. **(36) How much more is the upgraded room compared to the standard room?**

M：Well, it will cost an extra $50 a night. However, the room comes with a larger bed and a hot tub. I recommend you visit our website to see pictures and information.

W：OK. **(37) I'll look at your website and then call you back with my decision.**

35. Why is the man calling?
- [A] To request a payment
- [B] To confirm an order
- **[C] To offer a room upgrade**
- [D] To advertise a product

36. What does the woman inquire about?
- **[A] Difference in price**
- [B] Valet parking
- [C] Local entities
- [D] A warranty period

37. What does the woman say she will do?
- [A] Pay by credit card
- **[B] Compare options**
- [C] Take pictures
- [D] Rearrange her schedule

33. 女子無法做什麼？
- [A] 聯繫客戶
- [B] 寫電子郵件
- **[C] 取用檔案**
- [D] 購買筆記型電腦

34. 男子提議做什麼？
- **[A] 前往他的辦公室**
- [B] 報名參加課程
- [C] 更換零件
- [D] 閱讀使用手冊

35–37 對話

男：哈囉，透納女士。我是麥克・史密特從約克夏海濱飯店的來電。資料顯示，您希望海濱房間有空房時能收到通知。**(35) 嗯，剛剛有人取消訂房，因此如果您想要升級的話，是可以的。**

女：喔，太好了，很感謝你通知我。**(36) 與標準房相比，升級的房間要再加少錢？**

男：嗯，一晚要多 50 元。不過，房間的床比較大，還有一個浴缸。我建議您上我們的網站看看照片以及相關資訊。

女：好的。**(37) 我會上你們的網站然後回你電話，告知我的決定。**

35. 男子為何打電話？
- [A] 為了要請求付款
- [B] 為了確認訂單
- **[C] 為了提供房間升等**
- [D] 為了宣傳產品

36. 女子詢問什麼？
- **[A] 費用差額**
- [B] 代客泊車
- [C] 當地的公司行號
- [D] 保固期限

37. 女子說她將會做什麼？
- [A] 以信用卡付費
- **[B] 比較選項**
- [C] 拍攝照片
- [D] 重新安排行程

38-40 conversation

M： Hello. Since I bought an air conditioner from your store, I have never changed the air filter. **(38) Should I replace it soon?**

W： When did you buy it? **(39) We recommend changing the filter once a year at a minimum.** If you suffer from allergies, you should change it even more often.

M： **(39) Oh, I guess I'm due for a new filter then.** How can I purchase a replacement? Do you carry it there?

W： Yes, we do. **(40) All you need to tell us is the model number of your air conditioner.** Do you happen to know it?

38-40 對話

男： 哈囉，自從我在你的店裡買了一台冷氣機以後，還沒有換過濾網。**(38) 我是否得盡快更換？**

女： 你是何時購買的？**(39) 我們建議至少一年更換濾網一次。** 如果你會過敏，應該要更經常更換。

男： **(39) 喔，那麼我猜想我該換新的濾網了。** 我要怎麼購買替換的濾網呢？你們有賣嗎？

女： 是的，我們有。**(40) 你只需要跟我們說冷氣機的型號即可。** 你會不會剛好知道呢？

---

38. Why is the man calling?
- A To cancel an order
- **B To ask for advice**
- C To purchase an air conditioner
- D To schedule an appointment

38. 男子為什麼打電話？
- A 為了取消訂單
- **B 為了尋求建議**
- C 為了購買冷氣機
- D 為了安排會面

39. How long has the man most likely used the air conditioner?
- A About a day
- B About a week
- C About a month
- **D About a year**

39. 男子最有可能已使用這台冷氣機多久？
- A 大約一天
- B 大約一週
- C 大約一個月
- **D 大約一年**

40. What information does the woman request?
- A The year of production
- B Contact information
- **C A model number**
- D The date of purchase

40. 女子要求什麼資訊？
- A 製造年分
- B 聯繫方式
- **C 型號**
- D 購買日期

41-43 conversation

M： **(41) Katrina, I'm going to pick you up at 5 o'clock to go to the rock festival.** I had such a great time last year. I hope it's even better this year.

W： Yeah, I'm excited, too. **(42) However, are you sure if we leave at 5:00 we will still get there on time?** It starts at 5:30 and I think it takes at least an hour to get there.

M： Huh? **(43) Isn't it being held in Harpersville like last year?**

41-43 對話

男： **(41) 卡崔娜，我五點鐘會去接你參加搖滾音樂節。** 我去年玩得很愉快，希望今年會更棒。

女： 沒錯，我也很興奮。**(42) 但是你確定我們五點鐘離開還能夠準時到達嗎？** 音樂節五點半就開始，我認為到那裡至少需要一小時。

男： 什麼？**(43) 它不是像去年一樣在哈波斯威爾舉辦嗎？**

W : **(43) No, the festival is being held in Bristol this year.** The festival organizers are expecting more attendees this year. They were concerned that there wouldn't be enough parking spaces, so they moved it to Bristol.

女：**(43) 不，今年是在布里斯多舉辦。** 音樂節主辦單位預計今年會有更多人參與。他們擔心停車位不足，因此將地點改到布里斯多。

41. What type of event are the speakers discussing?
   A A fundraiser
   B A workshop
   C An anniversary
   D A music festival

41. 對話者們在討論哪一種活動？
   A 募款會
   B 研習會
   C 週年慶
   D 音樂節

42. What is the woman concerned about?
   A Reserving tickets
   B Finding a parking space
   C Arriving on time
   D Accommodating more attendees

42. 女子擔心什麼？
   A 訂門票
   B 找停車位
   C 準時到達
   D 容納更多參與者

43. How is the event different from the one held last year?
   A There will be a family ticket option.
   B A shuttle bus will be available.
   C No cameras will be allowed.
   D A different place will be used.

43. 今年的活動與去年辦的有何不同？
   A 將會有家庭票的選擇
   B 將會有接駁巴士可坐
   C 不准使用相機
   D 將使用不同的地點

44-46 conversation

M : **(44) Stephanie, did you see the flyer hanging on the bulletin board in the hallway?** It says a yoga class will be available to all employees free of charge. Are you planning on signing up?

W : Yeah, I saw that. **(45) It looks like a great opportunity, but the class is held on Wednesday nights, and that's the same day as my jazz dance class.**

M : Oh, I didn't know you took a dance class. You have so many talents I didn't know about. I would love to see you dance sometime.

W : **(46) Well, actually, we are putting on a performance next month at the Mond Theater.** I would be so happy if you and our team members came.

44-46 對話

男：**(44)** 史蒂芬妮，你看見貼在走廊布告欄上的傳單了嗎？它說所有員工都可以免費參加一門瑜伽課程，你打算要報名嗎？

女：對啊，我看見了。**(45)** 看起來是個不錯的機會，但課程是在星期三晚上，與我的爵士舞蹈課同一天。

男：喔，我不知道你在上舞蹈課。你有很多我不知道的才華，我改天想看你跳舞。

女：**(46)** 其實，我們下個月將在門德戲院演出。如果你和我們的團隊成員能來，我會很開心。

44. How did the man find out about the yoga class?
   A From a public posting
   B From a coworker
   C From the woman
   D From a company's website

44. 男子如何得知瑜伽課程的事？
   A 從公告
   B 從同事
   C 從女子
   D 從公司網站

45. Why can't the woman attend the yoga class?
- [A] She hurt her back.
- [B] She can't afford the fee.
- [C] She has to take care of her children.
- **[D] She must attend a different class.**

46. What will the woman do next month?
- [A] Apply for a new job
- [B] Watch the man's jazz dance
- **[C] Appear in a performance**
- [D] Register for a class

45. 女子為何無法上瑜伽課？
- [A] 她的背受傷
- [B] 她負擔不起費用
- [C] 她必須照顧孩子
- **[D] 她必須上另一堂課**

46. 女子下個月將會做什麼？
- [A] 應徵新工作
- [B] 觀賞男子的爵士舞蹈表演
- **[C] 參與演出**
- [D] 報名課程

47–49 conversation

M : Hello, this is Axel Fischer calling. I placed an order last week for a blouse that I was going to give to my wife as a present. However, I think I bought the wrong size. **(47) I'd like to cancel the order.**

W : **(48) I'm sorry, but that item has already been shipped.** You'll have to wait until it arrives and then return it. But don't worry. We can still refund your purchase.

M : Oh, thanks. Wow, I'm surprised it was shipped so soon after the order was placed. By the way, will I have to pay for shipping?

W : Unfortunately, yes. According to our policy, in this case you will have to pay for the return shipping. **(49) I'll send you a return shipping label via email.** What's your email address?

47–49 對話

男：哈囉，我是阿克塞爾·費雪。我上星期下了訂單要買一件女用襯衫，想送給我妻子當禮物。但我覺得我買錯尺寸了，**(47) 我想要取消訂單。**

女：(48) 很抱歉，但該商品已經出貨了，必須要等它送達後再退貨。但別擔心，我們仍可退款。

男：喔，謝謝。哇，我很驚訝下訂單後那麼快就出貨了。對了，我需要付運費嗎？

女：很遺憾，需要。根據我們的規定，在這種情況下，您必須要負擔退貨的運費。**(49) 我會透過電子郵件寄給您退貨的托運標籤。**您的電子郵件地址是什麼？

47. Who most likely is the woman?
- **[A] A customer service representative**
- [B] A travel agent
- [C] A fashion designer
- [D] An event coordinator

48. According to the woman, why can't the item be refunded immediately?
- [A] A computer system is not working.
- [B] A manager is absent.
- **[C] It has already been sent.**
- [D] The man is not eligible for a refund.

47. 女子最有可能是什麼人？
- **[A] 客服人員**
- [B] 旅行社代辦人員
- [C] 時裝設計師
- [D] 活動籌辦者

48. 根據女子所言，為何此商品不能立刻退款？
- [A] 電腦系統無法運作
- [B] 經理不在
- **[C] 商品已出貨**
- [D] 男子不符合退款資格

49. What does the woman say she will do?

    Ⓐ Offer a discount

    Ⓑ Send an email

    Ⓒ Provide a product catalog

    Ⓓ Contact a manager

50-52 conversation

W： Here is the office space you asked me about.**(50)** **It is hot inside because the air conditioners have been off, but usually the temperature is fine.** What do you think?

M： It's quite nice. There is a lot of natural sunlight, which I really like.

W： Me, too. It's a little small, but we only have five employees, so it would be fine.

M： Is there any public transport close by? Some of our employees take the subway to work.

W： Yes. Actually, the Brighton street stop is about a five-minute walk, so it's pretty close.

M： **(51) The only problem is the carpet.** It's quite dirty. Does the owner plan on changing it anytime soon?

W： **(52) Actually, we are having new carpets put in next week.** So don't worry about that. If you sign the contract, you won't move your stuff in for a month.

M： That's great. I think we will take it. When do we need to sign the contract?

W： I will prepare it when I get back to the office, and we can sign it all tomorrow afternoon.

50. Why is it hot inside the office?

    Ⓐ The air conditioner was on.

    Ⓑ The air conditioner was broken.

    Ⓒ There is no air conditioning.

    Ⓓ The air conditioner had been off.

51. What is the man's problem with the office?

    Ⓐ There is no public transport close by.

    Ⓑ The carpet is not clean.

    Ⓒ The contract is not signed.

    Ⓓ The office is too small.

---

49. 女子說她將會做什麼？

    Ⓐ 提供折扣

    Ⓑ 寄電子郵件

    Ⓒ 提供產品型錄

    Ⓓ 聯繫經理

50-52 對話

女： 這就是你先前向我詢問的辦公場所。**(50)** 裡面很熱，因為沒開空調。但是室溫通常還算適宜。您覺得如何？

男： 這地方很不錯，有很多的自然光，我很喜歡。

女： 我也是。這裡有點小，但我們只有五名員工，因此這不成問題。

男： 附近有任何大眾運輸嗎？我們有一些員工搭地鐵上班。

女： 有，其實，走路去布萊敦街車站大約只要五分鐘，因此很近。

男： **(51) 唯一的問題是地毯**，它很髒。屋主打算最近要換地毯嗎？

女： **(52) 實際上，我們下星期就會鋪新的地毯。** 所以別擔心這件事。如果您簽了合約，您也得等一個月後才能把東西搬進來。

男： 太好了，我想這個地方我們要了。我們什麼時候要簽合約？

女： 我回到辦公室後會去準備合約，然後我們明天下午就可以簽約。

50. 為何辦公室裡很熱？

    Ⓐ 空調開著

    Ⓑ 空調壞了

    Ⓒ 沒有裝空調

    Ⓓ 空調關了

51. 男子覺得辦公室有什麼問題？

    Ⓐ 附近沒有大眾運輸

    Ⓑ 地毯不乾淨

    Ⓒ 還沒有簽合約

    Ⓓ 辦公室太小了

52. How does the woman respond to the man's problem?

   Ⓐ She tells him they are putting in new carpets.

   Ⓑ She tells him that the carpets aren't dirty.

   Ⓒ She prepares the contract for tomorrow.

   Ⓓ She shows him another office.

53-55 conversation

M: **(53) OK, Ms. Florence, I have talked with my colleagues about purchasing your office building.** The total offer, including tax, is three hundred thousand dollars.

W: That's much lower than I had expected. **(54) I've had several other offers that are higher than that from other real estate agents.** One agent offered me three hundred and fifty thousand dollars.

M: Well, there is room for negotiation. We are very interested in the property, so I will pay more if you have other offers. We would like to sign a contract as soon as possible.

W: **(55) I'm pleased you can match their offer.** I will give you a call this afternoon and we can arrange the contract.

---

53. What are the speakers discussing?

   Ⓐ A real estate deal

   Ⓑ The condition of the property

   Ⓒ The terms of a contract

   Ⓓ Renovating the property

54. Why does the woman say "I've had several other offers that are higher than that from other real estate agents"?

   Ⓐ To offer a contract

   Ⓑ To negotiate a higher price

   Ⓒ To settle a deal

   Ⓓ To recommend a realtor

55. Why is the woman pleased?

   Ⓐ Because she completed her work.

   Ⓑ The renovations will go ahead.

   Ⓒ She found a new realtor.

   Ⓓ The buyer will pay more money.

---

52. 女子如何回應男子的問題？

   Ⓐ 她跟他說會鋪新的地毯

   Ⓑ 她告訴他地毯並不髒

   Ⓒ 她會備妥明天所需的合約

   Ⓓ 她帶他看另一間辦公室

53–55 對話

男：(53) 好的，佛羅倫斯女士，我已經與我的同事討論過購買你辦公大樓的事。含稅的總出價是 30 萬元。

女：那比我先前預期的低很多。**(54)** 其他幾位房仲報給我的價錢更高，其中一名房仲出價 35 萬元。

男：嗯，我們還有協商的空間。我們對這個房產很有興趣，因此如果你有其他的出價，我願意付更多錢。我們想要盡快簽署合約。

女：(55) 我很高興你願意比照抬高價碼。我今天下午會打電話給你，然後我們可以安排合約的事。

53. 對話者們在討論什麼？

   Ⓐ 房地產交易

   Ⓑ 該房地產的狀況

   Ⓒ 合約條款

   Ⓓ 翻修房產

54. 為何女子說「其他幾位房仲報給我的價錢更高」？

   Ⓐ 為了提供合約

   Ⓑ 為了談到較高的價格

   Ⓒ 為了成交

   Ⓓ 為了推薦房仲

55. 為何女子感到高興？

   Ⓐ 因為她完成了工作

   Ⓑ 翻修會繼續進行

   Ⓒ 她找到了新的房仲

   Ⓓ 買家會付更多的錢

56-58 conversation

W：Hi, Simon. I just got a phone call from Joseph Hardy at Datsio Construction. **(56) He is wondering why we have not started construction on the Marshall Tower yet.** He wants to begin construction as soon as possible because they are losing money while they wait.

M：I see. My lawyers are still going over some of the clauses in the contract that may need changing. **(57) I've been meaning to visit him, but I have been busy with the new mall we are building on West Point. I'll go down this afternoon and have a talk with him.**

W：OK, I understand. It's probably best we make sure that the contract is right before you sign it. **(58) I'll call Joseph and organize a meeting time, and I'll email and tell you what time to go and see him.**

56. Where do the speakers most likely work?
- Ⓐ A research facility
- Ⓑ A legal firm
- **Ⓒ A construction company**
- Ⓓ A pharmacy

57. What does the man mean when he says, "I've been meaning to visit him"?
- Ⓐ He has already visited him.
- **Ⓑ He knows that he should have visited him.**
- Ⓒ He will visit him tonight.
- Ⓓ He forgot about it.

58. What will the woman include in her email?
- **Ⓐ When to visit Joseph**
- Ⓑ The contract details
- Ⓒ Joseph's phone number
- Ⓓ The lawyer's documents

59-61 conversation

M1：OK, Ms. Mendez. **(59) The total cost to repaint the foyer will be around $4,000.** That includes after-service for six months if you have any problems with our work.

56-58 對話

女：嗨，賽門。我收到了達西歐建設公司約瑟夫・哈地的來電。**(56) 他想問我們為什麼還沒開始馬歇爾塔的建設工程。**他想要盡快開工，因為他們等候的同時也在虧錢。

男：我了解了。我的律師們正在審閱合約當中一些可能需要異動的條款。**(57) 我一直想要拜訪他，但我忙著處理我們在西點搭建新商場的事。我今天下午會過去並且與他談談。**

女：好的，我知道了。我們或許該在你簽署前確保合約是正確的。**(58) 我會打電話給約瑟夫並且安排會議時間，然後我會寄電子郵件給你，告訴你什麼時候去見他。**

56. 對話者們最有可能在哪裡工作？
- Ⓐ 研究機構
- Ⓑ 法律事務所
- **Ⓒ 建設公司**
- Ⓓ 藥局

57. 男子說「我一直想要拜訪他」，他指的是什麼？
- Ⓐ 他已經拜訪過他了
- **Ⓑ 他知道他早該拜訪他**
- Ⓒ 他今晚將會拜訪他
- Ⓓ 他忘了此事

58. 女子將會在電子郵件中包含什麼？
- **Ⓐ 何時要拜訪約瑟夫**
- Ⓑ 合約細節
- Ⓒ 約瑟夫的電話號碼
- Ⓓ 律師的文件

59-61 對話

男1：好的，曼德茲女士。**(59) 重新油漆門廳的總價大約是 4000 元。**這包含了六個月的售後服務，如果您對於我們的工作有任何問題的話。

W : Hmm . . . That's more expensive than I thought it would be. Our budget was $3,000. Why is the price so high?

M2 : **(60) I can explain why the price is over your budget.** It is because the old paint is peeling badly in some areas. We have to remove it all before repainting, which takes a long time. If you had repainted it earlier, it would be less expensive.

M1 : In the future I would recommend painting it every seven years.

W : OK. I thought I was being overcharged, but that makes sense. **(61) You can go ahead and begin painting on the first weekend of August.**

女：嗯……這比我先前想的還要貴。我們的預算是 3000 元。為何價格如此高？

男 2：**(60) 我可以解釋為何價格會超過你們的預算。**這是因為有幾個地方的老舊油漆嚴重剝落。重新粉刷之前我們必須將它全都清除乾淨，這要花很長的時間。如果你早一點重新油漆，就會比較便宜。

男 1：我會建議以後每七年油漆一次。

女：好的，我以為我被多收了，但你說得有道理。**(61) 你們可以從八月的第一個週末開始油漆。**

11

59. What kind of work are the men doing?
   A Remodeling the foyer
   B Renovating the bathrooms
   C Repainting the foyer
   D Renovating the kitchen

59. 男子們在做哪一種工作？
   A 改建門廳
   B 翻修浴室
   C 重新粉刷門廳
   D 翻修廚房

60. What does the man explain to the woman?
   A Why she has a low budget
   B Why the price is above her budget
   C Why the foyer isn't ready to be painted
   D Why the paint in the foyer is peeling

60. 男子對女子解釋什麼？
   A 為何她的預算很低
   B 為何價格超過她的預算
   C 為何門廳還不可以油漆
   D 為何門廳的油漆在剝落

61. When does the woman want the men to begin work?
   A The second week of September
   B Anytime during August
   C After August
   D The first Saturday of August

61. 女子想要男子們何時開始工作？
   A 九月的第二週
   B 八月的任何時候
   C 八月之後
   D 八月的第一個星期六

62-64 conversation

W : Excuse me? **(62) I'm on a diet at the moment, so I'm looking for some healthier food options.** I like to have cereal in the morning. Can you recommend something to me? My nutritionist said I should eat a lot of protein.

M : There are many different breakfast options. One of my favorites is the new Protein Plus range. It has oats, fruits, and extra protein added. Here, take a look.

62–64 對話

女：不好意思？**(62) 我正在節食，因此我在找尋比較健康的食物。**我喜歡早上吃玉米片，你可以幫我推薦嗎？營養師說我應該吃大量的蛋白質。

男：有很多不同的早餐選擇。我最喜歡的其中一項是新的「蛋白質加量」系列產品。它們有燕麥、水果，還添加了額外的蛋白質。拿去看看吧。

W：Hmm, this looks delicious! **(63) But my nutritionist said I should keep my sugar intake below 20 grams a day.** One serving of this cereal contains 28 grams!

M：Yes. In that case **(64) I recommend that you try having eggs in the morning with some coffee.** Then you can eat some sugar later in the day.

女：這看起來很美味，**(63) 但營養師說我應該將糖份攝取量保持在每日 20 公克以內。**這個玉米片一份就包含 28 公克！

男：是的。這樣的話，**(64) 我建議你試著早餐吃蛋並搭配咖啡，**然後可以在當天稍晚再吃一些糖。

Nutrition Information 營養資訊	
Serving Size: 150 g 每份份量：150 公克	
Calories 熱量	200 大卡
Fat 脂肪	5 g 公克
Protein 蛋白質	10 g 公克
Sugar 糖	28 g 公克

62. What is the woman trying to do?
   A Gain some weight
   B Eat foods with more sugar
   C Skip breakfast
   D Lose some weight

(NEW)
63. Look at the graphic. Which content is the woman concerned about?
   A Fat
   B Sugar
   C Protein
   D Eggs

64. What does the man recommend the woman do?
   A Have some bacon and eggs
   B Just drink coffee in the morning
   C Not to eat breakfast
   D Have coffee and eggs

62. 女子正嘗試做什麼？
   A 增加體重
   B 吃含有更多糖份的食物
   C 略過早餐
   D 減重

63. 參看圖表，女子擔心哪一個成分？
   A 脂肪
   B 糖
   C 蛋白質
   D 蛋

64. 男子建議女子做什麼？
   A 吃培根和蛋
   B 早上只喝咖啡
   C 別吃早餐
   D 喝咖啡和吃蛋

(NEW)
65-67 conversation

M：Hi, I need this suit cleaned. **(65) I'm going overseas on a business trip on the weekend, and all my suits are getting a bit old now.** How much would it cost to clean this?

65–67 對話

男：嗨，我需要清洗這件西裝。**(65) 我週末要到國外出差，而我所有的西裝都有點舊了。**清潔這個要多少錢？

W : Hmm . . . **(66) Usually twenty dollars.** But this one will cost a bit more.

M : Really? Why is that?

W : Well, you're very tall. This suit is going to take longer to clean and require more products. It will incur a surcharge.

M : Hmm . . . Maybe I will take it somewhere else. That doesn't seem fair.

W : **(67) OK. I will do it for twenty dollars.** And whenever you need a suit cleaned, please come back to me.

女：嗯……**(66) 通常是 20 元**，但這件要稍微貴一點。

男：真的嗎？為什麼？

女：嗯，你個頭很高。這件西裝要花比較久的時間清潔，而且要用較多的清潔產品，會導致費用增加。

男：嗯……也許我該將西裝帶去別的地方洗，這價格似乎並不公道。

女：**(67) 好吧，我幫你清洗，只收 20 元。** 以後無論你何時需要清潔西裝，請回來找我。

Frankie's Dry Cleaning 法蘭琪乾洗	
Fabric 布料	**Price 價格**
Polyester 聚酯纖維	$10
Cotton 棉	$12
Wool 羊毛	$20
Silk 蠶絲	$30

65. What does the man say he will do on the weekend?
  A Go on a vacation
  B Host a business lunch
  C Go on a business trip
  D Get some new suits

66. Look at the graphic. What is the suit made of?
  A Polyester
  B Silk
  C Cotton
  D Wool

67. What does the woman say she will do?
  A She won't do it for twenty dollars.
  B She will charge the man the original price.
  C She will do it for more than twenty dollars.
  D She will do it by next week.

65. 男子說他將在週末做什麼？
  Ⓐ 度假
  Ⓑ 舉辦商業午餐會
  C 出差
  Ⓓ 買新西裝

66. 參看圖表，這件西裝是用什麼材質製成的？
  Ⓐ 聚酯纖維
  Ⓑ 蠶絲
  Ⓒ 棉花
  D 羊毛

67. 女子說她將會做什麼？
  Ⓐ 她不會收 20 元就做此事
  B 她將收男子原價
  Ⓒ 她會收超過 20 元以做此事
  Ⓓ 她會在下星期前做此事

68-70 conversation

W： Hi, Jimmy. Just checking up on you. **(68) Have you finished installing wiring for the lighting in Olive Cosmetics?**

M： I've nearly finished. There were some problems with the electrical box, so I had to fix some old fuses. It took longer than expected.

W： **(69) OK. I'm nearly finished with the lighting on the first floor, but (70) I need help installing some cables on the roof.** Can you come downstairs when you are finished?

M： Sure. This will take me another 20 minutes. Then I will come down.

68-70 對話

女： 嗨，吉米，你好。我是來看看你的。**(68) 你安裝好奧利佛化妝品公司的照明線路了沒？**

男： 我快完成了。之前配電箱有些問題，因此我必須修理一些老舊的保險絲，所以花了比預期更久的時間。

女： **(69) 好的，我快要完成一樓的照明了，但是 (70) 我需要協助安裝天花板上的纜線。**你完成後可以到樓下來嗎？

男： 當然，這還要再花 20 分鐘，然後我就會下去了。

Franklin Towers 富蘭克林塔樓

First floor 一樓 :	Trinity Construction 三元建築
Second Floor 二樓 :	Mullberry & Co. 穆貝利公司
Third Floor 三樓 :	Olive Cosmetics 奧利佛化妝品
Fourth Floor 四樓 :	Torrenz Inc. 托倫茲公司

---

68. Who most likely are the speakers?
- [A] Plumbers
- [B] Office workers
- **[C] Electricians**
- [D] Carpet cleaners

(NEW)

69. Look at the graphic. Where is the woman currently working?
- **[A] Trinity Construction**
- [B] Mullberry & Co.
- [C] Olive Cosmetics
- [D] Torrenz Inc.

70. What does the woman ask the man to do?
- [A] Install some piping in the wall
- [B] Install some cables in the ground
- **[C] Install some cables in the roof**
- [D] Install some new software on the computers

68. 對話者最有可能是什麼人？
- [A] 水管工人
- [B] 辦公室員工
- **[C] 電工**
- [D] 地毯清潔人員

69. 參看圖表，女子目前正在哪裡施工？
- **[A] 三元建築**
- [B] 穆貝利公司
- [C] 奧利佛化妝品
- [D] 托倫茲公司

70. 女子要求男子做什麼？
- [A] 在牆壁安裝管線
- [B] 在地底安裝纜線
- **[C] 在天花板安裝纜線**
- [D] 在電腦安裝新軟體

71-73 telephone message

W：Hello, my name is Alice Keller. **(71) I'm calling to reserve some tables for a private party next Thursday. (72) I have been a loyal customer of your restaurant for years and trust it will be the perfect place for my wedding after-party.** We are expecting around 50 guests and will pay for food and drinks to be served to all guests. **(73) One of our requests is that vegetarian options be available for some of the guests.**

71-73 電話留言

女：哈囉，我的名字是愛麗絲·凱勒。**(71)** 我打電話是要為下星期四的一場私人派對訂位。**(72)** 我多年來一直是貴餐廳的忠實顧客，我相信貴餐廳會是我婚宴派對的最佳地點。我們預計大約有 50 名賓客。我們會付費購買食物和飲料提供給所有賓客。**(73)** 我們的要求之一是要為一些賓客提供素食的選擇。

71. Why is the speaker calling?
- [A] To order food delivery
- [B] To advertise a cooking class
- [C] To report a problem
- **[D] To make a reservation**

71. 發話者為什麼打電話？
- [A] 為了訂外送食物
- [B] 為了宣傳烹飪課
- [C] 為了提出問題
- **[D] 為了預訂場地**

72. What will the speaker celebrate next week?
- [A] A birthday
- [B] A promotion
- [C] A retirement
- **[D] A wedding**

72. 發話者下星期將會慶祝什麼？
- [A] 生日
- [B] 升遷
- [C] 退休
- **[D] 婚禮**

73. What does the speaker want the listener to do?
- [A] Contact some guests
- [B] Decorate a space
- **[C] Meet special dietary needs**
- [D] Prepare an estimate

73. 發話者想要聽者做什麼？
- [A] 聯繫賓客
- [B] 裝飾會場
- **[C] 滿足特殊的飲食需求**
- [D] 準備估價單

74-76 talk

M：Welcome to the Taylor Footwear factory. **(74) On this tour, you will see how shoes are made and packaged before they are shipped to our distributors. (75) One aspect that makes our factory special is that everything is done by hand.** Unlike most factories, where automated machines do all the work, at Taylor Footwear factory everything is done by a team of experienced shoemakers. **(76) Before this tour ends, everyone will get a chance to try making soles of leather sandals themselves, with the assistance of some of our staff members.**

74-76 談話

男：歡迎來到泰勒製鞋廠。**(74)** 在這次導覽中，你們會看到鞋子在運送到經銷商之前的製作和包裝過程。**(75)** 我們工廠很特別的一點是，所有一切皆為手工製成。有別於大部分工廠都是由自動化的機器進行所有工作，在泰勒製鞋廠，一切都是由經驗豐富的製鞋團隊完成的。**(76)** 在參觀行程結束之前，大家在我們一些員工的協助下，都有機會體驗親手製作皮製涼鞋的鞋底。

74. What does the factory produce?
  A Appliances
  B Clothes
  C Toys
  D Shoes

75. What is special about the factory?
  A Its size
  B Its production method
  C Its automated machines
  D Its location

76. What will listeners do at the end of the tour?
  A Participate in a hands-on experience
  B Receive a free product
  C Have refreshments
  D Return to the tour bus

77-79 announcement

W：(77) **The last item on today's meeting agenda is preparations for next week's business conference in Germany.** Linda Wong from marketing and Chris Owen from sales will be representing our company at the conference. (78) **This conference will connect us with more clients and more advantageous business opportunities.** (79) **Therefore, everyone is asked to email a departmental status report for the first quarter to both Ms. Wong and Mr. Owen before the end of the week to help them prepare.** Thank you.

77. What will happen next week?
  A A budget proposal
  B A business event
  C A performance evaluation
  D A shareholders' meeting

78. What benefit does the speaker mention?
  A Fewer complaints
  B Reduced travel time
  C Access to clients
  D Strengthened security

74. 這家工廠生產什麼？
  A 家電用品
  B 衣服
  C 玩具
  D 鞋子

75. 這家工廠有何特別之處？
  A 它的規模
  B 它的生產方式
  C 它的自動化機器
  D 它的地點

76. 聽眾在導覽結束時將會做什麼？
  A 親自動手做
  B 收到免費的產品
  C 享用茶點
  D 返回遊覽車

77–79 宣布

女：(77) 本日會議議程的最後一項，是為下週在德國商務會議做準備。行銷部門的琳達・王以及業務部門的克里斯・歐文，將代表公司出席會議。(78) 這場會議能讓我們有更多的客戶以及更有利的商業機會。(79) 因此，在這個星期結束以前，大家都要將第一季的部門狀況報告，以電子郵件寄給王女士及歐文先生，以協助他們做準備。謝謝。

77. 下星期將會發生什麼事？
  A 預算提案
  B 商務活動
  C 表現評量
  D 股東會議

78. 發話者提到有什麼好處？
  A 較少客訴
  B 縮短旅遊時間
  C 獲得客戶
  D 強化保全

79. What are the listeners asked to do?
 A Delete unnecessary data
 B Submit a report
 C Contact clients directly
 D Email an order confirmation

80-82 introduction

M : Welcome to the opening ceremony for this year's Young Novelists Seminar. **(80) This seminar is available to students from high school to university and will help aspiring novelists grow and develop into the masters of tomorrow. (81) The first thing we ask everyone to do is to fill out a name tag and attach it to your shirt.** There are over one hundred students here, and it's difficult to keep track of everyone. **(82) Next up, Natasha Marsh, the renowned literary critic, is going to give the opening speech for the ceremony.** Please listen up. She has some inspiring words for everyone today.

80. Who most likely are the listeners?
 A Professional novelists
 B University professors
 C Potential writers
 D Prospective clients

81. What are the listeners asked to do?
 A Fill out a questionnaire
 B Attach a name tag
 C Introduce themselves
 D Read a book

82. Who is Natasha Marsh?
 A An athlete
 B A children's author
 C An event organizer
 D A guest speaker

---

79. 聽眾被要求做什麼？
 A 刪除不必要的檔案
 B 繳交報告
 C 直接聯繫客戶
 D 以電子郵件寄送訂單確認信

80–82 介紹

男：歡迎來到今年「新鋭小説家研討會」的開幕典禮。**(80)** 從高中到大學的學生都可以參加，而且研討會能幫助有志成為小說家的人成長並發展成為明日的大師。**(81)** 我們要求大家所做的第一件事，就是填寫名牌並貼在衣服上。這裡有超過 100 名學生，要記得每個人是不容易的事。**(82)** 接下來，著名的文學評論家娜塔莎・馬歇將要發表開幕致詞。請仔細聆聽，她今天要給大家一些啟發性的話語。

80. 聽者最有可能是什麼人？
 A 專業小説家
 B 大學教授
 C 潛力作家
 D 潛在客戶

81. 聽者被要求做什麼？
 A 填寫問卷
 B 黏貼名牌
 C 自我介紹
 D 閱讀書籍

82. 娜塔莎・馬歇是什麼人？
 A 運動員
 B 兒童文學作家
 C 活動規劃者
 D 演講貴賓

83-85 news report

W : This is Sarah Brixton from CCR News. I'm here at the WingTip shoe store next to Hyde Park, where **(83) hundreds of people are waiting to buy the new running shoes the company will release tomorrow. (84) Some people have camped here overnight, while others have taken the day off work to be here. From the look of it, you'd think they were giving the shoes away.** The new shoe design is a huge upgrade from WingTip's last design because of their new Boost technology. The Boost technology is made with three strips of an innovative material the company has developed, which contains thousands of specially formulated foam pellets called "energy capsules". To show appreciation to its most loyal customers, **(85) WingTip is giving away a limited edition shoes to the first 100 customers on the first day of sales, featuring the signature of the Chicago Blue's star forward Jerry Halliwell.**

83-85 新聞報導

女 : 我是《CCR 新聞》的莎拉‧布萊克斯頓。現在我在海德公園旁的翼尖鞋店，在這裡 **(83)** 數以百計的人們已在等候要買這家公司明天上市的新款跑鞋。**(84)** 有些人已在此紮營過夜，也有些人請假前來。從這個情況看起來，你會以為他們在免費贈送鞋子。這款新鞋的設計是翼尖鞋店上代鞋款的大幅升級，因為有了新的 Boost 科技。Boost 科技是由三條該公司研發的創新材料製成，包含了數千個專門配製的膠粒，稱為「能量膠囊」。為了對最忠實的顧客表達感激之意，**(85)** 翼尖鞋店將在開賣首日送出一款限量版的鞋給前 100 名顧客，上面有芝加哥藍隊明星前鋒傑瑞‧哈利維爾的簽名。

---

83. According to the speaker, what is happening?
 A A new product is being released.
 B The store is closing down.
 C Their staff are all quitting.
 D The company is shooting a commercial.

84. What does the speaker mean when she says, "you'd think they were giving the shoes away"?
 A The store is giving the shoes away.
 B There are a lot of people waiting to buy the product.
 C They ran out of stock.
 D A few people were upset about the product.

85. According to the speaker, what is WingTip offering the first 100 customers?
 A 10% discount
 B A new pair of headphones
 C Free shoes
 D Special edition shoes

83. 根據發話者，即將發生什麼事？
 A 一項新產品即將上市
 B 這家店要歇業了
 C 他們的員工要全體辭職
 D 這家公司正在拍攝廣告

84. 發話者說「你會以為他們在免費贈送鞋子」，她指的是什麼？
 A 這家商店正在送鞋
 B 有很多人在等候購買此商品
 C 他們用盡庫存了
 D 有些人對此產品感到不高興

85. 根據發話者所言，翼尖鞋店會提供前 100 名顧客什麼？
 A 10% 的折扣
 B 一副新的耳機
 C 免費的鞋子
 D 特別版的鞋子

86-88 introduction

M：Our next guest speaker is Gary Hardwell, CEO of Broadbank Industries. His company is responsible for funding our latest work, building wells in Africa. **(86) The value of his contributions can be seen on the walls of his office, which are lined with pictures of the villages he has provided with clean drinking water.** In the last year, Broadbank Industries has donated over 12 million dollars and built over 3000 wells across the poorest regions of Africa. This has grown into Mr. Hardwell's greatest passion, and **(87) he now spends about six months of each year in Africa overseeing his workers and ensuring his money is being spent in the right places. I think it's safe to say that Mr. Hardwell should leave some room on his walls.** In the next year he intends to increase well production by 10 percent. He has written a book about his experiences titled *Water Is Life: Giving Back to the World.* **(88) Today he will preview the book and show us some video footage of the work he is doing in Africa.** Please put your hands together for Mr. Hardwell.

86. According to the speaker, how can we see the value of Mr. Hardwell's work?
- A By looking at all the paintings on his walls
- **B By looking at all the pictures on his walls**
- C By looking at all the fan mail in his office
- D By looking at all the special awards on his desk

(NEW)
87. Why does the speaker say, "I think it's safe to say Mr. Hardwell should leave some room on his walls"?
- A To discuss another issue
- **B To suggest he is going to continue doing more work**
- C To recommend a friend to him
- D To make sure the audience is familiar with him

88. What will Mr. Hardwell do today?
- A Share some of his business knowledge
- **B Preview the book and show some video**
- C Read some excerpts from his book
- D Read a chapter from his book

86-88 介紹

男：我們的下一位來賓講者是蓋瑞・哈德威爾，他是布洛德班克工業的總裁。他的公司負責資助我們最新的工程，要在非洲建造水井。**(86) 在他辦公室的牆上可以看見他的貢獻值，牆上排滿了他提供乾淨飲用水的村落照片。** 在過去一年，布洛德班克工業已經捐了超過 1200 萬元，並且建了超過 3000 座水井，遍及非洲最貧窮的地區。這已成為哈德威爾先生最大的愛好，而且 **(87) 他現在每年花大約六個月的時間在非洲，監督他的工人並且確保他的錢用得其所。我認為如此說並不為過，哈德威爾先生應該要在他的牆上留下一些空間。** 在接下來的一年，他打算要增加 10% 的水井建造量。他已經寫了一本關於他經驗的書，書名是《水即生命：回饋世界》。**(88) 今天他將會導讀這本書，並且讓我們觀賞他在非洲工作的影片。** 請大家鼓掌歡迎哈德威爾先生。

86. 根據發話者，我們如何看見哈德威爾先生做此事的價值？
- A 看他牆上的所有畫作
- **B 看他牆上的所有照片**
- C 看他辦公室裡所有的粉絲來信
- D 看他書桌上所有的特別獎項

87. 發話者為何說「我認為如此說並不為過，哈德威爾先生應該要在他的牆上留下一些空間」？
- A 為了討論另一項議題
- **B 為了暗示他即將繼續做更多事**
- C 為了向他推薦一名朋友
- D 為了確保觀眾熟悉他

88. 哈德威爾先生今天將會做什麼？
- A 分享他的商業知識
- **B 導讀這本書並且播放影片**
- C 朗讀他書中的摘錄
- D 朗讀他書中的一個章節

89-91 telephone message

W： Hello, Ms. Francis. **(89) This is Barry Walls from Calvin Fashion. We received your design portfolio last month. (90) I'm sorry I didn't call you sooner, I was out of town on a business trip.** I really liked your designs; it is exactly the kind of look we are going for in our summer collection. I would like to meet you for dinner in the next few days and show you the designs we are interested in. **(91) If you are happy with the arrangement, we can go back to my office and prepare a contract.** Please get back to me as soon as possible, so we can arrange a time. I really look forward to working with you.

89. Where does the speaker most likely work?
   A In a law office
   B In a fashion company
   C In an airline company
   D In an accounting firm

(NEW)
90. Why does the speaker say, "I was out of town on a business trip"?
   A To explain why she hadn't called
   B To arrange an appointment
   C To sign the contract
   D To discuss the building plan

91. What does the speaker offer to the woman?
   A A free plane ticket
   B Another portfolio
   C A deposit for rent
   D A possible contract

92-94 telephone message

M： Hello, this is George Benson from Winbox Computers. We made a catering order two weeks ago but we need to make some changes. **(92) We have added some additional businesses to the luncheon (93) so, we are going to need to increase the number of cold meat trays we ordered to 10, and the mixed salad plates to 8.** Everything else can

89–91 電話留言

女： 您好，法蘭西斯女士。**(89) 我是喀爾文時尚的巴莉・華爾斯。我們上個月收到你的設計作品集。(90) 很抱歉我沒有早一點打電話給您，我到城外出差了。** 我真的很喜歡您的設計作品，我們夏季商品想要尋找的款式就是這樣。我想要過幾天與你碰面吃晚餐，並且讓您了解我們感興趣的設計。**(91) 如果你滿意這樣的安排，我們就可以回到我的辦公室準備合約。** 請盡快回我電話，這樣我們就可以安排時間。我很期待與你合作。

89. 發話者最有可能在哪裡工作？
   A 在律師事務所
   B 在時尚公司
   C 在航空公司
   D 在會計事務所

90. 發話者為何說「我到城外出差了」？
   A 為了解釋她為何先前沒有打電話
   B 為了安排會面
   C 為了簽署合約
   D 為了討論建築平面圖

91. 發話者提供什麼給女子？
   A 免費機票
   B 另一份作品集
   C 租賃押金
   D 可能的合約

92–94 電話留言

男： 哈囉，我是 Winbox 電腦公司的喬治・班森。我們兩星期前訂了外燴服務，但我們需要做一些更動。**(92) 我們的午餐會多增加了幾家企業參與，(93) 因此，我們需要將原先訂購的肉品冷盤增加為十份、綜合沙拉盤增加為八份。** 其他部分可以維持原樣，我們的訂單號碼是

remain the same. Our order number is 5521673. **(94) Please give me a call back to confirm the changes. Thanks.**

5521673。**(94) 請回我電話確認這些更動，謝謝你。**

Order Form 訂購單 5521673	
Customer 客戶：Winbox Computers 電腦	
Item 項目	Quantity 數量
Cold meat tray 肉品冷盤	3
Mixed salad plates 綜合沙拉盤	5
12 pack bread rolls 麵包捲 12 包裝	2
Cutlery sets 餐具組	10

92. What type of event is being catered?
[A] A business dinner
[B] A business luncheon
[C] A corporate breakfast
[D] An annual picnic

93. Look at the graphic. Which items were not changed?
[A] Cold meat trays and mixed salad plates
[B] 12 pack bread rolls
[C] Cutlery sets
[D] Cutlery sets and bread rolls

94. What is the listener asked to do?
[A] Send an email confirmation
[B] Call the man to confirm the changes
[C] Not to change the order
[D] Cancel the whole order

92. 是什麼類型的活動要提供外燴？
[A] 商務晚餐
[B] 商務午餐會
[C] 公司早餐
[D] 年度野餐

93. 參看表格，哪些項目沒有更動？
[A] 肉品冷盤和綜合沙拉盤
[B] 麵包捲 12 包裝
[C] 餐具組
[D] 餐具組和麵包捲

94. 聽者被要求做什麼？
[A] 寄電子郵件確認信
[B] 打電話給男子確認更動
[C] 不更動訂單
[D] 取消整份訂單

95-97 tour guide

W：Hi, all. Welcome to the annual Florist Convention. It's a pleasure to see so many people here today. **(95) My name is Juliette White and I am the President of the Maryland Florist Association.** Today will be a great day filled with a lot of informative seminars and practical examples of how to improve your skills in all areas of floristry. **(96) First thing in the morning, everyone should meet**

95–97 旅遊導覽

女：嗨，各位好。歡迎來到年度的花卉業者大會，今天很高興看到這麼多人出席。**(95) 我的名字是茱莉葉·懷特，我是馬里蘭花卉業者協會的主席。** 今天將會是個很棒的日子，充滿許多資訊豐富的研討會以及實用案例，說明如何增進花藝各領域的技能。**(96) 早上的第一件事，大家上午九點要在鬱金香花園前面的**

at 9 a.m. on the road in front of the tulip garden. In the tulip garden we have the most diverse collection of tulips in England. At the moment, most are blooming, so it's a fantastic opportunity to see how you can make new and exciting arrangements. **(97) One more thing I suggest is that you visit the aviary before you go home. The combination of animal life and flowers is truly a sight to behold.**

那條路會面。在鬱金香花園裡種有英格蘭最多種類的鬱金香。現在大部分的鬱金香正在盛開，因此這是很好的機會，可以看看大家會插出什麼創新又令人興奮的花。**(97)** 我還想再建議一件事，就是在回家之前要參觀鳥園。動物和花卉的結合真的很值得一看。

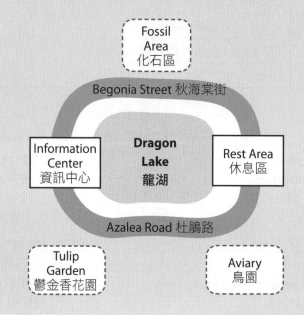

95. Who most likely is the speaker?
   A **President of the Maryland Florist Association**
   B President of the annual florist convention
   C President of Tulip Garden
   D President of the rest area

96. Look at the graphic. Where will the listeners go first?
   A The Aviary
   B Begonia Street
   C Dragon Lake
   D **Azalea Road**

97. What does the speaker encourage listeners to do before they leave?
   A Visit the Tulip Garden
   B Buy some flowers
   C Pick some roses
   D **Visit the Aviary**

95. 發話者最有可能是什麼人？
   A **馬里蘭花卉業者協會的主席**
   B 年度花卉業者大會的主席
   C 鬱金香花園的主席
   D 休息區的主席

96. 參看圖表，聽眾首先會去哪裡？
   A 鳥舍
   B 秋海棠街
   C 龍湖
   D **杜鵑路**

97. 發話者鼓勵聽眾離開之前做什麼？
   A 參觀鬱金香花園
   B 買花
   C 摘採玫瑰
   D **參觀鳥舍**

98-100 advertisement

M: Hello, Granville Produce shoppers. **(98) It's our first birthday, and we're commemorating it with a special offer this week through Sunday.** You'll be able to take advantage of our great savings. **(99) Make sure you stop by our heirloom tomato corner, where you can find our award-winning selection of heirloom tomatoes of every variety and color. (100) By far the best deal is the Brandywine this season. Normally at $2.50 per pound, the Brandywine won't last long.** Don't wait! Come into Granville Produce right away, before all of the fresh, delicious vegetables are gone. Thank you for being our loyal customers over the past year. We hope to make this birthday the first of many!

98-100 廣告

男：哈囉，格蘭威爾農產品的顧客們，**(98) 今天是我們開幕週年慶，為了慶祝，我們這週到週日提供特價優惠**，各位可以把握我們的超優價格。**(99) 請務必前往祖傳番茄一隅，各位可以在那裡看到我們各式各色的獲獎祖傳番茄。(100) 目前最划算的是這季的白蘭地番茄，平常要價每磅 2.5 元，白蘭地番茄產期很短。** 別再等了！立刻來到格蘭威爾農產品，以免所有新鮮美味的蔬菜都銷售一空。感謝您在過去一年成為我們的忠實顧客，我們希望以後還有許多週年慶！

HEIRLOOM TOMATOES! 祖傳番茄！
Prices are per pound — 價格為每磅——

Black Cherry 黑櫻桃番茄	$1.09 元
Brandywine 白蘭地番茄	$1.39 元
Black Krim 黑克里木番茄	$2.64 元
Amana Orange 阿馬納橙色番茄	$1.30 元

98. When will the special sale be over?
  A Monday
  B Saturday
  C Sunday
  D It is weekly.

99. What is indicated about Granville Produce?
  A They have a wide variety of potatoes.
  B They highlight their heirloom tomatoes.
  C They are an inexpensive grocer.
  D They have been in business for several years.

100. Look at the graphic. Why is the Brandywine such a good deal?
  A It is cheaper than the Black Krim.
  B It is a delicious tomato.
  C It is normally over a dollar more expensive per pound.
  D It is normally not in season.

98. 特賣會什麼時候結束？
  A 星期一
  B 星期六
  C 星期日
  D 每星期舉辦。

99. 關於格蘭威爾農產品有提到哪一點？
  A 他們有很多種類的馬鈴薯
  B 他們主打祖傳番茄
  C 他們是平價雜貨商
  D 他們已經營業了好幾年

100. 參看圖表，為何白蘭地番茄很划算？
  A 它比黑克里木番茄便宜
  B 它是美味的番茄
  C 它通常每磅要貴一塊多
  D 它通常不是當季

ACTUAL TEST ④

PART 1 P. 60-63 13

1. A There are a lot of other people at the park.
    B The boy is riding on his daddy's shoulders.
    C They are taking a walk in the park.
    D The boy is running on the path.

2. A The men are all wearing glasses.
    B One of the men is typing on his laptop.
    C The women are looking at each other.
    D They are having a business meeting.

3. **A She is putting air into her car tire.**
    B Someone is helping her fill the tire with air.
    C She is pumping gas into her car.
    D She is changing the tire on the car.

4. A She is cooking a steak in a frying pan.
    B She is tasting the food while cooking.
    C There are many fruits on the counter.
    D She is cutting vegetables.

5. **A They are running on the treadmills.**
    B They are using exercise bikes.
    C All of the treadmills are being used.
    D The man is pressing some buttons on the treadmill.

6. **A He is taking the hook out of the fish's mouth.**
    B There are several men in the boat.
    C He is cooking the fish.
    D He has a lot of fish in the boat.

PART 2 P. 64 14

7. When will the meeting be held?
    A After lunch.
    B Yes, it will be.
    C Next to the conference room.

8. Do you want me to sign this document?
    A The recent documentary.
    B Yes, right here.
    C I can't read them.

---

1. A 公園裡有很多其他的人。
    B 男孩騎坐在父親的肩膀上。
    C 他們在公園裡散步。
    D 男孩在路上奔跑。

2. A 男子們全都戴眼鏡。
    B 其中一名男子用筆記型電腦打字。
    C 女子們看著彼此。
    D 他們正在開商務會議。

3. **A 她正在為汽車輪胎打氣。**
    B 某人正在協助她為輪胎打氣。
    C 她正在為汽車加油。
    D 她正在換汽車輪胎。

4. A 她用煎鍋烹飪牛排。
    B 她一邊烹飪一邊品嚐食物。
    C 料理台上有很多水果。
    D 她在切蔬菜。

5. **A 他們正在跑步機上跑步。**
    B 他們正在使用健身車。
    C 所有的跑步機都有人在使用。
    D 男子正在按跑步機上的按鈕。

6. **A 他正從魚嘴裡取出魚鉤。**
    B 船上有數名男子。
    C 他正在烹煮這條魚。
    D 他船上有許多魚。

7. 會議將在何時舉行？
    A 午餐後。
    B 是的，它將會。
    C 在會議室旁邊。

8. 你要我簽署這份文件嗎？
    A 最近的紀錄片。
    B 是的，在這裡簽名。
    C 我讀不懂。

9. Who will be responsible for interviewing new job applicants?
   - A Before the New Year.
   - **B That's Jenny's duty.**
   - C Just apply online.

10. How many hotel rooms would you like to reserve?
   - **A I think at least five.**
   - B He stayed overnight.
   - C At the beginning of March.

11. Was that the last speaker of the conference?
   - A The conference schedule.
   - B At 5:00 p.m.
   - **C No, there will be another this afternoon.**

12. When will workshop registration happen?
   - A The shop opened last year.
   - B He is the new instructor.
   - **C It will begin next week.**

13. Where should I store these books?
   - A Yes, they are for sale.
   - **B Please put them in the closet.**
   - C He came in first place.

14. Could you pick up our client from the airport as soon as possible?
   - A It's a domestic flight.
   - B Check the contract.
   - **C Sure, I'll leave now.**

15. You locked the front door after you left, didn't you?
   - A No, she left early.
   - B It's in the front.
   - **C Yes, don't worry.**

16. Why was the quarterly training session canceled?
   - A He's undergoing intensive training.
   - **B Actually, it was rescheduled.**
   - C Because the pencil was broken.

17. Can you give me the email address for the sales department?
   - **A I'll forward it to you.**
   - B It's a sale price for a limited time.
   - C What a nice dress!

9. 誰要負責面試新的求職者？
   - A 在新年之前。
   - **B 那是珍妮的職責。**
   - C 只要上網申請即可。

10. 你想要訂幾間旅館的房間？
   - **A 我認為至少要五間。**
   - B 他在此過夜。
   - C 在三月初。

11. 那位是會議的最後一位演講人嗎？
   - A 會議時程表。
   - B 下午五點。
   - **C 不，今天下午還有另一位。**

12. 研討會將在何時開放報名？
   - A 這家店去年開張。
   - B 他是新的講師。
   - **C 將會在下週開始。**

13. 我應該將這些書收到哪裡？
   - A 是的，它們供販售。
   - **B 請將它們放在櫃子裡。**
   - C 他得了第一名。

14. 你可以盡快去機場接我們的客戶嗎？
   - A 那是國內航班。
   - B 檢查合約。
   - **C 當然，我現在就出發。**

15. 你離開的時候有鎖前門，對吧？
   - A 不，她提早離開了。
   - B 它在前面。
   - **C 是的，別擔心。**

16. 為何季度訓練課程被取消了？
   - A 他正在接受密集訓練。
   - **B 事實上，它被改期了。**
   - C 因為鉛筆斷了。

17. 你可以給我銷售部門的電子郵件地址嗎？
   - **A 我會將它轉寄給你。**
   - B 這是限時的拍賣價。
   - C 這件洋裝真不錯！

TEST 4

PART 2

13

14

18. Didn't you get my proposal?
 A It's not a new garbage disposal.
 B Yes, and I replied.
 C I didn't get there in time.

19. Are you interested in a year-long membership or something short-term?
 A I'll try just a month at first.
 B It's only available for members.
 C This loan offers low interest.

20. You can park your car in front of our building.
 A Oh, that's convenient.
 B I ran out of gas.
 C It overlooks an amusement park.

21. Is this laptop very portable?
 A Yes, it's small and lightweight.
 B It's comfortable to sit on.
 C No, it wasn't on my lap.

22. How can I find a roster of all the volunteers?
 A He volunteered to attend the conference.
 B Please register your complaint.
 C Just access the company database.

23. Please take a brochure before the presentation.
 A Thanks. I'll read it.
 B At the podium.
 C I forgot her present.

24. Ms. Schneider didn't call yet.
 A They did call for help.
 B Don't worry. She will soon.
 C Please transfer her call to me right away.

25. Shouldn't we inform our customers of the policy change soon?
 A Yes, it's custom furniture.
 B That was my application form.
 C I'll let them know.

26. You can fix my bicycle, can't you?
 A I ride the bus to work.
 B Sure, but it will take some time.
 C Yes, I can teach a graphics course.

18. 你沒有收到我的提案嗎？
 A 它不是新的廚餘粉碎機。
 B 有的，而且我回覆了。
 C 我沒有及時趕到那裡。

19. 你感興趣的是一年期的會員資格還是較短期的？
 A 我要先試用一個月。
 B 這只供會員使用。
 C 這個借款提供低利率。

20. 你可以將車子停在我們的大樓前面。
 A 喔，那真是方便。
 B 我的車沒油了。
 C 它俯瞰一座遊樂園。

21. 這台筆電易於攜帶嗎？
 A 是的，它又小又輕。
 B 坐在上面很舒服。
 C 不，它沒在我的腿上。

22. 我如何找到所有志工的名單？
 A 他自願參加這場會議。
 B 請提出你的投訴。
 C 只要進到公司的資料庫。

23. 請在簡報前拿一份手冊。
 A 謝謝，我會閱讀它的。
 B 在講台。
 C 我忘了她的禮物。

24. 史奈德女士還沒有打電話來。
 A 他們的確求救了。
 B 別擔心，她很快就會。
 C 請立刻將她的電話轉給我。

25. 我們不是該盡快告訴顧客這項政策的更動嗎？
 A 是的，這是客製化家具。
 B 那是我的申請表。
 C 我會告知他們的。

26. 你可以修好我的腳踏車，對不對？
 A 我搭公車上班。
 B 當然，但這要花一些時間。
 C 是的，我可以教一門影像設計課程。

27. I didn't turn in the assignment punctually.
- [A] Take a left turn at the corner.
- [B] We appreciate your punctuality.
- **[C] Maybe you should contact your professor.**

28. What kind of ink does the printer use?
- [A] He's a world-famous sprinter.
- **[B] Consult the manual.**
- [C] It's very kind of you to say so.

29. Would you like to go out for lunch?
- [A] It was tasty.
- [B] The lights will go out after 7:00 p.m.
- **[C] When is your break?**

30. Why was the manuscript I submitted rejected by the editor?
- [A] Submit the form online.
- **[B] It doesn't fit the style of writing he was looking for.**
- [C] It was written on the menu.

31. I need to confirm your reservation.
- **[A] I'll send the confirmation number.**
- [B] No, there is no room.
- [C] The seat was fairly firm.

27. 我沒有準時繳交作業。
- [A] 在街角左轉。
- [B] 我們感激你的準時。
- **[C] 也許你該聯絡你的教授。**

28. 這台印表機使用哪一種墨水？
- [A] 他是世界知名的短跑選手。
- **[B] 查詢這本手冊。**
- [C] 你這麼說真是太客氣了。

29. 你想外出用午餐嗎？
- [A] 那很美味。
- [B] 晚上七點後就會熄燈。
- **[C] 你什麼時候休息？**

30. 為什麼我交出去的稿子被編輯退回了？
- [A] 用網路提交表格。
- **[B] 這不符合他要的寫作風格。**
- [C] 它就寫在菜單上。

31. 我需要確認你的預訂。
- **[A] 我會寄送認證號碼。**
- [B] 不，沒有空間了。
- [C] 這個座位相當穩固。

PART 3 P. 65-69

32-34 conversation

M： Hello. **(32) Last Thursday, I arranged to have cable television installed at my house this Wednesday.** Unfortunately, I will have to be out of town that day because of some urgent matters and would like to reschedule the appointment for Friday afternoon.

W： OK, that shouldn't be a problem. **(33) However, I would like to warn you that there is a $5 rescheduling fee.** That's our company's policy. Can I have your name, please?

M： Oh, I see. My name is Charlie Kramer. I live in Hainesville. Do you know when I will have to pay this fee?

W： **(34) I'll email you soon about a user name and temporary password that you can use on our website.** Please check the email and pay all your bills through our website.

32-34 對話

男： 哈囉。**(32) 上週四，我安排了本週三要在我家安裝有線電視。** 不巧的是，我當天因為有些急事而必須要出城去，我想要將時間改到星期五下午。

女： 好的，那應該不成問題。**(33) 但是我想要提醒您，將會有五元的改期費用**，這是我們公司的規定。可以請您告訴我您的名字嗎？

男： 喔，我知道了。我的名字是查理·克萊門。我住在漢尼斯維爾。你知道我什麼時候要付這筆費用嗎？

女： **(34) 我很快就會將適用於我們網站的使用者名稱和暫用密碼，以電子郵件寄給你。** 請檢查電子郵件並透過網站繳付所有的帳款。

32. What did the man recently do?
- A Purchased a house
- B Went on a business trip
- **C Signed up for a service**
- D Installed a television

33. Why must the man pay a fee?
- **A He wants to change his schedule.**
- B He returned an item late.
- C He lost his membership card.
- D He needs an additional service.

34. What will the woman include in an email?
- A A receipt
- **B Log-in information**
- C A membership contract
- D Driving directions

35-37 conversation

M：Hi, Tiffany. Do you know what happened to the company car? I tried to reserve it today, but I was told it's being repaired.

W：**(35) When Mark was driving yesterday, he got a flat tire.** I just heard that the car should be out of the repair shop by this evening. I'll let you know when they call me.

M：Oh, that's good news. **(36) I was worried because I need it tomorrow morning to pick up an important client from the airport.**

W：Ah, isn't that Mr. Lee from Beijing? **(37) Just in case, why don't you call a local car rental business and reserve a car for tomorrow?** If the company car is fixed in time, you can cancel.

---

35. What does the woman say caused the problem?
- A A repair cost has increased.
- B A reservation has been canceled.
- C A client arrived too late.
- **D A tire needed to be replaced.**

36. Why is the man concerned?
- A He lost an important receipt.
- **B He needs a car to greet a client.**
- C He has to reschedule a meeting.
- D He was unable to contact a client.

---

32. 男子最近做了什麼？
- A 買房子
- B 出差
- **C 登記一項服務**
- D 安裝電視

33. 為何男子必須支付一筆費用？
- **A 他想要更改時間**
- B 他延遲退還一項物品
- C 他遺失會員卡
- D 他需要額外的服務

34. 女子將在電子郵件中包含什麼？
- A 收據
- **B 登入資訊**
- C 會員合約
- D 交通指引

35-37 對話

男：嗨，蒂芬妮。你知道公司的車發生了什麼事嗎？我今天試著預訂，但卻被告知它正在維修中。

女：**(35) 馬克昨天開車的時候爆胎了。** 我剛才聽說車子今晚前會出維修廠，他們打電話給我的時候，我會告知你。

男：喔，那真是好消息。**(36) 我本來很擔心的，因為我明天早上要用車，去機場接一名重要的客戶。**

女：啊，是來自北京的李先生嗎？**(37)** 為了預防萬一，你何不打電話給本地的租車行，並且預訂一輛明天要用的車？如果公司的車及時修好了，你可以取消預訂。

---

35. 女子說是什麼導致了這個問題？
- A 修理費用增加
- B 預約被取消
- C 客戶太晚到達
- **D 輪胎需要更換**

36. 男子為何擔心？
- A 他遺失了重要的收據
- **B 他需要車輛去迎接客戶**
- C 他必須重新安排會議時間
- D 他無法聯繫到客戶

37. What does the woman suggest?
A Preparing an alternative plan
B Ordering a replacement part
C Attending a conference
D Reserving a less expensive ticket

37. 女子提出什麼建議？
A 備妥備案
B 訂購替換零件
C 出席會議
D 訂較不昂貴的票

38-40 conversation

W: Hello, this is Kelly in the accounting department. **(38) The ink cartridge in the printer on the fourth floor has run out.** Do you think you could come to replace it today?

M: Sure. By the way, can I ask you a favor? **(39) I need you to let me know what model the machine is so I can bring the correct one.** Actually, I'm not in the office right now, so I can't see what it is.

W: OK. But how can I find that information? Do I have to open the printer cover or press some function buttons?

M: No, you don't. **(40) Just ask Mr. Hills in your department.** He should have a complete list of all the hardware on the fourth floor.

38-40 對話

女：哈囉，我是會計部門的凱莉。**(38) 四樓印表機的墨水匣沒墨水了**，你今天能過來更換嗎？

男：當然。對了，可以請你幫個忙嗎？**(39) 我需要你告訴我機器的型號，以便帶正確的墨水匣過去。** 我其實現在不在辦公室，因此無法知道是什麼型號。

女：好的，但我如何能找到這項資訊？我需要打開印表機的外殼或按下某些功能按鍵嗎？

男：不，你不需要。**(40) 只要問你部門的希爾斯先生。** 他應該有四樓所有硬體設備的完整清單。

---

38. What problem is the woman reporting?
A An accounting error has been made.
B A printer is out of order.
C Some office supplies have run out.
D A document has been lost.

38. 女子回報什麼問題？
A 犯了會計的錯誤
B 印表機故障
C 某些辦公用品已經用完
D 文件遺失了

39. What does the man ask the woman to do?
A Check some product information
B Install new equipment
C Update customer information
D Stop by his office

39. 男子要求女子做什麼？
A 查看某項產品資訊
B 安裝新設備
C 更新客戶資訊
D 去他的辦公室

40. What is mentioned about Mr. Hills?
A He is in charge of a new project.
B He is in the same department as the woman.
C He has recently ordered a new item.
D He wrote a hardware list.

40. 關於希爾斯先生有提到什麼？
A 他負責新專案
B 他與女子在相同的部門
C 他最近訂了新物品
D 他寫下硬體設備的清單

41-43 conversation

M: **(41) Hello, I saw your advertisement on TV promoting your grand opening.** Can you tell me about your clothing store?

41-43 對話

男：**(41) 哈囉，我在電視上看到宣傳你們盛大開幕的廣告。** 你可以跟我介紹你們的服飾店嗎？

W：Welcome to our store. Our store specializes in men's suits and formal wear. **(42) As a grand opening promotion, we are offering free delivery on all purchases this month.**

M：Wow, that's great. I need to buy a suit for my wedding, so I stopped by. Could you show me something I might like?

W：Sure. We have a variety of wedding suits. Please come here. **(43) First, I would like to have my assistant take your measurements so we can find a suit that fits you well.** It won't take much time.

41. How did the man learn about the store?
    A By watching television
    B By talking to a friend
    C By reading a brochure
    D By listening to the radio

42. According to the woman, what is being offered this month?
    A A discount coupon
    B A reduced membership fee
    C Free delivery
    D A lifetime warranty

43. What does the woman suggest doing?
    A Paying in advance
    B Getting measurements taken
    C Submitting a proposal
    D Hiring an assistant

44-46 conversation

W：Nice to meet you, Mr. Gomez. **(44) I'm sure after you hear about our business, you will want us to provide food and beverages for your company's various events.**

M：Nice to meet you, Ms. Gates. Thank you for coming today. I haven't inquired about your services because your company is located out of town. **(45) I didn't think you could provide services to us.**

W：Rose and Lily Co. is willing to travel anywhere within the state in order to meet our clients' needs. Our prices don't change depending on distance, so you don't need to worry about that.

女：歡迎光臨。本店專賣男士西服和正式穿著。**(42) 作為盛大開幕促銷，我們將為所有在本月購買的商品提供免運服務。**

男：哇，那真是太好了。我需要為我的婚禮買一套西裝，所以我才來。你可以讓我看看我可能會喜歡的衣服嗎？

女：當然可以。我們有各式婚禮西裝，請來這裡。**(43) 首先，我想請我的助理為你測量尺寸，這樣我們就可以為你找到合適的西裝。**這不會花太多時間。

41. 男子如何得知關於這家店的事？
    A 看電視
    B 與朋友談話
    C 閱讀手冊
    D 聽收音機

42. 根據女子，本月會提供什麼？
    A 折價券
    B 減收會員費
    C 免費運送
    D 終身保固

43. 女子提議要做什麼？
    A 事先付款
    B 進行尺寸測量
    C 繳交提案
    D 僱用助手

44–46 對話

女：很高興見到您，戈梅茲先生。**(44) 我相信當你了解我們公司的業務之後，會想要由我們來提供貴公司各種活動所需的食物和飲料。**

男：很高興見到你，蓋茲女士。感謝你今天過來。我尚未詢問關於貴公司的服務，因為貴公司位於城外。**(45) 我以為你們不能為我們提供服務。**

女：蘿絲和莉莉公司願意前往本州任何地方，以滿足我們客戶的需求。我們的價格不會因為距離而改變，因此您不需擔心這點。

M : Oh, I'm glad to hear that. In that case, we will consider your services. What are your specialties? **(46) Do you think I could sample some of the food and beverages you provide?**

男：我很高興聽你這麼説。這樣的話，我們將會考慮你們的服務。貴公司的特色是什麼？**(46) 我可以試吃你們提供的一些食物和飲料嗎？**

44. What kind of services are the speakers discussing?
   Ⓐ **Catering for company events**
   Ⓑ Business consultation
   Ⓒ Workforce training
   Ⓓ Delivery services

44. 對話者在討論何種服務？
   Ⓐ **公司活動的外燴**
   Ⓑ 商業諮詢
   Ⓒ 人力訓練
   Ⓓ 送貨服務

45. Why has the man not used Rose and Lily Co.'s services before?
   Ⓐ He was unaware of them.
   Ⓑ He was reluctant to pay a membership fee.
   Ⓒ He was on bad terms with the owner.
   Ⓓ **He did not realize their availability.**

45. 男子為何先前並未使用蘿絲和莉莉公司的服務？
   Ⓐ 他不知道有這家公司
   Ⓑ 他不想付會員費
   Ⓒ 他與業主關係不好
   Ⓓ **他不知道該公司能提供服務**

46. What does the man ask the woman to do?
   Ⓐ Try some food and beverages
   Ⓑ Send a catalog
   Ⓒ **Provide a sample**
   Ⓓ Expedite an order

46. 男子要求女子做什麼？
   Ⓐ 試吃食物和飲料
   Ⓑ 寄商品型錄
   Ⓒ **提供試吃品**
   Ⓓ 加速訂單處理速度

15

47-49 conversation

W : Hi, Josh. You work at Sentry Insurance, don't you? **(47) I heard from a friend they are expected to merge with another company.** Is your position secure?

M : Yes, no problem. I will be keeping my position. **(48) In fact, my company plans to expand internationally so that we can compete with other global corporations.** I'm certain it will be beneficial for both me and my company.

W : I'm glad to hear that. Actually, I've recently been thinking about changing my line of employment. Will there be any opportunities for getting hired at your company?

M : **(49) Well, you should visit my company's website because we are posting new job positions that will be available after the merger.**

47–49 對話

女：嗨，喬許。你在崗哨保全工作，對不對？**(47) 我聽一個朋友説，他們預計會與另一家公司合併。**你的職位有保障嗎？

男：是的，沒問題。我會保有我的職位。**(48) 實際上，我們公司計劃要拓展到國際市場，因此我們會與其他全球性的企業競爭。**我相信這對我和公司都會有好處。

女：我很高興聽你這麼説。其實我最近在考慮換工作，我有機會被你公司僱用嗎？

男：**(49) 嗯，你可以上我公司的網站，因為我們會在上面公告合併後的新職缺。**

47. What does the woman say she has heard about?
  Ⓐ The joining of two businesses
  Ⓑ The construction of a factory
  Ⓒ An international conference
  Ⓓ A highway expansion project

48. What benefit does the man mention?
  Ⓐ Lower insurance costs
  Ⓑ Increased vacation days
  Ⓒ International competitiveness
  Ⓓ Updated equipment

49. What does the man suggest the woman do?
  Ⓐ Visit his office
  Ⓑ Post an advertisement
  Ⓒ Submit a proposal
  Ⓓ Check job listings

47. 女子說她聽說了什麼？
  Ⓐ 兩家公司的合併
  Ⓑ 工廠的建造
  Ⓒ 國際會議
  Ⓓ 公路擴展計劃

48. 男子提到什麼好處？
  Ⓐ 較低的保險費
  Ⓑ 增加的休假天數
  Ⓒ 國際競爭力
  Ⓓ 更新的設備

49. 男子建議女子做什麼？
  Ⓐ 造訪他的辦公室
  Ⓑ 刊登廣告
  Ⓒ 繳交提案
  Ⓓ 查看工作職缺

(NEW)
50-52 conversation

M： Hi, Ms. Parker? This is Joseph Sterling, from Green Creek Realtors. **(50) We need to talk about an issue with the apartment you wanted.**

W： Oh, hi Joseph. Did you manage to find me a place in the Kahlua Apartment building?

M： Yes, that's the reason I'm calling. But there is a bit of an issue.

W： Really? What is it?

M： **(51) There is a major pest problem in the building, and they need to clear the whole building and carry out pest control.** It's going to take them at least three months to make sure the building is clean. So you would have to wait three months to get a place there.

W： I see.

M： There is a building just nearby called Graceville Towers. It's very close to the Kahlua building, so you could stay there for three months and then move over to the Kahlua building. **(52) I will arrange all of the moving for you.** Why don't you go online and check out Graceville Towers and get back to me?

W： Sure, that sounds good. Thanks, Joseph.

50–52 對話

男： 嗨，帕克女士嗎？我是綠溪房地產的約瑟夫・史特林。**(50) 我們來談談關於你想要的那間公寓。**

女： 喔，嗨，約瑟夫。你已幫我在卡魯哇公寓大樓找到住處了嗎？

男： 是的，這就是我打了這通電話的原因。但出了一些問題。

女： 真的嗎？什麼問題？

男： **(51) 大樓內有嚴重的蟲害問題，他們要淨空整棟大樓並且進行驅蟲。** 至少要三個月才能確保大樓乾淨。因此，你要等三個月才能入住。

女： 我知道了。

男： 在那裡附近有一棟叫做格瑞思維爾塔大樓。它很接近卡魯哇大樓，因此你可以在那裡住三個月，然後再搬到卡魯哇大樓。**(52) 我會為你安排所有的搬遷事宜。** 你可以上網看看格瑞思維爾塔，再回電話給我。

女： 當然，聽起來不錯。謝謝你，約瑟夫。

50. What is the reason for Joseph's call?

A **To relate a problem concerning the apartment**

B To sign the contract for the apartment

C To discuss another apartment

D To discuss the price of rent

51. What does Joseph say about the Kahlua Apartment?

A It's ready to be occupied anytime.

B There are renovations occurring.

C It is near a new fitness center.

D **There is a major pest problem.**

52. What does Joseph offer to do?

A Find a new apartment at Graceville Towers

B **Arrange all of the moving**

C Move her furniture personally

D Move into the Kahlua Apartment building

50. 約瑟夫打電話的原因為何？

A **為了說公寓的問題**

B 為了簽署公寓的租約

C 為了討論另一間公寓

D 為了討論租金價格

51. 關於卡魯哇公寓，約瑟夫說了什麼？

A 它隨時可以入住

B 正在進行翻修

C 在一家新的健身中心附近

D **有嚴重的蟲害問題**

52. 約瑟夫提議要做什麼？

A 在格瑞思維爾塔找新公寓

B **安排所有搬遷事宜**

C 親自幫她搬家具

D 搬進卡魯哇公寓大樓

53-55 conversation

W：Hi, Amos. This is Elizabeth Cox. **(53) Last year you helped find some office space for my company, and I was hoping you could help me find something in the same area.**

M：Hi, Elizabeth. It's good to hear from you. If I remember correctly, your office is in the Barnsbury area, right?

W：Yes. **(54) Actually, I recently left that company and I've opened my own legal firm.** I only have four staff members, so we don't need a big space. As long it is in good condition and the location is fine.

M：No problem. I have a few in the area I think you would like. **(55) What's your afternoon like?**

53–55 對話

🎧 15

女：嗨，阿摩司，你好。我是伊莉莎白‧考克斯。**(53) 去年你為我的公司找辦公室，我希望你可以在同一地區再幫我找個地方。**

男：嗨，伊莉莎白，您好。很高興接到您的來電。如果我沒記錯，您的辦公室是在巴恩斯伯里地區，對嗎？

女：是的。**(54) 其實，我最近才離開那家公司，開了自己的法律事務所。** 我只有四名員工，因此不需要很大的空間，只要狀況好、地點佳即可。

男：沒問題。我在該地區有些物件，我認為你會喜歡，**(55) 你下午忙嗎？**

---

53. Why is the woman calling the man?

A To ask a favor of him

B To order some flowers

C **To find a rental property**

D To rent a house

54. What does the woman say she has done recently?

A Been promoted at her company

B Closed down her business

C Got a new job

D **Opened her own business**

53. 女子為何打電話給男子？

A 為了請他幫忙

B 為了訂花

C **為了尋找出租的房子**

D 為了租屋

54. 女子說她最近做了什麼？

A 獲得公司的升遷

B 結束她的事業

C 找到新的工作

D **開立自己的公司**

55. Why does the man say, "What's your afternoon like"?
- [A] **To figure out when they can meet**
- [B] To ask her to dinner
- [C] To explain rental conditions
- [D] To get some keys for the office

55. 男子為何說「你下午忙嗎」？
- [A] **要知道他們何時可以會面**
- [B] 要邀請她吃晚餐
- [C] 要解釋出租的情況
- [D] 要拿辦公室的鑰匙

56-58 conversation

M：Hey Judy, (56) **did you see the new offices the company built?** They look fantastic.

W：(57) **Yeah it's about time!**

M：I know we had some slow years, but the last five years everyone has worked so hard, and now it's finally paying off.

W：(58) **Our company's growth has been fast, but there has been a lot of long nights and hard work.**

M：I agree with you. But it is nice to see it finally paying off. I can't wait to move into my new office!

56-58 對話

男：嗨，茱蒂，(56) 你看過公司蓋的新辦公室了嗎？看起來很棒。

女：(57) 是的，也該是時候了！

男：我知道我們有幾年成長緩慢，但大家在過去五年都很努力，現在也終有所回報了。

女：(58) 我們公司成長得很快，但都是許多夜晚加班和拚命工作的累積。

男：我同意。但看到終於有所回報真的很不錯，我等不及要搬進我的新辦公室了！

56. What did the company do recently?
- [A] Renovated the lobby
- [B] Built new research facilities
- [C] Hired new staff
- [D] **Built new offices**

56. 這家公司最近做了什麼？
- [A] 翻修大廳
- [B] 蓋了新的研究機構
- [C] 僱用新員工
- [D] **蓋了新辦公室**

57. What does the woman mean when she says, "it's about time"?
- [A] **She thinks the company deserves to have new offices.**
- [B] She thinks construction has taken too long.
- [C] She doesn't like the new offices.
- [D] She wants a raise in her salary.

57. 女子說「也該是時候了」，她指的是什麼？
- [A] **她認為公司該有新的辦公室**
- [B] 她認為工程花了太久的時間
- [C] 她不喜歡新的辦公室
- [D] 她想要加薪

58. What does the woman imply about the company?
- [A] They have been very lucky to grow so fast.
- [B] Some of the staff is not working hard.
- [C] **The company worked hard to grow fast.**
- [D] The new offices aren't very nice.

58. 關於這家公司，女子在暗示什麼？
- [A] 他們很幸運能成長得如此快速
- [B] 其中一些員工不努力
- [C] **公司很努力而成長快速**
- [D] 新的辦公室不太好

59-61 conversation

W：Hi, Roger. **(59) Is last month's sales report ready for our meeting today?**

M1：I have finished my section. Andrew, have you finished yours? **(60) I noticed you were at work late last night, so I assume you have finished.**

M2：My part is finished. Give me your part and I will get everything ready for the meeting. Sales are really high this quarter, so management will be very pleased.

W：Oh, that's great. We needed a good quarter after our last one. That was our lowest in history.

M1：**(61) Andrew, when you're finished send us an email and we can prepare for the meeting.**

59. What are the speakers mainly discussing?
   A Getting ready for a work party
   B Getting the sales report ready
   C Getting ready for a promotion
   D Getting ready to finish the quarter

60. What does the man say about Andrew?
   A That he left work early the night before
   B That he thinks Andrew isn't a hard worker
   C That he worked late the night before
   D That he had a good quarter

61. What does Roger tell Andrew to do?
   A Send a letter to Roger when he is finished
   B Bring the email to the meeting
   C Not to come to the meeting
   D Send an email when he is finished

62-64 conversation

M：Hello, this is Warren speaking. How can I help you today?

W：**(62) Hello, Warren. I purchased a work desk from your store.** I'm trying to put it together but there are some important parts missing.

59–61 對話

女：嗨，羅傑。**(59) 你準備好了上個月的銷售報告，供今日會議使用嗎？**

男 1：我的部分已經完成了。安德魯，你的部分完成了嗎？**(60) 我注意到你昨晚加班加到很晚，因此我猜你已經完成了。**

男 2：我的部分完成了。把你的部分給我，我就可以備妥開會所需的資料。本季銷售額很高，因此管理階層會很高興。

女：喔，太好了。這一季我們要表現亮眼一點。上一季是我們歷年來銷售最低迷的一季。

男 1：**(61) 安德魯，你做好之後寄電子郵件給我們，然後我們就可以為開會做準備。**

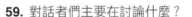

59. 對話者們主要在討論什麼？
   A 準備辦員工派對
   B 準備好銷售報告
   C 準備做促銷
   D 準備結束一季

60. 關於安德魯，男子說了什麼？
   A 他前一晚提早下班
   B 他認為安德魯工作不努力
   C 他前一晚工作得很晚
   D 他上季表現良好

61. 羅傑要安德魯做什麼？
   A 完成時寄信給羅傑
   B 將電子郵件帶去開會
   C 別去開會
   D 完成時寄電子郵件

62-64 對話

男：哈囉，我是華倫。今天有什麼需要我協助的嗎？

女：**(62) 哈囉，華倫。我從你的店買了一張工作桌。**我正在嘗試組裝，但有一些重要的零件不見了。

243

M : I'm sorry about that. Sometimes the manufacturer makes mistakes. What are you missing?

W : (63) **Well, the biggest problem is I don't have the tool to put in the bolts.** And I'm missing 3 barrel nuts.

M : OK, I have those parts in the shop. (64) **I have a lunch break at 2 p.m. I can bring them over to your place if you like.**

W : Oh, wow. That would be fantastic. Wait one moment and I will give you my address.

男：很抱歉，製造商有時候會出錯，你缺少了什麼？

女：(63) 最大的問題是，我沒有鎖上螺栓的工具，還少了三個圓柱帽。

男：好的，我店裡有這些零件。(64) 我下午兩點午休。如果你要的話，我可以把零件帶去給你。

女：喔，哇，那樣太棒了。請稍等，我給你我的地址。

Part A 部分 — 90 mm Bolts	90 厘米螺栓	
Part B 部分 — 25 mm Wood Screws	25 厘米木螺釘	
Part C 部分 — Barrel Nuts x 6	圓柱帽 *6	
Part D 部分 — Long Allen Key x 1	長的六角扳手 *1	

62. Where does the man most likely work?
   A At a university
   B At a furniture store
   C At a bedding store
   D At a technical college

(NEW)
63. Look at the graphic. What is the woman missing?
   A 90 mm Bolts
   B Wood Screws
   C Barrel Nuts
   D Allen Key

64. What does the man offer to do?
   A Deliver the parts to her house by post
   B Deliver the parts to her house in person
   C Have the parts delivered by his staff
   D Leave the parts at the front counter

62. 男子最有可能在哪裡工作？
   A 在大學
   B 在家具店
   C 在寢具店
   D 在技術學院

63. 參看圖表。女子缺少了什麼？
   A 90 厘米螺栓
   B 木螺釘
   C 圓柱帽
   D 長的六角扳手

64. 男子提議要做什麼？
   A 將零件郵寄到她家
   B 親自將零件送到她家
   C 請員工將零件送過去
   D 將零件留置在櫃台

65-67 conversation

M： Hi, Sandra. I'm so sorry I missed our meeting this morning. **(66) I didn't realize the Tower Bridge was closed for upgrading.** I had to go over the Brooklyn Bridge.

W： Don't worry about it, Rob. **(65) Most of the staff was late because of that. It's going to be annoying to have to go over the Brooklyn Bridge every day.** I might just take the Express Tunnel.

M： Yeah, I know. But the traffic is just so terrible in that tunnel. I can't really handle it.

W： I agree. **(67) I think we should all just take the subway until the Tower Bridge is open again.**

65-67 對話

男： 嗨，珊卓。很抱歉我錯過今天早上的會議。**(66) 我不知道高塔橋封閉進行改良工程，**我得繞道走布魯克林橋。

女： 別在意，羅伯。**(65) 大部分員工也都因此遲到了，以後每天要走布魯克林橋很令人困擾。**我可能會走快速隧道。

男： 是的，我知道。但那條隧道的交通很糟糕，我真的無法忍受。

女： 我同意。**(67) 我認為在高塔橋重新開放之前，我們應該都搭地鐵。**

Bridge closed until
Jan. 12 due to upgrade of infrastructure
因進行改善工程
橋梁封閉至 1 月 12 日

---

65. According to the woman, what is causing people to arrive late to work?

　Ⓐ A meeting was postponed.
　Ⓑ The bridge was very busy.
　Ⓒ The bridge was closed.
　Ⓓ They had car problems.

66. Look at the graphic. Where is the sign most likely located?

　Ⓐ The Brooklyn Bridge
　Ⓑ The Tower Bridge
　Ⓒ The East Bay Tunnel
　Ⓓ The Express Tunnel

67. What does the woman recommend to the man?

　Ⓐ Take the bus to work
　Ⓑ Share a taxi to work
　Ⓒ Take the subway to work
　Ⓓ Take the Express Tunnel

65. 根據女子，什麼導致員工上班遲到？

　Ⓐ 會議延後
　Ⓑ 橋梁壅塞
　Ⓒ 橋梁封閉
　Ⓓ 汽車故障

66. 參看圖表，這個標誌最有可能在哪裡？

　Ⓐ 布魯克林橋
　Ⓑ 高塔橋
　Ⓒ 東海岸隧道
　Ⓓ 快速隧道

67. 女子建議男子做什麼？

　Ⓐ 搭公車上班
　Ⓑ 共乘計程車上班
　Ⓒ 搭地鐵上班
　Ⓓ 走快速隧道

68-70 conversation

W: OK, your total bill comes to $75. **(68) I hope you enjoyed your food tonight.** Would you like to split the bill?

M: No, I will pay. I have a coupon for a 10 percent discount. It's in my wallet. Here it is.

W: OK. Hmm, it doesn't seem to work when I try to scan it. Let me get the manager.

M: **(69) Oh, never mind, I can see the problem. I didn't read it properly. I'm so careless sometimes. We should have ordered more drinks!**

W: Well next time you come in, you should bring a bigger group, and you will get a better discount that way anyhow. **(70) If you like I can put the coupon in our computer system so next time you come in you don't need to bring the card.**

68–70 對話

女： 好的。您的帳單總計為 75 元。**(68) 希望你們喜歡今晚的餐點。** 你們要分開結帳嗎？

男： 不，由我來付帳。我有九折優惠券。在我皮夾裡，在這裡。

女： 好的，嗯，我嘗試刷條碼，但似乎沒辦法刷。讓我去找經理來。

男： **(69) 喔，沒關係喔，我知道問題出在哪裡了，我沒看清楚。我有時候很粗心，我們應該多點一些飲料的！**

女： 下次你們來，應該多帶點人，這樣會折扣比較多。**(70) 如果您要的話，我可以把優惠券存在電腦系統裡。這樣你們下一次來就不用帶這張卡了。**

Fisherman's Wharf 漁人碼頭
Discount Coupon 優惠券

10% off any order above $100　超過 100 元打九折

Expires November 1st　有效期限至 11 月 1 日

68. Where most likely are the speakers?
- [A] In a hospital
- **[B] In a restaurant**
- [C] In a bar
- [D] In a hotel

 69. Look at the graphic. Why is the coupon rejected?
- [A] The order was above $100.
- [B] It is expired.
- **[C] Their order was below $100.**
- [D] The coupon didn't have credit on it.

70. What does the woman offer to do?
- [A] Give them a new card
- **[B] Put the coupon in the computer system**
- [C] Hold the card for them
- [D] Provide a refund

68. 對話者最有可能在哪裡？
- [A] 在醫院
- **[B] 在餐廳**
- [C] 在酒吧
- [D] 在旅館

69. 參看圖表，為何優惠券不能使用？
- [A] 餐點超過 100 元
- [B] 它過期了
- **[C] 他們的餐點未滿 100 元**
- [D] 優惠券上頭沒寫折扣額

70. 女子提議要做什麼？
- [A] 給他們新的卡片
- **[B] 將優惠券存在電腦系統**
- [C] 為他們保留這張卡片
- [D] 提供退費

71-73 announcement

W： Attention, conference attendees. Thank you for your patience while you wait for us to solve this delay. **(71) Unfortunately, the computer that is to be used during the keynote speaker's presentation is having problems.** As a result, we are currently transferring the necessary files onto a different computer. **(72) We plan to get underway with the presentation in half an hour.** In the meantime, feel free to enjoy some of the refreshments provided near the entrance. **(73) We will dim the lights in order to indicate that the presentation will be beginning.** Please return to your seats at that time.

71–73 宣布

女： 各位與會人士請注意，感謝你們耐心等候我們解決延誤的問題。**(71)** 很不巧地，主講演講時所需的電腦出了問題。因此，我們正在把必要的檔案傳輸到另一台電腦。**(72)** 我們打算在半小時後開始演講。同時，請儘情享用入口附近提供的茶點。**(73)** 我們會將燈光調暗以表示演講即將開始。屆時請各位回到座位。

71. What is causing the delay?
- [A] Bad weather
- [B] A canceled flight
- [C] A scheduling error
- **[D] A technical difficulty**

71. 什麼導致了延誤？
- [A] 惡劣的天氣
- [B] 取消的航班
- [C] 時間規劃錯誤
- **[D] 技術性問題**

72. According to the speaker, after how long will the presentation begin?
- [A] 5 minutes
- **[B] 30 minutes**
- [C] 45 minutes
- [D] 60 minutes

72. 根據發話者，演講將在多久之後開始？
- [A] 5 分鐘
- **[B] 30 分鐘**
- [C] 45 分鐘
- [D] 60 分鐘

73. What will happen when it's time for the presentation to begin?
- [A] An announcement will be made.
- **[B] Lighting will be adjusted.**
- [C] A keynote speaker will appear on the stage.
- [D] Refreshments will be served.

73. 當演講要開始時會發生什麼事？
- [A] 將會進行宣布
- **[B] 將調整光線**
- [C] 主講人將上台
- [D] 將提供茶點

74-76 radio broadcast

M： Welcome back to your local radio station WXFD 93.7 with the morning news update. **(74) Yesterday, the Clinton Town council passed a new law prohibiting pet owners from bringing their pets onto public beaches. (75) Tim Kellerman, who was newly elected to the town council last month, justified the decision by arguing that pets can bother other beach-goers.** Those who violate the law will have to pay a fine of $300. **(76) Up next, we will be taking calls from listeners to hear their reaction to this new measure.**

74–76 電台廣播

男： 歡迎回到本地廣播電台 WXFD 93.7，給您帶來最新的晨間新聞。**(74)** 昨天柯林頓鎮議會通過了一項新法律，禁止寵物主人將寵物帶到公有海灘。**(75)** 上個月剛當選進入鎮議會的提姆·克勒曼，主張這項決定是由於寵物可能會對其他海灘遊客造成困擾。違反這項法令的人將要支付 300 元的罰鍰。**(76)** 接下來我們要接聽眾的來電，聽聽大家對這項新措施的反應。

74. What is the radio broadcast about?
- [A] The opening of a pet store
- **[B] A newly introduced law**
- [C] A new council hall
- [D] An upcoming election

75. According to the speaker, what did Tim Kellerman do recently?
- **[A] He ran for office.**
- [B] He won an award.
- [C] He selected a pet.
- [D] He paid a fine.

76. What will listeners most likely hear next?
- [A] A weather forecast
- [B] Some breaking news
- **[C] Community members' opinions**
- [D] A telephone interview

77-79 advertisement

W：Welcome to our Holiday Sale here at Leeman's Department Store. We are currently running our Red Cart Savings Event. Pay just $100 for all the clothing that you can fit in a single red cart. **(77) You can get a cart immediately inside the main entrance to the store.** Make sure to take advantage of this sale. It only happens once a year! **(78) In order to accommodate the high volume of customers, we have extra staff located throughout the store. You can spot them easily because they are wearing green vests.** Also, you can enter your name into our raffle event by visiting the front desk. **(79) I will announce the results at the end of the day.**

77. Where should listeners get carts?
- [A] In the parking lot
- **[B] At the entrance**
- [C] Near the lobby
- [D] From a cashier

---

74. 這則電台廣播與什麼有關？
- [A] 寵物店開幕
- **[B] 新施行的法律**
- [C] 新議會廳
- [D] 即將舉行的選舉

75. 根據發話者，提姆·克勒曼最近做了什麼？
- **[A] 他競選公職**
- [B] 他獲獎
- [C] 他挑選了寵物
- [D] 他繳交罰款

76. 聽眾接下來最有可能聽到什麼？
- [A] 天氣預報
- [B] 突發新聞
- **[C] 公眾的意見**
- [D] 電話訪談

77–79 廣告

女：歡迎來到李曼百貨公司的節慶特賣。我們現在正在進行紅色購物車省錢活動。只要付 100 元，就可以買到你所有塞進一台紅色購物車的衣物。**(77)** 你現在就可以在百貨公司大門處取得推車。請務必把握這場特賣會，一年僅有一次！**(78)** 為了容納大量的顧客，我們在整間百貨公司都有增加員工。你很容易就能找到他們，因為他們穿著綠色的背心。此外，你也可以到櫃台報名抽獎。**(79)** 今天結束時我會宣布結果。

77. 聽眾應該從哪裡取得推車？
- [A] 停車場
- **[B] 入口處**
- [C] 大廳附近
- [D] 收銀員

78. According to the speaker, who is wearing green vests?
　Ⓐ Cashiers
　Ⓑ Store managers
　Ⓒ Additional staff
　Ⓓ Parking lot attendants

79. What will the speaker most likely do at the end of the day?
　Ⓐ Announce winners
　Ⓑ Collect donations
　Ⓒ Give a demonstration
　Ⓓ Purchase an item

80-82 advertisement

M：**(80) If you're looking for reasonable prices on ink toner, then stop by Quill Office Supplies in Rochester!** We have replacement ink toner to fit all models of printers and copy machines. **(81) During the month of April, we will send a technician to your location at no charge to help you remove an old ink cartridge and install a new one. (82) If you sign up for regular cartridge refills, you can receive a 5 percent discount on all of your purchases.** For more information, please visit our website at www.quillofficesupplies.com.

80. What business is being advertised?
　Ⓐ A computer retailer
　Ⓑ An electronics repair shop
　Ⓒ An office supply store
　Ⓓ A cosmetics store

81. What service is available in April?
　Ⓐ Installment payments
　Ⓑ Express shipping
　Ⓒ Online assistance
　Ⓓ Free installation

82. How can listeners get a discount?
　Ⓐ By bringing a coupon
　Ⓑ By buying in bulk
　Ⓒ By becoming a regular customer
　Ⓓ By signing up for a newsletter

78. 根據發話者，什麼人穿著綠色的背心？
　Ⓐ 收銀員
　Ⓑ 店經理
　Ⓒ 增設的員工
　Ⓓ 停車場服務員

79. 發話者在當天結束時最有可能做什麼？
　Ⓐ 宣布得獎者
　Ⓑ 收取捐款
　Ⓒ 進行演示
　Ⓓ 購買商品

80–82 廣告

男：**(80)** 如果您正在尋找價格公道的墨水匣，請來位於洛徹斯特的羽毛筆辦公用品店！我們有適合各種印表機和影印機型號的替換墨水匣。**(81)** 在四月期間，我們將會免費派遣技術人員到府，協助您拆下舊的墨水匣並安裝新的。**(82)** 如果您簽約定期補充墨水匣，就能享有 95 折的購買折扣。欲知詳情，請上我們的網站 www.quillofficesupplies.com。

80. 這是什麼行業的廣告？
　Ⓐ 電腦零售商
　Ⓑ 電子設備維修行
　Ⓒ 辦公用品店
　Ⓓ 化妝品店

81. 四月時會提供什麼服務？
　Ⓐ 分期付款
　Ⓑ 快遞送貨
　Ⓒ 線上支援
　Ⓓ 免費安裝

82. 聽眾要如何獲得折扣？
　Ⓐ 攜帶折價券
　Ⓑ 大量購買
　Ⓒ 成為常客
　Ⓓ 訂閱電子報

83-85 announcement

W: Hi, everyone, thanks for meeting with me today. **(83) I'd like to announce a few changes in our health and safety policy that are designed to conform to the new government regulations.** Firstly, we can no longer work a shift longer than six hours without taking a one-hour break. We'll be using a clock-in system that is automated to send you a text message once you reach six hours. You will also wear a device that monitors your time on the shift. **(84) It's a very simple device; you just attach it to your work belt and it will do the rest, so you won't need any training with that. (85) Sharing helmets and work boots is also now prohibited. You will have to buy your own equipment**, and then later you can claim the money back on your tax return.

83-85 宣布

女：嗨，大家好，感謝大家今天與我會面。**(83) 我要宣布在健康及安全政策方面的幾項變革，這是為了要符合政府的新規定。** 首先，不得再輪班六小時而沒有休息一小時。我們會使用打卡系統，能自動在工作滿六小時傳送簡訊給你。你們也要在輪班時穿戴監控工時的裝置，**(84) 這是個很簡單的裝置，你只需要將它繫在工作腰帶上，剩下的就交給它了，因此你不需要為此做任何訓練。(85) 現在也禁止共用安全帽和工作靴，你必須購買屬於自己的設備**，之後可以在退稅時領回這筆錢。

---

83. According to the speaker, why are changes being made?
- A The government took the company to court
- **B To conform to government regulations**
- C To enact a new labor law
- D To arrange lower-paying contracts

83. 根據發話者，變革的原因是什麼？
- A 政府控告這家公司
- **B 為了符合政府規定**
- C 為了施行新的勞動法案
- D 為了安排較低薪資的合約

84. What does the speaker imply when she says, "it's a very simple device; you just attach it to your work belt and it will do the rest, so you won't need any training with that"?
- **A The new system requires no training.**
- B She doesn't like the new system.
- C There is no budget for staff uniforms.
- D Everyone needs training.

84. 發話者說「這是個很簡單的裝置，你只需要將它繫在工作腰帶上，剩下的就交給它了，因此你不需要為此做任何訓練」，她暗示的是什麼？
- **A 新的系統不需要訓練**
- B 她不喜歡新的系統
- C 沒有預算可購買員工制服
- D 大家都需要受訓

85. What does the speaker tell the listeners they will have to start bringing to work?
- A Extra pairs of work pants
- B Other people's helmets
- **C Their own boots and helmets**
- D A new financial plan

85. 發話者告訴聽眾要開始帶什麼來上班？
- A 額外的工作褲
- B 其他人的安全帽
- **C 自己的靴子及安全帽**
- D 新的財務計劃

86-88 excerpt from a meeting

M：**(86) Well, it's only been a year since we began operating out of Beijing**, but our clothing has become a nationwide success. I got a call from a reporter at Phoenix Television, and they want to do a 30-minute story documenting our rise to success. They want to interview the designers about the clothing we are creating here. Also, *Xinhua Fashion* Magazine wants to come in next Thursday and do a full photo shoot of one our stores, so we need to book models for that day. **(87) They want to take photos of our new range of denim clothing.** The publicity is really going to get our name out. **(88) Our success is going to skyrocket! We should expect to get a lot busier soon.**

86-88 會議摘錄

男：**(86)** 嗯，自我們走出北京營運只有一年的時間，但我們的服飾已獲得全國性的成功。我收到鳳凰電視台記者的來電。他們想要進行一個 30 分鐘的報導，記錄我們的成功之路。他們想要訪問設計師，談論我們設計的服飾。此外，《新華流行雜誌》想要在下星期四來訪，並詳細拍攝我們其中一家店的照片。因此，我們需要預約當天的模特兒。**(87)** 他們想要拍攝我們新系列的牛仔服飾。這樣的宣傳能讓我們出名！**(88)** 我們的成功將會一飛衝天！我們預計業務很快會會更加繁忙。

---

86. According to the man, what did the company recently do?
   A **Began operating out of Beijing**
   B Began operating in India
   C Hired some new designers
   D Created some special dishes

86. 根據男子，這家公司最近做了什麼？
   A 開始在北京外營運
   B 開始在印度營運
   C 僱用新設計師
   D 創造特別的菜餚

87. What most likely will the *Xinhua Fashion* magazine do next Thursday?
   A Interview the models
   B Make a video of the street outside
   C **Photograph clothing**
   D Sign a new contract

87. 《新華流行雜誌》下星期四最有可能做什麼？
   A 訪問模特兒
   B 拍攝外面街道的影片
   C 拍攝服飾
   D 簽署新的合約

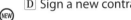

88. What does the man mean when he says, "our success is going to skyrocket"?
   A **Their business is going to grow quickly**
   B They will discuss the future plan
   C They will prevent the photo shoot
   D They will transfer some documents via mail

88. 男子說「我們的成功將會一飛衝天」，他指的是什麼？
   A 他們的生意將會快速成長
   B 他們將要討論未來的計劃
   C 他們將要避免拍攝相片
   D 他們將要透過郵件傳輸一些文件

89-91 announcement

W: Hi, everyone. **(89) There have been some new regulations sent in from Head Office.** Our productivity assessment was quite poor. They aren't very happy with our performance compared to last year. **(90) So we are going to have to put in some overtime to get ahead of schedule. We really need to stay on top of this**, or some people might get fired. **(91) We are going to need to make a roster and work some weekend overtime shifts.** We will have a rotation list, so each staff member works one Saturday every three weeks. I know this is a burden, but once we get high enough above our targets, things will go back to normal.

89-91 宣布

女：嗨，大家好。**(89) 總公司寄來一些新規定。** 我們的生產力考核相當差，與去年相比，我們的表現讓他們很不滿意。**(90) 因此，我們要加班將進度提前，我們真的必須表現優異**，否則有人會被開除。**(91) 我們需要製作一份執勤表，並且在週末進行加班輪值。** 我們會有輪值名單，每位員工每三週需在週六上班一次。我知道這會造成負擔，但是我們一旦超越目標夠多，就會回歸正常。

89. According to the speaker, who is introducing the new regulations?
   A The Board of Directors
   B Head Office
   C Management
   D The secretary

89. 根據發話者，誰推行新規定？
   A 董事會
   B 總公司
   C 管理階層
   D 秘書

90. What does the speaker imply when she says, "we really need to stay on top of this, or some people might get fired"?
   A There is a lot of work to do.
   B It isn't that important.
   C They can wait a week to start.
   D The project will begin soon.

90. 發話者說「我們真的必須表現優異，否則有人會被開除」，她暗示什麼？
   A 有很多工作要做
   B 這沒有那麼重要
   C 他們可以等一週後才開始
   D 這項計劃將很快開始

91. What does the speaker tell the listeners to do?
   A Bring their lunch to work
   B Occasionally work on Saturdays
   C Work every Sunday
   D Have some time off on Saturday

91. 發話者告訴聽眾要做什麼？
   A 帶午餐來上班
   B 偶爾在週六上班
   C 每週日上班
   D 週六休假

92-94 tour guide

M : Attention, passengers. **(92) (93) Welcome aboard Continental Lines, with bus service to Columbia, Charleston, and terminating in Eastport.** We will be spending the majority of our trip on the highways, so please make sure you have your seatbelts buckled. **(94) We will reach our first destination, Columbia, in approximately 2 hours, making our time at arrival 10:30 p.m., Friday the 15th.** We'll be getting on the road shortly, please make sure all of your luggage is secure and out of your neighbor's way. You can learn about attractions in Columbia, and all of our destinations, in the travel brochure located in the seat pocket. Now sit back, relax, and enjoy the scenery!

92-94 導遊

男：各位乘客請注意。**(92)(93)** 歡迎搭乘大陸幹線，本班巴士行經哥倫比亞市及查爾斯頓市，終點站在東港。我們的大半旅程會在公路上度過，因此請務必繫好安全帶。**(94)** 我們大約兩小時後會抵達第一個目的地：哥倫比亞市，到達時間為 15 號星期五晚上十點 30 分。我們很快將啟程，請確認你的行李都已放好且不會阻礙旁邊乘客的進出。你可以從座椅口袋內的旅行手冊中，了解哥倫比亞市的景點及其他的目的地。現在請坐好、放鬆，並且享受風景吧！

This Weekend's Events in Columbia
哥倫比亞的週末活動

Afternoon Theater 午後劇場
Columbia's own theater troupe stages short versions of classic plays for free in Central Park every Thursday at noon.
哥倫比亞的劇團每週四中午在中央公園免費演出經典戲劇的刪減版

Friday Night Concert in the Park Series
週五夜間公園音樂會
The show begins at 8:30 P.M. and lasts until 10:30 P.M.!
表演從晚上 8 點 30 分開始，持續到晚上 10 點 30 分！

Midnight Wine Tasting 午夜品酒
Regional wines sampled under the stars at the Black Cat, every Friday and Saturday night!
每週五和週六夜晚，在黑貓酒吧的星光下品嚐當地美酒！

Appropriate for all ages!
老少咸宜！

---

92. What kind of transportation company is Continental Lines?

- **A Bus**
- B Train
- C Limousine
- D Taxi

92. 大陸幹線是哪一種運輸公司？

- **A 公車**
- B 火車
- C 豪華轎車
- D 計程車

93. What is the last stop for Continental Lines this trip?

[A] Charleston
[B] Columbia
[C] Eastport
[D] Chesterville

94. Look at the graphic. What activity will still be available for the passengers to participate in when they arrive in Columbia?

[A] None
[B] Friday Night Concert in the Park
[C] Afternoon Theater
[D] Midnight Wine Tasting

93. 大陸幹線的旅途終點是哪裡？

[A] 查爾斯頓
[B] 哥倫比亞
[C] 東港
[D] 查斯特維爾

94. 參看圖表，乘客抵達哥倫比亞時，還有什麼活動可以參與？

[A] 沒有
[B] 週五夜間公園音樂會
[C] 午後劇場
[D] 午夜品酒

95-97 excerpt from a meeting

W：Hello everyone, **(95) I wanted to get you together to go over the recent failures in our customer service department here at Monster Telecom.** As you know, customer service is at the heart of everything we do. We receive on average 3,000 calls per week from customers with a wide range of needs. **(96) In order to prepare you all to handle the most frequently asked questions from our customers, I have distributed the graph in front of you.** Please go over this graph with your team leader and develop a plan to improve our customer service. Next quarter's reviews will be in two months. **(97) We aim to have half as many weekly calls by then.**

95–97 會議摘錄

女：哈囉，大家好，**(95) 我想把大家找來，檢視我們最近在怪物電信客服部門一些失敗的例子。** 各位都知道，客戶服務是我們所有事務的核心。我們平均每星期接到三千通的顧客來電，需求五花八門。**(96) 為了使各位都能準備好處理顧客的常見問題，我已發下各位眼前的圖表。** 請與你的小組長一起檢視這張圖表，並且想出計劃來改善我們的客戶服務。下一季的審核將在兩個月後舉行。**(97) 我們的目標是減少一半每週的顧客來電數。**

Customer Service FAQ Analysis 客服常見問題分析

Disputed Long Distance/Overcharges 有爭議的長途電話／超額收費	37%
Disputed Data Charges 有爭議的傳輸量費用	36%
Service Plan Change 服務方案異動	11%
Dropped Calls 通話中斷	9%
Replacement Phones 電話更換	5%
Miscellaneous 其他	2%

95. What is indicated about Monster Telecom?

[A] **They are having customer service problems.**

[B] There are too many calls for the number of employees.

[C] Customer service is not important to them.

[D] They need to hire more people.

96. Look at the graphic. What areas should the leaders focus their training on?

[A] **How to deal with upset customers by overcharges**

[B] Knowledge of all of the service plans

[C] Helping customers replace phones

[D] Knowledge of Monster Telecom's cellular coverage area

97. What is the goal for Monster Telecom?

[A] Reduce the number of dropped calls

[B] Expand their coverage area

[C] Add new cellular phone options

[D] **Reduce the number of customer calls they receive by 50%**

95. 關於怪物電信，有指出哪一點？

[A] **他們的客服出了問題**

[B] 電話太多，員工人數不足

[C] 客服對他們的公司並不重要

[D] 他們需要雇用更多人

96. 參看圖表，小組長應該將訓練重點放在哪些領域？

[A] **如何處理因超額收費而不悅的顧客**

[B] 對所有服務方案的了解

[C] 協助顧客更換電話

[D] 知道怪物電信訊號的涵蓋區域

97. 怪物電信的目標是什麼？

[A] 減少通話中斷的數量

[B] 拓展訊號涵蓋地區

[C] 增加新手機的選擇

[D] **將客戶來電減少 50%**

98-100 advertisement

M： (98) **Springdale Fitness Club has just expanded its swimming facilities to include a lap pool.** We are extremely excited to be able to build on our already impressive offerings of aquatic fitness! We'll be having a ribbon cutting ceremony this Saturday at noon, and to celebrate we will be holding a timed lap race! (99) **Because we created the lap pool for our members who are serious about training, we must enforce a policy that requires members to sign up for times to use the pool.** (100) **Additionally, the pool is not to be used for free style play.** Please come down to Springdale Fitness Club on Saturday and join us in the good time!

98–100 廣告

男： (98) 斯普陵代爾健身俱樂部剛擴建游泳設施，新增一個水道泳池。能以原本已經很棒的水中體適能設施為基礎進行擴建，我們感到很興奮。我們將在星期六中午舉行剪綵典禮，為了慶祝，我們將舉辦游泳計時賽。 (99) 由於我們興建此泳池是為了讓想認真訓練的會員使用，所以我們必須執行一項規定，要求會員登記使用泳池的時間。 (100) 此外，此泳池不得用於戲水。歡迎於星期六蒞臨斯普陵代爾健身俱樂部，與我們共度美好時光！

LAP POOL SIGN-UP SHEET 水道泳池登記表									
LANE 水道	9:00 a.m. 上午 9 點	10:00 a.m. 上午 10 點	11:00 a.m. 上午 11 點	12:00 p.m. 中午 12 點	1:00 p.m. 下午 1 點	2:00 p.m. 下午 2 點	3:00 p.m. 下午 3 點	4:00 p.m. 下午 4 點	5:00 p.m. 下午 5 點
1									
2									
3									

98. What is indicated about Springdale Fitness Club?
    A They have a tennis court.
    B They take pride in their customer service.
    C They specialize in children's pool parties.
    D They have a variety of swimming facilities.

99. Look at the graphic. What are the hours of the lap pool?
    A 8 a.m. to 5 p.m.
    B 9 a.m. to 5 p.m.
    C 9 a.m. to 6 p.m.
    D 8 a.m. to 6 p.m.

100. What does Springdale Fitness Club say about the new lap pool?
    A It is Olympic size.
    B It has four lanes.
    C It's for serious swimmers.
    D It will host weekly races.

98. 關於斯普陵代爾健身俱樂部,有提到哪一點?
    A 他們有網球場
    B 他們對於客戶服務感到自豪
    C 他們專營孩童泳池派對
    D 他們有各種游泳設施

99. 參看圖表,水道泳池的開放時間為何?
    A 上午八點到下午五點
    B 上午九點到下午五點
    C 上午九點到下午六點
    D 上午八點到下午六點

100. 關於新的水道泳池,斯普陵代爾健身俱樂部提到什麼?
    A 它符合奧運尺寸
    B 它有四個水道
    C 它是設置給想認真游泳的人士用
    D 它每週都會舉辦比賽

PART 1 P. 74-77

1. Ⓐ The man is pointing at the flowers.
Ⓑ She is picking some flowers.
Ⓒ The man is holding a flower.
Ⓓ They are all looking at the plants.

2. Ⓐ He is wearing a tool belt.
Ⓑ The man is loading a cart.
Ⓒ He is changing the tire in the garage.
Ⓓ The tire is brand new.

3. Ⓐ He is driving a car in the snow.
Ⓑ He has already shoveled the snow off the roof.
Ⓒ His car door is covered in snow.
Ⓓ He is playing with friends in the snow.

4. Ⓐ The lecture theater is full of students.
Ⓑ The lecture theater is empty.
Ⓒ All of the students are outside the lecture theater.
Ⓓ There is a man giving a lecture.

5. **Ⓐ The woman is looking at the computer.**
Ⓑ The woman is eating some fruits.
Ⓒ The woman has her hair down.
Ⓓ The woman is typing on the computer.

6. **Ⓐ She is holding a vegetable.**
Ⓑ She is looking at some fish.
Ⓒ She is checking her shopping list.
Ⓓ She is tasting some vegetables.

1. Ⓐ 男子正指著花朵。
Ⓑ 她正在採一些花。
Ⓒ 男子拿著一朵花。
Ⓓ 他們全都看著植物。

2. Ⓐ 他戴著工具腰帶。
Ⓑ 男子正在裝載手推車。
Ⓒ 他正在車庫更換輪胎。
Ⓓ 輪胎是全新的。

3. Ⓐ 他正在雪中開車。
Ⓑ 他已經剷掉車頂的雪。
Ⓒ 他的車門被雪覆蓋。
Ⓓ 他正在雪裡與朋友玩耍。

4. Ⓐ 演講廳擠滿了學生。
Ⓑ 演講廳是空的。
Ⓒ 所有的學生都在演講廳外頭。
Ⓓ 一名男子正在講課。

5. **Ⓐ 女子正在看著電腦。**
Ⓑ 女子正在吃水果。
Ⓒ 女子放下了頭髮。
Ⓓ 女子正在用電腦打字。

6. **Ⓐ 她正拿著蔬菜。**
Ⓑ 她正在看魚。
Ⓒ 她正在查看購物清單。
Ⓓ 她正在品嚐蔬菜。

PART 2 P. 78

7. Who's presenting the sales report at the next meeting?
Ⓐ I think Jason is.
Ⓑ It's already been sold.
Ⓒ At the nearest port.

8. Would you prefer an appointment today or tomorrow?
Ⓐ I arrived yesterday.
Ⓑ This afternoon is fine.
Ⓒ The office on the second floor.

7. 誰下次開會要由誰進行銷售報告的簡報？
Ⓐ 我想是傑森。
Ⓑ 它已經被賣掉了。
Ⓒ 在最近的港口。

8. 你想要約今天還或是明天？
Ⓐ 我昨天抵達。
Ⓑ 今天下午就可以了。
Ⓒ 二樓的辦公室。

9. How can you improve product quality?
   A **By using better materials.**
   B I can prove him wrong.
   C Production costs.

10. Which road is fastest?
    A Why don't I drive?
    B **Take the highway.**
    C Slow down.

11. Do you mind if I print a document?
    A It's black and white.
    B This is not mine.
    C **No problem. Go ahead.**

12. Who's welcoming our guest?
    A I think it's April 24.
    B Please reserve a room.
    C **Mary is responsible for that.**

13. That piano player played really well, didn't he?
    A **Yes, I was very impressed.**
    B It was rather expensive.
    C I bought the player online.

14. Why is the copy center closed today?
    A 300 copies, please.
    B In the storage closet.
    C **It's Sunday.**

15. Where can I apply for a job?
    A The application fee.
    B **On our website.**
    C Mr. Marshall will conduct an interview.

16. I signed up for the leadership workshop.
    A At the local community center.
    B I've been assigned the role.
    C **Oh, so did I.**

17. The wellness seminar is this afternoon, isn't it?
    A **Yes, don't be late.**
    B No, please register online.
    C It was quite informative.

18. Where can I find the client's phone number?
    A Before 5:00 P.M.
    B **The secretary should know.**
    C No, she never called back.

9. 你可以如何改善產品品質？
   A **藉由使用較好的材料。**
   B 我可以證明他是錯的。
   C 生產成本。

10. 哪條路最快？
    A 我何不開車？
    B **走公路。**
    C 減速。

11. 你介意我印一份文件嗎？
    A 這是黑白的。
    B 這不是我的。
    C **沒問題，印吧。**

12. 誰要歡迎我們的客人？
    A 我認為是 4 月 24 日。
    B 請訂一間房間。
    C **瑪莉負責此事。**

13. 那位鋼琴演奏者彈得真好，對吧？
    A **是的，我感到印象深刻。**
    B 它相當昂貴。
    C 我從網路上購買那台播放器。

14. 影印中心今天為何關閉？
    A 300 份，謝謝。
    B 在儲藏櫃裡。
    C **今天是星期天。**

15. 我可以在哪裡應徵工作？
    A 申請費用。
    B **在我們的網站上。**
    C 馬歇爾先生將進行面試。

16. 我報名了領導能力研習會。
    A 在當地的社區活動中心。
    B 我被指派了這個職務。
    C **喔，我也是。**

17. 健康研討會是在今天下午，不是嗎？
    A **是的，別遲到了。**
    B 不，請上網登記。
    C 它資訊豐富。

18. 我可以在哪裡找到客戶的電話號碼？
    A 下午五點以前。
    B **秘書應該知道。**
    C 不，她沒有回電。

19. The network system isn't functioning.
  A New login information.
  B For the corporate function.
  C It's being repaired.

20. Why are you still advertising this position?
  A The new advertising strategy.
  B We still haven't hired anyone.
  C Every other week.

21. When are membership fees due?
  A No, but you can upgrade.
  B A bank account number.
  C The last week of every month.

22. Are you scheduled for a private consultation?
  A No, I forgot to call ahead.
  B That was helpful.
  C She departed on schedule.

23. Weren't you going to purchase a large-screen television?
  A I bought a projector instead.
  B How much did it cost?
  C Turn down the volume.

24. Do you want to work on this task together?
  A I'll walk on the treadmill for half an hour.
  B A family get-together.
  C Sure. When do you want to start?

25. The manager expects everyone to arrive by 7:00 a.m.
  A I'll set the alarm.
  B What did you expect?
  C Leave it at the front desk.

26. Where do we store past years' sales records?
  A I'll inform a store manager.
  B Yes, it's an expense report.
  C They have all been digitized.

27. Would you be willing to organize the conference?
  A The keynote speaker.
  B Regarding consumer preferences.
  C Well, it depends on when it is.

19. 網路系統無法運作。
  A 新的登入資料。
  B 為了公司的聚會。
  C 已在修理中。

20. 你為何仍在徵才?
  A 新的廣告策略。
  B 我們還沒僱用任何人。
  C 每隔一個星期。

21. 什麼時候要交會費?
  A 還沒有,但是你可以升等。
  B 銀行帳號。
  C 每個月的最後一星期。

22. 你安排了私人晤談的時間嗎?
  A 不,我忘了提早打電話。
  B 那很有幫助。
  C 她依照計劃離開了。

23. 你不是要買一台大螢幕電視嗎?
  A 我改買了投影機。
  B 那要多少錢?
  C 將音量調低。

24. 你想要一起處理這件事嗎?
  A 我會在跑步機上走半小時。
  B 一場家族聚會。
  C 當然,你想要什麼時候開始?

25. 經理期望大家上午七點以前到達。
  A 我會設定鬧鐘。
  B 不然你以為是怎樣?
  C 把它放在櫃台。

26. 我們把過去幾年的銷售記錄存放在哪裡?
  A 我會通知一位商店經理。
  B 是的,這是一份費用報告。
  C 它們全都被數位化了。

27. 你願意籌劃這場會議嗎?
  A 主講者。
  B 關於消費者喜好。
  C 嗯,要視時間而定。

28. Have you found a new intern, or are you still searching?
   A The new intern starts tomorrow.
   B The sales department.
   C They will found a new company later this year.

29. Can I talk to Mr. Marquez in the finance department, please?
   A Yes, I'll transfer you.
   B He lives in a studio apartment.
   C No, he's a finance expert.

30. Is it possible to have this repaired today?
   A Yes, a pair of scissors.
   B Won't the event be held tomorrow?
   C No, we have to order new parts.

31. Why don't we send the parcel express?
   A It still won't arrive in time.
   B Throughout the press conference.
   C They deliver supplies to your doorstep.

28. 你已找到新的實習生,還是你仍在找人呢?
   A 新的實習生明天就會開始工作。
   B 銷售部門。
   C 他們今年稍晚將會成立新公司。

29. 我可以與財務部門的馬奎茲先生說話嗎,謝謝。
   A 好的,我幫你轉接。
   B 他住在套房。
   C 不,他是財經專家。

30. 今天有可能把這個修好嗎?
   A 是的,一把剪刀。
   B 明天不會舉辦這個活動嗎?
   C 不行,我們得訂購新的零件。

31. 我們何不用快遞寄這個包裹?
   A 這樣仍來不及送達。
   B 在整個記者會期間。
   C 他們會將貨品送到你家。

PART 3 P. 79-83 🎧19

32-34 conversation

W: Hi, James. This is Candice in the marketing department. **(32) I'm supposed to be leading a weekly meeting in Room 302 soon, but I just discovered that the room is already in use.**

M: I'm sorry, Candice. Actually, I have been getting calls like this all day. **(33) It looks like an error with our computer system is to blame for the mix-up.**

W: Oh, I see. Well, is there a currently vacant room that I could use for the meeting? The room will need to be equipped with a computer and a projector.

M: I'll need to check manually to determine which room will be available. **(34) I'll let you know as soon as I find another suitable room.** Please wait for a moment.

32-34 對話

女:嗨,詹姆士。我是行銷部門的凱蒂絲。**(32) 我本來不久後要在 302 室主持週會,但我剛發現那個會議室已經有人使用了。**

男:很抱歉,凱蒂絲。事實上,我已經接這樣的電話一整天了。**(33) 看起來是我們電腦系統出錯而造成混亂。**

女:喔,我懂了。那麼,現在有空的會議室讓我開會嗎?裡面將需要有電腦和投影機。

男:我得以人工方式查看,來確認哪間會議室可用。**(34) 我一找到合適的會議室就會通知你**,請稍等。

32. What is the woman's problem?
   A A meeting room is occupied.
   B A piece of equipment is out of stock.
   C An appointment has been canceled.
   D Some software is not installed.

32. 女子有什麼問題?
   A 會議室被占用
   B 設備缺貨
   C 預約被取消
   D 沒有安裝某些軟體

33. Why does the man mention a system malfunction?
    Ⓐ To apologize for an incorrect charge
    Ⓑ To explain a scheduling error
    Ⓒ To warn of security threats
    Ⓓ To change a company policy

34. What does the man say he will do?
    Ⓐ Fix a computer
    Ⓑ Provide an alternative
    Ⓒ Attend a meeting
    Ⓓ Check the employee manual

33. 男子為何提到系統故障？
    Ⓐ 為了錯誤的收費道歉
    Ⓑ 解釋時間安排的錯誤
    Ⓒ 警告安全威脅
    Ⓓ 改變公司政策

34. 男子說他將會做什麼？
    Ⓐ 修理電腦
    Ⓑ 提供替代方案
    Ⓒ 出席會議
    Ⓓ 查看員工手冊

35-37 conversation

W：Hi, Craig. **(35) I was expecting you to submit the market analysis report yesterday, but I still haven't received it.** Do you need more time to work on it?

M：Hi, Ms. Watson. I'm really sorry I didn't send it to you by the determined deadline. I have recently been very busy with another urgent task. **(36) I'll make sure I finish the report before doing anything else.** Is that OK?

W：**(37) Well, I really need that document for a meeting with a potential client tomorrow morning.** I'll stop by later today and help you so that we can finish it in time.

35-37 對話

女：嗨，克雷格。**(35) 我原本以為你昨天就會繳交市場分析報告，但我還沒有收到。**你需要更多時間處理它嗎？

男：嗨，華生女士。很抱歉我沒有在預定期限前把它寄給你。我最近在忙另一項緊急的工作。**(36) 我一定會在做任何其他事情前先完成那份報告，這樣可以嗎？**

女：**(37) 嗯，我明天早上與潛在客戶開會時很需要那份文件。**我今天稍後會去幫你，這樣我們就可以及時完成它。

35. What does the woman ask the man about?
    Ⓐ How to write a report
    Ⓑ Whether a document is finished
    Ⓒ How to reserve a meeting room
    Ⓓ Whether a client has been contacted

36. What does the man say he will do?
    Ⓐ Prioritize the woman's request
    Ⓑ Extend a deadline
    Ⓒ Draft a budget
    Ⓓ Visit the woman's office

37. What does the woman need?
    Ⓐ A list of clients
    Ⓑ A sample product
    Ⓒ Meeting materials
    Ⓓ A revised itinerary

35. 女子問男子什麼事？
    Ⓐ 如何寫報告
    Ⓑ 文件是否已完成
    Ⓒ 如何預約會議室
    Ⓓ 是否連繫了客戶

36. 男子說他將會做什麼？
    Ⓐ 優先處理女子的要求
    Ⓑ 延長截止期限
    Ⓒ 擬定預算
    Ⓓ 去女子的辦公室

37. 女子需要什麼？
    Ⓐ 客戶名單
    Ⓑ 產品樣本
    Ⓒ 會議資料
    Ⓓ 修改過的行程

38-40 conversation

W: Hello. **(38) I'm interested in enrolling in your school's vocational training program to become a dental assistant, but I couldn't find any information about tuition on your website.**

M: Thank you for your interest. We offer a two-semester training program to become a dental assistant at our community college. Tuition for a single semester is $6,500.

W: Oh, I see. Honestly, that is a little more than I expected. **(39) I will have to ask my bank about the possibility of getting a student loan.** Is there anything else you can tell me?

M: **(40) Well, one thing to keep in mind is that our community college offers night classes for all our programs.** This is very good for students who work during the day. And please remember that we are one of the top-ranked schools in the state, and so far more than 5,000 of our graduates have become dental assistants.

38-40 對話

女: 哈囉。**(38) 我想報名貴校牙醫助理的職業培訓課程,但我在你們網頁上找不到關於學費的資訊。**

男: 感謝您有興趣。我們社區大學提供兩學期的牙醫助理培訓課程,單一學期的學費是 6500 元。

女: 喔,這樣啊。老實説,這比我原先預期的高了一點。**(39) 我得問銀行讓我申請學生貸款的可能性。**你還有什麼可以告訴我的嗎?

男: **(40) 嗯,要記得,我們社區大學的所有課程都提供夜間課程。**這對於白天需要工作的學生很有益。還有請記得,我們是本州的頂尖學校,到目前為止,我們畢業生中超過 5000 人已經成為牙醫助理。

---

38. What career is the woman interested in?
- [A] College professor
- [B] Web programmer
- **[C] Dental assistant**
- [D] Financial adviser

38. 女子對於什麼工作有興趣?
- [A] 大學教授
- [B] 網路程式設計師
- **[C] 牙醫助理**
- [D] 財務顧問

39. What does the woman say she will do?
- [A] Submit an application
- **[B] Inquire about a loan**
- [C] Consult a doctor
- [D] Apply for a scholarship

39. 女子説她將會做什麼?
- [A] 繳交申請書
- **[B] 詢問貸款**
- [C] 請教醫師
- [D] 申請獎學金

40. According to the man, what advantage does the college offer?
- **[A] Convenient class times**
- [B] Small class sizes
- [C] Advanced level courses
- [D] Reduced tuition

40. 根據男子,這間大學提供什麼好處?
- **[A] 方便的上課時間**
- [B] 小班教學
- [C] 進階課程
- [D] 學費減免

41-43 conversation

M: Did you enjoy this afternoon's training session for the new software? **(41) I think it'll really help us improve the quality of our graphic design work.**

41-43 對話

男: 你喜歡今天下午為新軟體舉行的訓練課程嗎? **(41) 我認為那對於我們增進平面設計作品的品質很有幫助。**

W : I thought it was very informative, but there are still a lot of details that I'm unsure about. **(42) I wish the instructor had allowed some time for participants to ask questions.**

M : Yeah, I agree with you. However, I heard that the instructor of the training session left his contact information with the human resources department. **(43) Why don't you try contacting him via email?**

41. Where most likely do the speakers work?
    - A At a software company
    - B At a marketing firm
    - C At a travel agency
    - **D At a graphic design company**

42. What is the woman's complaint about the training session?
    - A There were not enough seats.
    - B The registration fee was too high.
    - **C There was no time for inquiries.**
    - D The instructor's presentation was lengthy.

43. What does the man suggest?
    - A Attending another training session
    - B Transferring to a new department
    - C Reviewing a training manual
    - **D Contacting the instructor**

44-46 conversation

M : Welcome back, Catherine. I hope you are feeling better after recovering from the flu. **(44) I wanted to make sure you know about the new policy concerning sick leave.**

W : I did hear that now we need to submit a doctor's note along with the sick leave form. **(45) Will I still be paid the same amount for my sick leave as I would a normal workday?**

M : Actually, the terms of compensation have changed as well. **(46) I'll print out a copy of the new policy and leave it on your desk later today.** If you have more questions, you should contact Jennifer in human resources.

女：我認為資訊很豐富，但還有許多我不確定的細節。**(42) 要是講師當時有留一些時間讓參與者提問就好了。**

男：是的，我同意你的看法。但是我聽說訓練課程的講師留下聯絡方式給人力資源部門。**(43) 你何不試著透過電子郵件與他聯繫？**

41. 對話者們最有可能在哪裡工作？
    - A 軟體公司
    - B 行銷公司
    - C 旅行社
    - **D 平面設計公司**

42. 女子對於訓練課程有何怨言？
    - A 座位不足
    - B 報名費太高
    - **C 沒有時間提問**
    - D 講師的簡報很冗長

43. 男子建議什麼？
    - A 參加另一場訓練課程
    - B 調至新的部門
    - C 檢視訓練手冊
    - **D 聯繫講師**

44-46 對話

男：歡迎回來，凱薩琳。我希望你從流感康復後身體有比較好了。**(44) 我只是想確認你知道病假的新作法。**

女：我的確聽說現在我們需要連同病假單一起附上醫師證明，**(45) 病假會跟正常工作日給付同樣的薪資嗎？**

男：實際上，薪資條款也更改了。**(46) 我今天會幫你印一份新的規定，稍晚時會放在你桌上。如果你還有其他的問題，你應該聯繫人力資源部門的珍妮佛。**

44. What is the topic of the conversation?
   A A pay raise
   B An upcoming deadline
   C A prescription for the flu
   D A new work procedure

45. What does the woman ask about?
   A Pay compensation
   B Promotion opportunities
   C Sick leave availability
   D Official forms

46. What will the man most likely do next?
   A Send an email
   B Revise a budget
   C Deliver a document
   D Call a doctor

47-49 conversation

W: Hello. **(47) I'm calling to ask about the landscaping services you advertised in the newspaper.** I moved into a new house two months ago and would like to have some work done on my front yard.

M: Thanks for calling us. Unfortunately, we are currently swamped with requests from a lot of customers. Summer is our busiest season. **(48) I'm afraid you will have to wait a month until we can help you.**

W: Oh, I understand. I heard your business is professional and reliable, so it's worth the wait. In the meantime, I can provide you with a plan of what I have in mind.

M: OK, that would be great. **(49) After reviewing your plan, I can send you an estimate of potential costs.**

---

47. Where most likely does the man work?
   A At a real estate agency
   B At a bank
   C At an art gallery
   D At a landscaping agency

---

44. 對話的主題是什麼？
   A 加薪
   B 接近的截止期限
   C 流感的處方箋
   D 新的工作流程

45. 女子詢問關於什麼事？
   A 薪資給付
   B 升遷機會
   C 是否可請病假
   D 正式表格

46. 男子接下來最有可能做什麼？
   A 寄電子郵件
   B 修改預算
   C 提供文件
   D 打電話給醫師

47–49 對話

女：你好。**(47) 我打電話是要詢問你們在報紙上刊登的造景服務廣告。** 我兩個月前搬進新家，想要打造前院的景觀。

男：感謝您的來電。很可惜我們目前有很多顧客的案子，忙得不可開交。夏天是我們最忙碌的季節。**(48) 恐怕你要等一個月，我們才能為你服務。**

女：喔，了解。我聽說你們公司專業又可靠，因此值得等候。在這期間，我可以提供你我心中的平面圖。

男：好的，那樣很好。**(49) 等我看過你的平面圖後，會把估價單寄給你。**

---

47. 男子最有可能在哪裡工作？
   A 房地產仲介公司
   B 銀行
   C 畫廊
   D 造景公司

48. How long does the man say the woman will have to wait?

- [A] For a day
- [B] For a week
- **[C] For a month**
- [D] For two months

49. What information will the man send the woman?

- [A] A job opening
- [B] An itinerary
- **[C] A price quote**
- [D] A meeting agenda

48. 男子說女子必須等候多久？

- [A] 一天
- [B] 一星期
- **[C] 一個月**
- [D] 兩個月

49. 男子將會寄什麼資訊給女子？

- [A] 職缺
- [B] 旅遊行程
- **[C] 估價單**
- [D] 會議議程

(NEW)

50-52 conversation

M：Hello, Charlotte. **(50) I'll be meeting a client for lunch next week. Do you know any great restaurants around here?**

W：Yes, Lament's Kitchen in Hildorf Hotel has a quiet atmosphere for meetings and the food is delicious.

M：That's good to know. I'll make a reservation today.

W：**(51) Oh and don't forget that Mr. Willis wants to meet you over dinner today to talk about this month's budget reports.**

M：I completely forgot. I'll need to cancel tonight's meeting then.

W：Don't worry about that. **(52) I'll inform everyone for you.**

M：Thanks!

50-52 對話

男：哈囉，夏洛特。**(50) 我下星期要與一位客戶吃午餐，你知道附近有什麼好餐廳嗎？**

女：是的，希朵夫飯店的拉曼廚房氣氛很適合開會，而且食物很美味。

男：那真是太好了。我今天就去訂位。

女：**(51)** 喔，別忘了威利斯先生今天想要與你碰面吃晚餐，討論這個月的預算報告。

男：我完全忘了，那麼我得要取消今晚的會議。

女：別擔心。**(52)** 我會幫你通知大家。

男：謝謝！

50. What does the man ask about?

- **[A] A lunch meeting location**
- [B] The schedule for the week
- [C] The budget reports
- [D] A client list

51. What does the woman remind the man about?

- **[A] A dinner meeting**
- [B] A restaurant reservation
- [C] A presentation
- [D] A client's demands

50. 男子詢問什麼事？

- **[A] 午餐會議的地點**
- [B] 這星期的行程表
- [C] 預算報告
- [D] 客戶名單

51. 女子提醒男子什麼事？

- **[A] 晚餐會議**
- [B] 餐廳訂位
- [C] 簡報
- [D] 客戶要求

52. What does the woman offer to do?
  [A] Meet with a colleague
  [B] Talk to a client
  [C] Call some coworkers
  [D] Organize the reports

52. 女子提議做什麼？
  [A] 與同事碰面
  [B] 與客戶談話
  [C] 致電給同事
  [D] 整理報告

53-55 conversation

W：Hi, this is Shelly from Bafta Airlines. **(53) Unfortunately your flight to Vancouver tomorrow has been canceled due to weather conditions.** The earliest we can fly you out is tomorrow night at 11 p.m.

M：Oh, I actually have an important meeting tomorrow. It won't be easy to reschedule. Is there any way you can get me on an earlier flight?

W：I'm sorry sir, but we are not allowed to fly under certain weather conditions. We understand the inconvenience and would like to offer your return ticket free of charge. **(54) There is an overnight bus that will get you there by the morning.** I can make the booking for you.

M：Hmm . . . **(55) That's not a bad idea.** Let me phone my client in Vancouver and I will call you back shortly.

53–55 對話

女：嗨，我是巴夫塔航空的雪莉。**(53) 很可惜地，您明天到溫哥華的航班因為天氣的原因而取消了。** 我們明天最早能飛的航班是在晚上 11 點。

男：喔，我明天其實有場重要的會議，不太容易重新安排時間。你有辦法能讓我搭早一點的班機嗎？

女：很抱歉，先生。但我們不被允許在某些特定的天候條件下飛航。我們了解這造成的不便，願意免費提供您回程機票。**(54) 您有夜車可搭，能在明天早上抵達目的地，我可以幫您訂位。**

男：嗯……**(55) 這樣還不錯。** 讓我打電話給溫哥華的客戶，我會很快會回你電話。

---

53. What is the problem?
  [A] The man forgot to book his plane ticket.
  [B] The flight is delayed.
  [C] The flight is canceled.
  [D] The man lost his ticket.

53. 有什麼問題？
  [A] 男子忘了訂機票
  [B] 班機延誤了
  [C] 班機取消了
  [D] 男子遺失了票券

54. What solution does the woman propose?
  [A] To book a bus for the man
  [B] To pay for his hotel room
  [C] To send him documents
  [D] To call his client in Vancouver

54. 女子提出什麼解決方法？
  [A] 為男子訂車票
  [B] 為男子支付旅館費用
  [C] 寄送文件給他
  [D] 致電給他在溫哥華的客戶

55. What does the man mean when he says, "that's not a bad idea"?
  [A] He wants a better solution.
  [B] He agrees with the proposed solution.
  [C] He would like to hear more options.
  [D] He wants to keep the plane ticket.

55. 男子說「這樣還不錯」，他指的是什麼？
  [A] 他想要更好的解決方法
  [B] 他同意提出的解決方法
  [C] 他想要聽到更多的選擇
  [D] 他想要保有機票

56-58 conversation

M: Hi, Carol. How was the recruitment fair in New York?

W: It was good. **(56) We recruited two new customer service managers, and I got to look around the city.** New York is a beautiful place! When did you start having flowers in your office?

M: Oh, you noticed them? I had them delivered today to freshen up the place a bit.

W: Um . . . **(57) Are they real?**

M: Of course! Go and smell them, they are beautiful. **(58) I can have some delivered to your office if you like.**

W: No, don't worry about it. That's too much bother, but I appreciate the offer!

56. What was the woman doing in New York?
- [A] Taking a vacation
- [B] Visiting family
- **[C] Looking for new staff**
- [D] Meeting clients

57. What does the woman imply when she says, "are they real"?
- [A] The flowers look really bad.
- **[B] The flowers look fake.**
- [C] She is surprised to see them.
- [D] She thinks they are real.

58. What does the man offer to do?
- [A] Give her a promotion
- [B] Send her a gift card
- **[C] Have flowers delivered to her office**
- [D] Send her to New York

56-58 對話

男：嗨，卡羅。在紐約的招募展進行得如何？

女：很不錯。**(56) 我們招募了兩名新的客服經理，而且我有去城裡四處逛逛。** 紐約是個美麗的地方！你什麼時候開始在辦公室裡擺花的？

男：喔，你注意到啦？我今天請人送過來的，讓辦公室變得更宜人一點。

女：呃……**(57) 它們是真花嗎？**

男：當然！你可以聞聞看，它們真美。**(58) 如果你要的話，我可以請人送一些到你的辦公室。**

女：不，不用了，那樣太麻煩了。但感謝你的提議。

56. 女子之前在紐約做什麼？
- [A] 度假
- [B] 拜訪家人
- **[C] 找新員工**
- [D] 與客戶會面

57. 女子說「它們是真的嗎」，她暗示的是什麼？
- [A] 花看起來狀況很差
- **[B] 花看起來很假**
- [C] 她很驚訝看見花
- [D] 她認為花是真的

58. 男子提議做什麼？
- [A] 給她升遷
- [B] 寄禮卡給她
- **[C] 送花到她的辦公室**
- [D] 派她去紐約

(NEW) 59-61 conversation

M： (59) **Hi Jennifer, this is Scott. Did you transfer some money to Mr. Woods yesterday?** He called me today and said they haven't received the funds yet. They are one of our most important clients and I don't want to upset them.

W1： Grace, did you do it? I asked you to go to the bank yesterday and take care of it.

W2： Yes, I did it at about 4 p.m. (60) **The bank said it might take an extra business day to go through because they are having some problems with their computer system.** Sorry, I should've told you.

M： I see. In the future please let me know. This client is quite strict about time so we need to be careful not to upset them. They bring us a lot of business. (61) **I need you to email me the transfer receipt so I can send them evidence of the payment.**

W2： I'm sorry. I'll email you the transfer receipt right away.

---

59. Why is the man calling Jennifer?
- A To ask about her vacation
- B To transfer her to another department
- **C To ask about a money transfer**
- D To talk to Mr. Woods

60. What does Grace say about the bank?
- A They were closed when she got there.
- **B They are having problems with their computers.**
- C She emailed the receipt.
- D She couldn't find the location.

61. What does the man say he needs?
- **A The transfer receipt**
- B The bank check
- C The company credit card
- D The transfer system

59–61 對話

男：(59) 嗨，珍妮佛，我是史考特。你昨天匯了錢給伍德斯先生了嗎？他今天打電話給我，説他們還沒有收到款項。他們是我們最重要的客戶之一，我不想讓他們生氣。

女 1：葛蕾絲，你匯錢了嗎？我昨天要你去銀行處理此事。

女 2：是的，我在下午四點左右匯了錢。(60) 銀行説可能需要多一個營業日才能匯過去，因為他們的電腦系統有點問題。很抱歉，我該早點告訴你的。

男：我知道了，以後請告知我。這名客戶相當注重時間，因此我們需要很小心別惹惱他們。他們為我們帶來許多生意。(61) 我需要你用電子郵件把匯款單寄給我，這樣我就可以把付款證明寄給他們。

女 2：很抱歉。我立刻就用電子郵件把匯款單寄給你。

---

59. 男子為什麼打電話給珍妮佛？
- A 詢問她的假期
- B 將她調到另一個部門
- **C 詢問匯款的事情**
- D 要與伍德斯先生談話

60. 關於銀行，葛蕾絲説了什麼？
- A 她抵達時銀行已經關門了
- **B 他們的電腦有問題**
- C 她用電子郵件寄了單據
- D 她找不到該地點

61. 男子説他需要什麼？
- **A 匯款單**
- B 銀行支票
- C 公司信用卡
- D 匯款系統

62-64 conversation

W：Did you see this notice? The subways will be out of service during peak time tomorrow morning.

M：I know. **(63) The line that we need to catch is closed during morning peak time. (62) They are having some problems with tracks and they need to fix them.** I think it's a safety issue.

W：It's very irritating. That's probably the busiest line at that time of the morning. I don't know why they decided to do that.

M：**(64) I think if we get a few other people together, I can drive my car into work.** Traffic will be bad, but it's much better than taking the bus.

W：Oh, great idea. I'll ask around the office and let you know later.

62–64 對話

女：你看見通知單了嗎？地鐵將在明天晨間高峰時段停止營運。

男：我知道。**(63) 我們要搭的路線在晨間高峰時段關閉。(62) 他們的軌道有問題，需要進行檢修。**我想這是安全問題。

女：這真煩人。那可能是早上該時段最繁忙的路線，我不懂他們為何決定要這麼做。

男：**(64) 我想如果我們找幾個人一起，我就可以開我的車上班。**交通狀況會很差，但比搭公車好得多。

女：好主意，我會在辦公室詢問，稍後再告訴你。

Subway Closures 地鐵封閉 September 24th 9 月 24 日	
Line 2 路線 2	6:00 a.m. 上午 6 點—10:00 a.m. 上午 10 點
Line 4 路線 4	10:00 a.m. 上午 10 點—11:00 a.m. 上午 11 點
Line 6 路線 6	11:00 a.m. 上午 11 點—12:00 p.m. 中午 12 點
Line 7 路線 7	1:00 p.m. 下午 1 點—2:00 p.m. 下午 2 點

62. Why is the subway being closed on September 24th?
   A To upgrade the audio system
   B Because the drivers are striking
   C There is a safety issue
   D Problems with the air conditioner

63. Look at the graphic. Which subway line do the speakers need to take?
   A Line 6
   B Line 7
   C Line 2
   D Line 4

62. 地鐵為何在 9 月 24 日關閉？
   A 為了升級音響系統
   B 因為駕駛罷工
   C 有安全上的問題
   D 冷氣機的問題

63. 參看圖表，對話者們需要搭乘的是哪個地鐵路線？
   A 路線 6
   B 路線 7
   C 路線 2
   D 路線 4

64. What does the man suggest doing?
- [A] Taking the subway
- [B] Using the taxi service
- [C] Taking the bus
- **[D] Driving his car**

64. 男子建議做什麼？
- [A] 搭乘地鐵
- [B] 使用計程車服務
- [C] 搭乘公車
- **[D] 開他的車**

65-67 conversation

M： Ms. Franklin, here is the inventory list in case we need to order anything. **(65) Please let me know by today because the supply company is closing for Christmas soon.**

W： I see. Well, Christmas is coming up, so we will need to wrap a lot of gifts for the staff presents. **(66) Also, I'm tired of holding my phone while typing, and we don't have anything for me to use. Can you please order me something?**

M： Yes, no problem. I will order that for you. Also, we are out of business cards, and we have some new employees beginning after Christmas. I suggest we have business cards ready when they arrive. Otherwise, we may look unprofessional.

W： Good idea. Go ahead and order those, too. **(67) Can you please send me the order form so I can double check it before you send it away?**

M： I'll email it to you soon.

65–67 對話

男：富蘭克林女士，這是物品存貨清單，看我們是否需要訂購任何東西。**(65) 請在今天以前告知我，因為用品公司很快就要休息過聖誕節了。**

女：了解，聖誕節快到了，因此我們需要包裝很多要送給員工的禮物。**(66) 此外，我很討厭打字時還要拿電話，又沒有什麼東西可以讓我用。可以請你幫我訂購嗎？**

男：好的，沒問題。我會幫你訂購。此外，我們的名片用完了，而有些新員工會在聖誕節後開始上班。我建議在他們上班之前把名片準備好，否則我們會看起來很不專業。

女：好主意，也一起訂購那些吧。**(67) 可以請你把訂購單寄給我嗎？這樣我可以在你把它寄出去之前再次確認。**

男：我馬上就用電子郵件寄給你。

Supply Cabinet Inventory 用品櫃物件存貨清單	
Item 品項	Quantity 數量
Carbon Paper 複寫紙	50
Tracing Paper 描圖紙	25
Wrapping Paper 包裝紙	5
Business Cards 名片	0
Headset 頭戴式耳機	0

65. Why do they need to send the order today?
- **[A] Because the company is closing for Christmas**
- [B] Because the company is closing for New Years
- [C] The company doesn't have the item.
- [D] They have delayed the order.

65. 他們為何今日就要寄出訂購單？
- **[A] 因為公司要休息過聖誕節**
- [B] 因為公司要休息過新年
- [C] 公司沒有該用品
- [D] 他們延誤了訂單

66. Look at the graphic. What will the man NOT order for the woman?
　Ⓐ Wrapping paper
　Ⓑ A headset
　Ⓒ Business cards
　Ⓓ Carbon paper

67. What does the woman ask the man to do?
　Ⓐ Send her the order form
　Ⓑ Send her a headset
　Ⓒ Revise the memo
　Ⓓ Send a receipt

68-70 conversation

M： Hi, **(68) I'm competing in a triathlon next week and I need some energy bars or drinks to have during the race.** It's a six-hour race so it will be exhausting. I'd like something that is low in fat and will give me a boost of energy quickly.

W： Wow! That sounds exhausting. We actually have a new range of energy gels. My personal favorite is this one, it's called Hammer Gel.

M： Oh wow! I've never heard of energy gels. That's convenient. **(69) Oh, this looks great. It is basically just sugar.** That's perfect!

W： It also has caffeine, which is really helpful. Our other products don't have that. **(70) But I suggest you don't have too much caffeine before you take this because this has quite a lot.**

---

66. 參看圖表，男子「不會」為女子訂購什麼？
　Ⓐ 包裝紙
　Ⓑ 頭戴式耳機
　Ⓒ 名片
　Ⓓ 複寫紙

67. 女子要求男子做什麼？
　Ⓐ 將訂購單寄給她
　Ⓑ 將頭戴式耳機寄給她
　Ⓒ 修改備忘錄
　Ⓓ 寄送收據

68–70 對話

男： 嗨，**(68) 我下星期要參加鐵人三項比賽，我需要一些能量棒或能量飲料，好在比賽期間補充。** 這場比賽耗時六小時，會讓人很疲倦。我想要低脂而且能快速為我提升能量的東西。

女： 哇！聽起來真累人。我們其實有新系列的能量凝膠。我個人最喜歡的是這個，叫做「猛槌凝膠」。

男： 我從來沒有聽過能量凝膠，真是方便。**(69) 這看起來很不錯，基本上只是糖而已。** 這太完美了。

女： 它還含有咖啡因，會很有幫助。我們其他的產品都沒有咖啡因。**(70) 但我建議在你吃之前別攝取太多咖啡因，因為這個咖啡因的含量很高。**

Nutrition Information 營養資訊	
Serving Size 每份：150 g（公克）	
Calories 熱量	**173 大卡**
Fat 脂肪	5 g（公克）
Protein 蛋白質	10 g（公克）
Sugar 糖	22 g（公克）
Sodium 鈉	60 mg（毫克）
Caffeine 咖啡因	80 mg（毫克）

68. Why is the man looking for a certain product?
- [A] He is on a diet.
- [B] He doesn't like sugar.
- **[C] He will compete in a race.**
- [D] He has a test soon.

69. Look at the graphic. Which of the ingredients is the man interested in?
- [A] Fat
- **[B] Sugar**
- [C] Caffeine
- [D] Protein

70. What does the woman suggest the man do?
- [A] Drink a lot of caffeine before taking the gel
- **[B] Don't drink a lot of caffeine before taking the gel**
- [C] Drink some caffeine before bed
- [D] Drink some caffeine in the morning

68. 男子為何在尋找某種產品?
- [A] 他正在節食
- [B] 他不喜歡糖
- **[C] 他將會參加比賽**
- [D] 他很快就要參加考試

69. 參看圖表,男子在意的是哪一個成分?
- [A] 脂肪
- **[B] 糖**
- [C] 咖啡因
- [D] 蛋白質

70. 女子建議男子做什麼?
- [A] 食用凝膠之前喝富含咖啡因的飲品
- **[B] 食用凝膠之前別喝富含咖啡因的飲品**
- [C] 睡覺之前喝一些含咖啡因的飲品
- [D] 早上喝一些含咖啡因的飲品

PART 4   P. 84-87   🎧 20

71-73 telephone message

M: Hello, Ms. Grayson. **(71) This is Michael Cook calling from Alliance Financial Bank. (72) It has recently come to my attention that some clients who renewed their credit card this month were sent the wrong card.** We have had multiple calls from bank members saying that they were sent a credit card with someone else's name on it. According to our records, you were also sent the wrong credit card. **(73) We ask that you please dispose of the credit card by cutting it with a pair of scissors.** In the meantime, we will issue a new credit card and have it delivered by express mail. We apologize for the inconvenience.

71-73 電話留言

男:哈囉,葛瑞森女士。**(71) 我是聯合金融銀行的麥可‧庫克。(72) 我注意到,最近有些本月換新信用卡的客戶被發放錯誤的卡片。**我們收到許多銀行會員的來電,說他們收到的信用卡上寫著別人的名字。根據我們的紀錄,寄給您的卡片也是錯誤的。**(73) 請您用剪刀將卡片剪掉,以將它廢止。**同時我們將會簽發新的信用卡,並用快遞寄送給您。我們為此不便向您道歉。

71. Where does the speaker work?
- [A] At a retail store
- **[B] At a bank**
- [C] At a gift shop
- [D] At a shipping company

72. What does the speaker apologize for?
- **[A] A delivery mistake**
- [B] An incorrect charge
- [C] A scheduling error
- [D] A defective product

71. 發話者在哪裡工作?
- [A] 零售店
- **[B] 銀行**
- [C] 禮品店
- [D] 貨運公司

72. 發話者為何道歉?
- **[A] 寄送錯誤**
- [B] 收費錯誤
- [C] 時間安排錯誤
- [D] 商品瑕疵

73. What does the speaker ask the listener to do?
- Ⓐ Return a call
- Ⓑ Renew his credit card
- **Ⓒ Get rid of the recently delivered card**
- Ⓓ Sign an application form

74-76 announcement

W：**(74) Attention, all shoppers. The West Point Mall will be closing in 10 minutes.** We thank you for shopping with us and greatly appreciate your business. **(75) To purchase items, please bring them to the cashier right now.** Also, we would like to inform you that a wallet that was found inside the store has been sent to the front desk. **(76) If your name is Catherine Goya, please stop by the front desk to claim the wallet.** Once again, we will be closing in 10 minutes. Please finish your shopping immediately.

74. Where is the announcement being made?
- Ⓐ In a subway station
- Ⓑ In a conference hall
- **Ⓒ In a shopping mall**
- Ⓓ In a baggage claim area

75. What are the listeners asked to do?
- **Ⓐ Proceed to the checkout immediately**
- Ⓑ Register for a workshop
- Ⓒ Search for a missing item
- Ⓓ Visit a different location

76. Why should Ms. Goya go to the front desk?
- Ⓐ To pay a membership fee
- **Ⓑ To recover a lost item**
- Ⓒ To receive a voucher
- Ⓓ To return an item

---

73. 發話者要求聆聽者做什麼？
- Ⓐ 回撥電話
- Ⓑ 換新信用卡
- **Ⓒ 處理掉最近寄來的卡片**
- Ⓓ 簽署申請表

74–76 廣播

女：**(74) 各位顧客請注意，西點購物中心將在十分鐘後打烊。** 我們感謝您前來購物，也很感激您的惠顧。**(75) 如需購買物品，請現在將商品帶到收銀員處。** 此外，我們想要通知各位，我們在店內撿到皮夾並已送到櫃台。**(76) 若您的名字是凱薩琳·戈雅，請到櫃台領取皮夾。** 再重申一次，我們即將於十分鐘後打烊。請立即結束購物。

74. 這則廣播是在哪裡進行的？
- Ⓐ 在地鐵車站
- Ⓑ 在會議廳
- **Ⓒ 在購物中心**
- Ⓓ 在行李提領區

75. 聽眾被要求做什麼？
- **Ⓐ 立刻前去結帳**
- Ⓑ 報名研習會
- Ⓒ 尋找遺失物品
- Ⓓ 去別的地點

76. 戈雅女士為何應該前往櫃台？
- Ⓐ 繳交會員費
- **Ⓑ 取回遺失物品**
- Ⓒ 收取禮券
- Ⓓ 辦理退貨

TEST 5

PART 4

20

77-79 recorded message

M：Thank you for calling Joyce Optical. If you are calling to check on the status of an order, press 1. **(77) Remember, we are the only glasses store in town that offers the services of our opticians free of charge. (78) That means you can get a complimentary eye examination as your vision changes. (79) If you would like to meet with one of our opticians, press 2 now.** We appreciate you choosing Joyce Optical and we hope to see you soon.

77. What business created the message?
   A A glassware factory
   B A pharmacy
   C An eyeglasses store
   D An insurance company

78. According to the speaker, what service does the business offer?
   A Free eye examinations
   B Online purchases
   C Special discounts for regular customers
   D Free delivery on large orders

79. Why would listeners press 2?
   A To cancel an order
   B To change delivery information
   C To schedule an appointment
   D To leave a message

80-82 advertisement

M：**(80) Would you like to own a high-powered laptop that is small enough to fit in your suit pocket or purse?** Then the new compact laptop Hypertop from Hyperline is the one you have been waiting for. The laptop also boasts impressive graphics and fast processing times. However, this is not available at our stores for now. **(81) To purchase this laptop, you need to visit our website and place an order. (82) If you order this laptop this week, we will provide a portable printer at no extra charge as a special promotion.** Don't hesitate. Take advantage of this amazing opportunity!

77-79 留言錄音

男：感謝您來電喬伊斯光學公司。如果您來電是為了要確認訂單狀況，請按 1。(77) 請記得，我們是鎮上唯一免費提供驗光服務的眼鏡行。(78) 也就是說，若您的視力改變了，可以到本店進行免費的視力檢查。(79) 若您想要與我們的驗光師會面，現在請按 2。我們感謝您選擇喬伊斯光學公司，希望很快能與您見面。

77. 這是哪個行業的留言？
   A 玻璃工廠
   B 藥局
   C 眼鏡行
   D 保險公司

78. 根據發話者，該企業提供什麼服務？
   A 免費的眼睛檢查
   B 線上購物
   C 常客的特別折扣
   D 大量訂購可免運

79. 聽者為何要按 2？
   A 取消訂單
   B 更改運送資訊
   C 預約時間
   D 留言

80-82 廣告

男：(80) 你想要擁有一台高性能又體積小，能放進你西裝口袋或女用皮包的筆記型電腦嗎？那麼超線公司的新型迷你筆記型電腦「超頂」，正是您所期待的產品。這台筆記型電腦號稱有很棒的影像處理元件以及高速處理效能，但是目前我們店內沒有貨。(81) 若要買這台筆記型電腦，您需要到我們的網站下訂單。(82) 如果您本週訂購這台筆記型電腦，我們將會免費贈送可攜式印表機作為促銷優惠。別猶豫，把握這個大好機會吧！

80. What special feature of the new laptop does the speaker mention?
- [A] It is the lightest in the market.
- [B] It has a built-in high-definition camera.
- [C] It is water resistant.
- **[D] It is convenient to carry.**

81. How can customers purchase the new laptop?
- **[A] By accessing a website**
- [B] By stopping by the speaker's office
- [C] By visiting a local store
- [D] By calling a customer service hotline

82. What can customers receive this week?
- [A] An additional battery
- [B] A carrying case
- [C] A portable speaker
- **[D] A small printer**

80. 發話者提到新筆記型電腦的哪個特點？
- [A] 它是市面上最輕的
- [B] 它內建高解析度相機
- [C] 它能防水
- **[D] 它很便於攜帶**

81. 顧客如何購買這台新的筆記型電腦？
- **[A] 使用網站**
- [B] 去發話者的辦公室
- [C] 去當地的店家
- [D] 撥打客服熱線

82. 顧客本週可以收到什麼？
- [A] 額外的電池
- [B] 隨身包
- [C] 可攜帶式喇叭
- **[D] 小型印表機**

83-85 excerpt from a meeting

W: Hi, thanks for coming to this special meeting today. **(83) The reason I called everyone is to announce our new partnership with Walker Studios.** As the CEO of Metro Studios, I'm pleased to witness this amazing opportunity to work with such a high-caliber company like Walker Studios. They possess a number of studios that are capable of producing cutting edge quality 3-D films. This will allow our company to begin producing 3-D films. **(84) And why wouldn't we?** The majority of our films are science fiction, and I believe a transition into 3-D is an excellent path for us. I have ensured that we will have full access to Walker Studio's equipment, and in return they will become a shareholder in our company. **(85) I suggest that our studio staff should spend the next following weeks studying how this new type of equipment works, so we can begin producing content as soon as possible.**

83-85 會議摘錄

女：各位好，感謝大家今天參加這場特別的會議。**(83) 我找大家來是要宣布我們與渥克電影公司的新合夥關係。** 身為都會電影公司的執行長，我很高興能見證這個極佳的機會，與渥克電影公司這麼強的公司合作。他們擁有數間工作室，能夠製作品質最先進的 3-D 電影，這能讓我們公司也開始製作 3-D 電影。**(84) 而這又有何不可呢？** 我們的電影絕大部分都是科幻片，我相信轉換成 3-D 對我們而言是極佳的做法。我已經確保我們能夠完全取用渥克電影公司的設備，而給他們的回報則是成為我們公司的股東。**(85) 我建議我們電影公司的員工，應該在接下來幾個星期學會使用這種新設備，這樣我們就可以盡快開始製作電影內容。**

TEST 5

PART 4

20

83. What is the reason for the meeting?
- **[A] To announce a new partnership**
- [B] To introduce a new manager
- [C] To propose a budget plan
- [D] To announce her retirement

83. 為何召開會議？
- **[A] 要宣布新的合夥關係**
- [B] 要介紹新經理
- [C] 要提出預算計劃
- [D] 要宣布她的榮退

(NEW)

84. What does the woman imply when she says, "and why wouldn't we"?

   A **To suggest the partnership is good**

   B To review some materials

   C To recommend a new method

   D To offer a training program

85. What does the woman suggest the studio staff do?

   A Go on vacation

   B Continue using the old equipment

   C Produce a movie

   D **Study the new equipment**

86-88 notice

M：Hi, everybody. This Saturday the fitness center will be upgrading our water-heating system in the bathrooms. **(86) Unfortunately, the hot water will be off from 9 a.m. to 12 p.m.** If anyone was planning to come in and exercise, **(87) you might want to hold off until later.** If the work gets delayed **(88) I will send a text message to all club members to notify you of any changes.**

---

86. What problem does the speaker mention?

   A A shipment was missed.

   B The order was wrong.

   C **The center will have no hot water.**

   D There will be no water.

(NEW)

87. What does the speaker imply when he says, "you might want to hold off until later"?

   A **Members of the center should come in the afternoon.**

   B Members of the center shouldn't come.

   C There will be a meeting in the morning.

   D The center is closed in the afternoon.

88. What does the speaker say he will do?

   A **Send a text message**

   B Send an email

   C Make a phone call

   D Post a letter

---

84. 女子說「而這又有何不可呢」，她暗示什麼？

   A **要表示合夥關係是好的**

   B 要檢視一些題材

   C 要推薦新的方法

   D 要提供訓練課程

85. 女子建議電影公司員工做什麼？

   A 去度假

   B 持續使用舊設備

   C 製作電影

   D **研究新設備**

86–88 通知

男：嗨，大家好。本週六健身中心將要改善浴室的熱水系統。**(86)** 麻煩的是，從上午九點到中午 12 點，熱水將會關閉。如果有人打算要來運動，**(87)** 可能要晚點再來。如果工程延誤了，**(88)** 我會傳簡訊給所有會員，告知任何異動。

---

86. 發話者提到了什麼問題？

   A 錯過了送貨

   B 訂單有誤

   C **健身中心將沒有熱水可用**

   D 將會停水

87. 發話者說「可能要晚點再來」，他暗示什麼？

   A **健身中心的會員應該下午再來**

   B 健身中心的會員不應該來

   C 早上要開會

   D 健身中心下午關閉

88. 發話者說他將會做什麼？

   A **傳簡訊**

   B 寄電子郵件

   C 打電話

   D 郵寄信件

89-91 telephone message

W：⁽⁸⁹⁾ **Hi, Chef Garder, this is Lauren Cole phoning from the restaurant kitchen.** The delivery just came in, and ⁽⁹⁰⁾ **there is a lot more meat and fish delivered that we don't usually have on our list.** I don't recall any special events coming up, and the calendar doesn't have anything on it. Did you make the order? I'm going to call the supplier but I want to check with you first in case you need the products. ⁽⁹¹⁾ **Give me a call back, and please bear in mind I have to finish the kitchen inventory by 11 a.m., and it's already 9:30.** Thanks, Chef.

89-91 電話留言

女：⁽⁸⁹⁾ 嗨，加德主廚，我是餐廳廚房的蘿倫‧科爾。貨剛送到了，⁽⁹⁰⁾ 送來的肉和魚比我們平常訂購的多出很多。我不記得近期有任何特別的活動，日曆上也沒有任何紀錄。是你訂貨的嗎？我會打電話給供應商，但我想先與你確認，看是否是你需要這些貨品。⁽⁹¹⁾ 請回電給我，請記得，我必須在上午 11 點前完成廚房存貨盤點，而現在已經九點半了。感謝你，主廚。

89. Where does the speaker work?
- A At a market
- B At a clinic
- **C At a restaurant**
- D At a factory

89. 發話者在哪裡工作？
- A 市場
- B 診所
- **C 餐廳**
- D 工廠

90. What problem does the speaker describe?
- **A Extra items were delivered.**
- B The delivery is late.
- C The business was closed.
- D There is a special event planned.

90. 發話者描述了什麼問題？
- **A 送來多餘的物品**
- B 運送延遲了
- C 商店關門了
- D 有規劃特別活動

(NEW)
91. What does the woman mean when she says, "I have to finish the kitchen inventory by 11 a.m."?
- **A She would like a response soon.**
- B She doesn't need to know soon.
- C She needs some help with the new menu.
- D They have the right ingredients.

91. 女子說「我必須在上午 11 點前完成廚房存貨盤點」，她指的什麼？
- **A 她想趕快得到回覆**
- B 她不需要盡快知道
- C 她需要有人幫忙處理新菜單的事
- D 他們有正確的食材

92-94 introduction

W： Welcome to your first training session at Jarret's! The next four days will be quite intense, as you will be shown a lot of different equipment you will be required to handle in your daily job. Try not to get too overwhelmed. **(92) Once you get used to the assembly process, your efficiency at working the line will grow rapidly within a year.** At Jarret's we pride ourselves on producing quality materials in a positive environment. We hold weekly team-building exercises and a monthly staff getaway. **(93) I'm sure you will enjoy our company events and become good friends with your colleagues.** Today we will have a tour of the factory and meet the workers. The next three days are spent on machine training. **(94) One of the days we will have a special team lunch and the president will be coming in to meet everybody.**

92-94 介紹

女： 歡迎來到你在傑洛特工廠的第一堂訓練課程。接下來的四天會很辛苦，因為你會看到許多不同的設備，這些都是妳往後日常工作要操作的，試著別被嚇著了。**(92) 一旦你習慣了裝配過程，你在裝配線的工作效率就會在一年內快速提升。** 在傑洛特工廠，我們很自豪能在積極的環境中生產出高品質的材料。我們每星期舉辦團隊凝聚運動，每個月還有員工出遊。**(93) 我相信你們會喜歡公司的活動，而且會與同事成為好朋友。** 今天我們要參訪工廠，並且和工人會面，接下來的三天要做機器操作訓練。**(94) 其中一天，我們會有特別的團隊午餐，董事長會來和大家見面。**

Training Schedule 訓練時間表

Monday 星期一	Tuesday 星期二	Wednesday 星期三	Thursday 星期四
Meet and greet 相見歡	Machine training 機器操作訓練	Machine training 機器操作訓練	Machine training 機器操作訓練
Factory tour 工廠參訪			Lunch meeting with president 與董事長午餐會

92. What are the listeners training to be?
  A Airline attendants
  B Military soldiers
  C Assembly line workers
  D Computer programmers

92. 聽眾正在受訓成為什麼？
  A 空服員
  B 士兵
  C 裝配線工人
  D 電腦程式設計師

93. According to the speaker, what will the listeners enjoy doing?
  A Learning their job
  B Assembling products
  C Producing quality materials
  D Going to company events

93. 根據發話者，聽眾將會喜歡做什麼？
  A 學習他們的工作
  B 裝配產品
  C 生產高品質的材料
  D 參加公司活動

94. Look at the graphic. On what day will the listeners meet with the company president?

A Monday

B Tuesday

C Wednesday

D Thursday

94. 參看圖表，聽眾在哪一天將與公司的董事長會面？

A 星期一

B 星期二

C 星期三

D 星期四

95-97 excerpt from a meeting

M：Alright everyone, here's the analysis of this year's microbrew market shares. The good news is, Alright Ales is still in the top five small breweries in the Northcut region. **(95) The bad news is, the newest entry into our market, Strange Brew Ales, has a directly competing beer and is making strong gains.** In order to stay competitive we must be able to introduce new styles of craft beer to our consumers. Our analysts agree, if the current trend continues, Strange Brew Ales will bump us out of the top five by this time next year. Our master brewers have come up with four new styles of beer that we will introduce to a focus group at the upcoming Northcut Beer Festival. **(96)(97) Once we get consumer feedback we will select the two most popular offerings and create an aggressive marketing campaign.** Our sales must increase by at least 5% over the next quarter in order to maintain our market share in Northcut.

95-97 會議摘要

男：好的，各位，這裡是今年小型釀酒廠市佔率的分析。好消息是，好呀麥芽啤酒廠仍然是諾斯卡特地區排名前五的小酒廠。**(95) 壞消息是，新加入的奇特釀麥芽啤酒廠有直接與我們競爭的啤酒，而且市場增長快速。** 為了維持競爭力，我們必須有能力為消費者推出新風味的精釀啤酒。我們的分析師都認為，如果目前的趨勢持續下去，奇特釀麥芽啤酒廠在明年此時會把我們擠出前五名。我們的釀酒師已經想出四種新風味的啤酒，我們會在近期的諾斯卡特啤酒節時介紹給焦點小組。**(96)(97) 只要一收到顧客的意見回饋，我們就會挑選最受歡迎的兩種啤酒，並進行積極的行銷活動。** 下一季我們的銷售量至少要增加5%，才能維持我們在諾斯卡特的市佔率。

FOCUS GROUP QUESTIONAIRE RESULTS: 焦點團體問卷調查結果：
Majority respondents selected the following 多數受訪者選擇如下

Alright Ales New Styles 好呀麥芽啤酒新風味	Do you like the label? 你是否喜歡此品牌？	Do you like the flavor? 你是否喜歡此口味？	Would you choose this again? 你是否會再次選擇此產品？	Would you recommend this beer? 你是否會推薦這款啤酒？
Dark Ale 黑麥芽啤酒	Yes 是	No 否	Maybe 也許	Maybe 也許
Red Ale 紅麥芽啤酒	No 否	Yes 是	Yes 是	Yes 是
Belgium Style 比利時風味啤酒	Yes 是	No 否	No 否	No 否
Wheat Ale 小麥芽啤酒	Yes 是	Yes 是	Yes 是	Yes 是

95. Why is Alright Ales worried?
- **A** **They have a new competitor.**
- B They are nervous about their new beers.
- C They are not in the top 5 of the market share in Northcut.
- D They will have to cut staff.

96. What will the company likely do with the results of the survey?
- A Change the label of the Red Ale
- B Work on the Belgium Style
- **C** **Begin marketing the chosen beers**
- D Start working on a new style of beer

97. Look at the graphic. What beer is least likely to be part of Alright Ales' new product line?
- A Wheat Ale
- B Dark Ale
- C Red Ale
- **D** **Belgium Style**

95. 好呀麥芽啤酒廠為何憂心？
- **A** **他們有新的競爭對手**
- B 他們對於自家的新啤酒感到緊張
- C 他們不在諾斯卡特市佔率的前五名
- D 他們將要裁員

96. 這份調查的結果很可能會讓這家公司做什麼？
- A 改變紅麥芽啤酒的標籤
- B 努力改進比利時風味啤酒
- **C** **開始行銷獲選的啤酒**
- D 開始研發新款的啤酒

97. 參看圖表，哪種啤酒最不可能是好呀麥芽啤酒廠推出的新產品？
- A 小麥麥芽啤酒
- B 黑麥麥芽啤酒
- C 紅麥芽啤酒
- **D** **比利時風味啤酒**

98-100 announcement

W：Welcome to Big Toys' warehouse orientation. As the industry leader in children's toys, **(98) it is essential that you understand the huge volume of merchandise that you will be dealing with as a stock room worker.** The worksheet in front of you is a map of our warehouse. Each section of the warehouse is divided into zones by the type of toy, and then arranged alphabetically by manufacturer. **(99) At the bottom of the map is a list of toys we would like you to collect and place on the designated pallet for shelving.** There will be a "Z" and a number before the name of the toy, to let you know what zone it is in. **(100) This is a timed exercise, and all toys should be collected within 1 hour.** I understand this is a trial by fire, but once you get the hang of our organization, you will be able to complete a task like this with ease.

98–100 介紹

女：歡迎來到大玩具公司倉儲新進人員訓練。身為兒童玩具業的領導者，**(98) 各位有必要知道，身為倉庫員工，你們將會處理大量商品。**你們眼前的作業單是我們倉儲的地圖。倉儲的每個部分都依據玩具的種類劃分成若干區域，然後再依製造商的字母順序排列。**(99) 地圖下方列出的玩具清單則是要各位去取來並且放在指定的貨板上，以供上架。**玩具的名稱前面會有個字母 Z 和數字，是要讓你知道它在哪個區域。**(100) 這是個計時訓練，所有玩具都要在一小時內蒐集完成。**我了解這是嚴酷的考驗，但是你一旦熟悉我們的安排，就能輕而易舉完成像這樣的任務。

Zone 1 第一區 — Board Games and Video Games 桌遊和電玩
Zone 2 第二區 — Action Figures and Dolls 可動公仔和洋娃娃
Zone 3 第三區 — Sports Equipment 運動器材
Zone 4 第四區 — Learning and Education Games 學習與教育遊戲

Toy List 玩具清單

Z1 Laughing Logs 大笑木頭、**Z2** Macho Man 猛男、**Z2** Lovely Lady 美麗女士、
Z3 Soccer Ball 足球、**Z3** Golf Clubs 高爾夫球桿、**Z4** Animal ID 動物識別證、
Z1 Business Tycoon 企業大亨、**Z1** Fighting Forces 戰鬥兵力。

98. What is indicated at the orientation?
- [A] Big Toys will be a boring job.
- **[B] Big Toys has a large selection of products.**
- [C] Their inventory system is confusing.
- [D] The managers will be very critical of mistakes.

(NEW)
99. Look at the graphic. Where will the trainees spend most of their time during the training exercise?
- **[A] Zone 1**
- [B] Zone 2
- [C] Zone 3
- [D] Zone 4

100. How quickly should the trainees complete their exercise?
- [A] 2 hours
- [B] 45 minutes or less
- [C] 1.5 hours
- **[D] 1 hour or less**

98. 新進人員訓練時提到了什麼？
- [A] 大玩具公司是個無聊的工作
- **[B] 大玩具公司有大量的產品**
- [C] 他們的存貨目錄系統很難懂
- [D] 經理對於錯誤很嚴苛

99. 參看圖表，受訓人員大部分的訓練時間都會在哪裡？
- **[A] 第一區**
- [B] 第二區
- [C] 第三區
- [D] 第四區

100. 訓練人員應該要多快完成任務？
- [A] 兩小時
- [B] 45 分鐘以內
- [C] 1.5 小時
- **[D] 1 小時以內**

ACTUAL TEST ⑥

PART 1 P. 88-91

1.
Ⓐ She has some grocery bags.
Ⓑ She is holding some flowers.
Ⓒ She is reaching out to pick up a vegetable.
Ⓓ She is washing the fruits.

2.
Ⓐ The boy is putting bait on the hook.
Ⓑ The father has his right arm around the boy.
Ⓒ The boy is reeling in a fish.
Ⓓ They are fishing on the pier.

3.
Ⓐ He is washing the fruits.
Ⓑ He is cutting up some vegetables.
Ⓒ There are some glasses of water on the table.
Ⓓ She is standing next to him.

4.
Ⓐ They are looking at some documents on the table.
Ⓑ They are wearing helmets.
Ⓒ There are some people working behind them.
Ⓓ One of the men is writing on the document.

5.
Ⓐ There are some building designs on the table.
Ⓑ The woman is drinking a cup of coffee.
Ⓒ The woman is writing a recipe.
Ⓓ The woman is talking on the phone.

6.
Ⓐ The man is typing on the computer.
Ⓑ They are both looking at the laptop.
Ⓒ The men are wearing ties.
Ⓓ The men are checking some blueprints.

PART 2 P. 92

7. Who's responsible for the report?
Ⓐ Sometime in the afternoon.
Ⓑ In the news report.
Ⓒ It's John Draper.

8. Where can I buy a ticket?
Ⓐ A round-trip ticket.
Ⓑ On the official website.
Ⓒ By 5:00 at the latest.

1.
Ⓐ 她拿著一些雜貨袋。
Ⓑ 她拿著一些花朵。
Ⓒ 她伸手去拿蔬菜。
Ⓓ 她正在洗水果。

2.
Ⓐ 男孩將魚餌放上魚鉤。
Ⓑ 父親用右手摟著男孩。
Ⓒ 男孩正在捲線拉魚。
Ⓓ 他們正在碼頭上釣魚。

3.
Ⓐ 他正在洗水果。
Ⓑ 他正在切蔬菜。
Ⓒ 桌上有幾杯水。
Ⓓ 她正站在他身邊。

4.
Ⓐ 他們看著桌上的文件。
Ⓑ 他們戴著安全帽。
Ⓒ 有些人在他們後面工作。
Ⓓ 其中一名男子在文件上寫字。

5.
Ⓐ 桌上有些建築物設計圖。
Ⓑ 女子正在喝咖啡。
Ⓒ 女子正在寫食譜。
Ⓓ 女子正在講電話。

6.
Ⓐ 男子正在用電腦打字。
Ⓑ 他們兩人都看著筆記型電腦。
Ⓒ 男子們都打領帶。
Ⓓ 男子們在檢視一些藍圖。

7. 誰負責這份報告？
Ⓐ 下午的時候。
Ⓑ 在新聞報導裡。
Ⓒ 是約翰・德瑞伯。

8. 我可以在哪裡買票？
Ⓐ 來回票一張。
Ⓑ 在官方網站。
Ⓒ 最晚五點。

9. Did Mr. Stacks show you the new work schedule?
   A Yes, he was.
   B It's behind schedule.
   C Actually, Ms. Dwain did.

10. When should I call the travel agency?
   A Sometime before Friday.
   B In my desk drawer.
   C We don't allow refunds.

11. How many tables should I set up?
   A It's a table for four.
   B There isn't enough time.
   C At least twenty.

12. Let's take a short break.
   A I'd like that.
   B It's a short-term contract.
   C I put the brakes on.

13. Why won't the television turn on?
   A Because of a scheduling conflict.
   B Maybe it isn't plugged in.
   C It was yesterday.

14. Would you rather eat out or pack a lunch?
   A It was delicious.
   B We're preparing for a new product launch.
   C Let's go to a restaurant.

15. Sam is a really great clerk, isn't he?
   A Yeah, he is very hard-working.
   B Well, the clock is a few minutes slow.
   C No, he just moved last week.

16. How often does this bus come?
   A I will come up with some ideas.
   B Every twenty minutes.
   C The train to Hemsville.

17. When is Mary due to give birth?
   A No, it was a baby toy.
   B Of course. I'd love to.
   C Sometime next month, I think.

9. 史達克先生給你看新的工作時間表了嗎？
   A 是的，他是。
   B 進度落後了。
   C 其實，是德溫女士給我看的。

10. 我應該什麼時候打電話給旅行社？
   A 星期五前。
   B 在我書桌的抽屜裡。
   C 我們不退款。

11. 我應該要擺幾張桌子？
   A 這是四人座的餐桌。
   B 時間不夠了。
   C 至少 20 張。

12. 我們短暫休息一下吧。
   A 我很樂意。
   B 這是短期合約。
   C 我踩煞車了。

13. 電視為何無法開啟？
   A 因為時程安排衝突。
   B 也許它沒有插電。
   C 是昨天。

14. 你要在外用餐或帶便當？
   A 那很美味。
   B 我們正在準備新產品上市會。
   C 我們去餐廳吧。

15. 山姆是很棒的店員，不是嗎？
   A 是的，他非常努力。
   B 時鐘慢了幾分鐘。
   C 不，他上星期剛搬家。

16. 公車多久來一班？
   A 我會想出一些點子。
   B 每 20 分鐘。
   C 開往荷姆斯維爾的火車。

17. 瑪莉何時要生小孩？
   A 不，那是個嬰兒玩具。
   B 當然，我很樂意。
   C 我猜想是下個月的時候。

18. Is this food enough, or should I prepare more?
 [A] The restaurant is busy.
 [B] That will be plenty.
 [C] I need a pair of gloves.

19. When will the manager be making the announcement?
 [A] At around 3:00 p.m.
 [B] Yes, that's what I heard, too.
 [C] In the auditorium.

20. Which shirt did you decide to buy for your sister?
 [A] I decided to hire more employees.
 [B] Actually, I bought a scarf instead.
 [C] How much is it?

21. Would you like me to return this book for you?
 [A] No, I haven't finished it yet.
 [B] I'll book a room for you.
 [C] Please help me lift this.

22. I'm having a hard time choosing what to wear.
 [A] I bought the clothes last week.
 [B] Where is the exit?
 [C] I can help you decide.

23. Isn't the museum closed on Mondays?
 [A] Sometime this morning.
 [B] You're right.
 [C] We will open a new branch.

24. Mr. Yamaoka will be dropping by today, won't he?
 [A] Can you pick it up for me?
 [B] No, he said he's too busy.
 [C] Yes, it was his first visit.

25. I think I need to fill the car up with gas.
 [A] Take a right turn here, then.
 [B] It's a natural gas company.
 [C] Don't forget to pack the truck.

26. Could you come to the office early tomorrow?
 [A] It's reflected on the surface.
 [B] Yes, I met him in the office.
 [C] What time?

27. Why hasn't the delivery arrived yet?
 [A] Let me call Ms. Anderson.
 [B] I've signed the contract.
 [C] A cardboard box.

18. 食物足夠嗎？或者我該多準備一些？
 [A] 餐廳很忙碌。
 [B] 這樣就很足夠了。
 [C] 我需要一雙手套。

19. 經理什麼時候會宣布？
 [A] 大約下午三點。
 [B] 是的，我也是聽說如此。
 [C] 在禮堂。

20. 你決定要買哪件襯衫給你的妹妹？
 [A] 我決定要僱用更多的員工。
 [B] 實際上，我改買圍巾。
 [C] 那要多少錢？

21. 你要我幫你還這本書嗎？
 [A] 不，我還沒看完。
 [B] 我會幫你訂房。
 [C] 請幫我抬起這個。

22. 我難以抉擇該穿什麼。
 [A] 我上星期買了這些衣服。
 [B] 出口在哪裡？
 [C] 我可以協助你做決定。

23. 博物館星期一不是休館嗎？
 [A] 今天上午某時。
 [B] 沒錯。
 [C] 我們將開新分店。

24. 山崗先生今天將會來訪，不是嗎？
 [A] 你可以幫我把它撿起來嗎？
 [B] 不，他說他太忙碌了。
 [C] 是的，他那次是第一次來訪。

25. 我想我需要為這輛車加滿油。
 [A] 那麼，在這裡右轉。
 [B] 這是一家天然氣公司。
 [C] 別忘了把東西裝上卡車。

26. 你明天可以提早到辦公室來嗎？
 [A] 它反射在表面上。
 [B] 是的，我在辦公室遇到他。
 [C] 幾點鐘？

27. 為什麼貨物還沒有送達？
 [A] 讓我打電話問安德森女士。
 [B] 我已經簽了合約。
 [C] 一個硬紙箱。

28. Were you at the workshop this weekend?
  [A] I'll visit her next weekend.
  [B] Yes, I attended with Jake and Melissa.
  [C] I was going to shop for groceries.

29. Would you prefer to meet this Wednesday or on Saturday?
  [A] I won't refer to the matter again.
  [B] We can meet the deadline.
  [C] I'm most free on the weekends.

30. Have you printed a copy of the itinerary for everyone?
  [A] Yes, right here.
  [B] A cup of coffee, please.
  [C] No one knows where she is.

31. This book is too difficult for me.
  [A] Then I'll pick out a different one.
  [B] The library is close by.
  [C] Try this hat on.

28. 你這個週末在研習會嗎?
  [A] 我下週末要去拜訪他。
  [B] 是的,我與傑克和瑪麗莎一起參加。
  [C] 我當時正要去購買雜貨。

29. 你比較想在這星期三或是星期六見面?
  [A] 我不會再提及此事。
  [B] 我們可以趕上最後期限。
  [C] 我週末最有空。

30. 你幫每個人印旅遊行程表了嗎?
  [A] 是的,就在這裡。
  [B] 一杯咖啡,謝謝。
  [C] 沒有人知道她在哪裡。

31. 這本書對我而言太難了。
  [A] 那麼我要挑選另一本。
  [B] 圖書館就在附近。
  [C] 試戴這頂帽子。

PART 3 P. 93-97   23

32–34 conversation

W: Hi, Mr. Joyce. This is Sally Walker calling from Frohman Publishing. **(32) My company has a three-page text that we need translated into Chinese. I know you sometimes do these kinds of smaller jobs for our company.**

M: Yeah, I would be happy to. **(33) However, you should know that it is my policy to be paid in advance.** Is that OK?

W: That's no problem. I'll transfer the money into your bank account immediately. **(34) The deadline for this translation hasn't been decided yet. Once I know, I will inform you.**

M: Thank you for your understanding. Please email me the document. I'll do my best.

32–34 對話

女:嗨,喬伊斯先生。我是弗羅曼出版社的莎莉 · 沃克。**(32) 我的公司有一份三頁的文件需要翻譯成中文,我知道你有時候會為我們公司做這種短期的工作。**

男:是的,我很樂意。**(33) 但是你應該要知道,我的作法是提前收費。**這樣可以嗎?

女:沒問題。我會立刻將錢匯入你的銀行帳戶。**(34) 這份翻譯的交件日期還沒有決定,我一知道就會通知你。**

男:感謝你體諒,請用電子郵件把文件寄給我,我會盡力做好。

32. Why is the woman calling?
  [A] To extend a rental period
  [B] To confirm an appointment
  [C] To offer an assignment
  [D] To accept a proposal

32. 女子為什麼打電話?
  [A] 要展延租賃時間
  [B] 要確認預約
  [C] 要提供兼職工作
  [D] 要接受提案

33. What does the man ask the woman to do?
  A Interpret for her supervisor
  B Send an advance payment
  C Submit an official request
  D Provide a work space

34. What will the woman inform the man about?
  A A requirement
  B A deadline
  C A meeting time
  D A company policy

35-37 conversation

W: Good morning, James. **(35) Here is a copy of your expense report from last month's business trip to Tokyo.**

M: Thanks, Mary. **(36) Oh, while you're here, can you leave a message in this get-well-soon card for Bryce?** He had knee surgery yesterday and I was thinking this card might cheer him up.

W: Oh, did he? I didn't even know he was in the hospital. I was out of town yesterday. Is it serious?

M: Not that I know of. But he said he had to stay in the hospital for a few days. **(37) I'm planning on visiting him this evening after work.**

35. What did the woman make a copy of?
  A A receipt
  B A meeting schedule
  C An expense report
  D A prescription

36. What does the man ask the woman to do?
  A Sign a contract
  B Write a message
  C Contact a receptionist
  D Go on a business trip to Tokyo

37. What does the man plan to do?
  A Visit his coworker
  B Submit a report
  C Make a new reservation
  D Work overtime

33. 男子要求女子做什麼？
  A 為她的主管進行口譯
  B 付預付款
  C 繳交正式的請求
  D 提供工作空間

34. 女子會告知男子什麼？
  A 要求條件
  B 交件日期
  C 會面時間
  D 公司政策

35-37 對話

女：早安，詹姆士。**(35)** 這裡是你上個月出差到東京的支出報告。

男：謝謝你，瑪莉。**(36)** 喔，既然你來了，你可以在這張慰問卡上留言給布萊斯嗎？他昨天膝蓋手術，我想這張卡片可能會讓他心情好一點。

女：喔，真的嗎？我甚至不知道他住院了。我昨天出城去了，很嚴重嗎？

男：就我所知並不嚴重。但他說他必須住院幾天，**(37)** 我打算今晚下班後去探視他。

35. 女子印了一份什麼？
  A 收據
  B 會議時程表
  C 支出報告
  D 處方箋

36. 男子要求女子做什麼？
  A 簽合約
  B 寫留言
  C 聯繫接待員
  D 到東京出差

37. 男子打算要做什麼？
  A 探視同事
  B 繳交報告
  C 重新訂位
  D 加班工作

38–40 conversation

W: **(38) I need to talk to you about the interior decoration we are doing at the Carletons' property.** They are a major client, so we need to make sure that they are completely satisfied. Have you consulted with them about the furniture for the master bedroom?

M: I have. They agreed on all of our plans except for the choice for the master bed. **(39) They're worried it is too big and will occupy too much space, so I'm looking for something smaller that still fits the color scheme of the room.**

W: OK. **(40) I was planning on ordering all the furniture today, but I think we'll have to wait until we get their permission.**

38–40 對話

女: **(38)** 我需要和你討論我們在卡爾頓房子的室內裝潢。他們是大客戶，因此我們需要確保他們完全滿意。你是否諮詢過他們關於主臥室的家具？

男: 是的。他們同意我們所有的規劃，除了主臥室床鋪的選擇。**(39)** 他們擔心床太大，會佔去太多空間。因此我在找比較小又能夠符合房間配色設計的床。

女: 好的。**(40)** 我原本打算今天要訂購所有的家具，但我想我們還是等到他們同意後再買。

---

38. What field do the speakers work in?
- [A] Education
- [B] Manufacturing
- [C] Product development
- **[D] Interior design**

39. What does the man plan to do?
- **[A] Choose different furniture**
- [B] Share a building plan
- [C] Change a color scheme
- [D] Place an order for wallpaper

40. According to the woman, why will the speakers have to wait?
- [A] A shipment has been delayed.
- [B] A contract has not been signed yet.
- **[C] Authorization must first be obtained.**
- [D] Some equipment is out of order.

38. 對話者在哪個領域工作？
- [A] 教育
- [B] 製造業
- [C] 產品開發
- **[D] 室內設計**

39. 男子打算要做什麼？
- **[A] 選擇不同的家具**
- [B] 分享建築計劃
- [C] 改變配色設計
- [D] 下訂單購買壁紙

40. 根據女子，對話者們為何必須等候？
- [A] 運送耽擱了
- [B] 尚未簽署合約
- **[C] 必須先取得授權**
- [D] 某些設備故障了

41–43 conversation

W: **(41) Hi, I'd like to adopt a pet.** I live alone and feel that a dog would be great company.

M: You came to the right place. **(41) We have many cute dogs here who were rescued from the street and don't have a home.** What kind of dog are you looking for specifically?

41–43 對話

女: **(41)** 嗨，我想要領養寵物。我獨居，覺得狗會是很好的夥伴。

男: 你來對地方了。**(41)** 我們這裡有很多可愛的狗，都是從街道上救回來的，還沒有家。你想找什麼特定的狗呢？

W：**(42) Well, my house is not that big, so I was hoping for a dog small enough to hold in my lap.**

M：All right. **(43) Before we can allow you to adopt a dog, we need you to complete some official paperwork.** If you have a seat in the lobby, I'll bring you the documents immediately.

女：**(42) 嗯，我的房子沒那麼大，因此我希望有一隻可以放在腿上的小型犬。**

男：好的。**(43) 在我們同意你領養小狗之前，我們有一些正式的文書需要你寫。** 請你在大廳就座，我會立刻幫你把文件帶過來。

---

41. Where most likely are the speakers?
    - A At a pet shop
    - B At a catering company
    - C At a fire station
    - **D At an animal shelter**

42. What aspect of the woman's needs is mentioned?
    - A The price
    - **B The size**
    - C The age
    - D The color

43. According to the man, what does the woman have to do?
    - A Make an advance payment
    - B Bring her identification
    - **C Fill out some documents**
    - D Submit a letter of reference

41. 對話者最有可能在哪裡？
    - A 寵物店
    - B 外燴公司
    - C 消防局
    - **D 動物收容所**

42. 對話中提及女子哪方面的需求？
    - A 價格
    - **B 大小**
    - C 年紀
    - D 顏色

43. 根據男子的說法，女子必須做什麼？
    - A 預先付款
    - B 帶來她的身分證明
    - **C 填寫一些文件**
    - D 繳交介紹信

44–46 conversation

M：Hello, this is David Wright. **(44) I represent the guitar player Joe Jackson, who will be performing at your venue this weekend. (45) I wanted to remind you that Mr. Jackson requests that no photography be allowed during the duration of his performance.**

W：Yes, I remember. We have posted flyers at the entrance prohibiting cameras and have asked our staff to remind guests that photography is not allowed.

M：Thank you for your cooperation. As you know, Mr. Jackson is very sensitive when he plays.

W：**(46) I'll make an announcement onstage before the show to inform the audience one more time about this restriction.**

44–46 對話

男：哈囉，我是大衛 · 萊特。**(44) 我代表吉他手喬 · 傑克森，他將在本週末到你們的場地表演。(45) 我想要提醒你，傑克森先生要求演出期間不得拍攝。**

女：是的，我記得。我們已經在入口處張貼禁止相機的傳單，並且要求工作人員提醒來賓禁止攝影。

男：感謝你們的合作。你知道的，傑克森先生在演奏時非常敏感。

女：**(46) 演出前我會上台宣布，再次告知觀眾這項限制。**

44. Who most likely is the man?
- [A] A photographer
- **[B] A talent agent**
- [C] A performer
- [D] A receptionist

45. Why is the man calling?
- [A] To buy a ticket in advance
- [B] To confirm a reservation
- **[C] To provide a reminder**
- [D] To inquire about an advertisement

46. What does the woman offer to do?
- [A] Restrict backstage access
- [B] Take pictures of Mr. Jackson
- [C] Show the man a list of guests
- **[D] Make an official announcement**

44. 男子最有可能是什麼人？
- [A] 攝影師
- **[B] 藝人經紀人**
- [C] 表演者
- [D] 接待員

45. 男子為何打電話？
- [A] 要提前購票
- [B] 要確認預約
- **[C] 要做出提醒**
- [D] 要詢問廣告的事

46. 女子提議做什麼？
- [A] 限制進入後台
- [B] 為傑克森先生拍照
- [C] 給男子看來賓名單
- **[D] 公開聲明**

47–49 conversation

M： Hi, Kelly. Did you see our advertisement in this month's issue of *Fishing Fanatic*? **(47) The accompanying graphic shows how our fishing rods are stronger than any other product on the market.**

W： Yeah, I saw it this morning. **(48) I'm hoping the advertisement will help convince customers to purchase our newest line of fishing rods.**

M： **(48) I'm sure it will. (49) I'll get in touch with the advertising agency and request that the ad be placed in other magazines as well.**

47–49 對話

男： 嗨，凱莉。你有看見我們的廣告，出現在本月出刊的《釣魚狂人》裡嗎？**(47)** 附圖顯示出我們的釣竿比市面上的其他產品都更堅固。

女： 有，我今天早上看到了。**(48)** 我希望這則廣告能有助於說服顧客購買我們最新系列的釣竿。

男： **(48)** 我相信它會的。**(49)** 我會與廣告公司聯繫，要求這則廣告也要刊登在其他的雜誌裡。

---

47. What is mentioned about the product?
- [A] It is affordable.
- **[B] It is superior to competitors'.**
- [C] It is safe for children to use.
- [D] It is simple to install.

48. According to the man, what will the advertisement help to do?
- **[A] Promote new products**
- [B] Increase stock value
- [C] Encourage innovations
- [D] Reduce customer complaints

47. 對話裡提到這項產品的哪一點？
- [A] 它不貴
- **[B] 它優於競爭者的產品**
- [C] 它可以讓孩童安全使用
- [D] 它很容易安裝

48. 根據男子，這則廣告將將有助於什麼？
- **[A] 推廣新產品**
- [B] 提高股票價值
- [C] 鼓勵創新
- [D] 減少顧客投訴

49. What will the man do next?
- A Create a website
- B Buy a magazine
- C Revise an article
- **D Contact an agency**

(NEW)

50–52 conversation

M1: Heights Department Store, Michael speaking, how can I help you?

W: Hi, (50) **this is Sarah. I purchased a Regan cashmere coat from you two weeks ago, but I still haven't received it yet. I was told that I'd get it in 2 to 3 days.**

M1: Hold on a second; (51) **you'll need to speak with a representative from the Regan boutique. I'll transfer your call.**

W: No problem.

M2: Hello, this is Regan Luxury Boutique. Brian speaking. What can I help you with?

W: Yes, Brian, this is Sarah. I bought a coat from you two weeks ago and I'm wondering what happened to the shipment.

M2: Oh, hello Sarah, I'm sorry to hear that you haven't received it yet. Let me check the computer here. (52) **Can you give me your full name?**

W: Sure, it's Sarah Jane Park.

50. Why is the woman calling?
- **A She hasn't received her product.**
- B She was overcharged for the item.
- C She wants a product exchanged.
- D She wants to return a product.

51. Why does Michael transfer the call?
- A He is busy with another customer.
- B The woman requested another representative.
- **C The woman called the wrong department.**
- D The manager is unavailable.

52. What does Brian ask the woman for?
- A The tracking number
- B Her receipt
- **C Her full name**
- D The product name

49. 男子接下來要做什麼？
- A 建構網站
- B 購買雜誌
- C 修改文章
- **D 聯繫代理商**

50–52 對話

男1：高地百貨公司，我是麥克。有什麼可以為您服務的地方嗎？

女：嗨，(50) 我是莎拉。我兩個星期前從你們那裡購買了一件里根喀什米爾羊毛大衣，但我都還沒收到。我被告知兩到三天就會收到。

男1：請稍等。(51) 請您與里根精品店的客服談談，我幫您轉接。

女：沒問題。

男2：哈囉，這裡是里根高級精品店。我是布萊恩。有什麼可以為您服務的地方嗎？

女：是的，布萊恩。我是莎拉。我兩週前從你們那裡買了一件大衣，我不知道運送出了什麼問題。

男2：喔，哈囉，莎拉。很抱歉您還沒有收到。讓我查電腦。(52) 可以告訴我您的全名嗎？

女：當然。全名是莎拉・珍・帕克。

50. 女子為何打電話？
- **A 她還沒收到產品**
- B 她買東西被多收錢
- C 她想要更換產品
- D 她想要退還產品

51. 麥克為何轉接電話？
- A 他忙著處理另一名顧客的事
- B 女子要求找另一名客服
- **C 女子打錯部門了**
- D 經理不在

52. 布萊恩向女子要什麼？
- A 追蹤號碼
- B 她的收據
- **C 她的全名**
- D 產品名稱

53–55 conversation

M： Hi, Mrs. West. **(53) Everything is set up for your anniversary party tonight.** If you can arrive at about 6 p.m. that would be great.

W： 6 p.m.? I have meetings until 8 p.m. tonight. You know we are merging with another company at the moment, so it's a very important time for our company.

M： Oh, no! I've scheduled the band to play from six to ten o'clock. And dinner will be served at seven o'clock.

W： Well, I wish you would have told me about this earlier.

M： **(54) But it's your fifth anniversary party.**

W： OK. **(55) I will cancel my last meeting tonight and arrive around 6:30.** So, don't worry; everything will be fine. I will just be a little late.

53–55 對話

男： 嗨，威斯特女士。**(53) 您今晚週年派對的一切都已經準備就緒。** 如果您可以在晚上六點抵達，那就太好了。

女： 晚上六點？我今晚要開會到八點。您知道我們正要與另一家公司合併，現在對於我們公司是很重要的時刻。

男： 糟了⋯⋯我已經安排樂團從六點演出到十點，晚餐會在七點上菜。

女： 要是你早一點告訴我就好了。

男： **(54) 但這是您的五週年派對耶。**

女： 好吧。**(55) 我會取消今晚最後一場會議，並在大約六點半時抵達。** 所以，別擔心，一切都會沒事。我只會稍微晚一點到。

---

53. What are the speakers mainly discussing?
　　Ⓐ Merging with another company
　　Ⓑ Last month's sales reports
　　Ⓒ The woman's anniversary party
　　Ⓓ When the band will arrive

54. What does the man mean when he says, "But it's your fifth anniversary party"?
　　Ⓐ He wants her to change her schedule.
　　Ⓑ He thinks it's not important.
　　Ⓒ He will tell the band not to come.
　　Ⓓ He wants her to go to the meetings.

55. What solution does the woman provide?
　　Ⓐ She will cancel the band.
　　Ⓑ She will cancel the dinner service.
　　Ⓒ She will cancel her meeting.
　　Ⓓ She will fire the man.

53. 對話者們主要在討論什麼？
　　Ⓐ 與另一家公司合併
　　Ⓑ 上個月的銷售報告
　　Ⓒ 女子的週年派對
　　Ⓓ 樂團何時會抵達

54. 男子說「但這是你的五週年派對耶」，他指的是什麼？
　　Ⓐ 他希望她改變行程
　　Ⓑ 他認為這不重要
　　Ⓒ 他會請樂團不要來
　　Ⓓ 他希望她去開會

55. 女子提出什麼解決方法？
　　Ⓐ 她將要取消樂團
　　Ⓑ 她將要取消晚餐服務
　　Ⓒ 她將要取消會議
　　Ⓓ 她將要開除男子

56–58 conversation

M：Hi, Susan. This is Rob. **(56) Did you get the flowers I sent you?**

W：Yes, I did. But unfortunately I'm allergic to sunflowers. I had to go to the hospital because they had been in my office for several hours.

M：**(58) Oh, I thought you would like them.**

W：You know I'm allergic to pollen, Rob. How could you forget? **(57) You should take me to dinner tomorrow night to apologize.**

M：OK. I will! I'll take you somewhere nice. Sorry about the flowers!

56. Why is the man calling the woman?
- A To check the sales figures
- **B To check if she received the flowers**
- C To check if she wanted to go to dinner
- D To check if the documents were ready

57. What does the woman say he should do?
- A Take her to the hospital
- B Pay her hospital bills
- **C Take her out for dinner**
- D Buy her more flowers

58. Why does the man say, "I thought you would like them"?
- **A To express disappointment**
- B To show appreciation
- C To show respect
- D To show he thinks it's funny

59–61 conversation

M1：Hi Bob. Hi Karen. The reason I called you in is to talk about the budget. **(59) This biggest issue is that our entertainment expenses are way too high.** I think we need to reduce the amount we are spending on company lunches and dinners.

W：**(60) Yes, I agree. I think we need to start paying for our own lunches.**

56–58 對話

男：嗨，蘇珊，我是羅伯。**(56) 你收到我送給你的花了嗎？**

女：有，我收到了。但很可惜，我對向日葵過敏。我得去就醫，因為它們放在我的辦公室裡好幾個小時。

男：**(58) 喔，我以為你會喜歡那些花。**

女：你知道我對花粉過敏，羅伯。你怎麼可以忘記？**(57) 你明天晚上該請我吃晚餐做為道歉。**

男：好，我會的。我會帶你去個好地方。關於那些花，我很抱歉！

56. 男子為何打電話給女子？
- A 確認銷售數字
- **B 確認她是否收到花**
- C 確認她是否想去吃晚餐
- D 確認文件是否備妥了

57. 女子說他應該做什麼？
- A 帶她去醫院
- B 支付她就醫的費用
- **C 請她吃晚餐**
- D 買更多花給她

58. 男子為何說「我以為你會喜歡那些花」？
- **A 為了表達失望**
- B 為了表示感激
- C 為了表示尊敬
- D 為了表示他認為這很好笑

59–61 對話

男1：嗨，鮑伯。嗨，凱倫。我找你們來的原因是要討論預算的事情。**(59) 最大的問題是，我們的交際費太高了。** 我認為我們需要減少公司午餐和晚餐的開銷。

女：**(60) 是的，我同意。我認為我們需要開始自費買自己的午餐。**

23

M2 : I agree with both of you, but I think we need to keep entertaining clients. I think if we pay for our own lunches, then that will leave money to take clients out for dinner.

M1 : That's a pretty good idea, Bob. Karen, does that sound OK with you?

W : I think that's a great compromise, Bob. **(61) I will make a monthly budget plan and email it to you this afternoon.**

男2：我的看法和你們兩人相同，但我認為需要繼續招待客戶。我想如果我們為自己的午餐付錢，這樣就能把錢省下來請客戶吃晚餐。

男1：那是個好點子，鮑伯。凱倫，你覺得這聽起來可行嗎？

女：我認為那是個很好的折衷方法，鮑伯。**(61) 我會做出每月的預算計劃，今天下午用電子郵件寄給你們。**

---

59. What is the main problem the speakers are discussing?
- A What they should eat for lunch
- B Going out for dinner
- **C High entertainment expenses**
- D Getting more customers

59. 對話者在討論的主要問題是什麼？
- A 他們午餐該吃什麼
- B 外出吃晚餐
- **C 高額的交際費**
- D 獲得更多顧客

60. What does the woman suggest they do?
- A Stop going out for dinner
- B Reduce client numbers
- C Stop having lunches
- **D Pay for their own lunches**

60. 女子建議他們做什麼？
- A 不再外出吃晚餐
- B 減少客戶人數
- C 不再吃午餐
- **D 午餐自費**

61. What does the woman say she will send the man?
- **A A monthly budget plan**
- B This month's sales report
- C The old budget plan
- D Last month's marketing materials

61. 女子說他會寄什麼給男子？
- **A 月度預算計劃**
- B 本月的銷售報告
- C 舊的預算計劃
- D 上個月的行銷資料

(NEW)
62–64 conversation

W : Do you know why the lifts will be out of order next week?

M : **(62) Last week, Harriet saw that there were some inspectors in the building next door.** Our maintenance checks aren't up to date, so if we get inspected, the building manager might be in trouble.

W : Oh, OK. But did you see the work schedule? **(63) The busiest wing in the hospital will be closed from 8 to 9 a.m.** So many people will be arriving to work at that time. I don't understand why they would schedule the repair at that time.

62–64 對話

女：你知道為何下星期電梯不能用嗎？

男：**(62) 上星期哈莉葉在隔壁大樓看見一群檢查員。**我們的維修檢查沒有更新，因此如果我們受檢，大樓經理會有麻煩。

女：喔，好吧。但是你看到工作時間表了嗎？**(63) 上午八點到九點，醫院最忙碌的一側會關閉。**那是很多人的上班時間，我不懂他們為何要在那時間安排維修。

M：Hmm . . . Yes, you're right. **(64) I think we should talk to Dr. Franklin about this.** I'm sure he can get the schedule changed.

W：I'd better do it now so the technicians have time to reschedule.

男：嗯……對，你說的沒錯。**(64) 我認為我們應該與富蘭克林醫師討論此事。** 我確定他可以更改時程。

女：我最好現在就去。這樣技術人員就有時間重新安排時程。

Lifts will be out of order 電梯將無法使用	
North Wing 北側	8:00 a.m.–9:00 a.m. 上午 8:00–9:00
East Wing 東側	11:00 a.m.–12:00 p.m. 上午 11:00 – 中午 12:00
South Wing 南側	1:30 p.m.–2:30 p.m. 下午 1:30–2:30
West Wing 西側	3:00 p.m.–4:00 p.m. 下午 3:00–4:00

62. What did Harriet see last week?
   A Technicians in the building next door
   B Technicians posting about lift repairs
   C Some technicians installing lighting
   D Her boss having a meeting with some technicians

63. Look at the graphic. Which is the busiest wing in the hospital?
   A West
   B East
   C North
   D South

64. What does the man suggest the woman do?
   A Cancel the repairs immediately
   B Talk to Dr. Franklin
   C Ask Dr. Franklin to lunch
   D Close the North Wing

62. 哈莉葉特上星期看見什麼？
   A 技術人員在隔壁大樓
   B 技術人員在張貼電梯維修的公告
   C 技術人員在安裝燈具
   D 她的老闆正與技術人員開會

63. 參看圖表，何者是醫院最忙碌的一側？
   A 西
   B 東
   C 北
   D 南

64. 男子建議女子做什麼？
   A 立刻取消維修
   B 與富蘭克林醫師談話
   C 請富蘭克林醫師吃午餐
   D 關閉北側

65–67 conversation

W：Good morning, this is Hardy's All Purpose. How can I help you?

M：**(65) Hello. I picked up a camping pack this morning, but it's missing some of the items.**

W：Do you know which items aren't there?

65–67 對話

女：早安，這裡是哈地全方位，有什麼需要服務的嗎？

男：**(65) 哈囉，我今天早上買了一個露營套裝組，但裡面缺了某些東西。**

女：你知道裡面缺了哪些物品嗎？

M : **(66) I have the mats, sleeping bags, and the carry bag. I thought there was supposed to be one more item in there.**

W : Ah yes, I know what it is. Are you able to drop in the store today? **(67) I will give you a 15% refund because of the mistake.**

M : Oh, really? That's very kind of you. I'll come this afternoon and pick it up.

男：**(66)** 裡面有墊子、睡袋和手提袋。我認為裡面應該還要有一項物品。

女：啊，沒錯，我知道是什麼了。你今天可以來到店裡嗎？ **(67)** 因為這項疏失，我會幫你打八五折。

男：喔，真的嗎？你真好。我今天下午會過去拿。

Camping Pack 露營套裝組

4 Rectangular Sleeping Bags 四個長方形睡袋
4 Camping Mats 四個露營墊
Carry Bag 手提袋
Portable Gas Stove 可攜式瓦斯爐

---

65. Where does the woman likely work?
   - **A A camping store**
   - B A hardware store
   - C A medical clinic
   - D A shipping company

(NEW)
66. Look at the graphic. What is the man missing?
   - A Carry bag
   - **B Portable gas stove**
   - C Camping mats
   - D Sleeping bags

67. What does the woman offer to do?
   - A Give him a full refund
   - B Give him a 15% discount voucher
   - **C Give him a 15% refund**
   - D Give him a free tent

65. 女子可能在哪裡工作？
   - **A 露營用品店**
   - B 五金行
   - C 醫療診所
   - D 貨運公司

66. 參看圖表，男子少了什麼？
   - A 手提袋
   - **B 可攜式瓦斯爐**
   - C 露營墊
   - D 睡袋

67. 女子提出要做什麼？
   - A 給他全額退款
   - B 給他八五折優惠券
   - **C 給他八五折**
   - D 給他免費的帳篷

(NEW)
68–70 conversation

M : Hi, I have a carpet that is identical to this one here. **(68) I need it cleaned as I'm going to be selling my office soon.** There are 3 rooms.

W : **(69) Three rooms of that carpet would cost 750.**

68–70 對話

男：嗨，我有和這邊這個一模一樣的地毯。**(68)** 我需要找人清理它，因為我很快就要出售我的辦公室了，辦公室有三個房間。

女：**(69)** 三房的那種地毯要 750 元。

M：Oh, really? I thought you were advertising a 15% discount on all your carpets?

W：That discount only covers our frieze and shag pile carpets.

M：Hmm . . . **(70) I see. OK. I will need some time to think about it, and I will come back.**

男：喔，真的嗎？我以為你們廣告説所有地毯都打八五折？

女：那項折扣只適用於起絨粗呢和長絨粗呢地毯。

男：嗯……**(70) 我知道了，好吧，我需要一些時間考慮，我會再回來的。**

Henson's Corporate Cleaners
韓森公司清潔人員
Carpet Cleaning 地毯清潔

Frieze 起絨粗呢	$100 per room（每個房間）
Shag Pilet 長絨粗呢	$150 per room（每個房間）
Velvet 絲絨	$250 per room（每個房間）
Woven Carpet 編織地毯	$400 per room（每個房間）

68. What does the man say he is planning on doing with his office?
A Renovate it
B Sell it
C Clean it
D Repaint it

(NEW)

69. Look at the graphic. What is the carpet made of?
A Frieze
B Shag Pile
C Velvet
D Woven Carpet

70. What does the man say he will do?
A Buy the carpet today
B Ask his wife about it
C Tell his manager
D Think about it and come back

68. 男子説他打算要如何處理辦公室？
A 翻修
B 出售
C 清潔
D 重新粉刷

69. 參看圖表，地毯是什麼材質？
A 起絨粗呢
B 長絨粗呢
C 絲絨
D 編織地毯

70. 男子説他將會做什麼？
A 今天購買地毯
B 詢問妻子
C 告訴經理
D 考慮後再回覆

71–73 radio broadcast

W：You are listening to the news for the town of Clinton on your local CCBN radio station. **(71) School district officials have announced that they will be extending the deadline for new candidates to register for the upcoming school board election this May. (72) Remember, you can find the location of your voting district by visiting the official website of the town of Clinton. (73) We encourage all of the citizens of Clinton to exercise their right to vote in the May election.**

71. What is the announcement about?
  A An opinion survey
  B An upcoming election
  C An election outcome
  D A website update

72. What can listeners do on the website?
  A Register as a candidate
  B Cast their vote
  C Find some information
  D Enter a contest

73. What are listeners encouraged to do?
  A Participate in an official occasion
  B Reserve a ticket in advance
  C Exercise on a daily basis
  D Listen to an upcoming announcement

74–76 radio advertisement

M：Hello, everyone. **(74) Help us celebrate the 10-year anniversary of Salem Furniture Outlet in downtown Marion. (75) From now until the end of the month, you can get a free 22-inch flat-screen television with a purchase of $1,500 or more!** So come on down and check out our fine selection of couches, chairs, dining room tables, and much more. **(76) This anniversary offer only lasts until the end of the month.** Don't miss this great opportunity. Come in today!

71–73 電台廣播

女：你正在收聽的是柯林頓鎮本地電台 CCBN 的新聞報導。**(71) 教育局官員宣布，他們將延長教育委員會新候選人的登記期限，選舉將在五月舉行。(72) 請記得，你可以上柯林頓鎮的官方網站，找到你選區的位置。(73) 我們鼓勵柯林頓鎮的所有市民，在五月這場選舉中行使投票權。**

71. 這則廣播與什麼有關？
  A 意見調查
  B 近期選舉
  C 選舉結果
  D 網站更新

72. 聽眾可以在網站上做什麼？
  A 登記為候選人
  B 投票
  C 找到某些資訊
  D 參加比賽

73. 廣播鼓勵聽眾做什麼？
  A 參加官方活動
  B 提前訂票
  C 每天運動
  D 聆聽接下來的公告

74–76 電台廣告

男：哈囉，大家好。**(74) 來幫我們慶祝馬里蘭市區薩倫家具直營店的 10 週年慶吧。(75) 從現在起到月底，購物消費滿 1500 元以上，就可以免費獲得 22 吋平面電視！**因此，請來店看看我們精選的沙發、椅子、餐桌，還有許多其他商品。**(76) 週年慶優惠只到本月底。**別錯過這個大好機會，今天就過來！

74. What is the outlet store celebrating?
A **An anniversary**
B A festival
C An opening
D A holiday

75. What must customers do to receive the promotional offer?
A Become a member
B **Purchase a certain amount**
C Recommend some brands
D Trade in a television

76. When does the promotion end?
A At the beginning of next month
B At the end of the year
C On the second Sunday of the month
D **At the end of the month**

74. 這家直營店在慶祝什麼？
A **週年慶**
B 節慶
C 開幕
D 國定假日

75. 顧客必須做什麼才能獲得促銷優惠？
A 成為會員
B **達到消費門檻**
C 推薦某些品牌
D 以電視換購

76. 促銷何時結束？
A 下個月初
B 今年底
C 本月的第二個星期日
D **本月底**

77–79 instructions

M： Thank you for attending today's safety workshop. My name is Tim Hines, and I'll be instructing everyone on how to maintain a safe work environment. **(77) As you know, a factory is full of safety hazards. (78) I have looked over the history of accidents for this factory, and it appears most accidents happen during the night shift. (79) Therefore, my first suggestion for everyone here is to make sure you are getting enough sleep before your night shift.** Sufficient rest is one of the best methods for avoiding work accidents.

77–79 說明

男： 感謝大家參加今天的安全研習，我的名字是提姆‧海恩斯，我會教大家如何維持安全的工作環境。**(77)** 各位都知道，工廠裡充滿了工安危害。**(78)** 我看過這家工廠歷年來發生的意外事件，大部分的事故似乎都發生在晚班期間。**(79)** 因此，我給大家的第一個建議是，上晚班前務必要有充足的睡眠。充分休息是避免工作意外的最佳方法。

---

77. Who most likely are the listeners?
A Environmentalists
B Instructors
C **Factory workers**
D Factory consultants

78. What document has the speaker reviewed?
A An employee roster
B An annual budget
C A project overview
D **Accident reports**

77. 聽眾最有可能是什麼人？
A 環保人士
B 講師
C **工廠工人**
D 工廠諮詢員

78. 發話者看過了什麼文件？
A 員工名冊
B 年度預算
C 企劃概述
D **意外報告**

79. What does the speaker suggest listeners do?
- **Ⓐ Get enough rest**
- Ⓑ Work a day shift
- Ⓒ Receive more training
- Ⓓ Read a handout

80–82 telephone message

W： Hello, Roger. This is Jenna speaking. According to an email I received from Tina Miller, our business trip to Moscow has been postponed until next month. **(80) The factory we were scheduled to tour is closed for some renovations. (81) We will have to wait until the construction at the factory is finished. (82) In the meantime, I'll send you the revised travel itinerary for you to review.** Let me know if you have any questions about this change.

---

80. What is the purpose of the trip to Moscow?
- Ⓐ To finalize a contract
- **Ⓑ To visit a factory**
- Ⓒ To give a product demonstration
- Ⓓ To renovate a building

81. What is the reason for the postponed departure?
- Ⓐ A necessary document is not ready.
- **Ⓑ Some construction is underway.**
- Ⓒ A company has gone out of business.
- Ⓓ Building materials have not arrived yet.

82. What does the speaker say she will send to the listener?
- Ⓐ A copy of her passport
- Ⓑ A plane ticket
- **Ⓒ An itinerary**
- Ⓓ A blueprint

---

79. 發話者建議聽眾做什麼？
- **Ⓐ 有足夠休息**
- Ⓑ 上白班
- Ⓒ 接受更多訓練
- Ⓓ 閱讀講義

80–82 電話留言

女： 哈囉，羅傑，我是珍娜。根據提娜‧米勒寄給我的電子郵件，我們到莫斯科的出差已經延後到下個月了。 **(80) 我們安排好要參訪的工廠已經關閉，要進行翻修。(81) 我們得要等到工廠的工程結束。(82) 在此同時，我會把修訂過的旅遊行程表寄給你看。** 若你對於這項更動有任何問題，請告訴我。

80. 莫斯科之行的目的是什麼？
- Ⓐ 敲定合約
- **Ⓑ 參訪工廠**
- Ⓒ 進行產品示範
- Ⓓ 翻修建築物

81. 延遲出發的理由是什麼？
- Ⓐ 必要的文件未備妥
- **Ⓑ 工程正在進行中**
- Ⓒ 公司停止營運
- Ⓓ 尚未送來建築材料

82. 發話者說她會寄什麼給聽者？
- Ⓐ 她的護照影本
- Ⓑ 機票
- **Ⓒ 旅遊行程表**
- Ⓓ 藍圖

83–85 speech

W：Thank you, thank you so much. **(83) I feel truly honored to be promoted to executive chef at such a prestigious establishment such as Gray's on High Street.** I have been here for five years, and during that time we have been able to achieve a two-star Michelin rating. **(85) We have spent hundreds of hours in the kitchen at night perfecting our recipes and working on new and exciting culinary techniques. (84) I have to say, this promotion is not just for me. I could not have done this without highly skilled crew.** Their diligence and hard work have led to our success. So, please join me in giving them a warm round of applause. To our future!

83–85 演說

女：謝謝，非常感謝。**(83) 我真的覺得非常光榮，能在高街上如此知名的的蓋瑞餐廳裡晉升為行政總廚。**我已經在此工作五年，期間我們獲得了米其林的二星評比。**(85) 我們在廚房裡度過了數百小時的夜晚，完善我們的食譜並且精進新穎又令人興奮的廚藝技巧。(84) 我必須說，這次升遷不只是給我個人，若沒有如此廚藝精湛的團隊，我無法有這樣的成就。**他們的勤奮努力造就了我們的成功，因此，請和我一同為他們熱烈鼓掌。敬我們的未來！

83. What is the purpose of the speech?
- Ⓐ To announce a discovery
- Ⓑ To announce a retirement
- **Ⓒ To accept a promotion**
- Ⓓ To accept an award

(NEW)

84. Why does the speaker say: "I could not have done this without highly skilled crew"?
- **Ⓐ She wants to thank her team.**
- Ⓑ She hasn't worked on a team before.
- Ⓒ She dislikes her coworkers.
- Ⓓ She wants to accept the award.

85. Where most likely does the speaker work?
- Ⓐ At a hotel
- Ⓑ At a travel agency
- **Ⓒ At a restaurant**
- Ⓓ At a warehouse

83. 演說的目的是什麼？
- Ⓐ 要公布一項發現
- Ⓑ 要宣布退休
- **Ⓒ 要接受升遷**
- Ⓓ 要接受頒獎

84. 發話者為何說「若沒有如此廚藝精湛的團隊，我無法有這樣的成就」？
- **Ⓐ 她想要感謝她的團隊**
- Ⓑ 她先前未曾在團隊工作
- Ⓒ 她不喜歡同事
- Ⓓ 她想要接受頒獎

85. 發話者最有可能在哪裡工作？
- Ⓐ 在旅館
- Ⓑ 在旅行社
- **Ⓒ 在餐廳**
- Ⓓ 在倉庫

86–88 telephone message

W：**(86) I'm just calling because I wanted to say thank you so much for helping with the catering at last week's gallery opening.** I really wouldn't have been able to do it alone, and I'm so grateful that you helped me on such short notice. The green curry you made was absolutely delicious! **(87) You have to show me**

86–88 電話留言

女：**(86) 我打電話是想要向你道謝，因為你上星期協助藝術館開幕的外燴。**我真的不可能獨力完成這件事，而我很感謝你能臨危受命來幫我。你做的綠色咖哩真的很美味！**(87) 你一定要讓我看看食譜！**我想在場沒有一位嘉賓不喜歡那道菜。

the recipe! I think there was not a single person who didn't love that dish. **(88) Anyway, I'll see you next week for the Charity Ball. I'm really excited to see what dishes you cook for us!**

86. Why is the woman calling?

[A] **To express her gratitude**

[B] To discuss a recipe

[C] To report some news

[D] To make a complaint

(NEW)

87. What does the woman imply when she says, "you have to show me the recipe"?

[A] She didn't enjoy it.

[B] She wants to recommend a different ingredient.

[C] **She wants to cook the dish herself.**

[D] She wants her friend to try it.

88. Why is the woman looking forward to next week?

[A] She is going to the movies.

[B] She is taking her son to school.

[C] Some new project will be completed.

[D] **They will work together again.**

---

(88) 總之，我們下週慈善舞會見，我真的很興奮想知道你會為我們烹調什麼菜餚。

86. 女子為何打電話？

[A] **要表達謝意**

[B] 要討論食譜

[C] 要報告消息

[D] 要客訴

87. 女子說「你一定要讓我看看食譜」，她暗示什麼？

[A] 她不喜歡那道菜

[B] 她想要建議不同的食材

[C] **她想要自己做那道菜**

[D] 她想要讓朋友試做看看

88. 女子為何期待下個星期？

[A] 她要去看電影

[B] 她要帶兒子上學

[C] 某個新案子即將結案

[D] **他們將再次合作**

89–91 news report

W : **(89) In other news . . .** Bernburg Studios, which is the studio responsible for such blockbuster hits as *Rolling Hills*, and *Standing Tall* is looking to film a movie in Westchester. **(90) The CEO has made an announcement requesting someone to allow them to film inside their home.** In the movie, the chosen place will be the home of the Oscar winning actor Robert Holloway. **(91) The CEO admitted that it is awkward to impose upon someone's private life, but he also said he has received hundreds of applications. After all, this is Robert Holloway we are talking about.** The studio has not chosen a location yet, so if you are still interested, visit Bernburg Studios' website.

89–91 新聞報導

女：**(89)** 其他新聞……曾拍攝過《綿延山丘》和《屹立不搖》等賣座電影的伯恩堡電影公司要在威徹斯特拍片。**(90)** 該公司總裁公開宣告，想請求民眾讓他們進屋內拍攝，被選中的地方將是曾獲奧斯卡獎的影星羅伯特‧哈洛威在片中的家。**(91)** 該總裁承認，打擾別人的私生活很令人尷尬，但他也表示，他們已收到數百件的申請。畢竟，我們說的是羅伯特‧哈洛威。電影公司還沒有選定地點，因此如果你仍然有興趣，可以上伯恩堡電影公司的網站。

89. Who most likely is the speaker?
- A A news editor
- B A filmmaker
- **C A news reporter**
- D A movie star

90. What is Bernberg Studios looking for?
- A An actress
- **B A filming location**
- C A new script
- D More ideas for movies

(NEW)
91. What does the speaker imply when she says, "After all, this is Robert Holloway we are talking about"?
- **A Robert Holloway is very famous.**
- B Robert Holloway owns the house.
- C She will interview him next.
- D She doesn't know who Robert Holloway is.

89. 發話者最有可能是什麼人？
- A 新聞編輯
- B 製片家
- **C 新聞記者**
- D 電影明星

90. 伯恩堡電影公司在尋找什麼？
- A 女演員
- **B 拍攝地點**
- C 新的劇本
- D 更多拍片的想法

91. 發話者說「畢竟我們說的是羅伯特‧哈洛威」，她暗示什麼？
- **A 羅伯特‧哈洛威非常有名。**
- B 羅伯特‧哈洛威擁有那間房子。
- C 她接下來要訪問他。
- D 她不知道羅伯特‧哈洛威是誰。

92–94 advertisement

M：Hello, Happy Day shoppers. **(92) It's our anniversary, and we're offering 50% off the prices advertised on everything until Friday night at midnight!** Save on everything in our store, including our premium selection of pillows. Collect the whole series of Mama San brand pillows for half off! **(93) At the end of our sale, we will be restocking our shelves with a brand-new inventory**, so everything must go! **(94) Be sure to stop by our stylists. Bring a picture of a room you want to redecorate, and we will help you decide what colors to choose. Make every day a Happy Day!** Thank you for being our loyal customers, and we look forward to making you smile!

92–94 廣告

男：哈囉，快樂日子的買家們。**(92)** 現在正值我們的週年慶，星期五晚上午夜以前，我們會提供所有廣告商品半價優惠！購買我們店內的各種商品省錢吧，包含我們的精選枕頭，現在只要半價就能收藏全系列「媽媽桑」品牌的枕頭！**(93)** 特賣會結束時，我們將上架全新商品，因此要清空全數現有商品！**(94)** 請務必來找我們的設計師，只要帶著你想要重新裝潢的房間照片，我們就會幫你挑選顏色，讓你的每一天都是「快樂日子」！感謝你對我們的忠實惠顧，我們期待能讓你開心微笑！

MAMA SAN premium pillows
媽媽桑高級枕頭

Beauty Sleep 美容睡眠	£30.00（英鎊）
Soft Night 輕柔之夜	£35.00（英鎊）
Dreamtime 夢幻時光	£42.00（英鎊）
Lovely Rest 美麗休憩	£50.00（英鎊）

92. Look at the graphic. How much can a shopper purchase the Dreamtime Pillow for before Friday?
- A £15.00
- B £11.50
- **C £21.00**
- D £50.00

93. What is indicated about Happy Day?
- A They have a wide variety of toys.
- **B They are bringing in more merchandise.**
- C They specialize in low-end furniture.
- D They are going out of business this Friday.

94. What service does Happy Day offer?
- **A Personalized interior design advice**
- B Free shipping
- C Home installation
- D Wall papering services

---

92. 參看圖表，買家在星期五之前可以用多少錢買到「夢幻時光」枕頭？
- A 15.00 英鎊
- B 11.50 英鎊
- **C 21.00 英鎊**
- D 50.00 英鎊

93. 關於快樂日子，廣告中有提到什麼？
- A 他們有各式各樣的玩具。
- **B 他們要進更多的商品。**
- C 他們專營廉價家具。
- D 他們本週五要結束營業。

94. 快樂日子提供什麼服務？
- **A 個人化的室內設計建議**
- B 免費運送
- C 居家安裝
- D 貼壁紙服務

95–97 telephone message

M： Hello, this is Trent Herrington from Blanders & Co. We recently received an order from you, and there are some missing items. **(95) On the invoice it clearly says we ordered 30 case binders, but we only received 20. We also did not receive any of the legal pads we ordered. (96) We have some important cases today, and we need those case binders to organize our client's defense professionally. (96) (97) As a law firm it is very important that we arrive to the court organized.** Is it possible for us to pick up the binders and legal pads this morning? Please call me back on 2612-4547 as soon as possible. Thanks.

95–97 電話留言

男： 你好，我是布蘭德斯事務所的特倫特・海靈頓。我們最近收到貴公司寄來的貨品，但有些東西遺漏了。**(95)** 發票上清楚顯示，我們訂了 30 個盒裝文件夾，但是我們只收到 20 個。我們也沒收到訂購的黃色橫條記事本。**(96)** 我們今天有幾個重要的案子，需要用到盒裝文件夾，才能專業地整理好委託人的辯護。**(96)(97)** 我們是法律事務所，上法庭時必須要條理分明。我們可以早上去拿文件夾和黃色橫條記事本嗎？請盡快回電給我，號碼是 2612-4547。謝謝。

ORDER FORM OF BLANDERS & CO. 布蘭德斯事務所的訂單 14 March 3 月 14 日	
Product 產品	**Quantity 數量**
Case binders 盒裝文件夾	30
Envelopes 信封	20
Flags & Tabs 指示標籤和索引標籤	40
Legal pads 黃色橫條記事本	10

95. Look at the graphic. How many items were not delivered in total?
- [A] 40
- [B] 30
- **[C] 20**
- [D] 10

96. According to the speaker, why are the case binders important?
- [A] To look professional in the office
- **[B] To look professional in court**
- [C] To organize their financial record
- [D] To maintain the deadline

97. Where does Trent Herrington most likely work?
- [A] At an accounting firm
- **[B] At a law firm**
- [C] At a patenting firm
- [D] At a catering business

95. 參看圖表，總共缺了多少件物品？
- [A] 40
- [B] 30
- **[C] 20**
- [D] 10

96. 根據發話者，盒裝文件夾為何很重要？
- [A] 要在辦公室裡表現得很專業
- **[B] 要在法庭上表現得很專業**
- [C] 要整理他們的財務紀錄
- [D] 要趕上截止期限

97. 特倫特・海靈頓最有可能在哪裡工作？
- [A] 會計事務所
- **[B] 法律事務所**
- [C] 專利事務所
- [D] 外燴公司

98–100 tour guide

W： Welcome aboard the Midnight Cruise, Loveport's most romantic evening! **(98) We will be spending the majority of our cruise in Billing's Bay, (100) but we will also be following the coastline of Eagle Island to Port Lewis for a champagne toast.** During our cruise, our host, **(99) Star Master Jenkins, will be directing you through the constellations that are in view, and with any luck we will be able to witness tonight's meteor shower!** While we are cruising, we ask that you wear your life jackets at all times when on deck for your safety. If you begin to feel sea sick at any time, I encourage you to visit our onboard clinic for some medication. Now I would like to ask everybody to join the captain in the stateroom for a rundown of this evening's services!

98–100 導覽

女： 歡迎登上午夜航行號，度過樂芙港最浪漫的夜晚！ **(98) 我們航行的大部分時間都會在比琳海灣，(100) 但是也會循著老鷹島的海岸線航行到路易斯港喝香檳。** 航行期間，我們的主持人 **(99) 史塔詹金斯會指引您欣賞今晚會出現的星座。運氣好的話，我們將能看到今晚的流星雨！** 航行期間，我們要求各位在甲板上時要隨時穿著救生衣，以策安全。若你在任何時候開始暈船，建議您去船上的醫務室取藥。現在我想請各位和船長一起進入船艙裡，聽取今晚各項服務的詳細報告！

MIDNIGHT CRUISE ITINERARY 午夜航行號的行程表

5 p.m. 下午 5 點	Captain's address 船長致詞
6 p.m. 下午 6 點	Cocktails and dinner 雞尾酒和晚餐
7 p.m. 晚上 7 點	Constellation orientation 星座介紹
8 p.m. – 10 p.m. 晚上 8–10 點	Social mixer 社交活動
10 p.m. 晚上 10 點	Port Lewis for champagne toast 路易斯港喝香檳
11 p.m. 晚上 11 點	Cast off and back to Billing's Bay 解纜啟返回到比琳海灣
12 a.m. 午夜 12 點	Midnight constellation lesson and meteor shower on Top Deck 頂層甲板的午夜星座課和流星雨

98. Where will the cruise spend most of its time?
[A] Eagle Island
[B] Port Lewis
[C] Billing's Bay
[D] Socializing

98. 航行的大部分時間會待在哪裡？
[A] 老鷹島
[B] 路易斯港
[C] 比琳海灣
[D] 社交活動

99. Who is Star Master Jenkins?
[A] Host
[B] Captain
[C] Bartender
[D] Security guard

99. 史塔詹金斯是什麼人？
[A] 主持人
[B] 船長
[C] 酒保
[D] 保全人員

100. Look at the graphic. How long will the cruise stop at Port Lewis?
[A] All evening
[B] 3 hours
[C] 2 hours
[D] 1 hour

100. 參看圖表，船將在路易斯港停留多久？
[A] 整個晚上
[B] 三小時
[C] 二小時
[D] 一小時

ACTUAL TEST ⑦

PART 1 P. 102-105   25

1. Ⓐ They are drinking cups of coffee.
   Ⓑ He is pointing at some information.
   Ⓒ The man is writing something on the document.
   Ⓓ All of the women are looking at the man.

2. Ⓐ He is mixing the snow.
   Ⓑ He is making snow for skiing.
   Ⓒ He is clearing some snow with a snow blower.
   Ⓓ He is cleaning the road with a broom.

3. **Ⓐ The cars are being transported in a truck.**
   Ⓑ The cars are being fixed.
   Ⓒ There are many people in the cars.
   Ⓓ There are cars on the top level of the truck.

4. **Ⓐ She is pumping gas into the car.**
   Ⓑ She is paying for the gas.
   Ⓒ She is changing the oil in her car.
   Ⓓ She is putting air into her tires.

5. Ⓐ They are fixing the computer.
   Ⓑ They are pointing at the computer screen.
   Ⓒ They are both holding documents.
   Ⓓ They are pointing at each other.

6. Ⓐ She is wearing long pants.
   Ⓑ She is paying the bill.
   Ⓒ Her reflection is in the mirror.
   Ⓓ She is looking at her reflection.

PART 2 P. 106   26

7. Who are you going to send on the business trip?
   Ⓐ I've picked Susan in accounting.
   Ⓑ It was a very rewarding trip.
   Ⓒ At the start of next year.

8. Why don't we go for a bike ride tomorrow?
   Ⓐ I gave Mr. Holland a ride to the airport.
   Ⓑ That sounds like fun.
   Ⓒ It was 3:30.

---

1. Ⓐ 他們正在喝咖啡。
   Ⓑ 他指著一些資料。
   Ⓒ 男子正在文件上寫字。
   Ⓓ 女子全都看著男子。

2. Ⓐ 他正在混合雪。
   Ⓑ 他正在造雪以供滑雪。
   Ⓒ 他正在用除雪機除雪。
   Ⓓ 他正在用掃帚清理道路。

3. **Ⓐ 汽車正被卡車運送。**
   Ⓑ 汽車在維修中。
   Ⓒ 很多人在車上。
   Ⓓ 汽車在卡車的上層。

4. **Ⓐ 她正在幫汽車加油。**
   Ⓑ 她正在付油錢。
   Ⓒ 她正在為汽車換油。
   Ⓓ 她正在為輪胎打氣。

5. Ⓐ 他們在修理電腦。
   Ⓑ 他們指著電腦螢幕。
   Ⓒ 他們兩人都拿著文件。
   Ⓓ 他們指著彼此。

6. Ⓐ 她穿著長褲。
   Ⓑ 她在付帳。
   Ⓒ 她的倒影在鏡子裡。
   Ⓓ 她看著她的倒影。

7. 你要派誰去出差？
   Ⓐ 我已選了會計部門的蘇珊。
   Ⓑ 這是一趟很有收穫的旅程。
   Ⓒ 在明年初。

8. 我們明天何不去騎腳踏車呢？
   Ⓐ 我載哈蘭德先生去機場。
   Ⓑ 聽起來很有趣。
   Ⓒ 當時是下午三點半。

9. Did Monica answer the phone, or was she away from the office?
  A I'll mark it on the calendar at the office.
  B Please leave a message.
  C She was meeting her client at that time.

10. Which theater is the movie showing at?
  A He's a famous actor.
  B I'll have to check.
  C She's over there.

11. Why is there a moving truck parked outside?
  A We're removing coffee stains.
  B Into a bigger office.
  C Because new neighbors are moving in.

12. What should I bring on the camping trip?
  A You'll need hiking boots.
  B He's on a business trip with his colleague.
  C Yes, we should.

13. You will receive five days off next month.
  A I had a great time at the resort.
  B I turned the equipment off.
  C Will it be paid or unpaid?

14. Did Olivia already return the rental car?
  A Yes, just this morning.
  B There are several different models.
  C I'm ready to order now.

15. Isn't this area off limits to motor vehicles?
  A It's fifty percent off today.
  B There is a walking path only.
  C Actually, it's a stolen vehicle.

16. I'd recommend using the stairs today.
  A Can you tell me why?
  B No, I didn't stare straight into the camera.
  C I usually use the copy machine at the corner.

17. When will I receive this month's paycheck?
  A The conference will be held next month.
  B Before March 3.
  C In the bottom drawer.

9. 是莫妮卡接的電話，還是她不在辦公室？
  A 我會將它標記在辦公室的日曆上。
  B 請留言。
  C 她當時正在與客戶會面。

10. 這部電影在哪個戲院播放？
  A 他是知名演員。
  B 我得查查看。
  C 她就在那裡。

11. 搬家公司的卡車為何停在外頭？
  A 我們正在清除咖啡污漬。
  B 搬進比較大的辦公室。
  C 因為新鄰居正要搬入。

12. 我應該帶什麼去露營？
  A 你會需要健行用的靴子。
  B 他和同事出差了。
  C 是的，我們應該要。

13. 你下個月會有五天休假。
  A 我在度假村玩得很愉快。
  B 我關掉了設備。
  C 有薪價還是無薪假？

14. 奧莉維亞已經歸還租賃的車子了嗎？
  A 是的，就在今天早上。
  B 有好幾種不同的型號。
  C 我已經準備好要點餐了。

15. 這個地區不是禁止汽車進入嗎？
  A 今天打五折。
  B 這裡只有步道。
  C 事實上，這是失竊車輛。

16. 我建議今天走樓梯。
  A 可以告訴我為什麼嗎？
  B 不，我沒有直視相機鏡頭。
  C 我通常使用角落的那台影印機。

17. 我何時會收到這個月的薪水？
  A 會議將在下個月舉行。
  B 三月三日之前。
  C 在最底層的抽屜裡。

18. Do we have enough gas to get to the airport?
    A Who arrived at the airport yesterday?
    B We don't have to worry about it.
    C She's the chief flight attendant.

19. Why hasn't the travel itinerary been sent out yet?
    A At Terminal 6.
    B He was a travel agent.
    C We haven't decided on the dates.

20. Who forgot to turn off the lights last night?
    A We were waiting at the traffic lights.
    B I'm guessing it was John.
    C Kelly will take a day off tomorrow.

21. We are offering a promotional deal at the moment.
    A Congratulations on your promotion.
    B What benefit can I get?
    C Jenny will deal with the complaint.

22. I can borrow your book for a few days, can't I?
    A A few coworkers.
    B Of course. It's no trouble at all.
    C They booked tickets in advance.

23. Didn't your team improve your sales figures compared to last month?
    A Yes, the budget proposal is due this Friday.
    B Actually, they were about the same.
    C I couldn't figure out how to use this product.

24. How can I find her contact information?
    A We negotiated a contract.
    B By Wednesday at the latest.
    C Check the client list.

25. Where is the coffee shop you recommended?
    A I usually wear a suit.
    B It's across from the post office.
    C It's 3 o'clock sharp.

26. Would you like to drive instead of me?
    A It looks like he missed the bus.
    B Yes, I'll call right now.
    C Sorry, I can't. I forgot my glasses.

18. 我們的油夠開到機場嗎？
    A 昨天是誰抵達機場了？
    B 我們不需要擔心這件事。
    C 她是座艙長。

19. 旅遊行程表為何還沒寄出？
    A 在第六航空站。
    B 他以前是旅遊業者。
    C 我們尚未決定好日期。

20. 昨晚誰忘了關燈？
    A 我們當時在等紅綠燈。
    B 我猜想是約翰。
    C 凱莉明天會請假一天。

21. 我們目前有提供促銷方案。
    A 恭喜升官。
    B 我可以得到什麼好處？
    C 珍妮會處理這起客訴。

22. 我可以把你的書借走幾天，可以嗎？
    A 幾位同事。
    B 當然，沒問題。
    C 他們提前訂票了。

23. 與上個月相比，你團隊的銷售額沒有提高嗎？
    A 是的，預算提案的期限是這星期五。
    B 實際上，銷售額大致相同。
    C 我不知道要如何使用這個產品。

24. 我要如何找到她的聯絡資訊？
    A 我們談了一項合約。
    B 最晚在星期三。
    C 去查客戶名單。

25. 你推薦的咖啡店在哪裡？
    A 我通常穿西裝。
    B 在郵局對面。
    C 現在三點整。

26. 你想要代替我開車嗎？
    A 他似乎錯過了公車。
    B 是的，我現在就打電話。
    C 抱歉，我不行。我忘了戴眼鏡。

27. Did you say you were stopping by today or tomorrow?
  A Actually, I said this weekend.
  B A nice day for a walk.
  C Yeah, I thought so, too.

28. Food will be catered for tonight's party, won't it?
  A It was my birthday party.
  B It's scheduled to arrive at 6 o'clock.
  C No, he isn't registered here.

29. Isn't Mr. Rolland away from the office this week?
  A Yes, he comes back next Monday.
  B This product will be released next week.
  C Don't throw the receipt away.

30. I fixed the printer in the break room this morning.
  A You're welcome.
  B Was it out of order?
  C I was in the meeting room.

31. What did the tennis instructor say?
  A She said to practice more.
  B Have you decided on a date?
  C I told you so.

27. 你是說你要今天還是明天來訪？
  A 實際上，我是說週末。
  B 很適合散步的日子。
  C 是的，我也這麼認為。

28. 今晚派對會提供餐點，對不對？
  A 那是我的生日派對。
  B 餐點預計會在晚上六點送達。
  C 不，他沒有被登記在這裡。

29. 羅蘭先生這星期不會來上班吧？
  A 是的，他下星期一會回來。
  B 這項產品下星期會上市。
  C 別丟了那份食譜。

30. 我今天早上在修理休息室的印表機。
  A 不客氣。
  B 它壞了嗎？
  C 我在會議室。

31. 網球教練說了什麼？
  A 她說要多練習。
  B 你決定好日期了嗎？
  C 我就說吧。

PART 3 P. 107-111

32–34 conversation

W：Hi, Mark. This is Julie in accounting. **(32) Our printer has broken down again, and nobody in our department knows how to fix it. Could you stop by and give us a hand?**

M：**(33) I wish I could help, but I have a meeting with an important client in half an hour.** I have to be fully prepared when he arrives.

W：I understand. **(34) I'll try to find an instruction manual. I hope it will help me figure out what exactly is wrong.**

M：All right. I'll check on you right after the meeting.

32–34 對話

女：嗨，馬克。我是會計部門的茱莉。(32) 我們的印表機又故障了，我們部門沒人知道如何修理。你可以過來幫我們嗎？

男：(33) 真希望我能幫忙，但我半小時後要與一位重要的客戶開會。我必須要做好充分準備等他來。

女：我了解。(34) 我會試著找使用手冊，我希望它能幫我找到問題所在。

男：好的，開完會後我就立刻去找你。

TEST 7

PART 3

309

32. What does the woman ask the man to do?
   A Introduce a new client
   B Help to prepare a presentation
   C Repair malfunctioning equipment
   D Look for an instruction manual

33. Why is the man unable to help?
   A He has to meet a major client soon.
   B He finds the problem too complicated.
   C He isn't nearby at the moment.
   D He doesn't have the necessary tools.

34. What will the woman do next?
   A Attempt to solve the problem herself
   B Cancel an appointment
   C Print out a document
   D Have a meeting with a client

35–37 conversation

W : **(35) Mr. Hawke, I just looked over our projected sales for this month and it looks like our current inventory of televisions won't be enough to meet demand.**

M : Do you think so? But I thought we increased our stock this month compared to last. How are we already running out?

W : Well, all of the advertisements we placed seem to be having the intended effect. **(36) Thanks to the promotional sale this month, we are selling a lot more televisions than usual.**

M : **(37) OK, if anyone tries to buy a television that is out of stock, tell them that they can still get the same promotional deal next month as well.**

35. What problem does the woman mention?
   A The advertisements are not widely circulated.
   B The store inventory is inadequate.
   C The discounted price is not competitive.
   D The product is not selling well.

36. What does the woman say about this month's sales figures?
   A They are beginning to decrease.
   B They are similar to last month's figures.
   C They are unusually high.
   D They are impossible to predict.

32. 女子要求男子做什麼？
   A 介紹新客戶
   B 協助準備簡報
   C 修理故障的設備
   D 尋找使用手冊

33. 男子為何無法幫忙？
   A 他很快要去見大客戶
   B 他覺得這個問題太複雜
   C 他現在不在附近
   D 他沒有必要的工具

34. 女子接著會做什麼？
   A 嘗試自己解決問題
   B 取消預約
   C 列印一份文件
   D 與客戶開會

35–37 對話

女：**(35) 赫克先生，我剛看過我們這個月的銷售預估，我們目前電視的庫存似乎供不應求。**

男：你這麼認為嗎？但我以為我們這個月的存貨跟上個月比已經增加了，怎麼會快不夠了呢？

女：嗯，我們買的所有廣告似乎達到預期的效果。**(36) 因為這個月的促銷活動，我們賣出的電視比平常多很多。**

男：**(37) 好的，如果有人要買缺貨的電視，告訴他們，下個月還是能享有相同的折扣價。**

35. 女子提到什麼問題？
   A 廣告並未廣泛散佈
   B 商品庫存不足
   C 折扣價沒有競爭力
   D 產品賣得不好

36. 關於這個月的銷售量，女子說了什麼？
   A 開始減少
   B 與上個月相似
   C 異常地高
   D 無法預測

37. What does the man ask the woman to do?
- **[A] Extend the length of the promotion**
- [B] Direct customers to the online store
- [C] Secure more advertising space
- [D] Offer customers a bigger discount

37. 男子要求女子做什麼？
- **[A] 延長促銷時間**
- [B] 指引顧客到網路商店
- [C] 取得更多廣告空間
- [D] 提供顧客更多的折扣

38–40 conversation

M: Ms. Simpson, can you tell me why you applied to work at our store? **(38) Judging from your résumé, it appears you have no retail experience. What do you think makes you qualified for selling apparel?**

W: You're right. I previously worked as a secretary at a hospital. **(39) At that time I learned that I really enjoy working with people.** So I thought working in retail would be a good fit for me.

M: Yes, that is very important. Here at our store, we expect all employees to be kind and helpful with each and every customer. **(40) Next, I'd like to ask about your availability during the week.**

38–40 對話

男： 辛普森女士，你可以告訴我為何你想來我們店裡工作呢？**(38)** 從你的履歷看起來，你似乎沒有零售的經驗。你認為你具備什麼賣服飾的條件呢？

女： 你說的對。我之前在醫院當秘書，**(39)** 當時我發現我真的很喜歡和人們往來，因此我認為零售業很適合我。

男： 是的，那很重要。在我們的店裡，我們期待所有員工都能親切並樂於協助彼此以及每位顧客。**(40)** 接下來，我想問你每週的空檔。

38. Where most likely does the man work?
- [A] At a hospital
- [B] At a factory
- **[C] At a clothing store**
- [D] At a restaurant

38. 男子最有可能在哪裡工作？
- [A] 醫院
- [B] 工廠
- **[C] 服飾店**
- [D] 餐廳

39. Why does the woman think she is qualified for the job?
- [A] She completed a training course.
- [B] She has worked similar jobs before.
- **[C] She likes interacting with people.**
- [D] She majored in a related field.

39. 女子為何認為她符合這個工作的資格？
- [A] 她完成了訓練課程
- [B] 她先前做過類似的工作
- **[C] 她喜歡與人們互動**
- [D] 她主修相關領域

40. What will the speakers discuss next?
- **[A] Work hours**
- [B] An annual salary
- [C] Job qualifications
- [D] Previous jobs

40. 對話者們接著會討論什麼？
- **[A] 工作時間**
- [B] 年薪
- [C] 工作資格
- [D] 先前的工作

41–43 conversation

W: Hello, this is Suzy Smith calling for Dan Harmon. I work at Danny Sweets. **(41) I'm calling to let you know that the wedding cake you ordered is ready to be picked up at any time.**

M: Oh, thanks for calling. **(42) I'm extremely busy making other preparations for the wedding tomorrow, and won't have time to stop by.** Can you deliver the cake instead?

W: I'm sorry, but we don't offer any delivery service. **(43) However, if you give us a name in advance, you could have someone else pick it up for you.**

M: **(43) OK, I'll try to find someone to do that for me.** I'll call back later.

41–43 對話

女：哈囉，我叫蘇西 · 史密斯，我要找丹 · 哈蒙。我在丹尼甜點店工作，**(41) 我打電話是要告訴您，您訂購的結婚蛋糕已經備妥，隨時可以來領取。**

男：感謝你的來電。**(42) 我現在正忙著為明天的婚禮作其他準備，沒空過去。**你可以把蛋糕送過來嗎？

女：很抱歉，但我們不提供運送服務。**(43) 不過，若您事先提供我們姓名，就可以請別人幫您領取。**

男：**(43) 好的，我會試著找人幫我拿。**我晚點再回電給你。

41. Where most likely does the woman work?
   Ⓐ At a wedding hall
   Ⓑ At a bakery
   Ⓒ At a clothing store
   Ⓓ At a shipping company

41. 女子最有可能在哪裡工作？
   Ⓐ 婚禮會場
   Ⓑ 烘焙坊
   Ⓒ 服飾店
   Ⓓ 貨運公司

42. Why is the man unable to visit the woman's workplace?
   Ⓐ He has urgent arrangements to make.
   Ⓑ He must attend a wedding today.
   Ⓒ He is not feeling well.
   Ⓓ He has to prepare an order.

42. 男子為何無法去女子的工作處？
   Ⓐ 他有緊急的事務要安排
   Ⓑ 他今天必須參加婚禮
   Ⓒ 他身體不適
   Ⓓ 他必須備妥訂單

43. What information will the man probably provide?
   Ⓐ Directions to a location
   Ⓑ An individual's name
   Ⓒ His home address
   Ⓓ His phone number

43. 男子可能會提供什麼資訊？
   Ⓐ 到某地點的路線指示
   Ⓑ 某人的名字
   Ⓒ 他家的地址
   Ⓓ 他的電話號碼

44–46 conversation

W: I have noticed that a lot of our customers are from all over the world. **(44) I think it's because we provide exotic and delicious food, and we are near very popular tourist attractions.**

44–46 對話

女：我注意到我們有很多來自於世界各地的顧客。**(44) 我認為那是因為我們提供有異國風情且美味的料理，而且我們位於熱門觀光景點附近。**

M：You're right. I have noticed that, too. **(45) I was thinking maybe it would be very helpful if some of our servers could speak other languages fluently.** That would make things much more comfortable for our customers.

W：**(46) Actually, I have already scheduled two interviews next week with potential employees.** I'm going to interview a woman who can speak Japanese and a man who can speak Spanish.

男：你說的對，我也注意到這點。**(45)** 我認為，我們的服務人員如果能夠流利地說其他語言，會很有幫助，這樣能讓我們的顧客更舒適。

女：**(46)** 實際上，我已經在下週安排兩場與應聘者的面試。我將面試一名會說日文的女子，還有一名會說西班牙文的男子。

TEST 7

PART 3

27

44. Where most likely do the speakers work?
   A At a souvenir shop
   B At a language school
   C At a restaurant
   D At a travel agency

45. What does the man recommend doing?
   A Hiring bilingual staff
   B Opening a second location
   C Taking language classes
   D Planning a vacation

46. What has the woman done?
   A Contacted a translation agency
   B Scheduled job interviews
   C Extended operating hours
   D Hired new employees

44. 對話者們最有可能在哪裡工作？
   A 紀念品店
   B 語言學校
   C 餐廳
   D 旅行社

45. 男子建議做什麼？
   A 僱用雙語員工
   B 開第二家店
   C 修語言課程
   D 計劃度假

46. 女子已經做了什麼？
   A 聯繫翻譯社
   B 安排工作面試
   C 延長營運時間
   D 僱用新員工

47–49 conversation

M：Hi, Lindy. **(47) Jessica just left to go home because she had a bad headache.** I told her to take the day off tomorrow as well to go to the hospital. **(48) Do you think you could come in to fill in for her tomorrow morning?**

W：Oh, I'm really sorry, but tomorrow I have to attend a close friend's wedding. **(49) However, I'll call around to see if any other employee is available to work tomorrow in place of Jessica.**

M：OK, thanks. Just let me know immediately if you find somebody.

47–49 對話

男：嗨，琳蒂。**(47)** 潔西卡剛下班回家，因為她頭很痛。我要她明天休假一天並且去醫院。**(48)** 你覺得你明天早上可以來幫她代班嗎？

女：喔，真的很抱歉，但明天我得參加一位好友的婚禮。**(49)** 但我會打幾通電話，看看別的員工明天是否可以來代潔西卡的班。

男：好的，謝謝。如果有找到人，請立刻告訴我。

47. Why did Jessica leave work early?
  [A] She had a prior engagement.
  [B] She wasn't feeling well.
  [C] Her doctor called.
  [D] She had to attend a wedding.

48. What does the man ask the woman to do?
  [A] Work another person's shift
  [B] Clean the store tomorrow morning
  [C] Deliver a presentation at a meeting
  [D] Calculate sales figures

49. What will the woman do next?
  [A] Fill out a form
  [B] Distribute paychecks
  [C] Go to the hospital
  [D] Call her coworkers

47. 潔西卡為何提早下班？
  [A] 她已經有約在先
  [B] 她身體不適
  [C] 她的醫生打電話來
  [D] 她必須參加婚禮

48. 男子要求女子做什麼？
  [A] 幫別人值班
  [B] 明天早上清理商店
  [C] 開會時做簡報
  [D] 計算銷售額

49. 女子接著會做什麼？
  [A] 填寫表格
  [B] 發工資
  [C] 去醫院
  [D] 打電話給同事

(NEW)
50–52 conversation

W：Wilmore Appliance customer service. How can I help you?

M：Hi, **(50) I'm having problems with the freezer part of my fridge. The temperature never goes below 5 degrees Celsius even when I set it below freezing.**

W：Do you know the model number?

M：Let me check. It's the Azura 783XB model.

W：**(51) Oh, I'm sorry, but we no longer make that model, so I can't help you over the phone.**

M：That's going to be a problem. I purchased several gallons of ice cream for a party tomorrow.

W：I'm so sorry. **(52) I'll send a technician over as soon as possible so that the problem is looked at.** Will anyone be home at around 5 p.m. tonight?

M：Yes, I'll be here.

W：Good. Our technician will be there between 5 and 6 tonight.

50–52 對話

女：威莫家電客服部，有什麼需要服務的嗎？

男：嗨，**(50) 我冰箱的冷凍庫有問題，即使我將溫度設定為零度以下，溫度仍無法低於攝氏五度。**

女：你知道產品型號嗎？

男：讓我看一下。是亞斯拉 783XB 型。

女：**(51) 喔，很抱歉，但我們不再生產該型號了，因此我無法透過電話協助你。**

男：這樣就麻煩了，我為了明天的派對買了好幾加侖的冰淇淋。

女：很抱歉。**(52) 我會派技術人員過去盡快處理問題。** 今天大約五點的時候有人在家嗎？

男：是的，我會在。

女：很好。我們的技術人員會在五點與六點之間抵達。

50. What problem does the man mention?
 A The fridge is not working.
 B The temperature is too low.
 C The freezer temperature is too high.
 D Water is leaking from the fridge.

51. What does the woman mention about the fridge?
 A It is a very old model.
 B It is no longer manufactured.
 C It is not from their company.
 D It is a popular model.

52. What does the woman offer to do?
 A Give him a new manual
 B Give him a link to a website
 C Let him get a replacement
 D Send a technician over to him

50. 男子提到什麼問題？
 A 冰箱故障
 B 溫度太低
 C 冷凍庫溫度太高
 D 冰箱漏水

51. 關於冰箱，女子提到什麼？
 A 它是很舊的機型
 B 它停產了
 C 它不是他們公司製造的
 D 它是暢銷的機型

52. 女子建議做什麼？
 A 給他新的手冊
 B 給他網路連結
 C 給他換貨
 D 派技術人員過去他那邊

53-55 conversation

M：Hi, Angela. I just got an email from UHP incorporated. **(53) They are asking about installing the plumbing systems in their new offices.** They want to know when we will begin.

W：**(54) I intended to call them today, but I'm waiting for a call from some workers.** They are at the building site now testing the ground. **(55) It seems as though there may be some problems installing the pipes underground. We may need to dig deeper than we expected.** I will let them know by this afternoon.

M：I see. I'll call UHP and let them know the situation. They didn't sound like they were angry; they were just curious to know what was going on. Let me know when you hear back from the workers.

53-55 對話

男：嗨，安琪拉。我剛收到 UHP 公司寄來的電子郵件。**(53) 他們在詢問要在新辦公室安裝配管工程的事情**，他們想知道我們何時會動工。

女：**(54) 我今天原本打算要打電話給他們，但我在等一些工人的來電。**他們正在工地那裡測試土地。**(55) 在地下安裝管線似乎會有些問題，我們可能需要挖得比先前預期還深。**我今天下午之前會告訴他們。

男：了解。我會打電話給 UHP 公司，讓他們知道情況。他們聽起來沒生氣，只是好奇發生了什麼事。工人回覆你之後，請告訴我。

53. Where do the speakers most likely work?
 A A plumbing company
 B An electrical company
 C A construction company
 D In an office

53. 對話者們最有可能在哪裡工作？
 A 配管工程公司
 B 電力公司
 C 建築公司
 D 辦公室

54. What does the woman mean when she says, "I intended to call them today"?

Ⓐ She wasn't going to call them back.

Ⓑ They were going to call her back.

Ⓒ She was going to call them that day.

Ⓓ She was going to send them an email.

55. What is the problem?

Ⓐ They can't install the electrical system.

Ⓑ The plumbing is already installed.

Ⓒ There is some problem with the payment.

Ⓓ They may need to dig deeper to install the plumbing.

56–58 conversation

W： OK, sir. Your total bill comes to $1,000. Would you like to pay with cash or card?

M： One thousand dollars? **(56) Are you serious?**

W： Yes, sir. You ordered a lot of room service over the last few days and spent a lot of money at the bar and restaurant downstairs. **(57) You stayed in Room 208, didn't you?**

M： No. I was in Room 207. I think you've made a mistake.

W： Oh, I'm sorry, sir. **(58) I will give you a 10% discount next time you stay with us.** I apologize for the confusion.

56. What does the man mean when he says, "Are you serious"?

Ⓐ He believes the woman is correct.

Ⓑ He thinks the woman made a mistake.

Ⓒ He is going to pay by card.

Ⓓ He will pay with cash.

57. What does the woman want to know?

Ⓐ How much room service he ordered

Ⓑ Which room he is staying in

Ⓒ His credit card number.

Ⓓ Whether he ordered room service

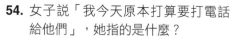

54. 女子說「我今天原本打算要打電話給他們」，她指的是什麼？

Ⓐ 她本來沒有要打電話給他們

Ⓑ 他們本來要回電話給她

Ⓒ 她當天本來就要打電話給他們

Ⓓ 她本來要寄電子郵件給他們

55. 有什麼問題？

Ⓐ 他們無法安裝電力系統

Ⓑ 管線已經安裝好了

Ⓒ 付款有些問題

Ⓓ 他們可能需要挖得更深，才能安裝配管工程

56–58 對話

女： 好的，先生。您的帳單總計是一千元。您要用現金或是信用卡付款呢？

男： 一千元？ **(56) 你是說真的嗎？**

女： 是的，先生。過去這幾天你點了很多次客房服務，而且在樓下的酒吧和餐廳花了很多錢。**(57) 您住 208 號房，對吧？**

男： 不，我住 207 房。我想你弄錯了。

女： 喔，很抱歉，先生。**(58) 下次您來住房，我會給您 10% 的折扣。**很抱歉弄錯了。

56. 男子說「你是說真的嗎」，他指的是什麼？

Ⓐ 他相信女子是對的

Ⓑ 他認為女子弄錯了

Ⓒ 他將要用信用卡付費

Ⓓ 他將要用現金付費

57. 女子想要知道什麼？

Ⓐ 他點了多少錢的客房服務

Ⓑ 他住在哪個房間

Ⓒ 他的信用卡卡號

Ⓓ 他是否使用客房服務

58. What does the woman offer to do?

    Ⓐ Give him his room for free

    Ⓑ Give him a discount on his next visit

    Ⓒ Give him free room service

    Ⓓ Give him a gift certificate

58. 女子提出要做什麼？

    Ⓐ 免費給他房間

    Ⓑ 他下一次住房時給他折扣

    Ⓒ 給他免費的客房服務

    Ⓓ 給他禮券

(NEW)

59–61 conversation

W1: Hi, can I please talk to Robert Porter? It's regarding the repairs to the office equipment at Baker & McKenzie. **(59) He is the head engineer, right?**

W2: Yes. May I ask who is calling?

W1: This is Susan Sherman. I'm the maintenance manager at Baker & McKenzie. **(60) Some of our equipment is missing, and I'd like to know where it is and when we will get it back.**

W2: OK, wait a moment. I will try to put you through to Robert. Please hold the line.

W1: Thank you.

M: Hello? Susan?

W1: Hi, Robert. I'm calling in regards to the missing office equipment you repaired at Baker & McKenzie yesterday. Where is it and when will we get it back?

M: Oh, I left a note with your receptionist. **(61) I told her we needed to take it away to our workshop for special repairs.** We should have it ready by the end of the week.

59–61 對話

女1：嗨，我找羅伯特・波爾特，這是有關貝克和麥肯錫公司的辦公設備維修一事。**(59) 他是總工程師，對嗎？**

女2：是的。請問您是？

女1：我是蘇珊・謝爾曼。我是貝克和麥肯錫公司的維修經理。**(60) 我們有些設備不見了，我想要知道它們在哪裡，以及什麼時候可以取回。**

女2：好的，請稍等。我會嘗試幫您轉接給羅伯特。請別掛斷。

女1：謝謝。

男：哈囉？是蘇珊嗎？

女1：嗨，羅伯特。我打電話來問遺失的設備，你昨天在貝克和麥肯錫公司修理的那些。請問現在在哪裡？我們什麼時候可以取回？

男：喔，我留了字條給你們的接待員。**(61) 我告訴她我們需要將設備帶回廠房，以進行特別維修。**這個星期結束前應該可以修好。

59. What is Robert Porter's position?

    Ⓐ Lead repairer

    Ⓑ Head engineer

    Ⓒ Main engineer

    Ⓓ Main repairer

59. 羅伯特・波爾特的職務是什麼？

    Ⓐ 主任修理員

    Ⓑ 總工程師

    Ⓒ 主工程師

    Ⓓ 主維修員

60. What problem does Susan Sherman describe?

    Ⓐ Some of the measurements weren't done.

    Ⓑ Some of their receipts are missing.

    Ⓒ Some of their equipment is missing.

    Ⓓ A piece of equipment is still in the office.

60. 蘇珊・謝爾曼描述什麼問題？

    Ⓐ 部分測量沒有完成

    Ⓑ 他們有些單據不見了

    Ⓒ 他們有些設備不見了

    Ⓓ 一件設備還在辦公室

61. Why did Robert take the equipment away?
- [A] To review it further
- **[B] For special repairs**
- [C] For replacement
- [D] To evaluate its condition

61. 羅伯特為何把設備帶走了？
- [A] 為了進一步檢視
- **[B] 為了特別的維修**
- [C] 為了替換
- [D] 為了評估其狀況

62–64 conversation

W：**(62) Ok, your total bill is $75. Did you enjoy your food tonight?**

M：Yes it was delicious! Oh, I have a voucher here. Let me find it. Here you go.

W：Hmm. I'm not sure if you can use this.

M：**(63) Oh! I see the problem. Never mind. (64) Can we sit back down and have some drinks so I can use the voucher?**

W：Certainly. I will find a table for you now.

62–64 對話

女：**(62) 好的，你的帳單總額是 75 元。你喜歡今晚的食物嗎？**

男：是的，很美味！對了，我有折價券。讓我找找看，在這裡。

女：嗯……我不確定你是否可以使用這個……

男：**(63) 喔，我知道是什麼問題了。沒關係。(64) 我們可以回座位再喝點飲料嗎？這樣我就可以使用折價券了。**

女：當然，我現在就為你們找座位。

Discount Voucher 折價券

10% off any order over $100
點餐超過 100 元折價 10%

Valid until December 31st 12 月 31 日前有效

---

62. Where most likely are the speakers?
- [A] At a stand
- [B] At a café
- **[C] At a restaurant**
- [D] At the airport

62. 對話者最有可能在哪裡？
- [A] 攤販
- [B] 咖啡店
- **[C] 餐廳**
- [D] 機場

63. Look at the graphic. Why is the voucher invalid?
- **[A] Their bill is under $100.**
- [B] The food was not good.
- [C] Their bill was over $100.
- [D] The voucher is expired.

63. 參看圖表，為何折價券無效？
- **[A] 他們的帳單未滿 100 元**
- [B] 食物不好吃
- [C] 他們的帳單超過 100 元
- [D] 折價券已經過期了

64. What does the man ask the woman?
- A If they can have more food
- **B If they can have more drinks**
- C If they can have a refund
- D If they can come back another time

65–67 conversation

W : I apologize for being late to work. **(65) The parking lot on Swan Street was closed for some reason.** I think they are moving to another location.

M : I understand. Most of the staff were late because of this issue. Where did you find a parking space? On Franklin Avenue?

W : Yeah. There was some parking on Franklin Avenue. So I parked there. **(66) The sign on Swan Street said I could not park there after nine o'clock in the morning.**

M : That's a good idea. Franklin Avenue has parking until ten o'clock.

W : **(67) I suggest you take the bus tomorrow; it took me 30 minutes to walk to the office from Franklin Avenue.**

No Parking After 9 A.M.
上午九點之後
禁止停車

64. 男子問女子什麼問題？
- A 他們是否可以吃更多食物
- **B 他們是否可以喝更多飲料**
- C 他們是否可以退費
- D 他們是否可以改天再來

65–67 對話

女： 很抱歉上班遲到了。**(65)** 天鵝街的停車場不知為何關閉了。我猜想他們要搬到另外的地點。

男： 我了解。大部分員工都因為這個問題而遲到了。你在哪裡找到停車位的？富蘭克林大道上嗎？

女： 是的，富蘭克林大道上有停車位，因此我把車停在那裡。**(66)** 天鵝街的告示牌說，上午九點之後不得在那裡停車。

男： 那是個好主意，富蘭克林大道的停車位十點前都可停車。

女： **(67)** 我建議你明天搭公車，從富蘭克林大道走到辦公室花了我 30 分鐘。

65. According to the man, why are people arriving late to work?
- **A The parking lot on Swan Street was closed.**
- B The Franklin Avenue parking lot was closed.
- C Everyone was feeling sick.
- D The traffic was bad.

65. 根據男子，為何大家上班都遲到了？
- **A 天鵝街的停車場關閉**
- B 富蘭克林大道的停車場關閉
- C 大家都身體不適
- D 交通不好

66. Look at the graphic. Where is the sign most likely located?
- A On Franklin Avenue
- **B On Swan Street**
- C In front of the building
- D On Swanson Avenue

67. What does the woman recommend to the man?
- A Take the subway
- **B Take a bus**
- C Take a taxi
- D Drive his car

66. 參看圖表，這個告示牌最有可能出現在哪裡？
- A 富蘭克林大道
- **B 天鵝街**
- C 大樓前面
- D 史文森大道

67. 女子建議男子做什麼？
- A 搭地鐵
- **B 搭公車**
- C 搭計程車
- D 開他的車

68–70 conversation

W：Hello, this is Will's Hi-Fi; Margaret speaking. How can I help you today?

M：(68) **Hi, I bought a laptop package from you today.** (69) **It was supposed to have a gift, but it wasn't in the bag.**

W：Oh, is this Graham? I served you today. I'm sorry that we left out the gift.

M：Yes, this is Graham. Do I need to come and pick up the gift?

W：No. (70) **We can send it to you by post. I will have the delivery driver drop it off tomorrow. Can you give me your address?**

M：Oh, that's great! My address is 1900 Forest Street, West Hampton.

68–70 對話

女：哈囉，這裡是威利高傳真，我是瑪格麗特。有什麼我可以幫忙的嗎？

男：(68) 你好。我今天從你們店裡買了一個筆記型電腦套件組。(69) 它應該要有個贈品，但袋子裡頭沒有。

女：喔，是葛拉罕嗎？今天是我為你服務的。很抱歉我們遺漏了贈品。

男：是的，我是葛拉罕。需要我過去拿贈品嗎？

女：不用。(70) 我們可以用郵件寄給你。我會請貨運司機明天送過去，可以給我你的地址嗎？

男：喔，太好了！我的地址是西漢普敦，森林街 1900 號。

Laptop Package 筆記型電腦套件組

1 laptop computer 一台筆記型電腦
Wireless mouse 無線滑鼠
Wireless keyboard 無線鍵盤
Office software 辦公室軟體
Detachable webcam 可拆卸式網路攝影機
Free 8 gigabyte USB stick 免費 8G USB 隨身碟

68. Where does the woman most likely work?
- [A] At a hardware store
- [B] At an online store
- [C] At a home appliance store
- **[D] At an electronics store**

 69. Look at the graphic. What is missing from the man's laptop package?
- [A] Office software
- **[B] An 8 gigabyte USB stick**
- [C] A wireless keyboard
- [D] A wireless mouse

70. What does the woman offer to do?
- **[A] Send a delivery driver the next day**
- [B] Give him a coupon
- [C] Have him come and pick the gift up
- [D] Deliver the gift in person

68. 女子最可能在哪裡工作？
- [A] 在五金行
- [B] 在網路商店
- [C] 在家電行
- **[D] 在電子用品店**

69. 參看圖表，男子的筆電組少了什麼？
- [A] 辦公軟體
- **[B] 8G USB 隨身碟**
- [C] 無線鍵盤
- [D] 無線滑鼠

70. 女子提議要做什麼？
- **[A] 隔天派貨運司機送過去**
- [B] 給他折價券
- [C] 要他過來領取贈品
- [D] 親自送贈品過去

PART 4　P. 112-115　28

71–73 radio advertisement

W：Are you feeling down this fall season? **(71) Then come down to Kim's tae kwon do center and energize yourself with the healthy and exciting sport of tae kwon do. (72) We are offering a special discounted membership to those with no prior experience.** So even if it's your first time, don't hesitate. Come sign up today. We are located on Main Street. **(73) You can come by bus and get off at the bus stop near Geller Bank.** Now is the time to refresh yourself with tae kwon do.

71–73 電台廣告

女：今年秋季心情不好嗎？ **(71) 那就快來金恩跆拳道中心，讓跆拳道這種健康又刺激的運動為自己充電。(72) 我們提供新手會員特別折扣價。**因此，即使這是你的第一次，也別猶豫，今天就來報名。我們的地址在緬恩街。**(73) 你也可以搭公車來，在靠近蓋勒銀行的車站下車，**現在正是用跆拳道振奮自己的好時機。

71. What is the advertisement about?
- **[A] A martial arts class**
- [B] An athletic contest
- [C] A city tour bus
- [D] A downtown festival

72. Who is the special offer directed at?
- [A] Senior citizens
- **[B] Beginners**
- [C] Children
- [D] Local residents

71. 這則廣告與什麼有關？
- **[A] 武術課**
- [B] 運動競賽
- [C] 市區導覽公車
- [D] 市中心的節慶

72. 特殊優惠是提供給什麼人的？
- [A] 老年人
- **[B] 初學者**
- [C] 孩童
- [D] 當地居民

73. What does the speaker say about the advertised location?
   A **It is accessible by public transportation.**
   B It has no parking space available.
   C It is near a train station.
   D It is in the same building as Geller Bank.

73. 關於廣告的地點，發話者說了什麼？
   A **可搭乘大眾運輸到達**
   B 沒有停車位
   C 在火車站附近
   D 與蓋勒銀行在同一棟大樓

74–76 introduction

M：**(74) Welcome to the Museum of Electronics.** Here you can see some of the earliest televisions, radios, and telephones ever made. This month we have a special exhibition that focuses on radar and other technologies developed during World War II. **(75) George Butler, an expert in the field, will be giving a short talk describing the history behind this marvelous technology. (76) There is also a workshop for students aged 13 to 19, where they can assemble their own radio transmitter.** It will be a good opportunity to learn a few basic principles of electronic engineering.

74–76 介紹

男：**(74) 歡迎光臨電子用品博物館。** 在這裡，你們可以看到一些最早期的電視機、收音機和電話。本月我們有一項特展，重點是雷達和其他第二次世界大戰期間研發的各種科技。**(75) 喬治 · 巴特勒是這個領域的專家，他會簡短地描述這項神奇科技背後的歷史。(76) 還有個供 13 到 19 歲的學生所使用的廠房，他們可以在那裡組裝自己的無線電傳輸器，** 這會是學習一些電子工程基本原理的大好機會。

---

74. Where is the introduction taking place?
   A At a school
   B **At a museum**
   C At a radio station
   D At a community center

74. 這則介紹在哪裡進行？
   A 學校
   B **博物館**
   C 廣播電台
   D 社區活動中心

75. Who is George Butler?
   A A computer technician
   B A mechanical engineer
   C An electrician
   D **A technology expert**

75. 喬治 · 巴特勒是什麼人？
   A 電腦技術人員
   B 機械工程師
   C 電工
   D **科技專家**

76. What is offered to teenage students?
   A **Hands-on experience**
   B A weekly after-school class
   C A complimentary souvenir
   D A discounted ticket price

76. 博物館提供什麼給青少年學生？
   A **手作體驗**
   B 每週的課後課程
   C 免費紀念品
   D 票價折扣

77–79 announcement

W：Attention, all conference attendees. **(77) Due to the late arrival of a shipment of food, the conference center cafeteria will not be able to serve lunch this afternoon.** We apologize for this inconvenience. **(78) We will be issuing meal vouchers that can be used at any restaurant in the surrounding neighborhood. (79) Please be back in the conference center by 1:00 p.m. in time for Janet Wallace's presentation on how to use the new client management software.**

77–79 廣播

女：所有與會人員請注意。**(77)** 因為食物延後送達，所以今天下午會議中心的自助餐廳將無法供應午餐。我們為此不便道歉。**(78)** 我們將會發放可用於附近任何一家餐廳的餐券。**(79)** 請在下午一點以前回到會議中心，參加珍娜特·華勒斯的簡報，主題是如何使用新的客戶管理軟體。

---

77. What has caused the change in plans?
- A Broken kitchen equipment
- B The absence of some clients
- **C A late delivery**
- D Traffic congestion

77. 什麼導致了計劃的異動？
- A 廚房設備損壞
- B 某些客戶缺席
- **C 運送延遲**
- D 交通阻塞

78. What will listeners receive?
- A A conference schedule
- **B A meal voucher**
- C A lunch menu
- D A name tag

78. 聽眾會收到什麼？
- A 會議時程表
- **B 餐券**
- C 午餐菜單
- D 名牌

79. What will begin at 1:00 p.m.?
- **A A software demonstration**
- B A leadership workshop
- C A luncheon
- D A client meeting

79. 什麼將於下午一點開始？
- **A 軟體示範**
- B 領導力研討會
- C 午餐會
- D 客戶會議

80–82 excerpt from a meeting

M：Hello, everyone. **(80) Welcome to the planning committee, which is in charge of overseeing the construction of a new elementary school here in Eagleton. (81) I'm looking for someone to volunteer as the note taker during this meeting. His or her duty will be to keep track of what is debated.** After this meeting, you will need to send a summary of it to all attendees. In order to perform this duty, he or she needs to be a careful listener. **(82) But for now, I would like you to give personal introductions.** That way, we can get to know each other better.

80–82 會議摘錄

男：哈囉，大家好。**(80)** 歡迎來到籌劃委員會，我們負責監督伊格頓本地一所新小學的建設工程。**(81)** 我在徵求自願者在開會期間當會議記錄，任務是記下辯論的內容。會後要將紀錄的摘要寄給每位與會者，為了要執行這項任務，會議記錄需仔細聆聽細節。**(82)** 但現在，我要各位自我介紹，這樣我們就能夠更認識彼此。

80. What is the purpose of the planning committee?
    A To tighten some regulations
    B To supervise a construction project
    C To review employee performance
    D To develop a new curriculum

81. What does the volunteer need to do?
    A Pick up a client
    B Introduce a guest
    C Write down an agenda
    D Give a presentation

82. What will listeners do next?
    A Go on a business trip
    B Participate in a workshop
    C Introduce themselves
    D Select a group leader

83–85 excerpt from a meeting

W：Hi, everyone. Let's start the weekly work meeting. **(83) Firstly, I want you to know that I've hired five more staff for the main factory. (84) I know that you have all been overworked**, I'm trying hard to push for funding to get two more people in over the next few months. The new staff will be here on Monday morning, and I want everyone to go out of their way to train them as quickly as possible. To do this efficiently, I'm going to have each of you train the new staff in a particular section of the factory. **(85) Please prepare some instructions and email them to me** so I can double check them.

---

83. Who most likely are the listeners?
    A Factory workers
    B Lawyers
    C Accountants
    D Web developers

(NEW)
84. What does the woman mean when she says, "I know that you have all been overworked"?
    A She recognizes the listeners concerns.
    B She doesn't really mind what they think.
    C She wants them to work less.
    D She is inviting them to a meeting.

---

80. 籌劃委員會的功能是什麼？
    A 使規定更嚴格
    B 監督建設案
    C 檢視員工表現
    D 發展新課程

81. 自願者需要做什麼？
    A 接送客戶
    B 介紹來賓
    C 寫下議程
    D 發表簡報

82. 聽眾接著會做什麼？
    A 出差
    B 參與研討會
    C 自我介紹
    D 選擇團體領導人

83–85 會議摘錄

女：嗨，大家好，我們開始每週工作會議吧。**(83) 首先，我要告訴你們，我已經為主要廠房多僱用五名員工。(84) 我知道你們的工作量超過負荷**。我正在努力爭取經費，要在接下來的幾個月多僱用兩個人。新進人員星期一早上會來，因此我要大家格外費心盡快訓練他們。為了有效率地進行此事，我要你們每人在工廠的特定區域訓練新進人員。**(85) 請備妥操作說明並以電子郵件寄給我**，以便我再次確認。

---

83. 聽者最有可能是什麼人？
    A 工廠工人
    B 律師
    C 會計師
    D 網路開發者

84. 女子說「我知道你們的工作量超過負荷」，她指的是什麼？
    A 她了解聽眾在意的事
    B 她不太在意他們的想法
    C 她想要他們工作得少一點
    D 她邀請他們去開會

85. What task does the speaker assign to the listeners?
- **A Prepare some instructions**
- B Prepare a new budget
- C Revise some training materials
- D Hire new staff

85. 發話者指派什麼任務給聽眾？
- **A 備妥操作說明**
- B 備妥新的預算
- C 修正訓練教材
- D 僱用新員工

86–88 talk

M： I appreciate the number of people who have attended the Westbridge Film Festival this evening. I hope that all the films have been enjoyable so far. The next film we are going to show is particularly special. The film is called *Beyond the Blue*, and is the debut release from documentary film maker Michael Harris. **(86) The film captures the deepest parts of the ocean, and explores the complex ecosystems that exist in the areas of the ocean that humans cannot survive in. (87) The film has already been nominated for multiple awards, most recently at the BAPTA Film Festival. Remember, this is the first film Mr. Harris has made. (88) After the film Mr. Harris will come to the front for a short Q&A session.** Anyway, please enjoy the show.

86–88 談話

男： 我感謝那麼多人參加今晚的西橋電影節。我希望目前為止大家都喜歡這些電影。接下來我們要放的影片尤其特別，片名叫做《越過蔚藍大海》」，是紀錄片製片人麥克・哈里斯首部公開放映的電影。**(86)** 電影拍攝了海洋的最深處，並在人類無法存活的區域，探索複雜的生態系。**(87)** 這部電影已經獲得多項獎項提名，最近的是在 BAPTA 電影節。請記得，這是哈里斯先生製作的第一部電影。**(81)** 電影結束後，哈里斯先生會到前面來進行簡短的問答時間。總之，請欣賞這部電影。

---

86. What is *Beyond the Blue* about?
- A Online bullying
- **B The ocean**
- C Whales and sharks
- D Sea water

87. Why does the speaker say, "Remember, this is the first film Mr. Harris has made"?
- **A To suggest that he is an impressive director**
- B To suggest the film will be poor
- C To recommend him as a good worker
- D To suggest they shouldn't watch the film

88. What is going to happen after the film?
- A They will give away free DVDs.
- B They will watch it again.
- **C The director will have a short Q&A.**
- D An actor will sign autographs.

86. 《越過蔚藍大海》與什麼有關？
- A 網路霸凌
- **B 海洋**
- C 鯨魚和鯊魚
- D 海水

87. 發話者為何說「請記得，這是哈里斯先生製作的第一部電影」？
- **A 要暗示他是令人印象深刻的導演**
- B 要暗示這部電影會很差
- C 要推薦他為優秀員工
- D 要暗示他們不該看這部電影

88. 電影放映後會發生什麼事？
- A 他們將發送免費的 DVD
- B 他們將再次觀賞電影
- **C 導演將會進行簡短的問答**
- D 一位演員將會舉辦簽名會

89–91 speech

M: **(89) Well, it's only been one year since I took over the position of company president. Since then our products have become the most sought-after watches in the world.** Our unique designs, excellent price point, and promotional campaigns have proven to be miraculous. This has led to a lot of media attention. The worldwide CNU Business channel wants to run a special story about our company next month. **(90) They are sending some reporters to interview me on Wednesday, and to take some video footage of our manufacturing processes. (91) You realize what this means. CNU is broadcasted globally, and this could cause our business to grow even more.**

89–91 演講

男: **(89)** 我自從開始接掌公司董事長職務也有一年了。從那時起,我們的手錶已經成為全世界最熱門的商品。我們的獨特設計、極佳價位以及促銷活動,都證實有奇蹟神效。這引起了媒體很大的關注,國際知名的的 CNU 商業頻道想在下個月特別專題報導我們的公司。**(90)** 他們星期三會派記者來訪問我,並且拍攝我們的生產過程。**(91)** 你們都了解此事的意義。CNU 在全球播出,這可能使我們的業績更加成長。

---

89. According to the speaker, what has happened to the company in the last year?
   A Their products have gained global success.
   B Their sales have gone down.
   C The quality of the products has changed.
   D Their CEO has changed many times.

89. 根據發話者,過去一年這家公司發生了什麼事?
   A 他們的產品在全球大獲成功
   B 他們的業績下滑
   C 產品品質改變
   D 他們的總裁換了很多人

90. What most likely are the CNU reporters doing on Wednesday?
   A Interviewing some office workers
   B Interviewing the president
   C Making a music video
   D Promoting their new web series

90. CNU 的記者最有可能在星期三做什麼?
   A 訪問一些辦公室員工
   B 訪問董事長
   C 製作音樂影片
   D 宣傳他們新的網路節目

(NEW)
91. Why does the man say, "you realize what this means"?
   A To discuss future renovations
   B To make a point clear
   C To highlight that the company will grow
   D To give staff some bonuses

91. 為何男子說「你們都了解此事的意義」?
   A 為了討論未來的創新
   B 為了使論點清楚
   C 為了強調公司將會成長
   D 為了給員工紅利

92-94 announcement

M：**(92) Sam's Salon is committed to helping aid the homeless.** If you have been a resident of Freewater over the last year, you have surely noticed the pop up salon on the corner of Cornwall Avenue and Dupont. **(92) This pop up is not for hipsters though. It's for the homeless. (92) (94) Sam's Salon has been volunteering to give the homeless in our community shampoos, shaves, and haircuts in order to help them get back on their feet.** To further this effort, Sam's Salon is having a Saturday-only haircut special, where half of all sales will go to help the local homeless shelter. This is a great opportunity to show that you care, support a local business, and to get a darn good haircut.

92-94 宣布

男：(92) 山姆美髮店致力於協助遊民。若你在過去一年曾經是自由水鄉的居民，那麼你一定曾注意到在康瓦爾大街與杜邦街角的行動美髮店。(92) 但這家行動美髮店並不是為了服務趕時髦的人，而是為了服務遊民。(92)(94) 山姆美髮店自願為社區的遊民洗髮、刮鬍及剪髮，幫助他們重新振作。為了更進一步推展這件事，山姆美髮店要舉辦僅限週六的剪髮優惠活動。期間一半的營業額，將用於幫助本地的遊民收容所。這是讓你表示關懷遊民、支持在地企業、又能剪一頭美髮的好時機。

SAM'S SALON PRICING FOR THE HOMELESS BENEFIT
山姆美髮店關懷遊民優惠活動價目表

Men's trim 男士修髮	$10
Men's full cut and shave 男士整頭理髮及刮鬍	$25
Women's trim 女士修髮	$20
Women's styling 女士造型	$45
Sorry! No coloring or perms for this Saturday's benefit! 抱歉！本週六優惠不提供染髮和燙髮！	

92. What is indicated in the announcement?

[A] Sam's Salon is just starting to interact with the homeless.

[B] Sam's Salon has been involved with improving the lives of homeless people.

[C] Sam's Salon employs a high quality manicurist.

[D] Sam's Salon is trying to make extra money from coloring and perms.

92. 這則宣布表示什麼？

[A] 山姆美髮店正要開始與遊民互動

[B] 山姆美髮店向來致力於改善遊民的生活

[C] 山姆美髮店僱用優秀的美甲師

[D] 山姆美髮店正試著從染髮和燙髮得到額外收入

93. Look at the graphic. What is true about the benefit?

Ⓐ **People should get their hair colored another time.**

Ⓑ Women's trim is expensive.

Ⓒ Most men will choose a trim.

Ⓓ Homeless people need to shave.

94. How much does Sam's Salon charge the homeless for a shampoo, shave, and a haircut?

Ⓐ $25

Ⓑ $45

Ⓒ $10

Ⓓ **Nothing; it's free**

93. 參看圖表，關於優惠活動，何者為真？

Ⓐ **人們應該找別的時間染髮**

Ⓑ 女士修髮很昂貴

Ⓒ 大部分男士會選擇修髮

Ⓓ 遊民需要刮鬍

94. 山姆美髮店會向遊民索取多少洗髮、刮鬍和理髮的費用？

Ⓐ 25 元

Ⓑ 45 元

Ⓒ 10 元

Ⓓ **不收，是免費的**

95–97 excerpt from a meeting

W：**(95) Hello everyone, and thank you for inviting me to speak with you all in this beautiful new conference room.** Our newest line of office security systems is really impressive, and I am sure it will meet your needs. We have developed four options to choose from. **(96) Let me just say that Option 1 is by far the best value because of the back-up system that we offer with this package.** It is not as expensive as Option 4, but don't let that fool you. Option 1 still offers all of the security that your business could want. All of our options include state-of-the-art video surveillance. **(97) Option 4 is more expensive because we offer 365 days of archived data.** After taking a tour of your facilities, I feel that this option would not be the best for your company.

95–97 會議摘錄

女：**(95) 哈囉，大家好，感謝各位邀請我來這個漂亮的新會議室與大家談話。** 我們最新系列的辦公室保全系統真的很令人印象深刻，我確信它能符合各位的需求。我們研發出四種方案。**(96) 在我看來，方案一最划算，因為我們在此套件提供了備份系統。** 它沒有方案四那麼貴，但別讓這點誤導了你。方案一仍提供貴公司所需的一切保全需求。我們所有選項都包含最先進的錄影監視器。**(97) 方案四比較昂貴，因為我們提供了 365 天的檔案儲存。** 參訪過你們的設施之後，我認為這個方案對你們公司而言並非最佳選擇。

	Option 1 方案一	Option 2 方案二	Option 3 方案三	Option 4 方案四
Price 價格	$1,000	$1,200	$1,300	$2,000
Back-up System 備份系統	yes 有	no 無	no 無	no 無
Data Archive 資料檔案庫	1 week （週）	10 weeks （週）	30 weeks （週）	52 weeks （週）

95. Where does the talk most likely take place?
- Ⓐ The cafeteria
- **Ⓑ The conference room**
- Ⓒ The new break room
- Ⓓ The new foyer

96. Look at the graphic. Which option does the speaker recommend?
- **Ⓐ Option 1**
- Ⓑ Option 2
- Ⓒ Option 3
- Ⓓ Option 4

97. Why is Option 4 more expensive than the others?
- Ⓐ It has state-of-the-art surveillance.
- Ⓑ It has video cameras.
- **Ⓒ It includes a one-year data archive.**
- Ⓓ It offers a back-up system.

95. 談話最有可能在哪裡進行？
- Ⓐ 自助餐廳
- **Ⓑ 會議室**
- Ⓒ 新的員工休息室
- Ⓓ 新的門廳

96. 參看圖表，發話者推薦哪個選項？
- **Ⓐ 方案一**
- Ⓑ 方案二
- Ⓒ 方案三
- Ⓓ 方案四

97. 為何選擇四比其他選擇貴？
- Ⓐ 它有最先進的監視設備
- Ⓑ 它有攝影機
- **Ⓒ 它包含了一年的資料檔案庫**
- Ⓓ 它提供了備份系統

98-100 excerpt from a meeting

M：**(98) Hello everyone, I wanted to get you together to go over the recent successes in our customer service here at Milton's Diner.** Milton's Diner is an institution here in Petersburg, and although we have always been complimented on our polite and timely service, the comments and tips we received over this long holiday weekend were extraordinary. I want to tell you all how proud I am of all of your hard work and dedication. **(98) It is my name on the sign, but this is really your business.** I have made a copy of a thank you letter that really touched my heart. We received it from a customer, and I wanted to share it with you so you could all see exactly how our hard work pays off. **(100) It moved me so much that I decided to give everyone who worked over the weekend an extra holiday bonus!** You all are the best!

98-100 會議摘錄

男：(98) 哈囉，大家好，我想要把大家聚在一起，逐一檢視我們最近在米爾頓餐廳客服方面的成功。米爾頓餐廳是彼得斯堡本地的一家機構，雖然我們向來因為禮貌和有效率的服務而廣受讚美，但在這週末的長假期間，我們收到的好評和小費更超乎平常。我想要告訴各位，我多麼為你們的努力和奉獻感到驕傲。(98) 招牌上面寫的是我的名字，但這實際上這是各位的事業。我印了一張令我感動的感謝函，它來自於一位顧客。我想要與你們分享，這樣你們就都能確切了解我們的努力是值得的。(100) 我覺得很感動，我決定要給該週末上班的每個人一份額外的假期津貼！你們全都是最棒的！

A LETTER TO MILTON'S DINER
致米爾頓餐廳的一封信

Dear Milton's Staff,
米爾頓餐廳的員工你們好：

My name is Jerome and I am a long haul trucker. I saw the sign from the highway, "Milton's Diner, home of classic pies," and thought, you know what, I am going to treat myself. I was exhausted, but as soon as I walked into the diner and smelled the pies, saw all the decorations, and was greeted by the hostess, I just felt so good. You really made my weekend special, and I wanted to thank you with all sincerity.

我的名字是傑洛米，我是長途卡車司機。我在公路上看見招牌寫著「米爾頓餐廳：經典派的家鄉」，我就想，對了，我要款待自己。我當時很累，但當我走進餐廳、聞到派的味道、看見所有裝飾品，還有女服務生和我打招呼，我就感覺很愉快。你們真的使我的週末變得特別。我想要誠心的向你們道謝。

Happy Holidays,
祝假期愉快

Jerome Simmons
傑洛米 ・ 西蒙斯

---

98. Who is speaking to the staff?
    A Milton
    B The manager
    C The chef
    D Jerome Simmons

99. Look at the letter. What do you think Milton's Diner prides itself on?
    A Cakes
    B Pies
    C Drinks
    D Steaks

100. What effect did Jerome's letter have?
    A The staff will get a day off.
    B Everyone will get to take home a pie.
    C Everyone will get holiday gift cards.
    D The staff will receive an extra holiday bonus.

98. 誰在對員工們說話？
    A 米爾頓
    B 經理
    C 廚師
    D 傑洛米 ・ 西蒙斯

99. 參看這封信，你認為米爾頓餐廳對什麼感到自豪？
    A 蛋糕
    B 派
    C 飲料
    D 牛排

100. 傑洛米的信有什麼影響？
    A 員工們將休假一天
    B 每個人都可以帶派回家
    C 每個人都會收到節日禮物卡
    D 員工會收到一份額外的假期津貼

ACTUAL TEST ⑧

1. **A One of the women is handing some paper to the man.**
   B They are all using laptops.
   C The lady is typing on the laptop.
   D The man is presenting in the office.

2. A The waiter is writing in his notepad.
   B The man is drinking a cup of coffee.
   C The woman is ordering some food.
   D The waiter is talking to the man.

3. A There are cleaners in the lecture hall.
   B The lecture hall is occupied.
   C There are many people in the lecture hall.
   D The lecture hall is unoccupied.

4. **A The man is holding the umbrella with his hand.**
   B The woman is strolling along the path.
   C They are boarding the train.
   D They are lined up against the wall.

5. A The woman is boiling water in the pot.
   B The woman is putting pepper into the pot.
   C The woman is pouring oil into the pan.
   D The woman is wearing a chef's hat.

6. A They are signing a contract.
   B They are shaking hands with each other.
   C They are sitting next to each other.
   D They are exchanging business cards.

7. How often should I replace the battery in this device?
   A It is in place.
   B At least once a year.
   C He often goes on business trips.

TEST 8

PART 2

1. A 其中一名女子將紙張拿給男子。
   B 他們全都在使用筆記型電腦。
   C 女子用筆記型電腦打字。
   D 男子在辦公室做簡報。

2. A 服務生正在記事本上寫字。
   B 男子正在喝一杯咖啡。
   C 女子正在點餐。
   D 服務生正在與男子說話。

3. A 演講廳裡有清潔人員。
   B 有人在使用演講廳。
   C 有許多人在演講廳裡。
   D 演講廳沒有人用。

4. **A 男子用手拿著傘。**
   B 女子沿著小路散步。
   C 他們正在上火車。
   D 他們靠著牆壁排隊。

5. A 女子正用鍋子煮水。
   B 女子正將胡椒粉倒入鍋子裡。
   C 女子正在倒油到平底鍋裡。
   D 女子戴著廚師帽。

6. A 他們正在簽署合約。
   B 他們正與彼此握手。
   C 他們正坐在彼此身旁。
   D 他們正在交換名片。

7. 我應該要多久更換一次這個儀器裡的電池？
   A 已經就定位了。
   B 至少一年一次。
   C 他經常出差。

8. Where do you keep the spare tire?
   A In the trunk of the car.
   B For an unexpected emergency.
   C Yes, I'm a little bit tired.

9. Weren't you going to send an email with corrections to the document?
   A Driving directions.
   B I'll change the format.
   C It's not finished yet.

10. Did you sign up for the special workshop on Monday?
    A Yes, I'm looking forward to it.
    B No, I didn't see the road sign.
    C He rescheduled the appointment.

11. Haven't you backed up your files yet?
    A She installed the hardware.
    B Actually, it does so automatically.
    C She'll be back soon.

12. When did I talk to you last?
    A No, not right now.
    B Sometime last winter.
    C I'll take you there immediately.

13. The reservation is for 8:00 p.m., isn't it?
    A The dinner was a vegetarian meal.
    B He worked all night.
    C Let me check the schedule.

14. We'd appreciate it if you would not park near the entrance.
    A The park closes before midnight.
    B I won't do that.
    C Between the two buildings.

15. Which paint would be best for these walls?
    A Probably three or four cans.
    B Yes, we ordered it already.
    C Light blue would look nice.

16. I can't find our tickets anywhere.
    A You should check your backpack.
    B She already boarded the airplane.
    C It's more expensive than expected.

8. 你把備胎放在哪裡？
   A 在汽車的後車箱裡。
   B 以備意外緊急之需。
   C 是的，我有點疲憊。

9. 你不是要寄一封附有修正文件的電子郵件嗎？
   A 行車路線。
   B 我要改變格式。
   C 還沒有完成。

10. 你報名參加星期一的特別研討會了嗎？
    A 是的，我很期待。
    B 不，我沒看見路標。
    C 他重新安排這項預約。

11. 你還沒有備份檔案嗎？
    A 她安裝了硬體。
    B 其實，它會自動。
    C 她很快就會回來。

12. 我上次什麼時候和你說話的？
    A 不，現在不行。
    B 去年冬天的時候。
    C 我立刻帶你過去。

13. 訂位是在晚上八點，不是嗎？
    A 晚餐是素食。
    B 他整夜工作。
    C 讓我查看行程表。

14. 若你不把車停在入口附近，我們會很感激的。
    A 公園在午夜之前關閉。
    B 我不會那麼做的。
    C 在兩棟建築物之間。

15. 哪種油漆最適合這些牆面？
    A 也許三或四罐。
    B 是的，我們已經訂購了。
    C 淺藍色看起來不錯。

16. 我到處都找不到我們的票。
    A 你該查看你的背包。
    B 她已經上飛機了。
    C 這比預期的還貴。

17. Who will be giving the keynote speech at the conference?

   A Mr. Franks wrote a reference letter.

   B It was very impressive.

   C A famous novelist.

18. How do you get to work each day?

   A I have to leave home before 8:00.

   B I ride my bike or walk.

   C The office on the first floor.

19. Will the contest be held in the courtyard or the auditorium?

   A On a stage would be preferable.

   B He will announce the winner.

   C I'm too tired to go.

20. Could you move the air conditioner to the other room?

   A Yes, I've moved into a new apartment.

   B What is the temperature?

   C I'll need help to do that.

21. Did you clean the meeting room for our clients?

   A The hotel is affordable.

   B No, but I will shortly.

   C They were satisfied with our proposal.

22. Why didn't the train arrive on time today?

   A It was delayed because of construction.

   B Yes, it's always punctual.

   C Actually, the tickets are non-refundable.

23. Should I put the clothes in the dryer or hang them outside?

   A No, this shirt is too small.

   B It's a brand-new hairdryer.

   C Either is fine with me.

24. How do you access the company database?

   A He will accompany you.

   B You need Mr. Harrison's permission.

   C At the annual conference.

25. Let's ask Mr. Miller to increase the budget for the business trip.

   A We're going to Atlanta.

   B Yes, I will right away.

   C I booked the airplane tickets.

17. 誰將在會議發表主要演說？

   A 法蘭克斯先生寫了一封介紹信。

   B 很令人印象深刻。

   C 一位知名的小說家。

18. 你每天如何上班？

   A 我必須在八點之前出門。

   B 我騎腳踏車或走路。

   C 在一樓的辦公室。

19. 比賽會在庭院還是禮堂舉行？

   A 在舞台上比較好。

   B 他將會宣布獲勝者。

   C 我太累了去不了。

20. 你可以將冷氣機搬到另一個房間嗎？

   A 是的，我已經搬進了新公寓。

   B 溫度是多少？

   C 我需要有人幫忙做這件事。

21. 你打掃要接見我們客戶的會議室了嗎？

   A 這個旅館不貴。

   B 還沒有，但我很快就去。

   C 他們對我們的提案很滿意。

22. 火車今天為何沒有準時抵達？

   A 它因為施工而延誤了。

   B 是的，它總是很準時。

   C 實際上，這些票不能退。

23. 我應該把衣服放進烘衣機裡，還是掛在外頭？

   A 不，這件襯衫太小了。

   B 這是全新的吹風機。

   C 我都可以。

24. 你如何進入公司的資料庫？

   A 他將會陪伴你。

   B 你需要哈里森先生的允許。

   C 在年度會議。

25. 我們要求米勒先生提高這次出差的預算吧。

   A 我們要去亞特蘭大。

   B 好的，我立刻就去。

   C 我訂了機票。

26. Can you make a reservation for the company dinner next week?

   A **Let me know how many people will attend.**

   B We ordered too much food.

   C Because Ms. Dean has recently been promoted.

26. 你可以為下週公司的聚餐訂位嗎？

   A **告訴我會有多少人參加。**

   B 我們點了太多食物。

   C 因為迪恩女士最近升遷了。

27. Who did you hire to fix your broken refrigerator?

   A I went grocery shopping this morning.

   B **This is his business card.**

   C A little bit higher.

27. 你僱用誰來修理壞掉的冰箱？

   A 我今天早上去買雜貨。

   B **這是他的名片。**

   C 再稍微高一點。

28. I've been reviewing several candidates for a vacant position.

   A **I hope you can find a qualified person.**

   B The election is next month.

   C Congratulations on your new job.

28. 我一直在審查職缺的應徵者。

   A **我希望你可以找到符合資格的人。**

   B 選舉是在下個月。

   C 恭喜你找到新工作。

29. Don't you want to see the apartment for rent next week?

   A I paid the rental fee.

   B **It's not close enough to the subway.**

   C Because of a population increase.

29. 你下個星期不是要去看出租的公寓嗎？

   A 我付了租金。

   B **它距離地鐵不夠近。**

   C 因為人口增加。

30. This television isn't still under warranty, is it?

   A We replaced the item at no cost to the customer.

   B A trusted brand for over 30 years.

   C **I believe it expired just a month ago.**

30. 這台電視已經過了保固期限，對吧？

   A 我們為顧客免費更換了此物件。

   B 一個超過 30 年的可靠品牌。

   C **我想它一個月前就過期了。**

31. I just spoke with Jonathan on the phone.

   A A spokesperson for Hines Tours.

   B **Oh, is he feeling better?**

   C I'll adjust the microphone.

31. 我剛與強納森講過電話。

   A 海恩斯旅遊的發言人。

   B **喔，他有好一點了嗎？**

   C 我會調整麥克風。

PART 3   P. 121-125   🎧 31

32–34 conversation

M: Hi. **(32) I was hired yesterday to work here on the night cleaning staff.** Today is my first day and I'm not sure who I need to talk to.

W: Oh, welcome to the staff of the Hampton Lodge Hotel. **(33) Mr. Carter is in charge of the cleaning staff, but he doesn't come into work for another hour.** I think you're here early.

32–34 對話

男： 嗨。**(32) 我昨天受僱成為夜班清潔人員。** 今天是我第一天上班，我不太確定我需要去找誰。

女： 喔，歡迎成為漢普敦旅館的工作人員。**(33) 卡特先生負責清潔人員的事宜**，但他還要一小時後才會來上班。我想你太早到了。

M : They told me to report to work at 11 o'clock. Then what should I do in the meantime?

W : I see. **(34) Well, normally new employees watch a series of training videos as part of their orientation.** Please follow me.

男：他們要我在 11 點報到，那麼，現在我該做什麼？

女：我了解。**(34)** 嗯，一般狀況下，新進員工會看一系列的訓練影片，當作新進人員訓練。請跟我來。

32. Who is the man?
- Ⓐ A hotel guest
- **Ⓑ A janitor**
- Ⓒ A night manager
- Ⓓ A receptionist

32. 男子是什麼人？
- Ⓐ 旅館房客
- **Ⓑ 清潔工**
- Ⓒ 夜班經理
- Ⓓ 接待員

33. Why is Mr. Carter unavailable?
- Ⓐ He is meeting a client.
- Ⓑ He is on vacation.
- **Ⓒ He has not arrived at work yet.**
- Ⓓ He is giving a presentation.

33. 卡特先生為何不在？
- Ⓐ 他在與客戶開會。
- Ⓑ 他在度假。
- **Ⓒ 他還沒來上班。**
- Ⓓ 他在發表簡報。

34. What will the man do next?
- **Ⓐ Watch training videos**
- Ⓑ Conduct an interview
- Ⓒ Contact Mr. Carter
- Ⓓ Fill out paperwork

34. 男子接著會做什麼？
- **Ⓐ 看訓練影片**
- Ⓑ 進行面試
- Ⓒ 聯繫卡特先生
- Ⓓ 填寫文書

35–37 conversation

W : Hi, Chris. Our client from Japan, Mr. Takahashi, just arrived at the airport. I'm going to leave in a few minutes to pick him up. **(35) Will everything be ready for the meeting once we arrive?**

M : **(36) Oh, that's good to hear. I was worried he wouldn't be able to arrive today because of the bad weather.** I have just about everything prepared. All I need to do is print out a blueprint for the new prototype.

W : OK, great. **(37) I'll call you 30 minutes before we arrive.** See you soon in the meeting room.

35–37 對話

女：嗨，克里斯。我們的日本客戶高橋先生剛抵達機場。我幾分鐘後要去接他。**(35)** 我們抵達時，會議所需的一切都會準備就緒嗎？

男：**(36)** 喔，很高興聽你這麼說。我還擔心他會因為天氣不佳而無法於今日到達。我幾乎準備好了所有的東西，只需要印出新原型的藍圖即可。

女：好的，很好。**(37)** 我會在到達前 30 分鐘打電話給你，待會會議室見。

35. What are the speakers discussing?
- **Ⓐ Preparations for a meeting**
- Ⓑ A keynote speech
- Ⓒ A seminar agenda
- Ⓓ Meeting locations

35. 對話者們在討論什麼？
- **Ⓐ 會議的準備工作**
- Ⓑ 主要演說
- Ⓒ 研討會議程
- Ⓓ 會議地點

36. What does the man say that he is relieved about?
- [A] A product is selling well.
- **[B] A trip was not delayed.**
- [C] A new employee was hired.
- [D] A meeting room is available.

37. What does the woman offer to do?
- [A] Act as an interpreter during a meeting
- **[B] Call before she arrives**
- [C] Call Mr. Takahashi's secretary
- [D] Listen to a weather report

36. 男子說他對什麼鬆了一口氣？
- [A] 產品賣得很好
- **[B] 旅程未受延誤**
- [C] 僱用新員工
- [D] 有會議室可以使用

37. 女子提議要做什麼？
- [A] 會議期間當口譯員
- **[B] 在到達前打給男子**
- [C] 致電給高橋先生的秘書
- [D] 聽氣象報導

38–40 conversation

W：**(38) Kevin, did you finish the billboard design for Frank's Tires Plus yet?** They want the advertisement to be up in time for their big sale next week.

M：**(39) I was just about to finish it this morning when my computer crashed suddenly.** Unfortunately, I lost some of my data, including the work I had done on the billboard design.

W：Oh, no. That's a shame. **(40) I'll call Frank's Tires Plus and ask for a few more days to complete the design.** In the meantime, I hope you can find a solution.

38–40 對話

女：**(38) 凱文，你完成法蘭克優級輪胎廣告看板的設計了嗎？** 他們希望廣告能趕在下星期的特賣會前刊登出來。

男：**(39) 我今天早上快要做完的時候，電腦突然當機了。** 不幸地，我失去了部分資料，包含我為廣告看版設計所做的部分。

女：糟了，真可惜。**(40) 我會致電法蘭克優級輪胎，並要求他們多給幾天來完成設計。** 在此同時，我希望你能夠找到解決方法。

---

38. What does the woman ask the man about?
- **[A] The status of a project**
- [B] The location of a store
- [C] The list of clients
- [D] The cause of a problem

39. Why was the man unable to complete his work?
- [A] He didn't have enough time.
- [B] His car wouldn't start.
- [C] He was busy with other projects.
- **[D] His computer malfunctioned.**

40. What is the woman planning to do?
- [A] Terminate a contract
- **[B] Ask for a deadline extension**
- [C] Meet with a company executive
- [D] Hire a new designer

38. 女子詢問男子什麼事？
- **[A] 一項企劃的狀況**
- [B] 商店的位置
- [C] 客戶名單
- [D] 問題原因

39. 男子為何無法完成工作？
- [A] 他時間不夠
- [B] 他的車發不動
- [C] 他忙著其他的案子
- **[D] 他的電腦故障了**

40. 女子打算做什麼？
- [A] 終止合約
- **[B] 請求延展期限**
- [C] 與公司行政主管會面
- [D] 僱用新設計師

41–43 conversation

M: Hello, this is Tim Mason speaking. I live on Maria Street. **(41) All the electricity at my house has gone out.**

W: I'm very sorry, sir. It looks like a tree fell on a power line and knocked out all the power on your street.

M: Yeah, that's what I expected. Do you know how long it will take to restore the electricity?

W: **(42) Because of all the storm damage, our repair teams are behind schedule. (43) In the meantime, I suggest you stay at a family member or friend's house.**

41–43 對話

男：哈囉，我是提姆 · 梅森。我住在瑪麗亞街。**(41) 我家完全停電了。**

女：很抱歉，先生。似乎有棵樹倒在電線上，並且切斷了你們街道上的所有電力供應。

男：是的，正如我所料。你知道要多久才能恢復電力嗎？

女：**(42) 因為暴風雨造成多起損壞，我們維修團隊的進度落後。(43) 在此期間，我建議你待在家人或朋友的家裡。**

🎧 31

41. What problem does the man report?
- [A] Internet access has been disconnected.
- [B] A delivery has not arrived yet.
- **[C] A power outage occurred.**
- [D] Some equipment has malfunctioned.

41. 男子提報什麼問題？
- [A] 網路連線被切斷
- [B] 貨品尚未送到
- **[C] 發生停電**
- [D] 某些設備故障了

42. Where most likely does the woman work?
- [A] At an electronics store
- **[B] At a power company**
- [C] At a toy factory
- [D] At a communications provider

42. 女子最有可能在哪裡工作？
- [A] 電器行
- **[B] 電力公司**
- [C] 玩具工廠
- [D] 通訊供應商

43. What does the woman suggest the man do?
- **[A] Take shelter elsewhere**
- [B] Report the incident to the police
- [C] Restart his computer
- [D] Arrive ahead of schedule

43. 女子建議男子做什麼？
- **[A] 到別處避難**
- [B] 向警方提報此事件
- [C] 重新開啟電腦
- [D] 提早抵達

44–46 conversation

W: Hello, I need to send a package to my brother who lives overseas in Germany. What delivery method would be best?

M: Well, it really depends on what you're sending. **(44) Because we are a public post office, we don't offer that many options.**

W: **(45) Actually, it was my brother's birthday last week, but I forgot. So I'm in a hurry to send this package.** Also, what I'm sending is somewhat fragile.

44–46 對話

女：哈囉，我需要寄一個包裹給住在德國的哥哥，什麼運送方式最好？

男：嗯，要視你所寄送的物品而定。**(44) 因為我們是公立郵局，所以我們提供的選擇並不多。**

女：**(45) 實際上，上星期是我哥哥的生日，但我忘了。因此我急著要寄這個包裹。**此外，我要寄的東西算是易碎品。

M：**(46) In that case, I suggest you use a private delivery service.** Private companies provide a larger variety of services that we don't offer.

男：**(46)** 那樣的話，我建議你使用私人貨運服務。私人公司提供我們沒有的多樣化服務。

44. Where does the man work?
    A At an immigration office
    B At a public school
    C At a post office
    D At a travel agency

44. 男子在哪裡工作？
    A 移民局
    B 公立學校
    C 郵局
    D 旅行社

45. Why is the woman in a hurry?
    A She is late to work.
    B She forgot an important event.
    C She must meet a deadline.
    D She has another appointment.

45. 女子為何匆忙？
    A 她上班遲到了
    B 她忘了一件重要的事
    C 她必須趕上截止期限
    D 她有另一項約會

46. What does the man recommend?
    A Making a phone call
    B Visiting a different business
    C Sending an email
    D Canceling a subscription

46. 男子建議什麼？
    A 打電話
    B 去另一家公司
    C 寄電子郵件
    D 取消訂閱

47–49 conversation

W：Hi, Mr. Winston. This is Sharon Smith. **(47) I was the person interested in buying the used Speedster sports car that you showed me last week.** I checked my financial situation, and I've decided to go ahead with the purchase.

M：Hi, Ms. Smith. Well, unfortunately, we already sold that car to somebody yesterday. However, I have a similar model that you could look at. The car is used, but it is in great shape and just had new tires put on it.

W：Oh, that's too bad that you already sold the model. **(48) That car had a really good safety rating, which is what I consider most important when buying a car.**

M：I see. Well, this similar model also has a five-star safety rating. **(49) Why don't you come here this week? You can take a look at it and take it for a test drive.**

47–49 對話

女：你好，溫士頓先生。我是雪倫・史密斯。**(47)** 我就是上週有意購買你向我展示的勁速二手跑車的那個人。我查看了我的財務狀況，決定要購買。

男：嗨，史密斯女士。很可惜，我們昨天已經將車賣給別人了。然而，我還有一個相似車款，你可以來看看。它是二手車，但車況很好，而且才剛換新輪胎。

女：喔，真可惜你已經賣了那款車。**(48)** 那輛車的安全評比很高，我認為這是購車時最重要的考慮因素。

男：我了解。嗯，這台相似車款也有五顆星的安全評比。**(49)** 你何不這週過來？你可以來看看這台車並且進行試駕。

47. What type of business does the man work for?
- [A] An auto repair shop
- [B] An insurance company
- **[C] An automobile dealership**
- [D] A construction contractor

48. What does the woman say is her top priority when she makes a purchase?
- [A] Affordability
- [B] Popularity
- [C] Design
- **[D] Safety**

49. What does the man suggest doing?
- [A] Replacing a broken part
- **[B] Evaluating a different model**
- [C] Visiting a new branch
- [D] Paying a deposit

47. 男子從事什麼行業？
- [A] 汽車修理廠
- [B] 保險公司
- **[C] 汽車經銷商**
- [D] 建築承包商

48. 女子說她購買時的首要考量是什麼？
- [A] 價格
- [B] 知名度
- [C] 設計
- **[D] 安全**

49. 男子建議做什麼？
- [A] 更換損壞的零件
- **[B] 評估另一款車**
- [C] 造訪新的分店
- [D] 付訂金

50–52 conversation

M：Hello, Judy. **(50) Have you got a moment to discuss last week's sales figures?**

W：**(51) I'm actually on my way to a meeting, but you can ask me something briefly.**

M：The sales figures for your branch are much lower than they have ever been. The board of directors is pretty upset about it. Is everything ok at the office?

W：Well, not really. There are some problems with my staff at the moment, and they aren't working like they used to. There is a conflict between some of the staff. I know it's affecting sales figures and it is a serious problem.

M：Really? **(52) Do you think we need to fire someone?**

W：I think that's the only solution. I'm going to see how they go in the next week and I will make a decision.

50–52 對話

男：哈囉，茱蒂。**(50) 你有空討論上星期的銷售業績嗎？**

女：**(51) 我其實正要去開會，但你可以簡短詢問。**

男：你分公司的銷售業績遠低於以往，董事會對此很不高興，辦公室一切都還好嗎？

女：嗯，不盡然。我的員工目前有些問題，他們工作狀況不如以往，部分員工之間起了衝突。我知道這影響了銷售業績，而且這是個嚴重的問題。

男：真的嗎？**(52) 你認為我們需要開除什麼人嗎？**

女：我認為這是唯一的解決方法，我要看看他們下星期的狀況，然後做出決定。

50. What are the speakers mainly discussing?
- [A] High sales figures
- [B] A staff conflict
- **[C] Low sales figures**
- [D] A new training manual

50. 對話者們主要在討論什麼？
- [A] 高的銷售業績
- [B] 員工衝突
- **[C] 低的銷售業績**
- [D] 新的訓練手冊

51. What does the woman mean when she says, "I'm actually on my way to a meeting"?
[A] **She doesn't have a lot of time to talk.**
[B] She can stay and chat for a long time.
[C] She is asking the man out to lunch.
[D] She will send him an email later on.

52. What possible solution does the man suggest?
[A] To employ more staff members
[B] That the woman should be fired
[C] They should have lunch together.
[D] **The woman might have to fire someone.**

53–55 conversation

W：Hello, Mr. Morgan. This is Debra. **(53) We have a bit of a problem.** The person that was supposed to give the keynote speech next week is sick. So we need to find a replacement. Would you be able to do it?

M：I'll be out of town for the next four days on business, and when I get back I'll be quite busy.

W：I see. **(54) The board of directors would love to have you do the speech.** They really liked it the last time you delivered it.

M：**(55) Thanks, but I'll have to pass on it.** I just have too much on my plate at the moment. If I had some more time to prepare, I would have considered it.

W：OK, I understand. I'll let the board know. I hope you have a safe trip.

M：Thanks for your understanding, Debra.

53. What is the problem?
[A] **The person who was supposed to give the speech is sick.**
[B] The person who was supposed to give the speech doesn't want to do it now.
[C] There is no keynote speech anymore.
[D] The keynote speaker is late.

---

51. 女子說「我其實正要去開會」，她指的是什麼？
[A] **她沒有太多可以講話的時間**
[B] 她可以留下來聊很久
[C] 她約男子去吃午餐
[D] 她之後會寄電子郵件給他

52. 男子提出什麼可能的解決方法？
[A] 僱用更多員工
[B] 應該開除女子
[C] 他們應該共進午餐
[D] **女子可能必須開除某人**

53–55 對話

女：哈囉，摩根先生。我是黛布拉。**(53) 我們有點問題。** 原定下星期要發表主題演講的人生病了。因此我們需要找人替補。您可以嗎？

男：我接下來四天要出城去洽公，回來後會很忙碌。

女：了解。**(54) 董事會很想邀您來演講，** 他們很喜歡您上次的演講。

男：**(55) 謝謝，但我必須放棄這次機會。** 我現在事情太多了。如果有多一些時間可以準備，我會考慮的。

女：好的，我懂。我會告訴董事會，祝您旅途平安。

男：感謝你的體諒，黛布拉。

53. 問題是什麼？
[A] **本來要發表演講的人生病了**
[B] 本來要發表演講的人現在不想演講了
[C] 沒有主題演講了
[D] 主講人遲到了

54. What does the woman say to the man?
- [A] To find someone to do the speech.
- [B] She will deliver the speech.
- **[C] To deliver the keynote speech.**
- [D] The board is not happy.

55. What does the man imply when he says, "thanks, but I'll have to pass on it"?
- [A] He will deliver the speech.
- **[B] He doesn't want to deliver the speech.**
- [C] He will talk to the board of directors.
- [D] He needs some more information.

56–58 conversation

W : Tristar Logistics, How can I help you?
M : Hello. **(56) I have a delivery coming today, but I won't be at the office.** Can you reschedule the delivery?
W : No problem. If you prefer, we can leave it with someone at your office?
M : **(57) That won't work for me.** The delivery contains some expensive pieces of art, so I want to personally receive it.
W : That's fine. When would you like it delivered?
M : Before midday would be perfect.
W : **(58) OK, if you could give me your cell phone number, I can have the delivery man call you when he is in your neighborhood.**

56. Why is the man calling Tristar Logistics?
- **[A] To reschedule a delivery**
- [B] To cancel his order
- [C] To change his address
- [D] To update his details

57. What does he imply when he says, "that won't work for me"?
- [A] The package contains important documents.
- [B] He will pay with a money order.
- **[C] He doesn't want them to leave the package with someone else.**
- [D] He wants it left at the office.

54. 女子對男子說什麼？
- [A] 找人演講
- [B] 她將要發表演講
- **[C] 發表主題演講**
- [D] 董事會不開心

55. 男子說「謝謝，但我必須放棄這次機會」，他暗示什麼？
- [A] 他將會發表演講
- **[B] 他不想要發表演講**
- [C] 他會與董事會討論
- [D] 他需要更多資訊

56–58 對話

女：三星物流，有什麼需要服務的嗎？
男：你好，**(56) 我今天會有貨物送達，但我不在辦公室。**你可以更改送貨時間嗎？
女：沒問題。如果您要的話，我們或許可以將貨品留給你辦公室的人？
男：**(57) 這對我而言行不通。**貨品包含幾件昂貴的藝術品，因此我想要親自收貨。
女：沒關係，您想要何時送達呢？
男：最好中午之前。
女：**(58) 好的，請你給我您的手機號碼，**這樣我可以請貨運人員到您附近時打給你。

56. 男子為何打電話給三星物流？
- **[A] 要重新安排送貨時間**
- [B] 要取消訂貨
- [C] 要更改住址
- [D] 要更新細節資料

57. 當他說「這對我而言行不通」時，他暗示什麼？
- [A] 包裹包含了重要的文件
- [B] 他會以匯票付款
- **[C] 他不想把包裹留給別人**
- [D] 他想要把包裹留在辦公室

58. What does the woman say she wants?

    Ⓐ The office address

    Ⓑ His cell phone number

    Ⓒ The order number

    Ⓓ His building number

58. 女子說她想要什麼？

    Ⓐ 辦公室地址

    Ⓑ 他的手機號碼

    Ⓒ 訂單編號

    Ⓓ 他的大樓編號

(NEW)

59–61 conversation

M1： Hi Ruth; hi Greg. **(59) Unfortunately, there is going to be a delay on the delivery of your computer equipment.** We won't be able to deliver it until tomorrow.

W： We needed that equipment today. **(60) We are going to miss some important deadlines without that equipment.**

M2： If we miss that deadline, we might lose some very important clients. Is there any possible way you can get it to us today?

M1： I'm sorry it's not possible. We haven't received the equipment at our distribution center yet.

W： OK. I know another supplier who can guarantee same day delivery. **(61) I'm going to call them and ask if they can supply us with the equipment.**

59–61 對話

男1： 嗨，露絲，嗨，格雷。**(59)** 很不幸地，你們電腦設備的運送將會延誤。我們要到明天才能送貨。

女： 我們今天就需要那項設備。**(60)** 沒有那項設備，我們會錯過一些重要的截止期限。

男2： 如果我們錯過截止期限，可能會失去一些很重要的客戶。你是否有可能今天就將設備交給我們？

男1： 很抱歉，這不可能。我們的配送中心尚未收到那項設備。

女： 好的，我知道另一家可以保證當天送達的供應商。**(61)** 我要打電話給他們，詢問是否能供應我們那項設備。

---

59. What are the speakers mainly discussing?

    Ⓐ The delivery of some furniture

    Ⓑ The signing of a rental contract

    Ⓒ The drafting of a document

    Ⓓ The delivery of computer equipment

59. 對話者們主要在討論什麼？

    Ⓐ 運送家具

    Ⓑ 簽署租約

    Ⓒ 草擬文件

    Ⓓ 運送電腦設備

60. What problem do Ruth and Greg have?

    Ⓐ They don't need the equipment.

    Ⓑ They could miss some important deadlines.

    Ⓒ They need to train their new staff.

    Ⓓ They haven't found the documents.

60. 露絲和格雷有什麼問題？

    Ⓐ 他們不需要這項設備

    Ⓑ 他們可能會錯過重要截止期限

    Ⓒ 他們需要訓練新進員工

    Ⓓ 他們尚未找到文件

61. What does the woman suggest she'll do?

    Ⓐ Accept the late order

    Ⓑ Cancel the order

    Ⓒ Call another supplier

    Ⓓ Rent some equipment

61. 女子說她會做什麼？

    Ⓐ 接受晚到的訂單

    Ⓑ 取消訂單

    Ⓒ 打電話給另一個供應商

    Ⓓ 租用某些設備

62-64 conversation

W: **(62) Hi, Aaron. How is the painting going? (63) Have you finished most of the work on level two?**

M: No, it is taking longer than we thought it would. We had to get some more paint delivered to the site, so we just started working again.

W: OK. When you finish on level two please come up to the fourth floor. We need your help to paint the ceiling. We don't have enough ladders. **(64) I suggest you bring at least three more ladders; there is a lot of work to be done here.**

M: Sure. We just have one more coat to put here, and then I will come up and help you finish.

62-64 對話

女：**(62) 嗨，亞倫。粉刷進行的怎麼樣了？(63) 你已經完成二樓大部分的工作了嗎？**

男：還沒有，這所需的時間比我們原先預期的還長。我們得請人多送一些油漆來這裡，所以才剛重新上工。

女：好的，等你完成二樓後請來四樓。我們需要你幫忙油漆天花板。我們梯子不夠。**(64) 我建議你至少再帶三個梯子過來，這裡有很多工作要做。**

男：好的，我們這裡只需要再上一層漆，然後我就上樓幫你完成。

Office Directory
公司行號一覽表

1st FL 一樓	Harlington Accounting 哈林頓會計事務所
2nd FL 二樓	Jersey Construction 澤西建設公司
3rd FL 三樓	Swanson and Sons 史文森氏公司
4th FL 四樓	Grounds Ltd. 地域有限公司

---

62. Who most likely are the speakers?
- [A] Store clerks
- [B] Artists
- **[C] Painters**
- [D] Electricians

63. Look at the graphic. Where is the man currently working?
- [A] Swanson and Sons
- [B] Harlington Accounting
- **[C] Jersey Construction**
- [D] Grounds Ltd.

64. What does the woman recommend to the man?
- [A] To bring more paint
- [B] To bring one ladder
- **[C] To bring at least three ladders**
- [D] To paint the roof first

62. 對話者最有可能是什麼人？
- [A] 店員
- [B] 藝術家
- **[C] 油漆工**
- [D] 電工

63. 參看圖表，男子正在哪裡工作？
- [A] 史文森氏公司
- [B] 哈林頓會計事務所
- **[C] 澤西建設公司**
- [D] 地域有限公司

64. 女子建議男子什麼？
- [A] 多帶一些油漆
- [B] 帶一個梯子
- **[C] 至少帶三個梯子**
- [D] 先粉刷屋頂

65–67 conversation

W： Good morning, I need this gown cleaned. **(65) I have to attend an award ceremony tomorrow night,** and I've only just noticed that there is a big stain on the back here. I need it cleaned by today. I know your service usually requires two days, but this is an emergency. Can you help me?

M： Yes, I can have it ready for you by 9 p.m. It will cost $36.

W： Are you serious? **(66) But your price list says $12.**

M： Well, yes, but if you need rush service, we charge three times the price. I have to delay other people's orders to clean yours, so it causes me some problems.

W： OK. I understand. That's fine. **(67) I'm busy this evening so I will send my daughter to pick it up tonight at 9 p.m.** Her name is Julie.

M： That sounds fine. I'll have it cleaned by 9 p.m.

65–67 對話

女： 早安，我需要送洗這件禮服。**(65) 我明晚要參加頒獎典禮，**而我剛才注意到在背後這裡有一塊很大的污漬。我今天就得把它清乾淨。我知道你們的服務通常需要兩天，但這是緊急情況，你可以幫我嗎？

男： 是的，我可以在晚上九點以前為你處理好，這樣是 36 元。

女： 你是說真的嗎？**(66) 但是你們價目表上寫的是 12 元。**

男： 是的，但是如果你需要緊急服務，我們會收三倍的價格。我必須延後其他人的訂單才能清潔你的衣服，因此這會造成一些問題。

女： 好，我了解，沒關係。**(67) 我今天晚上很忙，因此我會請我女兒今晚九點過來拿。**她的名字是茉莉。

男： 聽起來沒問題，我會在九點之前清洗好。

Harron Dry Cleaning 哈倫乾洗

Fabric 布料	Price 價格
Cotton 棉花	$10
Denim 牛仔布	$15
Wool 羊毛	$20
Silk 蠶絲	$12

65. What does the woman say she will do tomorrow?
- A Go out for dinner
- B Visit her family
- C Host an award show
- **D Attend an award ceremony**

66. Look at the graphic. What is the gown made of?
- A Cotton
- B Wool
- C Denim
- **D Silk**

65. 女子說她明天要做什麼？
- A 外出吃晚餐
- B 拜訪家人
- C 主持頒獎表演
- **D 參加頒獎典禮**

66. 參看圖表，這件禮服是由什麼製成的？
- A 棉花
- B 羊毛
- C 牛仔布
- **D 蠶絲**

67. What does the woman say she will do?

   A Pick it up at 9 p.m.

   B Send her husband to pick it up

   C Send her daughter to pick it up

   D Cancel the order

67. 女子説她將會做什麼？

   A 晚上九點來領取

   B 請她先生來領取

   C 請她女兒來領取

   D 取消訂單

68–70 conversation

W：I apologize for being late, Bruce. **(68) The Cranson Lot on Prunkel Street was shut because of water damage from the recent hurricane, so I couldn't find a parking spot.**

M：That's fine. Most of the staff is late today because of the Cranson Lot closure. Where did you park? Swinton Road?

W：**(69) There was a couple of spaces there but the sign said I couldn't park there past 8 p.m.** I think we will be working late tonight so I just parked on Menzies St.

M：Oh, that's a smart move. I think Menzies St. parking is 24 hours, **(70) so I suggest we have an early dinner** and then get this project finished tonight.

68–70 對話

女：很抱歉我遲到了，布魯斯。**(68) 普朗克街的克蘭森停車場因為最近颶風的水災而封閉了，因此我找不到停車位。**

男：沒關係，大部分員工今天都因為克蘭森停車場封閉而遲到。你車停在哪裡？是史文敦路嗎？

女：**(68) 那裡還有幾個停車位，但告示牌上寫晚上八點之後就不可以在那裡停車。我想我們今晚會工作到很晚，因此我就把車停在曼西斯街。**

男：喔，這招很聰明。我想曼西斯街停車場 24 小時開放，**(70) 因此我建議我們提早吃晚餐，然後今晚就完成這個案子。**

No Parking
After 8 P.M.
晚上八點之後禁止停車

68. According to the man, what is causing people to arrive late to work?

   A An electrical storm

   B A closed parking lot

   C A protest

   D Some new traffic rules

68. 根據男子，什麼導致人們上班遲到？

   A 雷暴

   B 關閉的停車場

   C 抗議遊行

   D 新的交通規則

69. Look at the graphic. Where is the sign most likely located?

    Ⓐ On Swinton Road

    Ⓑ At the Cranson Lot

    Ⓒ On Menzies Street

    Ⓓ On Prunkel Street

70. What does the man suggest they do?

    Ⓐ Go home

    Ⓑ Buy some parking tickets

    Ⓒ Have an early dinner

    Ⓓ Walk to work

69. 參看圖表，這個告示牌最有可能立在哪裡？

    Ⓐ 在史文敦路

    Ⓑ 在克蘭森停車場

    Ⓒ 在曼西斯街

    Ⓓ 在普朗克街

70. 男子建議他們做什麼？

    Ⓐ 回家

    Ⓑ 買停車票券

    Ⓒ 提早吃晚餐

    Ⓓ 走路上班

PART 4   P. 126-129   🎧 32

71–73 announcement

M： Hello, passengers. **(71) This is an announcement from your conductor.** Due to a freight train stalled at the next station, our departure will be delayed. The train ahead of us seems to be suffering a slight malfunction. **(72) Once we receive official permission from the traffic control center, we will proceed as normal.** Unfortunately, we will arrive a little bit later than the scheduled arrival time. We apologize for this inconvenience. **(73) Please adjust your plans accordingly.** Thank you for your patience. We should be on the move shortly.

71–73 宣布

男： 哈囉，各位乘客。**(71) 這是列車長的廣播。** 由於有列貨運火車在下一站拋錨，我們將延後發車。前方的火車似乎有些微故障。**(72) 一旦我們從交管中心獲得許可，就會恢復正常運行。** 很遺憾，我們會比預定抵達時間稍晚到達。我們為此不便道歉。**(73) 請依此調整你的計劃。** 感謝您的耐心，我們應該很快就會出發。

71. Where does the announcement most likely take place?

    Ⓐ On a train

    Ⓑ On a bus

    Ⓒ On a plane

    Ⓓ On a ship

72. What is the speaker waiting for?

    Ⓐ An itinerary

    Ⓑ Authorization to depart

    Ⓒ Some passengers to board

    Ⓓ A parking permit

73. What does the speaker suggest listeners do?

    Ⓐ Have their tickets reissued

    Ⓑ Transfer to another line

    Ⓒ Stay near a departure gate

    Ⓓ Modify their plans

71. 廣播最有可能是在哪裡播送？

    Ⓐ 火車上

    Ⓑ 公車上

    Ⓒ 飛機上

    Ⓓ 船上

72. 發話者在等什麼？

    Ⓐ 旅遊行程表

    Ⓑ 發車授權

    Ⓒ 一些乘客上車

    Ⓓ 停車許可

73. 發話者建議聽眾做什麼？

    Ⓐ 改車票

    Ⓑ 轉乘另一路線

    Ⓒ 待在登機口附近

    Ⓓ 修改他們的計劃

74–76 recorded message

W : **(74) Hello, you've reached Susan and Clare's Downtown Shop.** Beginning this Tuesday, we are closed for three days in order to expand the display space. **(74) (75) We will open this Friday with a much wider selection of women's pants and sweaters. (76) To celebrate our renovation, we will be offering 10% off all purchases on our first day back in business.** Thank you for your interest.

74–76 錄製語音

女：**(74)** 哈囉，你已來到蘇珊和克萊兒的市區分店。從本週二開始，我們要歇業三天，以拓寬展示區。**(74)(75)** 我們將於本週五恢復營業，屆時將有更多女性長褲和毛衣的款式。**(76)** 為了慶祝翻修，我們將在恢復營業的首日，提供所有商品九折優惠。感謝您的關注。

74. What type of business does the speaker work for?
- [A] An electronics store
- [B] A furniture outlet
- **[C] A clothing store**
- [D] A theater company

74. 發話者從事什麼行業？
- [A] 電子產品店
- [B] 家具直營店
- **[C] 服飾店**
- [D] 劇團

75. What improvement is mentioned?
- **[A] Product selection will be increased.**
- [B] More staff will be able to help.
- [C] Free parking will be offered.
- [D] Store hours will be extended.

75. 訊息中提到改善了什麼部分？
- **[A] 將會增加產品選擇性**
- [B] 將有更多員工能幫忙
- [C] 將提供免費停車
- [D] 將延長營業時間

76. When can customers receive a discount?
- [A] On Tuesday
- [B] On Wednesday
- [C] On Thursday
- **[D] On Friday**

76. 顧客何時能享有折扣？
- [A] 星期二
- [B] 星期三
- [C] 星期四
- **[D] 星期五**

77–79 radio advertisement

M : Every winter, families waste hundreds of dollars paying unreasonable prices to heat their homes. **(77) (78) By installing Garcia MX insulated windows in your home, you can add an extra layer of protection against dust and noise as well as lower your monthly heating costs. (79) You can get 20% off installation costs this month just by mentioning this radio advertisement when you call.** So why wait? Call today at 555-7263!

77–79 電台廣告

男：每年冬天，家家戶戶為了暖氣，浪費數百元支付不合理的價格。**(77) (78)** 只要在家裡安裝加西亞 MX 隔熱窗，你就可以增加一層保護來隔離灰塵和噪音，並降低每月的暖氣費。**(79)** 本月來電時，只要提及這則電台廣告就能享有八折安裝費的優惠。還在等什麼？今天就打 555-7263！

77. What is being advertised?
- [A] A security system
- [B] A rented house
- [C] A gardening tool
- **[D] An insulating product**

77. 這是什麼的廣告？
- [A] 保全系統
- [B] 出租房屋
- [C] 園藝工具
- **[D] 隔熱產品**

78.

78. What is mentioned about the product?

    Ⓐ It is domestically produced.

    Ⓑ It reduces the cost of living.

    Ⓒ It won several awards.

    Ⓓ It received positive reviews.

79. What must listeners do to receive a discount?

    Ⓐ Buy a certain amount of products

    Ⓑ Apply for a membership card

    Ⓒ Talk about the advertisement

    Ⓓ Make a payment in cash

80–82 instructions

W：**(80) This is the end of today's product demonstration for our newest model of cell phone.** If you would like to become a beta tester for this cell phone, please wait and talk to our representative, James Goldman. **(81) Volunteers must have worked in the consumer electronics industry for at least 5 years. (82) Remember, during the beta trial period, volunteers are strictly forbidden to release any details about the product.** Thank you very much for your interest in our brand-new model. I hope you enjoyed the presentation.

80. What event is ending?

    Ⓐ A grand opening

    Ⓑ A consumer electronics expo

    Ⓒ A product demonstration

    Ⓓ A museum tour

81. What is required of volunteers?

    Ⓐ Relevant experience

    Ⓑ A degree in engineering

    Ⓒ Availability to work on weekends

    Ⓓ Fluency in two languages

82. What are potential volunteers cautioned about?

    Ⓐ Missing a deadline

    Ⓑ Leaking confidential information

    Ⓒ Damaging a device

    Ⓓ Interrupting a presenter

---

78. 廣告中提到產品的什麼事？

    Ⓐ 它是國內生產的

    Ⓑ 它減少生活開銷

    Ⓒ 它贏得了數個獎項

    Ⓓ 它獲得好評

79. 聽眾要怎麼做才能獲得折扣？

    Ⓐ 買特定份量的產品

    Ⓑ 申請會員卡

    Ⓒ 提及這則廣告

    Ⓓ 用現金付款

80–82 指示

女：**(80)** 今日新款手機的產品示範會到此為止，若您想成為這款手機的試用者，請稍等並與我們的代表詹姆士・戈曼洽談。**(81)** 自願者必須在消費者電子產業有至少五年的工作經驗。**(82)** 請記得，在試用期間，將嚴格禁止自願者洩漏任何產品相關細節。感謝您對我們全新產品的關注，希望您喜歡今天的簡報。

80. 什麼活動快要結束了？

    Ⓐ 盛大開幕

    Ⓑ 消費者電子產品展

    Ⓒ 產品示範

    Ⓓ 博物館導覽

81. 自願者需要具備什麼？

    Ⓐ 相關經驗

    Ⓑ 工程學的學位

    Ⓒ 可在週末上班

    Ⓓ 能流利說兩種語言

82. 潛在的自願者被告誡什麼？

    Ⓐ 錯過截止期限

    Ⓑ 洩漏機密資訊

    Ⓒ 破壞裝置

    Ⓓ 打斷簡報人員

83–85 telephone message

M : Hi, Josephine, this is Robert Marcus calling from Human Resources. **(83) We're due to recruit some more interns for next year.** I've only been working here for a year, so I don't know the intern screening process. **(84) Have you seen the interview questions we use? (85) It would be great if you could just give me a quick rundown on what I need to do.** I can drop by your office anytime this week. Let me know a suitable time for you and I'll mark it in my calendar. Thanks.

83. What is the company recruiting?
- [A] Programmers
- [B] Chefs
- [C] **Interns**
- [D] Factory workers

(NEW)

84. What does the man imply when he says, "Have you seen the interview questions we use"?
- [A] He is postponing an appointment.
- [B] He needs a record of the report.
- [C] **He wants her to help him with the questions.**
- [D] He will recruit some accountants.

85. Why does the man want to meet with the woman?
- [A] **To get some assistance from her**
- [B] To ask her for some records
- [C] To get a new letterhead
- [D] To plan an orientation

86–88 talk

W : Welcome to the 2nd Annual Ball for Smith & Bradley. First of all, **(86) I'm pleased to announce that we have won Law Firm of The Year this year!** We had a win rate of 98% this year. We have beaten all the competition, with the second highest at 92%. This means a lot for us, since it will allow us to move into corporate law! Our success is due to the diligence and hard work of our legal team. **(87) So, let's keep**

83–85 電話留言

男： 嗨，約瑟芬，我是人力資源部的羅伯特 · 馬可斯。**(83) 我們要再多招募一些明年的實習人員。** 我只在這裡工作一年，不知道實習人員的篩選過程。**(84) 你看過我們面試時要用的問題了嗎？ (85) 若你能很快概述我需要做的事，那就太好了。** 我這週隨時可以去你的辦公室。請告訴我你可以的時間，我會將它標在我的日曆上。謝謝。

83. 這家公司在招募什麼？
- [A] 程式設計師
- [B] 廚師
- [C] **實習生**
- [D] 工廠工人

84. 男子説「你看過我們面試時要用的問題了嗎」，他暗示什麼？
- [A] 他要將會面延期
- [B] 他需要這份報告的紀錄
- [C] **他想要她協助擬定問題**
- [D] 他將要招募一些會計師

85. 男子為何想與女子會面？
- [A] **獲得她的協助**
- [B] 向她要求一些紀錄
- [C] 取得新的信頭
- [D] 籌劃新進人員訓練

86–88 談話

女： 歡迎來到第二屆史密斯和布萊德公司的年度舞會。首先，**(86) 我很高興宣布，我們今年被選為年度法律事務所！** 我們今年的贏率是98%。我們打敗了所有的競爭對手，第二高的是92%。這對我們來說意義重大，因為這能讓我們進展到公司法。我們的成功都是因為法務團隊的辛勞和努力。**(87) 因此，**

moving up! Corporate law is very technical, however. So I will be sending out a lot of information through email over the next several weeks. **(88) I'm going to need all of you to study this material, so we can maintain our win rate and continue growing as a firm.**

讓我們繼續努力吧！公司法非常的專業，因此在接下來的幾個星期中，我會透過電子郵件寄出大量資訊。**(88) 我要你們全體都研讀這些資料，這樣我們就可以保持贏率，讓事務所持續成長。**

86. What is the purpose of the announcement?
- **Ⓐ To announce an achievement**
- Ⓑ To announce a rise in sales
- Ⓒ To announce a new team member
- Ⓓ To complete a project

86. 這則宣布的目的是什麼？
- **Ⓐ 要宣布一項成就**
- Ⓑ 要宣布銷售的增加
- Ⓒ 要宣布一位新的團隊成員
- Ⓓ 要完成一項企劃

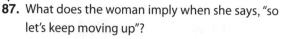

87. What does the woman imply when she says, "so let's keep moving up"?
- **Ⓐ They need to continue working hard.**
- Ⓑ They are moving buildings.
- Ⓒ She is renovating the office.
- Ⓓ They are going on a business trip.

87. 女子說「因此，讓我們繼續努力吧」，暗示什麼？
- **Ⓐ 他們需要持續努力工作**
- Ⓑ 他們要搬家
- Ⓒ 她正在翻修辦公室
- Ⓓ 他們要出差

88. What does the woman ask the staff to do?
- Ⓐ Study the new handbook
- Ⓑ Prepare a report
- **Ⓒ Study material on corporate law**
- Ⓓ Write a memo

88. 女子要求員工做什麼？
- Ⓐ 研讀新的手冊
- Ⓑ 備妥報告
- **Ⓒ 研讀公司法的資料**
- Ⓓ 寫備忘錄

89–91 phone message

W：Grace! **(89) Thank you so much for helping set up the Simpson wedding last weekend.** The centerpieces and floral arrangements you made were amazing! **(90) You have to show me the design sometime!** The bride and groom absolutely loved your work. **(91) Anyway, I'll see you on Tuesday. We have to go over the centerpieces and flower setups for the Grayson wedding next week.** I'm very excited to work with you again! Talk soon.

89–91 電話留言

女：葛瑞思！**(89) 很感謝你協助布置上週末辛普森的婚禮。**你所做的餐桌擺飾和插花真令人驚艷！**(90) 你一定要找時間讓我看看設計！**新娘和新郎真的很喜歡你的作品。**(91) 總之，我下星期二會見到你。我們要看下星期格瑞森婚禮的餐桌擺飾和花朵布置。**我很興奮能夠再與你合作！再聊囉。

89. Why is the woman calling?
- **Ⓐ To say thank you**
- Ⓑ To ask a favor
- Ⓒ To discuss travel plans
- Ⓓ To request a form

89. 女子為何打電話？
- **Ⓐ 道謝**
- Ⓑ 請求幫忙
- Ⓒ 討論旅遊計劃
- Ⓓ 要求表格

90. What does the woman imply when she says, "you have to show me the design sometime"?

A She wants to learn how to make it.

B She wasn't sure about the details.

C She needs a dentist recommendation.

D She is writing a design manual.

91. What will the women do next week?

A Plan for the Grayson wedding

B Plan for the Christmas party

C Design a new invitation

D Meet for coffee

90. 女子説「你一定要找時間讓我看看設計」,她暗示什麼?

A 她想要學習如何製作

B 她不確定細節

C 她需要牙醫的推薦

D 她正在寫設計手冊

91. 女子下星期要做什麼?

A 籌劃格瑞森婚禮

B 籌劃聖誕派對

C 設計新的邀請函

D 約會面喝咖啡

92-94 announcement

W : **(92) Springdale Music Club has just expanded its music selection to include world music artists.** We are extremely excited to be able to build on our already impressive offering of domestic recording artists! We'll be having a live performance of international sensation, Djubai Djinn this Saturday at 8 p.m. Come early for the cook out, too. Bring your own meats though, since we can't feed everyone! **(94) Djubai Djinn will be signing autographs and selling their own albums and merchandise to help promote their US tour, so be sure you bring your money** and your dancing feet! For those of you worried that we may be changing our focus too much, fear not! Springdale Music Club will still keep a healthy emphasis on rock and roll, and this Saturday's concert is no exception with 3 rockin' acts.

92-94 宣布

女 : **(92)** 春谷音樂俱樂部擴增其精選音樂,納入了世界音樂演奏家。能從原本就令人印象深刻的國內錄製歌手為基礎進行擴增,使我們很興奮!我們將舉辦一場充滿國際觀的現場演出,邀請到迪拜・狄金於本週六晚上八點開唱。也可以早點來參加野炊,但要自己帶肉來,我們無法餵飽每個人!**(94)** 迪拜・狄金將簽名並且販售他們的專輯和商品,以協助宣傳他們的美國之行,因此請務必帶錢,還有舞動的雙腳!擔心我們可能會大幅改變音樂重心的人,請別害怕!春谷音樂俱樂部仍然會持續以健康的方式把搖滾樂當成重點。本週六的音樂會也不例外,會有三場搖滾樂演出。

SPRINGDALE MUSIC CLUB'S SATURDAY CONCERT LINE UP
春谷音樂俱樂部週六音樂會陣容

5 p.m. to 8 p.m. 晚上 5 到 8 點	Barbeque Cookout, 烤肉野炊, bring your own meat! 帶自己的肉品!
8 p.m. to 9 p.m. 晚上 8 到 9 點	Djubai Djinn, 迪拜・狄金, all the way from East Timor 遠從東帝汶而來
9 p.m. to 10 p.m. 晚上 9 到 10 點	Swinging Devils 搖擺惡魔 touring from Memphis 從曼菲斯來此巡迴演出
10 p.m. to 11 p.m. 晚上 10 到 11 點	Rock or Die! 不搖滾就去死! Local Heroes 本地英雄
11 p.m. to 12 a.m. 晚上 11 到 12 點	Ferocious Four 兇猛四人組 all the way from New York City 遠從紐約市而來

92. What is indicated about Springdale Music Club?

    Ⓐ They love all music equally.

    Ⓑ They take pride in their location.

    Ⓒ They specialize in country music.

    Ⓓ They didn't carry world music before.

93. Look at the graphic. What can you infer about the bands?

    Ⓐ They will be great.

    Ⓑ They are jazz musicians.

    Ⓒ The acts following Djubai Djinn play rock and roll.

    Ⓓ They will be loud.

94. Why does Springdale Music Club ask you to bring your money?

    Ⓐ The concert will be expensive.

    Ⓑ There is a bar.

    Ⓒ To help support Djubai Djinn's US tour

    Ⓓ To pay for your meats

92. 關於春谷音樂俱樂部有提到哪一點？

    Ⓐ 他們同樣喜歡各種類型的音樂

    Ⓑ 他們對於地點很自豪

    Ⓒ 他們擅長鄉村音樂

    Ⓓ 他們先前從未有世界音樂

93. 參看圖表，關於這些樂團，你可以得到什麼推論？

    Ⓐ 他們將會很棒

    Ⓑ 他們是爵士音樂家

    Ⓒ 迪拜・狄金之後的演出是搖滾樂

    Ⓓ 他們會很大聲

94. 春谷音樂俱樂部為何要求帶錢？

    Ⓐ 音樂會很昂貴

    Ⓑ 有吧台

    Ⓒ 要協助支持迪拜・狄金的美國之旅

    Ⓓ 要為自己的肉品付錢

95–97 tour guide

W：Welcome to Lake Kitano National Park. **(95) I'm Jane Black, your guide for today.** If you look at your map, we'll start our tour from the Information Center and head to West Gate. **(96) Now, we usually continue our journey to South Gate after a short break, but that path is closed to the public this season.** Instead, we'll take the path to East Gate and hike up the Kilmore Cliff trail until we reach Lake Kitano. **(97) For those of you who are afraid of heights, Kilmore Cliff is a trail that goes along the 50 meter cliff drop.** If you have any concerns, please voice them now. Otherwise, we'll begin our tour.

95–97 旅遊導覽

女：歡迎來到北野湖國家公園。**(95) 我是珍・布萊克，你們今天的導遊。** 請參看地圖，我們的行程將由旅遊諮詢中心開始，並前往西側大門。**(96) 我們通常在短暫休息後會繼續行程前往南側大門，但本季那條小徑不開放給大眾通行。** 我們會改走通往東側大門的路，並且健行基墨峭壁的小徑，直到我們到達北野湖。**(97) 對於怕高的人，基墨峭壁是一條挨著 50 公尺峭壁走的山路。** 如果你有任何顧慮，請現在就說出來。否則我們將要開始行程。

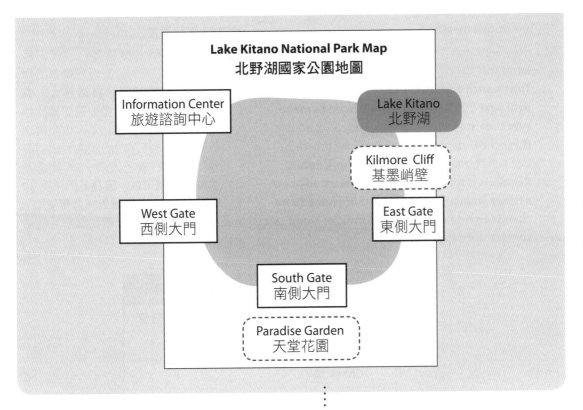

Lake Kitano National Park Map
北野湖國家公園地圖

Information Center
旅遊諮詢中心

Lake Kitano
北野湖

Kilmore Cliff
基墨峭壁

West Gate
西側大門

East Gate
東側大門

South Gate
南側大門

Paradise Garden
天堂花園

95. Who most likely are the listeners?

Ⓐ Residents

Ⓑ Tourists

Ⓒ Park employees

Ⓓ Forest rangers

96. Look at the map. What place are the listeners unable to go to?

Ⓐ Lake Kitano

Ⓑ East Gate

Ⓒ Kilmore Cliff

Ⓓ Paradise Garden

97. What does the woman mention about Kilmore Cliff?

Ⓐ It is dangerous.

Ⓑ The views are spectacular.

Ⓒ People who fear heights may not enjoy it.

Ⓓ It is 50 meters from the final destination.

95. 聽眾最有可能是什麼人？

Ⓐ 居民

Ⓑ 觀光客

Ⓒ 公園員工

Ⓓ 森林管理員

96. 參看地圖，聽者無法去什麼地方？

Ⓐ 北野湖

Ⓑ 東側大門

Ⓒ 基墨峭壁

Ⓓ 天堂花園

97. 關於基墨峭壁，女子提到什麼？

Ⓐ 它很危險

Ⓑ 景色很壯觀

Ⓒ 懼高的人可能不會喜歡

Ⓓ 它距離最終目的地 50 公尺

98–100 phone message

M: Hello Lima, this is George. I've faxed you the order forms that the different departments sent. **(99) The finance department has the largest order with over 100 items, but you'll need to make sure they stay within the budget.** Also, double check the IT department's form. They ordered a lot of electronic equipment. **(98) I think Public Relations is fine, since they only wanted about a dozen items. (100) Call me if there need to be changes made on the order forms, so that I can contact the departments.**

98–100 電話留言

男： 你好，莉瑪，我是喬治，我已經將各部門寄來的訂購表格傳真給你了。**(99) 財務部門的訂單最大，有超過 100 件物品，但你需要確認他們沒有超過預算。**此外，也要再次確認資訊科技部門的表格，他們訂購了大量的電子設備。**(98) 我認為公關部門還可以，因為他們只要 12 件物品。(100) 若訂單表格需要更動，請打電話給我，以便我聯繫各個部門。**

Order form 訂單表格	
Item 品項	Quantity 數量
Desks 書桌	1
Chairs 椅子	8
File Binders 檔案夾	3

98. Look at the graphic. Which department filled out the order form?
- A Finance
- B IT
- **C Public Relations**
- D Human Resources

99. What does the speaker anticipate may happen?
- **A Some departments may go over budget.**
- B The warehouse may not have enough supplies.
- C The orders may not arrive on time.
- D The departments may forget some items.

100. What does the speaker request of Lima?
- A To fax over the orders
- B To file the papers
- C To arrange a meeting
- **D To contact him**

98. 參看圖表，這張訂購表是哪個部門填寫的？
- A 財務
- B 資訊科技
- **C 公關**
- D 人力資源

99. 發話者預期可能發生什麼事？
- **A 一些部門可能超過預算**
- B 倉庫可能沒有足夠的辦公用品
- C 訂單可能不會準時送達
- D 各個部門可能忘了某些物件

100. 發話者要求莉瑪做什麼？
- A 傳真訂單給他
- B 將文件歸檔
- C 安排會議
- **D 與他聯繫**

PART 1 P. 130-133   33

1. Ⓐ There are many people in the store.
   Ⓑ She is purchasing a garment.
   Ⓒ She is looking at some clothing.
   Ⓓ There are clothes on all the coat hangers.

2. **Ⓐ One woman is raising her hand.**
   Ⓑ The presenter is looking at the watch.
   Ⓒ The presenter is using the microphone.
   Ⓓ The presentation is very boring.

3. Ⓐ She is wearing safety glasses.
   Ⓑ She is looking for some bacteria.
   Ⓒ She is looking through the microscope.
   Ⓓ She is using the microphone.

4. Ⓐ They are playing golf.
   Ⓑ They are carrying their golf clubs over their right shoulder.
   Ⓒ They are setting up the golf clubs.
   Ⓓ They are trading used golf clubs.

5. Ⓐ She is repairing the shoes.
   Ⓑ There are other people in the store.
   Ⓒ They are trying on some shoes.
   Ⓓ She has a sock on her left foot.

6. **Ⓐ The man is giving a presentation in front of a screen.**
   Ⓑ The man is typing on his laptop.
   Ⓒ The woman is writing some notes with her right hand.
   Ⓓ They all have computers.

1. Ⓐ 商店裡有許多人。
   Ⓑ 她正在買衣服。
   Ⓒ 她看著服飾。
   Ⓓ 所有的大衣衣架上都有掛衣服。

2. **Ⓐ 一名女子正在舉手。**
   Ⓑ 簡報者正在看手錶。
   Ⓒ 簡報者正在使用麥克風。
   Ⓓ 簡報非常無聊。

3. Ⓐ 她戴著護目鏡。
   Ⓑ 她正在尋找某些細菌。
   Ⓒ 她正在透過顯微鏡觀察。
   Ⓓ 她正在使用麥克風。

4. Ⓐ 他們正在打高爾夫球。
   Ⓑ 他們的右肩背著高爾夫球桿。
   Ⓒ 他們正在擺放高爾夫球桿。
   Ⓓ 他們在買賣二手高爾夫球桿。

 33
 34

5. Ⓐ 她正在修理鞋子。
   Ⓑ 商店裡有其他人。
   Ⓒ 她們正在試穿鞋子。
   Ⓓ 她的左腳有穿襪子。

6. **Ⓐ 男子正在螢幕前進行簡報。**
   Ⓑ 男子正用筆記型電腦打字。
   Ⓒ 女子正用右手寫筆記。
   Ⓓ 他們都有電腦。

TEST 9
PART 2

PART 2 P. 134   34

7. Is Mr. Johnson joining us for lunch?
   Ⓐ Yes, I'm hungry, too.
   Ⓑ No, he's occupied.
   Ⓒ I brought a sandwich.

7. 強森先生要和我們一起吃午餐嗎?
   Ⓐ 是的,我也餓了。
   Ⓑ 不,他有事要忙。
   Ⓒ 我帶了三明治。

8. When will the company release its newest video game console?
   A At midnight tonight.
   B He will renew his lease next month.
   C It's on the desk.

9. How did you get such great seats for the concert?
   A By winning tickets at a raffle.
   B At least once a week.
   C He's a world-renowned musician.

10. Why are the lights off in the conference room?
    A I was sitting there.
    B They are watching a video.
    C Yes, she's off duty.

11. Do you know where the employee break room is?
    A We will take a 10-minute break.
    B Have you worked here long?
    C On the second floor.

12. Who replaced the ink cartridge?
    A Suzy did this morning.
    B In the shopping cart.
    C It's a brand-new printer.

13. I'm so thankful for all your help in preparing this report.
    A You're welcome to stay.
    B Don't mention it.
    C I need a pair of gloves.

14. Would you like to make a reservation for tonight?
    A The dinner was delicious.
    B I would, for six people.
    C It's an expensive hobby.

15. Why did you open the window?
    A To let in some fresh air.
    B In the master bedroom.
    C Because the store will open next month.

16. Let's stop by the post office on the way.
    A A letter to my cousin.
    B OK, where is it?
    C The delivery arrived yesterday.

8. 這家公司何時會發表最新的電玩遊戲機？
   A 今天午夜。
   B 他下個月會簽新租約。
   C 在書桌上。

9. 你是怎麼得到位子那麼棒的演唱會門票？
   A 在抽獎活動中贏得門票。
   B 至少一星期一次。
   C 他是世界的知名的音樂家。

10. 會議室為什麼要關燈？
    A 我當時坐在那裡。
    B 他們正在看影片。
    C 是的，她下班了。

11. 你知道員工休息室在哪裡嗎？
    A 我們休息 10 分鐘。
    B 你在這裡工作很久了嗎？
    C 在二樓。

12. 誰換了墨水匣？
    A 蘇西今天早上換的。
    B 在購物推車裡。
    C 這是全新的印表機。

13. 我很感謝你幫忙備妥這份報告。
    A 很歡迎你留下來。
    B 別客氣。
    C 我需要一雙手套。

14. 您想要預約今天晚上的位子嗎？
    A 晚餐很美味。
    B 是的，六個人。
    C 這是個昂貴的嗜好。

15. 你為何打開窗戶？
    A 要讓新鮮空氣進來。
    B 在主臥室裡。
    C 因為這家商店下個月將會開幕。

16. 我們順便去郵局吧。
    A 一封給我表哥的信。
    B 好的，郵局在哪？
    C 貨運昨天送到了。

17. There's a name missing from the list of speakers.
    A **Oh, who is it?**
    B I'll make 20 copies.
    C Yes, he agreed to the contract.

18. What day are we hosting that party?
    A Yes, it's ready.
    B He requested a chocolate cake.
    C **Check the calendar in the office.**

19. You should sign up for a computer programming workshop.
    A Mr. Greene will assign more employees to the project.
    B **You don't think it would be too difficult for me?**
    C Please refund this purchase.

20. You've finished interviewing the candidates, haven't you?
    A It was in the meeting room.
    B **Yes, the last person just left.**
    C Where did you put the applications?

21. Would you like to be in charge of entertainment or catering?
    A **I'll take care of food and drinks.**
    B It was a great party.
    C The stage is too small.

22. Don't we need to check out soon?
    A **No, I reserved the room until tomorrow.**
    B The hotel doesn't provide room service.
    C Let's make a reservation for 6 o'clock.

23. I'm excited to start using this new software.
    A **Yes, it should make work easier.**
    B It's old, but still usable.
    C I was disappointed in him.

24. Why don't we hand out free samples to customers?
    A No, it's the customer service department.
    B Because we conducted a survey.
    C **Yeah, that's a good strategy.**

17. 講者名單上有個名字漏掉了。
    A **喔,是誰?**
    B 我要印 20 份。
    C 是的,他同意這個合約。

18. 我們要在星期幾辦那場派對?
    A 是的,已經準備好了。
    B 他要求有個巧克力蛋糕。
    C **查看辦公室的日曆。**

19. 你應該報名參加電腦程式設計研討會。
    A 格林先生將指派更多員工參與計劃。
    B **你不覺得這對我而言太困難了嗎?**
    C 請退還這個商品的款項。

20. 你已經結束應徵者的面試了,不是嗎?
    A 在會議室裡。
    B **是的,最後一人剛離開。**
    C 你把求職表放在哪裡?

21. 你想要負責娛樂或者是外燴?
    A **我來負責食物和飲料。**
    B 這是場很棒的派對。
    C 舞台太小了。

22. 我們不是很快就要退房了嗎?
    A **不,房間我訂到明天。**
    B 這家飯店不提供客房服務。
    C 我們訂六點鐘吧。

23. 我很興奮能開始使用這個新軟體。
    A **是的,它應該能讓工作更容易。**
    B 它很舊,但仍可使用。
    C 我對他很失望。

24. 我們何不發送免費試用品給顧客?
    A 不,這是客服部門。
    B 因為我們進行了一項調查。
    C **好啊,那是個好策略。**

25. The building site hasn't been selected, has it?

   A We are still considering multiple options.

   B It's a luxury apartment complex.

   C He will cite a passage from his book.

26. How did you hear about the meeting on Thursday?

   A Mr. Shepard told me at lunch.

   B My neighbor gave it to me.

   C I can't tell them apart.

27. Should I tell Susan for you, or do you want to tell her yourself?

   A She's a bank teller.

   B I want to do it directly.

   C I forgot the phone number.

28. The annual sales report is finished.

   A We should proofread it before printing.

   B I watched the weather report, too.

   C They raised the price by 10 dollars.

29. Is this used vehicle for sale?

   A Yes, and I changed the tires on it.

   B The price of gas is reasonable.

   C I used it for cooking.

30. What is needed to apply for this job?

   A Yes, she starts on Monday.

   B A bachelor's degree or higher in engineering.

   C The rule doesn't apply to children under 8.

31. Who's in charge of designing promotional handouts?

   A Mr. Wilson was promoted to sales manager.

   B The man wearing the blue shirt.

   C We don't charge for delivery.

---

25. 建築地點還沒有選定，不是嗎？

   A 我們還在考量多種選擇。

   B 這是一棟豪華公寓大樓。

   C 他將從他的書中引用一段話。

26. 你如何得知星期四的會議？

   A 薛帕森先生午餐時告訴我的。

   B 我鄰居給我的。

   C 我無法分辨他們。

27. 我應該幫你跟蘇珊說，還是你想親自跟她說？

   A 她是一名銀行櫃員。

   B 我想要直接跟她說。

   C 我忘了電話號碼。

28. 年度銷售報告完成了。

   A 我們應該在付印之前進行校對。

   B 我也看了氣象報導。

   C 他們把價格調漲十元。

29. 這輛二手車供販售嗎？

   A 是的，而且我已經為它換了輪胎。

   B 油價很合理。

   C 我用它來烹飪。

30. 應徵這份工作需要什麼資格？

   A 是的，她星期一開始工作。

   B 工程學學士或以上的學位。

   C 這項規則不適用於八歲以下的孩童。

31. 誰負責設計促銷的傳單？

   A 威爾森先生被晉升為銷售經理。

   B 穿藍色襯衫的男子。

   C 我們不收運費。

32–34 conversation

W: Hello, Mr. Penn. **(32) I wanted to ask about changing my work hours.** I will be entering university starting next month, and my availability is going to change.

M: Well, Nami, we really value you as a hard-working employee at this restaurant, so I want you to continue working here. What do you think your schedule will be?

W: Thank you for saying so. **(33) I haven't registered for classes yet, so I'm not completely sure.**

M: I see. **(34) Once you find out, please let me know.** I'm sure we can figure something out so that you can attend university and continue working here.

32–34 對話

女：哈囉，潘恩先生。**(32) 我想要詢問改變工時的事。**我下個月要上大學，我的空檔時間將會改變。

男：這樣啊，娜米，我們這家餐廳很看重你這位努力的員工，因此我希望你繼續在這裡工作，你認為你的時間表會是什麼樣子？

女：感謝您這麼說。**(33) 我還沒選課，所以我還不太確定。**

男：了解。**(34) 你一知道就請告訴我。**我們一定能想出方法，讓你能上大學又能繼續在這裡工作。

32. What is the woman requesting?
- A Time off from work
- B A recommendation letter
- **C A schedule change**
- D A pay raise

33. Why is the woman unsure about the man's question?
- A She wants to quit her job.
- B She is waiting for her exam results.
- C She got a job offer from another restaurant.
- **D She has not registered for classes.**

34. What does the man ask the woman to do?
- A Work overtime this week
- **B Inform him about her availability**
- C Recommend her acquaintance
- D Create a new menu design

32. 女子要求什麼？
- A 休假
- B 推薦函
- **C 班表更動**
- D 加薪

33. 關於男子的問題，女子為何不能確定？
- A 她想要辭職
- B 她在等候考試結果
- C 她找到另一家餐廳工作
- **D 她尚未註冊課程**

34. 男子要求女子做什麼？
- A 這週加班
- **B 告訴男子她有空的時間**
- C 推薦她認識的人
- D 設計新的菜單

35-37 conversation

M： Hello, my name is Jordan Briggs. **(35) I'll be getting married next week and we are looking for someone to photograph our wedding.** A friend of mine showed me photographs you took, and I was really impressed.

W： Thanks for calling me, Mr. Briggs. What type of photographs are you interested in exactly?

M： Well, we would want you to take photographs of everything including the guests, the food, the ceremony, and the after-party. **(36) How much would that cost?**

W： Well, it could be quite expensive. **(37) In order to photograph the event that extensively, I would need to hire two or three assistants.**

35. Why is the man calling?
- A To order a product
- B To postpone an appointment
- C To book a wedding hall
- **D To hire a photographer**

36. What does the man inquire about?
- **A A price quote**
- B A product sample
- C A list of employees
- D An event schedule

37. Why does the woman say the service might be quite expensive?
- A Her services are in high demand.
- **B She will need additional staff.**
- C She uses high-end equipment.
- D She has to meet a tight deadline.

38-40 conversation

M： We will have a new quality control inspector joining our staff as of tomorrow. **(38) His name is Nathan Gates, and he'll be examining products for any defects before being shipped.**

35-37 對話

男： 哈囉，我的名字是喬丹・布力格斯。**(35) 我下個星期就要結婚了，我們在找人為婚禮攝影。** 我的一個朋友讓我看你拍的照片，讓我留下深刻的印象。

女： 感謝您打電話給我，布力格斯先生。您對什麼類型的照片特別感興趣呢？

男： 我們想要你為所有東西拍照，包含賓客、食物、典禮以及婚禮後的派對。**(36) 這樣要多少錢？**

女： 這可能會很貴。**(37) 若要完整捕捉這場活動，我需要僱用兩或三名助理。**

35. 男子為何打電話？
- A 訂購產品
- B 延後預約
- C 預訂婚宴廳
- **D 僱用攝影師**

36. 男子詢問什麼事？
- **A 估價**
- B 產品樣本
- C 員工名單
- D 活動行程表

37. 女子為何說這項服務可能很貴？
- A 她的服務很熱門
- **B 她需要額外的工作人員**
- C 她使用高檔的設備
- D 她必須趕很緊迫的截止期限

38-40 對話

男： 明天開始將有一位新的品管員加入我們的團隊。**(38) 他的名字是納森・蓋茲，他會在出貨前查看產品以找出瑕疵品。**

W : I'm glad to hear that. We have had a lot of customers returning defective items lately. It's not good for our company's image and reputation.

M : **(39) When he comes to work tomorrow, please introduce him to everyone in the factory.**

W : Sure, I will. **(40) I'll also make sure to give him all the proper safety gear he needs to wear inside the factory.**

女：我很高興聽見這件事。我們最近有很多顧客退回瑕疵品，這有損我們公司的形象和名聲。

男：**(39)** 他明天上工時，請你把他介紹給工廠裡的所有人。

女：當然，我會的。**(40)** 我也一定會提供他在工廠裡面必須穿戴的合適安全裝備。

---

38. Who is Nathan Gates?
  Ⓐ A sales clerk
  Ⓑ A customer
  Ⓒ A private detective
  Ⓓ A product inspector

39. What does the man ask the woman to do?
  Ⓐ Run a training session
  Ⓑ Enforce safety measures
  Ⓒ Introduce a new employee
  Ⓓ Inspect a construction site

40. What will the woman give Mr. Gates?
  Ⓐ A training manual
  Ⓑ Safety gear
  Ⓒ A work schedule
  Ⓓ An identification card

38. 納森・蓋茲是什麼人？
  Ⓐ 銷售店員
  Ⓑ 顧客
  Ⓒ 私家偵探
  Ⓓ 品管員

39. 男子要求女子做什麼？
  Ⓐ 辦理訓練課程
  Ⓑ 加強安全措施
  Ⓒ 介紹新員工
  Ⓓ 檢查工地

40. 女子會給蓋茲先生什麼？
  Ⓐ 訓練手冊
  Ⓑ 安全裝備
  Ⓒ 工作時間表
  Ⓓ 識別證

41–43 conversation

M : We finally were able to pump all of the water from the basement today. **(41) Unfortunately, a lot of our inventory was damaged by the water.**

W : **(42) I've never seen a flood occur so fast like that.** Because of the damaged inventory, we won't be able to open for a few days.

M : Well, at least it didn't happen over the weekend when no one was in the office. The damage could have been much worse.

W : That's true. **(43) I heard from our supplier, and they said they can restock our storage room this Friday.** I guess we'll just have to wait patiently until then.

41–43 對話

男：我們今天終於能把地下室的水都抽掉。**(41)** 不幸的是，我們有很多存貨因水而受損。

女：**(42)** 我從來沒看過水淹得這麼快。因為存貨受損，我們有幾天都不能開店。

男：至少淹水不是發生在週末沒有人在辦公室的時候，不然損失可能更加慘重。

女：沒錯。**(43)** 我收到供貨商的消息，他們這星期五可以為我們的儲藏室補貨。我想在那之前，我們只能耐心等候。

41. What problem are the speakers discussing?
- Ⓐ Unsatisfied customers
- Ⓑ An unexpected drop in sales
- **Ⓒ Damaged inventory**
- Ⓓ A delayed shipment

42. What caused the problem?
- Ⓐ An electrical fire
- Ⓑ A burst water pipe
- **Ⓒ A sudden flood**
- Ⓓ A gas leak

43. What will happen on Friday?
- Ⓐ Construction will be completed.
- Ⓑ Stock prices will increase.
- **Ⓒ A shipment will arrive.**
- Ⓓ A supplier will be changed.

41. 對話者們在討論什麼問題？
- Ⓐ 顧客不滿
- Ⓑ 業績意外下跌
- **Ⓒ 存貨受損**
- Ⓓ 運送延遲

42. 是什麼導致這個問題？
- Ⓐ 電線走火
- Ⓑ 水管爆裂
- **Ⓒ 突發水災**
- Ⓓ 瓦斯漏氣

43. 星期五會發生什麼事？
- Ⓐ 工程將完工
- Ⓑ 股價將會上漲
- **Ⓒ 貨品將會送到**
- Ⓓ 供應商將被更換

44–46 conversation

M： **(44) Next week at Harrison University, Charlie Klein will be conducting an introductory lecture on creative writing. It's open to the public and it isn't very expensive.**

W： Charlie Klein? **(45) Doesn't he currently have a book on the bestseller list?** I heard his stories are very moving and powerful. I'd like to attend it.

M： Yes. I recently bought one of his books and was really impressed. That's why I don't want to miss this opportunity to learn from him. Would you like to read it before the lecture?

W： Sure. **(46) I'll stop by your home tomorrow and pick up the book from you.** Thanks for letting me know.

44–46 對話

男： (44) 下星期查理・克萊恩將在哈里森大學進行創意寫作介紹演講。演講會對大眾開放，而且並不會很昂貴。

女： 查理・克萊恩？ (45) 他現在不是有本書在暢銷書排行榜上嗎？我聽說他的故事很深刻感人，我想要參加。

男： 是的，我最近買了一本他的書，而且真的覺得印象深刻。這就是我為什麼不想錯過這次向他學習的機會。你想在演講前閱讀這本書嗎？

女： 當然。(46) 我明天會去你家拿那本書。謝謝你告訴我。

---

44. What are the speakers discussing?
- **Ⓐ A public lecture**
- Ⓑ An upcoming exam
- Ⓒ A graduation requirement
- Ⓓ A recent publishing trend

45. Who is Charlie Klein?
- Ⓐ A scientist
- Ⓑ An inventor
- Ⓒ A professor
- **Ⓓ A writer**

44. 對話者們在討論什麼？
- **Ⓐ 公開演講**
- Ⓑ 近期的考試
- Ⓒ 畢業要求
- Ⓓ 最近的出版趨勢

45. 查理・克萊恩是什麼人？
- Ⓐ 科學家
- Ⓑ 發明家
- Ⓒ 教授
- **Ⓓ 作家**

46. Why is the woman planning to visit the man tomorrow?
- A To return an item
- **B To borrow a book**
- C To meet Mr. Klein
- D To sign up for a course

46. 女子為何打算明天要拜訪男子？
- A 歸還物件
- **B 借書**
- C 與克萊恩先生會面
- D 報名參加課程

47–49 conversation

W: I saw an advertisement on the subway today for back pain relief at Frank Logan Hospital. The advertisement offers a free consultation to assess a patient's situation and suggest a course of treatment. I'm thinking of going.

M: **(47) Actually, I was treated by Dr. Moran at the hospital for back pain last year.** After five years of enduring the pain, my pain was drastically reduced under the care of Dr. Moran. In addition to medication, he showed me some useful stretching exercises. I really recommend seeing him.

W: You're right. I shouldn't hesitate anymore. **(48) My work is disrupted by my back pain almost every day.**

M: **(49) If you would like, I can give you the number for Dr. Moran's office.** That way you can set up an appointment with him directly.

47–49 對話

女：我今天在地鐵看到一則廣告，是法蘭克・羅根醫院的背痛緩解。廣告提供免費諮詢來評估病人的病況，並建議療程，我考慮要去。

男：(47) 實際上，我去年就是由該醫院的莫倫醫師治療背痛的。忍受疼痛五年之後，在莫倫醫師的照料下，我的疼痛大幅減輕。除了用藥以外，他還教我一些實用的伸展運動，我真心推薦你去看他。

女：你說的對，我不該再猶豫。**(48)** 我的工作幾乎每天都會受到背痛的干擾。

男：(49) 如果你要的話，我可以給你莫倫醫生辦公室的電話號碼。這樣你就可以直接跟他預約看診。

---

47. Who is Dr. Moran?
- A A university professor
- B A patient
- C A pharmacist
- **D A medical practitioner**

47. 莫倫醫生是誰？
- A 大學教授
- B 病人
- C 藥劑師
- **D 執業醫生**

48. What problem does the woman mention?
- A An incorrect diagnosis
- B A family problem
- **C Persistent pain**
- D An outstanding balance

48. 女子提到什麼問題？
- A 誤診
- B 家庭問題
- **C 持續性疼痛**
- D 未清償餘額

49. What does the man offer to do?
- **A Provide contact information**
- B Drive the woman to the hospital
- C Set up an appointment
- D Offer a free consultation

49. 男子提議要做什麼？
- **A 提供聯絡資訊**
- B 開車載女子去醫院
- C 預約掛號
- D 提供免費諮詢

50–52 conversation

M: Sarah, I need your help. **(50) There is something wrong with the phone transfer software.**

W: What exactly is the problem?

M: I can't get through to Human Resources and Accounting. When I try to call through to them, I just hear a strange noise and then the phone just goes silent.

W: Oh. They are on a different version now, I think. **(51) You might need to update your software so it's compatible with theirs.**

M: Oh. Yeah, I haven't updated for over a year.

W: That is definitely the problem then. **(52) I will send you the link for a free upgrade, and you shouldn't have any more problems.**

M: Great! Thanks, Sarah!

50. What is the man concerned about?
- [A] The messaging system
- [B] Cell phone reception
- **[C] Phone transfer software**
- [D] A new computer system

51. What does the woman suggest?
- [A] Deleting all his software
- [B] Getting a new computer
- [C] Downloading a movie
- **[D] Upgrading his software**

52. What does the woman say she will do?
- **[A] Send him a link for a free upgrade**
- [B] Upgrade his phone model
- [C] Revise the schedule
- [D] Check with management

53–55 conversation

M: I'm concerned about the output of some of our machinery. **(53) Production has slowed by 8% since June; I think there must be a problem with the software.** We are losing money over this, and I'm not sure who to ask about it.

50–52 對話

男: 莎拉，我需要你的幫忙。**(50) 電話轉接軟體有問題。**

女: 究竟出了什麼問題？

男: 我無法接通人資部門和會計部門，我試著與他們通話時，只會聽見奇怪的噪音，然後電話就沒有聲音了。

女: 我猜他們現在是用不同的版本。**(51) 你可能需要更新軟體，才能跟他們的相容。**

男: 喔，對耶，我超過一年沒有更新了。

女: 這肯定是問題所在。**(52) 我會寄免費升級連結給你，應該就不會再有問題了。**

男: 太好了！謝謝你，莎拉！

50. 男子擔心什麼事？
- [A] 訊息系統
- [B] 手機訊號
- **[C] 電話轉接軟體**
- [D] 新的電腦系統

51. 女子建議什麼？
- [A] 刪除所有軟體
- [B] 取得新的電腦
- [C] 下載電影
- **[D] 升級軟體**

52. 女子說她將會做什麼？
- **[A] 寄給他免費升級的連結**
- [B] 升級他的電話型號
- [C] 更正時程表
- [D] 與管理階層進行確認

53–55 對話

男: 我很擔心我們部分機器的產量。**(53) 從六月以來，生產量已減緩 8%。** 我認為軟體一定有問題。我們因此而虧損，我也不確定該向誰詢問此事。

W : We had it repaired once in the past, but it was so expensive we ended up just buying a new one. Now it is slowing down as well. Do you think we should just replace the machine again?

M : (54) **Yeah, it doesn't make sense to keep going like this.**

W : (55) **I'll call the machine repair shop and get a quote on the repairs, and we can decide what to do.**

M : OK, but let's get it done as quickly as possible, please.

女：我們以前曾經修理過機器，但太貴了，我們最後買了一台新的，現在它也變慢了。你認為我們應該再次更換機器嗎？

男：(54) 是的，繼續這樣下去沒有意義。

女：(55) 我會打電話給機器維修廠，進行維修估價，然後我們可以決定該怎麼辦。

男：好的，但請盡快完成此事。

53. What is the man worried about?
- A Buying new software
- **B The production rate of the machine**
- C Finding a repair shop
- D An increase in production

54. What does the man imply when he says, "It doesn't make sense to keep going like this"?
- **A He wants to take action immediately.**
- B He wants to continue business as usual.
- C He wants to repair the software.
- D He doesn't agree with the woman.

55. What does the woman say she will do?
- A Call the software engineer
- B Contact the IT department
- **C Call the machine repair shop**
- D Buy new software

53. 男子擔心什麼事？
- A 購買新軟體
- **B 機器的生產率**
- C 找到維修廠
- D 生產量增加

54. 男子說「繼續這樣下去沒有意義」，他暗示什麼？
- **A 他想要立即採取行動**
- B 他想要如往常般持續營業
- C 他想要修理軟體
- D 他不同意女子的話

55. 女子說她將會做什麼？
- A 打電話給軟體工程師
- B 聯繫資訊科技部門
- **C 打電話給機器維修廠**
- D 購買新軟體

56–58 conversation

W : Hey Joe! (56) **How did your presentation go last weekend?**

M : It was great! We sold a lot of books after the seminar.

W : (57) **Wow, sounds like you've really made it!** So what are your plans for the future?

M : (58) **I'm writing another book, which is due for release next year. In the meantime, I will just continue doing seminars and try to get more exposure.**

W : Excellent. If you need any help, let me know. I have a few connections in the publishing industry.

56–58 對話

女：嘿，喬！(56) 你上週末的演講進行得如何？

男：很好啊！研討會後我們賣了很多書。

女：(57) 哇，聽起來你真的很成功！那麼你未來有什麼計劃？

男：(58) 我正在寫另一本書，明年就會出版，在此期間，我會持續開研討會，並試著增加曝光率。

女：太好了。如果你需要任何協助，請告訴我。我在出版業有一些人脈。

56. What did the man do last weekend?

   A He went to a conference.

   B He finished his sales reports.

   C He gave a presentation.

   D He visited his family.

57. What does the woman imply when she says, "wow, sounds like you've really made it"?

   A He failed.

   B He was successful with his presentation.

   C His presentation wasn't well received.

   D His book didn't sell well.

58. What does the man plan on doing next year?

   A Retire from writing

   B Move to another country

   C Have a child with his wife

   D Release another book

59–61 conversation

M1： Hi, Mrs. Kraft? This is Logan from Yellow Bank Realtors. **(59) I am calling about some problems with the apartment you will be renting in the Swiss Tower Building.** Let me put you through to our manager and he will tell you.

W： OK, I'll wait.

M2： Hi, Mrs. Kraft. **(60) They are having some renovations done at the Swiss Tower Building, so we need to change your move-in date to the end of October.** Will that be OK with you?

W： Well, not really. I will have nowhere to live, and it's far too expensive to stay in a hotel.

M2： OK. **(61) We will be happy to pay for your hotel expenses until you can move into the apartment.** I'm really sorry for the inconvenience. We only found out about this today.

W： That sounds fine.

59. Why most likely is the man calling?

   A To discuss an issue with the apartment

   B To offer a lower rental price

   C To negotiate a contract

   D To make an appointment

---

56. 男子上週末做了什麼？

   A 他去參加會議

   B 他完成銷售報告

   C 他發表一場演說

   D 他去拜訪家人

57. 女子說「哇，聽起來你真的很成功」，她暗示什麼？

   A 他失敗了

   B 他的演說很成功

   C 他的演說不受歡迎

   D 他的書賣得不好

58. 男子明年打算做什麼？

   A 退休不再寫作

   B 搬到別的國家

   C 與妻子生小孩

   D 出另一本書

59–61 對話

男 1： 嗨，是克拉夫特女士？ 我是黃色河岸房地產的羅根。**(59) 我打這通電話，是為了要談您想要租賃瑞士塔大樓公寓的相關問題。** 讓我將電話轉接給我們的經理，他會向您說明。

女： 好的，我會等候。

男 2： 嗨，克拉夫特女士。**(60) 瑞士塔大樓正在進行翻修，因此我們需要將您的遷入日期更改到 10 月底。** 您可以接受嗎？

女： 不太行。我會沒有地方住，而住旅館太貴了。

男 2： 好的。**(61) 我們會很樂意為您支付旅館的費用，直到您可以搬入公寓為止。** 我為這項不便道歉，我們今天才得知此事。

女： 聽起來沒問題。

59. 男子最有可能為何而打這通電話？

   A 要討論公寓的問題

   B 要提供較低的租賃價格

   C 要協商合約

   D 要約定會面

60. What does the man say about the Swiss Tower building?
- [A] It is too far away from her office.
- **[B] It is being renovated at the moment.**
- [C] It is being closed down.
- [D] It is located close to a dry cleaner.

61. What does the man offer the woman?
- [A] Give her a lower rental price
- [B] Extend the lease
- **[C] Pay for her hotel costs**
- [D] Arrange to move her furniture

60. 關於瑞士塔大樓，男子説了什麼？
- [A] 距離她的辦公室太遠
- **[B] 現在正在進行翻修**
- [C] 正被封閉
- [D] 地點在乾洗店附近

61. 男子提議要為女子做什麼？
- [A] 給她較低的租賃價格
- [B] 延展租約
- **[C] 支付她的旅館花費**
- [D] 安排搬遷她的家具

(NEW)
62–64 conversation

W：OK, sir. **(62) This suit comes to $385. Would you like to pay cash or by card?**

M：I have a gift certificate here for a 10% discount. Wait, I can't find it. OK, here it is.

W：Thank you, sir. Hmm, unfortunately you won't be able to use this with this suit.

M：**(63) Ah, I see the problem. Well, I need some more dress pants for work; do you mind if I go and pick some items out so I can use my gift certificate?**

W：Of course, sir. Please follow me. **(64) I will help you pick out some pants I think will suit you well.**

62–64 對話

女：好的，先生。**(62) 這套西裝要價 385 元，您要付現金或者是用信用卡？**

男：我這裡有九折的禮券。等等，我找不到。好，在這裡。

女：謝謝您，先生。很可惜，您買這套西裝不能使用。

男：**(63) 啊，我知道是什麼問題了。我上班需要更多條西裝褲，你介意我再去挑選一些商品，以便使用禮券嗎？**

女：沒問題，先生。請跟我來。**(64) 我會幫您挑些我認為很適合的長褲。**

Bernard & Son's Tailors 巴納德父子裁縫店
Gift Certificate 禮券

10% off any purchase of $500 or more
消費滿 500 元可享九折優惠

Expires March 10
3 月 10 日到期

---

62. What is the woman doing?
- [A] Giving away free suits
- **[B] Helping a customer**
- [C] Updating software
- [D] Celebrating with friends

62. 女子在做什麼？
- [A] 贈送免費西裝
- **[B] 協助顧客**
- [C] 更新軟體
- [D] 與朋友慶祝

63. Look at the graphic. Why is the gift certificate rejected?
[A] It is expired.
[B] Because he is in the wrong store
[C] Because he didn't purchase enough
[D] The certificate is damaged.

64. What does the woman offer to do?
[A] Give him another certificate
[B] Help him try on a suit
[C] Show him some pants
[D] Give him a refund

63. 參看圖表，禮券為何不能使用？
[A] 過期了
[B] 因為他走錯商店了
[C] 因為他買得不夠
[D] 禮券遭到毀損

64. 女子提議做什麼？
[A] 給他另一張禮券
[B] 協助他試穿西裝
[C] 拿長褲給他看
[D] 退他錢

65-67 conversation

M： Excuse me? **(65) I've just started a new exercise program, and my trainer told me I should buy some protein powder to have after I work out.** Most importantly, I need something that is high in protein, but doesn't have a lot of carbohydrates. Do you have anything you can recommend?

W： We have a wide variety of protein powders, but there is one I particularly like the taste of. It is a protein drink made from milk and soy.

M： Oh. **(66) Actually, I'm lactose intolerant.** Are there any other options?

W： **(67) I suggest you purchase a powder that is only soy-based.** You won't have any problems with that.

65-67 對話

男： 不好意思？ **(65) 我剛開始進行一項新的運動計劃，而教練告訴我應該購買乳清蛋白，在健身之後服用。** 最重要的是，我需要含高蛋白質但碳水化合物成分不高的產品。你有什麼可以推薦的嗎？

女： 我們有各種的乳清蛋白，但其中有種口味我特別喜歡，是由奶類和黃豆做成的高蛋白飲。

男： **(66) 實際上，我有乳糖不耐症。** 有別種選擇嗎？

女： **(67) 我建議你購買主要成分只有黃豆的蛋白質粉。** 那種的對你就不會有問題。

Nutrition Information 營養資訊	
Serving Size: 1 Rounded Scoop (29.4 g) 每份：一圓匙（29.4 公克）	
Calories 熱量	**120大卡**
Fat 脂肪	10 grams（公克）
Carbohydrate 碳水化合物	3 grams（公克）
Protein 蛋白質	24 grams（公克）
Calcium 鈣質	10%
Contains milk and soy products 含奶類和大豆產品	

65. Why is the man looking for a certain product?
- [A] He stopped working out.
- **[B] His trainer told him to.**
- [C] Because he is a trainer.
- [D] He had a favorite brand.

66. Look at the graphic. Which content is the man worried about?
- [A] Carbohydrate
- [B] Fat
- **[C] Milk**
- [D] Protein

67. What does the woman suggest?
- [A] Purchasing a milk-based product
- [B] Getting a full refund
- [C] Using soy beans
- **[D] Buying a soy-based powder**

65. 男子為何要找某種產品？
- [A] 他停止健身
- **[B] 他的教練要他這麼做**
- [C] 因為他是教練
- [D] 他有最喜愛的品牌

66. 參看圖表，男子擔心哪種成分？
- [A] 碳水化合物
- [B] 脂肪
- **[C] 奶類**
- [D] 蛋白質

67. 女子建議什麼？
- [A] 購買以奶類為主要成分的產品
- [B] 全額退費
- [C] 使用黃豆
- **[D] 購買以黃豆為主要成分的乳清蛋白**

68–70 conversation

W：Hi, Harold. Just wanted to let you know I'm nearly finished with all of Farnod Computing's windows. **(68) I'm going to move up to the next floor in about 20 minutes.** Are you finished with Raptas' windows?

M：Hi, Batty. Yeah, I have finished Raptas' and I'm going upstairs to the next floor. The windows are already pretty clean up there, so I think we can get the job done pretty soon.

W：Great. Before you start on the 4th floor, can you please bring me some more window cleaner? I have run out.

M：Sure, I'll be up in about 20 minutes. It will be good to see how clean your windows are compared to mine. **(70) When we are finished with the windows we need to start on the carpets.**

68–70 對話

女：嗨，哈洛德。我只是想讓你知道我快完成法納德電腦公司的全部窗戶了。**(68) 我大約 20 分鐘後就要往上一樓了。** 你完成了銳普塔公司的窗戶了嗎？

男：嗨，芭蒂，你好。是的，我已經完成了銳普塔公司的窗戶，即將要往上一樓。上面的窗戶已經很乾淨了，因此我認為我們很快就可以把工作做完。

女：太好了。你開始四樓的工作之前，可否請你為我多帶一些窗戶清潔劑？我的已經用完了。

男：好的，我大約 20 分鐘後就會上去，能看看你的窗戶和我的比有多乾淨很不錯。**(70) 清洗完窗戶後，我們要開始清潔地毯。**

Park Tower 帕克塔大樓
Office Directory 公司行號一覽表

1st Floor 一樓	Farnod Computing 法納德電腦公司
2nd Floor 二樓	Chaims & Son 查姆斯父子公司
3rd Floor 三樓	Raptas 銳普塔公司
4th Floor 四樓	Hecadi Constructing 西卡蒂建設公司

68. Who most likely are the speakers?
- **A** **Office cleaners**
- B Computer repair technicians
- C Telephone operators
- D Athletes

68. 對話者們最有可能是什麼人？
- **A** **辦公室清潔工**
- B 電腦維修人員
- C 接線生
- D 運動員

(NEW)

69. Look at the graphic. Where is the woman going next?
- A Raptas
- B Farnod Computing
- **C** **Chaims & Son**
- D Hecadi Constructing

69. 參看圖表，女子接下來會去哪裡？
- A 銳普塔公司
- B 法納德電腦公司
- **C** **查姆斯父子公司**
- D 西卡蒂建設公司

70. What are the speakers going to do when they're finished with the windows?
- A Go home
- B Eat lunch
- **C** **Clean the carpets**
- D Leave the building

70. 對話者們在清洗完窗戶後接下來也許會做什麼？
- A 回家
- B 吃午餐
- **C** **清潔地毯**
- D 離開大樓

71–73 telephone message

M：Hello, this is Sam Booth calling from Crimson Realty. **(71) This message is for Jordan King. I'm happy to say that someone is interested in making an offer on your house. (72) I would like to stop by with the potential buyer this Thursday to discuss the sale in more detail.** Please let me know what time on Thursday you're available and I'll arrange a time with the potential buyer. **(73) In the meantime, I suggest you clean up the house so it looks as impressive as possible for Thursday.** Thank you.

71–73 電話留言

男：哈囉，我是克里門森房地產的山姆・伯斯。**(71) 我是要留言給喬登・金。我很高興告訴您，有人有意對您的房子出價。(72) 我這星期四想帶潛在買家過去，討論出售的詳細事宜。** 請告訴我您星期四何時有空，我會與潛在買家安排時間。**(73) 同時，我建議您打掃房屋，讓它在星期四時盡量有好賣相。** 謝謝您。

71. Who most likely is the speaker?
    A A potential buyer
    B A bank teller
    C A real estate agent
    D An architect

72. Why would the speaker like to arrange a meeting?
    A To discuss a sale
    B To renew a contract
    C To draw up a budget
    D To introduce his coworker

73. What does the speaker suggest doing?
    A Updating a website
    B Accepting an offer
    C Making the house neat
    D Lowering a price

71. 男子最有可能是什麼人？
    A 潛在買家
    B 銀行櫃員
    C 房地產仲介
    D 建築師

72. 發話者為何想要安排會面？
    A 討論買賣事宜
    B 續約
    C 規劃預算
    D 介紹同事

73. 發話者建議做什麼？
    A 更新網站
    B 接受出價
    C 清理乾淨房屋
    D 降低價格

74–76 news report

M： Good morning, radio listeners. This is Tim Lester with your Morning Newsflash. **(74) An hour ago there was a serious collision at the intersection of Smith Avenue and Main Street.** Traffic is extremely congested and it's almost impossible to get anywhere downtown. **(75) As a result, tonight's soccer match has been delayed by two hours to allow spectators time to make it to the stadium.** Oh, also remember, during half time there will be a hot dog eating contest. **(76) The winner will receive an airline ticket to Hawaii.**

74–76 新聞報導

男： 早安，廣播聽眾們。我是提姆・雷斯特，為您帶來晨間新聞快報。**(74)** 一小時前，在史密斯大道和緬恩街的路口發生一場嚴重車禍。交通嚴重壅塞，在市區幾乎無法動彈。**(75)** 因此，今晚的足球賽將延後兩小時，讓觀眾有時間到達體育場。喔，對了，也請記得，中場時間會有熱狗大胃王比賽。**(76)** 贏家將得到一張飛往夏威夷的機票。

---

74. What is the news report mainly about?
    A A weather forecast
    B A road construction project
    C A traffic accident
    D A cooking contest

75. What event has been delayed?
    A A sports game
    B A live concert
    C An opening ceremony
    D An orientation

74. 新聞報導主要與什麼有關？
    A 天氣預報
    B 道路修建工程
    C 交通意外
    D 烹飪比賽

75. 什麼活動受到耽擱？
    A 運動比賽
    B 現場演唱會
    C 開幕典禮
    D 新進人員訓練

76. What will the winner of the eating contest receive?
  - A A concert ticket
  - B A gift certificate
  - C A cash prize
  - **D A plane ticket**

76. 大胃王比賽的獲勝者能得到什麼？
  - A 一張演唱會門票
  - B 一張禮券
  - C 一筆獎金
  - **D 一張機票**

77–79 announcement

W：**(77) Welcome, spectators. Please listen to a short announcement before the match begins. (78) As of today, you are no longer allowed to bring food and drinks from outside into the stadium. Please adhere to this new regulation.** However, there are concession stands selling a variety of delicious snacks and beverages at reasonable prices. **(79) In addition, 5% of the proceeds made from concession stands will be donated to a charity that helps children with disabilities.** Thank you.

77–79 公告

女：(77) 歡迎光臨，各位觀眾。比賽開始之前，請先聽一則簡短的廣播。(78) 今天起不能再帶外食和飲料進體育場，請遵守這項新規定。然而，販賣部會用合理價格販售各種美味的零食和飲料。(79) 此外，販賣部收益的 5% 將會捐給幫助殘障孩童的慈善機構。感謝您。

---

77. Where is the announcement being made?
  - A At a campground
  - B At a movie theater
  - C At a concert hall
  - **D At a sports stadium**

77. 這則公告是在哪裡發布的？
  - A 營地
  - B 電影院
  - C 音樂廳
  - **D 體育場**

78. What is being announced?
  - **A A new restriction**
  - B Operating hours
  - C Price changes
  - D A discount policy

78. 公告的內容是什麼？
  - **A 新的限制**
  - B 營運時間
  - C 價格更動
  - D 折扣方案

79. What is said about some of the proceeds?
  - **A They will be used for a worthy cause.**
  - B They will be put toward updating facilities.
  - C They will be saved for a special event.
  - D They will be awarded to some spectators.

79. 提到什麼關於收益的事？
  - **A 將用在有意義的事上**
  - B 將用於更新設施
  - C 將留給特別活動使用
  - D 將頒發給某些觀眾

80–82 weather report

M：**(80) The National Weather Service has issued a tornado warning for Allison County beginning at 4:00 p.m. and lasting until 8:00 p.m. (81) Therefore, all after-school activities in Allison County have been canceled. (82) Local residents are urged to take shelter in a basement or windowless room and wait until the tornado has passed.** Please stay tuned for more updates.

80–82 氣象報導

男：**(80) 國家氣象局已對愛莉森縣發出下午四點到晚上八點的龍捲風警報，(81) 因此，所有愛莉森縣內的課後活動都已經取消。(82) 呼籲在地居民盡快前往地下室或沒有窗戶的房間避難，等候龍捲風過去。** 請持續收聽更多最新報導。

80. What is the speaker discussing?
  A A new curriculum
  B A weather warning
  C A quarterly report
  D A travel advisory

80. 發話者主要在談論什麼？
  A 新課程
  B 天氣警報
  C 季度報告
  D 旅遊忠告

81. What has been canceled?
  A Television programs
  B Graduation ceremonies
  C Educational programs
  D Fundraising events

81. 什麼事被取消？
  A 電視節目
  B 畢業典禮
  C 教育課程
  D 募款活動

82. What are local residents advised to do?
  A Update their anti-virus software
  B Wear protective gear
  C Go into a safe place
  D Take an alternative route

82. 在地居民應該要做什麼？
  A 更新防毒軟體
  B 穿戴防護裝置
  C 進入安全的地方
  D 走替代路線

83–85 speech

W：Thank you, thank you so much. **(83) It's an incredible honor to be nominated as sales manager of the year.** I have enjoyed working at Optimal Telecommunications since my first day and it's a privilege to be acknowledged for doing a job that I really love. **(85) This year our branch broke all the records for cell phone contracts,** and I have to say **(84) I couldn't have done this without my talented team.** Their passion and persistence has been vital to our success. So, I'd like to say I'm going to share my bonus amongst my team members as a sign of my appreciation for their hard work.

83–85 演講

女：謝謝，很感謝各位。**(83) 被提名為年度銷售經理，令我感到非常榮耀。** 從我第一天上班以來，我就很享受著在理想電信公司上班，能夠因為從事我真心熱愛的工作而獲得肯定，真是一種殊榮。**(85) 我們分店今年打破了手機合約的各項紀錄。** 我必須說 **(84) 沒有這才華洋溢的團隊，我無法有此成就。** 他們的熱情和堅持對於我們的成功至關重要。因此，我想宣布，我要將我的紅利與團隊成員分享，以表達我對他們努力工作的感激之意。

83.
What is the purpose of the speech?

A To accept a nomination

B To announce a retirement

C To announce a merger

D To request funding

(NEW) 84.
Why does the speaker say: "I couldn't have done this without my talented team"?

A She dislikes her team.

B She is asking for some extra awards.

C She wants to thank her colleagues.

D She wants to offer her services.

85.
Where most likely does the speaker work?

A At a cell phone shop

B At a computer shop

C At a shoe store

D At a flower shop

83.
演說的目的是什麼？

A 接受提名

B 宣布退休

C 宣布合併

D 要求資助

84.
發話者為何說「沒有這才華洋溢的團隊，我無法有此成就」？

A 她不喜歡她的團隊

B 她要求一些額外的獎賞

C 她想要感謝她的同事們

D 她想要提供服務

85.
發話者最有可能在哪裡工作？

A 在手機店

B 在電腦店

C 在鞋店

D 在花店

86–88 talk

M：Hi, everybody. This week we will be renovating the restaurant. The work will be taking place from 8 a.m. to 11:30 a.m. for one week. **(86) Unfortunately, we will not be offering breakfast service during this period.** If anyone was planning to come in and eat, **(87) you might want to come in the evening.** I know a lot of people really love our breakfast menu, so **(88) I will be giving a 10% discount on all dinner meals until renovations are complete.**

86–88 談話

男：嗨，大家好。本週我們餐廳將進行翻修，工程會從上午八點開始進行到 11 點半，持續一週。**(86) 可惜，在此期間我們將不提供早餐。**若有人原本打算來用餐，**(87) 可以選在晚上過來。**我知道許多人都很喜歡我們早餐的菜色，因此 **(88) 我將會提供所有晚餐餐點九折的折扣，直到翻修工程結束。**

86.
What problem does the speaker mention?

A No breakfast service

B No dinner service

C Missing extra items on the menu

D Rats in the kitchen

(NEW) 87.
What does the speaker imply when he says, "you might want to come in the evening"?

A He will offer free breakfast.

B The dinner menu is better.

C Don't come during the day.

D They are installing air conditioners.

86.
發話者提到什麼問題？

A 沒有供應早餐

B 沒有供應晚餐

C 菜單上沒有的餐點

D 廚房裡有老鼠

87.
發話者說「可以選在晚上過來」，他暗示什麼？

A 他將會提供免費早餐

B 晚餐菜色比較好

C 白天別過來

D 他們要安裝冷氣機

88. What does the speaker say he will do?
- A Serve breakfast at night
- B Charge more
- C Offer free breakfast
- **D Offer a discount**

88. 發話者說他會做什麼?
- A 在夜晚供應早餐
- B 多收費
- C 提供免費早餐
- **D 提供折扣**

89–91 telephone message

W: **(89) Hi, Trent, this is Fiona calling from the warehouse.** The delivery just came in, and **(90) there is a lot of clothing on here we don't usually order.** I don't recall any special fashion sale coming up, and I phoned Head Office and they said there is no reason why we received them. Did you make the order? I'm going to call the supplier, but I want to check with you first in case you ordered the products. **(91) Please call me back. I need to let Head Office know what to do by 1 p.m. and it's already midday.** Thanks, Trent.

89–91 電話留言

女: **(89) 嗨,特倫,我是倉庫的費歐娜。** 貨品剛送到了,然後 **(90) 有很多我們平常不會訂的衣服。** 我不記得最近有什麼時尚服飾特賣會,我打電話給總公司,他們說我們不應該收到這些衣服。這是你訂的嗎?我會打電話給供貨商,但我想先與你確認,以免這些產品是你訂的。**(91) 請回我電話,我需要在下午一點之前讓總公司知道該怎麼辦,而現在已經中午了。** 謝謝你,特倫。

89. Where does the speaker work?
- **A A fashion company**
- B A restaurant
- C A factory
- D A clinic

89. 發話者在哪裡工作?
- **A 時裝公司**
- B 餐廳
- C 工廠
- D 診所

90. What problem does the speaker describe?
- A The delivery driver is lost.
- B The delivery is late.
- C The order is not perfect.
- **D The order has extra items.**

90. 發話者描述什麼問題?
- A 貨運司機迷路了
- B 送貨延遲了
- C 訂貨不完整
- **D 訂貨有多出來的品項**

(NEW)
91. What does the woman imply when she says, "I need to let Head Office know what to do by 1 p.m., and it's already midday"?
- A She would like a response after midday.
- **B She would like a response as soon as possible.**
- C She would like extra time off.
- D She will call head office now.

91. 女子說「我需要在下午一點之前讓總公司知道該怎麼辦,而現在已經中午了」,她指的是什麼?
- A 她想在中午後得到回覆
- **B 她想盡快得到回覆**
- C 她想要額外的休假
- D 她現在要打電話給總公司

92–94 telephone message

M：Hello, is this Barry White? **(94) This is James Holden calling on behalf of the National Center for the Blind.** We noticed that you did not renew your yearly donation to our center. **(93) If you could give me a few moments of your time, I would like to share some information with you. I would appreciate the opportunity to tell you how we use the donations we receive to help the blind.** You should have received a brochure in the mail. If I could direct your attention to it while we talk, I am sure that you will see how valuable our service is.

92–94 電話留言

男：哈囉，是貝瑞・懷特嗎？ **(94) 我是詹姆斯・霍頓，代表國家盲人中心來電。** 我們注意到您今年並未繼續捐獻給本中心。**(93) 如果您可以給我一些時間，我想跟您分享一些資訊，** 感謝您讓我有機會訴說我們如何使用捐款以幫助盲人。您該已經收到郵寄給你的手冊。我們談話時，請您參閱那本手冊，我相信您會了解我們的服務是多麼地有價值。

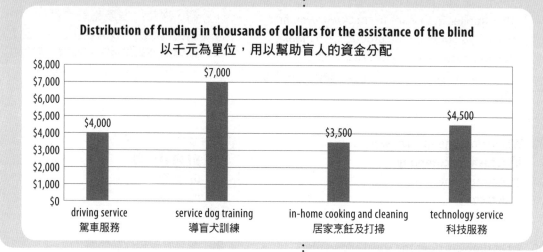

Distribution of funding in thousands of dollars for the assistance of the blind
以千元為單位，用以幫助盲人的資金分配

driving service 駕車服務	$4,000
service dog training 導盲犬訓練	$7,000
in-home cooking and cleaning 居家烹飪及打掃	$3,500
technology service 科技服務	$4,500

92. Look at the graphic. What is the largest expense?
- **A Dog training**
- B Technology
- C Meal preparation
- D Driving assistance

92. 參看圖表，哪一項的花費最大？
- **A 導盲犬訓練**
- B 科技
- C 備餐
- D 代駕

93. What is the listener asked to do?
- A Give more money than last year
- **B Listen to some information**
- C Become a volunteer
- D Become a member

93. 聆聽者被要求做什麼？
- A 比前一年捐更多錢
- **B 聆聽一些資訊**
- C 成為志工
- D 成為會員

94. Where does the speaker most likely work?
- A A hospital
- **B The National Center for the Blind**
- C A church
- D The local government

94. 發話者最有可能在哪裡工作？
- A 醫院
- **B 國家盲人中心**
- C 教會
- D 當地政府機構

95-97 speech

W: Hello, everyone. I would like to begin today's seminar by asking you all to consider a few questions. First, how many of you would like to be rich? Everyone? Exactly. Second, how many of you would like to be happy? Everyone? Of course! **(96) I can promise you all that if you follow a few simple steps, you will be able to make your financial and life goals a reality.** The Fast Forward Financial System, or FFFS, that I have developed, is an easy step-by-step guide to living the good life. **(97) Today's seminar is just an introduction of course. In order to fulfill your financial potential you will need to enroll in one of our immersion programs.**

95-97 演說

女：哈囉，大家好。今天研討會一開始，我想先要求大家思考幾個問題。首先，各位當中有多少人想變得富有？大家都是嗎？沒錯。第二，各位當中有多少人想要快樂？大家都是嗎？當然！**(96) 我可以向各位保證，如果你依循幾個簡單的步驟，就能夠實現你的財務和人生目標。**我所開發出來的快轉財務系統，或簡稱 FFFS，是個能使你過美好生活的簡易逐步指南。**(97) 今天的研討會當然只是基本介紹。要實現你的財務潛力，你需要報名參加我們其中一門深入課程。**

FFFS Seminar Schedule and Price Guide
研討會時間表及價格指南

Orlando 奧蘭多	"3 Weeks to Riches!" 三週致富！	3 weeks（週）	$1,500
New York 紐約	"The Big Apple is Yours" 大蘋果屬於你	5 days（天）	$750
Boston 波士頓	"Revolutionary Wealth" 革命性的財富	13 days（天）	$1,200
Seattle 西雅圖	"Prepare for Your Rainy Day" 未雨綢繆	20 days（天）	$3,000

95. Look at the graphic. Where will the longest course take place?
- **A Orlando**
- B Boston
- C New York
- D Seattle

96. Who most likely are the people attending the seminar?
- A Wealthy people
- **B People who wants to get rich**
- C Those who are bored
- D Those invited by friends

97. What is the speaker trying to do?
- A Sell real estate
- **B Sell seminar packages**
- C Sell vacations
- D Sell small businesses

95. 參看圖表，哪裡的課程時間最長？
- **A 奧蘭多**
- B 波士頓
- C 紐約
- D 西雅圖

96. 最有可能是什麼人參加研討會？
- A 富有的人
- **B 想變得富有的人**
- C 感到無聊的人
- D 受朋友邀約的人

97. 發話者試著要做什麼？
- A 賣房地產
- **B 賣研討會套裝課程**
- C 賣假期
- D 賣小型企業

98–100 excerpt from a meeting

W：Thank you all for coming to this meeting on such short notice. **(100) It has come to my attention that the human resource department has been overwhelmed lately with reports about messes in the common areas. (98) As your regional manager,** I feel it is my responsibility to take ownership of this problem before it gets completely out of control. Just so everybody is clear, the common areas include the kitchen, the foyer, recreation room A, and lounge C on the second floor. I don't know who is responsible for this recent run of uncleanliness, but from now on we are going to assign a staff member to monitor the condition of each area and sign off on it at the end of every day. We will do this until I feel everyone has learned to respect the space. Be sure to check the schedule to see which area you will be responsible for.

98–100 會議摘錄

女：感謝大家一接到臨時通知就來參加這場會議。**(100) 我注意到人資部門最近收到大量有關公共區域髒亂的報告，(98) 身為各位的區域經理，** 我覺得我有責任在這個問題完全失控之前加以處理。為了讓大家都清楚，我要說明：公共區域包含廚房、門廳、休閒室 A，以及二樓的休息室 C。我不知道誰要為最近的髒亂負責，但從現在起，我們將指派員工來監看每個區域的狀況，並且在每天下班時簽名。我們會持續這麼做，直到我覺得大家都已經學會重視這個空間。請務必確認時程表，以了解你將負責的區域。

Common Area Cleanliness Checklist 公共區域清潔檢核表					
Area 區域	Monday 星期一	Tuesday 星期二	Wednesday 星期三	Thursday 星期四	Friday 星期五
Kitchen 廚房	Scott W 史考特・W	Scott W 史考特・W	Scott W 史考特・W	Bill T 比爾・T	Bill T 比爾・T
Foyer 門廳	Bill T 比爾・T	Bill T 比爾・T	Hillary P 希拉蕊・P	Hillary P 希拉蕊・P	Hillary P 希拉蕊・P
Rec. A 休閒室 A	Lawrence P. 勞倫斯・P	Lawrence P. 勞倫斯・P	Lawrence P. 勞倫斯・P	Hillary P 希拉蕊・P	Scott W 希拉蕊・P
Lounge C 休息室 C	Hillary P 希拉蕊・P	Hillary P 希拉蕊・P	Bill T 比爾・T	Scott W 考特・W	Lawrence P. 勞倫斯・P

98. Who is speaking to the staff?
- A Human Resources
- **B The regional manager**
- C The CEO
- D The sales manager

(NEW)
99. Look at the graphic. Which employee was given responsibility for two common areas on the same day?
- A Lawrence P.
- **B Hillary P.**
- C Scott W.
- D Bill T.

98. 誰在對員工說話？
- A 人資部門
- **B 區域經理**
- C 總裁
- D 銷售經理

99. 參看圖表，哪位員工在同一天被指派要負責兩個共同區域？
- A 勞倫斯・P
- **B 希拉蕊・P**
- C 史考特・W
- D 比爾・T

100. What is indicated in the meeting?

    Ⓐ The staff will get reprimanded.

    Ⓑ The staff will need to work weekends.

    Ⓒ Everyone will get a holiday bonus.

    Ⓓ There have been a lot of complaints.

100. 會議中指出什麼？

    Ⓐ 員工將遭到責罵

    Ⓑ 員工將需要週末上班

    Ⓒ 員工將獲得假日津貼

    Ⓓ 近來有許多投訴

ACTUAL TEST ⑩

37

1. Ⓐ The woman is looking at the computer.
    Ⓑ The woman is typing on the computer.
    Ⓒ The woman is taking a phone call.
    Ⓓ The woman is talking on the cell phone.

2. Ⓐ He is looking at the laptop computer.
    Ⓑ They are having a discussion in a meeting room.
    Ⓒ They are all looking in the same direction.
    Ⓓ She is writing in her notepad.

3. Ⓐ He is selling the bread.
    Ⓑ The bread is in the oven.
    Ⓒ He is holding bread using a bread paddle.
    Ⓓ He is wearing safety gloves.

4. **Ⓐ She is walking her dog at the sea shore.**
    Ⓑ She is collecting sea shells at the shore.
    Ⓒ The dog is walking behind the girl.
    Ⓓ She is swimming in the water.

5. Ⓐ The man is wearing safety gloves.
    Ⓑ The man is using the remote control to move the pipe.
    Ⓒ There are many people in the factory.
    Ⓓ The man is moving the pipe with his hands.

6. Ⓐ The lady is looking away from the man.
    Ⓑ The man is touching the bench with his left hand.
    Ⓒ They are both holding the flower.
    Ⓓ The man is sitting with his legs crossed.

38

7. You've been to Japan before, haven't you?
    Ⓐ After 3:30 p.m.
    Ⓑ I prefer Japanese food.
    Ⓒ No, never.

8. Where's the light switch?
    Ⓐ We switched suppliers.
    Ⓑ On the back wall.
    Ⓒ It's too heavy.

---

1. Ⓐ 女子正在看著電腦。
    Ⓑ 女子正在用電腦打字。
    Ⓒ 女子正在講電話。
    Ⓓ 女子正在講手機。

2. Ⓐ 他正看著筆記型電腦。
    Ⓑ 他們正在會議室進行討論。
    Ⓒ 他們全都看著相同的方向。
    Ⓓ 她正在記事本上寫字。

3. Ⓐ 他正在賣麵包。
    Ⓑ 麵包在烤箱裡。
    Ⓒ 他正用麵包木鏟拿麵包。
    Ⓓ 他戴著安全手套。

4. **Ⓐ 她正在海邊遛狗。**
    Ⓑ 她正在海邊收集貝殼。
    Ⓒ 狗走在女子後面。
    Ⓓ 她正在水中游泳。

5. Ⓐ 男子戴著安全手套。
    Ⓑ 男子使用遙控器來移動水管。
    Ⓒ 工廠裡有許多人。
    Ⓓ 男子用手移動水管。

6. Ⓐ 女子轉頭不看男子。
    Ⓑ 男子用左手觸碰長椅。
    Ⓒ 他們兩人都拿著花。
    Ⓓ 男子雙腿交叉而坐。

7. 你以前曾去過日本，是嗎？
    Ⓐ 下午三點半後。
    Ⓑ 我偏好日式料理。
    Ⓒ 不，不曾。

8. 電燈開關在哪裡？
    Ⓐ 我們換了供應商。
    Ⓑ 在後面的牆上。
    Ⓒ 它太重了。

9. Would you like to return this item?
   A Yes, it doesn't fit.
   B A medium size, I think.
   C No, he left already.

10. How late did you work last night?
   A Past midnight.
   B Three times, I guess.
   C Don't be late again.

11. Why isn't the heater on?
   A A cold winter day.
   B It broke this morning.
   C Yes, it's on.

12. What's the name of the company?
   A A new CEO has been named.
   B Submit an application.
   C It's at the top of the page.

13. Are you picking up the client today or tomorrow?
   A She works in China.
   B A taxi driver.
   C This afternoon.

14. Who should I assign this task to?
   A Someone in marketing.
   B I'll finish it by Tuesday.
   C Please sign here.

15. You are planning to attend the concert on Wednesday, aren't you?
   A No, something urgent came up.
   B He tends to speak indirectly.
   C Yes, it was very good.

16. Isn't Mr. Moore married?
   A It's after the wedding.
   B No, it wasn't.
   C Yes, since last year.

17. Can I help you carry that?
   A That would be appreciated.
   B The box is full of paper.
   C I couldn't find an empty seat.

9. 你要退這件商品嗎？
   A 是的，它不合身。
   B 我猜想尺寸是中號。
   C 不，他已經離開了。

10. 你昨晚工作到多晚？
   A 午夜之後。
   B 我想是三次。
   C 別再遲到了。

11. 為何沒開暖氣？
   A 冬季寒冷的一天。
   B 它今天早上壞掉了。
   C 是的，它開著。

12. 這家公司叫什麼名字？
   A 已選定新的總裁。
   B 繳交一份申請書。
   C 名字在頁面的頂端。

13. 你是今天還是明天要去接客戶？
   A 她在中國工作。
   B 計程車司機。
   C 今天下午。

14. 我該把這項工作指派給誰？
   A 行銷部門的人。
   B 我星期二之前會完成。
   C 請在這裡簽名。

15. 你打算參加星期三的音樂會，不是嗎？
   A 不，有緊急的事情發生了。
   B 他傾向拐彎抹角的說話。
   C 是的，演出很精采。

16. 摩爾先生不是已婚了嗎？
   A 那是在婚禮之後。
   B 不，它不是。
   C 是的，去年結婚的。

17. 我可以幫你提嗎？
   A 太感謝了。
   B 箱子裡裝滿紙張。
   C 我找不到空的座位。

TEST 10

PART 2

37
38

18. When is the payment due?
    A You may use a credit card.
    B Before March 3.
    C Yes, I do.

19. Which pattern do you like best?
    A Let's choose the best idea.
    B I think the striped shirt is nice.
    C The store closes soon.

20. Do you want to take the bus or drive to the mall?
    A The price of gas.
    B Just look at a map.
    C I prefer public transportation.

21. How many new computers were purchased?
    A One for each employee.
    B It's an email attachment.
    C For the business conference.

22. I can't find the file on that client.
    A That's fine with me.
    B Look in this file cabinet.
    C Before the end of the day.

23. Why don't we rent bicycles?
    A Because Jake wants to.
    B Yes, just like the directions said.
    C That sounds fun.

24. Don't you live in the same neighborhood as Jim?
    A No, I don't leave until 6:00 p.m.
    B Yes, very close, in fact.
    C It's different from this new product.

25. Where's the nearest gas station?
    A It's toxic gas.
    B He is at the car show.
    C Just around the corner.

26. Why is nobody at the park today?
    A I forgot the picnic basket.
    B It is expected to rain.
    C No, he changed his mind.

27. Has your daughter decided on a wedding date?
    A No, that sounds too luxurious.
    B Yes, the last weekend in August.
    C She likes the white dress.

18. 付款截止日為何？
    A 你可以使用信用卡。
    B 三月三日之前。
    C 是的，我要。

19. 你最喜歡哪個樣式？
    A 我們選出最好的點子吧。
    B 我覺得這件條紋襯衫不錯。
    C 這家店很快就要關門。

20. 你想要搭公車或是開車到購物中心？
    A 油價。
    B 看地圖。
    C 我偏好大眾運輸。

21. 買了幾台新電腦？
    A 每位員工一台。
    B 它是電子郵件附件。
    C 供商務會議使用。

22. 我找不到那名客戶的檔案。
    A 我覺得可接受。
    B 在這個檔案櫃裡看看。
    C 在今天結束前。

23. 我們何不租用腳踏車？
    A 因為傑克想要。
    B 是的，就像指示所說的。
    C 聽起來很有趣。

24. 你不是和吉姆住在同一區嗎？
    A 不，我下午六點才會離開。
    B 是的，其實很接近。
    C 它與這個新產品不同。

25. 最近的加油站在哪裡？
    A 這是有毒氣體。
    B 他在車展。
    C 就在街角處。

26. 今天公園裡為什麼沒有人？
    A 我忘了野餐籃。
    B 預計會下雨。
    C 不，他改變主意了。

27. 你女兒決定好婚禮日期了嗎？
    A 不，那聽起來太奢華了。
    B 是的，八月的最後一個週末。
    C 她喜歡這件白色婚紗。

28. Should I park on the street or in the garage?
A **Wherever there is space.**
B You left your keys on the counter.
C They started from a garage band.

29. We are going to open a second location next month.
A **Your business is going well.**
B I often visit my cousins.
C No, it was on the third floor.

30. Why don't you ask for a few days off from work?
A **I guess I'll have to do that.**
B Yes, I'll turn it on.
C He received a promotion.

31. Who's most qualified for this position?
A Complete the form online.
B **Actually, I'll have to review their résumés.**
C They filed an official complaint.

PART 3 P. 149-153

32-34 conversation

M：Hello. Are you Ms. Joyce? **(32)** **I just started working here today and I was told to shadow you.** Is it OK if I follow you around and watch how you do things?

W：Nice to meet you. Of course you can shadow me today. And if you ever have any questions, don't hesitate to ask. **(33)** **I was just about to take inventory in the warehouse. Let's do it together.**

M：That sounds great. **(34)** **But before I do anything, I just need to change into my work uniform.** I'll join you in the warehouse in 10 minutes.

32. How do the speakers know each other?
A They met through a friend.
B They take a class together.
C They live in the same apartment complex.
D **They work at the same company.**

---

28. 我該把車停在街道上還是室內停車場中？
A **有空位的地方都可以。**
B 你把鑰匙遺留在櫃台了。
C 他們是從車庫樂團起家的。

29. 我們下個月即將開第二家店。
A **你們的生意很好。**
B 我經常拜訪我的表親們。
C 不，它在三樓。

30. 你何不請幾天假？
A **我想我得那麼做。**
B 是的，我會開啟它。
C 他獲得升遷。

31. 誰最符合這個職務的資格？
A 上網完成表格。
B **其實，我得檢視他們的履歷表。**
C 他們提出正式的客訴。

32-34 對話

男：哈囉。你是喬伊絲女士嗎？ **(32)** **我今天開始上班，有人告訴我要跟著你見習。** 我可以跟著你四處走動並看你做事嗎？

女：很高興見到你。當然，你今天可以跟著我見習。如果你有任何疑問，請別猶豫，儘管發問。 **(33)** **我正要去倉庫清點存貨，我們一起去吧。**

男：聽起來很不錯。 **(34)** **但我開始工作之前，需要換穿工作服。** 我十分鐘後到倉庫與你會合。

32. 對話者們如何認識彼此？
A 他們透過朋友認識
B 他們共同修一門課
C 他們住在同一棟公寓大樓
D **他們在同一家公司上班**

33. What does the woman suggest that the man do?
- [A] Introduce himself to his coworkers
- [B] Wear a work uniform
- **[C] Learn how to make a list of goods**
- [D] Have a house-warming party

34. What does the man need to do first?
- **[A] Change his clothes**
- [B] Attach a name tag
- [C] Contact a warehouse supervisor
- [D] Read an employee handbook

35–37 conversation

M： Hello, Tina. This is Michael Hall calling. **(35) I just left the office a minute ago and realized I forgot to email myself an important document.** It's a spreadsheet that I need for my presentation in Tokyo tomorrow. Are you still at the office?

W： Yes, I am. **(36) It's 6:00 p.m. now. I still have an hour left to leave work.** So, how can I help you?

M： Oh, great. If you turn my computer on, the spreadsheet document will be right on the desktop. If you could just email it to me, I would be so grateful.

W： No problem. Wait a moment. I'll look for the document and email it. **(37) Why don't you make sure that you receive it in about five minutes?**

---

35. Why is the man calling?
- [A] He forgot a document password.
- **[B] He needs an important document.**
- [C] He wants to apply for a job.
- [D] His computer is not working.

36. When will the woman leave work?
- [A] 4:00 p.m.
- [B] 5:00 p.m.
- [C] 6:00 p.m.
- **[D] 7:00 p.m.**

---

33. 女子建議男子做什麼？
- [A] 向同事們自我介紹
- [B] 穿工作服
- **[C] 學習如何列商品清單**
- [D] 舉辦喬遷派對

34. 男子需要先做什麼？
- **[A] 換衣服**
- [B] 掛上名牌
- [C] 聯繫倉庫管理人
- [D] 閱讀員工手冊

35–37 對話

男： 哈囉，提娜。我是麥可・霍爾。**(35)** 我一分鐘前離開辦公室後，才想起我忘了將一份重要文件用電子郵件寄給自己。那是我明天要在東京做簡報用的試算表，你還在辦公室嗎？

女： 是的，我在。**(36)** 現在是下午六點鐘。我還要一個小時才下班。那麼，我要如何幫你？

男： 喔，太好了。如果你開啟我的電腦，會看到試算表檔案就在電腦桌面上。請你將它用電子郵件寄給我，我會很感激的。

女： 沒問題。請稍等。我會尋找那份文件並且將它用電子郵件寄給你。**(37)** 你要不要在五分鐘後確認是否收到了？

---

35. 男子為何打電話？
- [A] 他忘了文件的密碼
- **[B] 他需要一份重要的文件**
- [C] 他想要應徵工作
- [D] 他的電腦故障了

36. 女子將於何時下班？
- [A] 下午四點
- [B] 下午五點
- [C] 下午六點
- **[D] 下午七點**

37. What does the woman suggest the man do?
　Ⓐ Extend a warranty
　Ⓑ Come to work early tomorrow
　Ⓒ Participate in a survey
　Ⓓ Check his email

38–40 conversation

M： Hello. This is Chris Holt calling on behalf of the World Science Fiction Convention. **(38) We reserved the conference center at your hotel for our event this weekend.** I visited the space today and noticed that there were no tables and chairs set up.

W： The seating will be ready in time for the event. **(39) Those items are currently needed for another convention in a different section of the hotel.** By the way, exactly how many attendees are you expecting?

M： **(40) We have 248 confirmed guests.** Therefore, we will need around 50 tables with 5 chairs each. Please let me know once these preparations are done.

38. Where does the woman work?
　Ⓐ At a restaurant
　Ⓑ At a hostel
　Ⓒ At a movie theater
　Ⓓ At a hotel

39. Why are the tables and chairs currently unavailable?
　Ⓐ A shipment has not arrived.
　Ⓑ The woman didn't permit their use.
　Ⓒ Other people are using them.
　Ⓓ The storage room is locked.

40. What does the man clarify?
　Ⓐ The expected number of guests
　Ⓑ The location of stored supplies
　Ⓒ The starting time of an event
　Ⓓ The necessary documents

---

37. 女子建議男子做什麼？
　Ⓐ 延長保固期
　Ⓑ 明天早點來上班
　Ⓒ 參與一項調查
　Ⓓ 查看電子郵件

38–40 對話

男： 哈囉。我是克里斯・霍爾特，代表世界科幻小說大會來電。**(38) 我們為了這週末的活動預訂了貴飯店的會議中心。** 我今天去看場地，注意到那裡沒有擺設桌椅。

女： 座位會在活動時準備好。**(39) 目前飯店別區正在進行另一場會議，需要使用那些桌椅。** 對了，你們預期會有多少與會者前來？

男： **(40) 我們有 248 名確認會出席的賓客。** 因此我們需要大約 50 張桌子，每張桌子搭配五張椅子，請在準備就緒後立即通知我。

38. 女子在哪裡上班？
　Ⓐ 餐廳
　Ⓑ 青年旅館
　Ⓒ 電影院
　Ⓓ 飯店

39. 現在為何沒有桌椅可用？
　Ⓐ 貨運尚未抵達
　Ⓑ 女子不允許他們使用桌椅
　Ⓒ 其他人正在使用桌椅
　Ⓓ 儲藏室被鎖上

40. 男子說明什麼事？
　Ⓐ 預計的賓客人數
　Ⓑ 儲存用品的地點
　Ⓒ 活動開始的時間
　Ⓓ 必要的文件

41-43 conversation

M：Hello, Ms. Morris. It's Marvin Gibson from *New York Eats*. **(41) I'm calling because I write a weekly column for the magazine and would like to profile your restaurant this week.**

W：Wow, I'm honored. **(42) We recently added some Mexican dishes to our menu.** Why don't you come by tonight and try some? Afterwards you can interview me and the chefs about the restaurant.

M：That sounds great. **(43) However, I'd like to come during the day so that I can take some nice pictures.**

W：All right, then. How about this Friday?

41-43 對話

男：哈囉，莫莉絲女士。我是《紐約美食》的馬文・吉普森。**(41) 我打這通電話是因為我為這本雜誌寫每週專欄，而這個星期我想介紹貴餐廳。**

女：哇，我很榮幸。**(42) 我們的菜單最近新增一些墨西哥菜。** 您何不今晚過來並試吃？然後您可以採訪我和廚師關於餐廳的事。

男：聽起來不錯。**(43) 然而，我想要在白天時過去，以便拍攝不錯的照片。**

女：好的。這星期五如何？

41. What are the speakers mainly discussing?
   A A new recipe
   B A grand opening
   C An interview
   D A detailed itinerary

41. 對話者們主要在討論什麼？
   A 新食譜
   B 盛大開幕
   C 一場訪談
   D 詳細的旅遊行程

42. What change does the woman mention about the restaurant?
   A A menu was expanded.
   B An address was changed.
   C A document was revised.
   D An opening date was delayed.

42. 關於餐廳，女子提到了什麼改變？
   A 新增菜色
   B 地址更動
   C 文件修訂
   D 開幕日延後

43. What does the man suggest doing?
   A Redecorating the space
   B Hiring a Mexican chef
   C Meeting at a different time
   D Making a reservation

43. 男子建議做什麼？
   A 重新裝飾場地
   B 僱用墨西哥廚師
   C 在另一時間會面
   D 預約訂位

44-46 conversation

M：Excuse me. **(44) I bought a fish tank and some goldfish here yesterday. (45) However, the water filter doesn't seem to be working properly.**

W：Ah, yes. I remember you from yesterday. I'm sorry to hear that. Could you tell me more?

44-46 對話

男：不好意思。**(44) 我昨天在這裡買了一個魚缸和幾條金魚，(45) 但是濾水器似乎沒有正常運作。**

女：啊，是的，我記得您昨天有來，很遺憾聽見這件事。您可以說得更詳細嗎？

M : Well, I turned it on, but it doesn't appear to be running. I'm worried the fish won't survive without the filter functioning. I brought it for you to take a look at.

W : Hmm, you're right. It appears to be broken. I'm so sorry about that. **(46) I'll give you a new one immediately.** Wait a moment, please.

男：嗯，我開啟濾水器時，它似乎沒有運轉。我擔心濾水器故障，魚就無法生存。我有把它帶來給你看。

女：嗯，您說的對，它壞掉了，我對此感到抱歉。**(46) 我馬上給您一個新的，請稍等。**

44. Where is the conversation taking place?
   A At a hardware store
   B At a fish market
   C At a pet store
   D At an animal shelter

45. What problem does the man mention?
   A A piece of equipment is out of order.
   B Some fish was not cooked properly.
   C A personal item has been lost.
   D An extra charge was added.

46. What does the woman say she will do?
   A Deliver an item
   B Fix a computer error
   C Replace a purchase
   D Offer a discount

44. 這則對話是在哪裡進行的？
   A 五金行
   B 魚市場
   C 寵物店
   D 動物收容所

45. 男子提到什麼問題？
   A 設備故障
   B 部分的魚肉烹調不當
   C 私人物品遺失
   D 增添了額外的收費

46. 女子說她會做什麼？
   A 運送一件物品
   B 修改電腦錯誤
   C 替換貨品
   D 提供折扣

39

47–49 conversation

M : **(47) My guest today is Donna Fuller, a famous singer-songwriter currently touring the United States.** Her newest album just came out this week. Thanks for joining us, Donna. First, could you describe your musical style for listeners who may be unfamiliar with you?

W : Well, my style has changed a lot over the years. **(48) Originally, I wrote and performed jazz music, but this new album is in the rock genre.** I think my fans will be a little surprised, but I hope they like it.

M : What can your fans expect if they come to see you live on this new tour?

W : **(49) There will be a lot more musicians on stage than before.** So, the stage will be full of energy and excitement.

47–49 對話

男：**(47) 今天的來賓是知名的創作型歌手唐娜‧富勒，她現在正在美國進行巡迴演出**，她的最新專輯本週才剛發行。感謝你來上節目，唐娜。首先，你可以向還不熟悉你的聽眾描述你的音樂風格嗎？

女：嗯，我的風格在這幾年改變很多。**(48) 我原本創作和演奏的是爵士樂，但這張新專輯是搖滾類型的。**我認為我的粉絲們會有些驚訝，但我希望他們會喜歡。

男：如果你的粉絲們來看你新的現場巡迴演出，他們可預期會看到什麼？

女：**(49) 舞台上將會比先前增加許多的樂手。**因此，舞台會充滿活力及興奮感。

47. Who most likely is the man?
- A A recording technician
- B A performer
- C A musician
- **D A radio host**

48. What kind of music does the woman currently play?
- A Pop
- **B Rock**
- C Folk
- D Blues

49. According to the woman, what will be different about her upcoming performance?
- A It will begin at midnight.
- B It is free to the public.
- C It will be broadcast live.
- **D It will include more performers.**

(NEW)

50–52 conversation

W1：Hi, can I speak with **(50) Thomas Hyatt? It's regarding the construction at Franklin Studios. He's the funds manager, right?**

W2：Yes. Can I ask who's calling?

W1：This is Sharon Jasmin, the studio director at Franklin's Studios. We are upgrading our studios but **(51) we're supposed to receive some funding today that didn't go through.** The builders have stopped construction until I can guarantee payment.

W2：OK, I'll put you through to Mr. Hyatt now. Hold, please.

M：Hello? Mrs. Jasmin?

W1：Good morning, Mr. Hyatt. Are those funds coming through today? I really want to stay on target with our project, so we need to keep construction going.

M：Definitely. I'm actually at the bank now doing all the transfers so the money should be in your account within half an hour. **(52) I'll send you a confirmation receipt via cellphone. Please message me back when you get it.**

---

47. 男子最有可能是什麼人？
- A 錄音師
- B 表演者
- C 音樂家
- **D 廣播主持人**

48. 女子現在演奏哪種類型的音樂？
- A 流行樂
- **B 搖滾樂**
- C 民謠
- D 藍調

49. 根據女子，她近期的演出會有何不同？
- A 將從午夜開始
- B 免費公開演出
- C 將現場直播
- **D 將包含更多演出者**

50–52 對話

女1：嗨，我可以找 **(50) 湯瑪士．海亞** 嗎？這是關於富蘭克林工作室工程的事。他是財務經理，對嗎？

女2：是的，請問您是誰？

女1：我是夏倫．茉莉，富蘭克林工作室的總監。我們要升級工作室，但 **(51) 我們今天應該要收到的款項還沒匯入。** 營建商已經停止工程，直到我確認付款。

女2：好的，我現在為您轉接海亞先生。請稍等。

男：哈囉，茉莉女士嗎？

女1：早安，海亞先生。資金今天會匯過來嗎？我很希望我們的計劃能朝目標前進，因此我們需要讓工程繼續進行。

男：當然。其實我正在銀行匯款，因此款項在半小時內就會進到你的帳戶。**(52) 我會透過手機將確認匯款收據寄給你，你收到後請傳訊息給我。**

50. Who is Mr. Hyatt?
　Ⓐ Building Manager
　Ⓑ Funds Manager
　Ⓒ Accountant
　Ⓓ Construction worker

51. What problem does Mrs. Jasmin mention?
　Ⓐ The main branch is closed.
　Ⓑ Construction is continuing.
　Ⓒ She didn't receive some funds.
　Ⓓ The timing was incorrect.

52. What does Mr. Hyatt ask Mrs. Jasmin to do?
　Ⓐ Not to message him back
　Ⓑ Send him a message back
　Ⓒ Review the receipt
　Ⓓ Cancel the transfer

50. 海亞先生是什麼人？
　Ⓐ 建築經理
　Ⓑ 財務經理
　Ⓒ 會計師
　Ⓓ 建築工人

51. 茉莉女士提到什麼問題？
　Ⓐ 主要分公司關閉
　Ⓑ 工程持續進行
　Ⓒ 她沒有收到某些資金
　Ⓓ 時機不對

52. 海亞先生要求茉莉女士做什麼？
　Ⓐ 別回傳訊息給他
　Ⓑ 回傳訊息給他
　Ⓒ 檢視收據
　Ⓓ 取消匯款

(NEW)
53–55 conversation

M： Here is the restaurant space I told you about last week. I think it's perfect for a small café. There is also a patio area out the back; you can see it from here.

W： **(53) Oh yeah, that look's nice. I think this is a little small, but I like the location.**

M： It is small, but with the patio space you could probably seat 20 people.

W： **(54) I've looked at another location up the street that is about 10% cheaper than this, so it's a tough choice.**

M： I see. **(55) Well, we can negotiate on the price.** I'll just have to talk to my manager first.

W： That would be great. If you can match their rental cost, I would probably take this location because of the patio.

M： OK. Let me talk to my manager and get back to you.

53–55 對話

男： 這就是我上星期和您說過的餐廳場地，我認為這很適合小型咖啡店。後面還有露台區，您從這裡就可以看見。

女： **(53)** 喔，對耶，那裡看起來很不錯。我認為場地有點小，但我喜歡這個地點。

男： 的確是小，但加上露台空間，也許可以容納 20 個人的座位。

女： **(54)** 我看過這條街的另一個地點，比這裡便宜一成左右。因此，很難做抉擇。

男： 了解。**(55)** 價格部分可做協商，但我得先和我們經理商量。

女： 那太好了。如果你的出租價格可以比照他們的，那麼我也許會因為露台而選這個地點。

男： 好的，讓我與經理談過後再回覆您。

53. What does the woman say about the restaurant space?
　Ⓐ She thinks it's too big.
　Ⓑ It has a good location.
　Ⓒ The location is not good.
　Ⓓ It's a bit far from her office.

53. 關於餐廳場地，女子說了什麼？
　Ⓐ 她認為場地太大
　Ⓑ 地點很好
　Ⓒ 地點不好
　Ⓓ 離她辦公室有點遠

54. Why does the woman say, "I've looked at another location up the street that is about 10% cheaper"?

  A **To get a lower rental price**
  B To buy the property
  C To prepare a new contract
  D To deny the request

55. What does the man say about the price?

  A He agrees to reduce it.
  B He has to ask his co-worker.
  C **He has to ask his manager.**
  D He refuses to reduce it.

56–58 conversation

W: Hi, Matthew. **(56)** **Any news on our sales results for last month?**

M: I am just finishing the report now. Looks like our sales are booming in our Woodsdale stores, but the Collingwood stores aren't doing well. Usually it's the other way around.

W: Hmm. **(57)** **That's interesting.**

M: **(58)** **Maybe we need to take a trip to Collingwood and talk to the management team about why their sales changed so quickly.**

W: Yep. Let's go this afternoon.

56. What are the speakers discussing?

  A Sales results of last quarter
  B **Sales results of last month**
  C Sales of the new range
  D Sales for the coming month

57. What does the woman imply when she says, "that's interesting"?

  A She wants to work at the Collingwood store.
  B She knows their sales are down.
  C She wasn't listening to the man.
  D **She wants to know why sales are down.**

58. What does the man suggest they do?

  A Visit Head Office
  B Visit the Woodsdale store
  C **Visit the Collingwood store**
  D Visit their manager

54. 女子為何説「我看過這條街的另一個地點，比這裡便宜大約一成」？

  A **為了獲得較低的出租價格**
  B 為了購買房地產
  C 為了準備新合約
  D 為了拒絕要求

55. 關於價格，男子説了什麼？

  A 他同意降低價格
  B 他必須詢問同事
  C **他必須詢問經理**
  D 他拒絕降低價格

56–58 對話

女：嗨，馬修。**(56)** 有任何關於我們上個月業績結果的新消息嗎？

男：我正要完成這份報告。看起來伍茲戴爾分店似乎生意興隆，但是科林伍德分店表現不好。通常情況是正好相反的。

女：嗯。**(57)** 那真是耐人尋味。

男：**(58)** 也許我們該去科林伍德一趟，並且與管理團隊討論為何他們業績變化如此迅速。

女：對。我們下午就去吧。

56. 對話者們在討論什麼？

  A 上一季的業績結果
  B **上個月的業績結果**
  C 新系列產品的業績
  D 下個月的業績

57. 女子説「那真是耐人尋味」，她暗示什麼？

  A 她想要在科林伍德分店上班
  B 她知道他們的業績下滑
  C 她沒在聽男子説話
  D **她想要知道為何業績下滑**

58. 男子建議他們做什麼？

  A 去總公司
  B 去伍茲戴爾分店
  C **去科林伍德分店**
  D 找他們的經理

59–61 conversation

M1： Harry, Anne, what kind of tools did you say we need?

M2： **(59) Look over there. We need a drill, and two hammers.** We don't need anything else because **(60) I'm getting all the small equipment delivered to the office today.**

W： What about paint?

M2： We don't need paint. We already have it.

M1： OK. **(61) But we do need some nails. I know you didn't order those. I saw the invoice.**

M2： Yes, you're right. Let's get what we need here and then go.

59–61 對話

男1： 哈利、安妮，你們說我們需要什麼工具？

男2： (59) 去那裡找找，我們需要一個鑽子和兩把鐵鎚。我們不需要其他別的東西，因為 (60) 小型工具今天會直接送到辦公室來。

女： 油漆呢？

男2： 我們不需要油漆，我們已經有了。

男1： 好的。(61) 但我們確實需要釘子，我知道你沒有訂購釘子，我有看到發票。

男2： 是的，你說得對。我們在這裡買所需的東西，然後就走吧。

---

59. Where most likely are the speakers?
- [A] At an office
- [B] At repair shop
- **[C] At a hardware store**
- [D] At an electrical appliance store

60. What does the man mention about the delivery?
- [A] He isn't getting any equipment delivered to the office.
- **[B] He is getting the small equipment delivered to the office.**
- [C] He is getting a drill delivered to the office.
- [D] He is getting some documents delivered to the office.

61. What does the man say he needs?
- [A] A saw
- [B] Some tapes
- [C] A shovel
- **[D] Some nails**

59. 對話者們最有可能在哪裡？
- [A] 辦公室
- [B] 修繕店
- **[C] 五金行**
- [D] 電子用品器材行

60. 關於貨品運送，男子提到什麼？
- [A] 他不要宅配任何用具到辦公室
- **[B] 他要宅配小型用具到辦公室**
- [C] 他要宅配鑽子到辦公室
- [D] 他要宅配一些文件到辦公室

61. 男子說他需要什麼？
- [A] 一把鋸子
- [B] 一些膠帶
- [C] 一把鏟子
- **[D] 一些釘子**

62-64 conversation

M： Hi Sally, how has your day been?

W： Really great, Jim. I have been busy, but productive. **(62) How was your meeting this morning?**

M： It went better than I expected. The interior design specialist just gave us some recommendations for our office layout. We don't need to purchase anything new, just rearrange a few things.

W： Oh really? What did he say?

M： **(63) He suggested that we move the help desk and the sales desk so that they are on opposite sides of the entrance. That way if we have people waiting in line they won't be crowded. (64) We will just slide the sales desk to where the waiting area is now.**

W： That is a good idea, and this way when people come into the office, they can see all of our products displayed against the back wall.

M： Exactly, and then after they purchase their items they can just step out the door. Glad we are already on the same page.

W： Well, I think we should start moving the sales desk right away, don't you?

62-64 對話

男： 嗨，莎莉，今天過得怎麼樣？

女： 很棒，吉姆。我一直很忙但很充實。**(62) 你今天早上的會議如何？**

男： 比我預期的還好。室內設計專家給我們一些辦公室空間規劃的建議。我們不用購買任何新東西，只要重新安排幾件物品就行了。

女： 喔，真的嗎？他說了什麼？

男： **(63) 他建議我們挪動服務台及銷售櫃台，讓它們在入口處對面兩側。這樣的話如果有人排隊等候也不會擁擠。(64) 我們只要將銷售櫃台推到現在等候區的位置。**

女： 那是個好主意，這樣人們進到辦公室時，就可以看見後牆展示著我們全部的產品。

男： 沒錯，然後在他們購買商品後就可以直接出門。很高興我們的意見一致。

女： 我認為我們該立刻移動銷售櫃台，不是嗎？

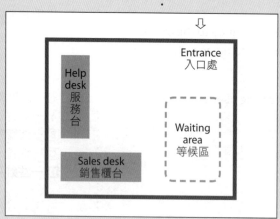

---

62. What did the man recently do?

    Ⓐ He met with a photographer.

    Ⓑ He met with a sales associate.

    Ⓒ He met with an interior decorator.

    Ⓓ He met with his supervisor.

62. 男子最近做了什麼？

    Ⓐ 他與攝影師會面

    Ⓑ 他與業務同事會面

    Ⓒ 他與室內裝潢師會面

    Ⓓ 他與主管會面

63. Why does the man want to move the sales desk?
- Ⓐ To increase the company's sales
- Ⓑ To make it look nicer
- Ⓒ To make more room for the woman to work
- **Ⓓ To give waiting customers more space**

64. Look at the graphic. Where will the sales desk be moved to?
- Ⓐ Where the help desk is now
- Ⓑ So it is to the right of the entrance
- **Ⓒ Where the waiting area is**
- Ⓓ They will move the help desk instead.

63. 男子為何想要搬動銷售櫃台？
- Ⓐ 為了增加公司業績
- Ⓑ 為了使它更為美觀
- Ⓒ 為了騰出空間讓女子工作
- **Ⓓ 為了給等候的顧客較多空間**

64. 參看圖表，銷售櫃台將會被搬動到哪裡？
- Ⓐ 現在服務台的位置
- Ⓑ 在入口處的右邊
- **Ⓒ 現在等候區的位置**
- Ⓓ 他們將會改為搬動服務台

(NEW)
65–67 conversation

M：Hi, Rosalie, did you hear about the fire drills next week?

W：Yeah. **(65) I can't believe they scheduled ours during our lunch break. (66) They need to reschedule our lunch break, or change the fire drill time to 1 to 2 p.m.** They shouldn't expect us to skip lunch and practice the fire drills.

M：I know. I don't think it is very fair. They should have had all the drills in the afternoon. The other departments actually get extra time off work, and we lose our lunch break.

W：**(67) I think we should go and speak to our supervisor.** What do you think?

M：I agree. Should we go now?

W：Yes. Let me quickly send an email and I will come with you.

65–67 對話

男：嗨，羅絲莉。你聽說下星期的消防演習了嗎？

女：是的。**(65) 我真不敢相信他們把我們的演習時段安排在午餐休息時間。(66) 他們需要重新安排我們的午休時間，或者是把消防演習時間改到下午一點到兩點。** 他們不該要我們不吃午餐進行消防演習。

男：我知道，我認為這樣並不公平，他們應該要把所有演習都安排在下午。其實其他部門在下班後會有額外時間，而我們卻沒了午餐休息時間。

女：**(67) 我認為我們該去與主管討論。** 你覺得呢？

男：我同意。我們要現在去嗎？

女：是的。讓我很快寄出一封電子郵件，然後我和你一起去。

Fire Drill Procedures 火警演習流程 January 21st 1 月 21 日		
Level 1 一樓	8 a.m. – 9 a.m. 上午 8 點 – 上午 9 點	Human Resources Department 人力資源部門
Level 2 二樓	9 a.m. – 10 a.m. 上午 9 點 – 上午 10 點	Accounting Department 會計部門
Level 3 三樓	11 a.m.– 12 p.m. 上午 11 點 – 上午 12 點	Customer Service Department 客戶服務部門
Level 4 四樓	12 p.m. – 1 p.m. 中午 12 點 – 下午 1 點	Legal Department 法務部門

65. What did the man say about next week?

[A] There will be an inspection.

[B] Some new computers will arrive.

[C] They will have fire drills.

[D] Someone called in sick.

66. Look at the graphic. What department do the speakers work in?

[A] Human Resources

[B] Accounting

[C] Customer Service

[D] Legal

67. What does the woman suggest they do?

[A] Don't say anything

[B] Print out some extra copies

[C] Speak to their supervisor

[D] Put up a sign

68–70 conversation

M : **(68) Mark's Models, this is Greg speaking. How can I help you today?**

W : Hi Greg. I bought a snap fit Mazda Mikado plastic model kit yesterday and I'm just starting to put it together now, but some of the pieces are missing.

M : Oh, that's not good. What exactly is missing?

W : **(69) Well, it seems like all the parts are here, but I have nothing to put them together with.**

M : Ah. It must be the snap fit tool. With our older model kits that's a pretty common problem. We have a lot in the store. **(70) I'll express-post one to you today if that's OK?**

W : Oh, that's great. Thanks for your help!

---

65. 關於下星期，男子說了什麼？

[A] 將會進行檢查

[B] 將會送來一些新電腦

[C] 他們將進行消防演習

[D] 某人請病假

66. 參看圖表，對話者們在哪個部門工作？

[A] 人力資源部門

[B] 會計部門

[C] 客戶服務部門

[D] 法務部門

67. 女子建議他們做什麼？

[A] 保持沉默

[B] 再多印幾份

[C] 與主管商談

[D] 設立標語

68–70 對話

男 : **(68)** 馬克模型店，我是格雷。您今天需要什麼服務呢？

女 : 嗨，格雷。我昨天買了一個馬自達天皇塑膠模型扣合組。我現在正要開始組裝，但有些物件不見了。

男 : 喔，真糟糕。究竟是什麼不見了？

女 : **(69)** 看起來全部零件都在，但我沒有組裝它們的工具。

男 : 一定是扣合工具，我們較舊款的模型組常常出現這個問題。我們店裡還有很多，**(70)** 我今天用快捷郵件寄給您好嗎？

女 : 喔，太好了。感謝你的幫忙！

1980 Mazda Mikado Plastic Model	**1980 年馬自達天皇塑膠模型組**
Part A 零件 A	- 1:25 scale plastic model kit 1:25 比例的塑膠模型組
Part B 零件 B	- Snap fit tool 扣合工具
Part C 零件 C	- Rubber tires 橡膠輪胎
Part D 零件 D	- Rub-on decals 感壓轉印貼紙

68. Where does the man most likely work?
- [A] At a stationery shop
- [B] At a hardware store
- **[C] At a model shop**
- [D] At a medical clinic

(NEW)
69. Look at the graphic. Which part is the woman missing?
- [A] Decals
- [B] Model kit
- **[C] Snap fit tool**
- [D] Rubber tires

70. What does the man offer to do?
- [A] Deliver it to her
- [B] Give her a refund
- [C] Cancel the order
- **[D] Express-post it to her**

68. 男子最有可能在哪裡工作？
- [A] 文具店
- [B] 五金行
- **[C] 模型店**
- [D] 醫療診所

69. 參看圖表，女子缺少了什麼？
- [A] 感壓轉印貼紙
- [B] 模型組
- **[C] 扣合工具**
- [D] 橡膠輪胎

70. 男子提議要做什麼？
- [A] 送去給她
- [B] 退款給她
- [C] 取消訂單
- **[D] 用快捷郵寄給她**

PART 4   P. 154-157   🎧40

TEST 10   PART 4   🎧40

71–73 telephone message

W：Hello, Ms. Jansen. It's Kate Douglas. **(71) I'm so grateful that you offered to babysit my son Michael this weekend.** As you know, something urgent came up and I have to be away on business this weekend. **(72) An important merger will take place in April, and I need to be in New York in order to lead a meeting between my company and NX Electronics. (73) Oh, and also, please let me know how much you expect to be compensated for babysitting.** Thanks again.

71–73 電話留言

女：哈囉，簡森女士，我是凱特‧道格拉斯。**(71) 我很感激你願意在這個週末當保母照顧我兒子麥克。**你知道的，由於有緊急事務，我週末必須出差。**(72) 四月將有重要的合併案，我需要在紐約主持我公司與 NX 電子的會議。(73)** 喔，對了，還要請你告訴我，你當保母想要的報酬。再次感謝你。

71. What did Ms. Jansen offer to do?
- [A] Attend a meeting
- [B] Go to New York
- **[C] Take care of the speaker's child**
- [D] Lend a personal item

72. What will happen in April?
- [A] An annual conference
- **[B] A business merger**
- [C] A budget review
- [D] A town meeting

71. 簡森女士欲提供什麼幫助？
- [A] 出席會議
- [B] 去紐約
- **[C] 照顧發話者的孩子**
- [D] 出借一項私人物品

72. 四月將會發生什麼事？
- [A] 年度會議
- **[B] 企業合併**
- [C] 預算審查
- [D] 小鎮會議

73. What will the listener most likely inform the speaker about?
- A The time of arrival
- **B The payment**
- C An event location
- D A weekend schedule

74–76 announcement

M： Good morning, ladies and gentlemen. **(74) On behalf of the staff, I regretfully announce that Flight 344 will be slightly delayed.** The fueling process is taking longer than expected but should be completed soon. **(75) Passengers who are hungry can receive complimentary snacks and fruit juices here at the counter. (76) However, we will be boarding relatively shortly, so we ask that passengers not leave the boarding area.** Thank you for your cooperation.

---

74. Where most likely is this announcement being made?
- A In a factory
- B On an airplane
- C At a bus terminal
- **D At an airport**

75. What can listeners receive at the counter?
- A A name tag
- B A receipt
- C A meal ticket
- **D Some refreshments**

76. What are listeners asked to do?
- A Form a line
- **B Stay nearby**
- C Sign a document
- D Present a ticket

---

73. 聆聽者最有可能告知發話者什麼事？
- A 抵達時間
- **B 薪資**
- C 活動場地
- D 週末行程

74–76 公告

男：早安，各位先生、女士。**(74) 謹代表全體員工很遺憾地宣布 344 號班機將會稍微延誤。** 加油的過程比原先預期的還要久，但應該很快就會完成了。**(75) 感到飢餓的乘客可以在櫃台這裡領取免費的零食以及果汁。(76) 但是我們很快就要登機，因此請乘客不要離開登機區。** 感謝各位的配合。

---

74. 這則公告最有可能在哪裡進行？
- A 工廠裡
- B 飛機上
- C 公車總站
- **D 機場**

75. 聽眾可以在櫃台領取什麼？
- A 名牌
- B 收據
- C 餐券
- **D 茶點**

76. 聽眾被要求做什麼？
- A 排隊
- **B 待在附近**
- C 簽署文件
- D 出示票券

77–79 tour guide

M：Hello, everyone. **(77) Welcome to the guided tour of the Giant Dinosaurs exhibit.** Today you will be able to see dinosaur skeletons that were excavated by Dr. Mark Simmons while on an expedition in South Africa. **(78) Dr. Simmons is one of the most respected scientists in the field and has discovered some of the oldest and most well-known fossils in the field.** These fossils here were found in layers of sedimentary rock dated back over 65 million years ago. **(79) Because these fossils are delicate, I remind everyone that if you want to take pictures, please turn the flash off on your camera.**

77–79 導覽

男：哈囉，大家好。**(77) 歡迎來到大型恐龍展的導覽，**今天各位將能見到馬克・西蒙斯博士在南非探險時挖掘出來的恐龍骨骼。**(78) 西蒙斯博士是這個領域最受推崇的科學家之一，他發現了這個領域最古老且最著名的一些化石。**這裡的化石是在超過 6500 萬年前的沉積岩層中發現的。**(79) 因為這些化石很脆弱，所以我要提醒大家，如果想要拍照，請關閉相機的閃光燈。**

77. Where most likely is the speaker?
 A In a museum
 B In a library
 C In a lecture hall
 D In a gift shop

77. 發話者最有可能身在何方？
 A 博物館
 B 圖書館
 C 演講廳
 D 禮品店

78. According to the speaker, what is Dr. Simmons famous for?
 A Writing best-selling books
 B Making important discoveries
 C Finding ancient buildings
 D Conducting groundbreaking experiments

78. 根據發話者，西蒙斯博士以何聞名？
 A 寫暢銷書
 B 提出重大發現
 C 找到古代建築物
 D 進行開創性的實驗

79. What does the speaker request that listeners do?
 A Purchase a day pass
 B Turn off a camera
 C Refrain from using a flash
 D Stay with the group

79. 發話者要求聽眾做什麼？
 A 購買一日通行票
 B 關閉相機
 C 不要使用閃光燈
 D 團體行動

80-82 excerpt from a meeting

W：Before this meeting concludes, I would like to mention a new opportunity available to all employees. **(80) As a benefit of our recent merger with TechSoft Solutions, you can now expand your medical insurance to include vision and dental coverage. (81) You can visit our company website to calculate exactly how much this change would increase your monthly payment. (82) If you have never accessed our website in the past, you will first need to contact Suzie Summers in order to get your login information.** Please make sure to keep your login information private.

80. What is the speaker mainly discussing?
 Ⓐ A company picnic
 Ⓑ A job opportunity
 Ⓒ A new benefit
 Ⓓ Overseas expansion

81. According to the speaker, what can listeners do online?
 Ⓐ Find out a new payment
 Ⓑ Register for a workshop
 Ⓒ Remit a monthly payment
 Ⓓ Review a proposal

82. Why should some listeners contact Suzie Summers?
 Ⓐ To request a schedule change
 Ⓑ To obtain personal information
 Ⓒ To cancel a subscription
 Ⓓ To congratulate a co-worker

80-82 會議摘要

女：會議結束之前，我想要提出一項所有員工都可以利用的新機會。**(80)** 這是我們最近與科技軟體公司合併所帶來的好處，各位可以增加醫療保險的項目，涵蓋視力和牙齒的保險給付。**(81)** 各位可以上公司網站試算這項改變究竟會增加多少你每月的保險費。**(82)** 如果你過去從未登入我們的網站，你需要先聯繫蘇西·薩默斯，以獲得你的登入資訊。請務必將你的登入資訊保密。

80. 發話者主要在討論什麼？
 Ⓐ 公司野餐
 Ⓑ 工作機會
 Ⓒ 新的福利
 Ⓓ 海外擴展

81. 根據發話者，聽眾可以上網做什麼？
 Ⓐ 了解新支付項目
 Ⓑ 報名研討會
 Ⓒ 匯寄每月的款項
 Ⓓ 檢視提案

82. 聽眾為何需要聯繫蘇西·薩默斯？
 Ⓐ 要求改變時程
 Ⓑ 獲得個人資訊
 Ⓒ 取消訂閱
 Ⓓ 祝賀同事

83–85 talk

W：Hi, everyone, we should get started with the monthly meeting. **(83) First of all, we have two knew interns starting next week. They are both accounting majors who specialize in auditing. (84) I know that you are all very busy**, but I really need you to help the interns settle in as quickly as possible. I'm going to give each of you a specific job that I want you to personally train the intern. I think it is the most efficient way to get them up to speed. I'm going to prepare a task for each of you and email it to you. When the interns arrive **(85) I want each of you to spend one full week with them and train them.** Thanks for your patience.

83–85 談話

女：嗨，大家好，我們應該開始進行月會了。**(83) 首先，我們下週將有兩位新的實習生。他們兩人都主修會計，專攻審計。(84) 我知道你們全都很忙**，但我真的需要各位協助實習生盡快適應新環境。我將會指派你們每個人一份特定的工作，我要你們親自訓練實習生，我認為這是使他們跟上進度最有效的方式。我會為你們每個人準備一項任務，並且用電子郵件寄送給你們。實習生到的時候，**(85) 我要你們每個人各花整整一週訓練實習生。**感謝你們的耐心。

---

83. Who most likely are the listeners?
- A Lawyers
- **B Accountants**
- C Bankers
- D Cashiers

(NEW)
84. What does the woman mean when she says, "I know that you are all very busy"?
- A She wants to organize a meeting.
- B She needs more printers.
- **C She is recognizing their concerns.**
- D She isn't sure what to do.

85. What task does the speaker assign to the listeners?
- **A Spend a week with the interns**
- B Not to speak to the interns
- C Write a training manual
- D Report on sales figures

83. 聽眾最有可能是什麼人？
- A 律師
- **B 會計師**
- C 銀行家
- D 收銀員

84. 女子說「我知道你們全都很忙」，她指的是什麼？
- A 她想要籌辦一場會議
- B 她需要更多的印表機
- **C 她了解他們的顧慮**
- D 她不確定該做什麼

85. 發話者指派什麼任務給聽者？
- **A 與實習生共度一星期**
- B 別與實習生交談
- C 寫訓練手冊
- D 提報銷售數據

86-88 announcement

W：As everyone knows, **(86) the line of keyboards and web cameras we produced this year are selling extremely well.** I'm not sure why, but our LCD monitors are not selling well at all. I suspect the price point might be too high when compared with other brands. Whatever the reason, we need to start selling more, **(87) so I have hired some marketing analysts that can help us try to figure out what the problem is. (88) I've arranged a meeting with them this afternoon after lunch, so please come to the boardroom on the 2nd floor and sit in on the meeting.**

86-88 宣布

女：大家都知道，**(86) 我們今年生產的系列鍵盤和網路攝影機賣得非常好。**我不確定為什麼，但我們的LCD螢幕賣得不太好。我猜想可能是零售價與其他廠牌相比太高了。不論是什麼原因，我們都需要增加銷量 **(87) 因此我已經僱用了幾位能幫助我們試圖了解問題所在的市場分析師。(88) 我已經安排今天下午午餐過後要與他們開會，因此請各位到二樓的會議室出席這場會議。**

86. What product does the speaker's company sell?
   A Electronics
   B Software
   C Wearable technology
   D Automobile

86. 發話者的公司販售什麼產品？
   A 電子產品
   B 軟體
   C 穿戴科技
   D 汽車

87. According to the speaker, what happened last month?
   A Someone was fired.
   B Some products sold well.
   C The company went bankrupt.
   D There was a merger.

87. 根據發話者，上個月發生了什麼事？
   A 有人被解僱
   B 有些產品銷售不佳
   C 公司破產
   D 公司併購案

88. What does the woman mean when she says, "sit in on the meeting"?
   A She will send employees an email.
   B She wants employees to prepare a report.
   C She wants employees to come to the meeting.
   D She will have a conference call.

88. 女子說「出席這場會議」，她指的是什麼？
   A 她將寄電子郵件給員工
   B 她想要員工準備一份報告
   C 她想要員工參加會議
   D 她將進行電話會議

89-91 speech

M : Great news, everybody. Our sales are up by 12 percent compared to last year. **(89) Our new range of electric blankets and space heaters sold more than we expected. The biggest seller was our new heated pillow inserts. (90) Last month we signed a special contract to have our pillows used exclusively in Charleston Hotels, which means a huge boost in sales figures.** We are expecting even more contracts like this in the future. **(91) How about that? Everyone should give themselves a pat on the back. I'm really proud of your efforts.**

89-91 演說

男： 各位，有好消息，我們的業績與去年相比提高了一成。**(89) 我們新系列的電毯和暖氣機賣得比預期的更好，銷售最好的是我們的加熱枕芯。(90) 我們上個月簽署了一份特別的合約，讓查斯頓旅館獨家使用我們的枕頭，這表示業績會大幅增加。** 我們預計未來會有更多像這樣的合約。**(91) 很棒吧？大家應該給自己一點鼓勵。我對於你們的努力感到非常的驕傲。**

---

89. What product does the speaker's company sell?
A Heating products
B Air conditioners
C Vacuum cleaners
D Magazines

90. According to the speaker, what happened last month?
A They signed a special contract.
B They bought out another company.
C They traded stocks.
D Their sales went down.

(NEW)
91. What does the man mean when he says, "How about that?"
A He is confused about the situation.
B He is pleased with the results.
C He isn't happy.
D He wants to try to upgrade their computers.

89. 發話者的公司販售什麼商品？
A 加熱產品
B 冷氣機
C 吸塵器
D 雜誌

90. 根據發話者，上個月發生了什麼事？
A 他們簽署了特別的合約
B 他們收購另一家公司
C 他們交易股票
D 他們的業績下滑

91. 男子說「很棒吧」，他指的是什麼？
A 他對於情況感到困惑。
B 他對於成果感到很滿意
C 他不高興
D 他想要試著升級他們的電腦

92–94 advertisement

M：**(92) Springfield Dance Troupe has just added a new hip-hop workshop to our winter schedule.** We are extremely excited to be able to offer more contemporary dance routines to the members of our community! **(94) We'll be having a live performance of some of the moves that we will be teaching people to master this Saturday at 12 p.m. We would like to invite all members of the community, young and old, boys and girls, to come down to the Recreational Center and enjoy the performance.** Springfield Dance Troupe will of course be continuing to teach the courses that we have always offered, with one exception. Sally Jones, whom many of you know from her fantastic *Nutcracker* performances, will be moving back to Westport. As a result, after this week we will not be offering ballet classes until we can find a teacher to replace her. I hope to see you all at the Recreation Center this Saturday at noon!

92–94 廣告

男：**(92)** 春田舞團剛為我們冬季的課程表新增了嘻哈工作坊。我們很興奮能為我們社區的居民提供更多當代舞步。**(94)** 我們將在本週六中午 12 點舉行現場演出，內容包含一些我們將在課程中教授的舞步。我們想邀請社區的所有居民，不論男女老少，都來休閒中心欣賞表演。春田舞團當然會持續教授已開設的課程，只有一項除外。在《胡桃鉗》中有精彩演出並一鳴驚人的莎莉‧瓊斯，將搬回威斯特波特。因此這星期後，我們就不會開芭蕾課，直到我們能找到代替她的老師。我希望本週六中午能在休閒中心看到各位！–

SPRINGFIELD DANCE TROUPE CLASS SCHEDULE 春田舞團課程表

Class 課程	Mon 星期一	Tue 星期二	Wed 星期三	Thu 星期四	Fri 星期五	Sat 星期六	Sun 星期日
Hip Hop 嘻哈	X	X	X	Tiffany 蒂芬妮 11–2	Tiffany 蒂芬妮 11–2	Owen 歐文 11–2	Owen 歐文 11–2
Swing 搖擺	Beth 貝絲 11–2	Beth 貝絲 11–2	Beth 貝絲 11–2	Beth 貝絲 11–2	Beth 貝絲 11–2	X	X
Jazz 爵士	Gwen 葛溫 5–8	X	Gwen 葛溫 5–8	X	X	Gwen 葛溫 5–8	X
Ballet 芭蕾	Sally 莎莉 1–4	Sally 莎莉 1–4	X	X	X	X	X

92. What is indicated about Springfield Dance Troupe?

A They are changing the music they like.

B They are moving to a new location.

C They want to find a new swing class instructor.

D They are changing the courses they will offer.

92. 關於春田舞團，廣告中有提到哪一點？

A 他們改變了音樂喜好

B 他們要搬到新地點

C 他們想找新的搖擺課老師

D 他們要更改提供的課程

93. Look at the graphic. What can you infer about the dance classes?
    Ⓐ They will be difficult.
    Ⓑ They are for beginners.
    Ⓒ Dance classes last for three hours.
    Ⓓ They are coed.

94. What does Springfield Dance Troupe invite the public to do?
    Ⓐ Come to their picnic
    Ⓑ See them in the concert hall downtown
    Ⓒ Watch them perform a hip-hop dance routine
    Ⓓ Say goodbye to Sally Jones

93. 參看圖表，關於舞蹈課程，你可以推論出什麼？
    Ⓐ 課程會很困難
    Ⓑ 課程是要給初學者的
    Ⓒ 舞蹈課要三個小時
    Ⓓ 課程是男女合班的

94. 春田舞團邀請大家做什麼？
    Ⓐ 參加他們的野餐
    Ⓑ 去市區的音樂廳看他們表演
    Ⓒ 觀賞他們表演嘻哈舞蹈
    Ⓓ 與莎莉・瓊斯道別

95–97 advertisement

W：**(97) Presidential Tailoring is committed to helping you look your best.** If you have been thinking about updating your wardrobe to include custom fit ensembles, we would like to invite you to stop by our shop on the corner of Lexington and Dupont for complimentary measurement. Our tailors have a combined 120 years of experience with men's and women's tailoring. **(95) Our master tailor, Jeffrey Frye, apprenticed in London for 15 years at the prestigious Lorde Homme Tailors before returning home here to the US.** Let us make you look presidential. You deserve it.

95–97 廣告

女：**(97) 老董裁縫店致力於為您打造最出色的樣貌。** 如果您在想要為衣櫥添加合身套裝，那麼我們想邀請您蒞臨我們位於列星頓和迪朋街角的店面，進行免費的套量。我們的裁縫師在男裝和女裝方面共計有 120 年的經驗，**(95) 我們的裁縫大師傑佛瑞・弗萊在返回美國家鄉之前，曾在倫敦知名的羅德・霍姆裁縫店當過 15 年的學徒。** 讓我們幫您看起來如董事長一般；因為您值得。

Presidential Tailoring Pricing Structure 老董裁縫店價目表 **FIRST MEASUREMENTS ARE FREE 首次套量免費**	
Men's trousers 男士長褲	$35*
Men's jackets 男士夾克	$150*
Women's ensembles 女士套裝	$130*
Women's gowns 女士禮服	$200*

*Prices may vary by choice and volume of fabric chosen or required.
* 價格可能因為所選或所需的布料種類或數量而異動。

95. What is indicated in the advertisement?

 A Presidential Tailoring is just getting started in their business.

 B Jeffrey Frye is an experienced American tailor trained overseas.

 C Presidential Tailoring is having a big sale.

 D They only have one tailor on staff.

(NEW)

96. Look at the graphic. What is true about the pricing?

 A It can change based on the material chosen.

 B Women's gowns are cheaper than women's ensembles.

 C Women's ensembles cost more than men's jackets.

 D All of the clothes are 10% off.

97. What can you infer about Presidential Tailoring?

 A They are a discount clothier.

 B They work with leather.

 C Their target market is children.

 D They take a lot of pride in their work.

---

95. 廣告中指出哪一點？

 A 老董裁縫店的生意剛起步

 B 傑佛瑞・弗萊是一名在海外受訓且經驗豐富的美國裁縫師

 C 老董裁縫店正要舉辦大拍賣

 D 他們員工中只有一名裁縫師

96. 參看圖表，關於定價，何者為真？

 A 定價會依所選擇的質料而變動

 B 女士禮服比女士套裝便宜

 C 女士套裝比男士夾克還貴

 D 所有服飾都打九折

97. 關於老董裁縫店，你可以推論什麼？

 A 他們是折扣服裝廠商

 B 他們用皮革製衣

 C 他們的目標市場是孩童

 D 他們對自家商品感到自豪

98–100 telephone message

M：Hello, Ms. Johnson, I am calling about the invoice that you sent me last week. **(99) I just have a few questions I need to ask you about the quantities and pricing of some of the supplies that I ordered. (98) I thought that you told me that if I ordered more than two dozen of any item that I would receive a discount of 5%.** Is this correct? Additionally, I want to just confirm the numbers with you. I ordered 36 foot stools, 12 chairs, 117 small end tables and NO large end tables. I believe there was some confusion. **(100) Can you change the invoice to reflect my requested items?**

98–100 電話留言

男：哈囉，強森女士。我打這通電話是要談關於你上週寄給我的發票。**(99)** 我想請教你幾個問題，是有關部分我所訂購的用品數量和價格。**(98)** 我以為你告訴我說，如果我任何品項的訂購數量超過兩打，就會得到 5% 的折扣，這是正確的嗎？此外，我想要與你確認這些數字。我訂了 36 張腳凳、12 張椅子、117 張小茶几、沒有大茶几。我認為有些地方弄錯了。**(100)** 你可以更改符合我訂購品項的發票？

INVOICE 發票

Item 品項	Quantity 數量	Volume discount 批量折扣
Foot Stools 腳凳	36	3%
Chairs 椅子	12	0%
Small End Tables 小茶几	117	5%
Large End Tables 大茶几	24	5%

(NEW)

98. Look at the graphic. Which item was incorrectly discounted?
 A **Foot stools 3%**
 B Chairs 0%
 C Small end tables 5%
 D Large end tables 5%

99. What is Ms. Johnson asked to do with the invoice?
 A Change the large end table orders to two dozen
 B **Make the invoice match the order**
 C Send the invoice to the factory for completion
 D Send the invoice to accounting

100. What does the speaker anticipate will happen next?
 A He will receive his order.
 B **He will receive a new invoice.**
 C He will have to place the order a third time.
 D He will need to use a different supplier.

98. 參看圖表，哪個數量折扣有誤？
 A **腳凳 3%**
 B 椅子 0%
 C 小茶几 5%
 D 大茶几 5%

99. 強森女士被要求如何處理發票？
 A 將大茶几的訂單改為兩打
 B **使發票與訂單相符**
 C 將發票寄到工廠以完成訂購物品
 D 將發票送交給會計部門

100. 發話者預期接下來會發生什麼事？
 A 他會收到訂購的物品
 B **他會收到新的發票**
 C 他必須下第三次的訂單
 D 他會需要使用不同的供應商

ANSWER KEY

Actual Test 01

1	(A)	26	(A)	51	(C)	76	(B)
2	(A)	27	(C)	52	(D)	77	(B)
3	(A)	28	(A)	53	(B)	78	(C)
4	(B)	29	(B)	54	(C)	79	(D)
5	(A)	30	(C)	55	(B)	80	(D)
6	(D)	31	(A)	56	(C)	81	(C)
7	(C)	32	(B)	57	(A)	82	(C)
8	(B)	33	(A)	58	(D)	83	(A)
9	(A)	34	(C)	59	(C)	84	(D)
10	(B)	35	(A)	60	(D)	85	(C)
11	(C)	36	(B)	61	(A)	86	(D)
12	(B)	37	(C)	62	(C)	87	(A)
13	(A)	38	(A)	63	(D)	88	(B)
14	(B)	39	(C)	64	(A)	89	(A)
15	(B)	40	(B)	65	(A)	90	(C)
16	(A)	41	(C)	66	(B)	91	(D)
17	(C)	42	(C)	67	(B)	92	(C)
18	(B)	43	(D)	68	(D)	93	(B)
19	(C)	44	(D)	69	(C)	94	(B)
20	(A)	45	(D)	70	(C)	95	(C)
21	(B)	46	(A)	71	(C)	96	(C)
22	(C)	47	(D)	72	(A)	97	(B)
23	(B)	48	(B)	73	(D)	98	(C)
24	(A)	49	(C)	74	(A)	99	(A)
25	(C)	50	(A)	75	(C)	100	(C)

Actual Test 02

1	(A)	26	(B)	51	(A)	76	(C)
2	(A)	27	(C)	52	(D)	77	(C)
3	(B)	28	(B)	53	(A)	78	(C)
4	(C)	29	(B)	54	(B)	79	(A)
5	(D)	30	(A)	55	(D)	80	(D)
6	(B)	31	(B)	56	(D)	81	(B)
7	(A)	32	(D)	57	(B)	82	(C)
8	(B)	33	(A)	58	(C)	83	(C)
9	(A)	34	(D)	59	(D)	84	(C)
10	(C)	35	(C)	60	(C)	85	(D)
11	(B)	36	(A)	61	(A)	86	(B)
12	(B)	37	(B)	62	(B)	87	(A)
13	(B)	38	(C)	63	(C)	88	(C)
14	(C)	39	(A)	64	(D)	89	(B)
15	(A)	40	(D)	65	(B)	90	(B)
16	(C)	41	(C)	66	(D)	91	(A)
17	(A)	42	(D)	67	(B)	92	(C)
18	(B)	43	(D)	68	(C)	93	(A)
19	(C)	44	(A)	69	(C)	94	(C)
20	(A)	45	(C)	70	(B)	95	(D)
21	(B)	46	(D)	71	(B)	96	(C)
22	(A)	47	(C)	72	(D)	97	(D)
23	(B)	48	(A)	73	(C)	98	(C)
24	(A)	49	(D)	74	(D)	99	(C)
25	(C)	50	(C)	75	(B)	100	(B)

Actual Test 03

1	(B)	26	(C)	51	(B)	76	(A)
2	(A)	27	(A)	52	(A)	77	(B)
3	(C)	28	(A)	53	(A)	78	(C)
4	(D)	29	(B)	54	(B)	79	(B)
5	(A)	30	(C)	55	(D)	80	(C)
6	(B)	31	(C)	56	(C)	81	(B)
7	(B)	32	(D)	57	(B)	82	(D)
8	(C)	33	(C)	58	(A)	83	(A)
9	(A)	34	(A)	59	(C)	84	(B)
10	(A)	35	(C)	60	(B)	85	(D)
11	(C)	36	(A)	61	(D)	86	(B)
12	(B)	37	(B)	62	(D)	87	(B)
13	(A)	38	(B)	63	(B)	88	(B)
14	(C)	39	(D)	64	(D)	89	(B)
15	(B)	40	(C)	65	(C)	90	(A)
16	(B)	41	(D)	66	(D)	91	(D)
17	(A)	42	(C)	67	(B)	92	(B)
18	(B)	43	(D)	68	(C)	93	(D)
19	(A)	44	(A)	69	(A)	94	(B)
20	(C)	45	(D)	70	(C)	95	(A)
21	(B)	46	(C)	71	(D)	96	(D)
22	(A)	47	(A)	72	(D)	97	(D)
23	(A)	48	(C)	73	(C)	98	(C)
24	(B)	49	(B)	74	(D)	99	(B)
25	(B)	50	(D)	75	(B)	100	(C)

Actual Test 04

1	(C)	26	(B)	51	(D)	76	(C)
2	(D)	27	(C)	52	(B)	77	(B)
3	(A)	28	(B)	53	(C)	78	(C)
4	(B)	29	(C)	54	(D)	79	(A)
5	(A)	30	(B)	55	(A)	80	(C)
6	(A)	31	(A)	56	(D)	81	(D)
7	(A)	32	(C)	57	(A)	82	(C)
8	(B)	33	(A)	58	(C)	83	(B)
9	(B)	34	(B)	59	(B)	84	(A)
10	(A)	35	(D)	60	(C)	85	(C)
11	(C)	36	(B)	61	(A)	86	(A)
12	(C)	37	(A)	62	(B)	87	(C)
13	(B)	38	(C)	63	(C)	88	(A)
14	(C)	39	(A)	64	(B)	89	(B)
15	(C)	40	(B)	65	(C)	90	(A)
16	(B)	41	(A)	66	(B)	91	(B)
17	(A)	42	(C)	67	(C)	92	(A)
18	(B)	43	(B)	68	(B)	93	(C)
19	(A)	44	(A)	69	(C)	94	(D)
20	(A)	45	(D)	70	(B)	95	(A)
21	(A)	46	(C)	71	(D)	96	(A)
22	(C)	47	(A)	72	(B)	97	(D)
23	(A)	48	(C)	73	(B)	98	(D)
24	(B)	49	(D)	74	(B)	99	(B)
25	(C)	50	(A)	75	(A)	100	(C)

Actual Test 05

#		#		#		#	
1	(A)	26	(C)	51	(A)	76	(B)
2	(C)	27	(C)	52	(C)	77	(C)
3	(C)	28	(A)	53	(C)	78	(A)
4	(B)	29	(A)	54	(A)	79	(C)
5	(A)	30	(C)	55	(B)	80	(D)
6	(A)	31	(A)	56	(C)	81	(A)
7	(A)	32	(A)	57	(B)	82	(D)
8	(B)	33	(B)	58	(C)	83	(A)
9	(A)	34	(B)	59	(C)	84	(A)
10	(B)	35	(B)	60	(B)	85	(D)
11	(C)	36	(A)	61	(A)	86	(C)
12	(C)	37	(C)	62	(C)	87	(A)
13	(A)	38	(C)	63	(C)	88	(A)
14	(C)	39	(B)	64	(D)	89	(C)
15	(B)	40	(A)	65	(A)	90	(A)
16	(C)	41	(D)	66	(D)	91	(A)
17	(A)	42	(C)	67	(A)	92	(C)
18	(B)	43	(D)	68	(C)	93	(D)
19	(C)	44	(D)	69	(B)	94	(D)
20	(B)	45	(A)	70	(B)	95	(A)
21	(C)	46	(C)	71	(B)	96	(C)
22	(A)	47	(D)	72	(A)	97	(D)
23	(A)	48	(C)	73	(C)	98	(B)
24	(C)	49	(C)	74	(C)	99	(A)
25	(A)	50	(A)	75	(A)	100	(D)

Actual Test 06

#		#		#		#	
1	(C)	26	(C)	51	(C)	76	(D)
2	(D)	27	(A)	52	(C)	77	(C)
3	(B)	28	(B)	53	(C)	78	(D)
4	(A)	29	(C)	54	(A)	79	(A)
5	(D)	30	(A)	55	(C)	80	(B)
6	(D)	31	(A)	56	(B)	81	(B)
7	(C)	32	(C)	57	(C)	82	(C)
8	(B)	33	(B)	58	(A)	83	(C)
9	(C)	34	(B)	59	(C)	84	(A)
10	(A)	35	(C)	60	(D)	85	(C)
11	(C)	36	(B)	61	(A)	86	(A)
12	(A)	37	(A)	62	(A)	87	(C)
13	(B)	38	(D)	63	(C)	88	(D)
14	(C)	39	(A)	64	(B)	89	(C)
15	(A)	40	(C)	65	(A)	90	(B)
16	(B)	41	(D)	66	(B)	91	(A)
17	(C)	42	(B)	67	(C)	92	(C)
18	(B)	43	(C)	68	(B)	93	(B)
19	(A)	44	(B)	69	(C)	94	(A)
20	(B)	45	(C)	70	(D)	95	(C)
21	(A)	46	(D)	71	(B)	96	(B)
22	(C)	47	(B)	72	(C)	97	(B)
23	(B)	48	(A)	73	(A)	98	(C)
24	(B)	49	(D)	74	(A)	99	(A)
25	(A)	50	(A)	75	(B)	100	(D)

Actual Test 07

#		#		#		#	
1	(B)	26	(C)	51	(B)	76	(A)
2	(C)	27	(A)	52	(D)	77	(C)
3	(A)	28	(B)	53	(A)	78	(B)
4	(A)	29	(A)	54	(C)	79	(A)
5	(B)	30	(B)	55	(D)	80	(B)
6	(C)	31	(A)	56	(B)	81	(C)
7	(A)	32	(C)	57	(B)	82	(C)
8	(B)	33	(A)	58	(B)	83	(A)
9	(C)	34	(A)	59	(B)	84	(A)
10	(B)	35	(B)	60	(C)	85	(A)
11	(C)	36	(C)	61	(B)	86	(B)
12	(A)	37	(A)	62	(C)	87	(A)
13	(C)	38	(C)	63	(A)	88	(C)
14	(A)	39	(C)	64	(B)	89	(A)
15	(B)	40	(A)	65	(A)	90	(B)
16	(A)	41	(B)	66	(B)	91	(C)
17	(B)	42	(A)	67	(B)	92	(B)
18	(B)	43	(B)	68	(D)	93	(A)
19	(C)	44	(C)	69	(B)	94	(D)
20	(B)	45	(A)	70	(A)	95	(B)
21	(B)	46	(B)	71	(A)	96	(A)
22	(B)	47	(B)	72	(B)	97	(C)
23	(B)	48	(A)	73	(A)	98	(A)
24	(C)	49	(D)	74	(B)	99	(B)
25	(B)	50	(C)	75	(D)	100	(D)

Actual Test 08

#		#		#		#	
1	(A)	26	(A)	51	(A)	76	(D)
2	(C)	27	(B)	52	(D)	77	(D)
3	(D)	28	(A)	53	(A)	78	(B)
4	(A)	29	(B)	54	(C)	79	(C)
5	(C)	30	(C)	55	(B)	80	(C)
6	(B)	31	(B)	56	(A)	81	(A)
7	(B)	32	(B)	57	(C)	82	(B)
8	(A)	33	(C)	58	(B)	83	(C)
9	(C)	34	(A)	59	(D)	84	(C)
10	(A)	35	(A)	60	(B)	85	(A)
11	(B)	36	(B)	61	(C)	86	(A)
12	(B)	37	(B)	62	(C)	87	(A)
13	(C)	38	(A)	63	(C)	88	(C)
14	(B)	39	(D)	64	(C)	89	(A)
15	(C)	40	(B)	65	(D)	90	(A)
16	(A)	41	(C)	66	(D)	91	(A)
17	(C)	42	(B)	67	(C)	92	(D)
18	(B)	43	(A)	68	(B)	93	(C)
19	(A)	44	(C)	69	(A)	94	(C)
20	(C)	45	(B)	70	(C)	95	(B)
21	(B)	46	(B)	71	(A)	96	(D)
22	(A)	47	(C)	72	(B)	97	(C)
23	(C)	48	(D)	73	(D)	98	(C)
24	(B)	49	(B)	74	(C)	99	(A)
25	(B)	50	(C)	75	(A)	100	(D)

Actual Test 09

1	(C)	26	(A)	51	(D)	76	(D)
2	(A)	27	(B)	52	(A)	77	(D)
3	(C)	28	(A)	53	(B)	78	(A)
4	(B)	29	(A)	54	(A)	79	(A)
5	(C)	30	(B)	55	(C)	80	(B)
6	(A)	31	(B)	56	(C)	81	(C)
7	(B)	32	(C)	57	(B)	82	(C)
8	(A)	33	(D)	58	(D)	83	(A)
9	(A)	34	(B)	59	(A)	84	(C)
10	(B)	35	(D)	60	(B)	85	(A)
11	(C)	36	(A)	61	(C)	86	(A)
12	(A)	37	(B)	62	(B)	87	(C)
13	(B)	38	(D)	63	(C)	88	(D)
14	(B)	39	(C)	64	(C)	89	(A)
15	(A)	40	(B)	65	(B)	90	(D)
16	(B)	41	(C)	66	(C)	91	(B)
17	(A)	42	(C)	67	(D)	92	(A)
18	(C)	43	(C)	68	(A)	93	(B)
19	(B)	44	(A)	69	(C)	94	(B)
20	(B)	45	(D)	70	(C)	95	(A)
21	(A)	46	(B)	71	(C)	96	(B)
22	(A)	47	(D)	72	(A)	97	(B)
23	(A)	48	(C)	73	(C)	98	(B)
24	(C)	49	(A)	74	(C)	99	(B)
25	(A)	50	(C)	75	(A)	100	(D)

Actual Test 10

1	(C)	26	(B)	51	(C)	76	(B)
2	(B)	27	(B)	52	(B)	77	(A)
3	(C)	28	(A)	53	(B)	78	(B)
4	(A)	29	(A)	54	(A)	79	(C)
5	(B)	30	(A)	55	(C)	80	(C)
6	(C)	31	(B)	56	(B)	81	(A)
7	(C)	32	(D)	57	(D)	82	(B)
8	(B)	33	(C)	58	(C)	83	(B)
9	(A)	34	(A)	59	(C)	84	(C)
10	(A)	35	(B)	60	(B)	85	(A)
11	(B)	36	(D)	61	(D)	86	(A)
12	(C)	37	(D)	62	(C)	87	(B)
13	(C)	38	(D)	63	(D)	88	(C)
14	(A)	39	(C)	64	(C)	89	(A)
15	(A)	40	(A)	65	(C)	90	(A)
16	(C)	41	(C)	66	(D)	91	(B)
17	(A)	42	(A)	67	(C)	92	(D)
18	(B)	43	(C)	68	(C)	93	(C)
19	(B)	44	(C)	69	(C)	94	(C)
20	(C)	45	(A)	70	(D)	95	(B)
21	(A)	46	(C)	71	(C)	96	(A)
22	(B)	47	(D)	72	(B)	97	(D)
23	(C)	48	(B)	73	(B)	98	(A)
24	(B)	49	(D)	74	(D)	99	(B)
25	(C)	50	(B)	75	(D)	100	(B)

答案紙

ACTUAL TEST 01

LISTENING SECTION

1	Ⓐ Ⓑ Ⓒ
2	Ⓐ Ⓑ Ⓒ
3	Ⓐ Ⓑ Ⓒ
4	Ⓐ Ⓑ Ⓒ
5	Ⓐ Ⓑ Ⓒ
6	Ⓐ Ⓑ Ⓒ
7	Ⓐ Ⓑ Ⓒ
8	Ⓐ Ⓑ Ⓒ
9	Ⓐ Ⓑ Ⓒ
10	Ⓐ Ⓑ Ⓒ

11	Ⓐ Ⓑ Ⓒ Ⓓ
12	Ⓐ Ⓑ Ⓒ Ⓓ
13	Ⓐ Ⓑ Ⓒ Ⓓ
14	Ⓐ Ⓑ Ⓒ Ⓓ
15	Ⓐ Ⓑ Ⓒ Ⓓ
16	Ⓐ Ⓑ Ⓒ Ⓓ
17	Ⓐ Ⓑ Ⓒ Ⓓ
18	Ⓐ Ⓑ Ⓒ Ⓓ
19	Ⓐ Ⓑ Ⓒ Ⓓ
20	Ⓐ Ⓑ Ⓒ Ⓓ

21	Ⓐ Ⓑ Ⓒ Ⓓ
22	Ⓐ Ⓑ Ⓒ Ⓓ
23	Ⓐ Ⓑ Ⓒ Ⓓ
24	Ⓐ Ⓑ Ⓒ Ⓓ
25	Ⓐ Ⓑ Ⓒ Ⓓ
26	Ⓐ Ⓑ Ⓒ Ⓓ
27	Ⓐ Ⓑ Ⓒ Ⓓ
28	Ⓐ Ⓑ Ⓒ Ⓓ
29	Ⓐ Ⓑ Ⓒ Ⓓ
30	Ⓐ Ⓑ Ⓒ Ⓓ

31	Ⓐ Ⓑ Ⓒ Ⓓ
32	Ⓐ Ⓑ Ⓒ Ⓓ
33	Ⓐ Ⓑ Ⓒ Ⓓ
34	Ⓐ Ⓑ Ⓒ Ⓓ
35	Ⓐ Ⓑ Ⓒ Ⓓ
36	Ⓐ Ⓑ Ⓒ Ⓓ
37	Ⓐ Ⓑ Ⓒ Ⓓ
38	Ⓐ Ⓑ Ⓒ Ⓓ
39	Ⓐ Ⓑ Ⓒ Ⓓ
40	Ⓐ Ⓑ Ⓒ Ⓓ

41	Ⓐ Ⓑ Ⓒ Ⓓ
42	Ⓐ Ⓑ Ⓒ Ⓓ
43	Ⓐ Ⓑ Ⓒ Ⓓ
44	Ⓐ Ⓑ Ⓒ Ⓓ
45	Ⓐ Ⓑ Ⓒ Ⓓ
46	Ⓐ Ⓑ Ⓒ Ⓓ
47	Ⓐ Ⓑ Ⓒ Ⓓ
48	Ⓐ Ⓑ Ⓒ Ⓓ
49	Ⓐ Ⓑ Ⓒ Ⓓ
50	Ⓐ Ⓑ Ⓒ Ⓓ

51	Ⓐ Ⓑ Ⓒ Ⓓ
52	Ⓐ Ⓑ Ⓒ Ⓓ
53	Ⓐ Ⓑ Ⓒ Ⓓ
54	Ⓐ Ⓑ Ⓒ Ⓓ
55	Ⓐ Ⓑ Ⓒ Ⓓ
56	Ⓐ Ⓑ Ⓒ Ⓓ
57	Ⓐ Ⓑ Ⓒ Ⓓ
58	Ⓐ Ⓑ Ⓒ Ⓓ
59	Ⓐ Ⓑ Ⓒ Ⓓ
60	Ⓐ Ⓑ Ⓒ Ⓓ

61	Ⓐ Ⓑ Ⓒ Ⓓ
62	Ⓐ Ⓑ Ⓒ Ⓓ
63	Ⓐ Ⓑ Ⓒ Ⓓ
64	Ⓐ Ⓑ Ⓒ Ⓓ
65	Ⓐ Ⓑ Ⓒ Ⓓ
66	Ⓐ Ⓑ Ⓒ Ⓓ
67	Ⓐ Ⓑ Ⓒ Ⓓ
68	Ⓐ Ⓑ Ⓒ Ⓓ
69	Ⓐ Ⓑ Ⓒ Ⓓ
70	Ⓐ Ⓑ Ⓒ Ⓓ

71	Ⓐ Ⓑ Ⓒ Ⓓ
72	Ⓐ Ⓑ Ⓒ Ⓓ
73	Ⓐ Ⓑ Ⓒ Ⓓ
74	Ⓐ Ⓑ Ⓒ Ⓓ
75	Ⓐ Ⓑ Ⓒ Ⓓ
76	Ⓐ Ⓑ Ⓒ Ⓓ
77	Ⓐ Ⓑ Ⓒ Ⓓ
78	Ⓐ Ⓑ Ⓒ Ⓓ
79	Ⓐ Ⓑ Ⓒ Ⓓ
80	Ⓐ Ⓑ Ⓒ Ⓓ

81	Ⓐ Ⓑ Ⓒ Ⓓ
82	Ⓐ Ⓑ Ⓒ Ⓓ
83	Ⓐ Ⓑ Ⓒ Ⓓ
84	Ⓐ Ⓑ Ⓒ Ⓓ
85	Ⓐ Ⓑ Ⓒ Ⓓ
86	Ⓐ Ⓑ Ⓒ Ⓓ
87	Ⓐ Ⓑ Ⓒ Ⓓ
88	Ⓐ Ⓑ Ⓒ Ⓓ
89	Ⓐ Ⓑ Ⓒ Ⓓ
90	Ⓐ Ⓑ Ⓒ Ⓓ

91	Ⓐ Ⓑ Ⓒ Ⓓ
92	Ⓐ Ⓑ Ⓒ Ⓓ
93	Ⓐ Ⓑ Ⓒ Ⓓ
94	Ⓐ Ⓑ Ⓒ Ⓓ
95	Ⓐ Ⓑ Ⓒ Ⓓ
96	Ⓐ Ⓑ Ⓒ Ⓓ
97	Ⓐ Ⓑ Ⓒ Ⓓ
98	Ⓐ Ⓑ Ⓒ Ⓓ
99	Ⓐ Ⓑ Ⓒ Ⓓ
100	Ⓐ Ⓑ Ⓒ Ⓓ

ACTUAL TEST 02

LISTENING SECTION

1	Ⓐ Ⓑ Ⓒ
2	Ⓐ Ⓑ Ⓒ
3	Ⓐ Ⓑ Ⓒ
4	Ⓐ Ⓑ Ⓒ
5	Ⓐ Ⓑ Ⓒ
6	Ⓐ Ⓑ Ⓒ
7	Ⓐ Ⓑ Ⓒ
8	Ⓐ Ⓑ Ⓒ
9	Ⓐ Ⓑ Ⓒ
10	Ⓐ Ⓑ Ⓒ

11	Ⓐ Ⓑ Ⓒ Ⓓ
12	Ⓐ Ⓑ Ⓒ Ⓓ
13	Ⓐ Ⓑ Ⓒ Ⓓ
14	Ⓐ Ⓑ Ⓒ Ⓓ
15	Ⓐ Ⓑ Ⓒ Ⓓ
16	Ⓐ Ⓑ Ⓒ Ⓓ
17	Ⓐ Ⓑ Ⓒ Ⓓ
18	Ⓐ Ⓑ Ⓒ Ⓓ
19	Ⓐ Ⓑ Ⓒ Ⓓ
20	Ⓐ Ⓑ Ⓒ Ⓓ

21	Ⓐ Ⓑ Ⓒ Ⓓ
22	Ⓐ Ⓑ Ⓒ Ⓓ
23	Ⓐ Ⓑ Ⓒ Ⓓ
24	Ⓐ Ⓑ Ⓒ Ⓓ
25	Ⓐ Ⓑ Ⓒ Ⓓ
26	Ⓐ Ⓑ Ⓒ Ⓓ
27	Ⓐ Ⓑ Ⓒ Ⓓ
28	Ⓐ Ⓑ Ⓒ Ⓓ
29	Ⓐ Ⓑ Ⓒ Ⓓ
30	Ⓐ Ⓑ Ⓒ Ⓓ

31	Ⓐ Ⓑ Ⓒ Ⓓ
32	Ⓐ Ⓑ Ⓒ Ⓓ
33	Ⓐ Ⓑ Ⓒ Ⓓ
34	Ⓐ Ⓑ Ⓒ Ⓓ
35	Ⓐ Ⓑ Ⓒ Ⓓ
36	Ⓐ Ⓑ Ⓒ Ⓓ
37	Ⓐ Ⓑ Ⓒ Ⓓ
38	Ⓐ Ⓑ Ⓒ Ⓓ
39	Ⓐ Ⓑ Ⓒ Ⓓ
40	Ⓐ Ⓑ Ⓒ Ⓓ

41	Ⓐ Ⓑ Ⓒ Ⓓ
42	Ⓐ Ⓑ Ⓒ Ⓓ
43	Ⓐ Ⓑ Ⓒ Ⓓ
44	Ⓐ Ⓑ Ⓒ Ⓓ
45	Ⓐ Ⓑ Ⓒ Ⓓ
46	Ⓐ Ⓑ Ⓒ Ⓓ
47	Ⓐ Ⓑ Ⓒ Ⓓ
48	Ⓐ Ⓑ Ⓒ Ⓓ
49	Ⓐ Ⓑ Ⓒ Ⓓ
50	Ⓐ Ⓑ Ⓒ Ⓓ

51	Ⓐ Ⓑ Ⓒ Ⓓ
52	Ⓐ Ⓑ Ⓒ Ⓓ
53	Ⓐ Ⓑ Ⓒ Ⓓ
54	Ⓐ Ⓑ Ⓒ Ⓓ
55	Ⓐ Ⓑ Ⓒ Ⓓ
56	Ⓐ Ⓑ Ⓒ Ⓓ
57	Ⓐ Ⓑ Ⓒ Ⓓ
58	Ⓐ Ⓑ Ⓒ Ⓓ
59	Ⓐ Ⓑ Ⓒ Ⓓ
60	Ⓐ Ⓑ Ⓒ Ⓓ

61	Ⓐ Ⓑ Ⓒ Ⓓ
62	Ⓐ Ⓑ Ⓒ Ⓓ
63	Ⓐ Ⓑ Ⓒ Ⓓ
64	Ⓐ Ⓑ Ⓒ Ⓓ
65	Ⓐ Ⓑ Ⓒ Ⓓ
66	Ⓐ Ⓑ Ⓒ Ⓓ
67	Ⓐ Ⓑ Ⓒ Ⓓ
68	Ⓐ Ⓑ Ⓒ Ⓓ
69	Ⓐ Ⓑ Ⓒ Ⓓ
70	Ⓐ Ⓑ Ⓒ Ⓓ

71	Ⓐ Ⓑ Ⓒ Ⓓ
72	Ⓐ Ⓑ Ⓒ Ⓓ
73	Ⓐ Ⓑ Ⓒ Ⓓ
74	Ⓐ Ⓑ Ⓒ Ⓓ
75	Ⓐ Ⓑ Ⓒ Ⓓ
76	Ⓐ Ⓑ Ⓒ Ⓓ
77	Ⓐ Ⓑ Ⓒ Ⓓ
78	Ⓐ Ⓑ Ⓒ Ⓓ
79	Ⓐ Ⓑ Ⓒ Ⓓ
80	Ⓐ Ⓑ Ⓒ Ⓓ

81	Ⓐ Ⓑ Ⓒ Ⓓ
82	Ⓐ Ⓑ Ⓒ Ⓓ
83	Ⓐ Ⓑ Ⓒ Ⓓ
84	Ⓐ Ⓑ Ⓒ Ⓓ
85	Ⓐ Ⓑ Ⓒ Ⓓ
86	Ⓐ Ⓑ Ⓒ Ⓓ
87	Ⓐ Ⓑ Ⓒ Ⓓ
88	Ⓐ Ⓑ Ⓒ Ⓓ
89	Ⓐ Ⓑ Ⓒ Ⓓ
90	Ⓐ Ⓑ Ⓒ Ⓓ

91	Ⓐ Ⓑ Ⓒ Ⓓ
92	Ⓐ Ⓑ Ⓒ Ⓓ
93	Ⓐ Ⓑ Ⓒ Ⓓ
94	Ⓐ Ⓑ Ⓒ Ⓓ
95	Ⓐ Ⓑ Ⓒ Ⓓ
96	Ⓐ Ⓑ Ⓒ Ⓓ
97	Ⓐ Ⓑ Ⓒ Ⓓ
98	Ⓐ Ⓑ Ⓒ Ⓓ
99	Ⓐ Ⓑ Ⓒ Ⓓ
100	Ⓐ Ⓑ Ⓒ Ⓓ

ACTUAL TEST 03

LISTENING SECTION

| 1 | Ⓐ Ⓑ Ⓒ | 11 | Ⓐ Ⓑ Ⓒ | 21 | Ⓐ Ⓑ Ⓒ Ⓓ | 31 | Ⓐ Ⓑ Ⓒ Ⓓ | 41 | Ⓐ Ⓑ Ⓒ Ⓓ | 51 | Ⓐ Ⓑ Ⓒ Ⓓ | 61 | Ⓐ Ⓑ Ⓒ Ⓓ | 71 | Ⓐ Ⓑ Ⓒ Ⓓ | 81 | Ⓐ Ⓑ Ⓒ Ⓓ | 91 | Ⓐ Ⓑ Ⓒ Ⓓ |

ACTUAL TEST 04

LISTENING SECTION

| 1 | Ⓐ Ⓑ Ⓒ | 11 | Ⓐ Ⓑ Ⓒ | 21 | Ⓐ Ⓑ Ⓒ Ⓓ | 31 | Ⓐ Ⓑ Ⓒ Ⓓ | 41 | Ⓐ Ⓑ Ⓒ Ⓓ | 51 | Ⓐ Ⓑ Ⓒ Ⓓ | 61 | Ⓐ Ⓑ Ⓒ Ⓓ | 71 | Ⓐ Ⓑ Ⓒ Ⓓ | 81 | Ⓐ Ⓑ Ⓒ Ⓓ | 91 | Ⓐ Ⓑ Ⓒ Ⓓ |

ACTUAL TEST 05

LISTENING SECTION

1 ⒶⒷⒸⒹ	11 ⒶⒷⒸⒹ	21 ⒶⒷⒸⒹ	31 ⒶⒷⒸⒹ	41 ⒶⒷⒸⒹ
2 ⒶⒷⒸⒹ	12 ⒶⒷⒸⒹ	22 ⒶⒷⒸⒹ	32 ⒶⒷⒸⒹ	42 ⒶⒷⒸⒹ
3 ⒶⒷⒸⒹ	13 ⒶⒷⒸⒹ	23 ⒶⒷⒸⒹ	33 ⒶⒷⒸⒹ	43 ⒶⒷⒸⒹ
4 ⒶⒷⒸⒹ	14 ⒶⒷⒸⒹ	24 ⒶⒷⒸⒹ	34 ⒶⒷⒸⒹ	44 ⒶⒷⒸⒹ
5 ⒶⒷⒸⒹ	15 ⒶⒷⒸⒹ	25 ⒶⒷⒸⒹ	35 ⒶⒷⒸⒹ	45 ⒶⒷⒸⒹ
6 ⒶⒷⒸⒹ	16 ⒶⒷⒸⒹ	26 ⒶⒷⒸⒹ	36 ⒶⒷⒸⒹ	46 ⒶⒷⒸⒹ
7 ⒶⒷⒸⒹ	17 ⒶⒷⒸⒹ	27 ⒶⒷⒸⒹ	37 ⒶⒷⒸⒹ	47 ⒶⒷⒸⒹ
8 ⒶⒷⒸⒹ	18 ⒶⒷⒸⒹ	28 ⒶⒷⒸⒹ	38 ⒶⒷⒸⒹ	48 ⒶⒷⒸⒹ
9 ⒶⒷⒸⒹ	19 ⒶⒷⒸⒹ	29 ⒶⒷⒸⒹ	39 ⒶⒷⒸⒹ	49 ⒶⒷⒸⒹ
10 ⒶⒷⒸⒹ	20 ⒶⒷⒸⒹ	30 ⒶⒷⒸⒹ	40 ⒶⒷⒸⒹ	50 ⒶⒷⒸⒹ
51 ⒶⒷⒸⒹ	61 ⒶⒷⒸⒹ	71 ⒶⒷⒸⒹ	81 ⒶⒷⒸⒹ	91 ⒶⒷⒸⒹ
52 ⒶⒷⒸⒹ	62 ⒶⒷⒸⒹ	72 ⒶⒷⒸⒹ	82 ⒶⒷⒸⒹ	92 ⒶⒷⒸⒹ
53 ⒶⒷⒸⒹ	63 ⒶⒷⒸⒹ	73 ⒶⒷⒸⒹ	83 ⒶⒷⒸⒹ	93 ⒶⒷⒸⒹ
54 ⒶⒷⒸⒹ	64 ⒶⒷⒸⒹ	74 ⒶⒷⒸⒹ	84 ⒶⒷⒸⒹ	94 ⒶⒷⒸⒹ
55 ⒶⒷⒸⒹ	65 ⒶⒷⒸⒹ	75 ⒶⒷⒸⒹ	85 ⒶⒷⒸⒹ	95 ⒶⒷⒸⒹ
56 ⒶⒷⒸⒹ	66 ⒶⒷⒸⒹ	76 ⒶⒷⒸⒹ	86 ⒶⒷⒸⒹ	96 ⒶⒷⒸⒹ
57 ⒶⒷⒸⒹ	67 ⒶⒷⒸⒹ	77 ⒶⒷⒸⒹ	87 ⒶⒷⒸⒹ	97 ⒶⒷⒸⒹ
58 ⒶⒷⒸⒹ	68 ⒶⒷⒸⒹ	78 ⒶⒷⒸⒹ	88 ⒶⒷⒸⒹ	98 ⒶⒷⒸⒹ
59 ⒶⒷⒸⒹ	69 ⒶⒷⒸⒹ	79 ⒶⒷⒸⒹ	89 ⒶⒷⒸⒹ	99 ⒶⒷⒸⒹ
60 ⒶⒷⒸⒹ	70 ⒶⒷⒸⒹ	80 ⒶⒷⒸⒹ	90 ⒶⒷⒸⒹ	100 ⒶⒷⒸⒹ

ACTUAL TEST 06

LISTENING SECTION

1 ⒶⒷⒸⒹ	11 ⒶⒷⒸⒹ	21 ⒶⒷⒸⒹ	31 ⒶⒷⒸⒹ	41 ⒶⒷⒸⒹ
2 ⒶⒷⒸⒹ	12 ⒶⒷⒸⒹ	22 ⒶⒷⒸⒹ	32 ⒶⒷⒸⒹ	42 ⒶⒷⒸⒹ
3 ⒶⒷⒸⒹ	13 ⒶⒷⒸⒹ	23 ⒶⒷⒸⒹ	33 ⒶⒷⒸⒹ	43 ⒶⒷⒸⒹ
4 ⒶⒷⒸⒹ	14 ⒶⒷⒸⒹ	24 ⒶⒷⒸⒹ	34 ⒶⒷⒸⒹ	44 ⒶⒷⒸⒹ
5 ⒶⒷⒸⒹ	15 ⒶⒷⒸⒹ	25 ⒶⒷⒸⒹ	35 ⒶⒷⒸⒹ	45 ⒶⒷⒸⒹ
6 ⒶⒷⒸⒹ	16 ⒶⒷⒸⒹ	26 ⒶⒷⒸⒹ	36 ⒶⒷⒸⒹ	46 ⒶⒷⒸⒹ
7 ⒶⒷⒸⒹ	17 ⒶⒷⒸⒹ	27 ⒶⒷⒸⒹ	37 ⒶⒷⒸⒹ	47 ⒶⒷⒸⒹ
8 ⒶⒷⒸⒹ	18 ⒶⒷⒸⒹ	28 ⒶⒷⒸⒹ	38 ⒶⒷⒸⒹ	48 ⒶⒷⒸⒹ
9 ⒶⒷⒸⒹ	19 ⒶⒷⒸⒹ	29 ⒶⒷⒸⒹ	39 ⒶⒷⒸⒹ	49 ⒶⒷⒸⒹ
10 ⒶⒷⒸⒹ	20 ⒶⒷⒸⒹ	30 ⒶⒷⒸⒹ	40 ⒶⒷⒸⒹ	50 ⒶⒷⒸⒹ
51 ⒶⒷⒸⒹ	61 ⒶⒷⒸⒹ	71 ⒶⒷⒸⒹ	81 ⒶⒷⒸⒹ	91 ⒶⒷⒸⒹ
52 ⒶⒷⒸⒹ	62 ⒶⒷⒸⒹ	72 ⒶⒷⒸⒹ	82 ⒶⒷⒸⒹ	92 ⒶⒷⒸⒹ
53 ⒶⒷⒸⒹ	63 ⒶⒷⒸⒹ	73 ⒶⒷⒸⒹ	83 ⒶⒷⒸⒹ	93 ⒶⒷⒸⒹ
54 ⒶⒷⒸⒹ	64 ⒶⒷⒸⒹ	74 ⒶⒷⒸⒹ	84 ⒶⒷⒸⒹ	94 ⒶⒷⒸⒹ
55 ⒶⒷⒸⒹ	65 ⒶⒷⒸⒹ	75 ⒶⒷⒸⒹ	85 ⒶⒷⒸⒹ	95 ⒶⒷⒸⒹ
56 ⒶⒷⒸⒹ	66 ⒶⒷⒸⒹ	76 ⒶⒷⒸⒹ	86 ⒶⒷⒸⒹ	96 ⒶⒷⒸⒹ
57 ⒶⒷⒸⒹ	67 ⒶⒷⒸⒹ	77 ⒶⒷⒸⒹ	87 ⒶⒷⒸⒹ	97 ⒶⒷⒸⒹ
58 ⒶⒷⒸⒹ	68 ⒶⒷⒸⒹ	78 ⒶⒷⒸⒹ	88 ⒶⒷⒸⒹ	98 ⒶⒷⒸⒹ
59 ⒶⒷⒸⒹ	69 ⒶⒷⒸⒹ	79 ⒶⒷⒸⒹ	89 ⒶⒷⒸⒹ	99 ⒶⒷⒸⒹ
60 ⒶⒷⒸⒹ	70 ⒶⒷⒸⒹ	80 ⒶⒷⒸⒹ	90 ⒶⒷⒸⒹ	100 ⒶⒷⒸⒹ

ACTUAL TEST 07

LISTENING SECTION

#				
1	Ⓐ	Ⓑ	Ⓒ	
2	Ⓐ	Ⓑ	Ⓒ	
3	Ⓐ	Ⓑ	Ⓒ	
4	Ⓐ	Ⓑ	Ⓒ	
5	Ⓐ	Ⓑ	Ⓒ	
6	Ⓐ	Ⓑ	Ⓒ	
7	Ⓐ	Ⓑ	Ⓒ	
8	Ⓐ	Ⓑ	Ⓒ	
9	Ⓐ	Ⓑ	Ⓒ	
10	Ⓐ	Ⓑ	Ⓒ	
11	Ⓐ	Ⓑ	Ⓒ	Ⓓ
12	Ⓐ	Ⓑ	Ⓒ	Ⓓ
13	Ⓐ	Ⓑ	Ⓒ	Ⓓ
14	Ⓐ	Ⓑ	Ⓒ	Ⓓ
15	Ⓐ	Ⓑ	Ⓒ	Ⓓ
16	Ⓐ	Ⓑ	Ⓒ	Ⓓ
17	Ⓐ	Ⓑ	Ⓒ	Ⓓ
18	Ⓐ	Ⓑ	Ⓒ	Ⓓ
19	Ⓐ	Ⓑ	Ⓒ	Ⓓ
20	Ⓐ	Ⓑ	Ⓒ	Ⓓ
21	Ⓐ	Ⓑ	Ⓒ	Ⓓ
22	Ⓐ	Ⓑ	Ⓒ	Ⓓ
23	Ⓐ	Ⓑ	Ⓒ	Ⓓ
24	Ⓐ	Ⓑ	Ⓒ	Ⓓ
25	Ⓐ	Ⓑ	Ⓒ	Ⓓ
26	Ⓐ	Ⓑ	Ⓒ	Ⓓ
27	Ⓐ	Ⓑ	Ⓒ	Ⓓ
28	Ⓐ	Ⓑ	Ⓒ	Ⓓ
29	Ⓐ	Ⓑ	Ⓒ	Ⓓ
30	Ⓐ	Ⓑ	Ⓒ	Ⓓ
31	Ⓐ	Ⓑ	Ⓒ	Ⓓ
32	Ⓐ	Ⓑ	Ⓒ	Ⓓ
33	Ⓐ	Ⓑ	Ⓒ	Ⓓ
34	Ⓐ	Ⓑ	Ⓒ	Ⓓ
35	Ⓐ	Ⓑ	Ⓒ	Ⓓ
36	Ⓐ	Ⓑ	Ⓒ	Ⓓ
37	Ⓐ	Ⓑ	Ⓒ	Ⓓ
38	Ⓐ	Ⓑ	Ⓒ	Ⓓ
39	Ⓐ	Ⓑ	Ⓒ	Ⓓ
40	Ⓐ	Ⓑ	Ⓒ	Ⓓ
41	Ⓐ	Ⓑ	Ⓒ	Ⓓ
42	Ⓐ	Ⓑ	Ⓒ	Ⓓ
43	Ⓐ	Ⓑ	Ⓒ	Ⓓ
44	Ⓐ	Ⓑ	Ⓒ	Ⓓ
45	Ⓐ	Ⓑ	Ⓒ	Ⓓ
46	Ⓐ	Ⓑ	Ⓒ	Ⓓ
47	Ⓐ	Ⓑ	Ⓒ	Ⓓ
48	Ⓐ	Ⓑ	Ⓒ	Ⓓ
49	Ⓐ	Ⓑ	Ⓒ	Ⓓ
50	Ⓐ	Ⓑ	Ⓒ	Ⓓ
51	Ⓐ	Ⓑ	Ⓒ	Ⓓ
52	Ⓐ	Ⓑ	Ⓒ	Ⓓ
53	Ⓐ	Ⓑ	Ⓒ	Ⓓ
54	Ⓐ	Ⓑ	Ⓒ	Ⓓ
55	Ⓐ	Ⓑ	Ⓒ	Ⓓ
56	Ⓐ	Ⓑ	Ⓒ	Ⓓ
57	Ⓐ	Ⓑ	Ⓒ	Ⓓ
58	Ⓐ	Ⓑ	Ⓒ	Ⓓ
59	Ⓐ	Ⓑ	Ⓒ	Ⓓ
60	Ⓐ	Ⓑ	Ⓒ	Ⓓ
61	Ⓐ	Ⓑ	Ⓒ	Ⓓ
62	Ⓐ	Ⓑ	Ⓒ	Ⓓ
63	Ⓐ	Ⓑ	Ⓒ	Ⓓ
64	Ⓐ	Ⓑ	Ⓒ	Ⓓ
65	Ⓐ	Ⓑ	Ⓒ	Ⓓ
66	Ⓐ	Ⓑ	Ⓒ	Ⓓ
67	Ⓐ	Ⓑ	Ⓒ	Ⓓ
68	Ⓐ	Ⓑ	Ⓒ	Ⓓ
69	Ⓐ	Ⓑ	Ⓒ	Ⓓ
70	Ⓐ	Ⓑ	Ⓒ	Ⓓ
71	Ⓐ	Ⓑ	Ⓒ	Ⓓ
72	Ⓐ	Ⓑ	Ⓒ	Ⓓ
73	Ⓐ	Ⓑ	Ⓒ	Ⓓ
74	Ⓐ	Ⓑ	Ⓒ	Ⓓ
75	Ⓐ	Ⓑ	Ⓒ	Ⓓ
76	Ⓐ	Ⓑ	Ⓒ	Ⓓ
77	Ⓐ	Ⓑ	Ⓒ	Ⓓ
78	Ⓐ	Ⓑ	Ⓒ	Ⓓ
79	Ⓐ	Ⓑ	Ⓒ	Ⓓ
80	Ⓐ	Ⓑ	Ⓒ	Ⓓ
81	Ⓐ	Ⓑ	Ⓒ	Ⓓ
82	Ⓐ	Ⓑ	Ⓒ	Ⓓ
83	Ⓐ	Ⓑ	Ⓒ	Ⓓ
84	Ⓐ	Ⓑ	Ⓒ	Ⓓ
85	Ⓐ	Ⓑ	Ⓒ	Ⓓ
86	Ⓐ	Ⓑ	Ⓒ	Ⓓ
87	Ⓐ	Ⓑ	Ⓒ	Ⓓ
88	Ⓐ	Ⓑ	Ⓒ	Ⓓ
89	Ⓐ	Ⓑ	Ⓒ	Ⓓ
90	Ⓐ	Ⓑ	Ⓒ	Ⓓ
91	Ⓐ	Ⓑ	Ⓒ	Ⓓ
92	Ⓐ	Ⓑ	Ⓒ	Ⓓ
93	Ⓐ	Ⓑ	Ⓒ	Ⓓ
94	Ⓐ	Ⓑ	Ⓒ	Ⓓ
95	Ⓐ	Ⓑ	Ⓒ	Ⓓ
96	Ⓐ	Ⓑ	Ⓒ	Ⓓ
97	Ⓐ	Ⓑ	Ⓒ	Ⓓ
98	Ⓐ	Ⓑ	Ⓒ	Ⓓ
99	Ⓐ	Ⓑ	Ⓒ	Ⓓ
100	Ⓐ	Ⓑ	Ⓒ	Ⓓ

ACTUAL TEST 08

LISTENING SECTION

#				
1	Ⓐ	Ⓑ	Ⓒ	
2	Ⓐ	Ⓑ	Ⓒ	
3	Ⓐ	Ⓑ	Ⓒ	
4	Ⓐ	Ⓑ	Ⓒ	
5	Ⓐ	Ⓑ	Ⓒ	
6	Ⓐ	Ⓑ	Ⓒ	
7	Ⓐ	Ⓑ	Ⓒ	
8	Ⓐ	Ⓑ	Ⓒ	
9	Ⓐ	Ⓑ	Ⓒ	
10	Ⓐ	Ⓑ	Ⓒ	
11	Ⓐ	Ⓑ	Ⓒ	Ⓓ
12	Ⓐ	Ⓑ	Ⓒ	Ⓓ
13	Ⓐ	Ⓑ	Ⓒ	Ⓓ
14	Ⓐ	Ⓑ	Ⓒ	Ⓓ
15	Ⓐ	Ⓑ	Ⓒ	Ⓓ
16	Ⓐ	Ⓑ	Ⓒ	Ⓓ
17	Ⓐ	Ⓑ	Ⓒ	Ⓓ
18	Ⓐ	Ⓑ	Ⓒ	Ⓓ
19	Ⓐ	Ⓑ	Ⓒ	Ⓓ
20	Ⓐ	Ⓑ	Ⓒ	Ⓓ
21	Ⓐ	Ⓑ	Ⓒ	Ⓓ
22	Ⓐ	Ⓑ	Ⓒ	Ⓓ
23	Ⓐ	Ⓑ	Ⓒ	Ⓓ
24	Ⓐ	Ⓑ	Ⓒ	Ⓓ
25	Ⓐ	Ⓑ	Ⓒ	Ⓓ
26	Ⓐ	Ⓑ	Ⓒ	Ⓓ
27	Ⓐ	Ⓑ	Ⓒ	Ⓓ
28	Ⓐ	Ⓑ	Ⓒ	Ⓓ
29	Ⓐ	Ⓑ	Ⓒ	Ⓓ
30	Ⓐ	Ⓑ	Ⓒ	Ⓓ
31	Ⓐ	Ⓑ	Ⓒ	Ⓓ
32	Ⓐ	Ⓑ	Ⓒ	Ⓓ
33	Ⓐ	Ⓑ	Ⓒ	Ⓓ
34	Ⓐ	Ⓑ	Ⓒ	Ⓓ
35	Ⓐ	Ⓑ	Ⓒ	Ⓓ
36	Ⓐ	Ⓑ	Ⓒ	Ⓓ
37	Ⓐ	Ⓑ	Ⓒ	Ⓓ
38	Ⓐ	Ⓑ	Ⓒ	Ⓓ
39	Ⓐ	Ⓑ	Ⓒ	Ⓓ
40	Ⓐ	Ⓑ	Ⓒ	Ⓓ
41	Ⓐ	Ⓑ	Ⓒ	Ⓓ
42	Ⓐ	Ⓑ	Ⓒ	Ⓓ
43	Ⓐ	Ⓑ	Ⓒ	Ⓓ
44	Ⓐ	Ⓑ	Ⓒ	Ⓓ
45	Ⓐ	Ⓑ	Ⓒ	Ⓓ
46	Ⓐ	Ⓑ	Ⓒ	Ⓓ
47	Ⓐ	Ⓑ	Ⓒ	Ⓓ
48	Ⓐ	Ⓑ	Ⓒ	Ⓓ
49	Ⓐ	Ⓑ	Ⓒ	Ⓓ
50	Ⓐ	Ⓑ	Ⓒ	Ⓓ
51	Ⓐ	Ⓑ	Ⓒ	Ⓓ
52	Ⓐ	Ⓑ	Ⓒ	Ⓓ
53	Ⓐ	Ⓑ	Ⓒ	Ⓓ
54	Ⓐ	Ⓑ	Ⓒ	Ⓓ
55	Ⓐ	Ⓑ	Ⓒ	Ⓓ
56	Ⓐ	Ⓑ	Ⓒ	Ⓓ
57	Ⓐ	Ⓑ	Ⓒ	Ⓓ
58	Ⓐ	Ⓑ	Ⓒ	Ⓓ
59	Ⓐ	Ⓑ	Ⓒ	Ⓓ
60	Ⓐ	Ⓑ	Ⓒ	Ⓓ
61	Ⓐ	Ⓑ	Ⓒ	Ⓓ
62	Ⓐ	Ⓑ	Ⓒ	Ⓓ
63	Ⓐ	Ⓑ	Ⓒ	Ⓓ
64	Ⓐ	Ⓑ	Ⓒ	Ⓓ
65	Ⓐ	Ⓑ	Ⓒ	Ⓓ
66	Ⓐ	Ⓑ	Ⓒ	Ⓓ
67	Ⓐ	Ⓑ	Ⓒ	Ⓓ
68	Ⓐ	Ⓑ	Ⓒ	Ⓓ
69	Ⓐ	Ⓑ	Ⓒ	Ⓓ
70	Ⓐ	Ⓑ	Ⓒ	Ⓓ
71	Ⓐ	Ⓑ	Ⓒ	Ⓓ
72	Ⓐ	Ⓑ	Ⓒ	Ⓓ
73	Ⓐ	Ⓑ	Ⓒ	Ⓓ
74	Ⓐ	Ⓑ	Ⓒ	Ⓓ
75	Ⓐ	Ⓑ	Ⓒ	Ⓓ
76	Ⓐ	Ⓑ	Ⓒ	Ⓓ
77	Ⓐ	Ⓑ	Ⓒ	Ⓓ
78	Ⓐ	Ⓑ	Ⓒ	Ⓓ
79	Ⓐ	Ⓑ	Ⓒ	Ⓓ
80	Ⓐ	Ⓑ	Ⓒ	Ⓓ
81	Ⓐ	Ⓑ	Ⓒ	Ⓓ
82	Ⓐ	Ⓑ	Ⓒ	Ⓓ
83	Ⓐ	Ⓑ	Ⓒ	Ⓓ
84	Ⓐ	Ⓑ	Ⓒ	Ⓓ
85	Ⓐ	Ⓑ	Ⓒ	Ⓓ
86	Ⓐ	Ⓑ	Ⓒ	Ⓓ
87	Ⓐ	Ⓑ	Ⓒ	Ⓓ
88	Ⓐ	Ⓑ	Ⓒ	Ⓓ
89	Ⓐ	Ⓑ	Ⓒ	Ⓓ
90	Ⓐ	Ⓑ	Ⓒ	Ⓓ
91	Ⓐ	Ⓑ	Ⓒ	Ⓓ
92	Ⓐ	Ⓑ	Ⓒ	Ⓓ
93	Ⓐ	Ⓑ	Ⓒ	Ⓓ
94	Ⓐ	Ⓑ	Ⓒ	Ⓓ
95	Ⓐ	Ⓑ	Ⓒ	Ⓓ
96	Ⓐ	Ⓑ	Ⓒ	Ⓓ
97	Ⓐ	Ⓑ	Ⓒ	Ⓓ
98	Ⓐ	Ⓑ	Ⓒ	Ⓓ
99	Ⓐ	Ⓑ	Ⓒ	Ⓓ
100	Ⓐ	Ⓑ	Ⓒ	Ⓓ

答案紙

ACTUAL TEST 09

LISTENING SECTION

ACTUAL TEST 10

LISTENING SECTION

新制 New TOEIC 聽力超高分
最新多益改版黃金試題1000題

作　　者	Ki Taek Lee
譯　　者	王傳明
編　　輯	Gina Wang
審　　訂	Helen Yeh
校　　對	黃詩韻
內文排版	林書玉（題目）／葳豐企業有限公司（聽力對白和翻譯）
封面設計	林書玉
製程管理	洪巧玲
發 行 人	黃朝萍
出 版 者	寂天文化事業股份有限公司
電　　話	+886-(0)2-2365-9739
傳　　真	+886-(0)2-2365-9835
網　　址	www.icosmos.com.tw
讀者服務	onlineservice@icosmos.com.tw
出版日期	2024 年 03 月 初版再刷 (0106)

ISBN 978-986-318-967-1 （寂天雲隨身聽 APP 版）